Praise for *Never*

"Urgent and fiercely compelling . . . *Never* is first-rate entertainment that has something important to say. It deserves the popular success it will almost certainly achieve." —*The Washington Post*

"Superstar novelist Ken Follett's what-if political thriller . . . is so exciting—and so plausible—you won't want to look away."
—Apple Books (Best Book of the Month)

"Settle in for a thrilling ride." —CNN.com

"Terrific . . . A powerful, commanding performance from one of the top writers in the genre."
—*Publishers Weekly* (starred review)

"A complex, scary thriller that feels too plausible for comfort. You'll be so absorbed in the story threads that you'll follow them anywhere—and you'll suddenly realize you've read hundreds of pages. . . . On one level, it's great entertainment; on another, a window into a sobering possibility." —*Kirkus Reviews* (starred review)

"Absolutely compelling . . . A smart, scary, and all-too-plausible thriller." —*Booklist*

"Bold in scale and meticulously researched."
—*The Sunday Times* (London)

"Stunning . . . One of the most compelling reads of the year." —*Daily Express* (London)

PENGUIN BOOKS

NEVER

KEN FOLLETT is one of the world's best-loved authors, selling more than 188 million copies of his thirty-six books. Follett's first bestseller was *Eye of the Needle*, a spy story set in the Second World War. In 1989, *The Pillars of the Earth* was published and has since become Follett's most popular novel. It reached number one on bestseller lists around the world and was an Oprah's Book Club pick. Its sequels, *World Without End* and *A Column of Fire*, and the prequel *The Evening and the Morning*, proved equally popular, and the Kingsbridge series has sold more than fifty million copies worldwide. Follett lives in Hertfordshire, England, with his wife, Barbara. Between them they have five children, six grandchildren, and three Labradors.

ALSO BY KEN FOLLETT

NEVER

PENGUIN BOOKS

PENGUIN BOOKS
An imprint of Penguin Random House LLC
penguinrandomhouse.com

First published in the United States of America by Viking,
an imprint of Penguin Random House LLC, 2021
Published in Penguin Books 2022
This edition published 2023

ISBN 9780593300046 (mass market)

THE LIBRARY OF CONGRESS HAS CATALOGED
THE HARDCOVER EDITION AS FOLLOWS:
Names: Follett, Ken, author.
Title: Never / Ken Follett.
Description: First edition. | New York: Viking, [2021]
Identifiers: LCCN 2021009867 (print) | LCCN 2021009868 (ebook) |
ISBN 9780593300015 (hardcover) | ISBN 9780593300022 (ebook)
Subjects: GSAFD: Suspense fiction.
Classification: LCC PR6056.O45 N48 2021 (print) |
LCC PR6056.O45 (ebook) | DDC 823/.914—dc23
LC record available at https://lccn.loc.gov/2021009867
LC ebook record available at https://lccn.loc.gov/2021009868

Printed in the United States of America
3   5   7   9   10   8   6   4   2

Book design by Daniel Lagin

When I was doing the research for *Fall of Giants* I was shocked to realize that the First World War was a war that *nobody wanted*. No European leader on either side intended it to happen. But the emperors and prime ministers, one by one, made decisions—logical, moderate decisions—each of which took us a small step closer to the most terrible conflict the world had ever known. I came to believe that it was all a tragic accident.

And I wondered: could that happen again?

Two tigers cannot share the same mountain.

Chinese proverb

MUNCHKIN
COUNTRY

PROLOGUE

For many years James Madison held the title of the shortest-ever United States president, at five feet four inches. Then President Green broke his record. Pauline Green was four feet eleven inches. She liked to point out that Madison had defeated DeWitt Clinton, who was six feet three.

She had twice postponed her visit to Munchkin Country. It had been scheduled once every year she had been in office, but there was always something more important to do. This time she felt she had to go. It was a mild September morning in the third year of her presidency.

This exercise was a Rehearsal of Concept Drill, used to familiarize senior government figures with what they had to do in an emergency. Pretending that the United States was under attack, she walked rapidly out of the Oval Office to the South Lawn of the White House.

Hurrying behind her was a handful of key people who were rarely far from her side: her national security advisor, her senior secretary, two Secret Service bodyguards, and a young army captain carrying a leather-covered briefcase called the atomic football, which contained everything she needed to start a nuclear war.

Her helicopter was part of a fleet, and whichever one she was aboard was called Marine One. As always, a marine in blue dress uniform stood at attention as the president approached and ran lightly up the steps.

The first time Pauline had flown in a helicopter, something like twenty-five years ago, it had been an uncomfortable experience, she recalled, with hard metal seats in a cramped interior, and so noisy it was impossible to talk. This was different. The inside of the aircraft was like a private jet, with comfortable seats upholstered in pale tan leather, air-conditioning, and a small bathroom.

The national security advisor, Gus Blake, sat next to her. A retired general, he was a big man, African American, with short gray hair. He exuded an air of reassuring strength. At fifty-five he was five years older than Pauline. He had been a key member of her team in the presidential election campaign, and now he was her closest colleague.

"Thank you for doing this," he said as they took off. "I know you didn't want to."

He was right. She resented the distraction and felt impatient to get it over with. "One of those chores that just has to be done," she said.

It was a short journey. As the helicopter descended she checked her appearance in a hand mirror. Her short blond bob was tidy, her makeup light. She had nice hazel eyes that showed the compassion she often felt, although her lips could set in a straight line that made her look remorselessly determined. She closed the mirror with a snap.

They landed at a warehouse complex in a suburb in Maryland. Its official name was U.S. Government Archive Overflow Storage Facility No. 2, but those few people who knew its real function called it Munchkin Country, after the place where Dorothy went during the tornado in *The Wizard of Oz*.

Munchkin Country was a secret. Everyone knew about the Raven Rock Complex in Colorado, the underground nuclear bunker where military leaders planned to shelter during a nuclear war. That was a real facility that would be important, but it was not where the president would go. A lot of people also knew that underneath the East Wing of the White House was the Presidential Emergency Operations Center, used in crises such as 9/11. However, that was not designed for long-term post-apocalypse use.

Munchkin Country would keep a hundred people alive for a year.

President Green was met by a General Whitfield. In his late fifties, he was round faced and plump, with an amiable manner and a marked lack of military aggression. Pauline felt quite sure he was not in the least interested in killing enemies—which was, after all, what soldiers were for. His lack of bellicosity would be why he had ended up in this job.

It was a genuine storage facility, and signs directed deliveries to a loading dock. Whitfield led the party through a small side door, and that was where the atmosphere changed.

They were confronted by a massive double door that would have looked appropriate at the entrance to a maximum-security prison.

The room it led to felt suffocating. It had a low ceiling, and its walls seemed nearer, as if they were several feet thick. The air had a bottled taste.

"This blast-proof room exists mainly to protect the elevators," Whitfield said.

As they entered the elevator, Pauline quickly lost the impatient sense that she was engaged in an exercise that was barely necessary. This began to feel portentous.

Whitfield said: "With your permission, Madam President, we'll go all the way down and work back up."

"That will be fine, thank you, General."

As the elevator descended he said proudly: "Ma'am, this facility offers you one hundred percent protection if the United States should suffer any of the following: a pandemic or plague; a natural disaster such as a large meteorite hitting the Earth; riot and major civil disorder; a successful invasion by conventional military forces; cyberattack; or nuclear war."

If this list of potential catastrophes was meant to reassure Pauline, it failed. It reminded her that the end of civilization was possible and she might have to shelter in this hole in the ground so that she could try to save a remnant of the human race.

She thought she might prefer to die on the surface.

The elevator was falling fast and seemed to go a long way down before slowing. When at last it stopped, Whitfield said: "In case of elevator trouble, there is a staircase."

It was a witticism, and the younger members of the party laughed, thinking about how many steps there might be, but Pauline remembered how long it had taken people to descend the stairs in the burning World Trade Center, and she did not crack a smile. Nor did Gus, she noticed.

The walls were painted restful green, soothing creamy white, and relaxing pale pink, but it was still an underground bunker. The creepy feeling remained with her as she was shown the Presidential Suite, the barracks with lines of cots, the hospital, gym, cafeteria, and supermarket.

The Situation Room was a replica of the one in the basement of the White House, with a long table down the center and chairs at the sides for aides. There were large screens on the walls. "We can provide all the visual data you get at the White House, and just as fast," Whitfield said. "We can look at any city in the world by hacking into traffic cameras and security surveillance. We get military radar in real time. Satellite photos take a couple of hours to reach the Earth, as you know, but we get them at the same time as the Pentagon. We can pick up any television station, which can be useful on those rare occasions when CNN or Al Jazeera get a story before the security services. And we will have a team of linguists to provide instant subtitles for news programs in foreign languages."

The facilities floor had a power plant with a diesel fuel reservoir the size of a lake, a heating and cooling system, and a five-million-gallon water tank fed by an underground spring. Pauline was not particularly claustrophobic, but she felt stifled by the idea of being stuck in here while the world outside was devastated. She became conscious of her own breathing.

As if reading her mind, Whitfield said: "Our air supply comes in from outside through a set of blast filters that, as well as resisting explosion damage, will capture airborne contaminants, whether chemical, biological, or radioactive."

Fine, Pauline thought, but what about the millions of people on the surface who would have no protection?

At the end of the tour Whitfield said: "Madam President, your office indicated that you would not wish to have lunch before leaving, but we have prepared something in case you should change your mind."

This always happened. Everyone liked the idea of an hour or so of informal conversation with the president. She felt a pang of sympathy for Whitfield, stuck underground in this important but unseen post, but she had to repress this urge as always and stick to her timetable.

Pauline rarely wasted time eating with people other than her family. She held meetings at which information was exchanged and decisions were made, then she moved on to the next meeting. She had slashed the number of formal banquets the president attended. "I'm the leader of the free world," she had said. "Why would I spend three hours talking to the king of Belgium?"

Now she said: "That's very kind of you, General, but I have to get back to the White House."

Back in the helicopter she fastened her seat belt, then took from her pocket a plastic container the size of a small wallet or billfold. This was known as the Biscuit. It could be opened only by breaking the plastic. Inside was a card with a series of letters and numbers: the codes for authorizing a nuclear attack. The president had to carry the Biscuit all day and keep it beside the bed all night.

Gus saw what she was doing and said: "Thank heaven the Cold War is over."

She said: "That ghastly place has reminded me that we still live on the edge."

"We just have to make sure it's never used."

And Pauline, more than anyone else in the world, had that responsibility. Some days she felt the weight on her shoulders. Today it was heavy.

She said: "If I ever come back to Munchkin Country, it will be because I have failed."

DEFCON 5

LOWEST STATE OF READINESS.

CHAPTER 1

Seen from a plane, the car would have looked like a slow beetle creeping across an endless beach, the sun glinting off its polished black armor. In fact it was doing thirty miles per hour, the maximum safe speed on a road that had unexpected potholes and cracks. No one wanted to get a flat tire in the Sahara Desert.

The road led north from N'Djamena, capital city of Chad, through the desert toward Lake Chad, the biggest oasis in the Sahara. The landscape was a long, flat vista of sand and rock with a few pale yellow dried-up bushes and a random scatter of large and small stones, everything the same shade of mid-tan, as bleak as a moonscape.

The desert was unnervingly like outer space, Tamara Levit thought, with the car as a rocket ship. If anything went wrong with her space suit she could die. The comparison was fanciful and made her smile. All the same she glanced into the back of the car, where there were two reassuringly large plastic demijohns of water, enough to keep them all alive in an emergency until help arrived, probably.

The car was American. It was designed for difficult terrain, with high clearance and low gearing. It had tinted windows, and Tamara was wearing sunglasses, but even so the light glared off the concrete road and hurt her eyes.

All four people in the car wore shades. The driver, Ali, was a local man, born and raised here in Chad. In the city he wore blue jeans and a T-shirt, but today he had on a floor-length robe called a galabiya, with a loose cotton scarf wound around his head, traditional clothing for protection from the merciless sun.

Next to Ali in the front was an American soldier, Corporal Peter Ackerman. The rifle held loosely across his knees was a US Army standard-issue short-barreled lightweight carbine. He was about twenty years old, one of those young men who seemed to overflow with chirpy friendliness. To Tamara, who was almost thirty, he seemed ridiculously young to be carrying a lethal weapon. But he had no lack of confidence—one time he had even had the cheek to ask her for a date. "I like you, Pete, but you're much too young for me," she had said.

Beside Tamara in the rear seat was Tabdar "Tab" Sadoul, an attaché at the European Union mission in N'Djamena. Tab's glossy mid-brown hair was fashionably long, but otherwise he looked like an off-duty business executive, in khakis and a sky-blue button-down shirt, the sleeves rolled to show brown wrists.

She was attached to the American embassy in N'Djamena, and she wore her regular working clothes, a long-sleeved dress over trousers, with her dark hair tucked into a headscarf. It was a practical outfit that complied with tradition, and with her brown eyes and olive skin she did not even look like a foreigner. In a high-crime country such as Chad it was safer not to stand out, especially for a woman.

She was keeping an eye on the odometer. They had been on the road a couple of hours but now they were close to their destination. Tamara was tense about the meeting ahead. A lot hung on it, including her own career.

"Our cover story is a fact-finding mission," she said. "Do you know much about the lake?"

"Enough, I think," Tab said. "The Chari River rises in central Africa, runs eight hundred and seventy miles, and stops here. Lake Chad sustains several million people in four countries: Niger, Nigeria, Cameroon, and Chad. They're small farmers, graziers, and fishermen. Their favorite fish is the Nile perch, which can grow to six feet long and four hundred pounds."

Frenchmen speaking English always sounded as if they were trying to get you into bed, Tamara thought. Perhaps they always were. She said: "I guess they don't catch many Nile perch now that the water is so shallow."

"You're right. And the lake used to cover ten thousand square miles, but now it's only about five hundred. A lot of these people are on the edge of starvation."

"What do you think of the Chinese plan?"

"A canal one thousand five hundred miles long, bringing water from the river Congo? Chad's president is keen on it, not surprisingly. It might even happen— the Chinese do amazing things—but it won't be cheap, and it won't be soon."

China's investments in Africa were regarded, by Tamara's bosses in Washington and Tab's in Paris, with the same mixture of awestruck admiration and deep mistrust. Beijing spent billions, and got things done, but what were they really after?

Out of the corner of her eye Tamara saw a flash in the distance, a gleam as of sunlight on water. "Are we approaching the lake?" she asked Tab. "Or was that a mirage?"

"We must be close," he said.

"Look out for a turning on the left," she said to Ali, and then she repeated it in Arabic. Both Tamara and Tab were fluent in Arabic and French, the two main languages of Chad.

"Le voilà," Ali replied in French. Here it is.

The car slowed as it approached a junction marked only by a pile of stones.

They turned off the road onto a track across gravelly sand. In places it was hard to distinguish the track from the desert around it, but Ali seemed confident. In the distance Tamara glimpsed patches of green, smudged by heat haze, presumably trees and bushes growing by the water.

Beside the road Tamara saw the skeleton of a long-dead Peugeot pickup truck, a rusting body with no wheels or windows, and soon there were other signs of human habitation: a camel tied to a bush, a mongrel dog with a rat in its mouth, and a scatter of beer cans, bald tires, and ripped polythene.

They passed a vegetable patch, plants in neat straight lines being irrigated by a man with a watering can, then they came to a village, fifty or sixty houses spread randomly, with no pattern of streets. Most of the dwellings were traditional one-room huts, with circular mud-brick walls and tall pointed roofs of palm leaves. Ali drove at walking pace, threading the car between the houses, avoiding barefoot children and horned goats and outdoor cooking fires.

He stopped the car and said: "Nous sommes arrivés." We have arrived.

Tamara said: "Pete, would you please put the carbine on the floor? We want to look like students of ecology."

"Sure thing, Ms. Levit." He put the gun by his feet, with its stock hidden under his seat.

Tab said: "This used to be a prosperous fishing village, but look how far away the water is now—a mile, at least."

The settlement was heartbreakingly poor, the poorest place Tamara had ever seen. It bordered a long, flat beach that had presumably been underwater once. Windmills that had pumped water to the fields now stood far from the lake, derelict, their sails turning pointlessly. A herd of skinny sheep grazed a patch of scrub, watched by a little girl with a stick in her hand. Tamara could see the lake glittering in the distance. Raffia palms and moshi bushes grew on the near shore. Low islets dotted the lake. Tamara knew that the larger islands served as hideouts for the terrorist gangs who plagued the inhabitants, stealing what little they had and beating any who tried to stop them. People who were already impoverished were made absolutely destitute.

Tab said: "What are those people doing in the lake, do you know?"

There were half a dozen women standing in the shallows, scooping the surface with bowls, and Tamara knew the answer to Tab's question. "They're skimming edible algae from the surface. We call it spirulina but their word is *dihé*. They filter it, then dry it in the sun."

"Have you tried it?"

She nodded. "It tastes awful but apparently it's nutritious. You can buy it in health food shops."

"I've never heard of it. It doesn't sound like the kind of thing that appeals to the French palate."

"You know it." Tamara opened the door and stepped out. Away from the car's air-conditioning, the atmosphere struck her like a burn. She pulled her scarf forward on her head to shade her face. Then she took a photo of the beach with her phone.

Tab got out of the car, putting a wide-brimmed

straw hat on his head, and stood beside her. The hat did not suit him—in fact it looked a bit comical—but he did not seem to care. He was well-dressed but not vain. She liked that.

They both studied the village. Among the houses were cultivated plots striped with irrigation channels. The water had to be brought a long way, Tamara realized, and she felt depressingly sure that it was the women who carried it. A man in a galabiya seemed to be selling cigarettes, chatting amiably with the men, flirting a little with the women. Tamara recognized the white packet with the gold-colored sphinx head: it identified an Egyptian brand called Cleopatra, the most popular in Africa. The cigarettes were probably smuggled or stolen. Several motorcycles and motor scooters were parked outside the houses, and one very old Volkswagen Beetle. In this country the motorcycle was the most popular form of personal transport. Tamara took more pictures.

Perspiration trickled down her sides under her clothes. She wiped her forehead with the end of her cotton headscarf. Tab took out a red handkerchief with white spots and mopped under the collar of his button-down.

"Half these houses are unoccupied," Tab said.

Tamara looked more closely and saw that some of the buildings were decaying. There were holes in the palm-leaf roofs and some of the mud bricks were crumbling away.

"Huge numbers of people have left the area," Tab said. "I guess everyone who has somewhere to go has gone. But there are millions left behind. This whole place is a disaster area."

"And it's not just here, is it?" said Tamara. "This process, desertification at the southern edge of the

Sahara, is happening all across Africa, from the Red Sea to the Atlantic Ocean."

"In French we call that region le Sahel."

"Same word in English, the Sahel." She glanced back at the car. Its engine was still turning over. "I guess Ali and Pete are going to stay in the air-conditioning."

"If they have any sense." Tab looked worried. "I don't see our man."

Tamara was worried, too. He could have been dead. But she spoke calmly. "Our instructions are that he will find us. Meanwhile we have to stay in character, so let's dip and look around."

"What?"

"Let's go and look around."

"But what did you say before? Dip?"

"Sorry. I guess it's Chicago slang."

"Now I could be the only French person who knows that expression." He grinned. "But first we should pay a courtesy call on the village elders."

"Why don't you do that? They never take any notice of a woman anyway."

"Sure."

Tab went off and Tamara walked around, trying to remain unflustered, taking pictures and talking to people in Arabic. Most villagers either cultivated a small piece of arid land or had a few sheep or a cow. One woman specialized in mending nets, but there were few fishermen left; a man owned a furnace and made pots, but not many people had any money to buy them. Everyone was more or less desperate.

A ramshackle structure of four posts holding up a network of twigs served as a clothes dryer, and a young woman was pinning up laundry, watched by a boy of about two. Her clothes were the vivid shades of orange and yellow that the people of Chad loved. She hung up

her last item, put the child on her hip, then spoke to
Tamara in careful schoolgirl French with a strong
Arabic accent and invited her into her house.

The woman's name was Kiah, her son was Naji, and
she was a widow, she said. She looked about twenty.
She was strikingly beautiful, with black eyebrows and
bold cheekbones and a curved nose, and the look in her
dark eyes suggested determination and strength. She
could be useful, Tamara thought.

She followed Kiah through the low arched doorway,
taking off her shades as she moved from the glare of the
sun into deep shadow. The inside of the hut was dim
and close and scented. Tamara felt a heavy rug under
her feet and smelled cinnamon and turmeric. As her
eyes adjusted she saw low tables, a couple of baskets for
storage, and cushions on the floor, but nothing she recognized as regular furniture, no chairs or cupboards.
To one side were two canvas palliasses for beds and a
neat pile of thick wool blankets, brightly striped in red
and blue, for the cold desert nights.

Most Americans would see this as a desperately poor
home, but Tamara knew that it was not only comfortable but a touch more affluent than the average. Kiah
looked proud as she offered a bottle of local beer called
Gala that she had cooling in a bowl of water. Tamara
thought it would be polite to accept hospitality—
and anyway she was thirsty.

A picture of the Virgin Mary in a cheap frame on
the wall indicated that Kiah was Christian, as were
some 40 percent of the people of Chad. Tamara said:
"You went to a school run by nuns, I suppose. That's
how you learned French."

"Yes."

"You speak it very well." This was not really true,
but Tamara was being nice.

Kiah invited her to sit on the rug. Before doing so,

Tamara went back to the door and glanced out nervously, screwing up her eyes against the sudden brightness. She looked toward the car. The cigarette vendor was bending down by the driver's-side window with a carton of Cleopatras in his hand. She saw Ali behind the window, his scarf wound around his head, making a contemptuous flicking-away gesture with his fingers, evidently not wanting to buy cheap cigarettes. Then the vendor said something that altered Ali's attitude dramatically. Ali jumped out of the car, looking apologetic, and opened the rear door. The vendor got into the car and Ali quickly closed the door.

So that's him, Tamara thought. Well, the disguise is certainly effective. It fooled me.

She was relieved. At least he was still alive.

She looked around. No one in the village had taken any notice of the vendor's getting into the car. He was now out of sight, hidden by the tinted windows.

Tamara nodded with satisfaction and went back inside Kiah's house.

Kiah asked her: "Is it true that all white women have seven dresses and a maid to wash a different one every day?"

Tamara decided to answer in Arabic, as Kiah's French might not be good enough. After a moment's thought she said: "Many American and European women have a lot of clothes. Exactly how many depends on whether the woman is rich or poor. Seven dresses wouldn't be unusual. A poor woman would have only two or three. A rich woman might have fifty."

"And do they all have maids?"

"Poor families don't have maids. A woman with a well-paid job, such as doctor or lawyer, will usually have someone to clean the house. Rich families have many maids. Why do you want to know all this?"

"I am thinking of going to live in France."

Tamara had guessed as much. "Tell me why."

Kiah paused, collecting her thoughts. She silently offered Tamara another bottle of beer. Tamara shook her head. She needed to stay alert.

Kiah said: "My husband, Salim, was a fisherman with his own boat. He would go out with three or four other men, and they would share the catch, but Salim took half, because it was his boat, and he knew where the fish were. That is why we were better off than most of our neighbors." She lifted her head proudly.

Tamara said: "What happened?"

"One day the jihadis came to take Salim's catch. He should have let them have it. But he had caught a Nile perch and he refused to let them take it. So they killed him and took it anyway." Kiah's composure was shaken, and her noble face twisted in grief. She paused, suppressing emotion. "His friends brought me his body."

Tamara was angered but not surprised. The jihadis were Islamist terrorists, but they were also criminal gangsters. The two things went together. And they preyed on some of the poorest people in the world. It made her mad.

Kiah went on: "When I had buried my husband I asked myself what I should do. I can't sail a boat, I can't tell where the fish are, and even if I could do both of those things the men would not accept me as their leader. So I sold the boat." She looked fierce for a moment. "Some people tried to get it for less than it's worth, but I wouldn't do business with them."

Tamara began to sense a core of steely determination within Kiah.

There was a touch of desperation in Kiah's voice as she went on: "But the money from the boat won't last forever."

Tamara knew that family was important in this country. "What about your parents?" she said.

"My parents are dead. My brothers went to Sudan—they work on a coffee plantation there. Salim had a sister, and her husband said that if I let him have my boat cheap he would always take care of me and Naji." She shrugged.

"You didn't trust him," said Tamara.

"I didn't want to sell my boat for a promise."

Determined, and no fool, Tamara thought.

Kiah added: "Now my in-laws hate me."

"So you want to go to Europe—illegally."

"People do it all the time," Kiah said.

This was true. As the desert spread southward, hundreds of thousands of desperate people left the Sahel looking for work, and many attempted the perilous journey to southern Europe.

"It's expensive," she went on, "but the money from the boat will pay my fare."

The money was not the real issue. Tamara could tell, from Kiah's voice, that she was frightened.

Kiah said: "They usually go to Italy. I can't speak Italian but I've heard that once you are in Italy you can easily go to France. Is that true?"

"Yes." Tamara was now in a hurry to get back to the car, but she felt she had to answer Kiah's questions. "You just drive across the border. Or take a train. But what you're planning is terribly dangerous. People smugglers are criminals. They may just take your money and disappear."

Kiah paused, thinking, perhaps seeking a way to explain her life to this privileged Western visitor. After a moment she said: "I know what happens when there is not enough food. I have seen it." She looked away, remembering, and her voice went quieter. "The baby gets thinner, but at first that doesn't seem too serious. Then he gets sick. It's a childhood infection such as many children catch, with spots or a runny nose or diarrhea, but the hungry child takes a long time to recover, then he gets another illness. He is tired all the time and grizzles a lot and he doesn't play much, just lies still and coughs. And then one day he closes his eyes and doesn't open them again. And sometimes the mother is too tired to weep."

Tamara looked at her through eyes full of tears. "I'm so sorry," she said. "I wish you luck."

Kiah became brisk again. "It is kind of you to answer my questions."

Tamara stood up. "I need to get going," she said awkwardly. "Thank you for the beer. And please try to find out more about the people smugglers before you give them your money."

Kiah smiled and nodded, responding politely to a platitude. She understands the need to be cautious about money better than I ever will, Tamara thought ruefully.

Tamara went outside and found Tab heading back toward the car. It was close to noon, and the villagers were no longer in sight. The livestock had found shade under makeshift shelters evidently built for that purpose.

When she stood close to Tab she noticed a light aroma of fresh sweat on clean skin, and a hint of sandalwood. She said: "He's in the car."

"Where was he hiding?"

"He was the cigarette vendor."

"He fooled me."

They reached the car and got in. The air-conditioning felt like an Arctic sea. Tamara and Tab sat on either side of the cigarette vendor, who smelled as if he had

not showered for many days. He held a carton of cigarettes in his hand.

Tamara could not contain herself. "So," she said,
"did you find Hufra?"

The cigarette vendor's name was Abdul John Haddad,
and he was twenty-five years old. He had been born in
Lebanon and raised in New Jersey, and he was an
American citizen and an officer of the Central Intelligence Agency.

Four days ago he had been in the adjacent country
of Niger, driving a battered but mechanically sound
off-road Ford up a long hill in the desert north of the
town of Maradi.

He wore thick-soled boots. They were new, but they
had been treated to look old, the uppers artificially
worn and scratched, the laces mismatched, and the
leather carefully stained to appear much used. Each
deep sole had a hidden compartment. One was for a
state-of-the-art phone, the other for a device that
picked up only one special signal. Abdul carried in his
pocket a cheap phone as a diversion.

The device was now on the seat beside him, and he
looked at it every few minutes. It confirmed that the
consignment of cocaine he had been following seemed
to have come to a halt somewhere ahead. It might
simply have stopped at an oasis where there was a gas
station. But Abdul hoped it might be at an encampment belonging to ISGS, the Islamic State in the
Greater Sahara.

The CIA was interested in terrorists more than drug
smugglers, but they were the same people in this part of
the world. A string of local groups, loosely associated

as ISGS, financed their political activities by the lucrative twin businesses of drug smuggling and people smuggling. Abdul's mission was to establish the route taken by the drugs in the hope that it would lead him to ISGS hideouts.

The man believed to be the leading figure in ISGS— and one of the worst mass murderers in the world today—was known as al-Farabi. This was almost certainly a pseudonym: al-Farabi was the name of a medieval philosopher. The ISGS leader was also called "the Afghan" because he was a veteran of the war in Afghanistan. His reach was long, if the reports were to be believed: while based in Afghanistan he had traveled through Pakistan into the rebellious Chinese province of Xinjiang, where he had made contact with the East Turkestan Independence Party, a terrorist group seeking autonomy for the ethnic Uighurs, who were predominantly Muslim.

Al-Farabi was now somewhere in North Africa, and if Abdul could find him it would strike a blow at ISGS that might even be mortal.

Abdul had studied fuzzy long-distance photographs, artists' penciled impressions, Photofit composites, and written descriptions, and he felt sure he would know al-Farabi if he saw him: a tall man with gray hair and a black beard, often described as having a piercing gaze and an air of authority. If Abdul could get close enough he might be able to confirm identification by al-Farabi's most distinctive feature: an American bullet had taken away half his left thumb, leaving a stump he often showed off proudly, telling people that God had protected him from death but at the same time warned him to be more careful.

Whatever happened, Abdul must not try to capture al-Farabi, just pin down his location and report. It was said the man had a hideout called Hufra, which meant

Hole, but its location was not known to anyone in the entire intelligence community of the West.

Abdul came to the top of the rise and slowed the car to a halt on the other side.

In front of him a long downslope led to a wide plain that shimmered in the heat. He squinted against the glare: he did not wear sunglasses, because local people thought of them as an unnecessary Western accessory, and he needed to look like one of them. In the distance, some miles away, he thought he could see a village. Turning in his seat, he removed a panel in the door and took out a pair of field glasses. Then he got out of the car.

The glasses brought the distance into sharp relief, and what he saw made his heart beat faster.

It was a settlement of tents and makeshift wooden huts. There were numerous vehicles, most of them in ramshackle shelters that would screen them from satellite cameras. Other vehicles were shrouded in covers patterned with desert camouflage, and by their shape might have been truck-mounted artillery. A few palm trees indicated a water source somewhere.

There was no mystery here. This was a paramilitary base.

And an important one, he felt. He guessed it would house several hundred men, and if he was right about the artillery, those men were formidably well armed.

This might even be the legendary Hufra.

He lifted his right foot to remove the phone from his boot so that he could take a photograph, but before he could do so he heard from behind the sound of a truck, distant but approaching fast.

Since leaving the made-up road he had seen no other traffic. This was almost certainly an ISGS vehicle heading for the encampment.

He looked around. There was nowhere to hide himself,

let alone a car. For three weeks he had risked being spotted by the people he was spying on, and now it was about
to happen.

He had his story ready. All he could do was tell it
and hope.

He looked at his cheap watch. It was now two o'clock
in the afternoon. He figured the jihadis might be less
likely to kill a man at his prayers.

He moved quickly. He returned the binoculars to
their hiding place behind the door panel. He opened
the trunk and took out an old, worn prayer rug, then
slammed the lid and spread the rug on the ground. He
had been raised Christian, but he knew enough about
Muslim prayer to fake it.

The second prayer of the day was called zuhr and
was said after the sun passed its zenith, which could be
stretched to mean any time from midday to midafternoon. He prostrated himself in the correct position,
touching the rug with his nose, hands, knees, and toes.
He closed his eyes.

The truck roared closer, laboring up the slope on the
far side of the ridge.

Abdul suddenly remembered the device. It was on
the passenger seat. He cursed: it would give him away
instantly.

He jumped to his feet, flung open the passenger-side
door, and snatched up the device. With a two-fingered
grip he released the catch of the hidden drawer in the
sole of his left boot. In his haste he dropped the device
onto the sand. He picked it up and lodged it in the
shoe. He closed the compartment and hurried back to
the rug.

He knelt down again.

Out of the corner of his eye he saw the truck climb
the rise and come to a sudden stop alongside his car.
He closed his eyes.

He did not know the prayers by heart, but he had heard them often enough to mumble an approximation.

He heard the doors of the truck open and close, then heavy footsteps approaching.

A voice said in Arabic: "Get up."

Abdul opened his eyes. There were two men. One held a rifle, the other had a holstered pistol. Behind them was a pickup truck loaded with sacks that might have been full of flour—food for the jihadis, no doubt.

The one with the rifle was younger, with a wispy beard. He wore camouflage trousers and a blue anorak that would have been more suited to a rainy day in New York. He said harshly: "Who are you?"

Abdul quickly assumed the hail-fellow-well-met persona of a traveling salesman. He smiled and said: "My friends, why do you disturb a man at prayer?" He spoke fluent colloquial Arabic with a Lebanese accent: he had lived in Beirut until age six and his parents had continued to use Arabic at home after they moved to the USA.

The man with the pistol had graying hair. He spoke calmly. "We ask God's forgiveness for interrupting your devotions," he said. "But what are you doing here, on this desert track? Where are you going?"

"I'm selling cigarettes," Abdul said. "Would you like to buy some? They're half price." In most African countries a pack of twenty Cleopatras cost the equivalent, in local currency, of a dollar. Abdul sold them for half that.

The younger man threw open the trunk of Abdul's car. It was full of cartons of Cleopatras. "Where did you get them?" he said.

"From a Sudanese army captain called Bilel." It was a plausible story: everyone knew the Sudanese officers were corrupt.

There was a silence. The older jihadi looked thoughtful. The younger man looked as if he could hardly wait to use his rifle, and Abdul wondered if he had ever before fired it at a human being. But the older man was less tense. He would be slower to shoot but more accurate.

Abdul knew that his life was at stake. These two would either believe him or try to kill him. If it came to a fight, he would go for the older man first. The younger one would fire, but he would probably miss. Then again, at this range he might not.

The older man said: "But why are you here? Where do you think you're going?"

"There's a village up ahead, isn't there?" said Abdul. "I can't see it yet, but a man in a café told me I would find customers there."

"A man in a café."

"I'm always looking for customers."

The older man said to the younger: "Search him."

The young man slung his rifle across his back, which gave Abdul a moment's relief. But the older man drew a nine-millimeter pistol and pointed it at Abdul's head while Abdul was patted down.

The young man found Abdul's cheap phone and handed it to his companion.

The older man turned it on and pressed buttons confidently. Abdul guessed he was looking at the contact directory and the list of recent calls. What he found would support Abdul's cover: cheap hotels, car repair workshops, currency changers, and a couple of hookers.

The older man said: "Search the car."

Abdul stood watching. The man began with the open trunk. He picked up Abdul's small traveling bag and emptied its contents onto the road. There was not much: a towel, a Koran, a few simple toiletries, a phone charger. He threw all the cigarettes out and lifted the floor panel to reveal the spare wheel and the tool kit. Without replacing anything, he opened the rear doors. He thrust his hands between the back and the flat of the seats and bent to peer underneath.

In the front he looked under the dashboard, inside the glove box, and into the door pockets. He noticed the loose panel in the driver's door and removed it. "Binoculars," he said triumphantly, and Abdul felt a chill of fear. Binoculars were not as incriminating as a gun, but they were costly, and why would a vendor of cigarettes need them?

"Very useful in the desert," Abdul said, beginning to feel desperate. "You're probably carrying a pair yourselves."

"These look expensive." The older man examined the glasses. "'Made in Kunming,'" he read. "They're Chinese."

"Exactly," said Abdul. "I got them from the Sudanese captain who sold me the cigarettes. They were a bargain."

Again his story was plausible. The Sudanese Armed Forces bought a lot from China, which was their country's biggest trading partner. Much of the equipment ended up on the black market.

The older man said shrewdly: "Were you using these when we came along?"

"I was going to, after my prayers. I wanted to know how big the village is. What do you think—fifty people? A hundred?" It was a deliberate underestimate, to give the impression that he had not looked.

"Never mind," said the man. "You're not going there." He gave Abdul a long, hard stare, probably making up his mind whether to believe Abdul or kill him. Suddenly he said: "Where's your gun?"

"Gun? I have no gun." Abdul did not carry one.

Firearms got an undercover officer into trouble more
often than they got him out, and here was a dramatic
example. If a weapon had been found now, they would
have felt sure Abdul was not an innocent vendor of cigarettes.

"Open the hood," the older man said to the younger.

He obeyed. As Abdul knew, there was nothing
hidden in the engine compartment. "All clear," he reported.

"You don't seem very scared," the older man said to
Abdul. "You can see we're jihadis. We might decide to
kill you."

Abdul stared back but allowed himself to tremble
slightly.

The man nodded, making a decision, and handed
the cheap phone back to Abdul. "Turn your car around,"
he said. "Go back the way you came."

Abdul decided not to look too relieved. "But I was
hoping to sell—" He pretended to think better of his
protest. "Would you like a carton?"

"As a gift?"

Abdul was tempted to agree, but the character he
was playing would not have been so generous. "I'm a
poor man," he said. "I'm sorry. . . ."

"Go back," the jihadi repeated.

Abdul gave a disappointed shrug, pretending to
give up hope of sales. "As you wish," he said.

The man beckoned his comrade, and the two of
them returned to the truck.

Abdul began to pick up his scattered possessions.

The truck roared away.

He watched it disappear into the desert. Then at last
he spoke, in English. "Jesus, Mary, and Joseph," he
breathed. "That was close."

Tamara had joined the CIA because of people like Kiah.

With all her heart she believed in freedom, democracy, and justice, but those values were under attack all around the world, and Kiah was one of the victims. Tamara knew that the things she cherished had to be fought for. She often thought of the words of a traditional song: "If I should die and my soul gets lost, it's nobody's fault but mine." Everybody was responsible. It was a gospel song, and Tamara was Jewish, but the message was for everyone.

Here in North Africa, American forces were fighting against terrorists whose values were violence, bigotry, and fear. The armed gangs associated with the Islamic State murdered, kidnapped, and raped Africans whose religion or ethnicity did not meet with the approval of fundamentalist warlords. Their violence, plus the southward creep of the Sahara Desert, was driving people like Kiah to risk their lives crossing the Mediterranean in inflatable dinghies.

The US Army, allied with the French and with national armies, attacked and destroyed terrorist encampments whenever they could find them.

Finding them was the problem.

The Sahara Desert was the size of the United States. And that was where Tamara came in. The CIA cooperated with other nations to provide intelligence for attacking armies. Tab was attached to the European Union mission but was in truth an officer of the DGSE, the Direction Générale de la Sécurité Extérieure, which was the French CIA. Abdul was a part of the same effort.

So far the project had had little impact. The jihadis continued to ravage much of North Africa more or less freely.

Tamara was hoping Abdul would change that.

She had never met him before, though she had spoken to him on the phone. However, this was not the first time the CIA had sent an undercover agent to spy out ISGS camps. Tamara had known Abdul's predecessor, Omar. She had been the one who discovered Omar's body, a corpse without hands or feet dumped in the desert. She had found the missing hands and feet a hundred yards away. That was how far the dying man had crawled on his elbows and knees while he bled to death. Tamara knew she would never get over that.

And now Abdul was following in Omar's footsteps.

He had been in touch intermittently, whenever he could get a phone signal. Then, two days ago, he had called to say he had arrived in Chad and had some good news that he would report in person. He had requested some supplies and given precise directions to this location.

And now they knew what he had been doing.

Tamara was electrified but keeping her excitement under control. "It might be Hufra," she said. "Even if not, it's a fantastic discovery. Five hundred men, with truck-mounted artillery? It's a major establishment!"

Abdul said: "When will you move?"

"Two days, three at the most," she said. The armed forces of the United States, France, and Niger would flatten the encampment. They would burn the tents and huts, confiscate the weapons, and interrogate any jihadis who survived the battle. In a matter of days the wind would blow away the ashes, the sun would bleach the garbage, and the desert would begin to reconquer the area.

And Africa would be a bit safer for people like Kiah and Naji.

Abdul gave precise directions to the encampment.

Both Tamara and Tab had notebooks on their knees and wrote down everything he said. Tamara was awestruck. She could hardly digest the fact that she was talking to a man who had taken such risks with his own life and achieved such a coup. As he talked, and she made notes, she took every chance of studying him. He had dark skin and a trim black beard and unusual light brown eyes that had a flinty look. His face was taut with strain, and he appeared older than twenty-five. He was tall and broad shouldered: she recalled that while attending the State University of New York he had been a mixed-martial-arts fighter.

It seemed strange that he was also the vendor of cigarettes. That man had been easygoing, garrulous, talking to everyone, touching the men on the arm, winking at the women, lighting everyone's cigarettes with a red plastic lighter. This man, by contrast, was quietly dangerous. She felt a bit afraid of him.

He gave full details of the route followed by the consignment of cocaine. It had passed through the hands of several gangs and had been transferred to different vehicles three times. As well as the paramilitary base, he had located two smaller encampments and several city addresses for ISGS groups.

"This is gold dust," Tab said. Tamara agreed. The results were more than she had hoped for, and she felt jubilant.

"Good," said Abdul briskly. "Did you bring my stuff?"

"Of course." He had asked for money in local currencies, pills for the gastric ailments that often afflicted visitors to North Africa, a simple compass—and one thing that had puzzled her: a yard of narrow-gauge titanium wire, fixed to wooden handles at each end, the whole ensemble sewn inside a cotton sash of the type worn by men as a belt around a traditional robe. She wondered if he would explain that.

She handed everything over. He thanked her but made no comment. He looked around, studying the view in every direction. "All clear," he said. "Are we done?"

Tamara looked at Tab, who said: "All done."

Tamara said: "Have you got everything you need, Abdul?"

"Yes." He opened the car door.

"Good luck," said Tamara. It was a heartfelt wish.

Tab said: "Bonne chance."

Abdul pulled his scarf forward to shade his face, then got out, closed the door, and walked back into the village, the carton of Cleopatras still in his hand.

Tamara watched him go and noticed his gait. He did not stride out the way most American men would, as if they owned the place. Instead he adopted the desert shuffle, keeping his face down and shaded, using minimum effort to avoid generating heat.

She was awestruck by his courage. She shuddered to think what would happen to him if he were caught. Beheading would be the best he could hope for.

When he had disappeared from sight she leaned forward and spoke to Ali. "Yalla," she said. Let's go.

The car left the village and followed the track to the road, where it turned south, heading back to N'Djamena.

Tab was reading his notes. "This is amazing," he said.

"We should do a joint report," Tamara said, thinking ahead.

"Good plan. Let's write it together when we get back, then we can submit it in two languages simultaneously."

They seemed to work together well, she thought. A lot of men would have tried to take charge this morning.

But Tab had not tried to dominate the conversation. She was beginning to like him.

She closed her eyes. Slowly her elation subsided. She had gotten up early, and the drive home would take two to three hours. For a while she just saw visions of the nameless village they had visited: the mud-brick homes, the pathetic vegetable gardens, the long walk to the water. But the drone of the car's engine and the tire noise reminded her of long trips in her childhood, driving in the family Chevrolet from Chicago to St. Louis to see her grandparents, slumping next to her brother in the wide backseat, and eventually, now as then, she dozed.

She fell into a deep sleep and was startled awake when the car braked sharply. She heard Tab say: "Putain," which was the French equivalent of "Fuck." She saw that the road ahead was obstructed by a truck parked sideways. Around it were half a dozen men wearing odd articles of army uniform mixed with traditional garments: a military tunic with a cotton headdress, a long robe over army pants.

They were paramilitaries, and they all had firearms.

Ali was forced to stop the car.

Tamara said: "What the hell?"

Tab said: "This is what the government calls an informal roadblock. They're retired or serving soldiers making money on the side. It's a shakedown."

Tamara had heard of informal roadblocks but this was her first experience of one. She said: "What's the price?"

"We're about to find out."

One of the paramilitaries approached the driver's window, yelling fiercely. Ali rolled down his window and yelled back in dialect. Pete picked up his carbine from the floor but kept it low in his lap. The man at the window waved his gun in the air.

Tab seemed calm, but to Tamara this looked like an explosive situation.

An older man in an army cap and a denim shirt with holes in it pointed a rifle at the windshield.

Pete responded by bringing his carbine to his shoulder.

Tab said: "Easy, Pete."

"I won't fire first," Pete said.

Tab reached over the back of the seat into the rear of the car and pulled a T-shirt out of a cardboard box. Then he got out of the car.

Tamara said anxiously: "What are you doing?"

Tab did not answer.

He walked forward, with several guns trained on him, and Tamara put her fist in her mouth.

But Tab did not seem scared. He approached the denim shirt, who pointed his rifle straight at Tab's chest.

Speaking Arabic, Tab said: "Good day to you, Captain. I am with these foreigners today." He was pretending to be some kind of guide or escort. "Please allow them to pass." Then he turned back to the car and shouted, still in Arabic: "Don't shoot! Don't shoot! These are my brothers!" Switching to English, he shouted: "Pete, lower the gun."

Reluctantly Pete moved the rifle butt from his shoulder and held the gun diagonally across his chest.

After a pause, the denim shirt lowered his rifle.

Tab handed the T-shirt to the man, who unfolded it. It was dark blue with a red-and-white vertical stripe, and after a moment's thought Tamara figured it was the uniform shirt of Paris Saint-Germain, the most popular soccer team in France. The man beamed delightedly.

Tamara had wondered why Tab had brought that cardboard box with him. Now she knew.

The man took off his old shirt and pulled the new one over his head.

The atmosphere changed. The soldiers crowded around, admiring the shirt, then looked expectantly at Tab. Tab turned to the car and said: "Tamara, pass me the box, please?"

She reached into the rear and picked up the box, then handed it through the open car door. Tab gave them all a shirt.

The soldiers all looked thrilled and several of them put the shirts on.

Tab shook the hand of the man he had called "Captain," saying: "Ma'a as-salaama," good-bye. He returned to the car with the nearly empty box, got in, slammed the door, and said: "Go, Ali, but slowly."

The car crept forward. The happy gangsters waved Ali to a prepared route along the verge of the road, skirting the parked truck. On the far side Ali steered back to the road.

As soon as the tires touched the concrete surface, Ali floored the pedal and the car roared away from the roadblock.

Tab put his box into the rear.

Tamara let out a long breath of relief. She turned to Tab and said: "You were so cool! Weren't you scared?"

He shook his head. "They're scary, but they don't usually kill people."

"Good to know," said Tamara.

CHAPTER 2

Four weeks earlier Abdul had been two thousand miles away in the lawless West African country of Guinea-Bissau, classified a narco state by the United Nations. It was a hot, wet place with a monsoon season that poured and dripped and steamed for half the year.

Abdul had been in the capital city, Bissau. He was in an apartment with a room overlooking the docks. There was no air-conditioning, and his shirt clung to his sweaty skin.

His companion was Phil Doyle, twenty years older, a senior officer of the CIA, a bald guy in a baseball cap. Doyle was based at the American embassy in Cairo, Egypt, and was in charge of Abdul's mission.

Both men were using binoculars. The room was in darkness. If they should be spotted they would be tortured and killed. By the light coming in from outside Abdul could just about make out the furniture around him: a sofa, a coffee table, a TV set.

Their glasses were focused on a waterfront scene. Three stevedores were working hard and sweating copiously, stripped to the waist under arc lights. They were unloading a container, lifting big sacks made of heavy-duty polythene and transferring them to a panel van.

Abdul spoke in a low voice even though there was no one other than Doyle to hear him. "How much do those sacks weigh?"

"Twenty kilos," said Doyle. He spoke with a clipped Boston accent. "Forty-five pounds, near as damn it."

"Hard work in this weather."

"In any weather."

Abdul frowned. "I can't read what's printed on the sacks."

"It says: 'Caution—dangerous chemicals,' in several languages."

"You've seen those sacks before."

Doyle nodded. "I watched them being loaded into that container by the gang that controls the Colombian port of Buenaventura. I tracked them across the Atlantic. From here on, they're yours."

"I guess the label's not wrong: pure cocaine is a very dangerous chemical."

"Bet your ass."

The van was not large enough to take all the contents of a full-size container, but Abdul guessed that the cocaine had been a part load, perhaps concealed within a hidden compartment.

The work was being supervised by a big man in a dress shirt who kept counting and recounting the sacks. There were also three black-clad guards carrying assault rifles. A limousine waited nearby, its engine idling. Every few minutes the stevedores stopped to drink from giant plastic bottles of soda pop. Abdul wondered whether they had any conception of the value of the cargo they were handling. He guessed not. The man who kept counting did, though. And so did whoever was in the limo.

Doyle said: "Inside three of those sacks are minia-
ture radio transmitters—three, just in case one or two
sacks get stolen or otherwise removed from the consignment." He took from his pocket a small black
device. "You switch them on remotely with this gizmo.
The screen tells you how far away they are and in what
direction. Don't forget to switch off, to save the batteries in the transmitters. You could do all that with a
phone, but you're going to places where there's no connectivity, so it has to be a radio signal."

"Got it."

"You can follow at a distance, but you'll have to get
close sometimes. Your mission is to identify the people
who handle the consignment and the places it goes.
Those people are terrorists, and the places are their
hideouts. We need to know how many jihadis are in a
place and how well armed they are, so that our forces
know what to expect when they go in there to wipe the
bastards out."

"Don't worry, I'll get close enough."

They were silent for a minute or two, then Doyle
said: "I guess your family doesn't really know what
you do."

"I have no family," Abdul said. "Both my parents
are dead, and my sister." He pointed at the waterfront
scene. "They've finished."

The stevedores closed up the container and the
truck, banging the metal doors cheerfully, clearly seeing
no reason to be surreptitious, having no fear of the
police, who were undoubtedly well bribed. They lit cigarettes and stood around, talking and laughing. The
guards shouldered their weapons and joined in the
conversation.

The driver of the limo got out and opened the passenger door. The man who emerged from the backseat
was dressed as if to go to a nightclub, with a T-shirt

under a tuxedo jacket that had a gold design on the back. He spoke to the man in the dress shirt, then they both took out their phones.

Doyle said: "Right now the money's being transferred from one Swiss bank account to another."

"How much?"

"Something like twenty million dollars."

Abdul was surprised. "Even more than I thought."

"It will be worth double that when it gets to Tripoli, double again in Europe, and double again on the street."

The phone calls ended and the two men shook hands. The one in the tux reached back into his car and drew out a plastic bag marked DUBAI DUTY FREE in English and Arabic. It appeared to be full of banknotes packed in banded bricks. He handed a brick to each of the three stevedores and three guards. The men were all smiles: clearly they were being paid well. Finally he opened the trunk of his car and gave each of them a carton of Cleopatra cigarettes—a kind of bonus, Abdul supposed.

The man disappeared into his limo and it drove off. The stevedores and the guards drifted away. The truck full of cocaine departed.

Abdul said: "I'm out of here."

Doyle held out his hand and Abdul shook it.

"You're a brave man," said Doyle. "Good luck."

For days Kiah agonized over her conversation with the white woman.

As a little girl Kiah had imagined that all European women were nuns, since nuns were the only white women she ever saw. The first time she had come across an ordinary French woman, wearing a knee-length dress and stockings and carrying a handbag, she had been as shocked as if she had met a ghost.

But she was used to them now, and she instinctively trusted Tamara, who had a frank, open face with no hint of guile.

She understood now that wealthy European women did man-type jobs and so did not have time to clean their own houses, so they paid maids, from Chad and other poor countries, to do the housework. Kiah was reassured. There was a role for her in France, a life she could live, a way she could feed her child.

Kiah was not sure why rich women would want to be lawyers and doctors. Why did they not spend their days playing with their children and talking to their friends? She still had much to learn about Europeans. But she knew the most important fact, that they wanted to employ migrants from Africa.

By contrast, what Tamara had said about people smugglers had been the opposite of reassuring. She had looked horrified. And this was what was causing Kiah to agonize. She could not deny the logic of what Tamara had said. She was planning to put herself in the hands of criminals: why would they not rob her?

She had a few minutes to reflect on these questions while Naji was taking his afternoon nap. She gazed at him now, naked on a cotton sheet, sleeping in tranquility, oblivious to care. She had not loved her parents or even her husband as much as she loved her son. Her feelings for Naji had overwhelmed all other emotions and taken control of her life. But love was not enough. He needed food and water, and clothes to protect his soft skin from the burning sun. And it was up to her to provide for his needs. But she would be risking his life too in the desert. And he was so little, and weak, and trusting.

She needed help. She could go on this dangerous

journey, but not alone. With a friend, perhaps she could manage.

As she watched Naji he opened his eyes. He did not wake slowly, as adults did, but all at once. He got to his feet, toddled to Kiah, and said: "Leben." He loved this dish, cooked rice with buttermilk, and she always gave him a little after his nap.

While feeding him she decided to speak to her second cousin Yusuf. He was her own age and lived in the next village, a couple of miles away, with his wife and a daughter the same age as Naji. Yusuf was a shepherd, but most of his flock had died for lack of grazing, and now he too was thinking of migrating before all his savings were spent. She wanted to talk over the problems with him. If he decided to go, she could travel with him and his family and feel a lot safer.

By the time Kiah had dressed Naji it was midafternoon, and the sun was past its height. She set off with the child on her hip. She was strong and could still carry him for considerable distances, but she was not sure how long that would continue. Sooner or later he would be too heavy, and when he had to walk, their progress would be slower.

She followed the shore along the edge of the lake, shifting Naji from one hip to the other every few minutes. Now that the heat of the day was over, people were working again: fishermen mending nets and sharpening knives, children herding goats and sheep, women fetching water in traditional jars and big plastic demijohns.

Like everyone else, Kiah kept an eye on the lake, for there was no knowing when the jihadis might get hungry and come to steal meat and flour and salt. They sometimes even kidnapped girls, especially Christian girls. Kiah touched the little silver cross on a chain that she wore under her dress.

After an hour she came to a village like her own

except that it had a row of six concrete houses, built in better times and now crumbling but still inhabited.

Yusuf's house was like hers, made of mud bricks and palm leaves. She paused at the door and called: "Anybody home?"

Yusuf recognized her voice and replied: "Come in, Kiah."

He was sitting cross-legged, mending a puncture in a bicycle tire, gluing a patch over a hole in the inner tube. He was a small man with a cheerful face, not as domineering as some husbands. He smiled broadly: he was always pleased to see Kiah.

His wife, Azra, was breast-feeding their baby. Her smile was not quite so welcoming. She had a thin face with a pinched look, but that was not the only reason she looked forbidding. The truth was that Yusuf was a little too fond of his cousin Kiah. Since the death of Salim, Yusuf had assumed a protective air that involved his touching her hand and putting his arm around her more often than was necessary. Kiah suspected that he would like to be married to her as well as Azra, and Azra probably shared that suspicion. Polygamy was legal in Chad, and millions of Christian and Muslim women were in polygamous marriages.

Kiah had done nothing to encourage this behavior by Yusuf, but nor had she rejected him, for she really did need protection and he was her only male relative in Chad. Now she worried that this triangular tension could threaten her plans.

Yusuf offered her a drink from a stone jar of sheep's milk. He poured some into a bowl and she shared it with Naji. "I talked to a foreigner last week," she said while Naji slurped from the bowl. "A white American woman who came asking about the shrinking of the lake. I questioned her about Europe."

"That was smart," said Yusuf. "What did she tell you?"

"She said the people smugglers are criminals and they might rob us."

Yusuf shrugged. "We could be robbed right here by the jihadis."

Azra put in: "But it's easier to rob people out there in the desert. You can just leave them to die."

"You're right," Yusuf said to his wife. "I'm just saying there's danger everywhere. We'll die here if we don't leave."

Yusuf was being dismissive, which suited Kiah's purpose. She reinforced his words by saying: "We'd be safer together, the five of us."

"Of course," said Yusuf. "I will take care of everybody."

That was not what Kiah had meant, but she did not contradict him. "Exactly," she said.

He said: "I have heard that in Three Palms there is a man called Hakim." Three Palms was a small town ten miles away. "They say Hakim can take people all the way to Italy."

Kiah's pulse quickened. She had not known about Hakim. This news meant that escape could be closer than she had imagined. The prospect suddenly became more real—and more frightening. She said: "The white woman I met told me you can easily go from Italy to France."

Azra's baby, Danna, had drunk enough. Azra wiped the child's chin with her sleeve and set her on her feet. Danna toddled to Naji and the two began to play side by side. Azra picked up a small jar of oil and rubbed a little on her nipples, then adjusted the bodice of her dress. She said: "How much money does this Hakim want?"

Yusuf said: "The usual price is two thousand American dollars."

"Per person, or per family?" Azra asked.

"I don't know."

"And do you have to pay for babies?"

"It probably depends on whether they're big enough to need a seat."

Kiah scorned arguments without facts. "I will go to Three Palms and ask him," she said impatiently. In any case she wanted to see Hakim with her own eyes, speak to him, and get a sense of what kind of man he was. She could walk ten miles there and ten miles back in a day.

Azra said: "Leave Naji with me. You can't carry him all that way."

Kiah thought she probably could, if she had to, but she said: "Thank you. That would be a great help." She and Azra often babysat one another's children. Naji loved coming here. He liked to watch what Danna did and imitate her.

Yusuf said brightly: "Now that you've walked this far, you might as well spend the night with us, and get an early start."

It was a sensible idea, but Yusuf was a little too keen on sleeping in the same room as Kiah, and she saw a frown briefly cross Azra's face. "No, thank you, I need to go home," she said tactfully. "But I'll bring Naji first thing in the morning." She got up and lifted her son. "Thank you for the milk," she said. "God be with you until tomorrow."

Filling station stops took longer in Chad than in the States. People were not in such a hurry to get in and out and back on the road. They checked their tires, put oil in their engines, and topped up their radiators. They needed to be cautious: you could wait days for roadside recovery. A gas station was also a social place. Drivers talked to the proprietor and to one another, exchanging news about roadblocks, military convoys, jihadi bandits, and sandstorms.

Abdul and Tamara had agreed on a rendezvous on the road between N'Djamena and Lake Chad. Abdul wanted to talk to her a second time before he headed into the desert and he preferred not to use phones or messaging if he could avoid it.

He reached the gas station ahead of her and sold a whole box of Cleopatras to the owner. He had the hood of his car up, and was putting water into the windshield washer reservoir, when another car pulled in. A local man was driving it but Tamara was the passenger. In this country embassy staff never traveled alone, especially if they were women.

At first sight she might have been taken for a local woman, Abdul thought as she got out of the car. She had dark hair and eyes, and she wore a long-sleeved dress over trousers plus a headscarf. However, a careful observer would know she was American by the confident way she walked, the level gaze she directed at him, and the way she addressed him as an equal.

Abdul smiled. She was attractive and charming. His interest in her was not romantic—he had been soured on romance a couple of years ago and he had not yet gotten over it—but he liked her joie de vivre.

He looked around. The office was a mud-brick hut where the proprietor sold food and water. A pickup truck was just leaving. There was no one else.

All the same he and Tamara played it safe and pretended not to know each other. She stood with her back to him as her driver filled his tank. She said quietly: "Yesterday we raided the encampment you discovered in Niger. The military men are kvelling: they destroyed the camp, captured tons of weaponry, and took prisoners for interrogation."

"But did they capture al-Farabi?"

"No."

"So the camp wasn't Hufra."

"The prisoners call it al-Bustan."

"The Garden," Abdul translated.

"It's still a great prize, and you're the hero of the hour."

Abdul had no interest in being a hero. He was looking ahead. "I need to change my tactics," he said.

"Okay . . . ," she said dubiously.

"It's going to become difficult for me to stay out of sight. The route now will be north across the Sahara to Tripoli, and from there over the Mediterranean to the nightclubs of Europe. Between here and the coast it's pretty much all naked desert, with little traffic."

Tamara nodded. "So the driver is more likely to notice you."

"You know what it's like out here: no smoke, no mist, no pollution—on a clear day you can see for miles. On top of that I'll have to stop overnight at the same oases as the vehicle with the consignment— there's never a choice in the desert. And most of those places are small, too small for me to hide. I'm bound to be spotted."

"We've got a problem," Tamara said worriedly.

"Fortunately, a solution has presented itself. In the last couple of days the consignment has been transferred again, this time to a bus that carries illegal migrants. This is not unusual—the two kinds of smuggling fit together well, and both are lucrative."

"It could still be difficult for you to track the vehicle without arousing suspicion."

"That's why I'm going to be on the bus."

"You'll travel as one of the migrants?"

"That's my plan."

Tamara said: "It's clever."

Abdul was not sure how Phil Doyle and the higher-ups in the CIA would take the news. But there was little they could do about it. The officer in the field had to act as he thought best.

Tamara asked a practical question. "What will you do with your car and all those cigarettes?"

"Sell them," he said. "Someone will be keen to take over the business. And I won't be holding out for a high price."

"We could sell the stuff for you."

"No, thanks, it's better this way. I should stay in character. The sale will explain how I got the money to pay the people smugglers. It reinforces my cover story."

"Good point."

"One more thing," he said. "More or less by accident I came across a useful asset. He's a disillusioned terrorist in Kousséri, Cameroon, just across the bridge from N'Djamena. He's in the loop, and he's willing to pass information to us. You should try him out."

Tamara said: "Disillusioned?"

"He's an idealistic young man who has seen too much senseless killing to believe in jihad any longer. You don't need to know his name, but he'll call himself Haroun."

"How do I contact him?"

"He'll get in touch with you. The message will mention a number—eight kilometers, or fifteen dollars—and the number will be the time he wants to meet you by the twenty-four-hour clock, so fifteen dollars would mean three p.m. The place of the first meeting will be Le Grand Marché." Tamara knew it—everyone did. It was the central market in the capital city. "At the first meeting you can agree on the location for the second."

"The market is huge," Tamara said. "Hundreds of people of all races. How will we know one another?"

Abdul reached inside his galabiya and pulled out a blue scarf with a distinctive pattern of orange circles. "Wear this," he said. "He'll recognize it."

Tamara took the scarf. "Thank you."

"You're welcome." Abdul's mind returned to the raid on al-Bustan. "I assume the prisoners have been questioned about al-Farabi."

"They've all heard about him, but only one claimed to have seen him in the flesh. He confirmed the usual description—gray hair, black beard, amputated thumb. The prisoner had been part of a group in Mali that was trained by al-Farabi in how to make roadside bombs."

Abdul nodded. "I'm afraid that's highly credible. From what little we know, it seems al-Farabi isn't interested in getting all the African jihadis to work together—he probably thinks they're more secure as disparate groups, and he would be right about that. But he does want to teach them to kill more people more efficiently. He gained a lot of technical expertise in Afghanistan and now he's sharing it, hence the training course."

"A smart guy."

Abdul said bitterly: "That's why we can't catch him."

"He can't hide from us forever."

"I sure as hell hope not."

Tamara turned around to face him. She stared, as if trying to understand something.

He said: "What?"

"You really feel this."

"Don't you?"

"Not the way you do." She held his gaze. "Something happened to you. What was it?"

"They warned me about you," he said, but he was smiling gently. "They said you could be a bit blunt."

"I'm sorry," she said. "I've been told I ask overly personal questions. You're not angry?"

"You'll have to work harder than that to offend me." He closed the hood. "I'm going to pay the man."

He strolled over to the hut. Tamara was right. For him this was not a job, it was a mission. It was not enough for him merely to damage ISGS, as he had with the intelligence on al-Bustan. He wanted to wipe them out. Completely.

He paid for the gas. "You need some cigarettes?" the proprietor joked. "Very cheap!"

"I don't smoke," said Abdul.

Tamara's driver came into the hut as he was leaving. Abdul returned to his car. For a couple of minutes he had her to himself. She had asked a good question, he thought. She deserved an answer.

He said: "My sister died."

He was six years old, almost a man, he thought, and she was still a baby, at four. Beirut was the only world he knew then: heat and dust and traffic, and bomb-damaged buildings spilling rubble into the street. It was not until later that he learned Beirut was not normal, that that was not how life was for most people.

They lived in an apartment over a café. In the bed-room at the back of the building, Abdul was telling Nura about reading and writing. They were sitting on the floor. She wanted to know everything he knew, and he liked instructing her, for it made him feel wise and grown-up.

Their parents were in the living room, which was in the front of the building, overlooking the street. Their grandparents had come for coffee, two uncles and an aunt had shown up, and Abdul's father, who was the pastry chef for the café, had made halawet el-jibn, sweet cheese rolls, for the guests. Abdul had already

eaten two and his mother had said: "No more, you'll
be sick."

So he told Nura to go and get some.

She hurried out, always eager to please him.

The bang was the loudest noise Abdul had ever
heard. Immediately afterward the world went completely silent, and there seemed to be something wrong
with his ears. He started crying.

He ran into the living room, but it was a place he
had never seen. It took him a long time to understand
that the entire outside wall had vanished, and the room
was open to the air. It was full of dust and the smell of
blood. Some of the grown-ups looked as if they were
screaming, but they made no noise; in fact there was no
sound at all. Others lay on the floor, not moving.

Nura too lay motionless.

Abdul could not understand what was wrong with
her. He knelt down, grabbed her limp arm, and shook
her, trying to wake her, though it seemed impossible
that she was sleeping with her eyes wide open. "Nura,"
he said. "Nura, wake up." He could hear his own voice,
albeit faintly; his ears must have been getting better.

Suddenly his mother was there, scooping Nura up
in her arms. A second later Abdul felt himself lifted by
the familiar hands of his father. The parents carried
the two children into the bedroom and put them down
gently on their beds.

Father said: "Abdul, how do you feel? Are you hurt?"

Abdul shook his head.

"No bruises?" Father ran a careful eye over him and
looked relieved. Then he turned to Mother and they
both stared at the still form of Nura.

Mother said: "I don't think she's breathing." She
began to sob.

Abdul said: "What's the matter with her?" His voice

came out as a high-pitched squeak. He felt very scared but he did not know what he was frightened of. He said: "She doesn't speak, but her eyes are open!"

His father hugged him. "Oh, Abdul, my beloved son," he said. "I think our little girl is dead."

It was a car bomb, Abdul learned years later. The vehicle had been parked at the curb immediately under the living room window. The target was the café, which was patronized by Americans, who loved its sweet pastries. Abdul's family was merely collateral damage.

Responsibility was never established.

The family managed to move to the United States, which was difficult but not impossible. Father's cousin had a Lebanese restaurant in Newark, and Father was guaranteed a job there. Abdul went to school on a yellow bus, muffled in scarves against unimaginably cold weather, and found that he could not understand a word anyone said. But Americans were kind to children, and they helped him, and soon he could speak English better than his parents.

Mother told him he might get another baby sister, but the years went by and it never happened.

The past was vivid in his mind as he drove through the dunes. America had not looked so different from Beirut—it had traffic jams and apartment buildings, cafés and cops—but the Sahara really was an alien landscape, with its scorched and thorny bushes dying of thirst in the barren ground.

Three Palms was a small town. It had a mosque and a church, a filling station with a repair shop, and half a dozen stores. All the signs were in Arabic except the one that said ÉGLISE DE SAINT PIERRE, Church of St.

Peter. There were no streets in desert villages, but here the houses were built in rows, with blank outside walls that turned the dusty dirt roads into corridors. Despite the narrowness of the streets, cars were parked along the sides. In the center, next to the gas station, was a café where men sat drinking coffee and smoking in the shade of three unusually tall fan palms, and Abdul guessed the trees had given the town its name. The bar was a makeshift lean-to at the front of a house, its palm-leaf canopy unsteadily supported by thin tree trunks roughly trimmed.

He parked his car and checked his tracking device. The consignment of cocaine was still in the same place, a few yards from where he stood.

He got out, smelling coffee. He took several cartons of Cleopatras from the trunk. Then he went to the café and switched into salesman mode.

He sold some single packets before the proprietor of the café, a fat man with a huge mustache, complained. After Abdul had worked his charm, the man bought a carton and then brought Abdul a cup of coffee. Abdul sat at a table under the palms; sipped the strong, bitter coffee already dosed with sugar; and said: "I need to speak to a man called Hakim. Do you know him?"

"It's a common name," the proprietor said evasively, but the way he glanced reflexively at the garage next door was a pantomime giveaway.

Abdul replied: "He is a man of great respect." This was code for an important criminal.

"I will ask one or two people."

A couple of minutes later the proprietor strolled, with a casual air that was not very convincing, to the repair garage. Soon afterward an overweight young man emerged from the garage and walked toward Abdul. He shuffled like a pregnant woman, with his feet splayed, knees apart, belly forward, and head back.

He had curly black hair and a vain little mustache but no beard. He was dressed in Western sports clothes, an outsize green polo shirt with grubby gray jogging pants, but around his neck he had some kind of voodoo necklace. He wore running shoes, although he looked as if he had not run for years. When he came within speaking distance Abdul smiled and offered him a carton of Cleopatras at half the normal price.

The man ignored the offer. "You are looking for someone." It was a statement, not a question: men such as this hated to admit there was anything they did not know.

Abdul said: "Are you Hakim?"

"You have business with him."

Abdul was sure this man was Hakim. "Sit down, let's be friendly," he said, though Hakim was as friendly as an overweight tarantula.

Hakim waved at the proprietor, presumably to indicate that he wanted coffee, then sat at Abdul's table without speaking.

Abdul said: "I have made a little money selling cigarettes."

Hakim made no response.

Abdul said: "I would like to go to live in Europe."

Hakim nodded. "You have money."

"How much does it cost? To go to Europe?"

"Two thousand American dollars per person—half when you board the bus, half when we reach Libya."

It was a huge sum of money in a country where the average wage was about fifteen dollars a week. Abdul felt the need to quibble. If he agreed too readily, Hakim might become suspicious. "I'm not sure I've got that much."

Hakim jerked his head at Abdul's vehicle. "Sell your car."

So he had checked Abdul out earlier. No doubt the

proprietor had pointed out his vehicle. "Of course I will sell my car before I go," Abdul said. "But I must pay my brother the money he lent me to buy it."

"The price is two thousand."

"But Libya is not Europe. The final payment should be due on arrival."

"Then who would pay it? People would just run away."

"It's not very satisfactory."

"This is not a negotiation. You trust me, or you stay at home."

Abdul almost laughed at the idea of trusting Hakim. "All right, all right," he said. "Can I see the vehicle in which we will travel?"

Hakim hesitated, then shrugged. Without speaking he stood up and walked toward the garage.

Abdul followed.

They entered the building by a small side door. The interior was lit by clear plastic skylights in the roof. There were tools on the walls, new tires racked on deep shelves, and a smell of motor oil. In one corner, two men in galabiyas and headscarves sat watching a television set, smoking, bored. On a table nearby were two assault rifles. The men glanced up, saw Hakim, and returned their attention to the television screen.

Hakim said: "They are my security guards. People try to steal gasoline."

They were jihadis, not security guards, and their indifferent attitude suggested that Hakim was not their boss.

Abdul remained in character and asked them brightly: "Would you like to buy some cigarettes for half price? I have Cleopatras."

They looked away without speaking.

Much of the garage space was taken up by a small Mercedes bus that would hold about forty people. Its appearance was not reassuring. Long ago it had been sky blue, but now that cheerful paintwork was blotched with rust. Two spare wheels were strapped to the roof, but their tires were not new. Most of the side windows had lost their glass. That might have been deliberate: the breeze would keep the passengers cool. He looked inside and saw that the upholstery was worn and stained, and ripped in places. The windshield was intact, but the driver's sunshade had come loose and hung at a drunken angle.

Abdul said: "How long does it take to reach Tripoli, Hakim?"

"You will find out when we get there."

"Don't you know?"

"I never tell people how long. There are always delays, then they become disappointed and angry. Better for them to be surprised and happy when they arrive."

"Does the price cover food and water on the journey?"

"Essentials are provided, including beds at overnight stops. Luxuries are extra."

"What kind of luxury can you get in the middle of the desert?"

"You'll see."

Abdul nodded toward the jihadi guards. "Are they coming?"

"They will protect us."

And the cocaine. "What route will you follow?"

"You ask too many questions."

Abdul had pushed Hakim far enough. "All right, but I need to know when you plan to leave."

"Ten days from today."

"So far ahead. Why the delay?"

"There have been problems." Hakim was getting annoyed. "What do you care? It's no business of yours. Just show up on the day with the money."

Abdul guessed that the problems had to do with the attack on al-Bustan. That could have disrupted other jihadi activities, with senior men killed or injured. "You're right, it's not my business," he said pacifically.

Hakim said: "One bag per person, no exceptions."

Abdul pointed at the bus. "These vehicles usually have a big luggage hold as well as racks inside."

Hakim became angry. "One person, one bag!"

So, Abdul thought, the cocaine is in the luggage hold.

"Very well," he said. "I'll be here ten days from today."

"First thing in the morning!"

Abdul went out.

Hakim reminded him of the Mafia back in New Jersey: touchy, bullying, and stupid. Just like an American gangster, Hakim would use bluster and the threat of violence in place of the brains he did not have. Some of Abdul's dumbest school friends had drifted into that world. Abdul knew how to deal with the type. However, he could not appear too sure of himself. He was playing a part.

And while Hakim might have been a fool, his guards looked serious.

Abdul returned to his car, opened the trunk, and put in the cigarettes he had not sold. His work for the day was done. He would drive to another village or town, sell some more cigarettes to maintain his cover, and find a place to spend the night. There were no hotels, but he could usually find a family willing to take in a stranger at a price.

As he shut the lid, he saw a face he knew. He had seen this woman before, in the village where he had met Tamara and Tab; in fact Tamara had gone into her house. He remembered her mainly because she looked so striking, with an arched nose that enhanced her beauty. Now the sculpted planes of her face were touched with weariness. Her shapely feet in their plastic flip-flop shoes were dusty, and he guessed she must have walked here from her home village, a distance of about ten miles. He wondered what her errand was.

He looked away, not wishing to meet her gaze. It was a reflex: an undercover operator did not want to make friends. Anything more than a distant acquaintanceship would lead to dangerous questions: Where do you come from? Who are your family? What are you doing here in Chad? Such innocent inquiries forced the operator to tell lies, and lies could be found out. The only safe policy was to make no friends.

But she had recognized him. "Marhaba," she said. Hello. Evidently she was happy to see him.

He did not want to draw attention to himself by being rude, so he said formally: "Salaam alaikum," peace be with you.

She stopped to talk to him, and he noticed a faint aroma of cinnamon and turmeric. She gave him a wide, alluring smile that made his heart skip a beat. Her curved nose was noble. An American woman would be embarrassed by such a nose and would have it altered surgically if she had the money, he thought, but on this woman it looked distinguished.

She said: "You're the vendor of cigarettes. You came to my village. My name is Kiah."

He resisted the impulse to stare. "I'm just leaving," he said coldly, and he moved to the car door.

She was not so readily discouraged. "Do you know a man named Hakim?"

He stopped with his hand on the door handle and looked back at her. The tiredness was only superficial, he saw. There seemed to be iron purpose in the dark eyes that looked at him from under the shade of her headscarf. "Why do you want him?"

"I've been told he can help people get to Europe."

Why was a young woman making this inquiry? Did she even have the money? Abdul adopted the condescending tone of a man advising a foolish woman. "You should leave that to your husband."

"My husband is dead. So is my father. And my brothers are in Sudan."

That explained it. She was a widow alone. She had a child, he recalled. In normal times she might have married again, especially as she looked so lovely, but on the shrinking shores of Lake Chad no man wanted to take on the burden of a woman with another man's child.

He admired her courage but, unfortunately, she might be even worse off in the hands of Hakim. She was too vulnerable. Hakim could take all her money and then cheat her somehow. Abdul's heart went out to her.

But this was none of his business. Don't be a fool, he told himself. He could not befriend and help an unfortunate widow, even if she was young and beautiful— especially if she was young and beautiful. So Abdul simply pointed to the garage and said: "In there." He turned his back on the widow and opened his car door.

"Thank you, and may I ask you another question?" she said. She was hard to shake off. Without waiting for consent she went on: "Do you know how much he charges?"

Abdul did not want to answer, did not want to get involved, but he could not be indifferent to her plight. He sighed and yielded to the impulse to help her just so far as to give her a little useful information. He turned back to her and said: "Two thousand American dollars."

"Thank you," she said, but he got the impression he had merely confirmed something she already knew.

She did not look dismayed by the amount, he saw with surprise. So she did have the money.

He added: "Half on departure and half in Libya."

"Oh." She looked thoughtful: she had not known about the installments.

"He says that includes food and water and overnight accommodation, but not luxuries. That's all I know."

She said: "I'm grateful for your kindness." She gave that smile again, only this time there was a hint of triumph in the curve of her lips. He realized that despite his efforts she had controlled the entire conversation. Furthermore, she had smoothly extracted the information she needed. She got the better of me, he thought ruefully as she turned away. Well, well.

He got in the car and shut the door.

He started the engine, then watched her walk past the tables under the palm trees, across the filling station, and up to the repair shop.

He wondered whether she would board the bus ten days from today.

He put the car in gear and pulled away.

The cigarette seller had clearly not wanted to engage with Kiah, for some reason, and he had acted cold and indifferent, but underneath that she suspected he had a good heart, and in the end he had answered her questions. He had told her where to find Hakim, he had confirmed the price, and he had told her the money was payable in two installments. She felt more confident now, not being completely ignorant.

She was puzzled by the man. Back at the village he had seemed a typical street vendor, ready to say anything, flatter and flirt and tell lies, just to separate people from their money. But today there had been none of that bonhomie. Obviously it was an act.

She walked to the garage behind the gas station. Three cars were parked outside, presumably being worked on, though one of them seemed beyond repair. There was a pyramid of old bald tires. A side door of the building stood open. Kiah looked in and saw a small bus with no glass in its windows.

Was this the vehicle that would take people across the desert? Kiah was seized by fear. The journey was long, and people could die. A puncture could be fatal. I must be mad even to think of this, she told herself.

A plump young man in grubby Western clothes slouched into view. She noticed his grigri necklace, made of beads and stones, some of them probably engraved with religious or magical words. It was supposed to protect him from evil and bring suffering to his enemies.

He looked her up and down with a greedy expression. "What can I do for this angelic vision?" he said with a grin.

She knew immediately that she would have to be careful how she dealt with him. Clearly he thought he was irresistible to women, despite his unprepossessing appearance. She spoke politely, hiding the contempt she felt. "I'm looking for a gentleman called Hakim. Would that be you, sir?"

"I am Hakim, yes," he said proudly. "And all this is mine—the filling station, the repair shop, and the bus."

She pointed at the vehicle. "May I ask if this is your desert transport?"

"It's a fine vehicle, just serviced and in perfect working order." He narrowed his eyes. "Why do you ask about the desert?"

"I'm a widow with no way of making a living and I want to go to Europe."

Hakim became expansive. "I will look after you, my dear." He put an arm around her shoulders. An unpleasant smell arose from his armpit. "You can trust me."

She moved away, dislodging his arm. "My cousin Yusuf will be with me."

"Excellent," he said, though he looked disappointed. "How much?"

"How much have you got?"

"Nothing," she lied. "But I might be able to borrow money."

He did not believe her. "The price is four thousand American dollars. You need to pay me now to be sure of a place on the bus."

He thinks I'm stupid, she said to herself.

It was a familiar feeling. When she had been selling the boat several men had tried to buy it for next to nothing. However, she had quickly realized that it was a mistake to pour scorn on an offer, no matter how derisory. The potential buyer would become offended at being spoken to that way by a woman, and he would walk away in a sulk.

So she said: "I don't have the money right now, unfortunately."

"Then you may get left behind."

"And Yusuf said you normally charge two thousand."

Hakim was getting annoyed. "Maybe Yusuf should take you to Tripoli, not me. He seems to know everything."

"Now that my husband is dead, Yusuf is the head of my family. I must be ruled by him."

For Hakim this was a truism. "Of course you must," he conceded. "He is a man."

"He told me to ask you when you expect to leave."

"Tell him ten days from today, at dawn."

"We will be three adults, including Yusuf's wife."

"No children?"

"I have a two-year-old son, and Yusuf has a daughter the same age, but they will not need seats."

"I charge half price for children who don't take seats."

"Then we cannot travel," Kiah said firmly. She moved a few steps, as if on her way out. "I'm sorry to have wasted your time, sir. We may be able to raise six thousand, by borrowing from all our family, but we will have taken everything they've got."

Hakim saw six thousand dollars disappearing and looked a shade less confident. "A shame," he said. "But why don't you come on the appointed day anyway? If the bus is not full I might make a special price."

It was a standoff and she had to accept it.

Naturally, Hakim wanted to fill every seat and make the maximum amount of money. With forty passengers he would get eighty thousand dollars. It was a fortune. She wondered what he would spend it on. But he probably had to share it with others. He must have been only one part of the organization.

She had to accept his terms. He was in the strong position. "Very well," she said, then she remembered to act like a mere woman and added: "Thank you, sir."

She had gathered the information she needed. She left the garage and set out on the long walk home.

Hakim had not surprised her, but all the same their conversation had discouraged her. He obviously felt superior to all women, but that was not unusual. However, the American woman's warning had been right: he was a criminal and could not be trusted. People sometimes said that thieves had their own code of honor, but Kiah did not believe it. A man such as Hakim would lie and cheat and steal whenever he could get away with it. And he might commit worse crimes against a defenseless woman.

She would be with others on the bus, of course, but

this did not give her much comfort. The other passengers might be scared and desperate too. When a woman was abused people sometimes looked away, making excuses for not getting involved.

Her only hope was Yusuf. He was family, and his honor would force him to protect her. With Azra there would be three adults in the group, so they would not be helpless. Bullies were often cowards too, and Hakim might hesitate to pick a fight with three people.

She felt that with the help of Yusuf and Azra she could face the journey.

The afternoon was cooling when she arrived at Yusuf's village. She was footsore but full of hope. She hugged Naji, who kissed her and immediately went back to playing with Danna. She was faintly disappointed that he had not missed her more, but it was a good sign, showing that he had spent a happy day and had felt safe.

Azra said: "Yusuf's gone to look at a ram, but he won't be long." Once again she was a little stiff with Kiah, not hostile but just somewhat less friendly than formerly.

Kiah wondered why Yusuf wanted to look at a ram when he no longer had a flock of sheep to be impregnated, but she supposed he was still interested in the work even though he had left it. She was keen to share all she had learned, but she forced herself to be patient. The two women watched their children at play until Yusuf appeared a few minutes later.

As soon as he sat down on the rug, Kiah said: "Hakim leaves ten days from today. We have to be at Three Palms at dawn if we want to go with him."

She was excited as well as scared. Yusuf and Azra seemed more calm. She told them about the price, and the bus, and the argument about children's fares. "Hakim is not a trustworthy man," she said. "We'll have to be careful how we deal with him. But between the three of us I think we can manage him."

Yusuf's normally smiling face looked thoughtful. Azra would not meet Kiah's eye. Kiah wondered if something was wrong. "What's the matter?" she said.

Yusuf adopted the expression of a man explaining the secrets of the universe to his women. "I have been thinking very much about this," he said ponderously.

Kiah had a bad feeling.

He went on: "Something tells me things may get better here at the lake."

They were going to drop out, Kiah realized with dismay.

"For the money it will cost to go to Europe, I could buy a fine flock of sheep."

And watch them all die, Kiah thought, just like the last lot; but she remained silent.

He read her mind. "There are risks both ways, of course. But I understand sheep. Whereas I know nothing about Europe."

Kiah felt let down and wanted to scorn his cowardice, but she held back. "You're not sure," she said.

"I am sure. I have decided not to go at this time."

Azra had made the decision, Kiah guessed. Azra had never been keen on migrating and she had talked Yusuf out of it.

And she was left high and dry.

"I can't go without you," she said.

Yusuf replied: "Then we will all stay here, and somehow we will get by."

Dumb optimism was not going to save anybody. Kiah was about to say so but held back again. It was not a good idea to challenge a man when he pronounced judgment in that formal way.

She was silent for a long moment. Then, for the sake

of good relations with her cousin, she said: "Well, then, so be it."

She stood up. "Come, Naji," she said. "Time to go home." To carry him the mile or so to their village suddenly seemed awfully hard. "Thank you for taking care of him," she said to Azra.

She took her leave. Trudging along the shore, shifting Naji from one aching hip to the other, she looked ahead to the time when all the boat money was spent. No matter how frugal she was, she could not make it last more than two or three years. Her only chance had just melted away.

Suddenly it was all too much. She put Naji down, then slumped down herself and sat on the sand, staring out over the shallow water to the muddy islets. Wherever she looked she saw no hope.

She put her head in her hands and said: "What am I going to do?"

CHAPTER 3

Vice President Milton Lapierre came into the Oval Office wearing a dark blue cashmere blazer that looked British. The drape of the double-breasted jacket did much to hide the gravid swell of his belly. Tall and slow-moving, he was a contrast with petite President Green, who had been a champion gymnast at the University of Chicago and was still slim and fit.

They were as different as President Kennedy, the classy Boston intellectual, had been from Vice President Lyndon Johnson, the rough diamond from Texas. Pauline was a moderate Republican, conservative but flexible; Milt was a white man from Georgia who was impatient with compromise. Pauline did not like Milt, but he was useful. He told her what the far right wing of the party was thinking, warned her when she was about to do something that would get them all in a lather, and defended her in the media.

Now he said: "James Moore has a new idea."

Next year was an election year, and Senator Moore was threatening to challenge Pauline for the Republican nomination. The crucial New Hampshire primary was five months away. A challenge from the sitting president's own party was unusual but not unknown: Ronald Reagan had done it to Gerald Ford in 1976 and failed, Pat Buchanan had challenged George H. W. Bush in 1991 and failed, but Eugene McCarthy had done so well against Lyndon Johnson in 1968 that Johnson had dropped out of the race.

Moore had a chance. Pauline had won the last presidential election in a backlash against incompetence and racism. "Commonsense conservatism" had been her slogan: no extremes, no abuse, no prejudice. She stood for low-risk foreign policy, low-key policing, and low-tax government. But millions of voters still hankered after a big-talking macho leader, and Moore was winning their support.

Pauline was sitting behind the famous Resolute desk, a gift from Queen Victoria, but she had a twenty-first-century computer in front of her. She looked up at Milt. "What now?"

"He wants to ban pop songs with obscene lyrics from being listed in the *Billboard* Hot One Hundred."

There was a burst of laughter from the other side of the room. Chief of Staff Jacqueline Brody was amused. A longtime friend and ally of Pauline's, she was an attractive forty-five-year-old with a brisk manner. She said: "If it wasn't for Moore, there'd be days when I wouldn't smile from breakfast to bedtime."

Milt sat down in the chair in front of the desk. "Jacqueline may think it's funny," he said grumpily, "but a lot of people are going to like this idea."

"I know, I know," Pauline conceded. "Nothing is too ridiculous for modern politics."

"What are you going to say about it?"

"Nothing, if I can avoid comment."

"And if you're asked a direct question?"

"I'll say the music that children listen to should not have dirty lyrics, and I would ban it if I were president of a totalitarian country like China."

"So you're comparing American Christians with Chinese Communists."

Pauline sighed. "You're right, it's too sarcastic. What do you suggest?"

"Appeal to singers, music companies, and radio stations to exercise good taste and remember their younger listeners. Then, if you must, you can say: 'But censorship isn't the American way.'"

"That won't make any difference to anything."

"No, but that's okay, as long as you appear sympathetic."

She looked appraisingly at Milt. He was not easily shocked, she thought. Could she ask him the question that was on her lips? She thought she could. She said: "How old were you when you and your friends started saying *fuck*?"

Milt shrugged, not shocked in the least. "Twelve, maybe thirteen."

She turned to Jacqueline. "You?"

"About the same."

"So what are we protecting our kids from?"

Milt said: "I'm not saying Moore is right. But I do think he's a threat to you. And he calls you a liberal in just about every speech."

"Smart conservatives know that you can't stop change but you can slow it down. That way people have time to get used to new ideas, and you don't suffer an angry reaction. Liberals make the mistake of demanding radical change now, and that undermines them."

"Try putting that on a T-shirt."

It was one of Milt's sayings. He believed that few voters understood anything that could not be put on a

T-shirt. The fact that Milt was so often right made him more obnoxious. Pauline said: "I want to win, Milt."

"Me too."

"I've been sitting at this desk for two and a half years and I feel I've hardly achieved anything. I want another term."

Jacqueline said: "Way to go, Madam President."

The door opened and Lizzie Freeburg looked in. Thirty years old with a mass of curly dark hair, she was the senior secretary. She said: "The national security advisor is here."

"Good," said Pauline.

Gus Blake entered, immediately making the room seem smaller. Gus and Milt nodded to one another: they did not get on.

The president's three closest advisors were now in the room. The chief of staff, the NSA, and the vice president all had offices a few steps away on this floor of the West Wing, and sheer physical proximity meant they saw more of the president than anyone else.

Pauline said to Gus: "Milt has been telling me about James Moore's appeal for censorship of pop songs."

Gus flashed his charming smile. "You're the leader of the free world, and you're worrying about pop songs?"

"I just asked Milt how old he was when he started saying *fuck*. He said twelve. How about you, Gus?"

The NSA said: "I was born in South Central Los Angeles. It was probably the first word I spoke."

Pauline laughed and said: "I promise I'll never quote you."

"You wanted to talk about al-Bustan."

"Yes. Let's be more comfortable." She got up from her desk. In the center of the room two couches faced each other across a coffee table. Pauline sat down. Milt and Jacqueline sat opposite and Gus beside her.

Gus said: "It's the best news we've had from that region for a long time. The Cleopatra project is paying off."

Milt said: "Cleopatra?"

Gus looked impatient. Milt was not conscientious about reading his briefings.

Pauline was. She said: "The CIA has an undercover officer who produced twenty-four-carat intelligence on an ISGS base in Niger. Yesterday a joint force of American, French, and local troops wiped the place out. It's in this morning's briefing papers, but you may not have had time to read them all."

Milt said: "Why did we bring in the French, for God's sake?"

Gus gave him a look that said, *Don't you know anything?* But he spoke politely enough. "A lot of those countries used to be French colonies."

"Okay."

As a woman, Pauline constantly suffered suggestions that she was too nice, too soft, too empathetic to be commander in chief of the US military. She said: "I'm going to announce this myself. James Moore has a big mouth when he talks about terrorists. It's time to show people that President Green actually kills the bastards."

"Good idea."

Pauline turned to the chief of staff. "Jacqueline, would you ask Sandip to arrange a press conference?" Sandip Chakraborty was the communications director.

"Sure thing." Jacqueline looked at her watch. It was midafternoon. "Sandip's going to suggest tomorrow morning, for maximum TV coverage."

"Fine."

Gus said: "Couple of details that weren't in the briefing because we've only just heard. First, the raid was led by Colonel Susan Marcus."

"The operation was commanded by a woman?"

Gus grinned. "Don't sound so incredulous."

"This is great. Now I can say: 'If brute force is what you need, get a woman to do what's necessary.'"

"Talking about Colonel Marcus, but also about yourself."

"I love it."

"Your briefing says that the terrorists' guns were a mixture of Chinese and North Korean."

Milt said: "Why does Beijing arm these people? I thought the Chinese hated Muslims. Don't they lock them up in re-education camps?"

Pauline said: "It's not ideological. Both China and North Korea make a lot of money making and selling weapons."

"They shouldn't sell them to ISGS."

"They'll say they don't. And there's a thriving second-hand market." Pauline shrugged. "What are you going to do?"

Gus surprised her by supporting Milt. "The vice president has a point, Madam President. Something else that wasn't in the morning briefing is that, as well as guns, the terrorists had three North Korean Koksan M-1978 self-propelled 170 millimeter field artillery pieces, based on a Chinese Type 59 tank chassis."

"Jesus. They didn't buy those in a flea market in Timbuktu."

"No."

Pauline was thoughtful. "I don't think we can let this pass. Rifles are bad enough, but the world is full of them, and no one can control the market. But artillery is different."

"I agree," said Gus, "but I'm not sure what we do about it. American arms manufacturers have to have government approval for overseas sales—I get their applications across my desk every week. Other countries should do the same, but they don't."

"Then maybe we can encourage them."

"Okay," said Gus. "What do you have in mind?"

"We could propose a resolution at the United Nations."

Milt said scornfully: "The UN! That won't do any good."

"It would put the spotlight on China. The debate on its own might constrain them."

Milt raised his hands in surrender. "All right. We'd be using the UN to draw attention to what the Chinese are up to. That's how I'll spin it."

Gus said: "There's no point in proposing a Security Council resolution—the Chinese would just veto it—so I presume we're talking about a General Assembly resolution."

"Yes," said Pauline, "but we won't just propose it. We should drum up support all around the world. US ambassadors should lobby their host governments to back the resolution—but quietly, not to forewarn the Chinese of how serious we are."

Milt said: "I still don't think it will change Chinese behavior."

"Then we can follow up with sanctions. But first things first. We need Chess in the loop." Chester Jackson was the secretary of state. His office was a mile away in the State Department building. "Jacqueline, arrange a meeting and we'll kick this around some more."

Lizzie looked in. "Madam President, the First Gentleman has returned to the Residence."

"Thank you." Pauline was still not used to her husband's being referred to as the First Gentleman—it sounded comical. She stood up, and the others did the same. "Thanks, everybody."

She left the Oval Office by the door that gave onto the West Colonnade. Trailed by two Secret Service men and the army captain with the atomic football, she walked around two sides of the Rose Garden and entered the Residence.

It was a beautiful building, fabulously decorated and expensively maintained, but it would never feel like a home. She thought regretfully of the Capitol Hill town house she had left behind, a narrow red-brick Victorian with small, cozy rooms full of pictures and books. It had had well-worn couches with bright cushions, a huge comfortable bed, and an out-of-date kitchen in which Pauline knew exactly where everything was kept. There had been bicycles in the hall, tennis rackets in the laundry room, and a bottle of ketchup on the sideboard in the dining room. Sometimes she wished she had never left.

She ran up the stairs without pausing for breath. At fifty she was still nimble. She went past the formal first floor and reached the family quarters on the second floor.

From the landing she looked into the East Sitting Hall, everyone's favorite place to hang out. She could see her husband sitting by the big arched window that looked over the East Wing to Fifteenth Street NW and the Old Ebbitt Grill. She walked along the short corridor into the small room, then sat on the yellow velvet couch beside him and kissed his cheek.

Gerry Green was ten years older than Pauline. He was tall, with silver hair and blue eyes, and he wore a conventional dark gray suit with a button-down shirt and a tie with a quiet pattern. He bought all his clothes at Brooks Brothers, although he could have afforded to fly to London and order suits in Savile Row.

Pauline had met him when she was at Yale Law School and he had been a guest lecturer, speaking on the subject of law as a business. He had been in his early thirties, and already successful, and the women in the class thought he was hot. But it was another fifteen years before she saw him again. By that time she was a congresswoman and he was a senior partner in his firm.

They had dated, gone to bed together, and taken a vacation in Paris. Their courtship had been exciting and romantic, but even then Pauline had known they had a friendship rather than a grand passion. Gerry was a good lover, but she had never wanted to tear his clothes off with her teeth. He was handsome and intelligent and witty, and she had married him for all those reasons and because she did not want to be lonely.

When Pauline was elected president he had retired from practice and had become head of a national charity, the American Foundation for the Education of Women and Girls, an unpaid part-time job that allowed him to play his role as the nation's First Gentleman.

They had one child, Pippa, fourteen. She had always gone happily to school and been an A student, so they had been startled when the principal had asked them to come to the school to discuss Pippa's behavior.

Pauline and Gerry had speculated about what the problem could be. Remembering herself at fourteen, Pauline guessed Pippa might have been caught kissing a tenth-grade boy behind the gym. In any event it was not likely to be serious, she thought.

Pauline could not possibly go. It would have made the papers. Then Pippa's problems, no matter how commonplace, would have been front-page news, and the poor girl would have been in the national spotlight. Pauline's dearest wish was a wonderful future for her child, and she knew the White House was an unnatural environment in which to grow up. She was determined to shield Pippa from the most bruising attentions of the media. So Gerry had quietly gone alone, this afternoon, and now Pauline was anxious to find out what had happened.

"I've never met Ms. Judd," Pauline said. "What's she like?"

"Smart and warmhearted," Gerry said. "Just the combination you want in a school principal."

"How old?"

"Early forties."

"What did she have to say?"

"She likes Pippa and thinks our daughter is a bright student and a valuable member of the school community. I felt quite proud."

Pauline wanted to say, *Cut to the chase*. But she knew Gerry would make his report in a thorough and logical way, starting at the beginning. Three decades as a lawyer had taught him to value clarity above everything else. Pauline controlled her impatience.

He went on: "Pippa has always been interested in history, studying in depth and contributing to class discussions. But lately her contributions have been disruptive."

"Oh, God," Pauline groaned. This was beginning to sound ominously familiar.

"So much so that the teacher has had to exclude Pippa from the room on three occasions."

Pauline nodded. "And when that's happened three times they send for the parents."

"Correct."

"What period of history is the class studying?"

"Several, but Pippa makes trouble when they talk about the Nazis."

"What does she say?"

"It's not the teacher's interpretation of history that Pippa disputes. Her complaint is that the class is studying the wrong subjects. The curriculum suffers from racist bias, she says."

"I know where this is heading. But go on."

"I think we should get Pippa to take over the story now."

"Good idea."

Pauline was about to get up and go in search of their daughter, but Gerry said: "Stay there. Take a minute. You're the hardest-working person in America. I'll find Pippa."

"Thanks."

Gerry left.

He was considerate, Pauline thought gratefully. It was how he showed his love.

Pippa's complaint had rung a bell with Pauline because she remembered challenging her teachers. Her beef, back then, had been that the lessons were all about men: male presidents, male generals, male writers, male musicians. Her teacher—a man—had foolishly argued that this was because women did not matter much in history. At that point the young Pauline had become superheated.

However, the older Pauline could not let love and empathy blur her vision. Pippa had to learn not to let an argument become a fight. Pauline had to steer her carefully. Like most political problems, this could not be solved by brute force, only by finesse.

Gerry returned with Pippa. She was short for her age and slim, like Pauline. She was not conventionally pretty, having a wide mouth and a broad jaw, but a sunny personality shone out of that plain face, and Pauline felt swamped by love every time Pippa walked into the room. Her school outfit, a loose sweatshirt and blue jeans, made her look quite childish, but Pauline knew that underneath she was rapidly becoming a woman.

"Come and sit by me, honey," Pauline said, and when Pippa sat down she put an arm round the girl's small shoulders and hugged her. "You know how much we love you, and because of that we need to understand what's happening at school."

Pippa looked guarded. "What did Ms. Judd say?"

"Forget about Ms. Judd for a minute. Just tell us what's troubling you." Pippa was silent for a few moments, so Pauline prompted her. "It's about history lessons, isn't it?"

"Yes."

"Tell us about it."

"We're studying the Nazis, all about how many Jews were murdered. We've seen pictures of the camps and the gas chambers. We learn the names: Treblinka, Majdanek, Janowska. But what about the people wiped out by us? There were ten million Native Americans when Christopher Columbus landed, but by the end of the Indian Wars there were only a quarter of a million left. Isn't that a holocaust? I asked when we would be studying the massacres at Tallushatchee, Sand Creek, Wounded Knee."

Pippa was indignantly defensive. That was what Pauline had expected. She did not think Pippa would crumble and apologize—not yet, anyway. "That sounds like a reasonable question," Pauline said. "How did the teacher answer?"

"Mr. Newbegin said he didn't know when we'd be studying that. So I asked, isn't it more important to know about atrocities committed by our own country than by other countries? I even think there's something in the Bible about that."

"There is," said Gerry, who had had a religious upbringing. "It's from the Sermon on the Mount. Before you try to take a speck out of your brother's eye, make sure you don't have a big piece of wood in your own eye, obstructing your vision, Jesus suggested. And he said 'Thou hypocrite,' so we know he was serious."

Pauline said: "What did Mr. Newbegin have to say about that?"

"He said the curriculum was not set by the pupils."

"That's a shame," said Pauline. "He chickened out."

"Exactly."

"How did you come to be excluded from the class?"

"I kept asking, and he got fed up. He said that if I couldn't sit and listen I should leave the room, so I did." Pippa shrugged, as if to say it was no big deal.

Gerry said: "But Ms. Judd told me this had happened three times. What were the second and third arguments about?"

"Same thing." Pippa's face took on a look of outrage. "I had a right to an answer!"

Pauline said: "So, even though you may have had right on your side, the result is that lessons continue as before, except that you're not in the class."

"And I'm in deep shit."

Pauline pretended not to notice the profanity. "Looking back, what do you think about the way you handled this?"

"I stood up for truth and got punished."

That was not the answer Pauline was looking for. She tried again. "Can you think of any alternative responses that might be worth trying?"

"Suck it up and shut my mouth?"

"Would you like to hear a suggestion?"

"Okay."

"Try to think of a way the class could learn about the genocide of Native Americans and the Nazi Holocaust too."

"But he won't—"

"Hold on. Suppose Mr. Newbegin would agree to devote the last lesson of the semester to the Native Americans, and let you make a presentation, which could be followed by a class discussion."

"He would never do that."

"He might." He would if I asked him, Pauline thought, but she kept that to herself. "If not, doesn't the school have a debate society?"

"Yes. I'm on the committee."

"Propose a motion about the Indian Wars. Were the pioneers guilty of a holocaust? Get the whole school involved in the discussion—including Mr. Newbegin. You need him to be your friend, not your enemy."

Pippa began to look interested. "Okay, that's an idea—a debate."

"Whatever you do, work it out with Ms. Judd and Mr. Newbegin. Don't dream something up, then spring it on them. The more they think it's their idea, the more they'll support it."

Pippa smiled. "Are you teaching me politics, Mom?"

"Maybe. But there's one more thing, and you probably won't like it."

"What?"

"Everything will go more smoothly if you begin by apologizing to Mr. Newbegin for disrupting his class."

"Do I really have to?"

"I think you do, honey. You've hurt his pride."

"I'm a kid!"

"Which makes it worse. Put a little ointment on his wound. You'll be glad you did."

"Can I think about it?"

"Sure. Now go and wash up while I call Ms. Judd and then we'll have dinner"—she looked at her watch—"in fifteen minutes."

"Okay."

Pippa left.

Gerry said: "I'll tell the kitchen." He went out.

Pauline picked up the phone. "Please call Ms. Judd, the principal of Foggy Bottom Day School," she told the switchboard operator.

"Certainly, Madam President." The staff of the White House switchboard were proud of their ability to find anyone in the world. "Are you expecting to stay in the East Sitting Hall for another minute or so?"

"Yes."

"Thank you, Madam President." ·

Pauline hung up and Gerry returned. Pauline asked him: "What do you think?"

"I think you handled that well. You persuaded her to make amends, but she's not mad at you. It was skillful."

It was loving too, Pauline thought with a touch of resentment. "You thought it was a bit cold?"

Gerry shrugged. "I'm wondering what this tells us about where Pippa is at right now, emotionally."

Pauline frowned, not really understanding what Gerry was trying to say, but the phone rang before she could ask him.

"I have Ms. Judd for you, Madam President."

Pauline said: "Ms. Judd, I hope I'm not disturbing your evening."

There were not many people in the world who would mind being disturbed by the president of the United States, but Pauline liked to be polite.

"Please don't worry, Madam President. I'm happy to speak to you, of course." The voice was low and friendly, though a little wary—which was hardly surprising in someone speaking to the president.

"First, I want to thank you for the concern you've shown for Pippa. It's appreciated."

"You're welcome, ma'am. It's our job."

"Pippa has to learn that she can't take control of lessons, obviously. And I'm absolutely not calling you to complain about Mr. Newbegin."

"Thank you for that." Ms. Judd began to relax slightly.

"However, we don't want to crush Pippa's idealism."

"Certainly not."

"I've had a talk with her, and I have strongly recommended that she apologize to Mr. Newbegin."

"How did she react to that?"

"She's thinking about it."

Ms. Judd laughed. "That's Pippa."

Pauline laughed too, and felt she had achieved a rapport. She said: "I've suggested that Pippa should look for a way to make her point without disrupting the class. For example, she might propose a motion in the Debate Society."

"What a good idea."

"Of course this is up to you, but I hope you agree with the general principle."

"I do."

"And I hope to send Pippa to school in the morning with a more conciliatory attitude."

"Thank you, Madam President. I appreciate that."

"Good-bye." Pauline hung up.

"Well done," said Gerry.

"Let's have dinner."

They left the room and walked through the long Center Hall and across the West Sitting Hall to the Dining Room on the north side of the building, with two windows onto Pennsylvania Avenue and Lafayette Square. Pauline had restored the antique wallpaper that showed battle scenes from the American Revolution, previously covered over by the Clintons.

Pippa came in, looking chastened.

Family dinners were eaten in this room, usually early in the evening. The food was always simple. Tonight they had a salad followed by pasta with tomato sauce, and fresh pineapple for dessert.

At the end of the meal Pippa said: "Okay, I'm going to tell Mr. Newbegin that I'm sorry I was a pain in the ass."

"Good decision," said Pauline. "Thank you for listening."

Gerry said: "But say 'pain in the neck' instead."

"You got it, Daddy."

When Pippa had gone, Pauline said: "I'll take my coffee in the West Wing."

"I'll tell the kitchen."

"What will you do tonight?"

"I have an hour's work to do for the foundation. When Pippa's finished her homework we'll probably watch TV for a while."

"Great." She kissed him. "I'll see you later."

She walked back around the colonnade, then through the Oval Office and out the other side. Next to the Oval Office was the study, a small informal room where Pauline preferred to work. The Oval Office was a ceremonial room that people walked into and out of all the time, but when the president was in the study she was mostly left alone, and no one came in without knocking and waiting for an answer. With a desk, two armchairs, and a TV screen, it was really quite cramped, but Pauline liked it, and most previous presidents had felt the same.

She spent three hours doing phone calls and preparing for the next day's business, then she returned to the Residence. She went straight to the master bedroom. Gerry was already in bed in his pajamas, reading *Foreign Affairs* magazine. As she undressed she said: "I remember being fourteen. I was a hellion. Hormones have a lot to do with it."

"You may be right," he said without looking up.

She could tell from his tone of voice that he meant the opposite. She said: "Do you have another theory?"

He did not answer the question directly. "I presume most of the kids in the class are going through hormonal changes. But Pippa is the only one acting up."

They did not actually know whether others in the class were misbehaving, but Pauline refrained from making a merely argumentative point. Mildly she said:

"I wonder why." She thought she knew the answer. Pippa was like her, a born crusader. But she waited for Gerry's opinion.

He said: "In a fourteen-year-old, behavior like this may be a sign that something is wrong."

Pauline said patiently: "And what do you think is wrong in Pippa's life?"

"She may want more attention."

"Really? She has you, she has me, she has Ms. Judd. She sees her grandparents."

"Maybe she doesn't see enough of her mother."

Pauline thought: So is it my fault?

Of course she did not spend enough time with her daughter. No one who had a demanding full-time job could be with their children as much as they would like. But when she was with Pippa it was quality time. Gerry's remark seemed unfair to her.

She was naked, and she could not help noticing that Gerry had not watched her undress. She slipped a nightdress over her head and got into bed beside him. She said: "Have you thought this for some time?"

"It's just an ongoing subterranean worry," he said. "I don't mean to criticize you."

But you did, she thought.

He put down his magazine and turned off his bedside lamp. Then he leaned over and kissed her lightly. "I love you," he said. "Good night."

"Good night." She turned out the light on her side. "I love you too."

It took her a long time to get to sleep.

CHAPTER 4

Tamara Levit worked at the American embassy in N'Djamena, in the suite of offices that formed the CIA station. Her desk was in the communal area: she was too junior to have a room of her own. She talked on the phone with Abdul, who told her that he had made contact with a people smuggler called Hakim, and she was writing a short report on this toward the end of the afternoon when she and all the staff were summoned to the conference room. The head of station, Dexter Lewis, had an announcement.

Dexter was a short, muscular man in a rumpled suit. Tamara thought he was clever, especially in operations involving deceit. But she thought he might be dishonest in everyday life too. He said: "We've had a great triumph, and I want to thank you all. I have a message here that I'd like to read to you." He was holding a single sheet of paper. "'To Colonel Susan Marcus and her squad, and to Dexter Lewis and his intelligence team. Dear colleagues, it is my pleasure to congratulate you all on your victory at al-Bustan. You have struck a vital blow against terror and saved many lives, and I am proud of you. Yours sincerely—'" He paused dramatically, then finished: "'Pauline Green, president of the United States.'"

The assembled team burst into cheers and applause. Tamara felt a flush of pride. She had done plenty of good work for the Agency, but this was the first time she had been involved in a big operation, and she was thrilled that it had been such a success.

But the person who most deserved President Green's congratulations was Abdul. She wondered whether the president even knew his name. Probably not.

And the mission was not over. Abdul was still in the field, still risking his life—and worse—by spying on the jihadis. Tamara sometimes lay awake thinking about him, and about the mutilated body of his predecessor, Omar, whose life's blood had soaked into the sand.

They returned to their desks, and Tamara recalled Pauline Green. Long before Pauline became president, when she was running for election as a Chicago congresswoman, Tamara had been a volunteer organizer in her campaign headquarters. Tamara was not a Republican but she admired Pauline personally. They had become quite close, Tamara had thought, but attachments formed in election campaigns were notoriously temporary, like cruise ship romances, and the friendship had not continued after Pauline got elected.

In the summer after Tamara got her master's she had been approached by the CIA. There had been nothing cloak-and-dagger about it. A woman had phoned and said: "I'm a recruiter for the CIA and I'd like to talk to you." Tamara had been hired by the Directorate of Operations, which meant working undercover. After her introductory briefing at Langley, she had done a residential training course at a place they called the Farm.

Most CIA officers went through their entire career

without ever using a gun. They worked in the US or
heavily guarded embassies and sat in front of screens,
reading foreign newspapers and scanning websites,
gleaning data and analyzing its significance. But there
were some, working in countries that were dangerous
or hostile or both, who went armed and occasionally
became involved in violence.

Tamara was no wimp. She had been captain of the
women's ice hockey team at the University of Chicago.
But until she joined the Agency she had known nothing
about firearms. Her father was a university professor
who had never held a gun. Her mother raised money for
a group called Women Against Gun Violence. When
the trainees were each given a nine-millimeter automatic pistol, Tamara had to watch the others to figure
out how to eject the magazine and rack the slide.

However, she was pleased to discover, after a little
practice, that she was an unusually good shot with any
kind of weapon.

She decided not to tell her parents this.

She soon realized that the Agency did not expect everyone to finish the combat course. The training was
part of the selection process, and a third of the original
group dropped out. One very ripped man turned out to
be terrified of physical violence. In a bomb threat simu-
lation using paintball ammunition, the toughest-looking
of the guys shot all the civilians. Several people simply
apologized and went home.

But Tamara passed everything.

Chad was her first overseas posting. It was not a
high-tension station like Moscow or Beijing, nor a
comfortable one like London or Paris, but though low-
key it was important because of ISGS, and Tamara had
been pleased and flattered to be sent here. And now
she had to vindicate the Agency's decision by doing a
great job.

Just being on the team supporting Abdul was a feather in her cap. If he found Hufra and al-Farabi, the whole team would bask in the glory.

Now the working day was coming to an end and, outside the window, the shadows of the palm trees were stretching longer. Tamara left the office. The heat of the day was easing.

The American embassy in N'Djamena was a thirteen-acre compound on the north bank of the Chari River. It occupied an entire city block in Avenue Mobutu, half-way between the Catholic Mission and the French Institute. The embassy buildings were new and modern, and the parking lots were shaded by palm trees. It looked like the Silicon Valley headquarters of a profit-able high-tech company, a look that nicely concealed the hard hand of American military power. But security was tight. No one got past the guards at the gate with-out a verified appointment, and visitors who arrived too early had to wait in the street until the proper time.

Tamara lived in the compound. The city outside was considered unsafe for Americans and she, along with others, had a studio apartment in a low-rise building that housed unmarried staffers.

Crossing the compound on the way to the apart-ment buildings, Tamara ran into the ambassador's young wife. Shirley Collinsworth was almost thirty, the same age as Tamara. She was dressed in a pink skirt suit that Tamara's mother might have worn. Shirley had to appear more conventional than she was, because of her role, but at heart she was like Tamara, and they had become friends.

Shirley was looking radiant, and Tamara said: "What are you so pleased about?"

"Nick has had a small triumph." Nicholas Collins-worth, the ambassador, was older than Shirley at forty. "He's just been to see the General."

The president of Chad was known as the General. He had come to power in a military coup. Chad was a fake democracy: elections were held, but the sitting president always won. Any opposition politician who began to gain popularity either found himself in jail or suffered a fatal accident. Elections were for show; change happened only by violence.

"Did the General summon Nick?" Tamara asked. This was an important detail and the kind of thing an intelligence officer always wanted to know.

"No, Nick asked to see him. President Green is proposing a resolution at the United Nations General Assembly, and all ambassadors have to lobby for support. That's not generally known, by the way, but I can tell you, you're CIA. Anyway, Nick went to the Presidential Palace with his head stuffed full of facts and figures about arms deals, poor lamb. The General listened for two minutes, then promised to back the resolution and started talking about soccer. Which is why Nick is triumphant and I'm happy."

"Good news! Another victory."

"It's minor compared with al-Bustan, of course."

"All the same, will the two of you have a party?"

"A glass of champagne, perhaps. We get the good stuff here, thanks to our French allies. You?"

"I'm having a celebratory dinner with Tabdar Sadoul, my opposite number from the Direction Générale de la Sécurité Extérieure."

"I know Tab. He's Arab, or partly."

"Algerian French."

"Lucky you. He's hot. 'All that's best of dark and bright.'"

"Is that a poem?"

"Byron."

"Well, we're just having dinner. I'm not going to sleep with him."

"Really? I would."

Tamara giggled.

Shirley said: "I mean, I would if I were not married to a wonderful husband, of course."

"Of course."

Shirley grinned. "Have a great time," she said, walking away.

Tamara headed for her apartment. She knew Shirley was kidding. If she seriously intended to cheat on her husband she would not joke about it.

Tamara had a single room with a bed, a desk, a couch, and a TV. It was only a little more comfortable than student accommodation. She had made it individual with local fabrics in bright shades of orange and indigo. She had a shelf of Arabic literature, a framed photograph of her parents on their wedding day, and a guitar that she still had not learned to play.

She showered, blow-dried her hair, made up her face lightly, then stood looking into the closet, considering what to wear. This was not an occasion for her working uniform of a long dress over trousers.

She was looking forward to the evening. Tab was a handsome and charming man who made her laugh. She wanted to look her best. She picked out a knee-length cotton dress with narrow navy and white stripes. The dress was short-sleeved, which was frowned upon by conservatives here, and anyway the nights could be cool, so she put on a blue bolero jacket to cover her arms. She stepped into low-heeled navy leather pumps: she never wore high heels. Looking in the mirror, she found her outfit too demure, but that was probably just as well in Chad.

She ordered a car. The embassy used a service whose drivers were all vetted. When she went out to meet the car, night had fallen. The summer rains were over, and there were no clouds, so the sky was crowded with

stars. A compact four-door Peugeot was waiting for
her. In front of it was an embassy limousine.

As she approached she saw Dexter coming the other
way, with his wife on his arm. They were in evening
dress. There was a reception at the South African embassy, Tamara recalled. The limo would be for them.
"Hi, Dexter," she said. "Good evening, Mrs. Lewis,
how are you?"

Daisy Lewis was pretty but she looked a bit cowed.
Dexter managed to make a tuxedo look disheveled.
"Hi, Tammy," he said.

He was the only person in the world who called her
Tammy.

She resisted the urge to correct him, and going too
far in the other direction, she said: "Thank you for
reading that message from President Green. I think it
was a great thing to do. Everyone was thrilled." She silently accused herself of being a suck-up.

"Glad you appreciated it." He looked her up and
down. "You're all dolled up. I don't believe you were
invited to the South African shindig."

"No such luck." She was too lowly. "I'm just going
out for a quiet dinner."

Dexter said bluntly: "Who with?" A normal boss
would have no right to ask such a question, but this was
the CIA and the rules were different.

"I'm celebrating al-Bustan with Tabdar Sadoul from
the DGSE."

"I know him. A steady guy." Dexter gave her a hard
look. "All the same, bear in mind that you have to tell
me about any 'close and continuing contact' with a foreign national, even an ally."

"I know."

Dexter replied as if she had disagreed with him. "It
would constitute an unacceptable security risk."

He enjoyed throwing his weight around. Tamara

caught a sympathetic look from Daisy. He badgers her like this too, Tamara thought. She said: "Got it."

He said: "I shouldn't need to remind you of that."

"We're just colleagues, Dexter. Don't worry."

"It's my job to worry." He opened the limousine door. "Just remember, 'close and continuing contact' means that one blow job is all right, but not two."

Daisy said: "Dexter!"

He laughed. "Get in the car, sweetie."

As the limo moved away, a dusty silver family sedan pulled out of a parking space and followed: Dexter's bodyguard.

Tamara got into her own car and gave the driver the address.

There was nothing she could do about Dexter. She might have spoken to Phil Doyle, the officer supervising the Abdul project, who was senior to Dexter, but complaining about your boss to his superiors was not the way to get on in any organization.

N'Djamena had been laid out by French planners, back in the days when it had been called Fort-Lamy, and it had marvelously wide Parisian-style boulevards. The car sped to the Lamy Hotel, part of a worldwide American chain. It was the top venue for an elegant evening, but Tamara really preferred local eateries that served spicy African food.

The driver said: "Shall I pick you up?"

"I'll call," said Tamara.

She entered the grand marbled lobby. The place was patronized by the wealthy Chad elite. The country was landlocked and mostly desert, but it had oil. Nevertheless, the people were poor. Chad was one of the most corrupt countries in the world, and all the oil money went to those in power and their friends. They spent some of it here.

A roar of conviviality came from the adjacent Inter-

national Bar. She went in: you had to pass through the bar
to reach the restaurant. Western oilmen, cotton brokers,
and diplomats mingled with Chadian politicians and
businessmen. Some of the women were spectacularly
well-dressed. Such places had died during the pandemic,
but this one had recovered and risen to new heights.

She was greeted by a Chadian man of about sixty.
"Tamara!" he said. "Just the person I wanted to see.
How are you?"

His name was Karim and he was very well-
connected. He was a friend of the General's, having
helped his rise to power. Tamara was cultivating Karim
as a source of information from inside the Presidential
Palace. Fortunately he seemed to have similar intentions toward her.

He wore a lightweight business suit, gray with a
faint pinstripe, probably bought in Paris. His yellow
silk tie was perfectly knotted and his thinning hair was
brilliantined. He kissed her twice on both cheeks, four
kisses in all, as if they were members of the same
French family. He was a devout Muslim and a happily
married man, but he had a harmless tendresse for this
self-confident American girl.

She said: "I'm glad to see you, Karim." She had
never met his wife, but she said: "How is the family?"

"Splendid, thank you, just marvelous, grandchildren coming along now."

"That's wonderful. You said you were hoping to see
me. Is there something I can do for you?"

"Yes. The General would like to give your ambassador's wife a gift for her thirtieth birthday. Do you know
what kind of perfume she likes?"

Tamara did. "Mrs. Collinsworth uses Miss Dior."

"Ah, perfect. Thank you."

"But, Karim, may I say something frankly?"

"Of course! We are friends, aren't we?"

"Mrs. Collinsworth is an intellectual with an interest in poetry. She might not be very pleased with a gift of perfume."

"Oh." Karim was taken aback by the notion of a woman who did not want perfume.

"May I suggest an alternative?"

"Please."

"How about an English or French translation of one of the classical Arab poets? That would please her much more than perfume."

"Would it?" Karim was still struggling with the idea.

"Perhaps al-Khansa." The name meant "gazelle." "One of the few female poets, I understand."

Karim looked dubious. "Al-Khansa wrote elegies for the dead. A bit gloomy for a birthday."

"Don't worry. Mrs. Collinsworth will be pleased that the General knows about her love of poetry."

Karim's face cleared. "Yes, of course, that would be flattering to a woman. More so than perfume. I understand now."

"I'm glad."

"Thank you, Tamara. You're so smart." He glanced toward the bar. "Would you like a drink? A gin and tonic?"

She hesitated. She was keen to develop her relationship with Karim, but she did not want to keep Tab waiting. And there was something to be said for playing hard to get. "No, thank you," she said decisively. "I'm meeting a friend in the restaurant."

"Then perhaps we could meet for coffee one day soon?"

Tamara was pleased by the invitation. "That would be great."

"May I call you?"

"Of course. You have the number?"

"I will get it from the secret police."

Tamara was not sure whether that was meant to be a joke. She thought not. She smiled and said: "We'll talk soon."

"Delightful."

She left him and walked through to the Rive Gauche restaurant.

This room was quieter. The waiters spoke softly, the tablecloths muted the sound of cutlery, and the customers had to stop talking while they ate.

The maître d' was French, the waiters were Arab, and the busboys clearing away dirty plates were African. There was color discrimination even here, Tamara thought.

She saw Tab right away, sitting at a table near a curtained window. He smiled and stood up as she approached. He was wearing a navy blue suit with a crisp white shirt and a striped tie. It was a traditional outfit but he wore it with panache.

He kissed her on one cheek, then the other, but did not double up, showing more decorum than Karim. They sat down and he said: "Shall we have a glass of champagne?"

"Sure." She waved a waiter over and ordered. She wanted to make it clear, to Tab and to anyone watching, that this was not a romantic date.

Tab said: "So—we had a win!"

"Our friend with the cigarettes is solid gold."

They were both being careful about what they said, not naming al-Bustan or Abdul, just in case there should be a recording device hidden in the small vase of white freesias at the center of the table.

The champagne arrived, and they were silent until the waiter went away.

Then Tab said: "But can he do it again?"

"I don't know. He's walking a tightrope, a hundred feet above the ground, with no safety net. He can't afford a single misstep."

"Have you talked to him?"

"Today. He met the organizer of the trip yesterday, declared his interest, found out the price, and established his cover story."

"They believed him."

"No suspicions expressed, apparently. Of course, they could be faking that to lure him into a trap. We don't know and he doesn't either." Tamara raised her glass and said: "All we can do is wish him luck."

Tab said seriously: "May his God protect him."

A waiter brought menus and they studied them in silence for a couple of minutes. The hotel served standard international cuisine with a few African additions. Tamara chose a tagine, a stew with dried fruits, cooked slowly in an earthenware pot with a cone-shaped lid. Tab ordered veal kidneys in mustard sauce, a favorite French dish.

Tab said: "Would you like some wine?"

"No, thanks." Tamara liked alcohol in small quantities. Much as she enjoyed wine and spirits, she hated being tipsy. The loss of judgment unnerved her. Did that make her a control freak? Probably. "But you go ahead."

"No. For a Frenchman I drink very little."

She wanted to get to know him better. "Tell me something about yourself that I don't know," she said.

"Okay." He smiled. "It's a good question. Er . . ." He thought for a long moment. "I was born into a family of strong women."

"Interesting! Go on."

"Years ago my grandmother opened a convenience store in a suburb of Paris called Clichy-sous-Bois. She still runs it. The suburb is a rough neighborhood now, but she refuses to move. Amazingly, she has never been robbed."

"A tough woman."

"Small and wiry, with hard hands. With the money she made from the store, she sent my father to college. Now he's on the main board of Total, the French oil company, and drives a Mercedes, or rather his chauffeur does."

"Great achievement."

"My other grandmother became the Marquise de Travers when she married my grandfather, a penniless aristocrat who owned a champagne house. It's difficult to lose money making champagne but he managed it. His wife, my grandmother, took the business in hand and turned it around. His daughter, my mother, expanded into luggage and jewelry. That's the company my mother runs, with an iron fist."

"The Travers company?"

"Yes."

Tamara knew the brand but could not afford any of its products.

There was more she wanted to know, but their food came, and for a while they talked little while they ate.

"How are the kidneys?" Tamara said.

"Good."

"I've never eaten kidneys."

"Would you like a taste?"

"Please." She passed him her fork. He speared a morsel and passed the fork back. The flavor was strong. She said: "Woo-hoo! Lots of mustard."

"That's how I like it. How's the tagine?"

"Good. Would you like some?"

"Please." He passed her his fork and she loaded it and gave it back. "Not bad," he said.

Tasting each other's food was intimate, she thought. It was the kind of thing you might do on a date. But this was a meeting between colleagues. At least, that was how she saw it. How did Tab see it?

Afterward Tamara had fresh figs for dessert and Tab had cheese.

The coffee came in tiny cups and Tamara took only a sip. They made coffee too strong here. She hankered after a big mug of weak American coffee.

She returned to the interesting topic of Tab's family. She knew that his heritage was Algerian, and she said: "Did your grandmother come from Algeria?"

"No. She was born in Thierville-sur-Meuse, where there is a major military base. You see, my great-grandfather fought in the Second World War, in the famous Third Algerian Infantry Division; in fact he won a medal, the Croix de Guerre. He was still in the army when my grandmother was born. But it's time I learned something about you."

"I can't compete with your fascinating ancestry," Tamara said. "I was born into a Jewish family in Chicago. My father's a history professor, and he drives a Toyota, not a Mercedes. My mother is a high school principal." She pictured the two of them, Dad in a tweed suit and a wool tie, Mom writing reports with her glasses on the end of her nose. "I'm not religious, but they go to a liberal synagogue. My brother, Simon, lives in Rome."

He smiled. "That's it?"

She hesitated to reveal too much in the way of intimate details. She had to keep reminding herself that this was a work occasion. She was not yet ready to tell him about her two marriages. Later, perhaps.

She shook her head. "No aristocrats, no medals, no luxury brands. Oh, wait. One of Dad's books was a bestseller. It was called *Pioneer Wives: Women on the American Frontier.* It sold a million copies. We were famous for almost a year."

"And yet this allegedly ordinary American family produced . . . you."

That was a compliment, she saw. And it was not just idle flattery. He seemed to mean it.

Dinner was over but it was too early to go home. She surprised herself by saying: "Do you want to dance?"

There was a club in the basement of the hotel. It was staid by comparison with clubs in Chicago or even Boston, but it was the hottest spot in N'Djamena.

Tab said: "Sure. I'm a terrible dancer, but I love it."

"Terrible? How?"

"I don't know. I've been told I look silly."

It was hard to imagine this poised and elegant man doing something silly. Tamara looked forward to seeing it.

Tab called for the bill and they split it.

They went down in the elevator. Before the doors opened they heard the seismic thud of bass and drums, a sound that always gave Tamara itchy feet. The club was packed with affluent young Chadians in skimpy clothing. The girls' short skirts made Tamara's outfit look middle-aged.

Tamara led Tab straight to the dance floor, moving to the beat even before they got there.

Tab was an endearingly bad dancer. His arms and legs flailed to no particular rhythm, but he clearly enjoyed it. Tamara liked dancing with him. The casually sexy atmosphere of a club put her in a mildly amorous mood.

After an hour they got Cokes and took a break. Reclining on a couch in the chill-out room, Tab said: "Have you ever tried marc?"

"Is that a drug?"

"It's a brandy made from the skins of the grapes after the juice has been squeezed out. It started as a cheap alternative to cognac, but it's become a refined tipple in its own right. You can even get marc de Champagne."

"Let me guess," she said. "You've got a bottle at home."

"You're telepathic."

"All women are telepathic."

"So you know that I want to take you home for a nightcap."

She was flattered. He had already decided that this was more than a professional relationship.

But she had not. "No, thank you," she said. "I've had a great time, but I don't want to stay up late."

"Okay."

They went out. She felt a bit down and wished she had not refused his offer of a nightcap.

He asked the doorman to fetch his car and offered her a lift. She declined and phoned the car service.

While they were waiting he said: "I enjoyed talking to you so much. Could we have dinner again? With or without marc de Champagne afterward?"

"Okay," she said.

"We could go somewhere more laid-back next time. A Chadian restaurant, perhaps."

"Nice idea. Call me."

"Okay."

Her car came and he held the door for her. She pecked his cheek. "Good night."

"Sleep well."

The car took her to the embassy and she went to her room.

She liked him a lot, she realized as she got undressed; then she reminded herself that she was very bad at picking men.

She had married Stephen while still at the Univer-

sity of Chicago. It was not until after the ceremony that
she discovered he did not feel the vows should stop him
from sleeping with anyone else he fancied, and they
had split after six months. She had not spoken to him
since and never wanted to see him again.

After Chicago she had done a master's degree in international relations, specializing in the Middle East,
at the Paris university called Sciences Po. There she
had met and married an American called Jonathan
who was a different kind of mistake. He was kind,
clever, and amusing. The sex had been a bit vanilla, but
they had been happy together. Eventually they both realized that Jonathan was gay. They had a friendly
divorce, and she was still fond of him. They talked on
the phone three or four times a year.

Part of her trouble was that so many men were attracted to her. She was nice looking and vivacious and
sexy, she knew, and it was easy for her to catch a man's
eye. Her difficulty was figuring out which were the
good ones.

She got into bed and turned out the light, still thinking about Tab. He certainly looked good. She closed
her eyes and pictured him. He was tall and slim, his
hair was made to be stroked, and he had deep brown
eyes that she wanted to stare into. His clothes seemed
to cling to him lovingly, whether he was dressed in a
suit, as tonight, or casually. Tamara had wondered
how he could afford such well-cut clothes, but he had
explained it: his family was wealthy.

Tamara mistrusted handsome men. Stephen had
been handsome. They could be vain and self-absorbed.
She had once gone to bed with an actor who had said
afterward: "How was I?" Tab could have been like
that, although she did not really think so.

Was Tab as good as he seemed, or would he turn

out to be another one of her ghastly errors? She had agreed to see him again, and she could not pretend that the second date would be purely business. So I guess I'll find out, she thought, and with that she went to sleep.

CHAPTER 5

Tamara swam in the embassy pool first thing in the morning, when the sun was low and the air was still cool and free of dust. She was normally alone. For half an hour she could think over everything that was on her mind: Abdul's courage, Dexter's hostility, Karim's fondness, and Tab's unconcealed interest in her. She had her second date with Tab tomorrow: drinks at his apartment and dinner at his favorite Arab restaurant.

When she got out of the water she found that Dexter was sitting on a poolside lounger, watching her. She felt irritated, especially when he stared at her wet swimsuit.

She wrapped a towel around herself and felt less vulnerable.

"Something I want you to check out," he said.

"Okay."

"You know the N'Gueli Bridge."

"Of course."

The N'Gueli Bridge crossed the Logone River, which formed the border between Chad and Cameroon, so the bridge was an international crossing. It connected N'Djamena with the Cameroonian town of Kousséri. In fact it was two bridges, a high viaduct for vehicles and an older bridge, lower and narrower, now used only for pedestrians.

Tamara shaded her eyes and looked south. "You can almost see the bridge from here—it's about a mile away as the crow flies."

"It's a frontier post, but not strictly policed," Dexter went on. "Most vehicles don't get stopped. As for the pedestrians, they all seem to be friends and relatives of the border guards. Only white people are detained. They're charged a fictional entry tax, or exit tax. The amount depends on how affluent they look, and the guards accept only cash. I assume I don't have to draw you a picture."

"No." Tamara was not surprised. Chad was notoriously corrupt. But this was not a CIA problem. "Why are we interested?"

"An informant of mine tells me the jihadis are taking over the pedestrian bridge. They have quietly insinuated armed men. They don't bother the local people, but they've taken over the shakedown. They increased the prices and they share the proceeds with the real border guards, who don't care."

"And do we? This sounds like an issue for the local police."

"You bet we care, assuming my informant is right. The bribes aren't the point. ISGS wants control of a frontier post."

Tamara remained unconvinced. Why would ISGS seek such a thing? She saw no advantage to the jihadis. "How reliable is your informant?"

"Good. All the same, we need to check out the story. I want you to go there and take a look."

"All right. I'll need protection."

"I doubt it. But take a couple of soldiers if it makes you feel better."

"I'll talk to Colonel Marcus."

She returned to her apartment, got dressed, then emerged into the heat of the morning. The military had their own building in the embassy compound. Tamara entered and found Susan Marcus's office. An assistant told her to go right in, the colonel would be there in a minute.

Tamara looked around the room. One wall was covered with maps that, joined edge to edge, formed a large-scale chart of all of North Africa. A sticker in the middle of Niger was marked AL-BUSTAN. On the opposite wall was a large screen. There were no family photographs. She had two computer workstations and a phone. A cheap plastic desk tidy contained pencils and paper and Post-its. Tamara thought Colonel Marcus must be obsessively neat, or determined not to reveal anything personal about herself, or both.

Colonel Marcus was part of what the military called a Tier 2 Combined Joint Special Operations Task Force, or, for short, Special Forces.

She came in a moment later. She had short hair and a brisk manner, like every other military officer Tamara had ever met. She wore a khaki uniform and a peaked cap, all of which made her look masculine, although Tamara could see that underneath she was pretty. Tamara understood both the look and the office: Susan needed to be treated equally in a man's world, and any hint of femininity could be used against her.

She took off her cap, they sat down, and Tamara said: "I've just been with Dexter."

"He must be pleased about your work with Abdul."

Tamara shook her head. "He doesn't like me."

"So I've heard. You need to learn the art of making men believe that every success is their doing."

Tamara chuckled, then said: "You're not kidding, though, are you?"

"Hell no. How do you think I made colonel? By always letting my boss take the credit. What did Dexter have to say to you today?"

Tamara explained about the N'Gueli Bridge.

When she had finished, Susan frowned, opened her mouth to speak, hesitated, then picked up a pencil from a side table and tapped it on her empty desk.

Tamara said: "What?"

"I don't know. How good is Dexter's informant?"

"Good, he says, but not so good that we don't need to check out this report." Tamara felt a little unnerved by Susan's anxiety. "What's bothering you? You're one of the smartest people around here. If you're unhappy I want to know why."

"Okay. Dexter says the jihadis are taking bribes from tourists, which is peanuts, and giving half back to the regular guards, so the monetary gain is half of peanuts. The real object of the exercise is therefore to gain control of a strategic frontier post."

"I know what you're thinking," said Tamara. "Is it really worth the effort for them?"

"Consider a few points. One: as soon as the local police realize what's going on, they will clear the jihadis off the bridge, which they can probably manage without breaking a sweat."

Tamara had not considered this point, but now she nodded. "ISGS have control only as long as they're tolerated—which isn't really control at all."

"Two," Susan went on. "The bridge is important only if a battle of some kind is imminent, for example an attempted coup, like the Battle of N'Djamena back in 2008, but that's improbable now, because opposition to the General is currently weak."

"The Union of Forces for Democracy and Development is certainly in no position to start a revolution."

"Exactly. And three: in the unlikely event that the jihadis are allowed to stay there, and the even more unlikely possibility that the UFDD is about to mount a coup against the General, they have the wrong bridge. The vehicle bridge is the crucial one. It permits tanks and armored cars and trucks full of troops to drive from a foreign country right into the capital city. The pedestrian bridge is nothing."

The analysis was very clear. Susan had a brain like a steel trap. Tamara wondered why she herself had not figured all this out. She said feebly: "Maybe this is a prestige thing."

"Like touching your toes. It does you no good, but you do it just to prove you can."

"In a way, everything the jihadis do is for prestige."

"Hmm." Susan was not convinced. "Anyway, you need a precautionary bodyguard."

"Dexter doesn't think so, but he said I should take a couple of soldiers if it makes me feel better."

"Dexter's full of shit. They're jihadis. You need protection."

They set off from the embassy compound the next day just as the sun edged up over the brick fields to the east of the city. Susan insisted that they all wear body armor, lightweight bulletproof vests. Tamara had a baggy blue denim trucker jacket over hers: later she would feel hot.

They went in two cars. The CIA had a three-year-old tan Peugeot station wagon with a dented fender, used for discreet operations because there were so many cars like it in the city. Tamara drove it and Susan sat beside her. The soldiers' transport was driven by Pete Ackerman, the cheeky twenty-year-old who had once asked Tamara for a date. That car was not so anonymous, a green sport utility vehicle with darkened window glass, a car some people might look at twice. However, they took off their caps and put their rifles on the floor, so that anyone glimpsing them casually through the windshield might not realize they were troops.

The streets were quiet as Tamara led the way along the north bank of the Chari River, then took a bridge to the southern suburb of Walia. The main road here led directly to the border crossing.

Tamara was nervous now. Last night she had lain awake thinking. She had now spent more than two years in Chad, gathering information about ISGS, but her work had consisted of things like studying satellite photos of distant oases, looking for signs of military force. She had not yet come into direct contact with men whose aim in life was to kill people like her.

She was carrying a gun, a neat small Glock nine-millimeter semiautomatic pistol in a holster that was built into the vest. CIA officers rarely saw action, even overseas. Tamara had passed the firearms course top of the class, but she had never fired a weapon outside the shooting range. She would be happy to keep it that way.

Susan's careful precautions made her worry more.

The twin bridges over the river Logone were about fifty yards apart, Tamara observed as they came within sight, and the vehicle bridge was higher. She turned off the main road onto a dusty track.

Twenty yards from the end of the pedestrian bridge was a scatter of parked vehicles: a minibus, presumably waiting to take people into the city center; a couple of taxis on a similar errand; and half a dozen jalopies. Tamara drove in among the cars and pulled up where she had a clear view of both bridges. She left the engine idling. The squad parked beside her.

At first glance the situation seemed normal. People were crossing the pedestrian bridge from the Cameroon side in a steady stream, very few traveling in the opposite direction. She knew that many residents of Kousséri, the small town on the far side, came to N'Djamena for work or business. Some rode bicycles or donkeys, and Tamara saw one camel. A few carried produce in baskets or homemade handcarts, presumably heading for markets in the city center. This evening they would return, and the stream would flow the other way.

She thought of commuters back home in the Chicago Loop. Apart from the clothes, the main difference was that in Chicago everyone would be rushing, whereas here they seemed to be in no great hurry.

No one was questioning people or asking for passports. There was little sign of officialdom. A small low building might have been a guard hut. At first she thought there was no barrier, but after a moment she spotted a long piece of wood, the trunk of a slender tree, lying on the ground next to a pair of trestles, and guessed that it could quickly be erected to form a flimsy hurdle.

This is Toytown, she thought. What am I doing here with a pistol under my jacket?

After a moment she realized that not everyone in view was moving purposefully. Two men dressed in incomplete army uniforms were lounging against the parapet at the near end, both with pistols in belt holsters. They wore camouflage trousers with civilian short-sleeved shirts, one orange and one bright blue.

The one in orange was smoking, the other eating his breakfast, a stuffed pancake roll. They were watching the commuters uninterestedly. The smoker glanced toward the parked cars and showed no reaction.

Finally Tamara spotted the enemy, and felt a chill of apprehension. A few yards farther across the bridge were two men who looked serious. One had a strap over his shoulder from which dangled something that was mostly covered by a cotton shawl—all but one end, which stuck out and looked exactly like the muzzle of a rifle barrel.

The other was staring straight at Tamara's car.

For the first time, she felt in real danger.

She studied him through the windshield. He was a tall man with a gaunt face and a high forehead. Perhaps it was her imagination, but he seemed to have an air of implacable purpose. He paid no attention to the people swarming around him, as if they were insects. He too carried a rifle that was partly wrapped in a cloth, as if he did not really care whether people saw it or not.

As she was looking he took out a phone, dialed a number, and put the device to his ear.

Tamara said: "There's a guy—"

"I see him," said Susan, beside her.

"On the phone."

"Exactly."

"But who to?"

"—is the sixty-four-thousand-dollar question."

Tamara felt like a target. He could shoot her through the windshield. The distance was close range for a rifle. She was clearly visible and she could hardly move, sitting in the driving seat. She said: "We should get out of the car."

"Are you sure?"

"I'm not going to learn anything sitting here."

"Okay."

They both got out.

Tamara could hear the traffic on the upper bridge but could not see the vehicles.

Susan went to the green car and conferred with the squad. When she came back she said: "I told them to stay in the car, as we're being discreet, but they'll jump out at any sign of trouble."

From somewhere there was a shout: "Al-Bustan!"

Tamara looked around, puzzled. Where had it come from and why would anyone shout those words?

That was when the first shots were fired.

There was a *rat-tat-tat* like a snare drum in a rock band, then a crash of breaking glass, and finally a shout of pain.

Without thought, Tamara threw herself under the Peugeot.

Susan did the same.

There were screams of terror from the people crossing the bridge. Looking that way, Tamara saw that they were all trying to run back the way they had come. But she could not see anyone firing.

The man Tamara had been watching had not deployed his weapon. Lying under the car, her heart thudding, Tamara said: "Where the fuck did that shot come from?" The uncertainty made her more scared.

Alongside her, Susan said: "From above. From the vehicle bridge."

Susan had a clear view of the high bridge when she poked her head out on her side, whereas Tamara could see the pedestrian bridge without moving.

"The shots smashed the windshield of the other car," Susan went on. "I think one of the guys got hit."

"Oh, Christ, I hope he's all right."

There was another roar of agony, this one longer.

"He doesn't sound dead." Susan looked to her right. "They're dragging him under their car." She paused. "It's Corporal Ackerman."

"Oh, hell, how is he?"

"I can't tell."

There was no more yelling, which Tamara thought was a bad sign.

Susan looked out and up, with her pistol in her hand. She fired once. "Too far away," she said with frustration. "I can see someone pointing a rifle over the parapet of the vehicle bridge, but I can't hit him at this distance with a damn handgun."

There was another burst of fire from the bridge, and a terrifying cacophony of breaking sounds as bullets tore into the roof and windows of the Peugeot. Tamara heard herself scream. She put her hands over her head, knowing it was useless but unable to resist the instinct.

However, when the burst ended she was unhurt, and so was Susan.

Susan said: "He's firing from the high bridge. Now would be a good time to draw your weapon, if you're ready."

"Oh, fuck, I forgot I had a gun!" Tamara reached into the holster attached to her vest under her left arm. At the same moment the soldiers began to fire back.

Tamara lay flat on her belly with her elbows on the ground, holding her pistol in both hands, taking care to point her thumbs forward so that they would be out of the way of the slide when it sprang back. She set her Glock to single-shot firing—otherwise she could run out of ammunition in seconds.

The soldiers paused their fire. Immediately there was a third burst from the bridge, but this time, within a split second the soldiers fired a returning burst.

Tamara could not see the high bridge from her position, so she kept an eye on the pedestrian bridge.

There was something like a riot as those desperately fleeing the near end, where the shooting was, shoved into less terrified people at the far end who probably were not sure what the bangs meant. The two border guards in camouflage trousers were at the back of the crowd and panicking just as much as the civilians, beating the people in front of them in their attempt to get away faster. Tamara saw someone jump into the river and start swimming for the far side.

At the near end, she saw the two jihadis clambering down to the riverbank. As she inched the sights of the Glock toward them, they took cover under the bridge.

The firing stopped, and Susan said: "I think we got him. Anyway, he's vanished. Oh—oh—he's back—no, this is another guy, different headdress. How the fuck many of them are up there?"

In the brief quiet Tamara again heard someone shout: "Al-Bustan!"

Susan used her radio to call for urgent reinforcements and an ambulance for Pete.

There was another exchange of fire between the soldiers and the high bridge, but both sides had good cover and it looked as if no one was hit.

They were pinned down and helpless. I'm going to die here, Tamara thought. I wish I'd met Tab a bit sooner. Like five years ago.

On the pedestrian bridge, the jihadi with the gaunt face reappeared, on the riverbank where the parapet ended and the roadbed of the bridge blended into the stony ground, only about twenty yards away. As she moved the sights toward him he got down on the ground, and she knew he was about to lie flat and take careful aim and shoot at all of them sheltering under the cars, something she felt sure he would do with no remorse.

She had only a second or two to do something about

it. Without thought she got the man's face in the sights of the pistol, looking through the notch of the rear sight and getting the white dot of the forward sight between his eyes. Some distant corner of her mind marveled at how calm she was. The barrel of her pistol followed the slow downward movement of the man's head as he settled to the ground, moving quickly but not hastily, knowing as she did that anything but a quietly calm shot was likely to miss. Finally he steadied himself and gripped his rifle and brought up the barrel, and then Tamara squeezed the trigger of her Glock.

The gun kicked up, as it always did. Calmly she brought the muzzle down and resighted on the head. She saw that there was no need for a second shot—the man's head was shattered—but she squeezed the trigger anyway, and her round smashed into a motionless body.

She heard Susan say: "Good shooting!"

Tamara thought: Was that me? Did I just kill a man?

The other jihadi appeared farther along the riverbank, running away with his rifle in his hand.

Tamara shifted her position so that she could see the high bridge, but there was no way to tell whether the shooters were still there. She could hear the sounds of trucks and cars continuing to pass. She noticed the throaty roar of a high-powered motorcycle: if there were only two shooters they might have fled on that.

Susan was thinking along the same lines. She spoke into her radio. "Before you deploy to the pedestrian bridge, check the road bridge in case any of the shooters are still there."

Then she spoke to the soldiers under the green car. "Stay where you are while we find out whether they've all gone."

Most of the commuters had now exited the pedestrian bridge on the far side. Tamara could see some of them clustered around a scatter of buildings and trees, peeping around corners, waiting to see what would happen next. The two border guards in their bright shirts appeared at that end of the bridge but hesitated to cross back.

Tamara began to think it might be over, but she was willing to lie here all day until she felt sure it was safe to move.

A US Army ambulance came racing along the dirt road and pulled up behind the green car.

Susan shouted: "All guns take aim at the high bridge parapet, now!"

The three soldiers who were still unhurt rolled from under their car and took cover behind other vehicles, aiming their rifles at the high bridge.

Two paramedics jumped out of the ambulance. "Under the green car!" Susan yelled. "One man with gunshot wounds."

No shots were fired.

The paramedics brought a stretcher.

Tamara stayed where she was. She watched the remaining jihadi running along the riverbank. He was almost out of sight and she guessed he was not coming back. The two border guards began cautiously to walk back across the bridge. They had their pistols out, too late. Tamara muttered: "Thanks for your help, guys."

Susan's radio squawked and Tamara heard a distorted voice say: "All clear on the road bridge, Colonel."

Tamara hesitated. Was she willing to bet her life on a fuzzy radio message?

Of course I am, she said to herself. I'm a professional.

She rolled out from under the car and got to her feet. She felt weak and would have liked to sit down but did not want to look like a wimp in front of the soldiers. She leaned on the fender of the Peugeot for a moment, staring at the bullet holes. She knew that some rifle ammunition could smash all the way through a car. She had been lucky.

She remembered that she was an intelligence agent and she needed to glean any available information from this incident. She said to Susan: "Ask if there are any bodies on the high bridge."

Susan put her radio to her mouth and asked the question.

"No bodies, but some bloodstains."

One or more wounded men had been driven away, Tamara concluded.

That left the one she had killed.

Determinedly, she stepped toward the pedestrian bridge. Her legs felt stronger. She walked up to the body. There was no doubt that the jihadi was dead: his head was a mess. She took his gun from his unresisting hands. It was short and surprisingly light, a bullpup rifle with a banana-clip magazine. There was a serial number on the left side of the barrel near the join with the frame. Tamara recognized the gun as having been made by Norinco, the China North Industries Group Corporation, a defense manufacturer owned by the Chinese government.

She pointed the gun at the ground, pulled the magazine release rearward, and disengaged the banana clip, then opened the bolt and took out the chambered round. She put the banana clip and the single round into the pockets of her trucker jacket, then she carried the unloaded rifle back to her ruined car.

Susan saw her and said: "You carry that like it's a dead dog."

"I just pulled out its teeth," said Tamara.

The paramedics were loading the stretcher into the ambulance. Tamara realized she had not even spoken to Pete. She hurried over.

Pete looked ominously still. She stopped and said: "Oh, Christ."

Pete's face was pale and his eyes stared upward.

A paramedic said: "Sorry, miss."

"He asked me for a date once," Tamara said. She began to cry. "I told him he was too young." She wiped her face with her sleeve but the tears kept coming. "Oh, Pete," she said to his lifeless face. "I'm sorry."

A switchboard operator said: "I have Corporal Ackerman's father on the line, Madam President. Mr. Philip Ackerman." Pauline hated this. Every time she had to speak to a parent whose child had died in the armed services, it wrenched at her heart. She was forced to think about how she would feel if Pippa died. It was the worst part of her job.

"Thank you," she said to the operator. "Put him on."

A deep male voice said: "This is Phil Ackerman."

"Mr. Ackerman, this is President Green."

"Yes, Madam President."

"I'm very sorry for your loss."

"Thank you."

"Pete gave his life, and you gave your son, and I want you to know that your country is profoundly grateful to you for your sacrifice."

"Thank you."

"I believe you're a firefighter, sir."

"That's right, ma'am."

"Then you know about risking your life for a good reason."

"Yes."

"I can't ease your pain, but I can tell you that Pete's

life was given for the defense of our country and our values of freedom and justice."

"I believe that." There was a catch in the man's voice.

Pauline judged it was time to move on. She said: "May I speak to Pete's mom?"

There was a hesitation. "She's very upset."

"It's up to her."

"She's nodding at me."

"Okay."

A woman's voice said: "Hello?"

"Mrs. Ackerman, this is the president. I'm very sorry for your loss."

She heard the sound of sobbing, and it brought tears to her own eyes.

In the background the husband said: "You want to give me the phone back, honey?"

Pauline said: "Mrs. Ackerman, your son died in a tremendously important cause."

Mrs. Ackerman said: "He died in Africa."

"Yes. Our military there—"

"Africa! Why did you send him to Africa to die?"

"In this small world—"

"He died for Africa. Who cares about Africa?"

"I understand your emotion, Mrs. Ackerman. I'm a mother—"

"I can't believe you threw his life away!"

Pauline wanted to say *I can't believe it, either, Mrs. Ackerman, and it breaks my heart.* But she remained silent.

After a pause Phil Ackerman came back on the line. "I'm sorry about that."

"No need to apologize, sir. Your wife is suffering terrible grief. She has my deep sympathy."

"Thank you."

"Good-bye, Mr. Ackerman."
"Good-bye, Madam President."

The debrief took the rest of the day.

The army suggested the whole thing had been a trap: false information lured them to the bridge, where an ambush had been laid. Susan Marcus was sure of it.

The CIA disagreed with that interpretation, which reflected badly on Dexter. The implication was that he had trusted an informant who had deceived him. On the contrary, Dexter argued, it had been a genuine tip-off and the jihadis on the pedestrian bridge had panicked when the army arrived in force and had called in reinforcements.

By six o'clock in the afternoon Tamara no longer cared which explanation was accepted. She felt mentally bruised. Back in her apartment she considered falling into bed, but she knew she would not sleep. She kept seeing Pete's lifeless body and the destroyed head of the gaunt-faced man she had killed.

She did not want to be alone. She remembered that she had a date with Tab. She felt instinctively that he would know what to do. She showered and put on fresh clothes, jeans and a T-shirt with a cotton shawl for decorum. Then she called for a car.

Tab lived in an apartment building near the French embassy. It was not very swanky, and she guessed he could have afforded better, but he would have been obliged to use diplomatic premises that could be vetted and monitored.

He opened the door and said: "You look dead beat. Come in and sit down."

"I was in a kind of shootout," she said.

"At the N'Gueli Bridge? We heard about that. You were there?"

"Yes. And Pete Ackerman died."

He took her arm and led her to the couch. "Poor Pete. And poor you."

"I killed a man."

"My God."

"He was a jihadi, and he was about to shoot me. I'm not sorry." She realized she could say things to Tab that she had not been able to say in the debrief. "But he was a human being, and one second he was alive, and moving, and thinking, and then I squeezed the trigger and he was dead, gone, a corpse, and I can't get him out of my head."

There was an open bottle of white wine in an ice bucket on the coffee table. He poured half a glass and gave it to her. She took a sip and put the glass down. She said: "Do you mind if we don't go out to dinner?"

"Of course not. I'll cancel."

"Thank you."

He took out his phone. While he was making the call she looked around. The apartment was modest but the furnishings were expensive, with deep soft armchairs and thick rugs. He had a large TV screen and some kind of fancy hi-fi setup with large floor-standing speakers. Her wineglass was crystal.

She was interested in two silver-framed photographs on a side table. One showed a dark-skinned man in a business suit with a chic middle-aged blond woman, undoubtedly Tab's parents. The other was of a fierce-looking little Arab woman standing proudly outside a shop front: that would be his grandmother in Clichy-sous-Bois.

When he got off the phone she said: "Talk about something else. What were you like as a boy?"

He smiled. "I went to a bilingual school called Ermitage International. I was a good student but I got into trouble sometimes."

"How? What did you do?"

"Oh, the usual stuff. One day I smoked a joint just before math. The teacher couldn't understand why I'd suddenly become completely stupid. He thought I was doing it to make the others laugh, a kind of stunt."

"What else?"

"I joined a rock band. Of course we had an American name: the Boogie Kings."

"Were you any good?"

"No. I was fired right after our first performance. My drumming was like my dancing."

She giggled, for the first time since the shootout.

He said: "After I left the band got better."

"Did you have girlfriends?"

"It was a mixed school, so yes."

She saw a faraway look in his eyes. "Who are you remembering?"

He looked embarrassed. "Oh . . ."

"You don't have to say. I don't want to pry."

"I don't mind, but if I tell you it might sound like boasting."

"Tell me anyway."

"It was the English teacher."

Tamara giggled—second time. She was starting to feel more normal. "What was she like?"

"About twenty-five. Pretty, blond. We used to kiss in the stationery store."

"Just kissing?"

"No, not just kissing."

"You bad boy."

"I was crazy about her. I wanted to run away from school and fly to Las Vegas and get married."

"How did it end?"

"She got a job in another school and disappeared from my life. I was heartbroken. But heartbreak doesn't last long when you're seventeen."

"A lucky escape?"

"Oh, yes. She was great, but look, you have to fall in and out of love a few times before you begin to understand what you're really looking for."

She nodded. He was quite wise, she thought. "I know what you mean."

"Do you?"

She blurted out: "I've been married twice."

"I wasn't expecting that!" He smiled, taking the edge off his expression of shock. "Tell me more—if you feel like it."

She did. She was glad to be reminded that there were important things in life other than guns and killing. "Stephen was just an adolescent mistake," she said. "We married in my first year at college and separated before the summer vacation. I haven't spoken to him for years and I no longer know where he lives."

"So much for Stephen," said Tab. "If it's any consolation, I feel the same way about a girl called Anne-Marie. I didn't marry her, though. Tell me about number two."

"Jonathan was serious. We were together for four years. We loved each other, and in a way we still do." She paused, thinking.

Tab waited patiently for a few moments, then prompted her gently. "What went wrong?"

"Jonathan is gay."

"Oh. That's awkward."

"I didn't know it at first, obviously, and I guess he didn't either, although at the end he admitted that he'd always been uncertain."

"But you parted friends."

"We haven't really parted. We're still close, or as

close as you can be to someone who lives thousands of
miles away."

"But you are divorced?" he said emphatically.

That seemed important to him for some reason.
"Yes, we're divorced," she said firmly. "He's married to
a man now." She wanted to know more about him.
"Have you ever been married? You must be, what,
thirty-five?"

"Thirty-four, and no, I've never been married."

"But you must have had at least one serious love
affair, after the English teacher."

"True."

"Why didn't you marry?"

"Um, I think my experience has been like yours
except that I never actually tied the knot. I've had one-
night stands and disastrous affairs and a couple of
really great women with whom I had relationships that
lasted a long time . . . but not forever."

Tamara took another sip of wine. It was delicious,
she noticed.

Tab was beginning to open his heart to her, and she
wanted desperately for him to go on. The morning's
deaths still lingered darkly at the back of her mind,
ghosts waiting to spring out at her, but this conversation was comforting. "Tell me about one of the great
women," she said. "Please."

"All right. I lived with Odette for three years in
Paris. She's a linguist, speaks several languages, and
makes her living translating, usually Russian to French.
She's really smart."

"And . . . ?"

"When I was posted here, I asked her to marry me
and come with me."

"Oh. So it was really serious." Tamara actually felt
dismayed that he had gone so far as to propose. Stupid
feeling, she told herself.

"Serious on my side, at least. And she could have carried on her translating work here in Chad—it's all done remotely anyway. But she said no. Okay, I said, let's get married and I'll refuse the posting. Then she told me that she didn't want to get married either way."

"Ouch."

He shrugged unconvincingly. "I was more serious than she was, and I found out the hard way."

He was only pretending to be insouciant. She could tell that he had been hurt. She wanted to hold him in her arms.

He made a brushing-away gesture. "Enough of ancient miseries," he said. "Would you like something to eat?"

"Yes," she said. "I haven't wanted food all day, but now I'm ravenous."

"Let's see if there's anything in the refrigerator."

She followed him into the little kitchen. He opened the fridge door and said: "Eggs, tomatoes, one large potato, and half an onion."

"Do you want to go out?" she said. She hoped he would say no: she did not yet feel ready for a restaurant.

"Heck no," he said. "There's enough here for a banquet."

He diced the potato and fried it, made a tomato-and-onion salad, then beat the eggs and made an omelet. They sat on stools at the small kitchen counter to eat. Tab poured more of the white wine.

He was right, it was a banquet.

Afterward she realized she felt human again. "I guess I should be going," she said reluctantly. She knew that when she went to bed alone in her apartment the ghosts would come out and she would have no defense.

"You don't have to leave," he said.

"I don't know."

"I know what you're thinking."

"Do you?"

"Let me just say that whatever you want will be okay with me."

"I don't want to sleep alone tonight."

"Then sleep with me."

"But I don't feel like sex."

"I didn't think you would."

"Are you sure that's all right? No kissing or any-thing? Will you just put your arms around me and hold me while I go to sleep?"

"I would love to do that."

And he did.

CHAPTER 6

The air in Beijing was breathable this morning. The weather girl said so, and Chang Kai trusted her, so he dressed in cycling gear. He confirmed her prognosis with his first breath when he stepped out of the building. All the same he put on his face mask before mounting his machine.

He had a Fuji-ta road bike with a lightweight aluminum alloy frame and a carbon-fiber front fork. As he set off, it seemed to weigh no more than a pair of shoes.

Cycling to work was the only form of exercise Kai had room for in his schedule. In Beijing's colossal traffic jams it took the same length of time as driving, so he did not lose any of the working day.

Kai needed to exercise. He was forty-five years old, and his wife, Tao Ting, was thirty. He was slim and fit, and taller than average, but he was always conscious of that fifteen-year gap, and he felt a duty to be as agile and energetic as Ting.

The street where he lived was a main artery with dedicated bike lanes to separate the thousands of cyclists from the hundreds of thousands of cars. All kinds of people rode: workers, school pupils, uniformed messengers, even smart office women in skirts. Turning off the main road onto a side street, Kai had to negotiate the four-wheeled traffic, winding between trucks and limousines, the yellow-sided taxis and the red-topped buses.

As he raced along he thought fondly about Ting. She was an actress, beautiful and alluring, and half the men in China were in love with her. Kai and Ting had been married five years, and he was still crazy for her.

His father disapproved. For Chang Jianjun, people who appeared on television were shallow and frivolous, unless they were politicians enlightening the masses. He had wanted Kai to marry a scientist or an engineer.

Kai's mother was equally conservative but not so dogmatic. "When you know her so well that all her faults and weaknesses are familiar to you, and you still adore her, then you can be sure it's true love," she had said. "That's how I feel about your father."

He cycled to the Haidian District in the northwest of the city and entered an extensive campus next to the Summer Palace. This was the headquarters of the Ministry of State Security, in Mandarin the Guojia Anquan Bu, or Guoanbu for short. It was the spy organization responsible for both foreign and domestic intelligence.

He parked his machine in a bike rack. Still breathing hard and sweating from his exertion, he entered the tallest of the campus buildings. Important though the ministry was, the lobby was shabby, with furniture in the angular style that had been excitingly modern in the Mao era. The doorman bowed his head deferentially. Kai was vice minister for international intelligence, in charge of the overseas half of China's intelligence operation. He and the vice minister for homeland intelligence were equals who reported to the security minister.

Kai was young for such a senior post. He was fiercely bright. After studying history at Peking University—which had the top history department in China—he had taken a PhD in American history at Princeton. But his brain was not the only reason for his rapid rise. His family was at least as important. His great-grandfather had been on the legendary Long March with Mao Zedong. His grandmother had been China's ambassador to Cuba. His father was currently vice chairman of the National Security Commission, the committee that made all the important foreign policy and security decisions.

In short, Kai was Communist royalty. There was a colloquial word for people like him, the children of the powerful: he was a princeling, tai zi dang, a phrase that was not used openly but spoken quietly, between friends, behind the back of the hand.

It was a derogatory name, but Kai was determined to use his status for the benefit of his country, and he reminded himself of this vow every time he entered Guoanbu headquarters.

The Chinese had thought they were in danger when they were poor and weak. They had been wrong. No one had seriously wanted to wipe them out then. But now China was on its way to becoming the richest and most powerful country in the world. It had the largest and smartest population and there was no reason why it should not be foremost. And so it was in serious danger. The people who had ruled the globe for centuries—the Europeans and the Americans—were terrified. They saw world domination slipping day by day out of their grasp. They believed they had to destroy China or be destroyed. They would stop at nothing.

And there was a dreadful example. The Russian Communists, inspired by the same Marxist philosophy that had driven China's revolution, had striven to become the world's most powerful country—and had been brought down with a seismic crash. Kai, like everyone else in the highest levels of the government, was obsessed with the fall of the Soviet Union and terrified that the same thing would happen to China.

Which was the reason for Kai's ambition. He wanted to be president, so that he could make sure China rose to its destiny.

It was not that he thought he was the smartest person in China. At the university he had met mathematicians and scientists a good deal cleverer. However, nobody was more capable than he of guiding the country to the achievement of its aspirations. He would never say this aloud, not even to Ting, for who could help regarding it as arrogant? But he secretly believed it, and he was determined to prove it.

The only way to approach a mammoth task was to divide it into manageable parts, and the minor challenge Kai had to deal with today was the United Nations resolution on the arms trade, proposed by the United States.

Countries such as Germany and Britain would support the US resolution routinely; others, such as North Korea and Iran, would equally automatically oppose it; but the outcome would depend upon the many nonaligned countries. Yesterday Kai had learned that American ambassadors in several third-world countries had petitioned their host governments to secure support for the resolution. Kai suspected that President Green was quietly mounting a massive diplomatic effort. He had ordered Guoanbu intelligence teams in every neutral country to find out immediately whether the government had been lobbied and with what success.

The results of that inquiry should be on his desk now.

He got out of the elevator on the top floor. There were three main offices here, belonging to the minister and the two vice ministers. All three had support staff in adjacent rooms. Below this level, the headquarters organization was divided into geographical departments called desks—the US desk, the Japan desk—and technical divisions such as the signals intelligence division, the satellite intelligence division, the cyberwar division.

Kai went to his own suite of rooms, greeting secretaries and assistants as he passed through. The desks and chairs were utilitarian, made of laminated plywood and painted metal, but the computers and phones were state-of-the-art. On his own desk was a neat pile of messages from heads of Guoanbu stations in embassies around the world, replying to yesterday's inquiry.

Before reading them he went into his private bathroom, took off his cycling clothes, and showered. He kept a dark gray suit here, one made for him by a Beijing tailor who had trained in Naples and knew how to achieve the relaxed modern look. He had brought with him in his backpack a clean white shirt and a wine-red tie. He dressed quickly and emerged ready for the day's work.

As he feared, the messages showed that the American State Department had unobtrusively conducted an energetic and comprehensive lobbying campaign with considerable success. He came to the alarming conclusion that President Green's UN resolution was on course to be passed. He was glad he had spotted this.

The UN had little power to enforce its will but the resolution was symbolic. If passed it would be used by Washington as anti-Chinese propaganda. By contrast, its defeat would be a boost for China.

Kai picked up the bundle of papers and crossed the

hallway to the minister's rooms. He went through the open-plan office to the personal secretary's room and said: "Is he free for something urgent?"

She picked up the phone and asked. After a moment she said: "Vice Minister Li Jiankang is with him, but you can go in."

Kai made a face. He would have preferred to see the minster alone, but he could not back out now. "Thank you," he said, and went in.

The security minister was Fu Chuyu, a man in his midsixties, a long-serving and reliable stalwart of the Communist Party of China. His desk was clear except for a gold-colored pack of cigarettes, Double Happiness brand, plus a cheap plastic lighter and an ashtray made of a military shell case. The ashtray was already half full and there was a burning cigarette perched on its rim.

Kai said: "Good morning, sir. Thank you for seeing me so quickly."

Then he looked at the other occupant of the room, Li Jiankang. Kai said nothing but his expression asked: *What's he doing here?*

Fu picked up his cigarette, drew on it, blew out smoke, and said: "Li and I were just talking. But tell me why you wanted to see me."

Kai explained about the UN resolution.

Fu looked grave. "This is a problem," he said. He did not thank Kai.

"I'm glad I learned of it early," Kai said, making the point that he had sounded the warning before anyone else. "I think there's still time to put matters right."

"We need to discuss this with the foreign minister." Fu looked at his watch. "The trouble is I've got to fly to Shanghai now."

Kai said: "I'll be happy to inform the Foreign Ministry, sir."

Fu hesitated. He probably did not want Kai to speak directly to the minister: it put Kai on too high a level. The downside of being a princeling was that others resented it. Fu favored Li, who was a traditionalist like himself. But he could not cancel a trip to Shanghai just to stop Kai from talking to the foreign minister.

Reluctantly, Fu said: "Very well."

Kai turned to leave, but Fu stopped him. "Before you go . . ."

"Sir?"

"Sit down."

Kai sat. He had a bad feeling.

Fu turned to Li. "Perhaps you'd better tell Chang Kai what you told me a few minutes ago."

Li was not much younger than the minister and he too was smoking. Both men had their hair cut like Mao's, thick on the top and sides but short. They wore the stiff boxy suits preferred by traditional old Communists. Kai had no doubt that they both regarded him as a dangerous young radical who needed to be kept in check by older, more experienced men.

Li said: "I've had a report from the Beautiful Films studio."

Kai felt a cold hand grip his heart. Li's job was to monitor discontented Chinese citizens, and he had found one in the place where Ting worked. It was almost certain to be someone close to Ting, if not herself. She was no subversive; in fact she was not very interested in politics. But she was incautious and sometimes said what came into her mind without pausing to reflect.

Li was getting at Kai through his wife. Many men would think it shameful to attack a man by threatening his family, but the Chinese secret service had never hesitated. And it was effective. Kai could withstand an assault on himself, but he could not bear to see Ting suffer on his account.

Li went on: "There have been conversations critical of the Party."

Kai tried not to let his distress show. "I see," he said in a neutral voice.

"I'm sorry to say that your wife, Tao Ting, participated in some of them."

Kai directed a look of hatred and contempt at Li, who was clearly not sorry in the least. In fact he was delighted to bring a charge against Ting.

This could have been handled differently. The comradely thing would have been for Li to tell Kai about the problem quietly, in private. But instead he had chosen to go to the minister, maximizing the damage. It was an act of naked hostility.

Kai told himself that such underhand tactics were the weapons of a man who knew he could not rise by merit. But this was small consolation. He was sick at heart.

Fu said: "This is serious. Tao Ting could be influential. She is probably more well-known than I am!"

Of course she is, you fool, Kai thought. She's a star, and you're a narrow-minded old bureaucrat. Women want to emulate her. No one wants to be like you.

Fu went on: "My wife watches every episode of *Love in the Palace*. She seems to pay it more attention than the news." He was clearly disgruntled about this.

Kai was not surprised. His mother watched the show, but only if his father was out of the house.

Kai pulled himself together. With an effort he remained courteous and unruffled. "Thank you, Li," he said. "I'm glad you informed me about these allegations." He gave a distinct emphasis to the word *allegations*. Without directly denying what Li had said, he was reminding Fu that such reports were not always true.

Li looked resentful at the implication but said nothing.

"Tell me," Kai went on. "Who made this report?"

"The senior Communist Party official at the studio," said Li promptly.

This was an evasive answer. All such reports came from Communist officials. Kai wanted to know the original source. But he did not challenge Li. Instead he turned to Fu. "Would you like me to talk to Ting about this, quietly, before the might of the ministry is officially brought to bear?"

Li bristled. "Subversion is investigated by the Domestic Department, not by the families of accused persons," he said in a tone of wounded dignity.

But the minister hesitated. "A degree of latitude is normal in such cases," he said. "We don't want prominent people brought into disrepute unnecessarily. It does the Party no good." He turned to Kai. "Find out what you can."

"Thank you."

"But be quick. Report to me within twenty-four hours."

"Yes, Minister."

Kai stood up and walked briskly to the door. Li did not follow him. He would stay behind and whisper more poison to the minister, no doubt. There was nothing Kai could do about that now. He went out.

He needed to talk to Ting as soon as possible, but to his frustration he had to put her out of his mind for now. First he had to deal with the UN problem. Back in his own suite he spoke to his principal secretary, Peng Yawen, a lively middle-aged woman with short gray hair and glasses. "Call the foreign minister's office," he said. "Say I would like to meet him to convey some urgent security information. Any time today that suits his convenience."

"Yes, sir."

Kai could not move until he knew when that would happen. The Beautiful Films studio was not far from the Guoanbu headquarters, but the Foreign Ministry was miles across town in the Chaoyang District, where many embassies and foreign businesses had their premises. If traffic was bad the journey could take an hour or more.

Fretting, he looked out of the window, across the assorted roofs with their satellite dishes and radio transmitters, to the highway that curved around the Guoanbu campus. The traffic appeared normal, but that could change quickly.

Happily the Foreign Ministry responded promptly to his message. "He'll see you at twelve noon," said Peng Yawen. Kai looked at his watch: he could make it comfortably. Yawen added: "I've called Monk. He should be outside by the time you reach the ground floor." Kai's driver had gone bald at a young age and had been nicknamed Heshang, Monk.

Kai stuffed the messages from the embassies into a folder and went down in the lift.

His car crawled through the center of Beijing. He could have made the journey faster by bike. On the way he mulled over the UN resolution, but his mind kept shifting to his worry about Ting. What had she been saying? He wrenched his thoughts back to the problem the Americans had created. He needed to have a solution to offer the foreign minister. Eventually he thought of something, and by the time he reached No. 2 Chaoyangmen Nandajie he had a plan.

The Foreign Ministry was a fine tall building with a curved façade. The lobby gleamed luxuriously. It was intended to impress foreign visitors, by contrast with the Guoanbu headquarters, which never received any visitors, ever.

Kai was ushered into the elevator and taken up to

the office of the minister, which was if anything more lavish than the lobby. His desk was a Ming Dynasty scholar's writing table, and on it stood a blue-and-white porcelain vase that Kai thought must be from the same period, and therefore priceless.

Wu Bai was an affable bon vivant whose main aim, in politics and life, was to avoid trouble. Tall and handsome, he wore a blue chalk-striped suit that looked made in London. His secretaries adored him but his colleagues thought he was a lightweight. Kai's view was that Wu Bai was an asset. Foreign leaders liked his charm and warmed to him in a way they never would to a more hidebound Chinese politician, such as Security Minister Fu Chuyu.

"Come in, Kai," said Wu Bai amiably. "It's good to see you. How's your mother? I used to have a crush on her when we were young, you know, before she met your father." Wu Bai would sometimes say things like this to Kai's mother and make her giggle like a girl.

"She's very well, I'm happy to say. So is my father."

"Oh, I know that. I see your father all the time, of course—I'm on the National Security Commission with him. Sit down. What's this about the United Nations?"

"I got a sniff of it yesterday and confirmed it overnight, and I thought I'd better tell you right away." It was always good for Kai to emphasize to ministers that he was giving them the very latest hot news. He now repeated what he had told the security minister earlier.

"It sounds as if the Americans have made a major effort." Wu Bai frowned disapprovingly. "I'm surprised my people haven't gotten wind of it."

"To be fair, they don't have the resources I've got. We focus on what is secret—that's our job."

"These Americans!" Wu said. "They know that we hate Muslim terrorists as much as they do. More."

"Much more."

"Our worst troublemakers are the Islamists in the Xinjiang region."

"I agree."

Wu Bai shrugged off his indignation. "But what are we going to do about it? That's the important question."

"We could push back against the American diplomatic campaign. Our ambassadors can try to change the minds of neutral countries."

"We can try, of course," Wu Bai said dubiously. "But presidents and prime ministers don't like to go back on their promises. It makes them look weak."

"May I make a suggestion?"

"Please do."

"Many of the neutral countries whose support we need are places where the Chinese government is making massive investments—literally billions of dollars. We could threaten to withdraw from those projects. You want your new airport, your railway, your petrochemical plant? Then vote with us—or go ask President Green for the money."

Wu Bai frowned. "We wouldn't want to carry out that threat. We're not going to cripple our investment program for the sake of a pesky UN resolution."

"No, but the threat alone might work. Or, if necessary, we could pull out of one or two minor projects symbolically. We could always restart them later anyway. But the news that a bridge or a school had been canceled would scare those who are expecting a highway or an oil refinery."

Wu Bai looked thoughtful. "This could work. Big threats, backed up by one or two token withdrawals that can be reversed later." He looked at his watch. "I'm seeing the president this afternoon. I'll put it to him. I think he'll like the idea."

Kai thought so too. In the maneuvering over the choice of a new Chinese leader—more secretive and byzantine than for a Pope—President Chen Haoran had given the traditionalists the impression that he was on their side, but since becoming leader he had generally made pragmatic decisions.

Kai stood up. "Thank you, sir. My kind regards to Madame Wu."

"I'll be sure to tell her."

Kai left.

Down in the swanky lobby he called Peng Yawen. She gave him several messages but none demanded his immediate attention. He felt he had done a good morning's work for his country, and now he could attend to a personal matter. He left the building and told Monk to take him to the Beautiful Films studio.

It was a long crosstown journey, almost all the way back to the Guoanbu. On the way he thought about Ting. He was passionately in love with her but sometimes baffled by her, and occasionally—as now—embarrassed. He had fallen for her partly because he was enchanted by the free-and-easy ways of film people. He loved their openness and lack of inhibition. They were always joking, especially about sex. But he also felt a conflicting impulse that was just as strong: he longed for a traditional Chinese family. He did not dare to mention this to Ting, but he wanted her to have a child.

It was something she never mentioned. She adored being adored. She liked it when strangers approached her and asked for her autograph. She drank up their compliments and fed off the excitement they showed just meeting her. And she enjoyed the money. She had a sports car and a room full of beautiful clothes and a vacation home on Gulangyu Island in Xiamen, twelve hundred miles from the polluted air of Beijing.

She showed no inclination to retire and become a mother.

But the need was becoming urgent. In her thirties it would slowly become less easy for her to conceive. When Kai thought of this he felt panicky.

He would say none of this today. There was a more immediate problem.

A small crowd of fans, all women, stood outside the studio gate, autograph books in hand, as Kai's car approached. His driver spoke to the guard while the women peered into the car, hoping to recognize a star, then saw Kai and looked away disappointed. Then the barrier was lifted and the car drove in.

Monk knew his way around the sprawl of ugly industrial buildings. It was early afternoon, and some people were taking a late lunch break: film workers could never rely on regular mealtimes. Kai saw a costumed superhero slurping noodles from a plastic bowl, a medieval princess smoking a cigarette, and four Buddhist monks sitting around a table playing poker. The car passed several outdoor sets: a section of the Great Wall, painted wood supported by modern steel scaffolding; the façade of a building in the Forbidden City; and the entrance to a New York City police station, complete with a sign saying: 78TH PRECINCT. Any fantasy could be realized here. Kai loved the place.

Monk parked outside a warehouselike building with a small door identified by a handwritten sign that read: LOVE IN THE PALACE. It could hardly have looked less like a palace. Kai went in.

He was familiar with the maze of corridors with dressing rooms, costume wardrobes, makeup and hairdressing studios, and stores of electric equipment. Technicians in jeans and headphones greeted him amiably: they all knew the star's lucky husband.

He learned that Ting was on the soundstage. He

followed a twisted plait of fat cables around the backs of tall scenery flats to a door where a red light forbade entry. Kai knew he could ignore the sign if he was quiet. He slipped in. The large room was hushed.

The show was set in the early eighteenth century, before the First Opium War, which had begun the destruction of the Qing Dynasty. People thought of it as a golden age, when the learning, sophistication, and wealth of traditional Chinese civilization were unchallenged. It was similar to the way French people harked back to Versailles and the court of the Sun King, or Russians glamorized St. Petersburg before the revolution.

Kai recognized the set, which represented the emperor's receiving chamber. There was a throne under a draped canopy, and behind it a fresco of peacocks and fantastic vegetation. It gave an impression of enormous wealth, until you looked closely and saw the cheap fabric and bare wood that the camera did not reveal.

The show was a family saga, disapprovingly called an idol drama by high-minded people. Ting was the emperor's favorite concubine. She was on set now, in heavy makeup, white powder and bright red lipstick. She wore an elaborate headdress studded with jewels, fake of course. Her dress was meant to be ivory silk exquisitely embroidered with flowers and birds in flight, though in reality it was printed rayon. The waist was tiny, as her own really was, and its smallness was exaggerated by a broad bustle.

Her look was innocent and precious, like something made of porcelain. The appeal of the character was that she was not as pure and sweet as she looked—not by a long way. She could be horribly spiteful, thoughtlessly cruel, and explosively sexy. The audience loved her.

Ting was the great rival of the emperor's senior wife,

who was not on the set. But the emperor was. He sat on the throne wearing an orange color silk coat with huge flared sleeves over a multicolored undergarment like a floor-length dress. His hat was a cap with a little spike, and he had a drooping mustache. He was played by Wen Jin, a tall, romantic-looking actor, the heartthrob of millions of Chinese women.

Ting was being angry, berating the emperor, tossing her head, her eyes flashing defiance. In this mode she looked supernaturally desirable. Kai could not quite make out what she was saying, for the room was large and she was speaking in low tones. He knew, because she had explained to him, that shouting did not play well on television and the microphones could easily pick up her quiet vituperation.

The emperor was alternatively conciliatory and stern, but he was always reacting to her, never taking the initiative, something about which the actor often complained. Finally he kissed her. The audience looked forward to such scenes, which happened infrequently: Chinese television was more prudish than the American equivalent.

The kiss was tender and lingering, something that might have made Kai jealous had he not known that Wen Jin was 100 percent gay. It went on for an unrealistically long time, then the director, a woman, shouted: "Cut!" in English, and everyone relaxed.

Ting and Jin immediately turned away from one another. Ting patted her lips with a tissue that Kai knew was a sanitizing wipe. He walked over to her. She smiled in surprise and embraced him.

He had never doubted her love, but if he had then a welcome such as this would have reassured him. She was obviously delighted to see him, even though it was only a few hours ago that they had had breakfast together.

"I'm sorry about the kiss," she said. "You know I didn't enjoy it."

"Even with that handsome man?"

"Jin's not handsome, he's pretty. You're handsome, my darling."

Kai laughed. "In a craggy sort of way, maybe, if the light's not too good."

She laughed and said: "Come to my dressing room. I've got a break. They have to move to the bedroom set."

She led the way, holding his hand. Once inside her dressing room, she closed the door. It was a small, drab room, but she had brightened it with some of her own stuff: posters on the wall, a shelf of books, an orchid in a pot, a framed photograph of her mother.

Ting climbed quickly out of her dress and sat down in her twenty-first-century bra and panties. Kai smiled with pleasure at the sight.

"One more scene and I think they'll wrap for the day," Ting said. "This director gets things done fast."

"How does she manage that?"

"She knows what she wants and she has a plan. But she works us hard. I'm looking forward to an evening at home."

"You're forgetting," Kai said with regret. "This is our night to have dinner with my parents."

Ting's face fell. "So it is."

"I'll cancel if you're tired."

"No." Ting's face changed, and Kai knew that she was acting Bravely Facing Disappointment. "Your mother will have prepared a banquet."

"I don't mind, honestly."

"I know, but I really want to be on good terms with your parents. They're important to you, so they're important to me. Don't worry. We'll go."

"Thank you."

"You do so much for me. You're the rock of stability in my life. Your father's disapproval is a small price to pay."

"I think my father secretly likes you, in his heart. He just has to keep up the façade of stern puritanism. And Mother no longer even pretends not to like you."

"I'll win your father over in the end. What brings you here this afternoon? Nothing much to be done at the Guoanbu? Americans being understanding and helpful to China? World peace imminent?"

"I wish. We've got a little problem. Someone has been saying that you criticized the Communist Party."

"Oh, for heaven's sake, what a stupid idea."

"Of course. But the report has reached Li Jiankang, and naturally he wants to make the most of it, to damage me. When the minister retires—which can't be long—Li wants his job, whereas everyone else wants me to have it."

"Oh, my darling, I'm so sorry!"

"So you're being investigated."

"I know who accused me. It's Jin. He's jealous. When this show started he was supposed to be the star. But now I'm more popular, and he hates me."

"Is there any basis for the accusation?"

"Oh, who knows? You know what film people are like, they mouth off all the time, especially in the bar after we wrap. I expect someone said that China isn't a democracy and I nodded in agreement."

Kai sighed. It was perfectly possible. Like all security agencies, the Guoanbu firmly believed there was no smoke without fire. Malicious people could use that to make trouble for their enemies. It was like the charge of witchcraft in the olden days: once the accusation had been leveled, it was easy to find something that looked like evidence. No one was really innocent.

However, the news that Jin was probably responsible gave Kai ammunition.

There was a knock at the door and Ting called: "Come in."

The floor manager, a young man wearing a Manchester United soccer shirt, looked in and said: "We're ready for you, Ting."

Neither he nor Ting seemed conscious that she was half naked. That was what it was like in the studio, Kai found: free and easy. He thought that was charming.

The floor manager left, and Kai helped Ting get back into her dress. Then he kissed her. "I'll see you back at home," he said.

Ting went off, and Kai walked to the administration building and went to the Communist Party office.

Every enterprise in China was shadowed by a Party group that monitored its activities, and anything to do with the media got special attention. The Party read every script and vetted every actor. Producers liked historical dramas because what had happened long ago had fewer political implications today, so they were less likely to suffer interference.

Kai went to the office of Wang Bowen, the secretary of the Party branch here.

The room was dominated by a large portrait of President Chen, a man with a dark suit and carefully combed black hair, looking like the portraits of a thousand other Chinese senior executives. On the desk was another picture of Chen, this one a photo in which he was shaking hands with Wang.

Wang was an unimpressive man in his thirties with grubby shirt cuffs and a receding hairline. Shadow executives tended to be smarter about politics than business. Nevertheless they were powerful and had to be appeased, like wrathful gods. Their wrong decisions could be disastrous. Wang was haughty with actors and technicians, Ting said.

On the other hand, Kai was powerful too. He was a princeling. Communist functionaries were often bullies but had to be subservient to their Party superiors. Wang began by fawning. "Come in, Chang Kai, sit down, it's a pleasure to see you, I hope you're well."

"Very well, thank you. I dropped by to see Ting and I thought I should have a word with you while I'm here. Just between ourselves, you understand."

"Of course," Wang said, looking pleased. He was flattered that Kai wanted to confide in him.

Kai's approach would not be to defend Ting. That would be taken as an admission of guilt. He took a different line. "You probably don't concern yourself with film-set tittle-tattle, Wang Bowen," he began. Of course tittle-tattle was exactly what Wang concerned himself with. "But it might help you to know that Wen Jin is insanely jealous of Ting."

"I had heard something to that effect," said Wang, unwilling to admit to ignorance.

"You're very well informed. So you know that when Jin took the part of emperor in *Love in the Palace* he was told he would be the star of the show, but now of course Ting has overtaken him in popularity."

"Yes."

"I mention it because the Guoanbu's investigation is likely to conclude that Jin's accusations are motivated by personal rivalry and otherwise unfounded. I thought it might help you to be forewarned." That was a lie. "Ting is fond of you." That was a bigger lie. "We don't want this to rebound on you."

Now Wang looked scared. "I was obliged to take the reports seriously," he protested.

"Of course. It's your job. We at the Guoanbu understand that. I just don't want you to be taken by surprise.

You may want to interview Jin again, and write a short addendum to your report emphasizing that animosity could be a factor."

"Ah. Good idea. Yes."

"It's not for me to interfere, of course. But *Love in the Palace* is such a success, so beloved by the people, that it would be a tragedy if some kind of shadow fell over the show—unnecessarily."

"Oh, I agree."

Kai stood up. "I mustn't linger. As always, there's much to be done. I'm sure it's the same for you."

"It is indeed," said Wang, looking around the room, which bore no evidence of any work at all.

"Good-bye, comrade," said Kai. "I'm glad we had this chat."

Kai's parents lived in a kind of villa, a spacious two-story house on a small plot of land in a new high-density suburban development for the affluent upper middle class. Their neighbors were leading government officials, successful businessmen, senior military officers, and top managers in large enterprises. Kai's father, Chang Jianjun, had always said he would never need a home larger than the compact three-room apartment in which Kai had been raised, but on this issue he had given in to his wife, Fan Yu—or perhaps he just used her as an excuse for changing his mind.

Kai would never want to live in such a boring neighborhood. His apartment had everything he needed, and he did not have to bother with a garden. The city was where things happened: government and business and culture. There was nothing to do in the suburbs, and the commute was even longer.

In the car on the way there Kai said to Ting: "Tomorrow morning I'll tell the security minister that the information against you came from an envious rival, and Wang will confirm that, so the investigation will be dropped."

"Thank you, my darling. I'm sorry you've had this worry."

"These things happen, but perhaps in the future you could be more discreet about what you say, and even what you nod about."

"I will, I promise."

The villa was full of the aroma of a spicy dinner. Jianjun was not home yet, so Kai and Ting sat on stools in the modern kitchen while Yu cooked. Kai's mother was sixty-five, a small woman with a lined face and strands of silver in her black hair. They talked about the show. Yu said: "The emperor likes his senior wife because she simpers and sweet-talks, but she's got a mean streak."

Ting was used to people talking about the fictional characters as if they were real. "He shouldn't trust her," she said. "She's only interested in herself."

Yu put out a plate of cuttlefish dumplings with paper-thin wrappers. "To keep you going until your father gets here," she said, and Kai tucked in. Ting took one to be polite, but she had to keep her waist small enough for the dresses of an eighteenth-century concubine.

Jianjun came in. He was short and muscular, like a flyweight boxer. His teeth were yellow from smoking. He kissed Yu, greeted Kai and Ting, and got out four small glasses and a bottle of baijiu, the vodkalike clear spirit that was the most popular form of booze in China. Kai would have preferred a Jack Daniel's on the rocks, but he did not say so and his father did not ask.

Jianjun poured four drinks and passed them around. Holding up his glass he said: "Welcome!" Kai took a sip. His mother touched her lips to the glass, pretending to drink so as not to offend her husband. Ting, who liked it, emptied her glass.

Yu deferred to Jianjun almost all the time, but then, once in a blue moon, she would say something sharp in a certain tone of voice, and Jianjun would be quelled. Ting found that amusing.

Jianjun topped up Ting's glass and his own, then said: "Here's to grandchildren."

Kai's heart sank. So this was going to be tonight's theme. Jianjun wanted a grandchild and thought he was entitled to insist. Kai too wanted Ting to have a baby, but this was not the way to raise the subject. She was not going to be bullied into it by his father or anyone else. Kai resolved not to have a row about it.

Yu said: "Now, dear heart, let the poor children alone." However, she was not using the special voice, so Jianjun ignored her. "You must be thirty now," he said to Ting. "Don't leave it too late!"

Ting smiled and said nothing.

"China needs more smart boys like Kai," Jianjun persisted.

"Or smart girls, Father," Ting suggested.

But Jianjun wanted a grandson. "I'm sure Kai would like a son," he said.

Yu took a steamer off the stove, filled a basket with bao buns, and handed the basket to her husband. "Put those on the table for me, please," she said.

She quickly dished up a platter of stir-fried pork with green peppers, another of homemade bean curd, and a bowl of rice. Jianjun poured more baijiu for himself; the others declined. Ting, eating sparingly, said to Yu: "You make the best buns ever, Mama."

"Thank you, dear."

To keep Jianjun off the grandchildren topic, Kai told him about President Green's UN resolution and the diplomatic contest over votes. Jianjun was inclined

to be scornful. "The UN never makes any real difference," he said. The traditionalists believed that conflict
was never really resolved by anything but fighting.
Mao had said that power grows out of the barrel of
a gun.

"It's good that young people should be idealists,"
Jianjun said with all the condescension that a Chinese
father felt entitled to.

"How kind of you to say so," said Kai.

The sarcasm went right over his father's head. Jianjun
said: "One way or another, we will have to break the
American ring of steel."

Ting said: "What's the ring of steel, Father?"

"The Americans encircle us. They have troops in
Japan, South Korea, Guam, Singapore, and Australia.
As well as that, the Philippines and Vietnam are friends
of the US. The Americans did the same thing to the
Soviet Union—they called it 'containment.' And in the
end the Russian Revolution was strangled. We have to
avoid the fate of the Soviets, but we won't do it at the
UN. Sooner or later we will have to smash the ring."

Kai agreed with his father's analysis but had an alternative solution. "Yes, Washington would like to
destroy us, but America isn't the world," he said.
"We're making alliances and doing business all around
the globe. More and more countries see that a friendship with China is in their interests, no matter that it
annoys the US. We're changing the dynamic. The
struggle between the US and China doesn't need to be
settled by a gladiatorial contest, winner takes all.
Better to move to a position where war isn't necessary.
Let the ring of steel rust and crumble."

Jianjun was immovable. "A pipe dream. No amount
of investment in third-world countries will change the
Americans. They hate us and they want to wipe us out."

Kai tried another approach. "It's the Chinese way

to avoid a battle whenever possible. Didn't Sun Tzu say the supreme art of war is to subdue the enemy without fighting?"

"Ah, you try to use my belief in tradition against me. But it won't work. We must always be ready for war."

Kai found himself becoming frustrated and annoyed. Ting saw this and put a restraining hand on his arm. He took no notice. Scornfully he said: "And do you think that we can defeat the overwhelming power of the United States, Father?"

Yu said: "Perhaps we should talk about something else."

Jianjun ignored her. "Our military is ten times stronger than it was. Improvements—"

Kai interrupted. "But who would win?"

"Our new missiles have multiple warheads that are independently targeted—"

"But who would win?"

Jianjun banged his fist on the table, rattling the crockery. "We have the nuclear bombs necessary to devastate American cities!"

"Ah," said Kai, sitting back. "So we come to nuclear war—very quickly."

Jianjun was angry too now. "China will never be the first to use nuclear weapons. But to avoid the total destruction of China—yes!"

"And what good would that do us?"

"We are never going back to the Era of Humiliation."

"In what circumstances, exactly, would you, Father, as vice chairman of the National Security Commission, recommend to the president that he attack the United States with nuclear weapons—knowing that annihilation would almost certainly follow?"

"Under two conditions," said Jianjun. "One: that American aggression threatens the existence, sovereignty, or integrity of the People's Republic of China.

Two: that neither diplomacy nor conventional weapons are adequate to counter the threat."

"You really mean it," said Kai.

"Yes."

Yu said to Jianjun: "I'm sure you're right, my dear." She picked up the bread basket. "Have another bun," she said.

CHAPTER 7

Kiah was bringing her laundry back from the lake shore, a basket on one hip and Naji on the other, when a large black Mercedes car drove into the village.

Everyone was astonished. A year could go by without a visit from a stranger, and now they had had two in a week. All the women came out of their houses to look.

The windshield reflected the sun as a burning disk. The car stopped for the driver to speak to a village man weeding a patch of onions. Then it went on to the house of Abdullah, the senior of the elders. Abdullah came out and the driver opened the rear door. Clearly the visitor had the good manners to speak to village elders before anything else. After a few minutes Abdullah got out, looking pleased, and went back into his house. Kiah guessed he had received some money.

The car returned to the center of the village.

The driver, wearing pressed trousers and a clean white shirt, got out and walked around the car. He slid open a rear passenger door, revealing a glimpse of tan leather upholstery.

The woman who emerged was about fifty. She was
dark skinned, but she wore expensive European clothes:
a dress that revealed her figure, shoes with heels, a
wide-brimmed hat to shade her face, and a handbag.
No one in the village had ever owned a handbag.

The driver pressed a button and the door closed
with an electric whirr.

The older village women stared from a distance, but
the youngsters crowded around the visitor. The teenage girls, barefoot in their hand-me-down dresses,
stared enviously at her clothes.

The woman took from her handbag a pack of
Cleopatra cigarettes and a lighter. She put a cigarette
between her red lips and lit it, then inhaled deeply.

She was the epitome of sophistication.

She blew out smoke and then pointed to a tall girl
with light-brown skin.

The older women moved close enough to hear what
was said.

"My name is Fatima," said the visitor in Arabic.
"What's yours?"

"Zariah."

"A lovely name for a lovely girl."

The other kids giggled but it was true: Zariah was
striking.

Fatima said: "Can you read and write?"

Zariah said proudly: "I went to the nuns' school."

"Is your mother here?"

Zariah's mother, Noor, stepped forward with a cock-
erel under her arm. She raised chickens and had
undoubtedly picked up the valuable bird to keep it safe
from the wheels of the car. It was grumpy and indignant, and so was Noor. She said: "What do you want
with my daughter?"

Fatima ignored the hostility and replied pleasantly:
"How old is your beautiful girl?"

"Sixteen."

"Good."

"Why is that good?"

"I have a restaurant in N'Djamena, on the Avenue Charles de Gaulle. I need waitresses." Fatima adopted a brisk, matter-of-fact tone of voice. "They must be intelligent enough to take food and drink orders without making mistakes, and they must also be young and pretty, because that is what customers want."

The crowd became even more interested. Kiah and the other mothers moved closer. Kiah noticed an aroma as if someone had opened a box of sweets, and realized the fragrance came from Fatima. She seemed like a creature from a folk tale, but she was here to offer something down-to-earth and much sought after: a job.

Kiah said: "What if the customers don't speak Arabic?"

Fatima looked hard at her, assessing her. "May I ask your name, young lady?"

"I'm Kiah."

"Well, Kiah, I find that bright girls can quickly learn the French and English words for the dishes they're serving."

Kiah nodded. "Of course. There wouldn't be many."

Fatima looked at her thoughtfully for a moment, then turned back to Noor. "I would never hire a girl without her mother's permission. I am a mother myself, and a grandmother too."

Noor looked less hostile.

Kiah asked another question. "What's the pay?"

"The girls get all their meals and a uniform, and a place to sleep. They can make up to fifty dollars American per week in tips."

Noor said: "Fifty dollars!" It was three times the normal wage. Tips could vary, everyone knew, but even half of that would be a lot for a week of carrying plates and glasses.

Kiah said: "But no wages?"

Fatima looked irritated. "Correct."

Kiah wondered whether Fatima could be trusted. She was a woman, which was a point in her favor, though not decisive. She was undoubtedly painting an attractive picture of the job she was offering, but that was natural and did not make her a liar. Kiah liked the frank speech and the undoubted glamour, but under all that she detected a hard vein of ruthlessness that made her uneasy.

All the same she envied the single girls. They could escape from the lakeside and find a new future in the city. She wished she could do the same. She thought she would be a perfectly good waitress. And she would be saved from the dreadful choice between Hakim and destitution.

Except that she had a child. She could not even wish for a life without Naji. She loved him too much.

Zariah said eagerly: "What's the uniform like?"

"European clothes," said Fatima. "A red skirt, a white blouse, and a red neck scarf with white polka dots." The girls made appreciative noises, and Fatima added: "Yes, it's very pretty."

Noor asked a mother's question. "Who is in charge of these young girls?" It was obvious that sixteen-year-olds needed to be supervised.

"They live in a little house behind the restaurant, and a lady called Mrs. Amat al-Yasu looks after them."

That was interesting, Kiah thought. The chaperone's name was Arabic Christian. She said: "Are you Christian, Fatima?"

"Yes, but my employees are a mixture. Are you interested in working for me, Kiah?"

"I can't." She glanced at Naji, who was in her arms,

staring in fascination at Fatima. "I couldn't leave my little boy."

"He's beautiful. What's his name?"

"Naji."

"He must be what, two years old?"

"Yes."

"Is his father handsome too?"

Salim's face flashed in Kiah's memory: the skin darkened by the sun, the black hair wet with spray, the folds around the eyes wrinkled from peering into the water looking for fish. The unexpected reminder filled her with sudden sadness. "I'm a widow."

"I'm so sorry. Life must be hard."

"That's true."

"But you could still be a waitress. Two of my girls have babies."

Kiah's heart leaped. "But how is that possible?"

"They spend all day with their children. The restaurant opens in the evening, and then Mrs. Amat al-Yasu watches the babies while the mothers are working."

Kiah was startled. She had been assuming she was not eligible. Now suddenly a new prospect opened up. She felt her heart racing. She was excited but intimidated. In her whole life she had been to the city only a handful of times, and now she was being asked to move there to live. The only restaurants she had ever entered were small cafés like the one in Three Palms, but she had been offered a job in a place that sounded terrifyingly luxurious. Could she make such a huge change? Did she have the nerve?

She said: "I need to think about this."

Noor asked another motherly question. "Those girls who have babies—what about their husbands?"

"One is a widow, like Kiah. The other, I'm sorry to say, was foolish enough to give herself to a man who ran away."

The mothers understood. They were a conservative group, but they had been flighty girls once.

Fatima said: "Think about it, take your time. I have other villages to visit. I'll pass through here again on my way back. Zariah and Kiah, if you want to work for me, be ready by midafternoon."

"We have to leave today?" said Kiah. She had thought she could consider the offer for a week or two, not a few hours.

"Today," Fatima repeated.

Kiah was frightened all over again.

Another girl said: "What about the rest of us?"

"Maybe when you're older," said Fatima.

Kiah knew that in truth the others were not pretty enough.

Fatima turned back to the car and the driver opened the door. Before getting in she dropped the end of her cigarette and trod on it. The whole conversation had been only as long as it took her to smoke it. She sat in the car and leaned out. "Make up your minds," she said. "I'll see you later." The driver shut the door.

The villagers watched the car drive away.

Kiah said to Zariah: "What do you think? Will you go to N'Djamena with Fatima?"

"If my mother will let me—yes!" Zariah's eyes gleamed with hope and enthusiasm.

Kiah was only four years her senior, but the age difference felt bigger. Kiah had a child to worry about, and she was more aware of hazards.

Then she thought of Hakim, with his dirty T-shirt and his grigri beads. She was now faced with a choice between Fatima and Hakim.

There was really nothing to think about.

Zariah said: "What about you, Kiah? Will you go with Fatima this afternoon?"

Kiah hesitated only a moment longer. "Yes," she said, then she added: "Of course."

The restaurant had an English name, Bourbon Street, displayed outside in red neon. Kiah arrived in Fatima's Mercedes late in the afternoon, along with Zariah and two girls she did not know. They all walked into a lobby with a thick carpet and walls painted the soft color of white orchids. It was even more luxurious than Kiah had imagined. She found that reassuring.

The girls made sounds of amazement and delight, and Fatima said: "Enjoy it. This is the last time you'll come in through the front door. There's a staff entrance at the back."

There were two big men in plain black suits in the lobby, doing nothing, and Kiah guessed they were security guards.

The main room was big. Along one side was a long bar with more bottles than Kiah had ever seen in one place. What could be in them all? There were sixty or more tables. On the side opposite the bar was a stage with red curtains. Kiah had not realized that restaurants might also put on a show. The room was carpeted but for a small circle of wood flooring in front of the stage that Kiah worked out must have been for dancing.

A dozen or so men were having drinks, and a couple of girls were serving them, but otherwise the place was empty, and Kiah guessed it must have just opened. The red-and-white uniforms were very smart, although she was shocked by how short the skirts were. Fatima introduced the new girls to the waitresses, who cooed over Naji, and to the barman, who was curt. In the kitchen six cooks were busy cleaning and chopping vegetables and making sauces. The space seemed too small for the task of preparing meals for all those tables.

At the far end a corridor led to a series of small rooms, each with a table and chairs and a long couch. "Customers pay extra for the private rooms," Fatima said. Kiah wondered why anyone would pay more to have dinner in secret.

She was awestruck by the scale of the enterprise. Fatima had to be very clever to manage it. Kiah wondered whether she had a husband to help her.

They passed through a small staff area with hooks for coats, then they went out by the staff door. Across a courtyard was a two-story concrete building, painted white, with blue shutters. An elderly woman sat outside enjoying the cool of the evening. She stood up when Fatima approached.

"This is Mrs. Amat al-Yasu," Fatima said. "But everyone calls her Jadda." It was the colloquial word for a nanny. She was a small, plump woman, but there was a look in her eye that gave Kiah the feeling that Jadda might have the same tough streak as Fatima.

Fatima introduced the new girls and said: "If you do as Jadda tells you, you won't go far wrong."

The house door was a sheet of corrugated iron nailed to a timber frame, not an unusual design in N'Djamena. Inside were a series of small bedrooms and a communal shower. The upper floor duplicated the lower. Each room had two narrow beds with a space between them just wide enough to stand up in, and two small wardrobes. Most of the residents were getting ready for the evening's work, doing their hair and putting on their waitress uniforms. Jadda announced that they were expected to shower at least once a week, which surprised the new girls.

Kiah and Zariah were given a room together. Their

uniforms were hanging up, one in each wardrobe, along with European-style underwear, brassieres and skimpy panties. There was no cot: Naji would have to sleep in Kiah's bed.

Jadda told them to get changed immediately as they would be working tonight. Kiah fought down panic: so soon! With Fatima, it seemed, everything happened faster than you expected. Fatima asked Jadda: "How will we know what to do?"

"Tonight you'll be paired with an experienced girl who will explain everything," the chaperone replied.

Kiah took off her outer robes and her plain shift underdress and went along to the shower. Then she put on her uniform and found Ameena, who was to be her tutor. In no time, it seemed, she was entering the restaurant, which was quickly filling up. A small band was playing and a few people were dancing. Although everyone was speaking Arabic or French, Kiah failed to recognize half the words, and she guessed they were talking about dishes and drinks she had never heard of. She felt like a foreigner in her own country.

However, as soon as Ameena started to take orders, Kiah began to understand. Ameena asked the customers what they would like, and they told her, sometimes pointing to items on a printed list, which made it easier to be sure what they were saying. Ameena wrote down their choices on a notepad, then went to the kitchen. There she called out the orders, then tore the sheet off the pad and put it on the counter. The drink orders she repeated to the taciturn barman. When the food was ready she took it to the table, and the same with the drinks.

After watching for half an hour Kiah took her first order and made no mistakes. Ameena gave her only one piece of advice. "Wet your lips," she said, licking her own lips to demonstrate. "Makes you look sexy."

Kiah shrugged and wet her lips.

She gained confidence rapidly and began to feel pleased with herself.

After a few hours the girls took turns to have a short break and a snack. Kiah hurried to the house and checked on Naji. She found him fast asleep. He was phlegmatic, Kiah thought gratefully; change interested him more than it scared him. She went back to work reassured.

Some customers went home after they had dined, but many stayed, and newcomers joined them for drinks. Kiah was amazed at how much beer, wine, and whisky people imbibed. She herself did not like the feeling she got from intoxicating drinks. Salim had enjoyed a glass of beer occasionally. Drinking was not prohibited—they were Christians, not Muslims—but all the same it played no big part in their lives.

The atmosphere began to change. The laughter got louder. Kiah noticed that the clientele was now mostly male. She was taken aback when men would put a hand on her arm while ordering drinks, or touch her back as they passed. One rested a hand on her hip, briefly. It was all done in a casual way, without leering smiles or murmured remarks, but it disconcerted her. Such things did not happen in the village.

It was midnight when she found out what the stage was for. The orchestra began to play an Arabic tune and the curtains opened to reveal an Egyptian belly dancer. Kiah had heard of such people but had never seen one. This woman wore an extraordinarily revealing costume. At the end of her dance she somehow slipped off her halter top to show her breasts, and a second later the curtains closed. The audience clapped enthusiastically.

Kiah did not know much about city life but she

suspected that not all restaurants had entertainment of this type, and she began to feel uneasy.

She checked her tables and a customer waved at her. It was the man who had put his hand on her hip. He was European, heavyset, wearing a striped suit with a white shirt open at the neck. He looked about fifty. "A bottle of champagne, chérie," he said. "Bollinger." He was a little drunk.

"Yes, sir."

"Bring it to me in the private room. I'll be in number three."

"Yes, sir."

"Bring two glasses."

"Yes, sir."

"Call me Albert."

"Yes, Albert."

She put ice in a silver-colored bucket and got a bottle of champagne and two glasses from the barman. She put them on a tray and the barman added a small bowl of dukkah, blended seeds and spices, and a plate of cucumber batons to dip. She carried the tray to the back of the restaurant. Another big guard in a black suit was standing by the door to the private corridor. Kiah found room number three, tapped on the door, and walked in.

Albert was sitting on the sofa. Kiah looked around the room but no one else was there. That made her nervous.

She put the tray on the table.

"You can open the champagne," said Albert.

Opening bottles of wine had not been part of Kiah's training. "I don't know how, sir, I'm sorry. This is my first day."

"Then I'll show you."

She watched carefully as he stripped away the foil

and loosened the wire closure. He grasped the cork, twisted it a little, then pressed down on it to let it come out slowly. There was a sound like a breath of wind. "Like the sigh of a satisfied woman," he said. "Only you don't hear that often, do you?" He laughed, and she realized he had made a joke, so she smiled, although she did not see what was funny.

He poured two glasses.

"You're waiting for someone," Kiah said.

"No." He picked up one of the glasses and offered it to her. "This is for you."

"Oh, no, thank you."

"It won't do you any harm, you little idiot." He patted his meaty thigh with his hand. "Come, sit on my lap."

"No, sir, I really cannot."

He began to look annoyed. "I'll give you twenty bucks for a kiss."

"No!" She did not know whether he meant dollars, euros, or something else, but in any currency it was a ridiculously large payment for a kiss, and she felt instinctively that more than that would be demanded of her. And she feared that, even though he seemed nice, he might become insistent and try to force her.

He said: "You drive a hard bargain. All right, a hundred for a fuck."

Kiah ran out of the room.

Fatima was right outside. "What happened?" she said.

"He wants sex!"

"Did he offer you money?"

She nodded. "A hundred. Bucks, he said."

"Dollars." Fatima took Kiah by the shoulders, leaning close, and Kiah breathed in her perfume, like scorched honey. "Listen to me. Have you ever been offered a hundred dollars before?"

"No."

"And you never will, unless you play the game. This is how you earn tips, though not all our customers are as generous as Albert. Now go back in there and take off your panties." She took a small, flat packet from a pocket. "And use a condom."

Kiah did not take the condoms. "I'm very sorry, Fatima," she said. "I don't like to go against you, and I really want to be a waitress, but I can't do what you ask, I just can't." Kiah was determined to keep her dignity, but to her dismay tears began to flow. "Please don't try to make me," she begged.

Fatima's face took on a determined look and she said: "You can't work here if you don't give the customers what they expect!"

Kiah found she was crying too much to reply.

The security guard appeared and said to Fatima: "Is everything all right, boss?"

Kiah realized that if they decided to force her, the guard could hold her down with little effort. The realization changed her mood. The worst thing she could do now was look helpless, an ignorant village girl who could be pushed around. She had to stand up for herself.

She took a step back and raised her chin. "I will not do this," she said firmly. "I'm sorry to disappoint you, Fatima, but it's your own fault—you deceived me." Speaking slowly and emphatically, she said: "So let us not have a fight."

Fatima looked angry. "Are you threatening me?"

Kiah looked at the guard. "Of course I can't fight against him." She raised her voice. "But I can make a terrible row in front of your customers."

At that moment a customer looked out of another private room and called out: "Hey, we need more drinks in here!"

Fatima said: "Coming, sir!" She seemed to relent. "Go to your room and sleep on it," she said to Kiah. "You will see things differently in the morning. You can try again tomorrow."

Kiah nodded without speaking.

Fatima said: "And for goodness' sake don't let the customers see you whimpering."

Kiah walked away immediately, before Fatima could change her mind.

She found her way to the staff door and crossed the courtyard to the girls' house. Jadda was sitting in the entrance lobby watching television. "You're back early," she said disapprovingly.

"Yes," Kiah said, and hurried upstairs without explanation.

Naji was still fast asleep.

Kiah stripped off the uniform she now thought of as a prostitute's clothing. She put on her shift underdress and lay down alongside Naji. It was past midnight, but she could hear the band and the roar of conversation from the club. She felt tired but she did not fall asleep.

Zariah came in at about three o'clock, her eyes sparkling, a fistful of money in her hand. "I'm rich!" she said.

Kiah was too tired to tell her she was doing wrong. In fact she was not even sure it was wrong. "How many men?" she said.

"One gave me twenty, and the other I did with my hand for ten," said Zariah. "Think how long it takes my mother to make thirty!" She took off her clothes and headed for the bathroom.

"Have a good wash," said Kiah.

Zariah returned shortly and was asleep a minute later.

Kiah lay awake until the morning light began to seep through the flimsy curtains and Naji stirred. She breast-fed him to keep him quiet a little longer, then she dressed them both.

When they left the room, no one else was stirring.

They crept out of the silent house.

The Avenue Charles de Gaulle was a broad boulevard in the center of the capital. Even at this hour there were people around. Kiah asked for directions to the fish market, the only place in N'Djamena that she knew. Every night, fishermen from Lake Chad drove through the dark to bring yesterday's catch into the city, and Kiah had accompanied Salim a few times.

When she got there the men were unloading their trucks in the half-light. The smell of fish was overpowering, but to Kiah it seemed more breathable than the atmosphere of Bourbon Street. They were arranging silvery displays on their stalls, spraying water to keep them cool. They would sell everything by midday and drive home in the afternoon.

Kiah walked around until she spotted a face she knew. She said: "Do you remember me, Melhem? I'm Salim's widow."

"Kiah!" he said. "Of course I remember you. What are you doing here, all on your own?"

"It's a long story," said Kiah.

CHAPTER 8

Four days after the shootout at the N'Gueli Bridge, four nights after Tamara slept with Tab without having sex, the American ambassador threw a party for his wife's thirtieth birthday.

Tamara wanted the party to be a success, both for Shirley's sake, because Shirley was her best friend in Chad, and for the sake of Shirley's husband, Nick, who was knocking himself out to organize everything. Shirley was normally in charge of parties—it was one of the duties of an ambassador's spouse—but Nick had decreed that she could not manage her own birthday celebration and that he would take charge.

It would be a big event. Everyone at the embassy was coming, including the CIA, who pretended to be ordinary diplomats. All the important staff of allied embassies had been invited, and many of the Chad elite. There would be a couple of hundred guests.

It would take place in the ballroom. The embassy rarely held actual dances there. The traditional European ball was now old-fashioned, with its stiff formality and bumpety-bumpety music. However, the room saw plenty of use for large receptions, and Shirley was always good at making people relax and enjoy themselves, even in formal surroundings.

In her lunch hour Tamara went across to the ballroom to see if she could help, and she found Nick floundering. There was a huge cake in the kitchen waiting to be decorated, twenty waiters hanging around for instructions, and a jazz band from Mali called Desert Funk sitting outside under the raffia palms smoking hashish.

Nick was a tall man with a big head, big nose, big ears, big chin. He had a relaxed, friendly manner and a sharp intelligence. He was a highly competent diplomat but he was no party organizer. He was keen to do it well, and he walked around with an eager look, having no idea why things were going so wrong.

Tamara got three cooks icing the cake, told the band where to plug in their amplifiers, and sent two embassy staff out to shop for balloons and streamers. She told the waiters to bring in huge containers of ice and set the drinks to cooling. She moved from one task to the next, chasing details and chivvying staff. She did not go back to the CIA office that afternoon.

And all the time Tab was in her thoughts. What was he doing right now? What time would he arrive? Where would they go after the party? Would they spend the night together?

Was he too good to be true?

She just had time to run to her room and put on her party frock, a dress made of silk in the vivid royal blue that was popular here. She was back in the ballroom minutes before the guests were due.

Shirley arrived a moment later. When she saw the decorations, the waiters with their trays of canapés and drinks, and the band holding their instruments ready, her face was suffused with happiness. She threw her arms around Nick and thanked him. "You've done so well!" she said, not hiding her surprise.

"I had crucial assistance," he admitted.

Shirley looked at Tamara. "You helped," she said.

"We were all driven by Nick's enthusiasm," Tamara said.

"I'm so glad."

Tamara knew that what made Shirley so happy was not so much the success of the arrangements as Nick's wish to do it for her. And he was happy because he had pleased her. That's how it should be, Tamara thought; that's the kind of relationship I want.

The first guest came in, a Chadian woman in robes of a bright red-and-blue print. "She looks so great," Tamara murmured to Shirley. "I'd be like a sofa in that."

"But she carries it off wonderfully."

California champagne was always served at embassy parties. The French politely said it was surprisingly good and put their glasses down unfinished. The British asked for gin and tonic. Tamara thought the champagne was delicious, but she was on a high anyway.

Shirley looked speculatively at her. "You're very bright eyed this evening."

"I enjoyed helping Nick."

"You look as if you're in love."

"With Nick? Of course. We all are."

"Hmm," said Shirley. She knew when she was getting an evasive answer. "I've learned to read what silent love hath writ."

"Let me guess," said Tamara. "Shakespeare?"

"Ten out of ten, and a bonus point for avoiding the original question."

More guests arrived. Shirley and Nick went to the doorway to meet them. It would take an hour to greet everyone.

Tamara circulated. This was the kind of occasion on which intelligence officers could casually pick up gossip. It was remarkable how quickly people forgot about confidentiality when the drinks were free.

The Chadian women had gotten out their brightest colors and most vibrant prints. The men were more somber, except for a few youngsters with a sense of fashion, wearing stylish jackets with T-shirts.

At such affairs Tamara sometimes suffered an uncomfortable flash of realism. Now, drinking champagne and making small talk, she pictured Kiah, desperate to find a way to feed her child, contemplating a life-threatening journey across the desert and the sea in the hope of finding some kind of security in a far country about which she knew so little. It was a strange world.

Tab was late. It was going to be weird, seeing him for the first time since their night together. They had gotten into his bed, he in a T-shirt and boxer shorts, she in her sweatshirt and panties. He had put his arms around her, she had cuddled up to him, and she had fallen asleep in seconds. The next thing she knew, he was sitting on the edge of the bed in a suit, offering her a cup of coffee, saying: "I'm sorry to wake you, but I have a plane to catch, and I didn't want you to wake up alone." He had flown to Mali that morning with one of his bosses from Paris, and he was due to return today. How was she to greet him? He was not her lover, but he was certainly more than a colleague.

She was approached by Bashir Fakhoury, a local journalist she had met before. He was bright and challenging, and she was immediately wary. When she asked how he was he said: "I'm writing an in-depth piece about the UFDD." He was talking about Chad's main rebel group, whose ambition was to overthrow the General. "What's your take on them?"

No reason why she should not make use of him, she

thought. "How are they financed, Bashir? Do you know?"

"A lot comes from Sudan, our friendly neighbor to the east. What do you think of Sudan? Washington surely believes that Sudan has no right to interfere in Chad?"

"It's not my job to comment on local politics, Bashir. You know that."

"Oh, don't worry, we're off the record. As an American, you must be in favor of democracy."

Nothing was ever truly off the record, Tamara knew. "I often think about America's long, slow road to democracy," she said. "We had to fight a war to free ourselves from the king, then another war to abolish slavery, and then it took a hundred years of feminism to establish that women are not second-class citizens."

This was not the kind of thing he was after. "Are you saying that Chadian democrats should be patient?"

"I'm not saying anything of the kind, Bashir. We're just chatting at a party." She nodded in the direction of a blond young American man conversing with a group in confident French. "Speak to Drew Sandberg, he's the press officer."

"I've talked to Drew. He doesn't know much. I want the CIA's opinion."

"What's the CIA?" said Tamara.

Bashir laughed ruefully, and Tamara turned away.

She immediately saw Tab. He was near the door, shaking hands with Nick. Tab was wearing a black suit tonight, with a gleaming white shirt and cuff links. His tie was a dark purple color with a faint pattern. He looked good enough to eat.

Tamara was not the only one to think so. She noticed several other women surreptitiously staring at Tab. Keep away, ladies, he's mine, she thought; but of course he was not hers.

He had given her comfort in distress. He had been charming and considerate and deeply sympathetic, but what did that tell her? Only that he was nice. During his trip to Mali he might have developed commitment panic; men did. He might give her the brush-off with some cliché: *It was fun while it was fun, let's leave it at that*; *I'm not looking for a relationship*; or—worst of all—*It's not you, it's me.*

And thinking about that, she realized that she wanted desperately to have a relationship with him and she would be completely devastated if he felt otherwise.

Tamara turned around again, and Tab stood there. His handsome face startled her as he smiled: it was radiant with love and happiness. Her doubts and fears vanished. She suppressed an urge to throw her arms around his neck. "Good evening," she said formally.

"What a great dress!" He looked as if he might be about to kiss her, so she put out her hand, and he shook it instead.

He was still beaming foolishly.

"How was Mali?" she said.

"I missed you."

"I'm glad. But stop smiling at me like that. I don't want people to know that we've become . . . close. You're an intelligence officer of another country. Dexter will kick up a fuss."

"I'm just very happy to see you."

"And I adore you, but fuck off now, before people begin to notice."

"Of course." He raised his voice a little. "I must congratulate Shirley on her birthday. Excuse me." He made a little bow and moved away.

As soon as he had gone Tamara realized she had just said *I adore you*. Oh, shit, she thought, that was too soon. And he didn't say it back. He'll be scared off.

She looked at the beautifully-fitting back of his suit jacket and wondered whether she had ruined it all.

Karim came to speak to her, in a new pearl-gray suit with a lavender tie. "I've heard all about your adventure," he said. He was looking at her in a particular way, as if he had never really seen her before. Since the shootout at the bridge she had seen a similar expression in other people's eyes. *We thought we knew you*, it said, *but now we're not sure*.

Tamara said: "What have you heard?"

"That when the US Army couldn't hit anybody, you were the one who shot a terrorist. Is that true?"

"I had an easy target."

"What was your victim doing at the time?"

"He was pointing an assault rifle at me from a distance of twenty yards."

"But you kept your nerve."

"I guess."

"And did you wound him, or what?"

"He died."

"My God."

Tamara realized she had joined some kind of elite. Karim was impressed. She did not find this gratifying: she wanted to be respected for her brains, not her marksmanship. She moved the conversation on. "What are they saying at the Presidential Palace?"

"The General is very angry. Our American friends have been attacked. The attackers may have been technically in Cameroon territory, or in a kind of no-man's-land on the border, but the US soldiers are our guests, so we are upset."

Tamara noted that Karim was making two points. First, the General was firmly distancing himself from the attackers by saying how angry he was. Second, he was implying that they were not necessarily Chadian. It was always best to blame trouble on outsiders. Karim was even suggesting they had not been on Chadian soil. Tamara knew this was crap, but she wanted to gather intelligence, not argue. "I'm glad to hear that."

"I'm sure you know that Sudan was behind the attack."

Tamara did not know any such thing. "The shouts of 'al-Bustan' suggest ISGS."

Karim waved a hand airily. "A ploy to confuse us."

"Then what's your thinking?" she said neutrally.

"The attack was mounted by the UFDD with support from Sudan."

"Interesting," Tamara said noncommittally.

Karim leaned closer. "After you killed your terrorist, you must have checked his gun."

"Of course."

"What type?"

"A bullpup rifle."

"Norinco brand?"

"Yes."

"Chinese!" Karim looked triumphant. "The Sudanese Armed Forces buy all their weapons from China."

ISGS had Norinco guns too, and they got them from the same source, the Sudanese army, but Tamara did not point this out. She doubted that Karim himself believed what he was saying. But it was the line that the government was going to take, and Tamara simply noted that as useful intelligence. "Will the General take any action?"

"He will tell the world who is responsible for this!"

"And how would he do that?"

"He is planning a major speech in which he will attack the role of the Sudan government in subversion here in Chad."

"A major speech."

"Yes."

"When?"

"Soon."

"You and the others must be working on the text already."

"Absolutely."

Tamara chose her words carefully. "The White House will be hoping that this situation isn't going to escalate. We don't want to see the region destabilized."

"Of course, of course, we feel the same, it goes without saying."

Tamara hesitated. Did she have the nerve for what she had in mind? Hell yes. "It would be a great help to President Green if she could see a draft of the speech in advance."

There was a long pause.

Tamara guessed that Karim was startled by the audacity of the request, but he was also thinking how useful it could be to get the Americans' approval.

She was amazed that he was even thinking about it.

Eventually he said: "I'll see what I can do," and turned away.

Tamara looked around and saw a riot of color. The room was now packed, with the women competing to be the brightest. The French doors were open so that people could go outside to smoke. Desert Funk were playing a rhythmic African version of cool jazz, but the roar of conversation in Arabic, French, and English drowned out the band. The air-conditioning struggled to cope. Everyone was having fun.

Shirley appeared by her side. "You didn't give Tabdar much time, Tamara."

That was perceptive. "He was in a hurry to tell you happy birthday."

"You were all over him a couple of weeks ago, at the Italian embassy reception."

Now that Tamara thought about it, she had talked to Tab for a long time that evening, though it had been mainly about Abdul. Had she been falling for Tab then, without knowing it? "I was not all over him," she said. "We were discussing work."

Shirley shrugged. "As you wish. I expect he's done something to offend you. You've quarreled." She looked hard at Tamara, then said: "No, wait—it's the opposite! You're pretending. You're covering it up." She lowered her voice. "Have you slept with him?"

Tamara did not know how to answer that. She would have to say *Yes and no*, which would only call for further explanation.

Shirley looked flustered, which was unusual for her. "How rude of me to ask. I'm sorry."

Tamara managed to put together a coherent sentence. "If it was true I wouldn't tell you, because then I'd have to ask you to keep it secret from Nick and Dexter, and that wouldn't be fair to you."

Shirley nodded. "I get that. Thank you." She saw something across the room. "I'm being summoned," she said. Tamara followed her gaze and saw Nick beckoning her from the entrance. Standing near him were two men in dark suits and sunglasses. They were plainly bodyguards, but whose?

Tamara followed Shirley across the room.

Nick talked urgently to an aide. As soon as Shirley reached him, he took her hand and moved to the door.

A moment later the General walked in.

Tamara had never seen Chad's president in the flesh, but she recognized him from photographs. He was a broad-shouldered man of about sixty, shaven headed, dark skinned. He wore a Western-style business suit and several chunky gold rings. A group of men and women followed him in.

He was in an affable mood, smiling. He shook hands with Nick, refused a glass of champagne offered by a waiter, and handed a small gift-wrapped parcel to Shirley. Then he began to sing, in English: "Happy birthday to you . . ."

His entourage joined in with the second line: "Happy birthday to you."

He looked around expectantly, and more people took the hint, singing: "Happy birthday, dear Shirley . . ." The band found the key and joined in.

By the end everyone in the ballroom was singing: "Happy birthday to you!" Then they applauded themselves.

Well, Tamara thought, he certainly knows how to dominate a room.

Shirley said: "May I unwrap my gift?"

"Of course, go ahead!" said the General. "I want to make sure it pleases you."

As if she'd tell him otherwise, Tamara thought.

She caught the eye of Karim, who was giving her a knowing look, and she realized what the gift was.

Shirley held up a book. "This is wonderful!" she said. "The works of al-Khansa—my favorite Arabic poet—translated into English! Thank you, Mr. President."

"I know you're interested in poetry," said the General. "And al-Khansa is one of the few female poets."

"This was such a clever choice."

The General was gratified. "Mind you, she's a bit gloomy," he said. "The poems are mostly elegies to the dead."

"Some of the greatest poetry is sad, though, isn't it, Mr. President?"

"True." He took Nick by the arm and turned him away from the group. "A quiet word, if I may, Ambassador," he said.

"Of course," said Nick, and they began to speak in low voices.

Shirley took the hint and turned to those around her, showing everyone the book. Tamara did not reveal her role in the choice of present. She would tell Shirley one day, perhaps.

The General talked to Nick for about five minutes, then left. The party became even livelier. Everyone was thrilled that the country's president had shown up.

Nick looked a bit solemn, Tamara thought, and she wondered what the General had said to him.

Bumping into Drew, she told him about her conversation with Bashir. "I didn't tell him anything he didn't already know," she said. "Of course, he could make something up, but that's an inevitable consequence of having embassy parties."

Drew said: "Thanks for letting me know. I don't think we need to worry."

Drew's fiancée, Annette Cecil, was by his side. She was part of the small British mission in N'Djamena. She said: "We're going to the Bar Bisous afterward. Do you want to come?"

"Maybe, if I can get away. Thanks."

Tamara caught Shirley's eye and saw that she looked cast down. What could have happened to spoil her birthday party? She went over to Shirley and said: "What is it?"

"You remember I told you that the General had agreed to support President Green's UN resolution about arms sales?"

"Yes—you said Nick was very pleased."

"The General came here to say that he's changed his mind."

"Shit. What brought that on?"

"Nick kept asking that question, and the General kept giving evasive answers."

"Has President Green done something to offend the General?"

"We're trying to figure that out."

Another guest came and thanked Shirley for the party. They were beginning to leave.

Karim approached Tamara. "Your gift suggestion was a big success!" he said. "Thank you for your advice."

"You're welcome. Everyone was so excited when the General arrived."

"I'll see you later in the week. We have a date for coffee."

He was leaving, but she stopped him. "Karim, you know everything that happens in this town."

He was flattered. "Perhaps not everything. . . ."

"The General won't vote for President Green's UN resolution, and we can't figure out why. He supported us at first. Do you know why he changed his mind?"

"I do," said Karim, but he did not volunteer the explanation.

"It would be so helpful to Nick to know."

"You should ask the Chinese ambassador."

That was a clue. Karim had weakened a little. Tamara pressed the point. "I realize that the Chinese are against our resolution, of course. But what kind of pressure could China bring to make a loyal friend switch sides?"

Karim rubbed the thumb of his right hand across the fingertips in the international gesture for money.

Tamara said: "They bribed him?"

Karim shook his head.

"What, then?"

Karim had to say something now, otherwise it would look as if he had only been pretending to know. "For more than a year now," he said carefully and quietly, "the Chinese have been working on a plan for a canal from the Congo River to Lake Chad. It will be the biggest infrastructure project in the history of the world."

"I've heard of it. And . . . ?"

"If we vote for the American resolution they will immediately drop the canal project."

"Ah," Tamara breathed. "That explains it."

Karim said: "The General is very keen on the canal."

As he should be, Tamara thought. It would save millions of lives and transform Chad.

But such projects could be used for political pressure. There was nothing wicked or even unusual about that. Other countries, including the US, would use their aid projects and foreign investments to strengthen their influence: it was part of the game.

But the ambassador needed to know.

"Don't say I told you." Karim winked at Tamara and walked away.

She looked around for Dexter or any of the senior CIA people she could report this to, but they had left.

Tab came up. "Thank you for a lovely party," he said loudly, then in a quieter voice: "Do you remember what you said to me an hour ago?"

"What?"

"You said: 'I adore you, but fuck off now.'"

She was embarrassed. "I'm really sorry. I was tense about the party." And about you.

"Don't apologize. Can we have dinner?"

"I'd love to, but we can't leave together."

"Where shall I meet you?"

"Could you pick me up at the Bar Bisous? I've been invited there by Drew and Annette."

"Of course."

"Don't come in. Phone me from outside and I'll leave right away."

"Good plan. That way we're less likely to be seen."
He smiled and left.

Tamara needed to pass on the news she had learned
from Karim. She could go in search of Dexter, but
Nick appeared so downhearted that she felt she should
tell him right away.

When she approached him he said: "Thank you for
your help this afternoon. The party was a huge success." He was sincere, but Tamara could tell he had a
weight on his mind.

"I'm glad," she said briskly, and went on: "I've just
been told something you may want to hear."

"Do tell."

"I've been wondering what made the General
change his mind about our UN resolution."

"So have I." Nick passed his hand through his hair,
ruffling it untidily.

"The Chinese have been dangling the possibility of
a multibillion-dollar canal from the river Congo to
Lake Chad."

"I know," said Nick. "Oh, I get it—they'll pull out if
Chad votes for the resolution."

"That's what I heard."

"It sounds right to me. Well, I'm glad we know, at
least. I'm not sure if we can do anything about it.
They've got us up against the wall." He drifted away.

The room was emptying and the waiters were clearing up. Tamara left Nick to brood. She felt she had
done well to provide intelligence on the General's
U-turn so quickly: the problem of what to do about it
belonged to Nick and President Green, not her.

She left the ballroom and crossed the compound. It
was evening: the sun had gone down and the air was
cooling. In her apartment the phone rang while she was
in the shower. Dexter left a message asking her to call

back. He was probably going to congratulate her. That could wait until morning: she was impatient to see Tab. She did not return the call.

She put on fresh underwear and dressed again in a purple shirt and black jeans. She put on a short leather jacket for warmth. Then she called for a car.

There was a handful of people waiting for cars: Drew and Annette, Dexter and Daisy, Dexter's deputy Michael Olson, and two juniors from the CIA station, Dean and Leila. Drew and Annette suggested sharing a car with Tamara, and she agreed readily.

Dexter was a bit red in the face from champagne. "I called you," he said accusingly.

"I was just about to call you back," she lied. It did not sound as if he was planning to congratulate her.

"I have a question for you," he said.

"Okay."

He raised his voice. "Who the hell do you think you are?"

She was so startled that she took a step back. She felt her neck flush red. The others standing nearby looked embarrassed. She said: "What have I done?" She spoke in a quiet voice in the hope that he would too.

It did not work. "You briefed the ambassador!" he raved. "That's not your job. I brief the ambassador, and if I can't Michael does. You're about twenty places down the goddamn line!"

How could he do this in front of so many of her colleagues? "I haven't briefed the ambassador," she said, but as soon as the words were out of her mouth she realized that she had, technically. "Oh, you mean about the General."

Wagging his head and putting on a silly voice he

said: "Yes, that's right, I mean about the motherfucking General."

Daisy said quietly: "Dexter, not here."

He ignored his wife. With his hands on his hips he
looked belligerently at Tamara and said: "Well?"

He was right, strictly speaking, but following protocol would have wasted time. "Nick was distressed and
puzzled, and I happened to find out what he needed to
know," she said. "I thought he should have the information right away."

"And you would be able to make judgments like
that if they made you head of station, which right now
you are not, and never will be if I have anything to do
with it."

It was true that intelligence needed to be assessed
before it was passed to politicians. Unfiltered reports
were untrustworthy and could be misleading. Senior
people in the Agency appraised what came in, checked
the past reliability of the source, compared one report
with another, and put things in context, then handed
the politician their best judgments. They rarely shared
raw data if they could avoid it.

On the other hand this was a simple case. Nick was
an experienced diplomat who hardly needed reminding that intelligence was not always right. No harm had
been done.

Tamara guessed that Dexter's rage was fueled by the
fact that his department had enjoyed a little triumph
but he was getting no credit. But there was no point in
arguing with Dexter. He was the boss and he had the
right to insist on protocol. She had to suck it up.

His limousine arrived and the driver opened the
door. Daisy got in, looking mortified.

"I'm sorry," Tamara said. "I acted impulsively. It
won't happen again."

"It better not," Dexter said, and he got into his car.

Three hours later Tamara had forgotten that Dexter existed.

She ran her fingertips along the line of Tab's jaw, a gracious curve from one earlobe to the other. She was glad he did not have a beard.

His apartment was dimly lit by a single table lamp. The couch was big and soft. A piano quartet played quietly; Brahms, she thought.

He took her hand and kissed it, his lips moving gently on her skin, tasting her, exploring the knuckles, the pads of the fingertips, the palm, and then the soft place at the wrist, where people cut themselves when they wanted to die.

She kicked off her shoes, and he did the same. He was not wearing socks. He had broad, shapely feet. It seemed that everything about him was elegant. There must be a flaw, she told herself. Within the next hour she was going to see him completely naked. Perhaps he has a big ugly navel, or . . . something.

I should be a bit nervous now, she thought. He might be a disappointment: inconsiderate, or too hasty, or peculiar in his desires. Sometimes when sex went wrong a man could become angry and abusive, blaming the woman. She had suffered a couple of bad experiences and heard about many more from women friends. But she felt relaxed. Instinct told her she did not need to worry about Tab.

She unbuttoned his shirt, feeling the crisp cotton and the warmth of his body underneath. He had taken off the tie hours ago. She smelled sandalwood, some old-fashioned cologne. She kissed his chest. It was not very hairy, just a few long black strands. She touched his dark brown nipples. She heard a faint sigh of pleasure, which she took as a sign, and she kissed them. He stroked her hair.

When she drew back he said: "I could take a lot more of that. Why are you stopping?"

She started to undo her purple shirt. "Because I want you to do the same to me," she said. "Is that all right?"

"Oh, boy," he said.

CHAPTER 9

President Green discussed the bad news with her secretary of state, Chester Jackson. He looked like a college professor, with his herringbone suit and knitted tie, but when he sat on the couch beside Pauline she noticed something white on his left wrist. "What's that watch, Chess?" she asked him. He normally wore a slim Longines with a brown alligator strap.

He pulled up his sleeve to reveal an all-white Swatch day-date with a plastic strap. "A present from my granddaughter," he explained.

"Which makes it so much more valuable than anything you could buy in a jewelry store."

"Exactly."

She laughed. "I like a man who has the right priorities."

Chess was a shrewd, practical statesman with a conservative bias toward letting sleeping dogs lie. Before going into politics he had been a senior partner in a Washington law firm specializing in international law. Pauline liked his dry, concise briefings, with not a word wasted.

He said: "We may lose the vote at the UN today.

You've already had the numbers in the report from Josh."
The American ambassador to the United Nations was
Joshua Woodward. "Our support has shriveled up. Most
of the neutral countries who originally promised to back
us have now said they'll abstain or even vote against.
I'm sorry."

"Damn," said Pauline. It had been looking dubious
over the weekend and she was dismayed to have her
fears confirmed.

Chess went on: "The Chinese have won a lot of
people over by threatening to cancel investments."

Vice President Milton Lapierre was sitting opposite
Pauline, fiddling with a purple scarf he had been wearing when he walked in. He spoke indignantly. "We
should do the same—use our overseas aid program as
a lever. People we help should help us!" In his Southern
accent, *help* came out as *hay-ulp*. "And if they don't,
they can go to hell." *Hail.*

Chess shook his head patiently. "Much of our aid
is tied to purchases from American manufacturers,
so if we pull the aid we get in trouble with our businessmen."

Pauline said: "This resolution wasn't such a bright
idea."

Chess said: "We all thought it was a good plan at the
time."

"Rather than lose the vote, I'd like to pull the resolution."

"Suspend it. We can say it's a postponement to discuss amendments. You can suspend for as long as you
like."

"Okay, Chess, but it breaks my heart, when a kid
from a salt-of-the-earth American family like the
Ackermans has just been killed by a terrorist with a
Chinese rifle. I'm not giving up on this. I want to make

sure China knows there's a cost to what they do. They won't get away with it scot-free."

"You could protest to the Chinese ambassador."

"I most certainly will."

"The ambassador will say that the Chinese sell guns to the Sudanese Armed Forces, and it's not really China's fault if the Sudanese sell them to ISGS."

"While the Chinese and Sudanese governments turn a blind eye."

Chess nodded. "Imagine what they'd say about us if Afghan army officers sold American rifles to the anti-Beijing rebels across the border in Xinjiang province."

"The Chinese government would accuse us of trying to bring them down."

"Madam President, if you want to punish China, why not tighten up the sanctions against North Korea?"

"That would cost the Chinese money, but not very much."

"No, but it would show the world that China ignores UN sanctions, and that would embarrass them. And if they protest, that will only prove our point."

"Very sly, Chess. I like it."

"And we wouldn't need a UN vote, because the UN has already imposed trade restrictions on North Korea. All we need to do is enforce existing rules."

"For example . . . ?"

"Import-export documents are published on the internet, and if we scrutinize them closely we can tell which are false."

"How?"

"I'll give you an example. North Korea makes piano accordions, good quality and cheap. In the past they exported them all over the world, now they can't. But you'll find that last year some province in China imported four hundred thirty-three of them, and in the same year China exported to Italy exactly four hundred thirty-three piano accordions marked *Made in China*."

Pauline laughed.

Chess said: "It's not rocket science, we just have to do the detective work."

"Anything else?"

"Lots. Monitor ship-to-ship transfers at sea—something we can do now by satellite. Make it difficult for North Korea to access its offshore hard currency reserves. Make trouble for nations suspected of sanctions busting."

"Heck, let's do it," said Pauline.

"Thank you, Madam President."

Lizzie opened the door and said: "Mr. Chakraborty would like a word."

Pauline said: "Come in, Sandip."

Sandip Chakraborty, the communications director, was a bright young Bengali American wearing a suit with sneakers, a current fashion among hip Washington staffers. He said: "James Moore is making a major speech tonight in Greenville, South Carolina, and I've heard he's going to talk about the UN resolution. I thought you might want to know."

Pauline said: "Put on CNN, please."

Sandip switched on the TV set, and Moore appeared.

He was sixty, ten years older than Pauline. He had craggy features and a graying blond crew cut. His suit jacket was western style, with V-shaped stitching on the shoulder yokes and pocket flaps.

Milt said disparagingly: "Just because you come from the South doesn't mean you have to dress like a shit-kicker."

Chess said: "He made his money from oil, not cattle."

"I bet he has a horse called Trigger."

"But look," said Pauline. "See how they love him?"

Moore was glad-handing shoppers in a sunlit street. They crowded around him, taking selfies with their phones. "This way, Jimmy! Look at me! Smile, smile!" The women in particular were thrilled to be with him.

He never stopped speaking, saying: "How are you? Good to see you. Hi. Thank you for your support—I sure appreciate it."

A young woman thrust a microphone in his face and said: "Are you going to condemn China for selling arms to terrorists when you speak tonight?"

"I'm sure fixing to discuss arms sales, ma'am."

"But what will you say?"

Moore gave her a roguish grin. "Well, ma'am, if I told you that now, no one would need to come out and hear me speak later, would they?"

Pauline said: "Turn it off."

The screen went dark.

Chess said: "The man's a walking joke!"

Milt said: "But he's got a great act."

Lizzie looked in and said: "Mr. Green is here, madam."

Pauline stood up, and the others did the same. She said: "I'm not finished with this. Let's have a meeting tomorrow morning in the conference room. Come with ideas for letting the Chinese know we haven't given up."

They all left, and Gerry came in. He was dressed for business in a navy suit and a striped tie. He rarely entered the Oval Office. Pauline said: "Is something wrong?"

"Yeah," he said, sitting opposite her. Milt had left his purple scarf behind on the seat, and Gerry picked it up and draped it over the arm of the couch. "The principal of Pippa's school came to my office this afternoon."

Gerry's retirement from the law was not total. His

old firm had given him a small but luxurious office on the partners' floor, theoretically for him to use for foundation work. But he often gave advice, informally and unpaid, and it was a boost for the firm to have the president's husband on tap. Pauline was not quite comfortable with this arrangement, but she had decided not to fight him over it.

She said: "Ms. Judd? You didn't tell me you were seeing her."

"I didn't know. She made an appointment using her married name of Mrs. Jenks."

It still seemed odd to Pauline, but that was not the important issue. "Is Pippa in trouble again?"

"Apparently she smokes marijuana."

Pauline was incredulous. "In school?"

"No. For that she would have been expelled instantly. They have a zero-tolerance policy, no exceptions. But it's not that bad. She did it off the premises and outside school hours, that time she went to Cindy Riley's birthday party."

"But I suppose Ms. Judd found out somehow, and she can't ignore the report, even though Pippa hasn't actually broken a school rule."

"Exactly."

"Fuck. Why can't kids go from cute child straight to responsible adult without the nasty in-between stage?"

"Some do."

Gerry probably had, Pauline thought. "What does Ms. Judd want us to do?"

"Make Pippa stop smoking weed," Gerry said.

"Okay," Pauline said, but she was thinking: How the hell am I going to do that? I can't even make her pick up her socks off the floor and put them in the laundry hamper.

Milt's voice said: "Pardon me, I left my scarf behind."

Pauline looked up, startled. She had not heard the door open.

Milton picked up the scarf.

Lizzie looked in and said: "Can I get you a cup of coffee or anything, Mr. Green?"

"No, thanks."

Lizzie caught sight of Milt and frowned. "Mr. Vice President! I did not see you come back." It was her job to police visitors to the Oval Office, and she was annoyed that someone had slipped in without her knowledge. "Is there anything I can do for you, sir?"

Pauline wondered how much Milt had heard of her conversation with Gerry. Not much, certainly. Anyway, there was nothing she could do about it.

Milt held up the purple scarf by way of explanation and said: "I'm sorry to have interrupted, Madam President." He left quickly.

Lizzie was embarrassed. "I'm so sorry about that, Madam President."

"Not your fault, Lizzie," said Pauline. "We'll go to the Residence now. Where is Pippa?"

"In her room, doing her homework." The Secret Service always knew where everybody was and they kept Lizzie informed.

Pauline and Gerry left the Oval Office together and took the winding path across the Rose Garden in the evening sunshine. At the residence they climbed the stairs to the second floor and went to Pippa's bedroom.

Pauline noticed that the poster of polar bears that had been over the head of her bed had been replaced by a picture of a cute boy with a guitar—probably a big star, though Pauline did not recognize the face.

Pippa was sitting cross-legged on the bed, wearing jeans and a sweatshirt, with her laptop open in front of her. She looked up and said: "What?"

Pauline sat on a chair. "Ms. Judd went to see your father this afternoon."

"What did old Judders want? To make trouble, I guess, by the looks on your faces."

"She says you've been smoking weed."

"How the fuck would she know a thing like that?"

"Don't swear, please. Apparently it happened at Cindy Riley's birthday party."

"What asshole told her?"

Pauline thought: How can she look so cute and talk so mean?

Gerald said calmly: "Pippa, you're asking the wrong questions. It doesn't matter how Ms. Judd found out."

"It's none of her business what I do outside school."

"She doesn't see it that way, and nor do we."

Pippa gave a theatrical sigh and closed the lid of her laptop. "What do you want me to do?"

Pauline remembered giving birth to Pippa. She had wanted the baby so badly, but it had hurt so much. She still loved her baby with all her heart, and it still hurt.

Gerry answered Pippa's insolent question. "Stop smoking marijuana."

"Everybody smokes it, Dad! It's legal in DC and half the world."

"It's bad for you."

"Not as bad as alcohol, and you drink wine."

Pauline said: "I agree. But your school bans it."

"They're stupid."

"They're not, but it would make no difference if they were. They write the rules. If Ms. Judd decides you're a bad influence on other pupils, she has the right to throw you out. And that's what will happen if you don't change your ways."

"I don't care."

Pauline stood up. "I guess I don't, either. You're

getting too old to be told, so I can't protect you from the consequences of your mistakes much longer."

Pippa looked scared. The conversation had taken a turn she had not expected. "What are you talking about?"

"If you get thrown out you'll have to be home-schooled. There's no point in sending you to another school where you can get in all the same kinds of trouble." Pauline had not planned to say this, but now she saw that it was necessary. "We'll hire a tutor, probably two, who will give you lessons right here and take you through your exams. You'll miss your friends, but that's too bad. In the evenings you may be allowed out, under supervision, if you behave well and study hard."

"That's so mean!"

"It's called tough love." She looked at Gerry. "I'm done here."

He said: "I'll spend a few more minutes with Pippa."

Pauline stared at him for several beats, then walked out of the room.

She went to the Lincoln Bedroom. This was the one she used if she had to come to bed late or get up early and did not want to disturb Gerry's sleep, which was quite often.

Why did she feel let down? Pippa had been defiant, so Pauline had spoken firmly to her. Yet Gerry had stayed behind, no doubt to soften the impact of Pauline's reprimand. They were not in accord. Was this new? When they first got together she had been struck by how much they thought alike. But now that she reflected on the past, she realized that they had often been at odds over Pippa.

It had started before she was born. Pauline had wanted to give birth in the most natural way possible. Gerry wanted his child to be delivered in a state-of-the-art maternity ward with all the high-tech equipment known to medical science. Pauline had had her way, initially, and Gerry had gone along with all the plans for home birth, but then when the contractions became severe he had called an ambulance, and Pauline had been too distressed to fight her corner. She had felt betrayed, but in the thrill and the challenge of caring for a new baby she had never confronted him about it.

Were they disagreeing more these days? Certainly this tendency to blame her for what went wrong seemed new.

A couple of minutes later he came in, saying: "I thought I might find you here."

She said immediately: "Why did you do that?"

"Comfort Pippa?"

"Undermine me!"

"I thought she needed a little tender loving care."

"Look. We can be strict or we can be indulgent, but the worst thing is to be divided. Mixed messages will just bewilder her, and a confused child is an unhappy child."

"Then we must agree in advance how we plan to deal with her."

"We did! You said we had to stop her from smoking dope, and I said okay."

"That's not how it was," he said with irritation. "I told you that Ms. Judd wanted her to stop, and you decided to make that happen. I wasn't consulted."

"Did you think we should let her carry on?"

"I would have liked to discuss it with her, rather than just give her a command."

"She's getting too old to obey us or listen to our advice. All we can do is warn her of consequences. And that's what I did."

"But you scared her."

"Good!"

Outside the door a voice said: "Dinner is ready, Madam President."

They walked along the Center Hall to the Dining Room, at the west end of the building next to the kitchen. There was a small round table in the middle and two tall windows looking over the north lawn with its fountain. Pippa came in a minute later.

As Pauline took her first mouthful of breaded shrimp, her phone rang. It was Sandip Chakraborty. She stood up, stepped away from the table, and turned her back. "What is it, Sandip?"

"James Moore got wind of the postponement of our resolution," he said. "He's on CNN now. You might want to take a look. He's hitting this hard."

"Okay. Stay on the line." She said to the others: "Excuse me for a minute."

Next door to the Dining Room was a small room known as the Beauty Salon, though Pauline did not use it as such. However, it had a TV, and she went in and turned it on.

Moore was in a basketball arena filled with his fans. He stood on a stage with a microphone in his hand and spoke without notes. He was wearing cowboy boots with pointed toes. Behind him was a backdrop of stars and stripes.

He was saying: "Now, how many of the good people in this room could have told President Green not to put her faith in the United Nations?"

The camera panned across the audience, most of them dressed casually, with "Jimmy" on their T-shirts and baseball caps.

"Oh!" said Moore. "All of you have your hands up!" They laughed. "So what we're saying is that anybody here could have set Pauline straight!" He came all the way downstage and looked into the auditorium. "I see

some little kids here in the front with their hands up."
The camera quickly moved to the front row. "Well,
maybe even they could have told her." He was like a
stand-up comic, with all the pauses in the right places.

"Now, if you choose to make me your president . . ."
There was a long round of applause for the modesty of
if you choose. "Let me tell you how I will speak to the
president of China." He paused. "Don't worry, it won't
take long." Pause for laughter.

"I'm going to say: 'You can do whatever you want,
Mr. President—but the next time you see me coming,
you better run!'"

The cheers were deafening.

Pauline muted the sound and spoke into her phone.
"What do you think, Sandip?"

"It's crap, but he's damn good."

"Should we respond?"

"Not immediately. It would just ensure that the clip
runs all day tomorrow. Wait till we have some good
ammunition."

"Thanks, Sandip. Good night." Pauline ended the
call and returned to the Dining Room. The appetizer
had been cleared away and a main course of fried
chicken was on the table. "I'm sorry," Pauline said to
Gerry and Pippa. "You know how it is."

Gerry said: "That cowboy giving you trouble?"

"Nothing I can't handle."

"Good."

After dinner they had coffee in the East Sitting Hall
and resumed the discussion.

Gerry said: "I still think what Pippa needs is to see
more of her mother."

Pauline was going to have to confront this. She said:
"You know how much I wish I could do that, and you
know just why I can't."

"Shame."

"You've said it twice now."

He shrugged. "I think it's true."

"I have to ask why you continue to say it when you know there's nothing I can do about it."

"Let me guess: you have a theory."

"Well, all you achieve is to shift the blame onto me."

"This isn't about blame."

"It's hard to see any other purpose."

"You're going to think what you like, but I believe Pippa needs more of her mother's attention." He finished his coffee and picked up the TV remote control.

Pauline returned to the West Wing and went to the study to work. She felt frustrated. A UN resolution was a little thing, really, but she had been unable to achieve it. She hoped Chess's plan of tightening sanctions on North Korea would do some good.

She had to review a summary of the annual defense spending bill but, alone in the little room, late in the evening, her mind wandered. Perhaps it was Gerry, not Pippa, who needed to see more of Pauline. He could be attributing to Pippa the feelings of rejection that he himself was experiencing. That was the kind of thing a shrink might say.

Gerry appeared self-sufficient, but Pauline knew he could be needy. Now perhaps he wanted more from her. It was not sex: soon after getting married they had settled into a routine of making love about once a week, usually on Sunday morning, and that was clearly plenty for him. Pauline would have liked more but she hardly had the time anyway. However, Gerry had needs other than sex. He wanted to be stroked mentally. He had to be told he was wonderful. I should do that more, Pauline thought.

She sighed. The whole world wanted more of her attention.

She wished Gerry could have been more positive.

Perhaps Pippa would be a supportive friend one day, but that time seemed a long way off.

I have to support everyone else, she thought, feeling sorry for herself.

Of course I do, that's why I'm president.

Stop being such a wimp, Pauline, she thought, and she returned her attention to the budget for defense.

CHAPTER 10

The Bourbon Street nightclub had been Kiah's last chance of making a living in Chad, she knew. But she had failed. I'm a failure as a prostitute, she thought; should I be ashamed of that, or proud?

She ought to have guessed what the job really was. Fatima had offered a home, food, a uniform, and even child care: no one would do that just to hire waitresses. Kiah had been naïve.

Should she have stuck it out? Young Zariah had. But Zariah had been happy with the work. She found it exciting and glamorous, and the money she made on that first night was probably more than she had ever held in her hand before. If Zariah could do it, Kiah asked herself, why not me? She had had sex before, many times, though only with Salim. It did not hurt. There were ways to avoid becoming pregnant. Prostitutes had to do it with unpleasant men as well as nice ones, but every woman at times had to smile and be charming to rude, ugly men. Had she been squeamish and cowardly? Had she thrown away the opportunity to provide for her child and herself? The questions were pointless: she could not do it and never would.

So her only hope was Hakim and his bus.

Her fastidiousness could kill her. She might die on the journey, long before reaching her dream destination of France. She could easily imagine Hakim's abandoning all his passengers if he thought he could get away with the money. Even if he proved honest, something as simple as a breakdown could be fatal in the desert. And people said the smugglers sometimes used dangerous small boats for the voyage across the Mediterranean Sea.

But if she was going to die, so be it. She could not do what she could not do.

She disposed of her few possessions to the other village wives: mattresses, cooking pots, jars, cushions, and rugs. She called them all into her house, announced who was to have what, and told them they could take the stuff as soon as she left.

That night she lay awake, thinking of all the things that had happened in this house. She had lain with Salim for the first time here. She had given birth to Naji on this floor, and everyone in the village had heard her crying out in pain. She had been here when they brought Salim's body home and gently laid it on the rug, and she had thrown herself on him and kissed him as if her love might bring him back to life.

On the day before the bus was due to leave she woke before dawn. She put a few clothes in a bag along with some food that would not spoil: smoked fish, dried fruit, and salted mutton. She looked around the room and said good-bye to her house.

She left home at the break of day, with the bag in one hand and Naji on the opposite hip. At the edge of the silent village she looked back at the roofs of palm leaves. She had been born here and had lived here for all of her twenty years. She looked at the shrinking lake. In the silver light its surface was as calm and still as death. She would never see it again.

She passed through the village of Yusuf and Azra without stopping.

After an hour Naji became heavy, and she had to stop for a rest. After that she stopped often and her progress was slow.

In the heat of the day she took a long break at another village and sat in the shade of a little grove of date palms. She breast-fed Naji, then drank some water and ate a slice of salted meat. Naji napped for an hour. They set off again in the cooling afternoon.

The sun was low when she reached Three Palms. She walked past the gas station by the café, almost hoping that Hakim would have departed early and left her behind. But she saw him, outside the door to the garage, talking with boastful assurance to a group of men who carried baggage of all shapes and sizes. Like her, they had arrived the day before departure, to be ready to go first thing tomorrow morning.

She walked slowly and tried to get a good look without appearing to stare. Those men were going to be her companions on a difficult journey. No one could say with confidence how long it would take, but it could not be less than a couple of weeks and might easily be twice that. The men were mostly young. They talked loudly and looked excited. She imagined that soldiers going to war might be like that, eagerly anticipating strange places and new experiences, knowing that they were risking their lives but not really taking it in.

There was no sign of the cigarette vendor. She hoped he would turn up. It would be a relief to have one person on the trip who was not a complete stranger.

There were no hotels in Three Palms. Kiah went to the convent and spoke to a nun. "Do you know a respectable family who might give me and my child a bed for the night?" she said. "I have a little money, I can pay."

As she had hoped, she was invited to stay at the convent. She was instantly taken back to her childhood by the atmosphere, an air of candle smoke and incense and old Bibles. She had loved school. She wanted to know more about the mysteries of math and French, past history and faraway places. But her education had stopped at thirteen.

The nuns made a great fuss of Naji and gave Kiah a hearty meal of spicy lamb with beans, all for the price of a hymn and a few prayers before bedtime.

That night she lay awake worrying about Hakim. He had demanded the full fare up front, and she feared he would repeat this demand tomorrow. She would not give him more than half, but what if he then refused to take her? And what if he made a fuss about Naji's traveling free?

Well, there was nothing she could do. She told herself that Hakim was not the only people smuggler in Chad. If the worst came to the worst she would look for another one. It would be better than doing something foolish like giving Hakim all her money.

On the other hand, she felt that if she did not go now she might lose her nerve forever.

In the morning the nuns gave her coffee and bread and asked her what she was planning. She lied, saying she was going to visit a cousin in the next town. She feared that if she told them the truth they would spend hours trying to talk her out of it.

Walking through the town, letting Naji toddle beside her, she realized that after today she would probably never again see Three Palms and soon she would say good-bye to Chad, and then to Africa. Migrants sent letters home; they seldom returned. She was about to

abandon her whole life so far, throw away her entire
past, and move to a new world. It was scary. She began
to feel lost and rootless in anticipation.

She was at the gas station before sunrise.

Several other passengers were there before her, some
accompanied by large families who were evidently
seeing them off. The café next door was open and doing
a lot of business while everyone waited for Hakim.
Kiah had already had coffee but she asked for some
sweetened rice for Naji.

The proprietor was hostile. "What are you doing
here? It doesn't look good, a woman alone at my café."

"I'm going on Hakim's bus."

"On your own?"

She made up a lie. "I'm meeting my cousin here.
He's coming with me."

The man walked away without replying.

However, his wife brought the rice. She remembered
Kiah from her last visit and told her to put her money
away as the rice was for the child.

There were kind people in the world, Kiah thought
gratefully. She might need the help of strangers on this
journey.

A minute later a family asked if they could sit with
her. There was a woman of Kiah's age called Esma,
and her parents-in-law, a kindly looking woman called
Bushra and an older man, Wahed, smoking a cigarette
and coughing.

Esma was immediately friendly with Kiah and asked
if her husband was with her. Kiah explained that she
was a widow.

"I'm so sorry," said Esma. "I have a husband in
Nice, that's a town in France."

Kiah was interested. "What work does he do there?"

"He builds walls for rich people's gardens. He's a
stonemason. There are many palaces in Nice. He works

all the time. As soon as he finishes one wall there is another to be built."

"Is it good money?"

"Amazing. He sent me five thousand US dollars so
I could join him. He's not a legal resident in France so
I have to take this route."

"Five thousand dollars?"

Bushra, the mother-in-law, explained. "It was supposed to be just for Esma. He said he would send more
later for his father and me. But my daughter-in-law is
such a good girl, she wants to take us with her."

Esma said: "I made a deal with Hakim, the three of
us for five thousand. It means we have nothing to spare,
but it was worth it, for soon we will all be together
again."

"God willing," said Kiah.

Abdul spent the night at the home of Anand, the man
who had bought his car. Abdul had haggled over the
price, to avoid arousing suspicion, but in the end it had
been a bargain, and he had thrown in his remaining
cartons of Cleopatras as a bonus. Anand had seemed
pleased and had invited Abdul to spend the night.
Anand's three wives had made a tasty dinner.

That evening two of Anand's friends had shown up,
Fouzen and Haydar, and Anand suggested a game of
dice. Fouzen was a thuggish young man in a dirty
shirt, and Haydar was small and mean looking, with
one eye half closed by some old injury. At best, Abdul
thought, Anand hoped to win back some of the money
he had paid for the car, but he feared their intentions
might be more sinister.

Abdul played carefully and won a little.

They asked him questions and he explained that he

had sold his car to pay his fare to Europe with Hakim. They could tell by the way he spoke Arabic that he was not from Chad. "I'm Lebanese," he said, which was the truth, and the accent would be recognized by anyone from there.

They asked him why he had left, and he gave them his standard reply. "If you were born in Beirut you'd want to leave too."

They were interested in what time the bus would depart and how early in the morning Abdul had to get to Hakim's gas station, and his misgivings strengthened. They were probably thinking of robbing him. He was a stranger and a drifter; they might even think they could get away with killing him. There was no police station in Three Palms.

Abdul would dodge a fight if he could, but in any event he was not worried. These men were amateurs. Abdul had been a high school wrestler and had fought in mixed-martial-arts contests to make money at college. He recalled an embarrassing moment in his CIA training. It was the unarmed combat course, and the trainer—a densely muscled man—had said the traditional words: "Okay, come at me and hit me."

"I'd rather not," Abdul had said, and the class had laughed, thinking he was afraid.

"Oh," the trainer sneered, "so you know all about unarmed combat?"

"I don't know all about anything. But I do know a little about fighting and I avoid it when I can."

"Well, let's see. Give me your best shot."

"Pick someone else, please."

"Just do it."

The man was stubborn. He wanted to strike awe into the students' hearts with a display of mastery. Abdul did not want to spoil his plan, but he would have to.

Abdul said: "Look, let's talk about this," then he kicked the trainer in the stomach, threw him to the ground, and got him in a chokehold.

"I'm really sorry," he said. "But you insisted." Then he released his hold and stood up.

The trainer struggled to his feet. His only visible injury was a bloody nose. He said: "Get the fuck out of here."

On the other hand, Fouzen and Haydar might have knives.

They left at around midnight, and Abdul lay down to sleep on a straw mattress. He woke at first light, thanked Anand and his wives, and said he was setting off immediately.

"Have some breakfast," Anand urged him. "Coffee, a little bread with honey, some figs. Hakim's garage is only a few minutes' walk from here."

Anand's enthusiasm made Abdul suspect they planned to rob him here in the house. The children could be gotten out of the way and the wives would say nothing. There would be no other witnesses.

He declined firmly, picked up his small leather bag, and set off, hoping he had foiled their plans.

The dusty streets of the little town were silent. Soon the shutters would be thrown open, the cooking fires would send up smoke from the courtyards, and the women would come out with their jars and plastic bottles to fetch water. The little mopeds and scooters would snarl irritably as they were woken up. But now it was quiet, so Abdul clearly heard the footsteps behind him, two men running to catch up.

He studied the ground, looking for a weapon. The street was littered with cigarette packets, vegetable peelings, small stones, and odd bits of wood. A fallen roof tile with a sharp edge would be perfect, but most of these roofs were made of palm leaves. He contemplated a rusty spark plug from a car engine, but it was too small to do much damage. In the end he settled for a stone about the size of his fist and walked on.

They came closer. Abdul stopped at a crossroads, where they might be distracted by having to look in four directions. He dropped his bag, then turned to face them. They wore sandals, which was useful: Abdul had boots. They both carried knives with six-inch blades, small enough to be passed off as kitchen equipment, large enough to reach the heart.

They walked toward him and stopped. Hesitation was a good sign. He said: "You're about to commit suicide. Don't you know that's a sin?"

He wanted them to turn around and go back, but they held their nerve, and he knew he would have to fight.

Raising the stone, he ran at Haydar, the smaller one, who backed away, but out of the corner of his eye Abdul saw Fouzen coming, and swiveled and threw the stone hard and accurately at near-point-blank range. It hit the man in the face. He cried out, one hand flew to his eye, and he dropped to his knees.

Abdul swiveled again and kicked Haydar in the balls with a booted foot. He had learned, in martial arts training, to make his kicks count, and Haydar howled with pain and bent over, staggering backward.

Abdul's instinct was to move in and hammer each of them as he would have in the ring, jumping on a fallen man and smashing punches into his face and body until the referee stopped the match. But there was no referee and he had to restrain himself.

He stared at them, looking from one to the other, daring them to move, but neither did.

He said: "If ever I see either of you again I will kill you."

Then he picked up his bag, turned around, and walked on.

He felt exultant, and was ashamed of the feeling. It was a familiar emotion. When in the ring he had taken a profound secret satisfaction in the aggression and violence it permitted, and afterward he always thought: What kind of man am I? He was like the fox in the henhouse, killing every bird, more than he could eat, more than he could ever carry back to his hole, biting and slashing for the sheer joy of it.

But I didn't kill Fouzen and Haydar, he thought, and they're not chickens.

A crowd of people filled the café next to the gas station. He saw Kiah, the woman who had questioned him last time he was here. She had the child with her. She was brave, he thought.

There was no sign of Hakim.

Kiah smiled at Abdul and waved, but he turned away and sat alone. He did not want to make friends with her or anyone else. An undercover operative had no friends.

He ordered coffee and bread. The men around him seemed both scared and eager. Some talked loudly, perhaps to mask their fear; some fidgeted impatiently; some sat silent, smoking and brooding. The older men and tearful women in the crowd seemed like relatives come to say farewell, knowing they would probably never see their loved ones again.

At last Hakim appeared, slouching along the street in his grubby Western sports clothes. He ignored the people waiting for him. He unlocked the side door of the garage, went in, and closed the door behind him. A few minutes later the up-and-over door opened and the bus was driven out.

The two jihadis came out after it, walking with a swagger, their assault rifles slung over their shoulders, staring hard at people, who quickly looked away. Abdul wondered what the passengers made of those two obvious terrorists. Only he knew that the bus contained millions of dollars' worth of cocaine. Did the others believe the jihadis were there to protect them? Perhaps they shrugged it off as a mystery.

Hakim got out of the bus and opened the passenger door, and the crowd surged forward.

Hakim shouted: "There is no place for luggage except the overhead rack. One bag per person. No exceptions, no arguments."

There were groans and shouts of indignation from the crowd, but the guards came and stood on either side of Hakim and the protests faded away.

Hakim said: "Get your money out now. One thousand American, one thousand euros, or the equivalent. Pay me, then you can get on the bus."

Some fought to be first aboard. Abdul did not join the crush: he would board last. Other passengers were trying to cram the contents of two suitcases into one. A few were hugging and kissing their weeping relatives. Abdul hung back.

He smelled cinnamon and turmeric, and found Kiah at his side. She said: "After I talked to you, I spoke to Hakim, and he said I had to pay the whole amount before leaving. Now he's asking everyone for half, as you said. Do you think he will still try to make me pay it all?"

Abdul would have liked to say something reassuring, but he held his tongue and gave an indifferent shrug.

"I'm going to offer him a thousand," she said. She joined the crush, with her child on her hip.

Eventually he saw her hand Hakim the money. He took it, counted it, pocketed it, and waved her aboard, all without speaking or even looking at her face. Clearly the demand for full fare up front had been a try-on, an attempt to exploit a woman alone, quickly abandoned when the woman turned out not to be so easy to push around.

Boarding took an hour. Abdul climbed the steps last, his cheap leather holdall in his hand.

The bus had ten rows of seats, four to a row, two each side of the aisle. It was crowded, but the front row was empty. However, there was a bag on each pair of seats, and a man in the row behind said: "The guards are sitting there. It seems they need two seats each."

Abdul shrugged and looked down the coach. One seat was left. It was next to Kiah.

He realized that no one wanted to sit next to the baby, who would undoubtedly fidget, cry, and vomit all the way to Tripoli.

Abdul put his bag in the overhead rack and sat next to Kiah.

Hakim got into the driving seat, the guards boarded, and the bus headed north out of town.

The smashed-out windows let in a cooling breeze as the vehicle picked up speed. With forty people on board they needed ventilation. But it was going to be uncomfortable in a sandstorm.

After an hour he saw in the distance what looked like a small American town, a sprawl of assorted buildings including several towers, and he realized he was looking at the oil refinery at Djérmaya, with its smoking chimneys, distillation columns, and squat white storage tanks. It was Chad's first refinery, and it had been built by the Chinese as part of their deal to exploit the country's oil. The government had earned billions in royalties from the deal, but none of the money had found its way to the destitute people on the shores of Lake Chad.

Ahead was mainly desert.

Most of Chad's population lived in the south, around Lake Chad and N'Djamena. At the far end of the journey, most of the towns of Libya were concentrated to the north, on the Mediterranean coast. In between these two population centers were a thousand miles of desert. There were a few made-up roads, including the Trans-Sahara Highway, but this bus with its contraband cargo and illegal migrants would not be taking the main routes. It would follow little-used tracks in the sand, doing twenty miles per hour, from one small oasis to the next, often seeing no other vehicle from dawn to dusk.

Kiah's child was fascinated by Abdul. He stared until Abdul looked at him, when he quickly hid his face. Gradually he decided that Abdul was harmless, and the looking and hiding became a game.

Abdul sighed. He could not be sulkily silent for a thousand miles. He gave in and said: "Hello, Naji."

Kiah said: "You remembered his name!" And she smiled.

Her smile reminded him of someone else.

He was working at Langley, the CIA headquarters on the outskirts of Washington, DC. He was using his middle name, John, for he had found that when he called himself Abdul he had to tell his life story to every white person he met.

He had been with the Agency for a year, and all he had done, apart from training, was to read Arabic newspapers and write summaries in English of any reports that touched on foreign policy, defense, or espionage. At first he had written too much, but he had soon developed a sense of what his bosses wanted, and now he was getting bored.

He had met Annabelle Sorrentino at a party in a Washington apartment. She was tall, though not as tall

as Abdul, and athletic: she worked out and ran mara-
thons. She was also strikingly beautiful. She worked at
the State Department, and they had talked about the
Arab world, which interested them both. Abdul had
quickly realized that she was very smart. But what he
liked best was her smile.

As she was leaving he had asked for her phone
number and she had given it to him.

They dated, then they slept together, and he discovered that she was wild in bed. Within a few weeks he
knew that he wanted to marry her.

After six months of spending most nights together,
in either his studio or her apartment, they decided to
move together to a larger home. They found a beautiful
place, but they could not afford the deposit. However,
Annabelle said she would borrow from her parents. It
turned out that her father was the millionaire owner of
Sorrentino's, a small chain of upmarket retail stores
selling expensive wine, prestige brands of spirits, and
specialty olive oils.

Tony and Lena Sorrentino wanted to meet "John."

They lived in a high apartment building on a gated
site at Miami Beach. Annabelle and Abdul flew there
on a Saturday and arrived in time for dinner. They
were given separate rooms. Annabelle said: "We can
sleep together—this is just for the benefit of the staff."

Lena Sorrentino looked shocked when she saw Abdul,
and he realized at that moment that Annabelle had not
told her parents that he was dark skinned.

"So, John," said Tony over the clams, "tell us about
your background."

"I was born in Beirut—"

"So, an immigrant."

"Yes—like the original Mr. Sorrentino, I imagine.
He must have come from Sorrento, I suppose."

Tony forced a smile. He was undoubtedly thinking,

Yeah, but we're white. He said: "In this country we're all immigrants, I guess. Why did your family leave Beirut?"

"If you'd been born in Beirut you'd want to leave too."

They laughed dutifully.

Tony said: "And how about religion?"

He meant: *Are you a Muslim?*

Abdul said: "My family are Catholics, which is not unusual in Lebanon."

Lena said: "Is Beirut in Lebanon?"

"Yes."

"Well, who knew?"

Tony, who was more knowledgeable than his wife, said: "But I believe they have a different type of Catholicism over there."

"True. We're called Maronite Catholics. We're in full communion with the Roman church, but we use Arabic in our services."

"A knowledge of Arabic must be useful in your work."

"It is. I'm also fluent in French, which is Lebanon's second language. But tell me about the Sorrentino family. Did you start the business?"

"My father had a liquor store in the Bronx," said Tony. "I saw him braving the bums and the junkies for a dollar profit on a bottle of beer, and I knew that wasn't for me. So I opened my own store in Greenwich Village and sold expensive wine for a profit of twenty-five dollars on a bottle."

Lena said: "His first ad showed a well-dressed guy with a glass in his hand saying: 'My, this tastes like a hundred-dollar bottle of wine!' And his buddy says: 'It does, doesn't it? But I got it at Sorrentino's and paid half that.' We ran that ad once a week for a year."

Tony said: "Those were the days when you could get a good wine for a hundred bucks," and they all laughed.

Abdul said: "Does your father still have the original store?"

"My father passed away," Tony said. "He was shot in his store by a guy who tried to rob him." Tony paused, then added: "An African American guy."

"I'm very sorry to hear that," Abdul said automatically, but he was thinking about Tony's afterthought: *an African American guy.* You had to say that, didn't you, Tony? he thought. It means *My father was murdered by a Black man.* As if no murders were committed by white people. As if Tony had never heard of the Mafia.

Annabelle took the pressure off by talking about her work, and for the rest of the evening Abdul mostly listened. That night Annabelle came to his room in her pajamas, and they spent the night in each other's arms, but they did not make love.

They never moved into an apartment together. Tony refused to lend them the deposit, but that was only the beginning of a family campaign to prevent her from marrying Abdul. Her grandmother stopped speaking to her. Her brother threatened to have Abdul beaten up by some people he was "connected" with—though he dropped the threat when he found out who Abdul worked for. Annabelle swore she would never give in to them, but the conflict poisoned their love. Instead of a romance, they were living through a war. When she could stand it no longer she ended the relationship.

And Abdul told the Agency he was ready for undercover work overseas.

CHAPTER 11

Tao Ting came out of the bathroom with a towel wrapped around her body and another around her head. Chang Kai, sitting in bed, looked up from reading the newspapers on his tablet. He watched her open the doors of all three closets and stand gazing at her clothes. After a few moments, she dropped both towels onto the carpet.

He drank in the sight of his naked wife and thought how lucky he was. There was a reason why millions of television viewers were in love with her. She was absolutely perfect. Her body was slim and shapely, her skin was the creamy color of ivory, and her hair was luxuriant and dark.

And she was fun.

Without turning around she said: "I know what you're looking at."

He chuckled. "I'm reading the *People's Daily* online," he said, pretending to protest.

"Liar."

"How do you know I'm lying?"

"I can read your mind."

"That's a miraculous power."

"I always know what men are thinking."

"But how?"

"They're always thinking the same thing."

She put on her panties and bra, then stood a little longer contemplating the racks of clothes. Kai felt guilty staying in bed watching her. There was so much he had to do, for himself and for his country. But it was hard to tear his gaze away.

He said: "It doesn't matter what you wear, does it? As soon as you get to the studio they're going to put you in some fantastic costume." Sometimes he suffered the dark suspicion that she dressed up for the handsome young male actors she worked with. She had so much more in common with them than with him.

Ting said: "It always matters what I wear. I'm a celebrity. People expect me to be special. Drivers, doormen, cleaners, and gardeners all tell their families and friends: 'You'll never guess who I saw today—Tao Ting! Yes, her, from *Love in the Palace*!' I don't want them to say that I'm not so beautiful in real life."

"Of course, I get it."

"Anyway, I'm not going straight to the studio. They're filming a big sword fight today. I'm not needed until two o'clock."

"What are you going to do with your free morning?"

"I'm taking my mother shopping."

"Nice."

Ting was close to her mother, Cao Anni, who was also an actor. They talked on the phone every day. Ting's father had died in a car crash when she was thirteen. The same crash had left her mother with a limp that had blighted her career. But Anni had found a new line of work doing voice-overs.

Kai liked Anni. "Don't make her walk too far," he said to Ting. "She hides it, but her leg still hurts."

Ting smiled. "I know."

Of course she knew. He was telling her to be thoughtful about her own mother. He always tried not to act like a parent with Ting, but sometimes it happened anyway. "Sorry," he said.

"I'm glad you care about her. She likes you too. She thinks you'll look after me when she's gone."

"I will."

Ting made a decision and pulled on a pair of faded Levi's blue jeans.

Without looking away from her, Kai turned his mind to the day ahead. He had a rendezvous with an important spy.

He was booked on a lunchtime flight to Yanji, a midsize city close to the border with North Korea. Although he was now the boss of the foreign intelligence department, he still personally ran a few of the most valuable spies, mostly those he had recruited when he was lower in the hierarchy. One such was a North Korean general called Ham Ha-sun. For some years now Ham had been the Guoanbu's best source of inside information about what was going on in North Korea.

And North Korea was China's great weakness.

It was the soft underbelly, the Achilles' heel, the kryptonite, and all the other images for a fatal weakness in a strong body. The North Koreans were key allies, and they were desperately unreliable. Kai met Ham regularly, and between scheduled meetings they could contact one another to request an emergency assignation. Today's meeting was routine but still important.

Ting put on a bright blue sweatshirt and stepped into a pair of cowboy boots. Kai looked at the clock beside the bed and got up.

He washed quickly and put on his office suit. While he was dressing, Ting kissed him good-bye and left.

There was smog over Beijing, and Kai took a mask in case he needed to walk anywhere. His overnight bag was packed, ready for the trip. He took out his heavy winter coat and carried it over his arm: Yanji was a cold city.

He left the apartment.

There were four hundred thousand people in Yanji, and almost half of them were Korean.

The city had expanded fast after the Second World War, and as Kai's plane descended he gazed at the ranks of modern buildings packed closely together on both sides of the wide Buerhatong River. China was North Korea's main trading partner, so thousands of people crossed the border every day in both directions to do business, and Yanji was an important entrepôt for such trade.

In addition hundreds of thousands of Koreans—perhaps millions—lived and worked in China. Many were registered immigrants; some were prostitutes; not a few were unpaid agricultural workers or purchased wives—never actually called slaves. Life in North Korea was so bad that to be a well-fed slave in China might not have seemed a terrible fate, Kai thought.

Yanji had the largest Korean population of any Chinese city. It had two Korean-language TV stations. One of the Korean residents of Yanji was Ham Hee-young, a bright and capable young woman who was the illegitimate daughter of General Ham, a fact known to no one in North Korea and very few people in China. As manager of a department store she earned a high salary plus commission on sales.

Kai landed at the domestic airport, Chaoyang-chuan, and took a cab to the city center. All road signs were bilingual, with Korean above Chinese. Some of the young women on the city streets wore the chic, sexy styles of South Korean fashion, he noticed. He checked into a large chain hotel, then immediately went out again, wearing his heavy coat against Yanji's bitter cold. He ignored the taxis at the hotel entrance, then walked a few blocks and hailed a cab on the street. He gave the driver the address of a Wumart supermarket in the suburbs.

General Ham was stationed at a nuclear base called Yeongjeo-dong, in the north of North Korea, near the border with China. He was a member of the Joint Border Oversight Committee, which met regularly in Yanji, so he traveled across the border at least once a month.

Many years ago he had become disillusioned with the regime in Pyongyang, the capital, and had begun to spy for China. Kai paid him well, channeling the money to Hee-young, Ham's daughter.

Kai's cab took him to a developing suburb and dropped him at the Wumart, two streets away from his actual destination. He walked to a building site where a large house was going up. This was where Ham spent the money he made from the Guoanbu. The land and the house were in Hee-young's name and she paid the builders out of the money Kai sent her. General Ham was close to retirement, and he planned to disappear from North Korea, adopt a new identity furnished by Kai, and spend his golden years with his daughter and grandchildren in their lovely new home.

Approaching the site, Kai did not see Ham, who took care never to be visible from the street. He was in the half-built garage, talking in effortlessly fluent Mandarin to a builder, probably the foreman. He broke off immediately, saying: "I must talk to my accountant," and shook Kai's hand.

Ham was a spry man in his sixties who had a doctorate in physics. "Let me show you around," he said enthusiastically.

All the plumbing had been installed and now carpenters were putting in doors, windows, closets, and kitchen cabinets. Kai found himself envying Ham as they toured the building: it was more spacious than any home Kai had lived in. Ham proudly pointed out a bedroom suite for Hee-young and her husband, two small bedrooms for their children, and a self-contained apartment for Ham himself. We gave him the money for all this, Kai thought. But he had been worth it.

When they had looked around they stepped outside, despite the cold, and stood at the back of the house, where they were hidden from anyone on the street and could not be overheard by the builders. There was a cold wind and Kai was glad of his coat. He said: "So how are things in North Korea?"

"Worse than you think," said Ham immediately. "You already know how completely dependent we are on China. Our economy is a failure. Our only successful industry is making and exporting armaments. We have a woefully inefficient agricultural sector that produces only seventy percent of our food needs. We lurch from crisis to crisis."

"So what's new?"

"The Americans have tightened up sanctions."

This was news to Kai. "How?"

"Just by enforcing existing rules. A shipment of North Korean coal destined for Vietnam was seized in Manila. Payment for twelve Mercedes limousines was refused by a German bank because of suspicion that they were destined for Pyongyang, even though the paperwork said Taiwan. A Russian ship was intercepted transferring gasoline to a North Korean ship at sea just off Vladivostok."

"Small things in themselves, but they get everybody scared of doing business," Kai commented.

"Exactly. But what your government may not realize is that we have only six weeks' supply of food and other essentials. That's how close we are to famine."

"Six weeks!" Kai was shocked.

"They're not admitting that to anyone, but Pyongyang is about to approach Beijing for emergency economic aid."

This was useful. Kai could forewarn Wu Bai. "How much will they ask for?"

"They don't even want money. They need rice, pork, gasoline, iron, and steel."

China would probably give them what they wanted, Kai thought; it always had, in the past. "What's the reaction of the Party hierarchy to yet another failure?"

"There are rumblings of discontent—there always are—but such murmurs will come to nothing as long as China props up the regime."

"Incompetence can be dreadfully stable."

Ham gave a short bark of laughter. "Too fucking true."

Kai had several American contacts, but the best was Neil Davidson, a CIA man at the American embassy in Beijing. They met for breakfast at the Rising Sun, on Chaoyang Park Road near the US embassy, convenient for Neil. Kai did not use his driver, Monk, because government cars looked official, and his meetings with Neil needed to be discreet, so he took a cab.

Kai got on well with Neil, even though they were enemies. They acted as if peace was possible even between such rivals as China and the US, given a little mutual understanding. It might even have been true.

Kai often learned something Neil had not intended to reveal. Neil did not always tell him the truth, but his evasions sometimes yielded clues.

The Rising Sun was a midpriced restaurant patronized by the Chinese and foreign workers in the central commercial district. It made no effort to attract tourists, and the waiters did not speak English. Kai ordered tea and Neil arrived a few minutes later.

Neil was a Texan but not much like a cowboy, except for his accent, which even Kai could detect. He was short and bald. He had been to the gym that morning—he was trying to lose weight, he explained—and he had not yet changed out of his worn sneakers and black Nike warm-up jacket. And my wife goes to work in blue jeans and cowboy boots, Kai thought. Funny world.

Neil spoke fluent Mandarin with atrocious pronunciation. He ordered congee, the rice porridge, with a soft-boiled egg. Kai asked for soy sauce noodles with tea eggs.

Kai said: "You won't lose much weight eating congee. Chinese food has a lot of calories."

"Not as much as American," said Neil. "Even our bacon contains sugar. Anyway, what's on your mind?"

That was direct. No Chinese person would be so blunt. But Kai had grown to like the way Americans got straight to the point. He replied equally plainly: "North Korea."

"Okay," Neil replied noncommittally.

"You're imposing sanctions."

"Sanctions were imposed a long time ago, by the United Nations."

"But now the US and its close friends are seriously

enforcing them, intercepting ships and interdicting cargoes and obstructing international payments that violate the sanctions."

"Perhaps."

"Neil, stop dicking me around. Just tell me why."

"Weapons in Africa."

Faking mild indignation, Kai said: "You're talking about Corporal Peter Ackerman. The killer was a terrorist!"

"It's a pity he used a Chinese gun."

"You don't normally blame the crime on the manufacturer of the weapon." Kai smiled as he added: "If you did, you would have shut down Smith and Wesson years ago."

"Maybe."

Neil was stonewalling, and Kai needed him to be more honest. He said: "Do you know which criminal enterprise is the largest in the world today, in money terms?"

"You're going to tell me it's the trade in illicit weapons."

Kai nodded. "Bigger than drugs, bigger than human trafficking."

"I'm not surprised."

"Both Chinese guns and American guns are easily available on the international black market."

"Available, yes," Neil conceded. "Easily? Not really. The gun that killed Corporal Ackerman was not bought in a regular black-market transaction, was it? When that sale was made, two governments looked the other way: the Sudanese, and the Chinese."

"Don't you understand that we hate Muslim terrorists as much as you do?"

"Let's not oversimplify. You hate Chinese Muslim terrorists. You're not so worried about African Muslim terrorists."

Neil was uncomfortably close to the truth.

Kai said: "I'm sorry, Neil, but Sudan is an ally and it's good business selling them guns. We're not going to stop. Corporal Ackerman is just one man."

"This is not really about poor Corporal Ackerman. It's about howitzers."

Kai was taken aback. He had not expected this. Then he recalled a detail from a report he had read two weeks ago. The Americans and others had raided a large and important ISGS hideout called al-Bustan that had truck-mounted howitzers.

So that was what had prompted the UN resolution.

The food came, giving Kai time to reflect. He felt tense, despite his façade of relaxed camaraderie, and he ate his noodles slowly, with little appetite. Neil was hungry after his workout and wolfed his congee. When they had finished Kai summed up. "So President Green is using the North Korea sanctions to punish China for the artillery at al-Bustan."

"More than that, Kai," said Neil. "She wants you to be more careful about the end users of the weapons you sell."

"I'll make sure that gets through to the highest levels," Kai said.

That meant nothing, but Neil seemed satisfied to have delivered the message. He changed the subject. "How is the lovely Ting?"

"Pretty good, thank you." Neil was one of the millions of men who found Ting devastatingly attractive. Kai was used to it. "Have you found an apartment yet?"

"Yes—at last."

"Good." Kai knew that Neil had been looking for a better place to live. He also knew that Neil had found one and moved in, and he knew the address and phone number. He also knew the identities and backgrounds of all the other residents of the building. The Guoanbu kept close track of foreign agents in Beijing, especially the American ones.

Kai paid for the breakfast and the two men left the restaurant. Neil headed for the embassy, walking, and Kai hailed a cab.

North Korea's demand for emergency aid was discussed at a small high-powered meeting called by the International Department of the Chinese Communist Party. The department's headquarters, at No. 4 Fuxing Road in the Haidian District, was smaller and less impressive than the Foreign Ministry but more powerful. The director's office overlooked the Military Museum of the Chinese People's Revolution, which had a giant red star on its roof.

Kai's boss, Minister for State Security Fu Chuyu, took Kai with him. Kai guessed that Fu would have preferred to leave Kai behind but did not have at his fingertips all the facts about the crisis in North Korea and was afraid of looking foolish. This way he could call on Kai for any details—and blame Kai for any gaps.

All those at the table were men, although some of the aides sitting around the walls were women. Kai thought the Chinese governing elite needed more women. His father thought the opposite.

The director, Hu Aiguo, asked Foreign Minister Wu Bai to outline the problem they had gathered to discuss.

"There is an economic crisis in North Korea," Wu began.

"As usual." The comment came from Kong Zhao, a friend and political ally of Kai's. It was mildly disrespectful to interrupt the foreign minister like this, but

Kong could get away with it. In a brilliant military career, he had completely modernized the army's communications technology, and now he was national defense minister.

Wu ignored him and went on: "The government in Pyongyang has asked for massive aid."

"As usual," Kong said again.

Kong was the same age as Kai, but he looked younger; in fact he looked like a precocious student, with his carefully disarranged hairstyle and his cheeky grin. In Chinese politics most people were careful to look conservative—as Kai was—but Kong allowed his appearance to advertise his liberal attitudes. Kai liked his nerve.

Wu said: "The demand arrived late yesterday, though I knew it was coming, thanks to advance intelligence from the Guoanbu." He looked at Fu Chuyu, who bowed his head in acknowledgment of the compliment, happy to take the credit for Kai's work.

Wu said in conclusion: "The message comes from Supreme Leader Kang U-jung to our president, Chen Haoran, and it is our task today to advise President Chen on his response."

Kai had thought in advance about this meeting and he knew how the discussion would go. There would be a clash between the Communist old guard on the one hand and the progressive element on the other. That much was predictable. The question was how the conflict would be resolved. Kai had a plan for that.

Kong Zhao spoke first. "With your permission, Director," he began, perhaps compensating for his earlier disrespectful attitude, and Hu nodded. Kong said: "In the past year or more the North Koreans have blatantly defied the Chinese government. They have mischievously provoked the South Korean regime in Seoul with minor incursions into their territory, both on land and at sea. Worse, they have continued to stir up international hostility by testing long-range missiles and nuclear warheads. This led to the United Nations' imposing trade sanctions on North Korea"—he held a finger up for emphasis—"those sanctions being one of the principal reasons for their continued economic crises!"

Kai nodded. Everything Kong said was true. The supreme leader was the author of his own problems.

Kong went on: "Our protests have been ignored in Pyongyang. We must now punish the North Koreans for defying us. If we do not, what conclusion will they draw? They will think they can continue their nuclear program, and thumb their noses at UN sanctions, because Beijing will always step in and save them from the consequences of their actions."

Hu said: "Thank you, Kong, for those characteristically trenchant comments." Across the table from Kong, General Huang Ling was drumming his blunt fingers on the polished woodwork, desperately impatient to speak. Hu noticed and said: "General Huang."

Huang was a friend of Fu Chuyu and of Kai's father, Chang Jianjun. All three were members of the powerful National Security Commission and shared a hawkish view of international affairs. "Allow me to make a few points," Huang said. His voice was an aggressive growl, and he spoke Mandarin with a harsh Northern Chinese accent. "One: North Korea forms a vital buffer zone between China and American-dominated South Korea. Two: if we refuse aid to Pyongyang the government there will collapse. Three: there will immediately be an international demand for so-called reunification of North and South Korea. Four: *reunification* is a euphemism for takeover by the capitalist West—remember what happened to East Germany! Five: China will end up with its implacable

enemy on its border. Six: this is part of the Americans'
long-term encirclement plan whose ultimate aim is to
destroy the People's Republic of China the way they
destroyed the Soviet Union. I conclude that we cannot
refuse aid to North Korea. Thank you, Director."

Hu Aiguo looked faintly baffled. "Both of these per-
spectives make a good deal of sense," he said. "Yet they
contradict one another directly."

Kai said: "Director, if I may, I do not have the experience or wisdom of my older colleagues around the
table, but it so happens that I debriefed a high-level
North Korean source just the day before yesterday."

"Go ahead, please," said Hu.

"North Korea has six weeks' supply of food and
other essentials. When that runs out, there will be mass
starvation and social breakdown—not forgetting the
danger of millions of starving Koreans walking across
the border and throwing themselves on our mercy."

Huang said: "So we should send them aid!"

"But we also would like to punish their bad behavior by withholding our help."

Kong said: "We have to, otherwise we lose all control!"

Kai said: "My suggestion is simple. Refuse help
now, to punish Pyongyang, but send aid in six weeks,
just in time to prevent the collapse of the government."

There was a moment of silence as they took this in.

Kong spoke first. "That's an improvement on my
proposal," he said generously.

"It might be," said General Huang reluctantly. "The
situation would have to be closely monitored, day by
day, so that if the crisis is worse than expected we can
bring forward the dispatch of aid."

Hu said: "Yes, that would be essential, thank you,
General."

Kai saw that his plan was going to be accepted. It was the right solution. He was on a roll.

Hu looked around the table. "If everyone is in agreement . . . ?"

No one demurred.

"Then we will propose this to President Chen."

CHAPTER 12

Tamara and Tab were both invited to the wedding, but separately: their relationship was still secret. They arrived in different cars. Drew Sandberg, head of the press office at the American embassy, was marrying Annette Cecil from the British mission.

The marriage took place at the palatial home of a British oilman who was a relative of Annette's, and the guests crowded into a large air-conditioned room with awnings shading the windows.

It was a humanist ceremony. Tamara was intrigued: she had never been to such a wedding before. The celebrant, a pleasant middle-aged woman called Claire, spoke briefly and sensibly about the joys and challenges of marriage. Annette and Drew had written their own vows and said them with such feeling that Tamara teared up. They played one of her favorite old songs, "Happy" by Pharrell Williams. She thought: If I ever get married again I want it to be like this.

Four weeks ago she would not have had that thought.

She glanced discreetly across the room at Tab. Did he like the ceremony? Did the vows touch his emotions?

Was he thinking about his own wedding? She could not tell.

The oilman had offered his house for the party, as well as the ceremony, but Annette had said that her friends were rowdy and might wreck the place. After the service, the bride and groom went to register their marriage and the guests were directed to a large local restaurant that had closed to the public for the day.

The place was owned by Christian Chadians who made North African food and had no problem serving alcohol. There was a big dining room fragrant with spicy cooking, plus a shaded courtyard where a fountain played. The buffet was mouthwatering: crisp golden sweet-potato fritters garnished with fragrant cut limes, a goat stew with okra that had the kick of chilies, fried millet dough balls called aiyisha with a peanut sauce dip, and more. Tamara particularly liked a brown-rice salad made with cucumber and banana slices in a spicy honey dressing. There was Moroccan wine and Gala beer.

The guests were mostly younger members of the N'Djamena diplomatic circuit. Tamara talked for a while to Nick Collinsworth's secretary, Layan, a tall, elegant Chadian woman who had studied in Paris, as Tamara had. Layan had a somewhat aloof manner, but Tamara liked her. They talked about the wedding ceremony, which they had both enjoyed.

At the same time Tamara was constantly aware of Tab and had to make an effort not to follow him around the room with her eyes, though she always knew where he was. She had not yet spoken to him. Every now and again she met his glance and looked away without acknowledging him. She felt as if she were walking around in a space suit, unable to touch or speak to him.

Annette and Drew reappeared dressed in party gear

and looking deliriously happy. Tamara stared, envying them.

A band started playing and the party began to swing. Tamara at last allowed herself to talk to Tab. "Boy, oh boy, this is difficult," she said quietly. "Pretending we're still no more than colleagues."

He had a bottle of beer in his hand, to look convivial, but he had drunk hardly any. "For me too."

"I'm glad you're suffering as well."

He laughed. "Just look at those two," he said, nodding at the bridal couple. "Drew can't keep his hands off Annette. I know just how he feels."

Most of the guests were dancing to the band. "Let's step into the courtyard," said Tamara. "Not quite so many people."

They went out and stood looking at the fountain. There were half a dozen other people out there, and Tamara wished they would go away.

Tab said: "We need more time together. We always meet and part, meet and part. I want us to be more intimate."

"More intimate?" she said with a grin. "Is there any part of me you don't know as well as you know your own body?"

His brown eyes looked at her in a way that always gave her a little internal twinge. "That wasn't what I meant."

"I know. I just enjoyed saying it."

But he was serious. "I want a whole weekend, somewhere else, without interruptions, without people we have to pretend to."

Tamara was beginning to find this exciting, but she did not see how it could be done. "You mean, like, take a vacation?"

"Yes. It's your birthday soon, I know."

She did not remember telling him that. But it would have been easy for him to find out. He was a spy, after all. "Sunday," she said. "I'll be thirty. I wasn't planning to make a big fuss."

"I'd like to take you away, as a birthday present."

She felt a warm flush of affection. Oh, God, I like this guy, she thought. There was a snag, though. "I love the idea," she said. "But where could we go? It's not like there's a resort where we could check into a hotel and be anonymous. Anywhere in this country other than here in the capital we'd stick out like a couple of visiting giraffes."

"I know a good hotel in Marrakech."

"Morocco? Are you serious?"

"Why not?"

"There are no direct flights from here. You have to go via Paris or Casablanca or both. It takes a day to get there. You can't do it for a weekend."

"Suppose I could solve that problem?"

"How else could we travel? Jet-propelled camel?"

"My mother has a plane."

She burst out laughing. "Tab! How will I ever get used to you? Your mother has a plane! My mother has never even flown first-class."

He smiled ruefully. "You'll find this hard to believe, I know, but I find the thought of your family intimidating."

"You're right, that's hard to believe."

"My dad is a salesman—a brilliant salesman, it's true—but he's no intellectual. Your father is a university professor who writes history books. My mom has a talent for creating watches and handbags that rich women will pay ridiculous prices for. Your mother runs a high school, responsible for the education of hundreds of young people, maybe thousands. I know your parents don't make any money, but in a way that's even more impressive. They're probably going to see me as a spoiled rich kid."

She noted two things in that little speech. One was his humility, which she thought was pretty unusual in men of his social group. The other, more important, was the assumption that he was going to meet her parents. He had a vision of his future, and she was in it.

She did not remark on either but said: "Could we really do it?"

"I'll have to ask if the plane is free."

"This is so romantic. I wish we could make love right now."

He raised an eyebrow. "I don't see why not."

"In the fountain?"

"Perhaps, but I don't want to draw the spotlight away from the bride and groom. It would seem discourteous."

"Oh, all right, you old stick-in-the-mud. Let's go back to your place."

"I'll go first. I'll slip out without saying good-bye. You could pay your respects to Drew and Annette and follow me a few minutes later."

"Okay."

"And that gives me a chance to make sure my apartment is reasonably clean and tidy. Unload the dishwasher, throw my socks in the laundry hamper, put out the garbage."

"All that, just for me?"

"Or I could take off my clothes and lie on the bed until you arrive."

"I like Plan B."

"Oh, boy," he said. "You got it."

Next morning Tamara woke up at her apartment in the embassy compound knowing that something had changed. Her relationship with Tab had moved up a gear. He was no longer just a boyfriend. He was more than a lover. They had become a couple, an item. They were going away together. And she had not pushed him into this. It was all his idea.

She lay in bed for a few minutes just enjoying the sensation.

When she got up she found a message on her phone:
Please get 14 bananas for your grandmother. Thank you—Haroun.

She flashed back to the half-abandoned village on the shore of the shrinking lake and the intense, dark-skinned Arab with the New Jersey accent who had said: *The message will mention a number—eight kilometers, or fifteen dollars—and the number will be the time he wants to meet you, by the twenty-four-hour clock. . . . The place of the first meeting will be Le Grand Marché.*

Tamara was excited, but she told herself not to expect too much. Abdul had not known a lot about Haroun. The man might have access to secrets, but he might not. It was possible he was a shyster who would hit her up for money. She should not get her hopes up.

She showered and dressed and ate a bowl of bran flakes. She put on the scarf Abdul had given her for identification, blue with a distinctive pattern of orange circles. Then she went out into the mild air of the desert morning. It was her favorite time of day in Chad, before the air became dusty and the heat oppressive.

She found Dexter at his desk drinking coffee. Today he was wearing a blue-and-white-striped seersucker suit. In this country of vivid Arab robes and chic French fashion, he was dressed in an American sartorial cliché. On the wall was a photograph of him with a college baseball team, proudly holding up a trophy.

"I have a meeting with an informant this after-noon," she said. "Le Grand Marché at two p.m."

"Who is it?"

"A disillusioned terrorist, according to Abdul. He's calling himself Haroun and he lives across the river in Kousséri."

"Reliable?"

"Nobody knows." It was important to manage Dexter's expectations. He found it hard to forgive un-fulfilled promises. "We'll see what he has to say."

"It doesn't sound auspicious."

"Perhaps."

"The Grand Marché is huge. How will you know each other?"

She touched the scarf at her neck. "This is his."

Dexter shrugged. "Give it a try."

Tamara turned to leave.

Dexter said: "I've been thinking about Karim."

She turned back. What now?

Dexter said: "He promised to get you a draft of the General's big speech."

"He promised nothing," Tamara said firmly. "He said he'd see what he could do."

"Whatever—"

"I don't want to pester him about it. If we let him know that it's important to us he may start to think he'd better keep it to himself."

Dexter said impatiently: "If he doesn't give us infor-mation, he's no use."

"I could give him a gentle hint next time I see him."

Dexter frowned. "He's a big fish."

Tamara wondered where Dexter was going with this. She said: "Yes, he's a big fish. That's why I'm so glad I've won his trust."

"You've been in the Agency now for what, five years?"

"Yes."

"And this is your first overseas posting."

Tamara began to see what he was getting at. She felt angry. "What are you trying to say, Dexter?" she said, not as respectful as she ought to be. "Spit it out."

"You're new and naïve." Her tone had given him an excuse to be harsh. "You aren't experienced enough to run a source as important as Karim, one who has such high-level access."

You asshole, Tamara thought. She said: "I was *experienced enough* to reel him in."

"Not the same thing, of course."

I should know better than to fence with him, she thought. You never win an argument with your boss. "So who will take over from me as Karim's contact?"

"I thought I might do it myself."

So that's it. You'll get the credit for my work. Like a professor who publishes a paper based on a discovery by his doctoral student. Classic.

Dexter said: "I assume his contact numbers are all in your written reports."

"You'll find everything you need in the computer files." Except for a few little things I didn't write down, such as the number of his wife's phone, which he carries when he wants to be hard to reach, but fuck you, Dexter, you're not getting that.

"Okay," he said. "That'll be all for now."

Dismissed, she left his office and went to her desk.

Later that morning she got a message on her phone:

Marrakech Express leaves early tomorrow, back in time for work on Monday. Okay?

Tomorrow was Saturday. They would have forty-eight hours. She replied:

You bet your cute little ass.

She decided she wanted to see Karim one more time. It would be a courtesy to let him know about Dexter's decision, and for the news to come from her personally. She would give Karim a sugared version, of course. She would have to say she was being shifted to different responsibilities.

She checked her watch. It was coming up to midday. Around this time Karim was often to be found in the International Bar at the Lamy Hotel. She had time to have a drink with him. If she went from the hotel straight to the market she could still get there by two o'clock.

She ordered a car.

She would have preferred to ride. There were thousands of large and small bikes on the broad boulevards of N'Djamena, motorcycles and scooters and mopeds and even the occasional classic Parisian VéloSolex, a bicycle with a little 50 cc engine the size of a concertina fixed over the front wheel. Back in DC she had ridden a Fat Boy, with a low seat and high handlebars and a massive V-twin engine. But it was too ostentatious for Chad. "Never attract attention" was a basic rule of diplomatic and intelligence work. So she had sold it when she was posted here. Perhaps one day she would get another one.

On the way she got the driver to stop at a little convenience store. She bought a box of breakfast cereal, a bottle of water, a tube of toothpaste, and a pack of tissues. She carried them out in a giveaway plastic bag. She asked the driver to keep them in the trunk and wait for her to come out of the hotel.

The lobby of the Lamy was busy. People were meeting for lunch here or leaving for dates at other restaurants. Tamara might have been in Chicago or Paris. This central district was an international island in an African city. People who traveled all the time wanted every place to look the same, she reflected.

She turned into the International Bar. It was time for pre-lunch drinks. The bar was busy, but quieter than at the evening cocktail hour, more businesslike. Most of the customers wore Western attire, though a few were in traditional robes. There was a preponderance of men, but she spotted Colonel Susan Marcus in civilian clothes. However, Karim was not there.

But Tab was.

She saw his face in profile; he was seated near a window and looking out. He was wearing a dark blue soft-shouldered jacket with a light blue shirt, which she now recognized as his favorite outfit. Her own face broke into a smile of surprise and pleasure. She took a step toward him, then stopped. He was not alone.

The woman with him was tall, almost as tall as Tab, and slim. She was somewhere in her middle forties, which made her ten years older than Tab. Her shoulder-length blond-streaked hair was expensively cut and colored, and she was lightly but expertly made up. She wore a simple linen shift dress in a summery shade of mid-blue.

They sat at a square table, not opposite one another as they would have at a business meeting, but on adjacent sides, suggesting friendship. On the table between them were two drinks. Tamara knew that Tab's glass would hold Perrier water and a slice of lime at that time of day. In front of the woman was a martini glass.

She was leaning toward him, looking into his eyes, talking intensely though quietly. He was saying little, just nodding and speaking monosyllables, though his body language was not embarrassed or rejecting. She was leading the conversation, but he was a willing participant. She put her left hand over his right on the table, and Tamara noticed that she wore no wedding ring. He let her touch his hand that way for a long moment, then he reached for his glass, making her release her hold.

She looked away from him briefly, her eyes scanning

the crowd in the room without curiosity. Her gaze
passed lightly over Tamara, showing no reaction: they
had never met. She returned her attention to Tab. She
had no interest in anyone else.

Suddenly Tamara felt self-conscious. She would feel
humiliated to be caught snooping. She turned and left
the bar.

In the lobby she stopped, thinking: Why am I embarrassed? What have I done to be ashamed of?

She sat on a couch, among a dozen or so people who
were waiting—for colleagues, for their rooms to be
ready, for their questions to be answered by the
concierge—and tried to compose herself. There were
twenty reasons why Tab would be having a drink with
someone. She could have been a friend, a contact, a
fellow officer in the DGSE, a salesperson, anything.

But she was poised, well-dressed, attractive, and
single. And she had put her hand over his on the table.

However, she had not been flirting. Tamara frowned,
thinking: How can I tell? The answer came immediately: They know each other too well for that.

The woman could have been a relative, an aunt perhaps, his mother's baby sister. But an aunt would not
have dressed so carefully for a drink with her nephew.
Thinking back, Tamara recalled diamond ear studs, a
tasteful silk scarf, two or three gold bracelets on one
wrist, high-heeled shoes.

Who was she?

I'll go back into the bar, Tamara thought. I'll just go
right up to their table and say: "Hi, Tab, I'm looking
for Karim Aziz, have you seen him?" Then Tab will
have to introduce me to her.

There was something she did not like about that scenario. She imagined Tab's being hesitant and the
woman's resenting the interruption. Tamara would be
cast in the role of the unwelcome intruder.

What the hell, she thought, and went back.

As she entered the bar she ran into Colonel Marcus, who was leaving. Susan stopped and kissed Tamara on both cheeks, French style. Her normal brisk manner was gone, and she was warm, almost affectionate. They had been in a deadly gunfight and had survived together, and that had made a bond. Susan asked: "How are you feeling?"

"I'm fine." Tamara did not want to be rude to Susan but she had something else pressing on her mind.

Susan went on: "It's a couple of weeks since our . . . adventure. These things sometimes have psychological effects."

"I'm okay, really."

"After something like that, you should talk to a counselor. It's standard."

Tamara forced herself to pay attention. Susan was being kind. Tamara had not thought about trauma counseling. When Susan had said "something like that," she had meant killing a man. No one at the CIA station had suggested that Tamara should seek help. "I don't feel the need of it," she said.

Susan put a hand lightly on Tamara's arm. "You may not be the best judge. Go once, at least."

Tamara nodded. "Thank you. I'm going to take your advice."

"You're welcome." Susan turned to go.

Tamara stopped her. "By the way . . ."

"What?"

"I'm sure I know the woman at the window table talking to Tabdar Sadoul. Is she in the DGSE?"

Susan looked, spotted the woman, and smiled. "No. That's Léonie Lanette. She's a big shot in the French oil company Total."

"Oh. Then she's probably a friend of his father's, who's a board director of Total . . . if I remember rightly."

"Maybe," said Susan, looking arch, "but either way she's a cougar."

Tamara felt a chill. A cougar was a middle-aged woman who preyed on young men sexually. She said: "You think she's after him?"

"Oh, it's way past that. They've been having an affair for months. I thought it was over, but apparently not."

Tamara felt as if she had been punched. I'm not going to cry, she told herself. She changed the subject quickly. "I was looking for Karim Aziz, but I guess he's not here."

"I haven't seen him."

They left the hotel together. Susan got into an army vehicle and Tamara found her driver. "Take me to Le Grand Marché," she said. "But drop me a couple of blocks away and wait, please."

Then she sat back and tried not to cry. How could Tab do this? Had he been two-timing her all along? It was hardly believable, but there was no mistaking the intimate body language. That woman felt she had the right to touch him, and he did not push her away.

The market was at the western end of the long Avenue Charles de Gaulle, in the district where most of the embassies were found. The driver parked and Tamara tied the blue-and-orange scarf around her head. She retrieved her plastic bag, lumpy with groceries, from the trunk of the car. Now she looked like an ordinary housewife doing her shopping.

At this point she should have been eager and hopeful, looking forward to meeting Haroun and finding out what he had to say, optimistic that it might be important intelligence useful to the military. But all she could think about was Tab and that woman, their heads close together, her hand covering his on the table, their voices low, in a conversation that was evidently emotional.

She kept reminding herself that there might be an innocent explanation. But she and Tab were now sharing a bed more often than not, and they had learned a lot about one another—Tamara even knew the name of Tab's parents' Great Dane, Flâneur, meaning Lazybones—but he had never mentioned Léonie.

"I thought it was the real thing," she said sadly, talking to herself as she walked along the street. "I thought it was love."

She reached the market and forced herself to concentrate on the task at hand. There was one conventional supermarket and at least a hundred stalls. The alleys between them were packed with brightly dressed Chadians plus a sprinkling of tourists in baseball caps and comfortable walking shoes. Vendors with trays or just a single item to sell mingled with the crowd, pouncing on likely customers, and Tamara half expected to see Abdul selling Cleopatra cigarettes.

Somewhere here was a man who wanted to betray a terrorist group.

She could not seek him out. She did not know what he looked like. She just had to remain alert and wait for him to make contact.

The displays of fresh fruit and vegetables looked gorgeous. Pre-owned electrical equipment seemed to be big business: cables, plugs, connectors, and switches. She smiled at a stall selling the shirts of European soccer teams: Manchester United, AC Milan, Bayern Munich, Real Madrid, Olympique de Marseille.

A man stepped in front of her with a length of brightly printed cotton. He held it up to her face and said in English: "This is perfect for you."

"No, thanks," she said.

He switched to Arabic. "I am Haroun."

Tamara looked hard at him, sizing him up. Under his headscarf, dark eyes stared candidly at her out of a narrow Arab face. By his wispy mustache and beard she guessed him to be about twenty years of age. He was draped in traditional robes, but under them was a lean and wide-shouldered body.

She took a fold of the cloth between her thumb and forefinger and pretended to feel the quality. "What can you tell me?" she said quietly in Arabic.

"Are you alone?"

"Of course."

He unrolled the cotton more, so that she could see a larger expanse of the print. It was vivid lemon and fuchsia. "ISGS is very happy about what happened at the N'Gueli Bridge," he said.

"Happy?" she said in surprise. "But they lost the fight."

"Two of their men died. But the dead are in paradise. And they killed an American."

This was the weird but familiar logic of the enemy. A dead American represented a triumph, a dead terrorist was a martyr. Win-win. Tamara knew all this already. She said: "What has happened since?"

"A man came to congratulate us. A hero of the struggle in many countries, we were told. He stayed five days, then went away again."

Tamara continued to examine the cloth while they talked, giving the impression they were discussing the fabric. "What was his name?"

"They called him the Afghan."

Tamara was suddenly on full alert. There might have been many Afghan men in North Africa, but the CIA had an interest in one in particular. "Describe him."

"Tall, with gray hair and a black beard."

"Anything special? Any visible wounds, for example?" She did not want to lead Haroun, but there was one crucial detail she needed to hear.

"The thumb," he said. "Shot off. He says it was an American bullet."

Al-Farabi, Tamara thought with mounting excitement. The leading figure in ISGS. The Most Wanted Man. Reflexively, she lifted her eyes from the length of cotton and looked to the south. Stalls and shoppers were all she saw, but she knew that the country of Cameroon was only a mile or so away in that direction—she could have seen it from the minaret of the nearby Grand Mosque. Al-Farabi had been that close.

"And something else," said Haroun. "Something more . . . spiritual."

"Tell me."

"He is a man on fire with hatred. He wants to kill, he longs to kill, and kill again, and again. It is the way some men are with alcohol, or cocaine, or women, or gambling. He has a thirst that is never satisfied. He will not change until the day someone kills him, may God bring that day soon."

Tamara was silent for a long moment, stunned by what Haroun had said and the intensity with which he had said it. At last she broke the spell and said: "What did he do, for five days, other than congratulate your group?"

"He gave us special training. We would assemble outside the town, sometimes several miles away, then he would arrive, with his companions."

"What did you learn?"

"How to make roadside bombs and suicide bombs. All about telephone discipline and coded messages and security. How to disable the phones in an entire neighborhood."

Even I don't know how to do that, Tamara thought. She said: "When he left, did he say where he was headed?"

"No."

"Was there any hint?"

"Our leader asked him the question directly, and he answered: 'Where God leads me.'"

Translation: *I'm not saying*, Tamara thought.

Haroun said: "How is the vendor of cigarettes?"

Was this genuine friendly interest or an attempt to get information? She said: "Fine, last I heard."

"He told me he was going on a long journey."

"He is often out of touch for days."

"I hope he's all right." Haroun looked around nervously. "You have to buy the cloth."

"All right." She took some notes from her pocket.

Haroun seemed intelligent and honest. Such judgments were guesswork, but her instinct told her to see him at least once more. "Where shall we meet next time?" she asked.

"At the National Museum."

Tamara had been there. It was small but interesting. "Okay," she said, handing over the money.

Haroun added: "By the famous skull."

"I know it." The museum's prize exhibit was the partial cranium of an ape that was seven million years old, and a possible ancestor of the human race.

Haroun folded the cotton and handed it to her. She put it in her plastic grocery bag. He turned away and vanished into the crowd.

Tamara returned to the car and rode back to the embassy, where she went to her desk. She had to put all thoughts of Tab out of her head until she had written her report on the meeting with Haroun.

She made her report low-key, emphasizing that this was her first contact with Haroun and he had no record with the Agency that might indicate whether he was reliable. But she knew that the glimpse of al-Farabi was electrifying news and would be relayed to every CIA station in North Africa and the Middle East immediately—no doubt with Dexter's signature at the end of the message.

When she finished, the CIA staff were beginning to leave for the day. She returned to her apartment. Now there was nothing to take her mind away from Léonie Lanette.

A message from Tab appeared on her phone:

See you tonight? Early start tomorrow.

She had to decide what to do. She could not go on a vacation, even a short one, with a man whom she suspected of cheating. She had to confront him about Léonie. Why was she hesitating? She had nothing to fear, did she?

Of course she did. She feared rejection, humiliation, and the dreadful sense of having made a stupid misjudgment.

But it could all be a misunderstanding of some kind. That seemed unlikely, but she had to ask.

She sent:

Where are you now?

He replied immediately:

At home, packing.

She sent:

On my way.

After that she had to go.

She felt shaky as she walked up the stairs to his apartment and knocked on the door. In a moment of nightmarish fantasy she imagined that the door would be opened by Léonie, wearing perfectly pressed lounging pajamas.

But it was Tab, and much as she hated him for deceiving her, she could not help noticing how alluring he looked in a white T-shirt and faded jeans, with his feet bare.

"My darling!" he said. "Come in—it's time I gave you a key. But where's your bag?"

"I haven't packed," she said. "I'm not going." She walked in.

He went pale. "What on earth is wrong?"

"Sit down and I'll tell you."

"Of course. Do you want some water, a coffee, wine?"

"Nothing."

He sat opposite her. "What's happened?"

"I looked in at the International Bar today at about midday."

"I was there! I didn't see you—ah. But you saw me, with Léonie."

"She's attractive and single, and you're clearly intimate with her. I could tell, anyone could tell just by looking at the two of you together. She even held your hand at one moment."

He nodded, saying nothing. Any second now, she thought, he will break out into indignant denials.

But he did not.

She went on: "I happened to be with someone who told me who she is and explained that you've been having an affair with her for months."

He gave a deep sigh. "This is my fault. I should have told you about her."

"Told me what, exactly?"

"I had an affair with Léonie for six months. I'm not ashamed of it. She's intelligent and charming and I still like her. But the affair ended a month before you and I took that trip to Lake Chad."

"A whole month! My goodness. What made you wait so long?"

He smiled wryly. "You're entitled to be sarcastic. I've never lied to you or cheated, but I didn't tell you everything, and that counts as deception, doesn't it? The truth is, I was embarrassed that I fell for you so soon and got serious so quickly. I'm still embarrassed. It makes me feel like a Casanova, which I'm not, and really, I don't respect those men I know who count up their conquests like goals in the soccer season. All the same, I should have confessed."

"Who ended the affair, you or her?"

"I did."

"Why? You liked her, and you still do."

"She told me a lie, and when I found out I felt betrayed."

"What lie?"

"She told me she was single. She's not, she has a husband in Paris, and two boys at boarding school—the one I went to, Ermitage International. She goes home in the summer to be with them."

"That's why you broke up—because she's married."

"I can't feel good about sleeping with a married woman. I don't condemn other people who do it, but it's not for me. I don't want to have a shameful secret."

She remembered how he had been concerned to establish that she and Jonathan were definitely divorced, that first time she had talked to him about her past.

If this was all an elaborate lie, it was a very plausible one.

She said: "So you finished the affair two months ago. Why were you holding hands today?" She immediately regretted saying that. It was a cheap shot, for they had not really been holding hands.

But Tab was too mature to quibble about that. "Léonie asked to see me. She wanted to talk." He shrugged. "It would have been unkind to refuse."

"What did she want?"

"To resume our affair. I said no, of course. But I tried to be gentle."

"So that's what I saw. You being gentle."

"I can't honestly say I regret that. But I sure as hell regret not telling you everything beforehand. Too late now."

"Did she say she loved you?"

He hesitated. "I'll tell you anything," he said. "But are you sure you want me to answer that?"

"Oh, God," she said. "You're so decent you should have a fucking halo."

He chuckled. "Even when you're breaking up with me you can make me laugh."

"I'm not breaking up with you," she said, and she felt warm tears on her face. "I love you too much."

He reached across and took her hands. "I love you too," he said. "In case you haven't already guessed. In fact . . ." He paused. "Look, you and I have both loved people before. But I'd like you to know that I have never felt this way about anyone. Never. Ever."

"Would you just come here and hug me?"

He did as she asked and she held him hard.

She said: "Don't scare me like that again, okay?"

"I swear to God."

"Thank you."

CHAPTER 13

Saturday was not a day off for the American president, but it was different from other days. The White House was a little quieter than usual, and the phone did not ring quite so often. Pauline welcomed the chance to deal with documents that demanded time and concentration: long international reports from the State Department, pages of tax numbers from the Treasury, technical specifications for billion-dollar weapons systems from the Pentagon. Late on Saturday afternoons she liked to work in the Treaty Room, an elegant traditional space in the Residence, much older than the Oval Office. She sat at Ulysses Grant's massive Treaty Table, with the tall grandfather clock ticking loudly over her shoulder, like the spirit of a previous president reminding her that there was not much time for all she wanted to do.

But she was never alone for very long, and today her peace was interrupted by Jacqueline Brody, her chief of staff. Jacqueline laughed a lot and never seemed tense, but she had a steel core. Her thin, muscular body came from a disciplined combination of a strict diet and regular hard workouts. She was a divorcée with grown-up children and seemed to have no romantic life, indeed no life at all outside the White House.

Jacqueline sat down and said: "Ben Riley came to see me this morning."

Benedict Riley was director of the Secret Service, the agency responsible for bodyguarding the president and other senior figures thought to be at risk. Pauline said: "What did Ben have to say?"

"The people guarding the vice president have reported a problem."

Pauline took off her reading glasses and put them down on the ancient table. She sighed. "Go on."

"They think Milt is having an affair."

Pauline gave a so-what shrug. "He's a single man, I guess he's entitled. It doesn't sound like a problem. Who's he sleeping with?"

"That's the problem. Her name is Rita Cross, and she's sixteen."

"Oh, fuck."

"Exactly."

"How the hell old is Milt?"

"Sixty-two."

"Dear Christ, he ought to know better."

"The age of consent is sixteen in DC, so at least he's not committing a crime."

"But still . . ."

"I know."

Pauline suffered an unpleasant vision of the portly Milt on top of a slender teenager. She shook her head to get rid of it. "She's not . . . Milt doesn't pay her for sex, does he?"

"Not exactly . . ."

"What does that mean?"

"He gives her presents."

"Such as?"

"He bought her a ten-thousand-dollar bicycle."

"Oh, dear. This is bad. I can just see it in the *New York* fucking *Mail*. Could Milt be persuaded to end the relationship, I wonder?"

"Probably not: Milt's bodyguards say he's infatuated. But I doubt if it would help. One way or another she'll probably end up selling her story."

"So a scandal is more or less inevitable."

"And that could happen early next year, just as the primaries are starting."

"So we have to get out in front of it."

"I agree."

"Which means I have to fire Milt."

"As soon as possible."

Pauline put her glasses back on, a sign that the meeting was coming to an end. "Find out where Milt is, please, Jacqueline. Ask him to come in and see me—" Pauline turned and looked at the grandfather clock "—first thing tomorrow morning."

"Will do." Jacqueline stood up.

"And brief Sandip. We'll have to do a press release. It will say that Milt has resigned for personal reasons."

"With a quote from you, thanking him for his years of service to the people of the United States and to the president—"

"And we need to choose a new veep. Make me a list of names, please."

"I'm on it." Jacqueline left the room.

Pauline had read only a few more pages about the shortcomings of inner-city schools when she heard a sound in the hall. Her parents were visiting Washington and spending the night at the White House, and it seemed they had arrived. The voice she heard was that of her mother, reedy and pathetic, saying: "Pauline? Where are you?"

Pauline got up and went outside.

Her mother was in the Center Hall, a big, pointless

space with furniture that was never used: an octagonal
desk in the middle, a grand piano with a locked lid,
sofas and chairs that no one sat on. Mother looked lost.

Christine Wagner was seventy-five. She wore a
tweed skirt and a pink cardigan. Pauline remembered
her half a lifetime ago: she had been briskly competent,
making breakfast while at the same time ironing a
clean white shirt, finding Pauline's homework, brushing the shoulders of Daddy's gray flannel suit as he
headed out the door, and listening for the honk of the
school bus. Once a smart and strong-willed woman,
she had become timid and anxious in the last few years.
"So there you are," she said, as if Pauline must have
been hiding.

Pauline kissed her. "Hello, Mother. Welcome. It's
good to see you."

Her father appeared. Keith Wagner's hair was white
but his neat mustache was black. A businessman who
had worn navy and gray suits for half a century, he had
taken to shades of brown. He had on a new-looking
outfit, a tan sport coat with chocolate-colored pants
and a matching tie. Pauline kissed his cheek, and they
moved into the East Sitting Hall. Gerry joined them.

They talked about the parents' hobbies. Keith was
on the board of the Commercial Club, Chicago's elite
business group, and Christine was a volunteer reader
at two local schools.

Pippa came in and kissed her grandparents.

Keith said: "So, Pauline, what global crisis have you
resolved lately?"

"I've been trying to get the Chinese to be more careful who they sell guns to."

Pauline was ready to explain the problem, but her
father was more interested in his own reminiscences.
"I did business with the Chinese, now and again, back
in the day. Bought millions of polythene bags from

them and sold them to hospitals. A very clever race, the Chinese. When they decide to do something, they get it done. There's something to be said for authoritarian governments."

Pauline said: "They make the trains run on time."

Gerry said pedantically: "Actually, that's a myth: Mussolini never did get Italian trains to run on time."

Keith was not listening. "They don't have to pander to every little group that stands in the way of progress because they want to protect the nesting grounds of the lesser spotted tit warbler"—Christine said: "Keith!" and Pippa sniggered but Keith ignored them both—"or they think the ground is holy because that's where the spirits of their ancestors gather under the full moon."

Pippa said: "And the other amazing thing about authoritarian governments is that if they want to murder six million Jewish people, no one can stop them."

Pauline considered whether to silence Pippa and decided that her father had asked for it.

But Keith was untroubled. "I recall, Pippa, that your mother also knew all the smart answers when she was just fourteen years old."

Christine said: "Don't pay attention to your grandfather, Pippa. Over the next three or four years you'll do things you'll remember later with deep embarrassment. But when you're old you'll wish you'd done all of them twice."

Pauline laughed happily. It was a flash of her mother as she used to be, feisty and funny.

Keith said grumpily: "Pearls of wisdom from the geriatric ward."

The conversation was becoming too combative. Pauline stood up. "Let's have dinner," she said, and they all walked along the Center Hall to the Dining Room.

Pauline no longer regarded her parents as people

she could lean on for support. This had happened gradually. Their horizons had narrowed, they had lost touch with the modern world, and their judgment had deteriorated. One day Pippa will feel like that about me, Pauline mused as they sat down to eat. How far ahead was that moment? Ten years? Twenty? She found the thought unsettling: Pippa out in the world, making decisions for herself, and Pauline sidelined as incapable.

Her father was talking to Gerry about business, and the three women did not interrupt. Gerry had once been Pauline's close confidant. When had that ceased? She could not tell exactly. It had petered out, but why? Was it just because of Pippa? Pauline knew, from observing other parents, that disagreements over child rearing created some of the worst marital conflicts. They involved people's most deeply held convictions about morals, religion, and values. They brought out the truth about whether the couple was compatible or not.

Pauline thought young people should challenge established ideas. It was how the world made progress. She was a conservative because she knew that change had to be introduced cautiously and managed judiciously, but she was not the type who thought nothing needed changing. Nor was she the even worse kind who hankered after a golden age in the past when everything was so much better. She did not yearn for the good old days.

Gerry was different. He said that young people needed to achieve maturity and wisdom before they tried to change the world. Pauline knew that the world was never changed by people who waited for a more suitable moment.

People like Gerry.

Ouch.

What could she do? Gerry wanted her to spend

more time with her family—which meant him—but she could not. A president was given everything she needed except time.

She had been committed to public service long before she married him: he could hardly have been surprised. And he had been keen for her to run for president. He had said frankly that it would be good for his career, win or lose. If she won he would retire for four years or eight, but after that he would be a legal superstar. But then, when she was elected, he had begun to resent how little time she had for him. Maybe he had thought that he would be more involved in her work, that as president she would consult him about decisions. Maybe he should not have retired. Maybe—

Maybe she should not have married him.

Why did she not share Gerry's yearning for them to spend more time together? Some busy couples looked forward to a regular date night, when they devoted themselves to one another, and had a romantic dinner or went to a movie or listened to music together on the couch.

The thought depressed her.

Looking at Gerry as he agreed with her father about labor unions, she realized that the trouble with Gerry was that he was a bit dull.

She was being harsh now. But it was true. Gerry was boring. She did not find him sexy. And he was not very supportive of her.

So what was left?

Pauline always faced the facts.

Did all this mean she no longer loved him?

She was afraid it did.

Next morning she had breakfast with Dad, just as she had when he was working and she was at the University of Chicago. They were both larks, up early. Pauline had muesli and milk while Dad ate toast and drank coffee. They did not say much: now as then, he was deep in the business section of the newspaper. But it was a companionable silence. With a twinge of reluctance she left him and went to the West Wing.

Milt had suggested an early hour for their appointment so that he could come to the White House on his way to church. Pauline would see him in the Oval Office. Its formal air was suitable for firing someone.

Milt arrived in a brown tweed suit with a vest, looking like a country gentleman. "What has James Moore done now, to require a meeting early in the morning of the Lord's Day?"

"This is not about James Moore," Pauline said. "Sit down."

"What is it about?"

"Our problem is Rita Cross."

Milt sat up straighter, tilted his chin, and looked haughty. "What are you talking about?"

Pauline could not bear to listen to bullshit: life was too short. She said: "Don't for Christ's sake pretend you don't know."

"It sounds like something that's no one's business but mine."

"When the vice president is fucking a sixteen-year-old it's everyone's business, Milt—stop acting dumber than you are."

"Who's to say it's more than a friendship?"

"Spare me the crap." Pauline was getting angry. She had thought that Milt would be realistic and mature about this, accept that he had been caught out breaking the rules and retire graciously. No such luck.

"She's not underage," Milt said, with the air of a card player who lays an ace.

"Tell the reporters that, when they call to ask you about your relationship with Rita Cross. Do you think they'll say that in that case there's no scandal? Or what?"

Milt was looking desperate. "We can keep this secret."

"No, we can't. Your bodyguards know, and they told Jacqueline, who told me and Sandip, all in the last twenty-four hours. And what about Rita? Doesn't she have sixteen-year-old friends? What do they think she's doing with a sixty-two-year-old man who gave her a ten-thousand-dollar bicycle? Playing Scrabble?"

"All right, Madam President, you've got a point." Milt leaned forward, lowered his voice confidentially, and spoke as one colleague to another. "Leave this with me, please. I'll work things out, I promise."

The proposal was outrageous, and he should have known that. "Fuck you, Milt. I'm not going to leave anything with you. This is a scandal that will hurt every one of the people here who have been working so hard for a better America. The least I can do is minimize the damage, and to that end I will control when and how the news comes out."

Milt looked as if he was beginning to see that there was no hope for him. He said miserably: "What do you want me to do?"

"Go to church, confess your sin, and promise God you won't do it again. Go home, call Rita, and tell her it's all over. Then write me a resignation letter, citing personal reasons—don't lie and invent health problems or anything else. Make sure that letter is on this desk by nine o'clock tomorrow morning."

Milt stood up. "I'm serious about her, you know," he said quietly. "She's the love of my life."

Pauline believed him. It was absurd, but against her will she felt a twinge of sympathy. She said: "If you really love her, you'll break up with her, and let her go back to the life of a normal teenager. Now go and do the right thing."

He looked sad. "You're a hard woman, Pauline."

"Yeah," she said. "But I have a hard job."

CHAPTER 14

O n Monday morning Tamara began to suspect that the General was up to something. It might have been trivial, but she had a bad feeling.

She was too euphoric, after Marrakech, to go straight to her desk, so she dropped her bag at her room and went to the canteen. She got a big cup of weak black coffee, American style, and a slice of toast, and picked up a copy of the government-subsidized French-language daily newspaper, *Le Progrès*.

It was when she turned to page three of the paper that an alarm bell rang faintly in the distant back of her mind. There was a photograph of the General, bald and smiling, dressed as if for sport in jogging pants and a warm-up jacket. He was pictured in the Atrone slum in northeast N'Djamena. News from Atrone usually focused on delays in extending the city's fresh water and sewage network. However, today there was a positive story. The General, pictured against a shanty-town background, was surrounded by a crowd of happy children and teenagers, and he was handing out free Nike sneakers.

As she mulled over the story her mind kept wandering to Tab.

She had traveled discreetly. Tab had ordered cars from the French embassy to take them to and from the airport, where they used the private aviation terminal to board the Travers company jet. Tamara had filed the required notification that she would be out of the country, but had not included the information that she was traveling with Tab. Dexter never read that kind of paperwork anyway.

The weekend had been a success. They had been inseparable for forty-eight hours without getting irritated or bored by one another. Tamara knew that domestic intimacy could cause quarrels. Men were never as hygienic as you thought they should be, and they in turn accused you of being a fusspot. People had long-established habits that they hated to change. "We'll tidy up in the morning," men would say, but they never did. However, Tab was not like the rest.

She kept reminding herself how badly she had judged men previously, especially the two she had married, immature Stephen and gay Jonathan. But surely she must have learned better? Jonathan had been an improvement on Stephen, and Tab was better still. Perhaps Tab was the One.

She thought: Perhaps? Bullshit. He is. I know it.

As they drove back into town on Monday morning, Tab said: "Now we have to get ready to pretend we're not madly in love."

She smiled. So he was *madly* in love with her. He had not used that phrase before. She was pleased.

But they now had a problem. Their countries were allies but had secrets from one another just the same. In principle, there was no CIA rule that forbade her to have a relationship with an officer of the DGSE, and vice versa. In practice, it would blight her career, and probably his too. Unless one of them found another job . . .

She looked up from the paper and saw the ambassador's secretary, Layan, carrying a tray. "Come and join me," Tamara said. "You don't usually have time for breakfast."

"Nick's having breakfast at the British embassy," Layan explained.

"What's he plotting with the Brits?"

"We think Chad might be furtively doing business with North Korea, selling them oil in violation of sanctions." Layan spooned yogurt over fresh figs. "Nick wants the Brits and others to pressure the General to sell his oil elsewhere."

"He probably gets a higher price from Pyongyang."

"I expect so."

Tamara showed Layan the newspaper. "What do you think this is all about?"

Layan studied the page for a few moments. "It's pretty good," she said. "For the price of a few hundred pairs of shoes, the General gets the whole nation thinking he's Santa Claus. A cheap way to win popularity."

"Agreed, but why does he need to chase that kind of publicity? He doesn't need popularity, he has the secret police."

"Maybe, up to a point. Being a beloved dictator is probably easier than being a hated dictator."

"I guess." Tamara was not convinced. "I'd better go to work." She stood up.

"Um . . ."

Layan had something on her mind. Tamara waited, standing by her chair.

"Tamara, would you like to come to my house for dinner? Sample some genuine Chadian cooking?"

Tamara was surprised but pleased. "I'd love that,"

she said. It was the first time she had been invited to a Chadian home in N'Djamena. "I'm honored."

"Oh, don't say that. It will be a pleasure for me. How about Wednesday night?"

"Wednesday is good." I'll go to Tab's place after, she thought.

"You know that we don't eat at a table. We sit on a rug on the floor for dinner."

"That's okay, no problem."

"I look forward to it."

"I can't wait!"

Tamara left the canteen and headed for the CIA office.

She was very curious about the General. Why did he suddenly feel the need to work on his image?

The two youngest agents at the station had the chore of reading every newspaper published in N'Djamena and watching every news show on TV, in both French and Arabic. The French expert was Dean Jones, a bright blond-haired kid from Boston; the Arabic speaker was Leila Morcos, a savvy New Yorker with dark hair in a bob. They sat opposite one another, with the day's papers on the desk between them. Tamara spoke to both. "Have you noticed any criticism of the General in any of the media?"

Dean shook his head and Leila said: "Nothing."

"Even slight hints and murmurs? Something like *On reflection, this could have been better handled*, or maybe *It's a shame this was not foreseen*, that sort of coded remark?"

They both thought harder, then repeated their earlier replies. Leila added: "But we'll look out for such comments especially, now that we know you're interested."

"Thanks. I've just got a feeling the General is a bit worried about something."

She sat at her desk. A few minutes later Dexter summoned her and she went into his office. He had his tie pulled loose and his shirt collar unbuttoned, even though the air-conditioning kept the place cool. He probably thought it made him look like Frank Sinatra. "About Karim Aziz," he said. "I think you misjudged him."

She had no idea what he was talking about. "How so?"

"He's really not as important or well-connected as you imagined."

"But—" She was about to argue, then stopped herself. She did not yet know where this was going. She would let him speak, and garner as much data as she could before responding. "Go on," she said.

"He never produced that speech of the General's that he said was going to be so important."

So, Karim would not give Dexter the draft he had half promised to Tamara. She wondered why.

Dexter went on: "And no such speech has been made."

The General might have abandoned the speech— but it was equally likely that he was simply waiting for the right moment. However, Tamara said nothing.

Dexter said: "I'm going to hand him back to you to run."

Tamara frowned. Why was he doing this?

He responded to her frown. "Karim doesn't merit the attention of a senior officer," he said. "Like I said, you overrated him."

But this man works in the Presidential Palace, Tamara thought. He's almost certain to have useful intelligence. Even a cleaner at the palace can pick up secrets from the wastepaper bins. "Okay," she said. "I'll give him a call."

Dexter nodded. "Do that." He looked down at the document on his desk. Tamara took that for dismissal and went out.

She busied herself with routine work, but she was

worried about Abdul. She hoped he would make contact soon. There had been no word from him for eleven days. This was not completely unexpected, just worrying. On American highways, a thousand-mile journey would be a two-day trip, Chicago to Boston; Tamara had driven it once, to visit a boyfriend at Harvard. One time she took the bus: thirty-six hours, a hundred and nine dollars, free wi-fi. Abdul's trip would be very different. There were no speed limits because none were needed: it was not possible to go more than about twenty miles per hour on stony unpaved desert tracks. Punctures and other breakdowns were likely, and if the driver could not fix the problem they might wait days for help to arrive.

But Abdul faced hazards worse than punctures. He was pretending to be a desperate migrant, but he had to talk to people, watch Hakim, identify the men Hakim contacted, and learn where they hung out. If suspicion fell on him . . . Tamara saw again the body of Abdul's predecessor, Omar, and she recalled like a nightmare how she had knelt in the sand and picked up his severed hands and feet.

And there was nothing she could do other than wait for Abdul to call.

A few minutes after twelve noon Tamara got a car to take her to the Lamy Hotel.

Karim was standing at the bar in a white linen suit, drinking what looked like a nonalcoholic cocktail, talking to a man Tamara vaguely recognized as being from the German embassy. She asked for Campari with ice and soda, a cocktail so weak that a gallon of it would hardly make her tipsy. Karim left his German acquaintance and came to talk to her.

She wanted to know why the General was giving out free sneakers, and whether his popularity was slipping, but a blunt question would put Karim on his guard, and he would deny everything, so she had to approach the subject carefully. "You know the US supports the General as the basis of stability in this country."

"Of course."

"We're a little concerned to hear rumors of discontent with him." She had heard no such rumors, of course.

"Don't worry about rumors," Karim said, and Tamara noticed that he had not contradicted her. "It's nothing," he went on, making her think it was definitely something. "We're dealing with it."

Tamara chalked up a point to herself. Karim had already confirmed something that had been no more than speculation on her part. She said: "We can't understand why this has started just now. There's nothing wrong. . . ." She let the unasked question hang in the air.

"There was that incident at the N'Gueli Bridge that you were involved in."

So that was it.

He went on: "A few people are saying that the General should have responded quickly and decisively."

Tamara was excited. This was a new insight. But she frowned, as if dispassionately calculating dates, and said: "Well, it was more than two weeks ago."

"People don't understand that these things are complicated."

"That's true," she said, showing sympathy by agreeing with an empty platitude.

"But we will respond very firmly, and soon."

"I'm glad. You spoke of a speech. . . ."

"Yes. Your friend Dexter was very curious about that." Karim looked offended. "He almost seemed to think he had the right to approve the draft."

"I'm sorry about Dexter. You and I help one another, don't we? That's what our relationship is about."

"Exactly!"

"Dexter may not have realized that."

"Well, perhaps that's all it was," said Karim, somewhat mollified.

"When will the General deliver his speech, do you think?"

"Very soon."

"Good. That should put a stop to the mutterings."

"Oh, it will, you'll see."

Tamara was desperate to see a draft, but she could not ask, after Dexter had caused offense by making the same request. Could she pick up a hint? She said: "What has delayed the speech, I wonder?"

"We are still making final preparations."

"Preparations?"

"Yes."

Tamara was genuinely mystified. "What preparations?"

"Ah," said Karim with an enigmatic smile.

Tamara said ruefully: "I'm trying to imagine what preparations you could need that would be so elaborate they would delay a speech for more than two weeks."

"I can't say," said Karim. "I mustn't reveal state secrets."

"Oh, no," said Tamara. "Heaven forbid."

That evening, before going to meet Tab for dinner, Tamara phoned her ex-husband Jonathan. He was wise and loving, and he was still her best friend. It was time she told him about Tab.

San Francisco was nine hours behind N'Djamena, so he would probably be having breakfast. He picked up right away. "Tamara, sweetheart, how nice to hear your voice! Where are you? Still in Africa?"

"Still in Chad. How about you? Is this a good time to talk?"

"I have to go to work in a few minutes, but I have time for you, always. What's happening? Are you in love?"

His intuition was good. "Yes, I am."

"Congratulations! Tell me all about him. Or her, but if I know you it's a boy."

"You know me." Tamara described Tab in glowing terms and recounted their trip to Marrakech.

"You lucky girl," was Jonathan's comment. "You're crazy about him, I can tell."

"But it's been less than a month. And you have to admit that in the past I've fallen for men who weren't right for me."

"So have I, darling, so have I, but you have to keep trying."

"I'm not sure what to do next."

"I know what you should do, if he's anything like your description," said Jonathan. "Lock him in the cellar and keep him there as a sex slave. I would."

She laughed. "Seriously, though."

"Seriously?"

"Yes."

"All right, I'll tell you, and I'm as serious as a heart attack."

"Go on."

"Marry him, you fool," said Jonathan.

An hour later Tab said: "How would you like to meet my father?"

"I'd love to," Tamara said immediately.

They were in a quiet Arab restaurant called al-Quds, which meant Jerusalem. The place had become their favorite haunt. They were not worried about being spotted: it did not serve alcohol, so Europeans and Americans did not go there.

"My father comes to Chad on business occasionally. The Total oil company is Chad's biggest customer."

"When will he be here?"

"In a couple of weeks."

She glanced at a reflective window and touched her head. "I need to get my hair cut."

Tab laughed. "Papa's going to love you, don't worry."

She wondered whether his parents met all his girl-friends. Before she could stop herself she blurted out: "Did your father meet Léonie?"

Tab winced.

"I'm sorry, what a rude question," Tamara said, embarrassed.

"I don't really mind. That's you, you're direct. No, Papa never met Léonie."

Tamara moved on hastily. "What's he like?" She was genuinely curious. Tab's father was Algerian French, the child of a shopkeeper, now a high-powered executive.

"I adore him, and I think you will too," Tab said. "He's smart and interesting and kind."

"Just like you."

"Not quite. But you'll see."

"Will he stay in your apartment?"

"Oh, no. A hotel is more convenient for him. He'll be at the Lamy."

"I hope he likes me."

"How could he not? You make a stunning first impression: you're absolutely gorgeous, plus you have the kind of simple chic style that French people prize." He made a gesture toward her outfit: she was wearing a mid-gray shift dress with a red belt, and she knew it looked great. "And then he'll love you for speaking

French. Of course he speaks English, but French people hate having to do so all the time."

"Politics?"

"Middle of the road. Socially liberal, financially conservative. He would never vote for the French Parti Socialiste, but if he was American he'd be a Democrat."

Tamara understood: in Europe the political center was somewhat to the left of its American equivalent.

There was nothing about Tab's father to bother her. All the same she said: "I'm nervous."

"Don't worry. You'll charm his socks off."

"How can you be sure?"

He gave a very French shrug. "It's what you did to me."

The General's plan was revealed the next afternoon in a press release that went to all embassies as well as the media. He was going to make a major speech at a refugee camp.

There were a dozen such camps in the east of Chad. The refugees came across the border from Sudan. Some were opponents of the government there; others were simply collateral damage, families escaping from violence. These camps enraged the government of Sudan in Khartoum, which angrily accused Chad of sheltering insurgents, and used that as an excuse to send its army over the border in hot pursuit of fugitives.

The Chad government made mirror-image accusations. The Chinese guns supplied to the army of Sudan found their way into the hands of rebel Chadians such as the Union of Forces for Democracy and Development, as well as assorted other North African troublemakers.

With each side accusing the other, the upshot was

fraught relations and the constant danger of trouble at the border.

All the agents crowded into Dexter's office to discuss the announcement. Dexter said: "The ambassador will want to know what this is about, and he'll expect the CIA to have some ideas. Right now, all we know for sure is the surprise location."

Leila Morcos spoke first. She was junior, but she never let that hold her back. "It's ninety-nine percent certain that the speech will be an attack on the government in Khartoum."

Dexter said: "But why now? And why such a big production?"

Tamara said: "Yesterday I picked up a rumor that the speech is a response to the shooting at the N'Gueli Bridge."

"Your big drama," Dexter said patronizingly. "But that was nothing to do with Sudan."

Tamara shrugged. The guns had come from Sudan, as everyone knew, but she did not bother to state the obvious.

A secretary came in and handed Dexter a sheet of paper. "Another message from the Presidential Palace," she said.

He read quickly, grunted with surprise, read again more slowly, then said: "The General is inviting favored allies to send one person from each embassy to accompany the media to the refugee camp for his speech."

Dexter's deputy, Michael Olson, said: "Which camp?"

Dexter shook his head. "It doesn't say."

Olson was a rangy, laid-back guy with a sharp eye for detail. "They're all about six hundred miles from here," he said. "How are people going to get there?"

"It says transport arrangements will be made by the military. There will be a plane to Abéché."

"That's the only airport in that part of the country," Olson said. "But it's still a hundred miles from the border."

Tamara recalled that Abéché was the hottest town in Chad, with temperatures in the thirties centigrade, nineties Fahrenheit, all year round.

Dexter went on: "From Abéché the army will organize road transport. The trip will include a tour of refugee camps and will involve two nights' stay at a hotel." Dexter frowned. "Two nights?"

Olson said: "That airport only operates in daylight. I guess that makes the logistics difficult."

These must be the preparations that Karim had said were taking a long time, Tamara realized. A press trip into the desert was a big project to organize. On the other hand, did it really take nearly three weeks?

Dexter said: "The party leaves tomorrow."

Leila said: "I suppose Nick will be our representative."

"No way." Dexter shook his head. "He'd have to go unprotected. The rule of one person per embassy will be strictly applied because of transport limitations, which means there's not enough room for bodyguards."

"So who will go?"

"I guess that has to be me—without my personal protection team." He did not look pleased. "Thanks, everyone," he said. "I'll brief the ambassador."

It was the end of the afternoon. Tamara went to her apartment, showered, and put on fresh clothes, then got a car to Tab's apartment.

She had her own key now. She walked in, calling: "It's me."

"I'm in the bedroom."

He was in his underwear. He looked cute, and she giggled. "Why are you in your tighty-whities?"

"I took off my suit and I haven't got dressed yet."

She saw that he was packing a small bag, and her heart turned cold. "Where . . . ?"

"I'm going to Abéché."

It was what she had feared. She swallowed. "I wish you weren't. It's practically a war zone."

"Not really."

"A combat zone, then."

"We accepted the possibility of a certain amount of danger when we became intelligence officers, didn't we?"

"That was before I fell in love with you."

He put his arms around her and kissed her, and she knew he had liked her saying that she had fallen in love with him. A minute later he broke the kiss and said: "I'll take care, I promise."

"When do you leave?"

"Tomorrow."

She could not help thinking that this might be their last evening together, ever.

She told herself not to be melodramatic. He was going with the General. He would be protected by half the National Army.

He said: "What would you like for supper? Or shall we go out?"

Suddenly she wanted to hold him in her arms. "Let's go to bed first," she said. "We can have supper later."

"I like your priorities," said Tab.

The General made the speech the next day. The late afternoon television news showed him in full military regalia, surrounded by heavily armed troops, haranguing a crowd of reporters, watched from a distance by a dismal cluster of gaunt, dusty-haired refugees.

The speech was inflammatory.

The government press office circulated the text while the General was speaking. It was more provocative than anyone had anticipated, and Tamara wished she had been successful in getting an advance draft. Perhaps she would have if not for Dexter's interference.

The General began by blaming Sudan for the killing of Corporal Ackerman. This had already been hinted at by the government media, but now for the first time the accusation was explicit.

He went on to say that the incident was part of a pattern of Sudanese sponsoring of terrorism throughout the Sahel. That too was no more than a bold statement of something that was believed by many, including the White House.

"Look at this camp," he said, waving his arm to indicate what was all around him, and the camera obediently panned across a settlement that was bigger than Tamara had imagined—not just a few dozen tents but several hundred makeshift dwellings, with a cluster of scrawny trees indicating a pond or well at the center. "This camp," the General said, "shelters refugees from the viciousness of the regime in Khartoum."

Tamara wondered how far he would go. The White House did not want anything to destabilize Chad, because it was a useful ally in the war against ISGS. President Green would not like this speech.

"We in Chad have a humanitarian duty to our neighbors," the General said, and Tamara felt he was reaching the main point. "We help those fleeing from tyranny and brutality. We must help them, and we do help them, and we will continue to help them. We will not be intimidated!"

Tamara sat back. That was the meat of it. He had issued an open invitation to opponents of the Sudan government to make their headquarters in the refugee

camps in Chad. She muttered: "This is going to infuriate Khartoum."

Leila Morcos heard her and said: "In spades."

The speech came to an end. There had been no trouble, no violence. Tab was all right.

As Tamara was leaving she passed Layan, who said:
"About seven this evening?"

"Perfect," said Tamara.

Layan's home was northeast of the city center in the
neighborhood called N'Djari. She lived on a litter-
strewn street. On both sides, dwellings hid behind
crumbling concrete walls and high metal gates, blank
and rusty. Tamara was surprised at how poor the
neighborhood was. Layan always came to work in
smart tailored clothes, wearing a little makeup expertly applied, her hair pinned up elegantly. She never
looked as if she had come from a slum.

As in most N'Djamena houses, the high gate opened
onto a courtyard. When Tamara walked in, Layan was
cooking over a fire in the middle of the open space,
watched by an elderly woman who resembled her. The
adjacent building had cinder-block walls and a tin
roof. Layan's motor scooter was parked in a corner. To
Tamara's surprise there were four small children playing in the dust. Layan had never mentioned them, and
there was no photograph on her office desk.

Layan welcomed Tamara, introduced her mother,
and then, waving vaguely at the children, reeled off
four names that Tamara immediately forgot. "All your
children?" Tamara said, and Layan nodded.

There was no sign of a man.

This was not at all how Tamara had imagined
Layan's home.

CHAPTER 14 279

The mother gave Tamara a glass of a lemony drink that was refreshing. "Dinner's almost ready," Layan said.

They sat cross-legged on a rug in the main room of the house, with the bowls of food in front of them. Layan had made a vegetable stew called daraba, flavored with peanut paste; a dish of red beans in a spicy tomato sauce; and a bowl of lemon-tinged rice. The children sat apart from the grown-ups. Everything was delicious and Tamara ate heartily.

"I know why Dexter gave Karim back to you," Layan said, speaking French so that her mother and the children would not understand.

"Do you?" Tamara was intrigued: she had not yet worked this out.

"Dexter had to tell the ambassador, and Nick told me."

"What did he say?"

"He said that Karim didn't like him and wouldn't give him any information."

Tamara smiled. So that was it. She was not surprised. She had worked hard at charming Karim. Dexter probably had not troubled to make nice, but had simply taken Karim's cooperation for granted. "So Karim wouldn't give Dexter the speech."

"Karim said there was no such speech."

"Well, well."

"Dexter told Nick that Karim would talk only to you because he had a thing for white girls."

"Dexter will say anything except that he made an error of judgment."

"That's what I think."

Layan's mother brought coffee and took the children away, presumably to their bedroom.

Layan said: "I want to thank you for being friendly to me. It means a lot."

"We talk," Tamara said. "It's not a big thing."

"My husband left me four years ago," Layan said. "He took all the money and the car. I had to leave the house because I couldn't pay the rent. My youngest was one year old."

"That's terrible."

"The worst of it was that I thought it was my fault, but I couldn't understand what I'd done wrong. I had kept his house spotless and beautiful. I did everything he wanted in bed, and I gave him four beautiful children. How had I failed?"

"You didn't fail."

"I know that now. But when it happens . . . you cast about for reasons."

"What did you do?"

"I moved in here with my mother. She was a poor widow living alone. She was pleased to have us, but she couldn't afford to feed and clothe six people. So I had to get a job." She looked directly at Tamara and repeated with emphasis: "I *had* to get a job."

"I understand."

"It was difficult. I'm educated, I can read and write in English and French and Arabic. But Chadian employers don't like to hire a divorcée. They think she must be a scarlet woman who will cause trouble. I was at my wits' end. But my husband was American and he gave me one thing he couldn't take back: my American citizenship. And so I got a job at the embassy. A good job, with American wages, enough even for me to send the children to school."

"That's a heck of a story," said Tamara.

Layan smiled. "With a happy ending."

Next day there was a major sandstorm at Abéché. Such storms sometimes lasted only a few minutes, but this one went on longer. The airport was closed and the press tour of refugee camps was postponed.

The day after, Tamara had a rendezvous with Karim, but she suggested they meet somewhere other than the Lamy Hotel, for fear that people would begin to notice how often they were there together. Karim said they were unlikely to be seen at the Café de Cairo and gave her an address outside the city center.

It was a clean but basic coffeehouse patronized entirely by local people. The chairs were plastic and the tables were covered with a wipe-clean laminate. On the walls were unframed posters of the sights of Egypt: the Nile, the pyramids, the mosque of Muhammad Ali, and the necropolis. A waiter in a spotless apron welcomed Tamara effusively and showed her to the corner table at the back where Karim was waiting. As usual he was immaculately dressed in a business suit and an expensive tie.

"This isn't the kind of place where I'd expect to see you, my friend," Tamara said with a smile as she sat down.

"I own the place," Karim said.

"That explains it." She was not surprised that Karim owned a café. Everyone at the top in Chad politics had money to invest. "The General's speech was exciting," she said, getting down to business. "I hope you're prepared for reprisals by Sudan."

"We would not be surprised," Karim said with an air of complacency.

There was an implication in there somewhere that disturbed Tamara. She said: "The Sudanese army might even attack across the border, using the excuse that they are pursuing subversives."

"Let me tell you," he said, and his expression became smug. "If they come, they will get a surprise."

Tamara concealed her alarm. Aiming to harmonize

with his mood, she tried to grin, and hoped it did not look as fake as it felt. "A surprise, eh?" she said. "They will meet more resistance than they're expecting?"

"And how."

She wanted more and continued to act the awe-struck ingenue. "I'm glad the General has anticipated this attack, and the National Army of Chad is ready to repel it."

Fortunately Karim was in a boastful mood. He loved to drop portentous hints. "With overwhelming force," he said.

"This is very . . . strategic."

"Exactly."

She flew a kite. "The General has prepared an ambush."

"Well . . ." He was not quite willing to assent to that. "Let's just say that he has taken precautions."

Tamara's mind was in a whirl. This was beginning to sound like serious conflict brewing. And Tab was out there. So was Dexter.

She tried to keep the tremor of fear out of her voice as she said: "If there is a battle, I wonder when it will begin."

Karim seemed to realize that his bragging had al-ready given away more than he had intended. He shrugged. "Soon. Could be today. Could be next week. It depends how ready the Sudanese are—and how angry they get."

He was not going to come up with any more infor-mation, she realized. Now she needed to get back to the embassy and share the news. She stood up. "Karim, it's always a pleasure to talk to you."

"For me too."

"And good luck to the army if the battle happens!"

"Believe me, they will not need luck."

She tried not to hurry out of the café and into her waiting car. As the driver pulled away she debated who she should report to. Obviously the CIA needed to get this news immediately. But so did the military. If there was a battle, the US Army might need to get involved.

When she got to the embassy she made a snap decision and went to Colonel Marcus's office. Susan was there. Tamara sat down and said: "I've just had a disturbing conversation with Karim Aziz. The government here is expecting the army of Sudan to launch a raid on a refugee camp, in retaliation for the General's speech, and the Chad National Army is at the border in force to ambush the Sudanese if they come."

"Wow," said Susan. "Is Karim reliable?"

"He's not a blowhard. Of course no one can be sure what Khartoum will do, but if they attack there will surely be a battle. And if they attack today, there's a group of media and embassy civilians who may get caught up in the fighting."

"We may need to do something about that."

"I think we will, especially as one of the embassy civilians is the head of the CIA station here."

"Dexter went?"

"Yes."

Susan got up and went to her map wall. She pointed to a group of red dots between Abéché and the Sudan border. "These are the refugee camps," she said.

"They're scattered across a big piece of territory," Tamara said. "What is it, a hundred square miles?"

"About that." Susan returned to her desk and tapped her keyboard. "Let's look at the latest satellite photographs," she said.

Tamara turned her attention to the large screen on the wall.

Susan muttered: "This could be the one day of the

year when there's cloud cover over the eastern
Sahara . . . but no, thank God." She touched more
keys, and the satellite showed a town with a long,
straight airstrip on its northern edge. "Abéché," she
said. She changed the picture, and a tan wasteland appeared. "All these photos were taken in the last
twenty-four hours."

Tamara had experience looking at satellite images.
It could be frustrating. "A whole army could hide in
that much desert," she said.

Susan kept changing the picture, showing different
sections of desert landscape. "If they're stationary, yes.
Everything gets covered with dust and sand in no time.
But when they're moving they're easier to see."

Tamara half hoped there would be no sign of the
Sudanese army. Then Tab would return in safety to
Abéché this afternoon and fly back to N'Djamena to-
morrow morning.

Susan grunted.

Tamara saw what looked like a column of ants on
the sand. It reminded her of a TV program she had
watched about swarming. She narrowed her eyes.
"What are we looking at?"

Susan said: "Christ Jesus, there they are."

Tamara remembered thinking that Tuesday evening
might be her last with Tab. No, she thought, please, no.

Susan was copying coordinates off the screen. "An
army of two or three thousand men, plus vehicles, all
in desert camouflage," she said. "On an unpaved road,
it looks like, so they'll be slow."

"Ours or theirs?"

"No way to be sure—but they're east of the camps,
toward the border, so they're probably Sudanese."

"You found them!"

"You tipped us off."

"Where's the Chad army?"

"There's a quick way to find that out." Susan picked up the phone. "Get me General Touré, please."

"I have to tell the CIA," Tamara said. "Let me write down those coordinates." She grabbed a pencil and tore a sheet from Susan's notepad.

Susan began to speak French, presumably talking to General Touré, using the familiar tu rather than the formal vous. She rattled off the coordinates of the Sudanese army's location and paused for him to write them down. Then she said, "Now, César," using his first name, "where is your army?"

Susan repeated the numbers aloud as she wrote them down, and Tamara noted them too.

Susan said: "And where did you take the press party?"

When Tamara had the three sets of coordinates she grabbed a Post-it pad from Susan's desk tray and went to the map wall. She put stickers at the positions of the two armies and the press party. Then she stared at the map. "The press party is between the two armies," she said. "Fuck."

Tab was in mortal danger. This was no longer her morbid imagination: it was plain fact.

Susan thanked the Chadian general and hung up. She said to Tamara: "You did incredibly well to get this warning to us."

"We have to rescue the civilians," Tamara said, thinking mainly of Tab.

"We sure do," said Susan. "I'll need authorization from the Pentagon, but that won't be a problem."

"I'm coming with you."

This was logical, as she had supplied the key information, and Susan nodded. "Okay."

"Let me know when you're leaving and where to meet you."

"Of course."

Tamara went to the door.

Susan said: "Hey, Tamara."

"Yes?"

"Bring a weapon."

CHAPTER 15

Tamara put on body armor and requisitioned the
Glock nine-millimeter pistol that had saved her life
at the N'Gueli Bridge. The CIA station was being
managed by Michael Olson, in Dexter's absence, and
Michael did not raise any petty objections of the kind
Dexter would surely have dreamed up. Tamara drove
with Susan to the military base at the N'Djamena airport, where they met up with a platoon of fifty soldiers
and boarded a giant Sikorsky helicopter that held
them all and their gear. Tamara was given a radio with
a microphone and a headset so that she could talk to
Susan over the noise of the rotors.

The aircraft was full. "How are we going to take
forty civilians on board for the return journey?"
Tamara asked Susan.

"Standing room only," she replied.

"Will the chopper take the weight?"

Susan smiled. "Don't worry. This is a heavy-lifting
machine, originally designed for recovering downed
aircraft in Vietnam. It can hover with another helicopter the same weight strapped underneath it."

The journey across the Sahara took four hours.

Somehow Tamara was not scared for herself, but she was tortured by the thought that she could lose Tab now, today. Just imagining it, she felt nauseous, and for an instant she feared she might throw up in front of fifty tough soldiers. The helicopter flew at a hundred miles an hour, but it seemed so slow as to be almost stationary over the unchanging landscape of sand and rock, and before the end of the journey she came to realize that she wanted to spend her life with Tab. She wanted never again to be separated from him like this, ever.

This was a life-changing thought, and she played out its consequences in her mind. She was sure that Tab's feelings were similar to her own. Despite her record of marrying men who were wrong for her, she thought she could not be mistaken about him. But there were a hundred questions for which she had no answers. Where would they go? How would they live? Did Tab want children? They had never talked about that. Did Tamara want children? She had never thought much about it. But I do, she realized; I do now. With other men I was lukewarm, but with him, yes.

She had so much to think about that the journey seemed too short, and she was surprised when they descended over Abéché. The distance they had covered had been close to the limit of the helicopter's range, and they needed to refuel before they began to search for the media party.

Abéché had once been a great city, a stopping place on the trans-Saharan route used for centuries by Arab slave traders. Tamara imagined the camel trains plodding tirelessly across the vast desert, the great mosques with hundreds of kneeling worshippers, the opulent palaces with their harems of bored beauties, and the human misery of the teeming slave markets. After the French had colonized Chad, the population of Abéché had been nearly wiped out by disease. Now it was a small town with a cattle market and some factories making blankets out of camel hair. Empires rise, she thought, and then they fall.

There was a small US Army base at the airport, staffed on a revolving six-week rotation, and the current shift had the refueling truck ready on the runway. Within minutes the helicopter was lifting again.

It turned east, heading for the last known location of the media group. Finally Tamara was getting near to Tab. Soon she would know if he was in trouble, and whether she could help him.

After a quarter of an hour they saw a grim encampment: rows of improvised dwellings; dusty, lethargic inhabitants; and dirty children playing with stones in the littered pathways. The pilot flew the length and breadth of the place three times; there was no sign of a media party.

Susan studied her map, identified the next nearest camp, and gave the co-pilot directions. The machine lifted fast and headed northeast.

A few minutes later they flew over a large military force moving east. "Troops of the Chad National Army," said Susan over the headset. "Five or six thousand men. Your information was correct, Tamara. They've got the Sudanese outnumbered two to one."

Hearing this, the soldiers looked at Tamara with new respect. Good intelligence could save their lives, and they valued anyone who provided it.

The next camp looked similar to the first except that it was located in a shallow dip, with slight rises to the east and west. Tamara looked for signs of people from the city: Western-style clothes, bare heads and dark glasses, camera lenses flashing in the sunlight. Then she spotted two buses, their paintwork layered with dust, parked in a row in the center of the encampment.

Nearby she noticed a purple blouse, then a blue shirt, then a baseball cap. "I think this is it," she said.

Susan said: "So do I."

A small helicopter, which Tamara had previously not spotted, suddenly rose from the camp. It tilted and veered away from the Sikorsky, then headed west, going fast.

Tamara said: "My God, what's that?"

"I recognize the aircraft," Susan said. "It's the General's personal transport."

That was ominous, Tamara thought. "I wonder why he's leaving."

Speaking to the pilot, Susan said: "Gain enough height for us to survey the surroundings."

The aircraft rose up.

It was a clear day. To the east they could see an army approaching, trailing a cloud of dust: the Sudanese.

Susan said: "Fuck."

Tamara said: "How far away are they—a mile?"

"Less."

"And how far in the other direction is the Chadian force?"

"Three miles. On these unpaved desert tracks they're moving at about ten miles an hour. They'll be here in twenty minutes."

"That's how long we've got to rescue our people— and get the refugees out of the way of the battle."

"Yes."

"I was hoping we'd get in and out before the Sudanese arrived."

"That was the plan. Now for the new plan."

Susan ordered the pilot to land near the buses, then spoke to the troops as the chopper was descending. "Squads One and Two, deploy to the east ridge immediately. Fire as soon as the enemy is within range. Try to look like ten times the number you are. Squad

Three, go through the camp telling the media to gather by the buses and the refugees to run into the desert. Hold on." She asked Tamara what the Arabic was for *The Sudanese are coming, run away!* and Tamara said it over the radio so they all could hear. Susan finished: "We'll hover so that I can see everything. I'll tell you when to fall back and where to regroup."

The helicopter touched down, and a ramp was lowered at the rear.

Susan said: "Go, go!"

The soldiers ran down the ramp. As ordered, most of them turned east, up the slope, and hit the ground near the ridge. The rest fanned out around the camp. Tamara went looking for Tab.

As the soldiers gave their message, a few refugees began leaving the camp at a desultory pace, apparently skeptical of the urgency.

Most of the visitors were wandering around and conducting interviews and they too responded sluggishly to the orders. Others had gathered around a hospitality table, where people from the government press office were handing out drinks from an icebox and snacks in plastic containers.

"There's going to be trouble," Tamara yelled at the government people. "We're here to pull you out. Tell everyone to get ready to board that chopper."

She recognized one of the reporters, Bashir Fakhoury, with a bottle of beer in his hand. He said: "What's going on, Tamara?"

She did not have time to brief the press. Ignoring the question, she said: "Have you seen Tabdar Sadoul?"

"Just a minute," said Bashir. "You can't just order us around. Tell us what's happening!"

Tamara said: "Fuck you, Bashir." She hurried away.

She had seen from the air that there were two long, fairly straight paths through the camp, one going roughly north-south and the other east-west, and she now decided the best way to search for Tab was to run the length of both. She would not be able to stop and look inside buildings; that would take too long, and she would still be searching when the Sudanese got here.

Running east, toward the soldiers on the ridge, she heard a single rifle shot.

There was a silence like a stunned pause. Then she heard a crackle as the rest of the American soldiers began shooting. Finally, more distant gunfire told Tamara that the surprised Sudanese had begun shooting back. Her heart thudded with fear, but she ran on.

The noise galvanized the people in the camp. Everyone came out of the tents to see what was going on. The sound of shooting was more effective than spoken instructions: refugees began running away from the camp, many carrying children or other precious possessions—a goat, an iron cooking pot, a rifle, a sack of flour. The journalists abandoned their interviews and ran for the buses, clutching cameras and trailing microphone leads.

Tamara scanned the faces without seeing Tab.

Then the shelling began.

A mortar exploded to Tamara's left, destroying a house, and it was quickly followed by several more. The Sudanese artillery were firing over the heads of the American soldiers into the camp. She heard cries of fright and screams of pain as refugees were wounded. Medical orderlies among the American troops broke out collapsible stretchers and began to attend to casualties. The rush to leave the camp turned into a stampede.

Stay cool, Tamara said to herself. Stay calm. Find Tab.

She found Dexter.

She almost missed him. Lying on the ground across the open entrance to a dwelling she saw what looked like a pile of rags, but something made her take a second glance, and she realized it was Dexter's blue-and-white seersucker suit, and Dexter was wearing it.

She knelt beside him. He was breathing, but shallowly. He showed little sign of outward harm—just scratches—but he was unconscious, so he must have been hurt.

She stood up and yelled: "Stretcher here!"

None of the medical orderlies was in sight and there was no response. She ran twenty yards toward the center but still did not see anyone. She returned to Dexter. It was risky to move an injured person, she knew, but clearly it would be more dangerous to leave him at the mercy of the Sudanese. She made a quick decision. She rolled him onto his front, lifted his torso, got her back under his belly, and heaved herself upright with his limp body over her right shoulder. Once she was standing she could bear the weight more easily, and she walked toward the helicopter and the buses.

She had gone a hundred yards when she saw two medics. "Hey!" she yelled. "Check this guy—he's from our embassy." They took the unconscious Dexter and laid him on a stretcher, and Tamara went onward.

She noticed that some of the journalists were filming, and she had to respect their courage.

Almost every refugee had now left. An elderly woman was helping a limping man, and a teenage girl was struggling to carry two bawling toddlers, but all the others were already outside the camp, heading across the desert as fast as they could go, putting distance between themselves and the weaponry.

How long could thirty or so American soldiers hold off an army of two thousand? Tamara guessed there was very little time left.

The helicopter was descending. Susan was about to pick everyone up. Where was Tab?

Then she spotted him. He was running along the north-south path, chasing the fleeing refugees, with a large child held unceremoniously under his left arm. It was a girl of about nine years, Tamara saw, and she was screaming her head off, probably more scared of the stranger who had grabbed her than of the mortars exploding behind her.

The chopper touched down. Over her headphones, Tamara heard Susan say: "Squad Three, board the civilians."

Tab reached the outskirts of the camp, caught up with the last of the fleeing refugees, and set the child on her feet. She immediately ran on. Tab turned around and headed back.

Tamara ran to meet him. He embraced her, grinning. "Why did I feel sure you'd be involved in this rescue?" he said.

She had to admire his cool nerve, joking on the battlefield. She was not so calm. "Let's get going!" she yelled. "We have to board that chopper!" She broke into a run, and Tab followed.

Susan's voice in her ear said: "Squad Two, fall back and board."

Tamara glanced up at the ridge and saw half the soldiers there crawling backward on their bellies, then getting up and running into the camp. One man was carrying a comrade, wounded or dead.

As the soldiers reached the chopper, Susan ordered: "Squad One, retreat and board. Run like hell, guys."

They followed her advice.

Tamara and Tab reached the chopper and boarded just ahead of Squad One. Everyone else was aboard. A hundred people were crammed into the passenger space, some of them on stretchers.

Tamara looked out of the helicopter window and saw

the Sudanese army coming over the ridge. They thought they smelled victory, and their discipline was failing. They were firing, but hardly bothering to aim, and their bullets were wasted on the ramshackle shelters standing between them and the retreating Americans.

The doors were slammed shut and the floor beneath Tamara's feet rose suddenly. She glanced out of the window and saw that all the Sudanese were now aiming their weapons at the helicopter.

She was almost overcome by terror. Although bullets might not penetrate the armored underside of the aircraft, it could be brought down by a well-aimed mortar or a rocket from a shoulder-mounted launcher. The engines could be disabled, or a lucky shot might hit the rotors, and then . . . She remembered a grimly humorous saying dear to pilots: *A helicopter glides like a grand piano.* She felt herself shaking as the machine lifted and the rifle muzzles followed its trajectory up. Despite the noise of the engines and the rotors she thought she heard a rattle of bullets hitting the armor. She imagined this massive aircraft with a hundred people aboard falling to Earth, smashing to smithereens, and bursting into flames.

Then she saw the Sudanese switch their attention. They stopped watching the helicopter and looked away. She followed their gaze up the western slope. There she saw the Chad army coming over the ridge. It was a battle charge rather than an orderly advance, the soldiers running and firing at the same time. Some of the Sudanese fired back, but it quickly became clear that they were outnumbered, and they began to flee.

The passengers on the helicopter broke into cheers and applause.

The pilot flew directly north, away from both armies, and in seconds the helicopter was out of range.

"I think we're safe," said Tab.

"Yeah," said Tamara, and she took his hand in hers and squeezed it very hard.

On the following morning the CIA station in N'Djamena was busy. Overnight the CIA director in Washington had fired a series of questions: What had sparked the battle? How many casualties? Were any Americans killed? Who won? What had happened to Dexter? Where in hell was Abéché? And, most important, what would the consequences be? He needed answers before briefing the president.

Tamara went in early and sat at her desk writing her report. She began with her meeting yesterday with Karim, whom she described as "a source close to the General." She would give his name if asked, but she would not put it in a written report if she could help it.

As the others arrived, each of them asked her what had happened to Dexter. "I don't know," she said each time. "I found him unconscious with nothing to indicate what had knocked him out. Perhaps he fainted with fright."

Along with other stretcher cases, Dexter had been taken to the hospital in Abéché when the chopper stopped to refuel. Tamara suggested to Mike Olson that he send a junior officer, maybe someone like Dean Jones, on the next plane to Abéché to visit the hospital and get a firsthand diagnosis from the doctor, and Olson said: "Good idea."

With Olson in charge the atmosphere was more pleasant, and yet all the work got done just as well, if not better.

The General was on the morning news, crowing like a rooster. "They have been taught a lesson!" he said.

"Now they will think twice about sending terrorists to the N'Gueli Bridge."

The interviewer said: "Mr. President, some people were saying that you were slow to respond to that incident."

The General was clearly ready for this question. "The Chinese have a proverb," he said. "'Revenge is a dish best eaten cold.'"

It was not a Chinese proverb, Tamara knew, but a quote from a French novel, but the message was clear in any language. The General had planned carefully and waited for this moment, then he had struck, and he was sure he had been very clever indeed.

Tamara put all the details into her report, then sat back and thought about how to sum up the significance of the battle. Her conversation with Karim confirmed the General's claim that he had laid an ambush in retaliation for the shooting at the bridge. His statement that the Sudanese had been "taught a lesson" was confirmed by a report from General Touré, which Susan had passed to Tamara, saying that the Sudanese had been soundly defeated.

That meant the government in Khartoum would be furious. They would try to put a spin on the battle that made them look less like losers, but they and the world would know the truth. And so they would feel humiliated, and want to retaliate.

Sometimes international politics was just like a Sicilian vendetta, Tamara thought. People took revenge for what had been done to them, as if they did not know that their rivals were sure to take revenge for the revenge. As the tit-for-tat went on, escalation was inevitable: more rage, more vengeance, more violence.

That was the weakness of dictators. They were so used to getting their own way that they did not expect the world outside their domain to refuse them anything.

The General had started something he might not be able to control.

And there lay the significance for President Green. She wanted Chad to be stable. The US had backed the General as a leader who could keep order, but now he was threatening the stability of the region.

She finished the report and sent it to Olson. A few minutes later he came to her desk with a printed copy in his hand. "Thank you for this," he said. "It makes exciting reading."

"Too damn exciting," she said.

"Anyway, it says most of what Langley needs to know, so I've sent it as it is."

"Thank you." Dexter would have rewritten it, Tamara thought, then sent it over his own signature.

Mike said: "If you want to take the rest of the day off, I'd say you've earned it."

"I'll do that."

"Enjoy a rest."

Tamara returned to her apartment and called Tab. He too had spent the morning at the office, writing his report for the DGSE, but he had almost finished and would then leave for the day. They agreed to meet at his place, and maybe go out for lunch.

She took a car to his apartment and got there before him.

She let herself in with her key. It was the first time she had been there without him. She walked around, exploring the sensation of being at home in his private world. She had seen it all already, and he had said: "Look at everything, I have no secrets from you," but now she could stare at something as long as she liked without fearing he might say: "What's so interesting about my bathroom cabinet?"

She opened the closet and gazed at his clothes. He had twelve light blue shirts. She noticed several pairs of shoes that she had never seen him wear. The whole closet smelled of sandalwood, and she eventually figured out that his wooden coat hangers and shoe trees were impregnated with the scent.

He had a small cupboard of medical supplies: aspirin, Band-Aids, a cold remedy, indigestion tablets. She had not known he suffered from indigestion. On his bookshelf was an eighteenth-century edition of the plays of Molière, six volumes, in French of course. She opened a tome and a card fell out. It was inscribed: "Joyeux anniversaire, Tab—ta maman t'aime." Your mother loves you. Nice, she thought.

In a drawer he had a folder containing personal papers: a copy of his birth registration, certificates for both his degrees, and an old letter from his grandmother, in the careful script of someone who does not write often, evidently sent when he was a boy. The letter congratulated him on passing his exams. Tamara found that brought tears to her eyes; she did not really know why.

He arrived a few minutes later. She sat cross-legged on his bed and watched him take off his office suit, wash his face, and put on casual clothes. But he seemed in no hurry to go out. He sat on the edge of the bed and looked at her for a long moment. She was not embarrassed by his stare; in fact she loved it.

Eventually he spoke: "When the shooting started . . ."

"You picked up that little girl."

He smiled. "The minx. She bit me, you know." He looked at his hand. "No blood, but look at that bruise!"

She took his hand and kissed the bruise. "You poor thing."

"This is nothing, but I did think I might die. And then I thought: I wish I'd spent more time with Tamara."

She stared at him. "That was your, like, dying thought."

"Yes."

"On the way there," she said, "that long trip across the desert in the helicopter, I was thinking about us, and I had a similar feeling. I just didn't want to be apart from you ever again."

"So we both feel the same."

"I knew we would."

"But what do we do about it?"

"That's the big question."

"I've been thinking about it. You're committed to the CIA. I don't feel that way about the DGSE. I've enjoyed working in intelligence, and boy, have I learned a lot, but I have no ambition to rise to the top. I've served my country for ten years, and I'd like to move into the family business now, and maybe take charge of it when my mother wants to retire. I love fashion and luxury, and we French are so good at it. But that means living in Paris."

"I figured that out."

"If the Agency would transfer you . . . would you move to Paris with me?"

"Yes," said Tamara. "In a heartbeat."

CHAPTER 16

The temperature rose mercilessly as the bus groaned slowly across the desert. Kiah had not realized that her old home, on the shore of Lake Chad, was one of the cooler areas of her country. She had always imagined that the whole of Chad was the same, and she was unpleasantly surprised to discover that the sparsely inhabited north was hotter. At the start of the journey she had been bothered by the open glassless windows, which let in an irritating dusty breeze, but now, sweaty and uncomfortable with Naji on her lap, she was glad of any wind, even if it was hot and gritty.

Naji was fidgety and cranky. "Want leben," he kept saying, but Kiah had no rice and no buttermilk and no way of cooking anything. She put him to her nipple, but he quickly became dissatisfied. She suspected that her breast milk was becoming thin because she herself was hungry. The food Hakim had promised was all too often just water and stale bread, and not much bread. The "luxuries" for which he charged extra included blankets, soap, and any food other than bread or porridge. Was there anything worse for a mother than to know that she could not feed her hungry child?

Abdul glanced across at Naji. Kiah was not as embarrassed as she should have been at his seeing her
breast. After more than two weeks of sitting side by
side all day, every day, a weary intimacy had set in.

Now he spoke to Naji. "There was once a man called
Samson, and he was the strongest man in the whole
wide world," he said.

Naji stopped grizzling and went quiet.

"One day Samson was walking in the desert when,
suddenly, he heard a lion roar nearby—really near."

Naji put his thumb in his mouth and snuggled up to
Kiah, at the same time staring at Abdul with big eyes.

Abdul was everyone's friend, Kiah had found. All
the passengers liked him. He often made them laugh.
Kiah was not surprised: she had first seen him as the
vendor of cigarettes, joking with the men and flirting
with the women, and she had recalled that the Lebanese
were said to be good businessmen. At the first town
where the bus stopped for a night, Abdul had gone to
an open-air bar. Kiah went to the same place, with
Esma and her parents-in-law, just for a change of scene.
She had seen Abdul playing cards, not winning or
losing much. He had a bottle of beer in his hand,
though he never seemed to finish it. Most of all he
talked to people, apparently inconsequential chatter,
but later she realized he had found out how many wives
the men had and which shopkeepers were dishonest
and who they were all frightened of. Thereafter it was
similar at every town or village.

Yet she felt sure this was an act. When not making
friends with everyone, he could be withdrawn, aloof,
even depressed, like a man with worries in his life and
sorrows in his past. This had at first led her to think he
disliked her. In time she had started to believe he had
two personalities. And then, beneath all that, there

was a third man, one who would take the trouble to soothe Naji by telling a story that a two-year-old boy would understand and like.

The bus was following tracks that were hardly marked and often invisible to Kiah. Most of the desert consisted of flat, hard rock with a thin layer of sand, an adequate driving surface at low speeds. Every now and again a discarded Coca-Cola can or a ruined tire confirmed that they were in fact following the road and not lost in the wilderness.

Every village was an oasis: people could not live without water. Each little settlement had an underground lake, often showing itself on the surface as a small pond or a well. Sometimes they dried up, like Lake Chad, and then the people had to go somewhere else, as Kiah was doing.

One night there was nowhere to stop, and they all slept in their seats on the bus until the morning sun woke them.

Early in the trip some of the men had pestered Kiah. It always happened in the evenings, after dark, when all the passengers were lying on the floor of some house or in a courtyard, on mattresses if they were lucky. One night one of the men climbed on top of her. She fought him off silently, knowing that if she screamed, or humiliated the man in any other way, his friends would take revenge on her, and she would be accused of being a whore. But he was too strong for her, and he managed to pull aside her blanket. Then, suddenly, he jerked away, and she realized that someone strong had pulled him off her. In the starlight she saw that Abdul had the man pinned to the ground with one hand gripping his neck, preventing him from making any noise or, perhaps, even breathing. She heard Abdul whisper: "Leave her alone or I will kill you. Do you understand? I will kill you." Then he was gone. The man lay gasping for breath for a minute, then crept away. She was not even sure who it was.

After that she began to figure Abdul out. She guessed that he did not want to be seen as her friend, so she treated him like a stranger in front of others, not chatting to him or smiling at him or seeking his help as she struggled to perform everyday tasks with a wriggling two-year-old in her arms. But sitting beside him on the bus, she talked. Quietly and undramatically she told him about her childhood, her brothers in Sudan, life beside the shrinking lake, and the death of Salim. She even related the story of the nightclub called Bourbon Street. He said nothing about himself, and she never asked him questions, because she sensed that would be unwelcome, but he often commented on the stories she told, and she felt a growing sympathy.

Now she listened to his soothing low voice, with its Lebanese accent. "She took a lock of his hair between her finger and thumb, and he did not wake up, but just snored on. She cut off the lock of hair with the scissors, and still he did not wake up. Then another lock. Snip, snip, went the scissors, and snore, snore, went Samson."

Her mind went back to the nuns' school, where she had first heard the Bible stories—Jonah and the whale, David and Goliath, Noah and his ark. She had learned to read and write, divide and multiply, and speak a little French. She had gathered knowledge from the other girls too, some of whom knew more than she did about adult mysteries such as sex. It had been a happy time. In fact her whole life had been happy until that awful day when they brought Salim's cold body home to her. Since then it had been all disappointment and hardship. Would that ever come to an end? Would there be happy days again? Would she get to France?

Suddenly the bus slowed. Looking forward, Kiah

saw steam coming out of the front of the vehicle. "What now?" she muttered.

Abdul said: "And when he woke up in the morning, his head was nearly bald, and his lovely long hair was on the pillow all around him. And what happened next, we shall find out tomorrow."

"No, now!" said Naji, but Abdul did not answer him.

Hakim stopped the bus and turned off the engine. "The radiator has boiled," he announced.

Kiah felt scared. The bus had broken down twice before—which was the main reason the trip was already taking longer than expected—but the third time was no less frightening. There was no one nearby, phones did not work, and they rarely saw another vehicle. If the bus could not be fixed, they would all have to walk. Then they would either reach an oasis or drop dead, whichever came first.

Hakim picked up a tool kit and got out of the bus. He opened the hood to look at the engine. Most of the passengers got off to stretch their legs. Naji ran around, getting rid of surplus energy. He had only recently learned to run, and he was proud of his speed.

Kiah and Abdul and several others looked over Hakim's shoulder at the steaming motor. Fixing old cars and motorcycles was an important activity in the poorer areas of Chad and, although it was a male responsibility, Kiah had picked up some knowledge.

There was no sign of a leak.

Hakim pointed to a snakelike piece of rubber dangling from a pulley. "The fan belt has broken," he said. Gingerly, he reached into the hot machinery and drew out the rubber. It was black with brownish patches, worn and cracked in places. Kiah could see that it should have been replaced long ago.

Hakim returned to the bus and pulled a large tin box from under his seat. He had produced this during the previous breakdowns. He put the box down on the sand, opened it, and rummaged through assorted spare parts: spark plugs, fuses, a selection of cylinder seals, and a roll of duct tape. Hakim frowned and looked through again.

Then he said: "There is no spare fan belt."

In a low voice Kiah said to Abdul: "We're in trouble."

"Not quite," he replied, equally quietly. "Not yet."

Hakim said: "We will have to improvise." He looked at the passengers around him and fixed his eyes on Abdul. "Give me that sash," he said, pointing to the cotton strip around Abdul's waist.

"No," said Abdul.

"I need to use it as a temporary fan belt."

"It won't work," said Abdul. "You need something with more grip."

"There is a spring pulley that acts as a tensioner."

"The cotton would still slip."

"I am ordering you!"

One of the guards intervened. Their names were Hamza and Tareq, and it was Tareq, the taller one, who spoke. He addressed Abdul in a voice that quietly indicated that no discussion was invited. "Do as he says."

Kiah would have been terrified, as would most men, but Abdul just ignored Tareq and spoke to Hakim. "Your belt would grip better," he said.

Hakim's jeans were held up with a worn brown leather belt.

Abdul added: "It's certainly long enough," and everyone laughed, because Hakim's waist was big.

Angrily, Tareq said to Abdul: "You must do as he says!"

Kiah was amazed that Abdul seemed to have no fear of the man with the assault rifle slung over his shoulder. "Hakim's belt will work better," Abdul said calmly.

For a moment it looked as if Tareq would unshoulder his rifle and threaten Abdul, but then he seemed to think better of it. He turned to Hakim. "Use your belt," he said.

Hakim took off his belt.

Kiah wondered why Abdul was so attached to his cotton sash.

Hakim wound the belt around the pulleys, buckled it, then tightened it. He took a five-liter plastic demijohn of water from inside the bus and topped up the radiator, which hissed and bubbled and then calmed. He got back inside the bus and started the motor, then returned outside to look under the hood. As Kiah could already see, the belt was doing its work, rotating the cooling mechanism.

Hakim slammed the hood shut. He was in a furious temper.

He returned to the bus, holding his jeans up with one hand. He sat in the driving seat and started the engine. The passengers reboarded. Hakim revved the engine impatiently. When Esma's father-in-law, Wahed, hesitated before putting a foot on the steps, Hakim suddenly moved the bus forward, then braked hard. "Come on, hurry up!" he snarled.

Kiah was already in her seat, with Naji on her lap and Abdul next to her. "Hakim is in a rage because you got the better of him," she said.

"I've made an enemy," Abdul said regretfully.

"He's a pig."

The bus pulled away.

Kiah heard a low buzzing sound. Looking surprised, Abdul took out his phone. "We have a connection!" he said. "We must be getting near Faya. I didn't realize they had connectivity." He seemed inordinately pleased.

The phone was bigger than she remembered, and

she wondered if he had two. "You can phone your girl-friends now," she said teasingly.

He looked at her for a moment, not smiling, and said: "I don't have any girlfriends."

He busied himself on the phone, and seemed to be sending messages he had written earlier and stored. Then he hesitated, made a decision, and called up some pictures, and she realized he had surreptitiously photographed Hakim, Tareq, Hamza, and some of the people they had met on the way. She watched out of the corner of her eye as he tapped the screen for a minute or two. He made sure no one could see his hands except Kiah.

She said: "What are you doing?"

He tapped again, then turned off the phone and put it back inside his robes. "I sent some photos to a friend in N'Djamena with a message saying: 'If I get killed, these men are responsible.'"

She whispered: "Aren't you worried that Hakim and the guards might find out what you sent?"

"On the contrary, it would warn them off."

She thought he was speaking the truth, but at the same time she felt sure it was not the whole truth. Today she had discovered another surprising fact about him: of all the people on the bus, he was the only one who was not afraid of Tareq and Hamza. Even Hakim obeyed them.

Abdul had a secret, she had no doubt about that, but she could not imagine what it might be.

Soon the town of Faya came within sight. She asked Abdul if he knew how many people lived here—he often knew that kind of thing—and sure enough he did. "About twelve thousand," he said. "It's the main town in the north of the country."

It looked more like a large village. Kiah saw a lot of trees and many irrigated fields. There had to be a good

deal of underground water to sustain so much agriculture. The bus passed an airstrip but she saw no planes
and no sign of activity.

Abdul said: "We've come about six hundred miles
in seventeen days. That's only thirty-five miles a day—
even slower than I expected."

The bus stopped outside a substantial house in the
middle of the town. The passengers were shown into a
broad courtyard and told this was where they would
eat and sleep. The sun was going down now, and there
was plenty of shade. Some young women appeared
with cold water for them to drink.

Hakim and the guards went off in the bus, presumably to buy a new fan belt—plus a spare, Kiah hoped.
She knew from previous stops that they would park
somewhere safe, and either Tareq or Hamza would
stay in the bus all night. Surely, she thought, no one
would want to steal such a rattletrap? But they seemed
to regard it as precious. She did not care, as long as it
turned up in the morning to continue the journey.

Abdul too left the house. He would go to a bar or
café, she guessed, and he might also keep an eye on
Hakim and the guards.

In a corner of the courtyard was a hand-pumped
shower behind a screen, and the men were able to wash.
Kiah asked one of the serving girls if the women and
Naji could wash in the house. The girl went inside, then
came to the entrance and nodded. Kiah beckoned
Esma and Bushra, the only other women on the bus,
and they all went inside.

The underground water was very cold, but Kiah
was grateful for it, and for the soap and towels generously provided by the invisible owner of the house—or,
more likely, his senior wife, she guessed. She washed
her underwear and Naji's clothes. Feeling better, she
returned to the courtyard.

When it got dark, torches were lit. Then the serving girls brought out mutton stew with couscous. Hakim would probably try to charge everyone for this in the morning. She did not let that thought spoil her pleasure. She fed Naji the couscous in the salty sauce, with some of the vegetables mashed, and he ate heartily. So did she.

Abdul returned as the torches were being extinguished. He sat a couple of yards from Kiah with his back to the wall. She lay down with Naji, who fell asleep instantly. Another day, she thought, a few miles closer to France, and we're still alive; and with that thought she went to sleep.

CHAPTER 17

Pauline said: "Am I the only person who's worried about what's happening in Chad?" No one answered the question, of course. "It shows every sign of escalating," she went on. "Sudan has now asked its ally Egypt to send troops to help combat aggression by Chad."

It was a formal meeting of the National Security Council, with the national security advisor, the secretary of state, the chief of staff, and other key officials, plus their aides. Pauline had called them all in at seven o'clock in the morning. They were in the Cabinet Room, a long, high-ceilinged space with four large round-arched windows looking onto the West Colonnade. There was an oval mahogany conference table with twenty leather-upholstered chairs on a red carpet with gold stars. Up against both long walls were smaller chairs for aides. At the far end was a fireplace that was never used. A window was open, and Pauline could hear faintly the traffic on Fifteenth Street, a soft sound like a wind in distant trees.

Chester Jackson, the secretary of state, said: "The Egyptians haven't yet agreed. They're annoyed with

the Sudanese for not supporting them over the building of that dam."

"They will agree, though," Pauline said. "The
squabble about the dam is minor. Neighbor Sudan is
claiming it was invaded. They explain their defeat by
saying it was a sneak attack across the border. It's not
true, but that doesn't matter."

Gus Blake, the national security advisor, said: "The
president is right, Chess. Yesterday in Khartoum there
were hysterical nationalist demonstrations against
Chad."

"Demonstrations organized by the government,
probably."

"True, but it tells us where they're headed."

"Okay," said Chess. "You're right."

Pauline said: "And Chad has asked France to double
its forces there. Don't tell me France won't help them.
France is committed to protecting the territorial integrity of Chad and other allies in the Sahel. And there are
a billion barrels of oil under the sand in Chad, much
of which belongs to the French oil company Total.
France doesn't want to quarrel with Egypt, and may
not want to send more troops to Chad, but I think
they'll have to."

Chess said: "I see what you mean about escalation."

"Before long we will have French and Egyptian
troops nose to nose across the Chad-Sudan border,
each daring the other to shoot first."

"It looks that way."

"And it could get worse. Sudan and Egypt might ask
China for reinforcements, and Beijing might comply—
the Chinese are very serious about getting a foothold
in Africa. Then France and Chad will ask the US for
help. France is our ally in NATO, and we already have
troops in Chad, so it becomes difficult for us to stay out
of the fighting."

"That's a big jump," said Chess.

"But am I wrong?"

"No, you're not wrong."

"And at that point we're on the brink of a super-power war."

The room went quiet for a moment.

The memory of Munchkin Country popped into Pauline's mind. It was like a nightmare that would not go away even after the dreamer woke up. She saw again the ranks of cots in the barracks, the five-million-gallon water tank, and the Situation Room with its lines of phones and screens. She was haunted by the thought that one day she might find herself living in that underground hideout, the only person who could save the human race. And if the apocalypse happened, it would be her fault. She was the American president. There would be no one else to blame.

And she had to make sure James Moore never became the one with that dreadful duty. Aggression was his default mode, and that was what his supporters liked. He pretended that no one could ever stand against America—forgetting Vietnam, Cuba, Nicaragua. He talked tough and it made his fans feel big. But violent talk led to violent action in the world just as it did in the school playground. A fool was just a fool, but a fool in the White House was the most dangerous person in the world.

She said: "Let me see if I can pour oil on the waters before they become too troubled." She turned to her chief of staff. "Jacqueline, schedule a call with the pres-ident of France, as soon as he's available but in any event before the end of the day."

"Yes, ma'am."

"I must speak to the president of Egypt too, but we need to lay some groundwork first. Chess, talk to the Saudi ambassador here—Prince Faisal, isn't it?"

"One of several Saudis called Prince Faisal, yes."

"Ask him to talk to the Egyptians and encourage them to listen to what I have to say to them. The Saudis are allies of Egypt and should have some influence."

"Yes, ma'am."

"Maybe we can put a stop to this before they all get too angry." Pauline stood up, and everyone else followed suit. She said to Gus: "Walk with me as far as the Residence."

He followed her out.

As they went along the West Colonnade he said: "You know, you were the only person in that room who perceived the extent of the danger. Everyone else was still seeing it as a little local fracas."

Pauline nodded. He was right. That was why she was the boss. She said: "Thank you for sending me that eyewitness report of the battle at the refugee camp. It made vivid reading."

"I thought you'd enjoy it."

"I know the woman who wrote it, Tamara Levit. She's from Chicago. She volunteered in my congressional campaign." Pauline conjured a memory. "Dark-haired girl, well-dressed, very attractive; all the boys fell for her. She was good too—we made her an organizer."

"And now she's an agent with the CIA station in N'Djamena."

"And not easily scared. Reading between the lines, Sudanese shells were exploding all around her while she was carrying her unconscious boss over her shoulder."

"I could have used her in Afghanistan."

"I'll call her later."

They arrived at the Residence. She left Gus and ran up the stairs to the family floor. Gerry was in the Dining Room, eating scrambled eggs and reading *The Washington Post*. Pauline sat down next to him and unfolded her napkin. She asked the cook for a plain omelet.

Pippa came in. She looked sleepy, but Pauline made no comment: she had read recently that teenagers needed a lot of sleep because they were growing so fast, and they were not just lazy. Pippa was wearing an over-size flannel shirt and distressed jeans. There was no uniform at Foggy Bottom Day School, but students were expected to wear clothes that were clean and reasonably neat. Pippa was clearly on the borderline, but Pauline remembered that she, at that age, had always tried to dress in a way that would offend the teachers without quite breaking the rules.

Pippa poured Lucky Charms into a bowl and added milk. Pauline thought of suggesting that she mix in a few blueberries, for the sake of the vitamins, then decided that that too was better left unsaid. Pippa's diet was not ideal, but her immune system seemed to be working perfectly anyway.

What she did say was: "How's school, my darling?"

Pippa looked surly. "I'm not smoking weed, don't worry."

"I'm very glad to hear it, but I was thinking more about the lessons."

"Same shit, different day."

Pauline thought: Do I really deserve this?

She said: "It's only three years until you have to start applying to colleges. Do you have any ideas about where you might go and what you might study?"

"I don't know if I want to go to college. I don't really see the point."

Pauline was taken aback but she recovered quickly. "Apart from learning for its own sake, I guess the point is to widen the life choices available to you. I can't imagine what kind of job you'd get at the age of eighteen with only a high school diploma."

"I might be a poet. I like poetry."

"You could study poetry at college."

"Yeah, but then they want you to have what they call a *broad general education*, which means I'd have to study, like, chemistry and geography and shit."

"Which poets do you like?"

"Modern ones, who experiment. I don't care about rhyme and meter and all that stuff."

Pauline thought: Why am I not surprised?

She was tempted to raise the question of how Pippa would earn a living as an eighteen-year-old experimental poet, but she restrained herself yet again. The point was really too obvious to make. Let Pippa come to that realization on her own.

Pauline's omelet arrived, giving her an excuse to end the conversation, and she picked up her fork with relief. Soon afterward Pippa finished her cereal, grabbed her bag, said: "Later," and disappeared.

Pauline waited for Gerry to say something about Pippa's mood but he remained silent, turning to the business section. There had been a time when he and Pauline would have commiserated with one another, but that had not happened much lately.

They had always talked about having two children. Gerry had been keen. But after Pippa arrived he became less enthusiastic about a second child. Pauline was a congresswoman by then, and Gerry had seemed to resent his share of the child care. Nevertheless they had tried, even though Pauline was by then in her late thirties. She had become pregnant again but miscarried, and after that Gerry did not want to try again. He had said he was worried about Pauline's health, but she wondered if the real reason was that he did not want any more arguments about who was going to take the baby to the doctor. She had felt this decision like a body blow, but she had not fought him: it was a mistake to have a child that one parent did not want.

She noticed that he was wearing suspenders and a dress shirt, and she asked him: "What's on your calendar today?"

"A board meeting. Nothing too taxing. You?"

"I have to make sure war doesn't break out in North Africa. Nothing too taxing."

He laughed, and for a moment she felt close to him again. Then he folded the newspaper and stood up. "I'd better put on my tie."

"Enjoy your board meeting."

He kissed her forehead. "Good luck with North Africa." He went out.

Pauline returned to the West Wing but instead of going to the Oval Office she made her way to the press office. A dozen or so people, mostly quite young, sat at workstations, reading or keying. There were television screens around the walls, all showing different news shows. Copies of the morning's papers were scattered everywhere.

Sandip Chakraborty had a desk in the middle of the room, which he preferred to a private office: he liked to be in the thick of things. He stood up as soon as Pauline entered. He was wearing his trademark suit-and-sneakers.

"The trouble in Chad," she said to him. "Has that story had any traction?"

"Until a few minutes ago, no, Madam President," Sandip said. "But James Moore just commented on NBC. He said you should not send American troops to intervene."

"We already have a counterterrorism force of a couple of thousand soldiers there."

"But he doesn't know things like that."

"Anyway, on a scale of one to ten?"

"It just went up from one to two."

Pauline nodded. "Talk to Chester Jackson, please," she said. "Agree on a short statement pointing out that we already have troops in Chad and other North African countries combating the Islamic State in the Greater Sahara."

"Perhaps hinting at Moore's ignorance? 'Mr. Moore doesn't seem to realize . . .' That sort of thing?"

Pauline thought for a moment. She did not really like that kind of sniping in politics. "No, I don't want Chess to come on like a smartass. Aim for the tone of one who patiently and kindly explains simple facts."

"Got it."

"Thank you, Sandip."

"Thank you, Madam President."

She went to the Oval Office.

She met with the Treasury secretary, spent an hour with the visiting Norwegian prime minister, and received a delegation of dairy farmers. She had her lunch on a tray in the study: cold poached salmon with a salad. While eating her lunch she read a briefing note on the water shortage in California.

Next was her phone call with the president of France. Chess came to the Oval Office and sat with her, listening on an earpiece. Gus and several others were listening in remotely. There were also interpreters at each end, in case of need, although Pauline and President Pelletier normally got by without them.

Georges Pelletier had a relaxed, easygoing manner, but when push came to shove he would ask himself what was in France's interests and do it ruthlessly, so there was no guarantee that Pauline would get her way.

Pauline began by saying: "Bonjour, monsieur le president. Comment ça va, mon ami?"

The French president replied in perfect colloquial

English. "Madam President, it's very kind of you to pretend to speak French, and you know how much we appreciate it, but in the end it's easier if we both speak English."

Pauline laughed. Pelletier could be charming even when he was scoring a point. She said: "In any language, it's a pleasure to talk to you."

"And for me."

She pictured him in the Élysée Palace, sitting at the vast president's desk in the gilded Salon Doré, looking as if he were born there, elegant in a cashmere suit. She said: "It's one o'clock in the afternoon here in Washington, so it must be seven in the evening in Paris. I guess you're drinking champagne."

"My first glass of the day, obviously."

"Salut, then."

"Cheers."

"I'm calling about Chad."

"I guessed."

Pauline did not need to go over all that had happened. Georges was always well briefed. She said: "Your army and mine work together in Chad, combating ISGS, but I don't think we want to get involved in a squabble with Sudan."

"Correct."

"The danger is that if there are troops on both sides of the border, sooner or later some fool is going to fire a rifle, and we'll end up fighting a battle no one wants."

"True."

"My idea is a twenty-kilometer-wide demilitarized zone along the border."

"Excellent idea."

"I believe the Egyptians and the Sudanese will agree to keep their forces ten kilometers from the border if you and I do the same."

There was a pause. Georges was no pushover and

now, as she had anticipated, he was making unsentimental calculations. "On the face of it that sounds like a good idea," he said.

Pauline waited for him to say *but*.

However, he did not. Instead he said: "Let me run it past the military."

"I'm sure they'll approve," Pauline said. "They won't want an unnecessary war."

"You may well be right."

"One other thing," Pauline said.

"Ah."

"We have to go first."

"You mean we impose a limit on ourselves *before* the Egyptians agree to do the same?"

"I think they will probably agree in principle but will not actually make the commitment until they have seen us do it."

"The snag."

"But your troops are nowhere near the border right now, so you merely need to announce that you're going to observe the demilitarized zone as a gesture of goodwill, in the firm hope that the other side will reciprocate. You will look like the sensible peacemaker, which of course you are. Then you can see what happens. If the other side doesn't do their bit, then you can move your troops to the border any time you like."

"My dear Pauline, you're very persuasive."

"I hate to blight your evening, Georges, but could you talk to the military right away? Perhaps even before dinner?" It was a bold request, but she hated delay: an hour turned into a day, and a day turned into a week, and bright ideas died from lack of oxygen. "If you could give me an okay before you retire for the night, I could progress this with the Egyptians, and you might wake up to a safer world in the morning."

He laughed. "I like you, Pauline. You have something. There's a Yiddish word. Chutzpah."

"I'll take that as a compliment."

"It is. You will hear from me this evening."

"I really appreciate that, Georges."

"You're welcome."

They both hung up.

Chess said: "Let me tell you something, Madam President. You're very good. Incredibly good."

"Let's see if it works," said Pauline.

She had a similar conversation with the president of Egypt. It was not as warm, but the result was the same: a favorable response without definite agreement.

That evening Pauline had to make a speech at the Diplomats' Ball, an annual shindig organized by a committee of ambassadors to raise funds for literacy charities. Big companies doing business overseas bought tables to gain access to important envoys.

The dress code was black tie. The clothes Pauline had chosen earlier had been put out by the Residence staff, a Nile-green dress with a wrap in dark green velvet. She added an emerald teardrop pendant with matching earrings while Gerry put cuff links in his shirt.

Much of the evening's conversation would be small talk, but a few powerful people would be among the guests, and Pauline intended to progress her plan for Chad and Sudan. In her experience, real decisions were made at events such as this just as often as in formal meetings around conference tables. The relaxed atmosphere, the booze, the sexy clothes, and the rich food all made people ease up and put them in a compliant frame of mind.

She would circulate during the predinner cocktails, chatting to as many people as possible, then make a speech and leave before the meal, sticking to her principle of not wasting time eating with strangers.

On the way out she was intercepted by Sandip. "Something you might like to know before you get to the ball," he said. "James Moore has spoken again about Chad."

Pauline sighed. "He may be relied upon to be unhelpful. What has he said?"

"I guess he's responding to our statement that we already have troops in Chad. Anyway, he's said they should be withdrawn, to make sure they don't get involved in a war that has nothing to do with America."

"So we would no longer be part of the struggle against ISGS?"

"That's the implication, but he didn't mention ISGS."

"Okay, Sandip, thanks for the heads-up."

"Thank you, Madam President."

She got into the tall black car with the armored doors and inch-thick bulletproof windows. In front was an identical car with Secret Service bodyguards; behind was another with White House staffers. As the convoy pulled away she controlled her irritation. While she was urgently pushing forward a peace plan, Moore was giving Americans the impression that she was thoughtlessly drifting into another foreign war. There was a saying: A lie goes halfway round the world while the truth is getting its boots on. It was infuriating that her efforts could be so easily undermined by a blowhard such as Moore.

Motorcycle police held up the traffic for her at every road junction, and it took only a few minutes to get to Georgetown.

As they drew up to the entrance to the hotel she said

to Gerry: "We'll separate soon after we walk in, as usual, if that's okay with you."

"Sure," he said. "That way, some of the people who are disappointed that they didn't get to speak to you can have the consolation prize of a conversation with me." But he smiled as he said it, so she felt he did not really mind.

The hotel manager met her at the door and led her downstairs, preceded and followed by members of her Secret Service detail. A roar of conversation came from the ballroom. She was pleased to see the broad-shouldered figure of Gus waiting at the foot of the stairs, looking devastatingly handsome in a tuxedo. "Just so you know," he murmured, "James Moore showed up."

"Thank you," she said. "Don't worry, I'll deal with him if I run into him. What about Prince Faisal?"

"He's here."

"Bring him to me if you get a chance."

"Leave it to me."

She entered the ballroom and declined a glass of champagne. There was an atmosphere of warm bodies, fishy canapés, and empty wine bottles. She was welcomed by the chair of one of the charities, a millionaire's wife in a turquoise silk sheath and impossibly high heels. Then Pauline was on the merry-go-round. She asked bright questions about literacy and showed interest in the answers. She was introduced to the main sponsor of the ball, the CEO of a huge paper-manufacturing company, and she asked how the business was doing. The Bosnian ambassador buttonholed her and begged for help dealing with unexploded land mines, of which his country had eighty thousand. Pauline was sympathetic, but the land mines had not been put there by Americans and she did not plan to spend taxpayers' money removing them. She was not a Republican for nothing.

She was charming and interested with everyone, and managed to conceal how impatient she was to get on with her priorities.

She was approached by the French ambassador, Giselle de Perrin, a thin woman of sixty-something in a black dress. What would the news from Paris be? President Pelletier could make or break this deal.

Madame de Perrin shook Pauline's hand and said: "Madam President, I spoke to Monsieur Pelletier an hour ago. He asked me to give you this." She took a folded paper from her clutch bag. "He said you would be pleased."

Pauline eagerly unfolded the single sheet. It was a press release from the Élysée Palace, with one paragraph highlighted and translated into English. "The government of France, concerned about tensions on the Chad-Sudan border, will immediately send 1,000 troops to Chad to reinforce its existing mission there. Initially at least, French forces will remain at least ten kilometers from the border, hoping that forces on the other side will reciprocate, thereby creating a twenty-kilometer separation between the armies, for the avoidance of accidental provocation."

Pauline was delighted. "Thank you for this, Ambassador," she said. "It's very helpful."

"You're welcome," the ambassador said. "France is always pleased to assist our American allies."

That wasn't true, Pauline thought, but she kept smiling.

Her attention was drawn away as Milton Lapierre appeared. Oh, shit, she thought, I don't need this now. She had not expected him to be here—there was no reason for it. He had resigned, and Pauline had nominated a replacement vice president, who was now going through the process of being approved by both houses of Congress. But the story of his affair with sixteen-year-old Rita Cross had not yet hit the media, and she guessed he was trying to maintain a pretense that everything was all right.

Milt did not look good. He had a whisky glass in his hand and he seemed to have sipped quite a lot from it. His tuxedo was expensive, but his cummerbund was slipping and his bow tie was loose.

Pauline's bodyguards came closer.

Pauline had learned early in her career to remain cool during embarrassing encounters. "Good evening, Milt," she said. She recalled that he had been made a director of a lobbying firm, and she said: "Congratulations on your appointment to the board of Riley Hobcraft Partners."

"Thank you, Madam President. You did your best to ruin my life, but you didn't quite succeed."

Pauline was startled by the intensity of his hatred. "Ruin your life?" she said with what she hoped was a friendly smile. "Better people than you and me have been fired and gotten over it."

He lowered his voice. "She left me," he said.

Pauline could not feel sorry for him. "It's for the best," she said. "Best for her and best for you."

"You know nothing about it," he hissed.

Gus stepped in and put a protective arm between Pauline and Milt. "Here's His Excellency Prince Faisal," he said, and with a light touch he turned her around so that her back was to Milt. She heard one of her bodyguards distracting Milt by saying pleasantly: "Good to see you again, Mr. Vice President, I hope you're well."

Pauline smiled at Faisal, a middle-aged man with a gray beard and a wary expression. "Good evening, Prince Faisal," she said. "I talked to the president of Egypt, but he wouldn't make any promises."

"That's what they said to us. Our foreign minister likes the idea of a demilitarized zone between Chad and Sudan, and he immediately called Cairo. But the Egyptians only said they would think about it."

Pauline had the French note in her hand. "Look at this," she said.

Faisal read it quickly. "This might make a difference," he said.

Her spirits rose again. "Why don't you show it to your friend the Egyptian ambassador?"

"That's just what I was thinking."

"Please do."

Gus touched her arm and eased her toward the podium. It was almost time for her speech. One television crew had been allowed in to film her speaking. A script about literacy would be displayed for her on screens that could not be seen by the audience. However, she was thinking of diverting from the script, or at least adding to it, with a few remarks about Chad. She just wished she had some concrete good news to report, instead of mere hopes.

She had brief exchanges with people as the Secret Service men made a way for her through the crowd. Just before she reached the short flight of steps, James Moore greeted her.

She spoke politely but kept her face expressionless. "Good evening, James, and thank you for the interest you're taking in Chad." She felt she was close to the line where courtesy turned into hypocrisy.

Moore said: "It's a dangerous situation."

"Of course, and the last thing we want to do is get American troops involved."

"Then you should bring them home."

Pauline smiled thinly. "I think we can do better than that."

Moore was puzzled. "Better?"

He did not have the brains to entertain several options and weigh their pros and cons. All he could do was think of something aggressive and then say it.

But Pauline did not have an alternative to his proposal, she only had the hope of one. "You'll see," she said with more confidence than she felt, and she moved on.

As she reached the steps she met Lateef Salah, the Egyptian ambassador, a small man with bright eyes and a black mustache. He was not much taller than Pauline. In his tuxedo he made her think of a chirpy blackbird. She liked his energy. "Faisal showed me the French announcement," he said without preamble. "This is an important step."

"I agree," Pauline said.

"It's very late in Cairo now, but the foreign minister is still awake, and I talked to him a few moments ago." He looked pleased with himself.

"Good for you! What did the foreign minister say?"

"We will agree to the demilitarized zone. We were only waiting for French confirmation."

Pauline hid her exultation. She wanted to kiss Lateef. "That's wonderful news, Ambassador. Thank you for letting me know so quickly. I may mention your announcement in my speech, if you don't mind."

"We would be glad, thank you, Madam President."

The millionaire's wife in the turquoise silk caught her eye. Pauline nodded to indicate that she was ready. The woman made a short speech of welcome, then introduced her, and Pauline moved to the lectern as the audience applauded. She took a printed copy of her speech from her clutch bag and unfolded it, not because she needed it, but so that she could do something theatrical with it later.

She spoke about the achievements of the literacy charities and the work that remained to be done by them and the federal government, but at the back of her mind was Chad. She wanted to trumpet her achievement, acknowledge the role played by ambassadors, and put James Moore down without seeming vindictive. She would have liked an hour to work on the speech, but this was too good an opportunity to miss, so she would improvise.

She said everything necessary about literacy, then spoke about the diplomats. At this point she ostentatiously folded up her speech and put it away, so that they knew she was going off script. She leaned forward, lowered her voice, and spoke in a more intimate tone, and the place went quiet. "I want to tell you about something important, an agreement that will save lives, that was achieved today by the Washington diplomatic corps, in fact by some of the people in this room. You've heard on the news about border tensions between Chad and Sudan, you know there has already been loss of life, and you're aware of the danger that escalation will draw the armies of other nations into the conflict. But today our French and Egyptian friends, with help and encouragement from the Saudis and from the White House, have agreed on a demilitarized zone twenty kilometers wide along the border, in a first step toward easing the tension and reducing the risk of further casualties."

She paused to let them digest that, then went on: "This is how we work for a peaceful world." She tried a little joke. "Diplomats do it quietly." There was a small appreciative laugh. "Our weapons are forethought and sincerity. And so to finish, as well as thanking our wonderful literacy charities, I'd like to ask you to thank the Washington diplomats, the quiet negotiators who save lives. Let's give them a round of applause."

A great cheer went up. Pauline clapped and the

audience followed suit. She looked around, catching the eyes of one ambassador after another, nodding special acknowledgment to Lateef and Giselle and Faisal; then she came down from the podium and was escorted by the Secret Service through the crowd, getting out of the door before the applause began to fade.

Gus was right behind her. "Brilliant," he enthused. "I'll call Sandip and give him the details, if you like. He should press-release this right away."

"Good. Do it, please."

"I have to go back inside," Gus said ruefully. "Only the privileged few get to avoid the chili-glazed salmon. But I'll drop by the Oval Office later, if that's okay?"

"Of course."

When she got into the car Gerry was already there. "Well done," he said. "It went well."

"The DMZ should be on tomorrow's front pages."

"And people will realize that while Moore is shooting off his mouth, you're actually solving problems."

She smiled ruefully. "That might be too much to hope for."

At the White House they went straight to the Residence and entered the Dining Room. Pippa was already at the table. Looking at their clothes she said: "There was no need to dress formally just for me, but all the same I appreciate the gesture."

Pauline laughed happily. This was the Pippa she liked best, smart-funny rather than smart-sulky. They ate steak with a rocket salad and had a lighthearted conversation. Then Pippa returned to her homework, Gerry went to watch golf on TV, and Pauline asked for her coffee to be served in the small study next to the Oval Office.

This was a more private space, and people did not walk in without permission. For the next two hours Pauline was mostly undisturbed. She worked her way through a stack of reports and memoranda. Gus came in at ten thirty, having escaped from the ball. He had changed out of his tux, and looked relaxed and almost cuddly in a dark blue cashmere sweater and jeans. She pushed aside her briefings with relief, glad to have someone with whom to chew over the day's events. "How was the rest of the ball?" she said.

"The auction did well," Gus said. "Someone paid twenty-five thousand dollars for a bottle of wine."

She smiled. "Who could ever drink it?"

"They loved your speech—they talked about it all evening."

"Good." Pauline was glad, but she had been preaching to the saved. Few of the people at the Diplomats' Ball would vote for James Moore. His supporters belonged in a different stratum of American society. "Let's see how it plays in the tabloids." She turned on the TV. "In a few minutes there'll be reviews of the first editions on the news channels." She muted a sports report.

Gus said: "How was the rest of your evening?"

"Nice. Pippa was in a happy frame of mind for a change, and then I had a few quiet hours for reading. With all the information I have to digest, I wish I had a bigger brain."

Gus laughed. "I know that feeling. My head needs one of the RAM upgrades you can get for your laptop."

The newspaper review began, and Pauline turned up the volume.

The front page of the *New York Mail* made her heart stop.

The headline read:

PIPPA THE
POTHEAD

Pauline said: "Oh, no! No!"

The anchor said: "The president's daughter, Pippa Green, aged fourteen, is in trouble for smoking pot at a party in the home of a fellow pupil at her elite private high school."

Pauline was stunned. She stared at the screen, mouth open in bewilderment, both hands held against her cheeks, hardly able to believe this was real.

The front page filled the screen. There was a faked color photo of Pauline and Pippa together: Pauline was looking furious and Pippa wore an old T-shirt and needed to wash her hair. The two images came from different shots that had been melded to show a scene that had never happened, with Pauline apparently berating her drug-addicted daughter.

Shock was replaced by rage. Pauline stood up, yelling at the TV: "You fucking shits!" she screamed. "She's a child!"

The door opened and an anxious Secret Service agent looked in. Gus waved him away.

On the screen, the anchor moved on to other newspapers, but every tabloid led with Pippa.

Pauline could accept any insult to herself and laugh it off, but she could not bear the humiliation of Pippa. She was so enraged that she wanted to kill someone: the reporter, the editor, the proprietor, and all the brain-dead fools who read this kind of trash. Her eyes filled with tears of rage. She was possessed by the primal instinct to protect her child, but she could not, and the frustration made her want to tear out her hair. "This is not fair!" she cried. "We conceal the identities of children who commit murder—but they're crucifying my daughter just for smoking a fucking joint!"

The serious press had other priorities but nevertheless Pippa was on every front page. The conflict in

Chad, and Pauline's success in establishing a demilitarized zone, was not mentioned by the anchor.

Pauline said: "I can't believe this."

The summary of the papers came to an end and the
anchor threw to a film reviewer. Pauline switched off
and turned to Gus. "What am I going to do?" she said.

Gus said quietly: "I think James Moore is responsible. He did this to push your DMZ off the front page."

"I don't care who leaked it," Pauline said, and she
could hear the shrill tone in her own voice. "I just need
to figure out how to handle this with Pippa. It's the
kind of mortification that makes teenage girls suicidal." Her tears flowed again, and now they were tears
of grief.

"I know," said Gus. "My girls were adolescents only
a decade or so ago. It's a sensitive time. They can be depressed for a week because someone criticized their
nail polish. But you can help her through it."

Pauline checked her watch. "It's after eleven, she'll
be asleep, she won't have heard the news. I'll see her as
soon as she wakes up in the morning. But what am I
going to say?"

"You'll say that you're sorry this happened, but you
love her, and together you'll get through it okay. It's
nasty, but on the other hand no one died, no one caught
a deadly virus, and no one is going to jail. Most of all,
you're going to tell her that this is not her fault."

She stared at him. Already she was feeling calmer.
In a more normal voice she said: "How did you get so
wise, Gus?"

He paused. "Mostly by listening to you," he said
quietly. "You're the wisest person I've ever met."

She was embarrassed by the unexpected strength of
his feeling. She passed it off with a quip. "If we're so
smart, how come we're in so much trouble?"

He took the question seriously. "Everyone who does

good acquires enemies. Think how they hated Martin Luther King. I have a different question, though I believe I know the answer. Who told James Moore that Pippa had smoked marijuana?"

"You're thinking about Milt."

"He hates you enough—he showed that earlier this evening. I don't know how he found out about her smoking weed, but it's not hard to imagine—he was around here all the time."

Pauline was thoughtful. "I believe I know exactly how and when he found out." She recalled the moment. "It was about three weeks ago. I had been discussing North Korea with Milt and Chess. Then Gerry came in, Milt and Chess left, and Gerry told me about the dope-smoking. While we were having that conversation, Milt came back to pick up something he'd left behind." She recalled looking up, startled, to check who it was, and seeing Milt grab that purple scarf. "I wondered then how much he'd overheard. Now we know. At any rate he gathered enough to put the *Mail* on the story."

"I'm pretty sure you won't do this, but I have to mention it: if you want to punish Milt you have a means at hand."

"You mean reveal the secret of his affair? You're right, I won't do it."

"I didn't think it was your style."

"Besides, let's not forget that there's another vulnerable teenage girl in the middle of this mess: Rita Cross."

"You're right."

Her phone rang. It was Sandip. He skipped the preliminaries and got right to the point. "Madam President, may I suggest how we might respond to the story in tomorrow's *New York Mail*?"

"We should say very little. I'm not going to discuss my daughter with those jackals."

"Exactly. I propose the following: 'This is a private matter and the White House has no comment to make.' What do you think?"

"Perfect," she said. "Thank you, Sandip."

She saw that Gus was smoldering. He had not erupted suddenly, as she had, but instead burned under the surface, but now he was about to burst into flame. "What do these motherfuckers want?" he said.

She was mildly startled. In the high-tension zone of the West Wing people were allowed to use profanity, but she did not think she had ever heard him use that particular swear word.

He went on: "You do something constructive, instead of shooting off your mouth, and they ignore that and target your kid. Sometimes I think we deserve to have an asshole like Moore for president."

Pauline smiled. His anger heartened her. As he showed his rage, she was able to become more rational. "Democracy is a terrible way to run a country, isn't it?" she said.

He knew that saying, and he delivered the punch line: "But all the other ways are worse."

"And if you expect gratitude, you shouldn't be in politics." Suddenly Pauline was tired. She stood up and went to the door.

Gus also stood. "What you did today was a small masterpiece of diplomacy."

"I'm pleased, regardless of what the media say."

"I hope you know how much I admire you. I've watched you for three years. Time and time again you've come up with the solution, the right approach, the telling phrase. I realized some time ago that I have the privilege of working with genius."

Pauline stood with her hand on the doorknob. "I never did anything on my own," she said. "We're part of a good team, Gus. I'm lucky to have you and your intelligence and friendship to support me."

He had not finished. Emotions chased one another across his face until she lost track. Then he said: "On my side, it's a little more than friendship."

What did that mean? She stared at him, confused. What amounted to more than friendship? An answer came to the edge of her consciousness but she could not accept it.

Gus said: "I shouldn't have said that. Please forget it."

She looked at him for a long moment, not knowing what to say or do. Finally she just said: "Okay."

She hesitated a moment longer, then went out.

She walked quickly back to the Residence, followed by her Secret Service detail, thinking about Gus. His statement had sounded like a confession of love. But that was ridiculous.

Gerry had retired and the bedroom door was closed, so she went to the Lincoln Bedroom again. She was glad to be alone. She had a lot to think about.

She brooded, planning her conversation with Pippa as she moved mechanically through the bedtime chores that required no thought: brushing her teeth, taking off her makeup, putting her jewelry in its box. She hung up her dress and dropped her tights into the laundry hamper.

She set the alarm for six o'clock, a full hour before Pippa would wake. They would talk for as long as necessary. If Pippa did not make it to school tomorrow, no one would mind.

Pauline put on a nightdress, then went to the window and looked out over the South Lawn to the Washington Monument. She thought about George Washington, the first person to have the job she now held. There had been no White House when he was inaugurated. He had never had children, and in any case the newspapers of that time were not interested in the behavior of their leaders' offspring: they had more important things to say.

It was raining. There was a nighttime vigil on Constitution Avenue, a protest against the killing of a Black man by a white cop, and the demonstrators stood in the rain with hats and umbrellas. Gus was Black. He had grandsons; one day they would have to be told that they were in special danger from the police and needed to obey strict rules to stay safe: no running in the street, no shouting, rules that did not apply to white kids. It made no difference that Gus held one of the highest offices in the land, and dedicated his intelligence and wisdom to his country; he was defined by his race just the same. Pauline wondered how long it would be before that kind of injustice disappeared from America.

She slipped between cold sheets. She turned out the light but did not close her eyes. She had had two shocks. She was beginning to know what to say to Pippa, but she had no idea how to handle Gus.

The trouble was, they had a history.

Gus had been foreign policy advisor to her presidential campaign. For a year they had been on the road together, days of intense work and nights of not enough sleep. They had become close.

And there was more. It was not much, but she had not forgotten, and she felt sure he had not either.

It had happened at the height of the campaign, when Pauline was looking like a winner. They had come back from a hugely successful rally, thousands of people cheering in a baseball stadium and a brilliant speech by her. Still on a high, they had gotten into a slow elevator in a tall hotel and found themselves alone. He had put his arms around her and she had tilted her face and they had kissed passionately, their mouths open, their hands all over one another, until the elevator had stopped and the doors had opened and they had turned in different directions and gone to their rooms without saying a word.

They had never spoken of it since.

She struggled to remember the last time someone had fallen in love with her. Of course she recalled her romance with Gerry, but that had been a slowly growing friendship rather than a grand passion. That was usually the way with her. She had never tried to be alluring or flirtatious—there was too much else to do. Men did not fall for her at first sight, although she was nice looking. No, people who became fond of her did so gradually, as they got to know her. Nevertheless there had been men who eventually threw themselves at her feet—and one woman, come to think of it. She had dated some of them and gone to bed with a few, but she had never been able to feel as they did, overwhelmed, helpless with love, desperate for intimacy. She had never experienced a passion that had changed her life, unless it had been the drive to make the world a better place.

And now Gus had made a declaration.

Nothing could possibly come of it, obviously. An affair between the two of them could not be kept secret, and when it came out the story would wreck his career and hers. It would also destroy her little family. In fact it would ruin her life. It was not even to be considered. No decision was required: there was no choice.

That said, how did she feel, theoretically, about a romance with Gus?

She liked him a lot. He was compassionate and tough, a difficult trick to pull off. He had mastered the art of giving advice without insisting on his point of view. And he was sexy. She found herself imagining the first exploratory touches, the loving kisses, the stroking of hair, the closeness of warm bodies.

You'd look ridiculous, she told herself: he's taller than you by a foot.

But it was not ridiculous. It was something else. It made her warm inside. Just thinking about it felt pleasant.

She tried to dismiss all such thoughts. She was the president: she could not fall in love. It would be a hurricane, a train crash, a nuclear bomb.

Thank God it could never happen.

CHAPTER 18

The bus drove northwest from Faya into a zone known as the Aouzou Strip. Here the travelers faced a new danger: land mines.

The Aouzou Strip, sixty miles wide, had been the issue in a border war in which Chad had beaten back its northern neighbor, Libya. After the fighting was over, thousands of land mines were left behind in the territory Chad had won. In some places there were warnings: rows of roadside stones painted red and white. But many remained hidden.

Hakim claimed to know where they all were, but he looked more and more scared as the bus advanced, and he slowed down nervously, checking and double-checking that he was following the road, which was not always clearly distinguishable from the surrounding desert.

They were now in the burning heart of the Sahara. Even the air had a singed taste. No one could get comfortable. Little Naji was naked and grizzly; Kiah kept giving him sips of water, to make sure he did not become dehydrated. Mountains loomed in the far distance, their heights offering a false promise of cooler

weather; false, because the mountains were impassable
to wheeled vehicles and would have to be skirted, so
the bus could not escape from the baking oven of the
desert floor.

Abdul reflected that the Arabs of earlier times would
not have traveled all day. They would have awakened
the camels before dawn, and strapped on the baskets of
ivory and gold by starlight, and roped the naked slaves
together in long, miserable lines, so that they could set
off at first light and rest during the scorching middle of
the day. Their modern descendants, with their gasoline-
fueled vehicles and their cargoes of costly cocaine and
desperate migrants, were not so smart.

As the bus drew nearer to the border with Libya,
Abdul wondered how Hakim would deal with frontier
controls. Most of the migrants had no passports, let
alone visas or other travel permits. Many Chadians
lived their whole lives without being issued any kind of
identity document. How would they get through immigration and customs? Clearly Hakim had some system,
presumably involving bribery, but that could be haz-
ardous. The man who took a backhander last time
might double his price. Or his supervisor might be
present, watching every move. Or he might have been
replaced by a zealot who refused to be corrupted.
These things were not predictable.

The last village before the border was the most
primitive place Abdul had ever seen. The main building material consisted of thin tree branches, as
bleached and dry as the sun-whitened bones of ani-
mals that had died of thirst in the desert. The
sticks—for that was all they were—were fixed to cross-
pieces to form walls that stood precariously upright.
Ragged lengths of cotton and canvas formed the roofs.
There were half a dozen or so better dwellings, tiny
one-room buildings made of cinder blocks.

Hakim stopped the bus, turned off the engine, and announced: "Here we meet our Toubou guide."

Abdul knew about the Toubou. They were nomadic herdsmen living around the borders between Chad, Libya, and Niger, ceaselessly moving their flocks and cattle in search of scarce pasture. They had long been regarded as primitive savages by the governments of all three countries. The Toubou returned that contempt: they recognized no government, obeyed no laws, and respected no borders. Many of them had discovered that smuggling people and drugs was easier and more lucrative than raising livestock. National governments found it impossible to police people who never stopped moving—especially when their habitat was hundreds of desert miles from the nearest administrative building.

However, their Toubou guide was not here.

"He will come," said Hakim.

In the center of the village was a well that gave clear, cold water, and everyone drank their fill.

Meanwhile Hakim had a long conversation with a resident, an older man with a look of intelligence, probably an informal village headman. Abdul could not hear what was said.

The travelers were shown into a compound with lean-to shelters around the sides. Abdul guessed by the smell that it had been used for sheep, probably to protect the beasts from the sun in the middle of the day. It was now late afternoon: clearly the bus passengers were to spend the night here.

Hakim called for everyone's attention. "Fouad has given me a message," he said, and Abdul assumed Fouad was the man who looked like the village leader. "Our guide has doubled his price, and he will not come until he is paid the extra. It will cost twenty dollars per person."

There was an outburst of protest. The passengers said they could not afford it, and Hakim said he was not going to pay it for them. What followed was a more intense repeat of an argument that had raged several times already on the trip, as Hakim tried to extort extra money. In the end people had to pay.

Abdul got up and left the compound.

Looking around the village, he decided that no one here was involved in smuggling either drugs or people: they were all too poor. At earlier stops he had usually been able to figure out who the local criminals were because they had money and guns, as well as the stressed-out air of men who lived on the violent fringes, always ready to run away. He had carefully noted names and descriptions and relationships, and had sent a long report to Tamara from Faya. There seemed to be no such men in this pathetic settlement. However, the mention of the Toubou people had given him the explanation: in this area the smuggling must have been run by them.

He sat on the ground near the well, his back up against an acacia tree that gave him shade. From here he could see much of the village, but a spreading thicket of tamarisk hid him from people who came to the well: he wanted to observe, not to talk. He wondered where the guide was, if not in the village. There were no other settlements for many miles around. Was the mysterious Toubou tribesman just beyond the hill, in a tent, waiting to be told that the migrants had found the extra money? It was quite possible that he had not even asked for more money: that could have been just another extortion ploy by Hakim. The guide might have been in one of these village huts, eating stewed goat with couscous, resting up before tomorrow's journey.

Abdul saw Hakim come out of the compound looking cross. He was followed by Wahed, the father-in-law of Esma. Hakim stopped and the two men had a conversation, Wahed pleading and Hakim refusing. Abdul could not hear the words but guessed they were arguing about the extra money for the guide. Hakim made a dismissive gesture and walked away, but Wahed followed him, hands spread out in supplication; then Hakim stopped and turned around and spoke aggressively before walking away again. Abdul made a grimace of distaste: Hakim's behavior was brutish and Wahed's was undignified. Abdul was offended by the entire scene.

Hakim slouched across the dusty ground toward the well, and Esma came out of the compound and walked briskly after him.

They stood at the well to talk, as people had done for thousands of years. Abdul could not see them, but he could hear their conversation clearly, and he was practiced at understanding their rapid colloquial Arabic.

Esma said: "My father is very upset."

Hakim said: "What's that to me?"

"We can't pay the extra. We have the money we must give you when we get to Libya, the balance of the fare. But no more."

Hakim pretended to be indifferent. "Then you will just have to stay here in this village," he said.

"But that doesn't make sense," she said.

Of course it didn't, Abdul thought. What was Hakim up to?

Esma went on: "In a few days' time we will pay you two thousand five hundred dollars. Would you really lose that for twenty?"

"Sixty," he said. "Twenty for you, twenty for your mother-in-law, and twenty for the old man."

A quibble, Abdul thought.

Esma said: "We don't have it, but we can get it when we reach Tripoli. We will ask my husband to send more money from Nice—I promise."

"I don't want promises. The Toubou don't accept them as payment."

"Then we have no choice," she said in baffled exasperation. "We will have to stay here until someone comes along who can give us a ride back to Lake Chad. We will have wasted the money my husband earned building all those walls for rich French people." She sounded utterly miserable.

Hakim said: "Unless you can think of another way to pay me—you pretty little thing."

"What are you doing? Don't touch me like that!"

Abdul tensed. His instinct was to intervene. He suppressed the impulse.

Hakim said: "As you wish. I'm just trying to help you. Be nice to me, why not?"

This has been Hakim's agenda all along, Abdul thought. I should not be surprised.

Esma said: "Are you trying to tell me that you will accept sex instead of money?"

"Don't speak so crudely, please."

The prudishness of the sexual bully, Abdul thought. He doesn't like to hear the name of what he wants to make her do. A dismal irony.

Hakim said: "Well?"

There was a long silence.

This was what Hakim really wanted, Abdul thought. He did not really care about the sixty bucks. He was insisting on it only as a way of getting her to accept the alternative.

Abdul wondered how many other women had been offered this grim choice.

Esma said: "My husband would kill you."

Hakim laughed. "No, he wouldn't. He might kill you."

At last Esma said: "All right. But only with my hand."

"We'll see."

"No!" She was insistent. "Nothing else."

"All right."

"Not now. Later, when it gets dark."

"Follow me when I leave the compound after the meal."

With a note of desperation in her voice Esma said, "I could pay you double when we get to Tripoli."

"More promises."

Abdul heard Esma's footsteps walking away. He stayed where he was. A little later he heard Hakim leave.

He watched the village for another couple of hours, but nothing happened, except that people came to the well and went away.

As the sky darkened he returned to the compound. Some of the village inhabitants were preparing the evening meal, supervised by Fouad, and there was a pleasant aroma of cumin. He sat on the ground near to where Kiah was nursing Naji.

Kiah, who was sharp-eyed, said: "I noticed Esma talking to Hakim."

Abdul said: "Yes."

"Did you hear them?"

"Yes."

"What was said?"

"He told her that if she didn't have money she could pay him another way."

"I knew it. That pig."

Unobtrusively, Abdul reached inside his robes and opened his money belt. He had notes in several currencies, and he kept them in order so that he could take money out without looking. In Africa, as in the US, it was foolish to let people see that you were carrying a lot of cash.

Gently he drew out three American twenty-dollar bills. Hiding them behind his hands, he glanced down to check the denomination, then folded them into a small packet. He passed the packet to Kiah, saying: "For Esma."

She stashed it somewhere in her robe. "God bless you," she said.

A little later, when they lined up to get their supper, Abdul saw Kiah slip something into Esma's hand. A moment later, Esma hugged and kissed her in happy gratitude.

The meal was flatbread and a vegetable soup thickened with millet flour. If there was meat in it, Abdul did not get any.

Abdul went out of the compound just before going to sleep. He washed his hands and face with water from the well. As he returned he passed the bus, where Hakim was standing with Tareq and Hamza. "You're not from this country, are you?" Hakim said, as if it was a challenge.

Hakim had been looking forward to his hand job and was disappointed to get sixty bucks instead, Abdul assumed. He had probably noticed Esma hugging and kissing Kiah, and guessed that Kiah had given her the money. Kiah might have had a secret stash of her own, of course, but if she had gotten it from someone else, then Hakim figured Abdul was the likely source. Sly crooks sometimes had good instincts.

Abdul said: "What do you care where I come from?"

"Nigeria?" Hakim said. "You don't sound Nigerian. What is that accent?"

"I'm not Nigerian."

Hamza took out a pack of cigarettes and put one in his mouth—a sign that he was getting nervous, Abdul thought. Almost automatically, Abdul took out the red plastic lighter he had always used with customers and lit Hamza's cigarette. He no longer needed the lighter, but he had kept it with a vague feeling that one day it

might be useful. In return, Hamza offered him a cigarette from the pack. Abdul declined.

Hakim resumed the attack. "Where was your father
from?"

This was a trial of strength. Hakim was challenging
Abdul in front of Hamza and Tareq. "Beirut," Abdul
said. "My father was Lebanese. He was a cook. He
made very good sweet cheese rolls."

Hakim looked scornful.

Abdul went on: "He's dead now. To God we belong,
and to God we all return." This pious saying was the
Muslim equivalent of *Rest in peace*. Abdul noticed that
Hamza and Tareq heard it with approval.

He continued, making his voice slow and serious.
"You should be careful what you say about a man's
father, Hakim."

Hamza blew out smoke and nodded.

"I'll say what I like," Hakim blustered. He looked at
the two guards. He relied on them to defend him, but
he realized that Abdul was weakening their loyalty.

Abdul spoke to the guards rather than to Hakim. "I
was a driver in the army, you know," he said conversationally.

Hakim said: "So what?"

Abdul ignored Hakim pointedly. "I drove armored
cars first, then tank carriers. The tank carriers were
difficult on desert roads." He was making this up. He
had never driven a tank carrier, never served in the
National Army of Chad or indeed any other military
force. "I was in the east, mostly, near the Sudan border."

Hakim was bewildered. "Why are you saying this?"
he said in a voice shrill with frustration. "What are you
talking about?"

Abdul jerked a thumb rudely at Hakim. "If he dies,"
he said to the guards, "I can drive the bus." It was a

thinly disguised threat on Hakim's life. Would Hamza and Tareq react?

Neither guard spoke.

Hakim seemed to recall that the guards' job was to protect the cocaine, not him, and he realized he had lost face. Feebly he said: "Get out of my sight, Abdul," then turned his back.

Abdul felt he might have brought about a subtle shift of loyalties. Men such as Hamza and Tareq respected strength. Their allegiance to Hakim had been undermined by his failed attempt to bully Abdul. It had been an effective stroke to say: "To God we belong, and to God we all return." As jihadis in the Islamic State in the Greater Sahara, the two guards must often have murmured those words over the bodies of slain comrades.

They might even have begun to think of Abdul as one of them. At any rate, given a choice between him and Hakim, they might at least hesitate.

Abdul said no more. He went into the compound and lay down on the ground. Waiting for sleep to come, he reflected on the day. He was still alive, still accumulating priceless intelligence for the war against ISGS. He had deflected Hakim's challenging questions. But his position was weakening. He had begun this trip as a stranger to everyone, a man about whom they knew nothing and cared less. But he had not sustained that role, and now he saw that it had been impossible, given the length of time for which this group had remained intimately close. He was a person to them now, a foreigner and a loner, yes, but also a man who helped vulnerable women and one who was not afraid of bullies.

He had made a friend in Kiah and an enemy in Hakim. For an undercover officer, that was two mistakes.

The Toubou guide was there in the morning.

He came into the compound early, while the day was still cool, as the passengers were having a breakfast of bread and weak tea. He was a tall dark-skinned man in white robes and a white headdress, and he had an aloof look that made Abdul think of a proud Native American. Under his clothes, on his left side between his ribs and his hip, was a bulge that might have been a long-barreled revolver, perhaps a Magnum, in an improvised holster.

Hakim stood with him in the middle of the yard and said: "Listen to me! This is Issa, our guide. You must do everything he tells you."

Issa spoke briefly. Arabic was evidently not his first language, and Abdul recalled that the Toubou spoke a tongue of their own called Teda. "You do not have to do anything," Issa said, enunciating carefully. "I will take care of it all." There was no warmth in his tone; he was coldly factual. "If you are questioned, say that you are prospectors going to the gold mines in the west of Libya. But I do not think you will be questioned."

Hakim said: "Right, you've got your instructions, now board the bus quickly."

Kiah remarked to Abdul: "Issa seems reliable, at least. I'd trust him more than Hakim, anyway."

Abdul was not so sure. "He has a competent air," he said. "But I can't tell what's in his heart."

That made Kiah thoughtful.

Issa was the last to board, and Abdul watched with interest as he surveyed the interior and saw that there was no spare seat. Tareq and Hamza were as usual sprawled over two seats each. Seeming to make a decision, Issa stood in front of Tareq. He said nothing and his expression was impassive, but he stared unblinkingly.

Tareq stared back as if waiting for him to say something.

Hakim started the engine.

Without turning around, Issa said calmly: "Engine off."

Hakim looked at him.

Issa continued gazing at Tareq and just said: "Off."

Hakim turned the key in the ignition and the engine stopped.

Tareq sat upright, lifted his backpack off the seat beside him, and scooted over, making room.

Issa simply pointed to the other double seat, the one occupied by Hamza.

Tareq got up, crossed the aisle with his backpack in one hand and his assault rifle in the other, and sat next to Hamza, both of them with their packs on their knees.

Issa looked at Hakim and said: "Go."

Hakim once again started the engine.

It soon became clear to Abdul that this contest of wills had not merely been to establish who was the alpha male. Issa actually needed both halves of that front seat. He watched the road with unflagging concentration, often moving to the window seat to look out and back to the aisle seat to look ahead. Every few minutes he gave Hakim some direction or other, mostly using gestures, telling him where the road was when its edges were imperceptible, ordering him to steer to one side, making him slow down when the surface was strewn with stones, encouraging him to go faster when the road was clear.

In one place Issa guided him right off the road and onto rough ground in order to give a wide berth to a Toyota pickup that lay upside down and burned out at the roadside, presumably destroyed by a land mine. The Libya-Chad war was a long time in the past, but the mines were still operative, and where there had been one there might be more.

They stopped every two or three hours. The passengers got out to relieve themselves, and when they reboarded Hakim doled out stale bread and bottles of water. The bus drove on through the heat of the day: there was no shelter outside, and they were less hot moving than staying still.

As the afternoon wore on and the bus neared the border, it occurred to Abdul that he was about to commit a crime for the first time in his life. Nothing he had so far done for the CIA, or in any other sphere of activity, had actually been against the law. Even when he had been posing as a vendor of stolen cigarettes, all of his stock had in fact been bought at full price. But now he was about to enter a country illegally, accompanied by other illegitimate migrants, escorted by men armed with illicit rifles, and traveling with several million dollars' worth of cocaine. If things went wrong he would end up in a Libyan jail.

He wondered how long it would take the CIA to get him out.

As the sun slid down the dome of the western sky, Abdul looked ahead and saw a makeshift shelter like the ones in the last village: just a wall of sticks with a roof improvised from an old worn carpet. There was also a small tanker truck that Abdul guessed might contain water. Beside the road were stacked dozens of oil drums.

This was an informal filling station.

Hakim slowed the bus.

Three men in white and yellow robes appeared brandishing high-powered rifles. They stood in a line, stone-faced, menacing.

Issa got out of the bus, and the atmosphere was transformed. The armed men greeted him like a brother, embraced him, kissed him on both cheeks, and shook his hand vigorously, chattering all the time in an incomprehensible tongue that was presumably Teda.

Hakim got out next, and was introduced by Issa, whereupon he too was welcomed, though less demonstratively, being a collaborator but not of their tribe.

Tareq and Hamza followed.

The water tanker was evidence that there was no oasis here. What then was the reason for there to be a gas station, or for that matter anything at all, here in the middle of nowhere?

Abdul murmured to Kiah: "I think we have arrived at the border."

The passengers got off the bus. It was evening, and clearly this was where they would spend the night. There was only the one building, and that hardly worthy of the name.

One of the Toubou men began to refuel the bus from a metal drum.

The passengers went into the shelter and made themselves more or less comfortable for their stay. Abdul himself could not relax. They were surrounded by heavily armed men, all of whom were violent criminals. Anything was possible: kidnapping, rape, murder. There was no law here. Nobody was safe. And who would care if every passenger on the bus were murdered? The migrants were criminals too. Good riddance, people would say.

After a while, two teenage boys served a meal of stew with bread. Abdul thought the boys had probably done the cooking themselves. He suspected that the chewy meat was camel, but he did not ask. Afterward the boys cleaned up in a perfunctory way, leaving scraps on the ground. Men without women were slobs every-where, Abdul thought.

When it was dark he sneaked a look at the tracking device hidden in the sole of his boot. He checked it at least once a day to make sure the cocaine had not been removed from the bus and taken elsewhere. Tonight, as usual, the device reassured him.

When they all wrapped themselves in their blankets for sleep, Abdul sat up, eyes open, watching. He let his mind wander, and for hours he thought about his child-hood in Beirut, his teenage years in New Jersey, his college career as a mixed-martial-arts fighter, and his failed romance with Annabelle. Most of all he thought about the death of Nura, his baby sister. In the end, he thought, she was the reason he was here, in the Sahara Desert, staying awake all night to avoid being murdered.

Men like this had killed Nura. The armies of the civilized world were trying to wipe these men out. And he was a crucial part of that effort. If he survived, he would enable the armies of the US and its allies to in-flict a terrible defeat on the forces of evil.

In the small hours he saw one of the Toubou men go outside to piss. On coming back the man stood and looked contemplatively at the sleeping Kiah. Abdul stared until the tribesman felt his gaze and met his eye. They glared at one another for a long hostile moment. Abdul could imagine the calculations going on in that cruel brain. The man knew he would be able to over-power Kiah, and with luck she might not scream, for women were always blamed, and she would know that people were sure to think—or pretend to think—that she had lured him. But the man could see that Abdul was not going to look away. He could fight Abdul, but he was not sure of winning. He could fetch his rifle and shoot Abdul, but that would wake everyone.

In the end the man turned away and went back to his blanket.

Not long afterward, Abdul saw shadowy movement out of the corner of his eye. He turned to look. There was no sound, and it took a moment to locate what he had glimpsed. There was no moon, but the starlight was bright, as usual in the desert. He saw a creature with silvery fur moving so smoothly that it seemed to glide, and he suffered a moment of superstitious dread. Then he realized that something like a dog had entered the compound, a dog with a light-colored coat and black legs and tail. It crept silently past oblivious sleepers in their blankets. It was cautious but confident, as if it had been here before, a regular night visitor haunting this crude encampment in the wilderness. It had to be some kind of fox, and he saw that it had a pup at its heels. Mother and child, he thought, and he knew he was seeing something rare and special. When one of the bus passengers suddenly snored loudly, the vixen was alerted. Turning her head in the direction of the sound, she pricked up her ears, which were remarkably long and stood upright, almost like rabbit ears, and as Abdul stared, mesmerized, he realized this was a creature he had heard of but never seen: a bat-eared fox. She relaxed, understanding that the snorer was not going to wake. Then vixen and pup began to scavenge the ground, noiselessly swallowing scraps of food and licking dirty bowls. After three or four minutes they left as silently as they had arrived.

Soon afterward, dawn broke.

The migrants got up wearily. Today began their fourth week on the road, and every night was more or less uncomfortable. They rolled up their blankets, drank water, and ate dry bread. There was no water for washing. None of them except Abdul had been raised in houses with hot showers, but just the same they were used to regular washing, and they all found it depressing to be so dirty.

However, Abdul's spirits lifted as the bus drove away from the gas station. The Toubou must get paid a hefty fee for safe passage of the drugs and migrants, he thought, enough to motivate them to keep their word and hope for another shipment soon, instead of killing everyone and stealing everything.

As the sun rose, they left the mountains behind and entered a vast flat plain. After an hour Abdul realized that the sun had been consistently behind them. He stood up and went to the front of the bus. "Why are we heading west?" he said to Hakim.

"This is the way to Tripoli," said Hakim.

"But Tripoli is due north of here."

"This is the way!" Hakim repeated angrily.

"Okay," said Abdul, and he returned to his seat.

Kiah said: "What was that about?"

"Nothing," Abdul said.

It was not his mission to get to Tripoli, of course. He had to stay with the bus wherever it went. His mission was to identify the people running the smuggling, learn where they hid out, and pass that information to the Agency.

So he shut up, sat back, and waited to see what would happen next.

CHAPTER 19

The incident in the South China Sea could become a crisis, Chang Kai thought, if it was not handled carefully.

Satellite photos on Kai's desk showed an unknown vessel near the Xisha Islands, which Westerners called the Paracel Islands. Aircraft surveillance revealed it to be a Vietnamese oil exploration ship called the *Vu Trong Phung*. This was dynamite, but the fuse did not have to be lit.

Kai was familiar with the background, as was just about everybody in the Chinese government. Chinese boats had fished these waters for centuries. Now China had dumped millions of tons of earth and sand onto a group of uninhabitable rocks and reefs and then built military bases. Kai thought any fair-minded person would concede that this made the islands part of China.

No one would care much about it except that oil had been discovered beneath the seabed near the islands, and everybody wanted some. The Chinese considered the oil to be theirs and were not planning to share.

That was why the voyage of the *Vu Trong Phung* was a problem.

Kai decided to brief the foreign minister himself. His boss, Security Minister Fu Chuyu, had gone out of town, to Urumqi, capital of the Xinjian region, where millions of Muslims stubbornly adhered to their religion despite the Communist government's energetic efforts to repress it. Fu's absence gave Kai the opportunity to discuss the *Vu Trong Phung* quietly with Foreign Minister Wu Bai and agree on a diplomatic course of action to be suggested to President Chen. But when he arrived at the Foreign Ministry in Chaoyangmen Nandajie, he was dismayed to find General Huang there.

Huang Ling was short and wide, and looked like a box in his square-shouldered uniform. He was a proud member of the Communist old guard, like his friend Fu Chuyu. Also like Fu, he smoked all the time.

Huang's membership of the National Security Commission made him very powerful. Like the gorilla at the dinner party, he sat where he liked, and he had the right to muscle in anywhere in the Foreign Ministry. But who had told him about this meeting? Perhaps Huang had a spy in the Foreign Ministry—someone close to Wu. I must remember that, Kai thought.

Despite his irritation, Kai greeted Huang with the respect due to an older man. "We're privileged to have the benefit of your knowledge and expertise," he said insincerely. The truth was that he and Huang were on opposite sides in the rancorous ongoing struggle between the old school and the young reformers.

As they sat down, Huang immediately went on the attack. "The Vietnamese keep provoking us!" he exclaimed. "They know they have no right to our oil."

Huang had an assistant with him, and an aide sat close to Wu. There was no real need for assistants at this meeting, but Huang was too important to travel without an entourage, and Wu probably felt the need for defensive reinforcement. Kai had slightly lost face by showing up alone. Such bullshit, he thought.

However, it was true that the Vietnamese had twice already attempted to explore the seabed for oil. "I agree with General Huang," Kai said. "We must protest to the government in Hanoi."

"Protest?" Huang was scornful. "We have protested before!"

Kai said patiently: "And, in the end, they have always backed down, and withdrawn their ship."

"So why do they do it again?"

Kai suppressed a sigh. Everyone knew why the Vietnamese kept repeating their incursions. It was all right for them to withdraw when threatened, for that meant only that they had been bullied, but to stop trying would be like accepting that they had no right to the oil, and they were not willing to do that. "They're making a point," he said, simplifying.

"Then we must make a stronger point!" Huang leaned forward and tapped cigarette ash into a porcelain bowl on Wu's desk. The bowl was ruby red with a double-lotus pattern and probably worth ten million dollars.

Wu carefully picked up the delicate antique bowl, threw the tobacco ashes on the floor, and silently put the bowl at the other end of the desk, out of Huang's reach. Then he said: "What did you have in mind, General?"

Huang answered without hesitation. "We should sink the *Vu Trong Phung*. That will teach the Vietnamese a lesson."

Huang wanted to turn the heat up—as usual.

Wu said: "It's a bit drastic. But it might put an end to these repeated offenses."

Kai said: "There's a snag. My intelligence says that the Vietnamese oil industry is advised by American geologists. There may well be one or more Americans aboard the *Vu Trong Phung*."

Huang said: "So?"

"I merely ask whether we want to kill Americans."

"Undeniably," Wu said, "to sink a ship that has Americans aboard would escalate the incident."

That infuriated Huang. "For how long must we allow the motherfucking Americans to dictate what will happen in our territory?" he raged.

This was impolite. The strongest Chinese swear words all had to do with fucking someone's mother. Such language was not normally used in foreign policy discussions.

"On the other hand," Kai said mildly, "if we're going to start killing Americans there is more to consider than merely oil under the sea. We would need to gauge their likely response to the murders and prepare for it."

"Murders?" said Huang with rising indignation.

"That is how President Green would see it." Kai judged it was time to make a concession, to calm Huang down. He went on quickly: "I don't rule out the possibility of sinking the *Vu Trong Phung*. Let's keep that option open. But we would need to say it was a last resort. We should first send Hanoi a protest—"

Huang gave a derogatory snort.

"—then a warning, then a plain threat."

"Yes, that's the way to do it," said Wu. "A ladder."

"Then, after all that, if we sink the ship, it will be clear that we did everything we could to seek a peaceful solution."

Huang was not happy but he knew he was beaten. Making the best of it, he said: "Then let us at least station a destroyer in the vicinity ready to attack."

"Excellent proposal," said Wu, standing up to indicate that the meeting was over. "This is what I will suggest to President Chen."

Kai went down in the elevator with Huang, who was silent as they descended seven floors. Outside, Huang and his assistant were met by a gleaming black Hongqi limousine, while Kai got into a silver-gray Geely family sedan with Monk at the wheel.

Kai wondered whether he should pay more attention to these status symbols. The marks of affluence and prestige were more important in Communist countries than in the decadent West, where a guy in a battered leather jacket might be a billionaire. But Kai, like the American students he had met at Princeton, felt status symbols were a waste of effort. And today he had proved that, for the foreign minister had followed his advice, not Huang's. So maybe the assistant and the limousine did not count for much after all.

Monk pulled out into the traffic and headed for the Beautiful Films studio. This evening there was a party to celebrate the one hundredth episode of *Love in the Palace*. The show was a hit. It attracted a huge audience and the two leads were celebrities. Ting was paid a lot more than Kai—which was fine with him.

Kai took off his tie to look less formal among the actors. When he arrived the party was just getting under way on the soundstage with the sets all around, great and small rooms furnished and decorated in the lavish style of the late Qing Dynasty.

The actors had removed their heavy television makeup and changed out of their costumes, and now they flooded the room with a sea of color. In Kai's world the men wore suits to make themselves look serious, and the few women wore gray and dark blue to look like the men. Here it was different. The actors and actresses wore fashionable clothes in all colors.

Kai saw Ting across the room, looking cute in black jeans and a pink sweatshirt. She was enchanting the show's producer. Kai had taught himself not to be jealous. This kind of behavior was part of her job, and half the men she was flirting with were gay anyway.

Kai took a bottle of Yanjing beer. The technicians and the extras were guzzling free booze as fast as they could, but the actors were more circumspect, Kai noticed. Ting's co-star Wen Jin, who played the emperor, was talking seriously to the studio boss, a subtle piece of self-positioning. Jin was tall and handsome and authoritative, and the boss was a little awestruck, treating him somewhat as if he were in reality the all-powerful ruler he merely played. Other actors seemed more relaxed, chatting and laughing, but they were being charming to the producers and directors who had the power to give them jobs. Like so many parties, this one was work for a lot of the guests.

Ting spotted Kai, came to him, and gave him a long kiss on the mouth, probably to make sure everyone knew this was her husband and she loved him. Kai basked in it.

However, he could see that her happy party smile was masking a different emotion, and he knew her well enough to understand that something was troubling her. "What's wrong?" he said.

Just then the boss of the studio, wearing a black suit, got up on a chair to make a speech, and everyone went quiet. Ting murmured: "I'll tell you in a minute."

"Congratulations to the most talented group of people I have ever worked with!" said the boss, and they all cheered. "We have now filmed one hundred episodes of *Love in the Palace*—and they get better all the time!" This kind of hyperbole was normal in show business, Kai knew. They probably talked that way in Hollywood, he thought, though he had never been to

Los Angeles. "And I have some special good news," the boss went on. "We have now sold the show to Netflix!"

This really was good news, and there was an eruption of cheers.

There were fifty million Chinese people living in other countries, and many of them loved to watch television shows that came from their home country. The best Chinese-made shows were broadcast in the original Mandarin with subtitles in the local language, and made good money for the producers. The traffic was two-way, sort of. Some foreign-made shows were broadcast in China, to help people learning English, but more usually Chinese studios produced shameless imitations of hit American programs—without paying royalties to the creators. Hollywood complained bitterly about this. Kai, like most Chinese people, laughed at that. The West had exploited China mercilessly for hundreds of years, so Western protests against exploitation struck the Chinese as hilarious.

As soon as the boss stepped down, Ting spoke to Kai in a low voice. "I've been with one of the writers," she said.

"What's the matter?"

"My character is going to fall ill."

"With what?"

"A mystery ailment, but serious."

Kai did not immediately see the problem. "Big drama," he said. "Your enemies rejoicing spitefully, your friends in tears, your lovers kneeling at the bedside. Gives you the chance to be tragic."

"You've learned a lot about television scripts, but not about the politics of the studio," she said with a touch of irritation. "This is what they do when they're thinking of writing the character out."

"You think your character might die?"

"I asked the writer that, and he was evasive."

Kai had a dishonorable thought. If Ting left the show she might retire and have a baby. He dismissed the idea right away. She loved being a star and he would do everything he could to help her keep the job. If she retired it had to be her wish. He said: "But you're the most popular character."

"Yes. When that complaint was made, a month ago, about me criticizing the Party, I felt sure Wen Jin did it out of jealousy. But Jin doesn't have the power to have me written out. Something else is going on, and I don't know what."

"I think I do," said Kai. "This is probably nothing to do with you. It's directed at me. My enemies are trying to get at me through you."

"What enemies?"

"The usual ones: my boss, Fu Chuyu; General Huang, who I clashed with today; all the old guys with bad haircuts and bad suits. Let me have a word with Wang Bowen." Kai knew Wang, the official of the Communist Party responsible for supervising the studio. He looked around and saw Wang's balding head in the bedroom of the emperor's number one wife. "I'll see what I can find out," he said.

Ting squeezed his arm. "Thank you."

Kai made his way through the crowd. In Ting's world, all conflicts were imaginary, he reflected. She was not really going to die, it was only the fictional person she played. Perhaps that was what he liked about show business. In his world, the discussion of the *Vu Trong Phung* was about real people dying.

He buttonholed Wang Bowen.

Wang's shirt was crumpled, and what little hair he had needed cutting. Kai wanted to say: You represent the greatest Communist Party in the world—don't you think you should look smart? But he had a different mission. After a few pleasantries, he said: "I'm sure you know that Ting's character is about to fall ill."

"Yes, of course," said Wang, looking wary.

That confirmed it. Kai then said: "Perhaps fatally."

"I know," said Wang.

So Ting's suspicion was right.

Kai said: "I'm sure you've thought about the political issue that might be raised by that story line?"

Wang looked completely baffled and a bit scared. "I'm not sure what you mean."

"Medicine in the eighteenth century was primitive."

"Yes, of course," Wang said. "Almost barbaric."

"She could have a miraculous recovery, of course." Kai shrugged and smiled. "Miracles can happen in idol dramas."

"Yes, indeed."

"But you will have to take great care."

"I always do," said Wang, still bewildered and troubled. "But what, in particular, are you thinking of?"

"The danger of the story being seen as a satire on health care in contemporary China."

"Oh, my God!" This suggestion frightened Wang. "How could that happen?"

There was even a tremor in his voice, Kai noticed.

It was not difficult to scare such men. They were terrified of seeming unfaithful to the Party line. Kai said: "There are only two ways this story could go. Either the doctors are incompetent and she dies, or the doctors are incompetent but she survives by a miracle. Either way, the doctors are incompetent."

"But doctors knew nothing in the eighteenth century."

"All the same, I don't think the Party wants to see the subject of incompetent doctors raised in a popular television drama." In township health centers only 10 percent of doctors had formal medical education. "I think you know what I mean."

"Yes, I do, of course." Wang was now in more familiar territory, and he cottoned on fast. "Someone might post on social media: 'I had a lousy doctor once.' And another person could say: 'Me too.' And before you know it there's a national discussion about the competence of our doctors, with people reporting personal experiences on the internet."

Kai said: "You're a very intelligent thinker, Wang Bowen, and you have immediately seen the dangers."

"Yes, I have."

"The production team look to you for guidance on such questions, and you're well able to help them. It's a good thing the Party has you to rely on."

"It's always helpful to talk to you, Chang Kai. Thank you for your input."

Pride was satisfied. Wang had saved face. Kai went back to Ting. "I don't think they will use that story line," he said. "Wang has realized that it has unwelcome political implications."

"Oh, thank you, my darling," she said. "But do you think they'll try something else?"

"I'm hoping my enemies will decide that it's simpler to go straight for me, rather than attack me through you." He did not have high hopes of this. The use of threats to the family as a way of keeping people in line was a standard Communist Party tactic. It was how the government controlled Chinese people abroad. Threats to the individual himself were much less effective.

"People are starting to leave," Ting said. "Let's slip out."

They left the studio and got into the car, and Monk pulled away. Ting said: "We'll buy something nice for dinner and have a quiet evening."

"Sounds wonderful."

"We could get deep-fried rabbit ears. I know you love them."

"My favorite." Kai's phone sounded the bell-like tone that indicated a text message. He looked at the screen and saw that the caller was unidentified. He frowned: few people had his number, and even fewer were allowed to contact him anonymously. He read the message. It was one word: *IMMEDIATE*.

He knew right away that it was from General Ham in North Korea. It meant that Ham wanted a meeting as soon as possible.

Ham had been quiet for almost three weeks. Something important must have happened. The country's economic crisis was old news: there must have been a new development.

Spies often exaggerated the significance of their information in order to pump up their own importance, but Ham was not like that. Perhaps Supreme Leader Kang U-jung was about to test a nuclear warhead, which would infuriate the Americans. Perhaps he was planning some violation of the demilitarized zone between North and South Korea. He had many ways to make life difficult for the Chinese government.

There were three scheduled flights per day from Beijing to Yanji, and in an emergency Kai could use an air force plane. He called his office. His senior secretary, Peng Yawen, was still at her desk. He said: "What time is the first flight to Yanji tomorrow?"

"It's early. . . ." Kai heard her tapping her keyboard. "Six forty-five, and it's nonstop."

"Book me on it, please. What time does it land?"

"Eight fifty. Can I order a car to meet you on arrival at the Chaoyangchuan airport?"

"No." Kai preferred to be unobtrusive. "I'll get a taxi."

"Will you stay overnight?"

"Not if I can help it. Book me on the next flight back. We can change it if necessary."

"Yes, sir."

Kai hung up and calculated timings in his head. Meetings were held at Ham's unfinished house, unless otherwise agreed. Kai should be there at about half past nine.

He replied to Ham's message with one equally terse. It said simply: *9:30 a.m.*

A cold, hard rain was falling on the airport at Yanji next morning. Kai's plane had to circle for fifteen minutes while an air force jet landed. Civilian and military terminals shared the runway, but the military had priority—as always in China.

It was only mid-October, but Kai was glad of his winter coat as he stepped outside the terminal and queued for a taxi. As usual he gave the address of the Wumart supermarket. The driver had the radio tuned to a Korean-language station that was playing "Gangnam Style," a familiar K-pop classic. Kai sat back and enjoyed the music.

From the supermarket Kai walked to Ham's house. The site was a sea of mud and little work was getting done.

"I'm risking my life by seeing you," said Ham. "But I'm probably going to get killed in the next few days anyway."

This was startling. Kai said: "Are you serious?"

The question was superfluous. Ham was always serious. He said: "Let's get inside out of the rain."

They entered the unfinished building. A decorator and his apprentice were working in the grandchildren's bedrooms, using bright pastel colors, and the distinctive smell of fresh paint filled the house, pungent and caustic, but also pleasantly suggestive of newness and smartness.

Ham led Kai into the kitchen. On the counter stood an electric kettle, a jar of tea leaves, and some cups. Ham switched the kettle on and closed the door so that their conversation could not be overheard.

The house was cold. The two men kept their coats on. There were no chairs: they leaned on the newly installed kitchen counters.

Kai said impatiently: "What is it? What's the emergency?"

"This economic crisis is the worst since the North-South war."

Kai already knew that. He was partly responsible for it. "And . . . ?"

"The supreme leader has squeezed the military budget. The vice marshals protested, and he fired them all." Ham paused. "That was a mistake."

"So now the military is run by a new, younger generation of officers. And . . . ?"

"For a long time the military has had a strong ultra-nationalist reformist element. They want North Korea to be independent of China. We should decide our own fate, they say; we should not be China's lapdog. I hope I don't offend you, my friend."

"Not in the least."

"In order to sustain independence they would have to reform agriculture and industry, loosening the constraints of Communist Party control."

"As China did under Deng Xiaoping."

"Their views have always been muted—if they were openly critical of the supreme leader they wouldn't be officers very long. Such opinions are always stated in hushed voices, among trusted friends. But that means the supreme leader doesn't always know who his enemies are. And many of the new cohort of leaders secretly belong to the ultra-nationalist group. They think nothing will ever improve under Kang U-jung."

Kai began to see where he was going, and he was worried. "What are they going to do about it?"

"They're talking about a military coup."

"Hell." Kai was rocked. This was serious, much more so than a Vietnamese ship near the Xisha Islands or a United Nations resolution about arms sales. North Korea had to be stable: that was a keystone of China's defense. Any threat to Pyongyang was a threat to Beijing.

The kettle boiled and switched itself off. Neither man moved to make tea. "A coup when?" said Kai. "How?"

"The ringleaders are my colleagues, the officers at Yeongjeo-dong. They will certainly be able to take control of their own base."

"Which means they will have nuclear weapons."

"They consider that essential."

Worse and worse. "How much support do they have elsewhere?"

"I don't know. You must understand that I'm not part of the core group. They consider me a supporter, reliable but peripheral. I probably would be an enthusiastic ally, except that I chose my own route years ago."

"But if the conspirators are serious they must be spread fairly widely."

"I assume they're in touch with like-minded senior officers at other army bases—but I don't know for certain."

"So you probably don't know when they will make their move."

"Soon. The army is running out of food and fuel. Perhaps next week. Or it could be tomorrow."

Kai had to get this news to the Chinese president fast.

He considered giving the information to Beijing over the phone but immediately rejected that idea as a panic reaction. His calls to the Guoanbu were encrypted, but no code was unbreakable. Anyway, if the coup was today he was already too late, and if it was even as soon as tomorrow he had time to give warning. He would go back to Beijing immediately and report within hours.

He said: "You'd better give me some names."

Ham stood still for a long moment, looking down at his feet on the newly tiled floor. After a while he said: "The government of North Korea is brutal and incompetent, but that's not the problem. It's that they lie. Everything they say is propaganda, nothing they say is true. A man can be loyal to bad leaders, but not to dishonest ones. I have betrayed the leaders of my country because they lied to me."

Kai did not want to listen to this. He was in a hurry. But he sensed that Ham had to say it, so he remained silent.

"A long time ago I resolved to take care of my family and myself," Ham said in the heavy tones of an older man reflecting on the choices that had decided the course of his life. "I encouraged my daughter to move here, to China. I began to spy for you and accumulate money. Eventually I started to build my retirement home. In all of that, I did nothing that made me feel ashamed. But now . . ."

Kai said: "I get that. But you're following your destiny now. As you said, you made the key decisions long ago."

Ham ignored that. "Now I'm about to betray my comrades in arms, men who only want their country to be truly independent." He paused, then said sadly: "Men who have never lied to me."

"I understand how you feel," Kai said quietly. "But we have to stop this coup. We can't tell how it will end. We must not allow North Korea to spin out of control."

Still Ham hesitated.

Kai said: "What was the point of telling me about the plot, if not to put a stop to it?"

"My comrades will be executed."

"How many people do you think they would kill in their coup?"

"There would be casualties, of course."

"You bet. Thousands. Unless you and I prevent it by taking action today."

"You're right. We're all in the army, we signed up for battle. I must be going soft in my old age." Ham shook himself. "The rebel leader is the base commander, my immediate superior, General Pak Jae-jin."

Kai wrote the name in his phone's clipboard.

Ham gave him six more names, and Kai noted each one.

Then Kai said: "You'll return to Yeongjeo-dong today?"

"Yes. And I probably won't be able to come to China for the next few days at least."

"If you need to report to me, we may have to talk openly on the phone."

"I'll take precautions."

"What precautions?"

"I'll steal someone else's phone."

"And after you've called me?"

"I'll throw the phone in the river."

"Good enough." He shook Ham's hand. "Be careful,

my friend. Survive the emergency, then retire and come back here." He looked around the gleaming modern kitchen. "You deserve this."

"Thank you."

He left the site and walked toward the supermarket. On the way he called a cab. Stored in his phone he had a list of all the taxi firms in Yanji, and he had never used one twice. No driver got the chance to notice the pattern of his movements.

He dialed the Guoanbu and spoke to Peng Yawen. "Call the office of the president," he said.

"Yes, sir," she said crisply. Nothing flustered her. She probably could have done Kai's job.

"Say it's vital that I speak to him today. I have extraordinary intelligence that cannot be mentioned over the phone."

"Extraordinary intelligence, yes."

Kai could imagine her pencil racing across the page of her notebook. "Then call the air force and tell them I must have an immediate flight to Beijing. I'll be at the air base within half an hour."

"Mr. Chang, I'd better tell the president's office that you need an appointment this afternoon or this evening. You won't be back before then."

"Good thinking."

"Thank you, sir."

"As soon as the president's people give you a time when he can meet me, call the Foreign Ministry and say I would like Wu Bai to attend the meeting."

"Yes."

"Keep in touch with your progress."

"Of course."

Kai hung up. A minute later he arrived at the Wumart store to find a taxi waiting for him. The driver was watching a South Korean television drama on his phone.

Kai got into the back and said: "Longjing air base, please."

The headquarters of the Chinese government was a fifteen-hundred-acre compound known as Zhongnanhai. In the old heart of Beijing, it was adjacent to the Forbidden City and had once been the emperor's park. Kai's driver, Monk, went in by the south entrance, called the Gate of the New China. The view from the gate to the interior was hidden from prying eyes by a screen wall with the giant slogan SERVE THE PEOPLE written in the distinctive calligraphy of Mao Zedong, a stylish cursive hand that was recognized by a billion people.

The public had been admitted to Zhongnanhai for a brief period in the let-it-all-hang-out atmosphere of the Cultural Revolution, but now security was massive. The firepower at the Gate of the New China might have withstood an invasion. Helmeted troops with bullpup rifles stared menacingly while guards examined the underside of the car with mirrors. Even though Kai had visited the president before, his Guoanbu identity card was carefully scrutinized and his appointment double-checked. When his bona fides had at last been established, tire-shredding obstacles sank back into the tarmac so that the car could go forward.

Two lakes took up more than half the area of Zhongnanhai. The water bleakly reflected the gray sky. Just looking at it made Kai shiver. It would freeze in a hard winter. Kai's car circled the southernmost lake clockwise to the northwest quarter, where most of the land was. The buildings were traditional Chinese palaces and summer houses with swooping pagoda roofs, suitable to the pleasure garden this had once been.

The compound was the official home of members of the Politburo Standing Committee, including the president, but they were not obliged to live there, and some chose to stay in their homes outside. The grand reception rooms were now used for conferences.

Monk parked outside Qinzheng Hall, on the far side of the first lake. This was a new building on the site of what had once been an imperial palace. The office of the president was here. There were no helmeted infantry, but Kai noticed several burly young men in cheap suits that bulged with ill-concealed weapons.

In the lobby Kai stood at a desk where his face was compared with an image on record. He then stepped into a security booth and was scanned for concealed weapons.

On the other side he met the head of presidential security, who was on his way out. Wang Qingli was a crony of Kai's father, and they had met at Chang Jianjun's house. Qingli was part of the conservative old guard but smarter, perhaps because he was often with the president. He was well groomed, his hair brushed back and neatly parted, his navy blue suit well cut in the European style—in fact, very like the man he guarded. He greeted Kai with a smile and a handshake and escorted him up the stairs. He asked after Ting and said that his wife never missed an episode of *Love in the Palace*. Kai had heard that from a hundred men, but he did not mind: he was happy that Ting was so successful.

The building was furnished in a style Kai liked. Traditional Chinese sideboards and screens were carefully mixed with comfortable modern seating so that neither looked out of place. This contrasted with many of the other buildings, which were still stuck with the splayed-leg furniture and atom-inspired fabrics that had once been chic and now looked awkward and shabby.

In the president's waiting room Kai saw Foreign Minister Wu Bai, lounging on a couch with a glass of sparkling water. He was immaculate in a black suit with a herringbone weave, a gleaming white shirt, and a dark gray tie with a faint red stripe. "I'm glad you showed up," he said sarcastically. "In a few more minutes I would have had to tell President Chen that I don't know why the fuck I'm here."

He was Kai's superior, so Kai should have been here before him, not the other way around. "I just flew back from Yanji," Kai said. "I apologize for keeping you waiting."

"You'd better tell me what the hell you're up to."

Kai sat down and explained, and by the time he had finished Wu's attitude had been transformed. "We have to act on this right away," he said. "The president will have to call Pyongyang and warn the supreme leader. It could already be too late."

An aide appeared and invited them to follow him into the president's office. As they walked, Wu said: "I will open the discussion." That was correct protocol: the spymaster served the politician. "I'll tell him that a coup is being plotted, and you will give him such details as we have."

"Very good, sir," said Kai. It was important to defer to older men. Anything else would offend both Wu and Chen.

They went in. The president's room was wide and long, with a large window looking out over the water. President Chen in real life was a bit different from the formal portraits that hung in so many government offices. He was quite short and had a slightly protruding belly that did not appear in photographs. But he was more friendly than his public image suggested. "Minister Wu!" he said amiably. "A pleasure to see you. How is Mrs. Wu? I know she had a minor medical procedure."

"The operation was a success and she has fully re-covered, Mr. President, thank you for asking."

"Chang Kai—I knew you as a child, and now every time I see you I want to say how much you've grown."

Kai laughed, though Chen had made the same joke the last time they met. The president took care to be af-fable. It was his policy to be everyone's friend. Kai wondered whether he had read Machiavelli, who said it was better to be feared than loved.

"Sit down, please. Lei will bring you tea." Kai had not noticed the silent middle-aged woman in the back-ground who now poured tea into small cups. "So," Chen went on, "tell me what this is all about."

As agreed, Wu gave him the headlines and then in-vited Kai to fill in the details. Chen listened in silence, twice making a note with a gold Travers fountain pen. The woman called Lei brought each person a delicate little cup of fragrant jasmine tea. When Kai had fin-ished, Chen said: "And this comes from a source you can trust."

"He's a general in the Korean People's Army and he has been giving us reliable information for many years, sir."

Chen nodded. "By its nature a plot such as this is secret, so we're unlikely to get confirmation. But it might be right, and that dictates our response. Your source doesn't know the strength of the rebels outside of Yeongjeo-dong?"

"No. Perhaps we may assume that the ringleaders at least believe they have strong support. They wouldn't move otherwise."

"Agreed." Chen thought for a moment. "As I recol-lect, there are eighteen military bases in North Korea—is that right?"

Kai glanced at Wu, who clearly did not have that

information at his fingertips. Kai said: "Yes, Mr. President, that's exact."

"Twelve of them are missile bases and two of those have nuclear weapons."

"Yes."

"It's the missile bases that really count, and the nuclear ones that are paramount."

Chen had gotten to the heart of the matter in no time, Kai reflected.

Chen looked at Wu, who nodded.

Chen said: "And your recommendation?"

Wu said: "At all costs we have to prevent the destabilization of the North Korean government. I think we should warn Pyongyang immediately. If they act now they could crush the rebellion before it gets started."

Chen nodded. "Much as we'd all like to see the back of Supreme Leader Kang, he's better than chaos. As the proverb says, if you're offered two bad apples you pick the least rotten one. And that's Kang."

"That would be my advice," said Wu.

Chen picked up the phone. "Call Pyongyang," he said. "I need to speak to Kang before the end of the day. Tell them it's most urgent." He put the phone down, then stood up. "Thank you, comrades. You've done a good day's work."

Kai and Wu shook hands and left the room.

"Well done," Wu said as they walked down the stairs.

"Let's hope we're in time," said Kai.

Kai's phone rang the next morning while he was shaving. The caller ID was in Korean. Kai could not read or speak Korean but he guessed who it was, and he tensed. "So soon?" he said aloud, then he picked up the call.

"It's started," said a voice that he recognized as belonging to General Ham.

"What's happened?" Kai put down his electric shaver and picked up a pencil.

Ham spoke quietly, obviously concerned about being overheard. "Just before dawn Yeongjeo-dong was raided by the Special Operation Force," he said.

He was talking about the elite division of the Korean People's Army.

Ham went on: "I assume this was the supreme leader's response to information from Beijing."

"Good," said Kai. Kang had acted fast. "And . . . ?"

"They attempted to take over the base and arrest the senior officers."

Kai did not like the sound of that. "Attempted, you say?"

"There was a shootout." Ham reported concisely but calmly, as he had been trained. "The rebels were on home ground, with easy access to all the resources of the base. The attackers arrived in vulnerable helicopters and were not familiar with the territory. Also, I think they were surprised by the number and strength of the rebels. Anyway, the Special Operation Force was repelled and the rebels are now in complete control of the base."

"Hell," said Kai. "We were too late."

Ham went on: "Most of the attackers are dead or locked up—a few got away. I took this phone from a dead one. Officers that are not supporters of the conspiracy have been imprisoned also."

"This is bad news. What's next?"

"The two missile bases nearest to here both have rebel groups. They have been told to move now, and reinforcements have been sent to them to make sure.

There may be other rebellions around the country—we haven't heard yet. The one the ringleaders are most interested in is the other nuclear missile facility, Sangnam-ni, but there's no word yet."

"Call me as soon as you know more."

"I'll steal a phone from another corpse."

Kai hung up and looked out of the window. It had been daylight for only an hour or so, and already things were going wrong. It was shaping up to be a long day.

He left brief messages for President Chen and Minister Wu, simply saying what had happened and promising more details shortly. Then he called the office.

He reached the overnight manager, Fan Yimu. "There's been a coup attempt in North Korea," he said. "Result undecided. Get the team in as soon as possible. I'll be there in less than an hour." It was a Sunday, but his staff would have to cancel their plans to wash their cars and do their laundry.

He finished shaving in a hurry.

Ting came into the bathroom naked, yawning. She had heard his half of the conversation. Speaking English, she said: "We got a situation."

Kai smiled. She must have heard that phrase in a movie or something. "I have to skip breakfast," he said in Mandarin.

She replied with another Americanism. "Knock yourself out."

Kai laughed. She had an ear for this kind of thing. "In the middle of a crisis, you can make me smile," he said.

"You bet your ass." She wiggled her own at him, then stepped into the shower.

Kai dressed quickly in his office clothes. By the time he was ready, Ting was rubbing her hair dry. He kissed her good-bye.

"I love you," she said in Mandarin. "Call me later."

Kai went out. On the street the air quality was poor. It was still early but the traffic was heavy, and the taste of car exhaust was in his mouth.

In the car he thought about the day ahead. This was the most important crisis since he had become vice minister for international intelligence. The entire government apparatus would be looking to him for information on what was happening.

After half an hour of thought, still stuck in traffic, he called the office again. By this time Peng Yawen was at her desk. "Three things," he said. "Get someone to check the signals intelligence from Pyongyang." The Guoanbu had long ago broken into North Korea's secure communications system, which used Chinese-made equipment. They did not have access to everything, of course, but what was available would be useful. "Second, make sure someone is listening to the news on South Korean radio. They're often the first to find out what's happening in the north."

"Jin Chin-hwa is already doing that, sir."

"Good. Third, see if we can arrange for our people at the Chinese embassy in Pyongyang to attend our planning meeting remotely."

"Yes, sir."

Kai reached the Guoanbu campus at last. He took off his coat as he went up in the elevator.

He was waylaid in his outer office by Jin Chin-hwa, who was a Chinese citizen of Korean ancestry, young and eager and, more important, fluent in the Korean language. Jin was casually dressed today, as was permitted for weekend working, in black jeans and an Iron Maiden hoodie. He had an audio bud in one ear. "I'm listening to KBS1," he said.

"Good." Kai knew that this was the principal news

channel of the Korean Broadcasting System, based in Seoul, the capital of South Korea.

Jin went on: "They're saying there has been an 'incident' at a military base in North Korea. They cite unconfirmed rumors that a detachment of the Special Operation Force attempted to arrest a group of anti-government conspirators in a dawn raid."

Kai said: "Can we put on North Korean TV news in the conference room?"

"North Korean television doesn't start broadcasting until the afternoon, sir."

"Oh, shit, I'd forgotten that."

"But I'm monitoring Pyongyang FM, the radio station, switching between that and KBS1."

"Good. We'll gather in the conference room in half an hour. Tell the others."

"Yes, sir."

Kai went to his desk and reviewed the information that had come in so far. There was nothing at all on social media, because North Koreans were forbidden access to the internet. Signals intelligence confirmed what was already known or suspected. The embassy in Pyongyang had nothing.

Ting phoned. "I think I've done something wrong," she said.

"What?"

"Do you have a friend called Wang Wei?"

There were hundreds of thousands of men in China called Wang Wei, but as it happened Kai did not have a friend of that name. "No, why?"

"I was afraid of that. I was learning a long speech, and I picked up the phone. He asked for you and I told him you'd gone to the office. I was distracted and I just didn't think. After I hung up I realized I shouldn't have told him anything. I'm so sorry."

"No harm done," he said. "Don't do it again, but don't worry about it."

"Oh, I'm glad you're not mad at me."

"Is everything else all right?"

"Yes, I'm about to leave for the market. I thought I'd make dinner tonight."

"Wonderful. See you later."

The call had been from a spy, probably American or European. Kai's home phone number was secret, but spies discovered secrets; it was their job. And the caller had learned something. He now knew that Kai had gone to the office on a Sunday morning. That told him there must be some kind of crisis.

Kai went to the conference room. His five senior men were there, plus four North Korea specialists, including Jin Chin-hwa, and the Guoanbu office in Pyongyang was attending remotely. Kai briefed them on the events of the last twenty-four hours, and each individual reported what information he had been able to glean in the past hour.

Then Kai said: "For today and probably the next few days it's imperative that we have real-time information about what's happening in North Korea. Our president and our entire foreign policy establishment will be following events minute by minute, and considering whether China needs to intervene, and if so what form the intervention will take—and they will be depending on us for reliable data.

"All sources of intelligence must be milked. Satellite reconnaissance must focus on the military bases. Signals intelligence must monitor all the North Korean traffic we can access. Any sudden flurry of phone calls and messages could indicate a rebel attack.

"The Guoanbu office in the Chinese embassy at Pyongyang will be working twenty-four/seven, as will our consulate at Chongjin. They ought to be able to

provide some information. And don't forget the dias-
pora. There are several thousand Chinese citizens
living in North Korea—some businessmen, a few students, plus people married to Koreans. We should have
phone numbers for all of them. This is the moment for
them to prove their patriotism. I want every one
called."

Jin interrupted him. "Pyongyang is making an announcement." He translated as he listened. "They say
they have arrested a number of American-controlled
saboteurs and traitors at a military base this morning. . . . They don't say which base . . . nor how many
people were arrested. . . . Nothing about violence or
gunfire. . . . And that's it. The announcement is over."

"This is surprising," Kai said. "They normally take
hours or even days to respond to events."

Jin said: "This has got the Pyongyang government
agitated."

"Agitated?" said Kai. "I think they're more than agitated. I think they're scared. And you know what? So
am I."

DEFCON 4

ABOVE NORMAL READINESS.

HEIGHTENED INTELLIGENCE WATCH AND
STRENGTHENED SECURITY MEASURES.

CHAPTER 20

President Green hated the cold. Growing up in Chicago, she might have gotten used to it, but she never had. As a little girl she had loved school but hated getting there in the winter. One day, she had vowed, she would live in Miami, where, she had heard, you could sleep on the beach.

She had never lived in Miami.

She put on a big puffy down coat to walk from the Residence to the West Wing at seven o'clock on Sunday morning. As she passed through the colonnade, she thought about sex. Gerry had felt amorous last night. Pauline liked sex, but she was not driven by it, not since her early twenties. Gerry was the same, and their sex life had always been pleasant but undramatic, like the rest of their relationship.

Not anymore, she thought sadly.

Something had gone wrong in her feeling toward Gerry, and she thought she knew why. In the past she had always felt the reassuring sense that he had her back. They had occasionally disagreed, but they had never undermined one another. Their arguments were not angry because their conflicts did not run deep.

Until now.

Pippa was at the bottom of it. Their cute little baby had turned into a mutinous adolescent, and they could not agree on what to do. It was almost a cliché: there were probably articles about it in the women's magazines that Pauline never read. She had heard that marital rows about how to raise the children were said to be the worst.

Gerry did not just disagree with Pauline, he argued that the problem was her fault. "Pippa needs to see more of her mother," he kept saying, when he knew perfectly well it was not possible. It made her feel sorry for them both.

Until now they had faced issues together and taken joint responsibility. She had been on Gerry's side, and he on hers. Now he seemed to be against her. And that was what she had been thinking about last night, as Gerry lay on top of her in the four-poster bed that stood in the Queen's Bedroom, once used by Queen Elizabeth II of England. Pauline had felt no affection, no intimacy, no arousal. Gerry had taken longer than usual, and she guessed that meant he too was feeling estranged.

Pippa would get through this phase, Pauline knew, but would the marriage survive? When she asked herself that question she felt despair.

She arrived at the Oval Office shivering. Chief of Staff Jacqueline Brody was waiting for her, looking as if she had been up for hours. "The national security advisor, the secretary of state, and the director of national intelligence are hoping to speak to you urgently," Jacqueline said. "They've brought the CIA's deputy director for analysis."

"Gus and Chess, the DNI, and a CIA nerd, while it's still dark on a Sunday morning? Something's up."

Pauline took off her coat. "Show them in right away." She sat at the desk.

Gus wore a black blazer and Chess a tweed jacket, Sunday clothes. The director of national intelligence, Sophia Magliani, was more formal in a short jacket and black pants. The CIA man looked like a street person, in jogging pants and well-used running shoes with a peacoat. Sophia introduced him as Michael Hare, and Pauline recalled that she had heard of him: he spoke both Russian and Mandarin, and his nickname was Micky Two-Brains. She shook his hand and said: "Thank you for coming to see me."

"Morning," he said blearily.

He gave the impression of having less than one brain, Pauline thought.

Sophia noticed her cool reaction. "Michael has been up all night," she said apologetically.

Pauline did not comment. "Sit down, everyone," she said. "What's going on?"

Sophia said: "It might be best if Michael explains."

"My opposite number in Beijing is a man called Chang Kai," Hare began. "He's vice minister for foreign intelligence at the Guoanbu, the Chinese secret service."

Pauline did not have time for a lengthy narrative. "You can cut to the chase, Mr. Hare," she said.

"This is the chase," he said, showing a touch of irritation.

Such a sharp reply to the president came close to rudeness. Hare was charmless, to say the least. There were people in the intelligence community who thought all politicians were fools, especially by comparison with themselves, and it seemed that Hare was one of them.

Gus spoke in his most emollient voice. "Madam

President, if I may say so, I think you will find the narrative helpful."

If Gus said so, it was true. "All right. Carry on, Mr. Hare."

Hare continued as if he had hardly noticed the interruption. "Yesterday Chang flew to Yanji, a town near the border with North Korea. We know this because the CIA station in Beijing has hacked the airport computer system."

Pauline frowned. "He used his own name?"

"For the flight out, yes. However, when he came back he either used a false name or took an unscheduled flight; either way his return doesn't appear in the system."

"Perhaps he didn't come back."

"But he did. This morning at eight thirty Beijing time, one of our agents there called his home, posing as a friend, and Chang's wife said he'd gone to the office."

Pauline was interested, despite her dislike of Hare. "So," she said thoughtfully, "yesterday he made a trip that at first seemed routine but became either urgent or high security or both, and he went to his office early this morning, a Sunday. Why? What else do you know?"

"I'm getting to that." Again the irritation. He was like a college professor who did not like his lecture to be interrupted by students with foolish questions. Sophia looked embarrassed but did not say anything. Hare went on: "Earlier today South Korean radio reported that North Korea's elite Special Operation Force had raided an unnamed military base in an attempt to seize antigovernment protestors. Later, Pyongyang announced that a number of American-controlled traitors had been arrested at a military base, again not identified."

"This is partly our doing," Pauline said.

Chess spoke for the first time. "Because we tightened up sanctions on North Korea, after the Chinese defeated our resolution on arms sales."

"Which damaged the North Korean economy."

"That's the purpose of sanctions," Chess said defensively. It had been his idea.

"And it worked better than we expected," Pauline said. "The North Korean economy was weak in the first place, and we made it fall off a cliff."

"If we didn't want that to happen we shouldn't have taken the action."

Pauline did not intend for Chess to see this as an attack on him. "I made the decision, Chess. And I'm not saying it was a wrong move. But none of us thought it would trigger a rebellion against the Pyongyang government . . . if that's what this is." She turned back to the CIA analyst. "Carry on, please, Mr. Hare. You were saying that there was a conflict in the reports over whether any arrests had actually taken place."

"A conflict that was resolved two hours ago—late afternoon Korean time, predawn here," said Hare. "A reporter for KBS1, the most important South Korean news channel, is in touch with the so-called traitors—who, by the way, are not American controlled."

"More's the pity," Gus interjected.

"The station broadcast an interview, filmed over the internet, with a North Korean army officer who claimed to be one of the rebels. He was not named, but we have since identified him as General Pak Jae-jin. He said that no one had been arrested, the Special Operation Force had been driven off, and the rebels were in control of the base."

"Did the report say which base?"

"No. And there are no satellite pictures of this morning's skirmish, because it's winter and there's cloud cover over the entire region. But he was filmed in the open air, with buildings behind him, so we compared what we could see with existing photographs and other information about North Korean army bases, and we were able to establish that this one is called Sangnam-ni."

"That name rings a bell," Pauline said. "Isn't it a nuclear missile base?" Enlightenment dawned. "Oh, Christ," she said. "The rebels have nuclear weapons."

Gus said: "That's why we're here."

Pauline was silent for a few moments while the news sunk in. Then she said: "This is very serious. Actions? I think my first move should be to speak to President Chen of China."

The others nodded.

She looked at her watch. "It's not yet eight p.m. in Beijing, he won't be asleep. Jacqueline, please book that call." The chief of staff went into the next room to make the arrangements.

Chess said: "What are you going to say to Chen?"

"That's the next big question. What do you suggest?"

"First of all, he could give us his assessment of the danger."

"I'll certainly ask. He should have more information than we do. He must have talked to Supreme Leader Kang at least once in the last twelve hours."

Hare said scornfully: "He won't have gotten much out of Kang. They hate each other. But Chen's intelligence service has been working hard all day, just as we've been doing all night, and they're just as smart as we are, so he should have learned something from his man Chang Kai. Whether he'll share it with you is another question."

That did not require a response from Pauline. She said: "What else, Chess?"

"Ask him what he plans to do about it."

"What are his options?"

"He could propose a joint Chinese and North Korean attack force to retake the Sangnam-ni base for the Pyongyang government in a lightning raid."

Hare spoke again, uninvited. "Kang won't go for that," he said dismissively.

Unfortunately, Pauline thought, he's right. She said: "All right, Mr. Hare, what can the Chinese president do, in your opinion?"

"Nothing."

"And what makes you think that?"

"I don't think it, I know it. Anything the Chinese do will escalate the situation."

"Regardless of that, I'm going to ask him if there's anything the United States or the international community can do that he would find helpful."

Hare said: "So long as you first say: 'I do not wish to interfere in the internal affairs of another country, but . . .' The Chinese are obsessive about that."

Pauline did not need a lesson in diplomacy from him. "Mr. Hare, I think we can let you go and get some sleep."

"Yeah, sure." Hare slouched to the door and went out.

Sophia said: "I apologize for his manners. No one likes him, but he's too smart to fire."

Pauline had no interest in discussing Hare. She said: "We need to make a decision about putting the US military on alert."

Gus said: "Yes, ma'am. Right now everything is on DEFCON 5, normal readiness."

"We should raise that to DEFCON 4."

"Heightened intelligence watch and strengthened security measures."

"I don't like doing this, because the media overreact, but in this instance it's inevitable."

"I agree. And we may need to move South Korea up to DEFCON 3. Last time it was used in the US was on 9/11."

"Remind me, what's the difference between four and three?"

"Crucially, in DEFCON 3 the air force must be ready to mobilize in fifteen minutes."

Jacqueline came back in. "The translators are in place, and we're getting Chen on video."

Pauline looked at her computer screen. "That's quick."

"I guess he was expecting your call."

Pauline scribbled notes on a pad—*Sangnam-ni, nuclear, Special Operation Force, no arrests, regional stability, international stability*—then there was a chime and Chen appeared. He was in his office, seated at a vast desk, with China's red-and-yellow flag over his shoulder and a painting of the Great Wall behind him.

Pauline said: "Good day to you, Mr. President, and thank you for taking my call."

Through the interpreter he replied: "I'm glad to have the opportunity to talk to you."

In informal situations Chen had chatted to Pauline in English quite comfortably, but in a conversation such as this they had to be absolutely sure they were not misunderstood.

Pauline said: "What's going on in Sangnam-ni?"

"I'm afraid an economic crisis has been caused by the American sanctions."

They were United Nations sanctions, and there would have been no crisis if not for the lousy Communist economic system, Pauline thought, but she did not say it.

Chen continued: "In response, China is sending emergency economic aid to North Korea in the form of rice, pork, and gasoline."

So we're the bad guys and you're the good guys,

Pauline thought; yeah, yeah, yeah. But let's get down to business. "We understand that the Special Operation Force was defeated with no arrests. Doesn't that tell us that the rebels are in control of nuclear weapons?"

"I cannot confirm that."

Which means yes, Pauline thought, and her heart sank. Chen would have denied it if he possibly could. "If it turns out to be true, Mr. President, what will you do?"

"I will not interfere in the internal affairs of another country," Chen said sternly. "This is a cardinal principle of Chinese foreign policy."

It was cardinal bullshit, Pauline thought, but she put her point more subtly. "If a rogue group has nuclear weapons, there is surely a threat to regional stability, which must concern you."

"At present there is no threat to regional stability."

Stone wall.

Pauline tried a shot in the dark. "What if the rebellion spreads to other military bases in North Korea? Sangnam-ni is not the only nuclear facility there."

Chen hesitated for several moments, then said: "Supreme Leader Kang has taken firm action to prevent such a development."

That statement, woodenly formulaic, actually contained a hidden revelation, but Pauline suppressed her excitement. She decided to bring the conversation to a close. Chen had been closemouthed, but—as often happened—he had inadvertently told her something she needed to know. She said: "Thank you for your help, Mr. President. As always, a conversation with you is a pleasant duty. Let us stay in close touch."

"Thank you, Madam President."

The screen went dark and Pauline looked at Gus and Chess. Both looked animated. They had drawn the conclusion too.

She said: "If the rebellion was confined to one base, he would have said so."

"Exactly," said Gus. "But Kang took firm action, which means that firm action was called for, because the rebellion has spread."

Chess agreed. "He must have sent troops to the base at Yongdok, where nuclear warheads are stored. And rebels there must have fought back. Chen did not say that government forces had prevailed, he said merely that Kang had taken steps. That suggests the situation is unresolved."

Gus said: "Kang is focused on the most important bases—but those are the places the rebels have targeted too."

Pauline judged it was time to move on. "I'd like more information. Sophia, make sure our signals intelligence people are reading everything we can pick up from North Korea. Gus, check our latest information on North Korea's nukes—how many, how big, things like that. Chess, talk to the foreign minister of South Korea in case she has insights—she may know things we've missed. And I need to put out some kind of announcement about this—Jacqueline, get Sandip in here, please."

They all left. Pauline thought about how best to explain the situation to the American people. Everything she said would be misrepresented and distorted by James Moore and his cheerleaders in the media. She needed to be crystal clear.

Sandip appeared a couple of minutes later, padding into the room in his sneakers. Pauline briefed him on Sangnam-ni.

"This can't be kept under wraps," he said. "The South Korean media are too good. Everything will come out."

"I agree. So I need to show Americans that their government is on top of the situation."

"Will you say that we are ready for nuclear war?"

"No, that's too alarmist."

"James Moore will ask the question."

"I can say we're ready for anything."

"Much better. But tell me what you're actually doing."

"I spoke to the president of China. He's concerned but says there's no danger of regional destabilization."

"What action is he taking?"

"Sending aid to North Korea—food and fuel—because he thinks the economic crisis is the real problem."

"Okay, practical if undramatic."

"It won't do any harm, at least."

"What else are you doing?"

"I don't think this will have immediate repercussions for the US, but as a precaution I'm raising the alert level to DEFCON 4."

"It's all very low-key."

"That's how I want it."

"When would you like to talk to the media?"

She looked at her watch. "Is ten o'clock too soon? I want to be out in front on this."

"Ten it is."

"Okay."

"Thank you, Madam President."

Pauline enjoyed press conferences. By and large, the White House correspondents were intelligent men and women who understood that politics was rarely simple. They asked her challenging questions and she tried to

give them honest answers. She enjoyed the cut and
thrust of debate when it was genuinely about the issues
and not just posturing.

She had seen historic photos of past press conferences, when the correspondents were all men in suits
with white shirts and ties. Now the group included
women, and the dress code was more relaxed, with the
TV crews in sweatshirts and sneakers.

Pauline had been nervous at her very first press conference, twenty years ago. She had been a Chicago city
alderman. Chicago was a Democratic city, and
Republican aldermen were almost unknown, so she
had run as an independent. Because of her record as a
champion gymnast, she had become an advocate for
better athletic facilities, and that was what her first
press conference had been about. Her nervousness had
not lasted long. As soon as she'd gotten into discussion
with the journalists, she'd relaxed, and before long she
had made them laugh. After that she was never nervous again.

Today's event went according to plan. Sandip had
told the correspondents that Pauline would not answer
questions about her daughter, and that if anyone asked
such a question, the press conference would immediately come to an end. Pauline half expected that
someone would break the rule, but no one did.

She talked about her conversation with Chen, she
told them about DEFCON 4, and she finished with the
words she wanted them to take home: "America is
ready for anything."

She answered questions from the senior correspondents and then, with just a minute or two left, she
called on Ricardo Alvarez from the hostile *New York
Mail*.

He said: "Earlier today James Moore was asked
about the crisis in North Korea and he said that in

these circumstances America needs to be led by a man. What do you say to that, Madam President?"

There was a chuckle around the room, though Pauline noticed that the women were not laughing.

The question did not surprise her. Sandip had told her about Moore's misogynist remark. She had said it was a blunder that would deprive Moore of many women's support, and Sandip had said: "My mother thinks he's right." Not all women were feminists.

Anyway, she did not want to get into a discussion with the press corps about whether a woman could be a war leader. That would allow Moore to define the terms of the argument. She needed to bring it back to her own territory.

She thought for a long moment. An idea came to her, but it was a little off-the-wall. However, she decided to go with it. She leaned forward and spoke in a more informal voice. "Have you folks noticed," she said, "that James Moore never does this?" With a broad sweep of her hand she indicated the correspondents massed in the room. "Here I have the networks and the cable channels, the broadsheets and the toxic tabloids, the liberal and the conservative media."

She paused and pointed at the questioner. "Right now I'm responding to a question from Ricky, whose paper has never had a good word to say about me. What a contrast with Mr. Moore! Do you know when he last gave an in-depth interview on network television? The answer is never. He has never facilitated a profile of himself in *The Wall Street Journal* or *The New York Times* or any of the mainstream newspapers, to the best of my knowledge. He takes questions only from his friends and supporters. Ask yourself why that is."

She paused again. She had thought of a zinger to finish with. Did she want to be aggressive? Yes, she decided. She resumed before anyone could interrupt. "I'll tell you what I think. James Moore is scared. He's frightened that he won't be able to defend his policies against a serious interrogator. And that brings me right back to your question, Ricky." Here comes the zinger, she thought. "When the chips are down, do you want America to be led by Timid Jim?"

She paused again, briefly, then said: "Thank you, everyone." And she left the room.

Pauline had dinner with Gerry and Pippa in the Residence that Sunday evening, looking out at the streetlights of Washington, while people in Beijing and Pyongyang were getting up in the dark on a winter Monday morning.

The Residence cook had made curried beef, Pippa's new favorite dish. Pauline ate the rice and the salad. Food did not excite her, nor did booze. Whatever was put in front of her, she would eat or drink a little.

She asked Pippa: "How are you getting on with Ms. Judd now?"

"Old Judders is off my case, thank God," Pippa said.

If Pippa was no longer attracting the attention of the school principal, it probably meant that her behavior had gotten better. It was the same at home: there had been no more rows. Pauline thought the improvement might be due to the threat of home schooling. Regardless of how much Pipa rebelled, school was the center of her social life. Pauline's talk of a tutor had served as a reality check.

Gerry said irritably: "Amelia Judd is not old and she doesn't judder. She's forty, and an extremely competent and capable woman."

Pauline looked at him in mild surprise. He did not often reprimand Pippa, and this was an odd issue to choose. The thought crossed her mind that Gerry might have developed a little crush on "Amelia." Perhaps it was not surprising. The head teacher was an authoritative woman in a leadership role, like Pauline but ten years younger. A more recent edition of the same book, Pauline thought cynically.

Pippa said to her father: "You wouldn't like Judders so much if it was you she was trying to push around."

There was a tap at the door and Sandip came in. It was unusual for staffers to disturb family meals at the Residence; in fact it was forbidden except in an emergency. Pauline said: "What's up?"

"I'm very sorry to interrupt, Madam President, but two things have happened in the last few minutes. CBS has announced a long interview with James Moore, live at seven thirty."

Pauline looked at her watch. It was a few minutes after seven.

Sandip said: "He's never done an interview with network television."

"As I pointed out this morning," Pauline said.

"It's a scoop for CBS, which is why they're rushing it."

"Do you think he was stung by my calling him Timid Jim?"

"I'm sure of it. A lot of the broadcasters used those words in their reports of the press conference. That was very clever of you. It's forced Moore to try to prove you wrong, and for that he has to stick his neck out."

"Good."

"He'll probably make a fool of himself on CBS. All they have to do is put up an interviewer with a brain."

Pauline was not so sure. "He may surprise us. He's slippery. Pinning him down is like trying to pick up a live fish with one hand."

Sandip nodded. "In politics, the only thing that's certain is that nothing is certain."

That made Pippa laugh.

"I'll watch the interview here, then come over to the West Wing," Pauline said to Sandip. "What was the second thing?"

"The media in East Asia have woken up, and South Korean television is saying that the rebels in North Korea now have control of both nuclear bases and two regular missile bases, plus an unknown number of ordinary military bases."

Pauline was perturbed. "This is no longer just an incident," she said. "This is a real rebellion."

"Do you want to say anything about it?"

She considered that. "I don't think so," she said. "I've raised the alert level, and I've told Americans that we're ready for anything. I see no reason to add to that message, for now."

"I agree, but perhaps we should talk again after we see Moore's interview."

"Of course."

"Thank you, Madam President."

Sandip left. Gerry and Pippa both looked thoughtful. They often heard hot political news, but this was more dramatic than usual. The family finished dinner in silence.

Just before seven thirty Pauline went into the former Beauty Salon and turned on the TV set there. Pippa followed her, but Gerry said: "I can't bear to spend half an hour in the company of that fool Moore," and disappeared.

Pauline and Pippa sat on the couch. Before the interview began, Pauline asked Pippa: "What does Ms. Judd look like?"

"Small and blond, with big tits."

So much for nonbinary gender descriptions, Pauline thought.

The interview took place in the studio, on a set that had been dressed to look like an anonymous lounge, with lamps and side tables and flowers in a vase. Moore did not look at ease.

He was introduced by an experienced television journalist, Amanda Gosling. She was perfectly groomed, as they all were. She had carefully styled blond hair and a blue-gray dress that showed her perfect calves, but she was also smart and tough. She would not give Moore an easy ride.

Moore had moderated his appearance. His jacket still had Western stitching, but he wore a white dress shirt and a regular tie.

Gosling began sympathetically. She asked him about his career as a baseball star, then a commentator, and finally a radio host. Pippa got impatient, saying: "Who cares about this crap?"

"She's softening him up," Pauline said. "Just wait."

Gosling quickly got around to the issue of abortion. "Some critics say that your policy on abortion means that women will be forced to have babies they don't want. Do you think that's fair?"

"No one forces a woman to get pregnant," he said.

Pippa said: "What? What?"

It was obviously untrue, but Gosling did not say so. "I'd like to make sure we get your views perfectly clear for our audience," she said with sweet reasonableness.

Pippa said: "Good idea—then everyone will see what an asshole he is."

Gosling went on: "In your opinion, when a husband asks his wife for physical intimacy, does she have the right to say no?"

"A man has needs," Moore said in a voice that

suggested profound wisdom. "And marriage is God's way of satisfying those needs."

Gosling allowed her scorn to show. "So when the wife gets pregnant, is that God's fault or her husband's?"

"It's certainly God's will, ma'am, don't you think?"

Gosling avoided discussion of God's will. "Either way," she said dismissively, "you seem to believe the woman should have no say in the matter."

"I believe that husbands and wives should discuss such things in a loving and caring way."

Gosling was not going to be brushed off that easily. "But in the end the man is the master, you say."

"Well, I think that's in the Bible, isn't it? Do you read your Bible, Ms. Gosling? I sure do."

Pippa said: "What century is he from?"

Pauline said: "He's saying what a lot of Americans believe. If he wasn't, he wouldn't be on TV."

Gosling took Moore on a tour of hot-button issues, from immigration to gay marriage. In each case, without seeming to oppose him, she dug down past his sound bites and brought him to state the extreme views to which he was driven. Millions of viewers were squirming on their couches with embarrassment and disgust. But, unfortunately, millions more were cheering.

Gosling left foreign policy to the end. "Recently you advocated sinking Chinese ships in the South China Sea," she said. "How do you imagine the Chinese government would react to that? What action would they take in retaliation?"

"None at all," Moore said boldly. "The last thing the Chinese want is a war with the US."

"But how could they overlook the deliberate sinking of one of their ships?"

"What else can they do? If they attack us, China will be turned into a nuclear wasteland within hours."

"And in those hours, what damage would be done to us?"

"None, because it isn't going to happen. They won't attack us while I'm president, because they know for gosh-darn certain that I'll wipe them out."

"That's your judgment, is it?"

"For sure."

"And you're willing to gamble the lives of millions of Americans on your judgment."

"It's what the president does."

It was almost unbelievable—until Pauline recalled the words of a previous president: *If we have nuclear weapons, why can't we use them?*

Gosling said: "For our last question, tell us what you would do today about the antigovernment rebels in Korea who have nuclear weapons."

"I see that the president of China is sending the North Koreans some rice and pork. President Green seems to think that's going to solve the problem. I'm skeptical."

"The president raised the alert level today."

"From five to four. That's not enough."

"So what would you do?"

"I would take simple and decisive action. A single nuclear bomb would destroy that entire North Korean base and all the weapons in it. And the world would give the US a great big round of applause for getting rid of a menace."

"And what do you think the North Korean government would do in response?"

"Thank me."

"Suppose they regarded the bombing as an attack on their sovereign territory?"

"What are they going to do? I've wiped out their nukes."

"They may well have nuclear arms launchers underground somewhere that we don't know about."

"They know that if they fire them at us, their country will be a radioactive desert for the next hundred years. They're not going to risk that."

"You're quite sure of that."

"I'm sure."

"Could we sum up your approach to foreign policy by saying that America can always get its own way simply by threatening nuclear war?"

"Isn't that what the nukes are for?"

"James Moore, hopeful candidate in the Republican primaries and next year's presidential election, thank you for being with us tonight."

Pauline switched off the TV. Moore had done better than she had expected. He had never seemed weak or uncertain, despite the utter rubbish he was talking.

"I have homework," Pippa said, and she left.

Pauline returned to the West Wing. "Ask Sandip to drop by, please," she said to Lizzie. "I'll be in the study."

"Yes, ma'am."

She turned on CNN for a discussion of Moore's performance. The pundits were full of scorn, quite reasonably, but Pauline felt they should pay more attention to his strengths.

She muted the sound when Sandip arrived. "What did you think?" she asked him.

"The guy is crazy," Sandip said. "Some voters will see that. Others won't."

"I agree."

"So no further action by us?"

"Not tonight." Pauline smiled. "Go home and sleep well."

"Thank you, Madam President."

As usual, Pauline spent these quiet hours catching up on briefings that required her to concentrate without interruption for at least a few minutes. Just after eleven p.m. Gus showed up, wearing the blue cashmere sweater she liked. "The Japanese are going ballistic about Sangnam-ni," he said.

"I'm not surprised," Pauline said. "They're close neighbors."

"Three hours on the ferry from Fukuoka to Busan. Longer to North Korea, but still very close bombing range."

Pauline left the desk and they sat on the two armchairs. In the small room their knees were close together. Pauline said: "Japan and Korea have a bad history."

"In Japan there's a lot of hatred of Koreans. Social media is full of racist attacks."

"So, just like America."

"Different color scheme, same abuse," said Gus.

Pauline found herself relaxing. She liked her occasional late-night chats with Gus. They roamed over issues randomly, and there was generally nothing they could do about them until the morning, so they did not feel pressured to act. "Help yourself to a drink," she said. "You know where the hooch is."

"Thanks." He went to a cupboard and took out a bottle and glass. "This is very good bourbon."

"I had no idea. I don't even know who chose it."

"I chose it," he said with a grin. For an uncharacteristic moment he looked like a naughty schoolboy. He sat down again and poured an inch of liquor into the glass.

She said: "What is the Japanese government doing?"

"The prime minister has called a meeting of their National Security Council, which will certainly order the military to some level of alert. It's easy to imagine how Japan and China could come into conflict over this, and the Japanese commentators are already worrying about the possibility of war."

"China is way stronger."

"Not as much as you'd think. Japan has the fifth-largest defense budget in the world."

"However, they have no nuclear weapons."

"But we do, and we have a military treaty with Japan that obliges us to come to their aid if they're attacked. To back up that promise, we have fifty thousand troops there, plus the Seventh Fleet, the Third Marine Expeditionary Force, and one hundred thirty USAF fighter planes."

"And back here at home we have about four thousand nuclear warheads."

"Half ready to use, half in reserve storage."

"And we're pledged to the defense of Japan."

"Yes."

The facts were not new to Pauline, but she had never seen the implications so clearly. "Gus," she said, "we're as committed as hell."

"I couldn't have put it better. And there's one more thing. Have you heard of what the North Koreans call Residence No. 55?"

"Yes, it's the official home of the supreme leader, in the suburbs of Pyongyang."

"It's actually a complex covering five square miles. It has a lot of high-end leisure facilities, including a pool with a waterslide, a spa, a shooting range, and a horse-racing track."

"These Communists don't stint themselves, do they? Why don't I have a horse-racing track?"

"Madam President, you have no use for leisure facilities, because you have no leisure."

"I should have been a dictator."

"No comment."

Pauline giggled. She knew they joked about her being a tyrant.

Gus said: "The National Intelligence Service in

South Korea says the Pyongyang regime has repelled an attack on Residence No. 55. It's a fort with an underground nuclear bunker, and it's probably the most heavily defended place in North Korea. The fact that the rebels have even tried to take it suggests that they're a lot stronger than any of us imagined until now."

"Could they win?"

"It's looking possible."

"A military coup!"

"Exactly."

"We'd better find out more about these people. Who are they, and what do they want? I could be dealing with them as a government in a few days' time."

"I've asked the CIA those questions. They will be working all night on a briefing that you should get in the morning."

"Thanks. You know what I need before I do."

He dropped his eyes, and she realized that her remark might have been interpreted as flirtatious. She felt embarrassed.

He took a sip of his drink.

Pauline said: "Gus, what happens if we fuck this up?"

"Nuclear war," he said.

"Indulge me," she said. "Walk me through it."

"Well, both sides would defend themselves with cyberattacks and anti-missile missiles, but all the evidence suggests that these methods would be only partially successful, at best. Therefore some nuclear bombs would reach their targets in both the warring countries."

"What targets?"

"Both sides would try to destroy the enemy's missile-launching facilities and also target major cities. At a minimum, China would bomb New York, Chicago, Houston, Los Angeles, San Francisco, and the town we're sitting in, Washington DC."

As he named the cities, Pauline saw them in her mind: the Golden Gate Bridge in San Francisco, the Houston Astrodome, Fifth Avenue in Manhattan, Rodeo Drive in LA, her parents' home in Chicago, and the Washington Monument outside her window.

"More likely," said Gus, "they would aim at between ten and twenty major cities."

"Remind me what the explosion is like."

"In the first one millionth of a second, a fireball is formed two hundred yards wide. Everyone within it dies instantly."

"Perhaps they're the lucky ones."

"The blast flattens buildings for a mile around. Almost everyone in that area dies from the impact or from falling debris. The heat sets fire to anything that will burn, including people, within a radius of two to five miles. Cars crash, trains come off the rails. The blast and the heat go upward too, so planes fall out of the sky."

"How many casualties?"

"In New York, about a quarter of a million people die more or less immediately. Another half a million are injured. More die of radiation sickness in the following hours and days."

"Jesus."

"But that's just one bomb. They would aim more than one missile at each city, in case of malfunctions. And China now has multiple warheads, so a single missile can carry up to five separate bombs, each seeking a different target. No one knows what the effect would be of ten, twenty, fifty nuclear explosions in a city, because it has never happened."

"It's unimaginable."

"And this is only the short term. With every major city in the US and China on fire, imagine how much soot is released into the atmosphere. Enough, some scientists think, to weaken sunlight and lower temperatures on the Earth's surface—leading to poor harvests, shortage of food, and starvation in many countries. It's called nuclear winter."

Pauline felt as if she had swallowed something cold and heavy.

"I'm sorry to be so bleak," Gus said.

"I asked for it."

She leaned forward and reached out with both her hands. Gus took them in his and held them.

After a long moment she said: "It must never happen."

He squeezed her hands gently. "Please God."

"And you know who's in charge of preventing it: you and me."

"Yeah," said Gus. "Especially you."

CHAPTER 21

Tamara thought they might have lost Abdul.

It was now eight days since he had called and said the bus was about to cross the border into Libya. He might have been arrested by the Libyans, though that part of the world was so lawless it seemed improbable. More likely he had been kidnapped or murdered by tribesmen who had nothing to do with any government. Perhaps a ransom demand was on its way.

And perhaps Abdul had disappeared, never to be seen again.

Tab called a meeting to discuss what to do. Such meetings were hosted by the Americans and the French alternately, and this one was held in the French embassy. As the discussion would be in the French language, Dexter did not attend.

It was chaired by Tab's boss, Marcel Lavenu, a big man whose bald head rose above his shoulders like a dome on a church. "I saw the Chinese ambassador last night," he said, speaking conversationally as the group took their seats. "He's mad as hell about the rebellion in North Korea. But the Chinese don't mind arming rebels in North Africa. Imagine the reaction if the nuclear base at Sangnam-ni had been taken over by men with Bugles!"

Tamara did not understand the reference, and Tab explained: "The Bugle is the nickname for the bullpup rifle made by the French company FAMAS."

Tab was spreading a large map on the conference table. He wore a white shirt with the sleeves rolled, and his brown arms had a light covering of hair. Leaning over the map with a pencil in his hand and his forelock tumbling over his eyes, he looked irresistibly attractive, and Tamara wanted to take him to bed there and then.

He was oblivious to the effect he had. One time she had laughingly accused him of deliberately dressing to make women's pulses race, and he had given a vague smile that showed he did not really understand what she was talking about. Which made him even more alluring.

"This is Faya," he began, pointing with his pencil to a place on the map. "A thousand kilometers from here by road. It's where Abdul called from, eight days ago, when he gave us a mass of priceless data. Since then he has presumably been out of telephone range."

Monsieur Lavenu was a smart man, if a little pompous. He said: "What about the radio signal from the consignment? Can't we pick that up?"

"Not from here," said Tab. "Its range is only about a hundred and fifty kilometers."

"Of course. Carry on."

"The military aren't proposing to take any action yet against the terrorists Abdul has identified, for fear of alerting others, possibly more important, farther along the road. But we'll pounce before too long."

Lavenu spoke again. "And how was the morale of Monsieur Abdul, eight days ago?"

"He spoke to our American colleague." Tab indicated Tamara.

Lavenu looked at her expectantly.

"He was in good spirits," she said. "Frustrated by the breakdowns and delays, naturally, but learning an enormous amount about ISGS. He knows he's in terrible danger, but he's brave and tough."

"There is no doubt about his courage."

Tab picked up the story. "We assume the bus went northwest from Faya to Zouarké, then due north, with the mountains on its right and the Niger border on its left. There are no paved roads there. Somewhere to the north of Wour the bus will have crossed the border, we assume. Abdul is probably in Libya now, though we have no way to be sure."

Lavenu said: "This is not quite satisfactory. Of course we must accept that we may lose sight of an undercover operative, but are we doing all we can to find him?"

Tab said politely: "I don't know what else we could do, sir."

"Presumably the radio signal from the consignment could be picked up by a helicopter overhead, following the most likely route of the bus?"

"Possibly," said Tab. "It's a huge area to cover, but it would be worth a try. We could assume that the bus took the shortest route to a paved highway, which is more or less due north. The problem is that the chopper would be seen and heard by the people on the bus, and the smugglers would realize that they are under surveillance, and then they would take some kind of evasive action."

"How about a drone?"

Tab nodded. "A drone is quieter than a helicopter and can fly much higher. Far better for clandestine surveillance."

"Then I will request the French air force to send one of our drones to try to pick up the radio signal from the consignment."

Tamara said: "That would be great!" She would feel much relieved by a sighting of Abdul's bus.

The meeting wound up soon after that, and Tab walked Tamara out to her car. The French embassy was a long, low modern building that gleamed white in the strong sunlight. Tab said: "You remember that my father is arriving today?" He was smiling, but he seemed nervous—which was unusual for him.

"Of course," Tamara said. "I can't wait to meet him."

"Slight change of plan."

She sensed that this was what he was nervous about. He said: "My mother will be with him."

"Oh, my God, she's coming to inspect me, isn't she?"

"No, of course not." He looked at Tamara's skeptical expression and said: "Well, yes."

"I knew it."

"Is that so bad? I've told them about you, and naturally she's curious."

"Has she visited you here before?"

"No."

What had Tab said, to bring his mother to Chad for the first time ever? He must have let his parents know that Tamara was likely to become a long-term part of his life—and theirs. She should have been pleased, not anxious.

Tab said: "It's ironic. Here in this lawless country you face danger every day without flinching, but you're scared of my mother."

"It's true." She laughed at herself. All the same she was anxious. She brought to mind the photograph in Tab's apartment. His mother was blond and well-dressed, but that was all she could remember. She said: "You've never told me their names. I can't very well call them Papa and Maman."

"Not yet, anyway. He's Malik. She's Marie-Anatole, but she's always called Anne, which works in many languages."

Tamara noticed that phrase *not yet* but did not comment. She said: "When do they arrive?"

"The flight gets in around midday. We could have dinner this evening."

Tamara shook her head. People were often cranky after flying. She preferred they should have a night's rest before she met them. "You should spend the first evening alone with them," she said. Not wanting to suggest that they might be ill-tempered, she said: "You'll need to catch up on all the family news."

"Maybe . . ."

"Why don't you and I meet them for lunch tomorrow?"

"You're right, that's a better idea. But we don't want to be seen, do we, the four of us in public? I'm not ready to confront my superiors with the news that I'm in love with a Yankee spy."

"I didn't think of that. And I can't invite them to my little studio apartment. What are we going to do?"

"We'll have to take one of the private dining rooms at the Lamy. Or we could have lunch in their suite. Papa always takes a single room, when he's on his own, but Maman will have booked the Presidential Suite."

So, no problem, Tamara thought, somewhat bemused. She still had not gotten used to Tab's family's wealth.

Tab said: "On our first date you wore a striped dress, navy blue and white, with a little blue jacket and blue leather shoes."

"Wow, you really noticed."

"You looked wonderful."

"It made me seem demure, but you saw through the disguise pretty quickly."

"It would be a great outfit to wear on Tuesday."

She was taken aback. He had never before told her what to wear. It was not like him to be controlling. She guessed it was only trepidation, but all the same she was irked that he should worry about the impression she was going to make on his mother. "Have faith, Tabdar," she said. She used his full name only when she was teasing him. "I probably won't embarrass you at all. These days I hardly ever get drunk and grab the waiter's ass."

"I'm sorry," he said with a laugh. "Papa is laid-back, but Maman can be critical."

"I sympathize. Wait till you meet my mother, the schoolteacher. If you annoy her she'll make you stand in the corner."

"Thank you for understanding."

She pecked his cheek and got into the waiting car.

She thought about Tab's *not yet*. He was assuming the time would come when she called his parents Papa and Maman, which meant she and Tab would be married. She already knew she wanted to spend her life with him, but the wedding was not high on her to-do list. She had married twice already, both times with unsatisfactory results. She was not in a hurry to do it again.

In five minutes she was back in the leafy grounds of the US embassy. At her desk she wrote a note about the meeting for Dexter, then she went to the canteen and got a Cobb salad and a diet soda for lunch.

Susan Marcus joined her, putting her tray on the table and taking off her uniform cap, shaking her short hair to restore its natural bounce. She sat down, but she did not begin to eat her steak. "Abdul's intelligence is priceless," she said. "I hope he gets a medal."

"If he does we may never know. CIA honors are usually secret. They're called jockstrap medals."

Susan grinned. "Because they're not visible, and they're not necessary for women."

"Got it in one."

Susan became serious again. "Listen, there's something I want to ask you about."

Tamara swallowed a mouthful and put down her fork. "Go ahead."

"You know that training the National Army of Chad is a big part of our mission here."

"Of course."

"You probably don't know that we've been teaching some of their best people how to use drones."

"I did not know that."

"Of course this is under tight control, and the local boys aren't allowed to operate drones without American supervision."

"Good."

"Sometimes the aircraft are destroyed in exercises. One that had a warhead blew up when it struck its target, which is what's supposed to happen. Another was downed—shooting them down is part of the training. Naturally we keep a meticulous tally of how many we have."

"Of course."

"But one has gone missing."

Tamara was surprised. "How could that happen?"

"A lot of drones crash; this is new technology. The official story is 'guidance system malfunction.'"

"And you can't find it? How big is it?"

"Drones that carry weapons over long distances are not small. This one has the wingspan of a corporate jet and needs a runway to take off. But it's a big desert."

"You think it might have been stolen?"

"The drone is normally flown by a three-man team: pilot, sensor operator, and mission intelligence coordinator. However, one man could do it in a pinch. But he could do nothing without the control station."

"How big is that?"

"It's a van. In the back, the drone pilot sits in a virtual

cockpit with screens showing the view from the drone, maps, and aircraft instrumentation. There's a conventional throttle and joystick. A satellite dish on the roof communicates with the aircraft."

"So the thief has to steal the van too."

"He might be able to buy one on the black market."

"You want me to put out some feelers?"

"Yes, please."

"The drones might have been put up for sale. Alternatively, the General may have the drones under cover at some remote airstrip. Maybe someone is trying to buy a control station on the black market. I'll see what I can find out."

"Thank you."

"Can I eat my salad now?"

"Go for it."

Tamara had a date with Karim for coffee on Tuesday morning.

She dressed carefully, because she had to go straight from Karim's coffee shop to lunch with Tab's parents. She did not put on the outfit prescribed by Tab: it would have made her feel like his puppet. However, she was not going to be mulish and dress in ripped jeans. She remembered his saying that she had the kind of simple chic that French people admired, and in truth that was her favorite style. She put on the outfit she had been wearing when he said that, a mid-gray shift dress with a red belt.

She hesitated over jewelry. Marie-Anatole Sadoul owned and ran the Travers company, which produced high-class bling, among other things. Nothing in Tamara's jewel box was expensive enough to compete with whatever Tab's maman might have on. Tamara decided to be contrarian and wear something she had made herself. She picked out a pendant of an ancient Tuareg arrowhead. In places the Sahara was littered with such relics, so it was not precious, but it was interesting and different. It was carved of stone and carefully shaped, with serrated edges. Tamara had simply drilled a hole in its wide base and threaded it with a narrow piece of rawhide that she slung around her neck. The stone was dark gray and toned nicely with her dress.

Karim's eyes widened appreciatively when he saw how smart she looked, though he did not comment. Tamara sat opposite him at what was evidently the proprietor's table and accepted a cup of bitter coffee. They talked about the battle at the refugee camp eleven days earlier. Karim said: "We're pleased that President Green did not believe the Sudanese lies about us invading their territory."

"The president had an eyewitness report."

Karim raised his eyebrows. "From you?"

"I got a personal phone call from her thanking me."

"Well done! Have you met her?"

"I worked on her congressional election campaign, years ago."

"Very impressive." His congratulations were tinged with something else, and she realized she needed to be careful. Karim was a big shot because he knew the General, and he would not like to feel that Tamara might be an even bigger shot because she knew the American president. She decided to play it down a bit. "She does this all the time, calls ordinary people, a driver, a cop, a reporter on a local paper, and thanks them for doing a good job."

"She gets good publicity from it!"

"Exactly." Tamara felt she had reduced herself back to normal size, and she was ready to ask her difficult question. "By the way, one of our drones is missing—did you know?"

Karim hated to admit ignorance. He would always pretend he already knew. The only time he would claim unawareness was when he wanted to hide the fact that he really did know something. So she reckoned that if he now said: "Yes, I heard about that," he probably knew nothing; whereas if he said: "I had no idea," it meant he knew all about it.

He hesitated for a significant fraction of a second, then he said: "Really? A drone missing? I had no idea."

So you knew, she thought. Well, well. Pushing for confirmation, she said: "We thought maybe the General had it."

"Certainly not!" Karim tried to look indignant. "Why, what would we do with it?"

"I don't know. He might think it's just nice to have one, like . . ." She pointed to the large complicated diving watch on Karim's left wrist. "Like your watch." If Karim was being honest he would laugh now and say: "Yes, of course, a drone is nice to have in your pocket, even if you never use it."

But he did not. Solemnly he said: "The General would never wish to have such a powerful weapon without the approval of our American allies."

This sanctimonious bullshit verified Tamara's instinct. She had the information she needed, so she changed the subject. "Are the armies observing the demilitarized zone along the border with Sudan?" she asked.

"So far, yes."

As they chatted about Sudan, Tamara pondered Karim's question: what would the General do with an American drone? He might just keep it as a superfluous trophy, never to be used, just as Karim, living in the landlocked desert country of Chad, was never going to need a watch that was water resistant to a depth of one hundred meters. But the General was a sly schemer, as he had proved with his ambush, and he might well have a more sinister purpose.

Tamara had all the intelligence she had been hoping to get from Karim today. She took her leave and returned to her car. She would report this conversation later. First she had to be assessed by Tab's parents.

She told herself not to be oversensitive. This was not an exam, it was a social lunch. All the same she felt apprehensive.

At the Lamy she went first to the restroom to freshen up. She combed her hair and retouched her makeup. The arrowhead pendant looked good in the mirror.

She had a message on her phone giving her the room number. As she got into the elevator, Tab stepped in right behind her. She kissed him on both cheeks, then wiped her lipstick off his face. He was dressed formally, in a suit and a spotted tie, with a white handkerchief peeking out of his breast pocket. "Let me guess," she said, speaking French. "Your mother likes her men to dress up."

He smiled. "The men like it too. And you look perfect."

They reached the room door, which was open, and went in.

Tamara had never been in a presidential suite. They passed through a small lobby into a spacious sitting room. A door to one side gave a glimpse of a dining room, where a waiter was putting napkins on a table. On the opposite side of the room was a double door that presumably led to the bedroom.

Tab's parents were sitting on a pink-upholstered couch. His father stood up and his mother remained sitting. Both wore glasses that had not appeared in the photo Tamara had seen. Malik's looks were craggy and dark, but he was well-dressed in a navy blue cotton blazer with off-white trousers and a striped tie, a Frenchman doing the English style but with more flair. Anne was pale and slim, a beautiful older woman in a cream-colored linen dress with a mandarin collar and flared sleeves. They looked like what they were, an affluent couple with good taste.

Tab performed the introductions, continuing in French. Tamara said a prepared sentence: "I'm so glad to meet the parents of this wonderful man." In response, Anne smiled, but coolly. Any mother should have been pleased by such a remark about her son, but she was unimpressed.

They all sat down. On the coffee table was an ice bucket with a bottle of champagne and four glasses. The waiter came in and poured, and Tamara noticed that the champagne was vintage Travers. She said to Anne: "Do you always drink your own champagne?"

"Often, yes, to check on how it's surviving," Anne replied. "Normally we taste in the cellars, and the same is true for buyers and wine writers who come from all over the world to our winery in Reims. But our customers have a different experience. Before they drink the wine it travels perhaps thousands of miles, and then it may be kept for years in unsuitable conditions."

Tab interrupted her. "When I was a student in California I used to work at a restaurant where the wine was kept in a cupboard next to the oven. If someone ordered champagne we had to put the bottle in the freezer for fifteen minutes." He laughed.

His mother did not see the funny side. "So, you see, champagne needs one quality that will never show at a cellar tasting: fortitude. We must make a wine that can survive ill treatment and still taste good despite conditions that are less than ideal."

Tamara had not expected a lecture. On the other hand, she found it interesting. And she had learned that Tab's mother was remorselessly serious.

Anne tasted the champagne and said: "Not too disappointing."

Tamara thought it was delicious.

As they chatted, Tamara checked out Anne's jewelry. The flared sleeves of her dress revealed a pretty Travers watch on her left wrist and three gold bangles on her right. Tamara was not planning to talk about jewelry, but Anne commented on her pendant. "I haven't seen anything quite like that before."

"It's homemade," Tamara said, and she explained what a Tuareg arrowhead was.

"How original," Anne said.

Tamara had met American matrons who could say something like *How original* when they really meant *How dreadful*.

Tab asked his father about the business side of his trip. "All the important meetings will take place here in the capital," Malik said. "The men who run this country are all here—I don't suppose I need to tell you that. But I will have to fly to Doba and look at oil wells." He turned to his wife to explain. "The oil fields are all in the far southwest of the country."

Tab said: "But what will you actually do in Doba and N'Djamena?"

"Business is very personal in Africa," Malik said. "Being on friendly terms with people can be more important than giving them generous terms in a contract. The most effective thing I do here is find out whether people are discontented—and take the action necessary to keep them on our side."

By the end of lunch Tamara had a vivid picture of this couple. Both were smart businesspeople, knowledgeable and decisive. But Malik was amiable and laid-back, whereas Anne was lovely but cold, like her champagne. In a lucky roll of the genetic dice, Tab had inherited his father's easygoing personality and his mother's good looks.

Afterward Tamara and Tab left together. "They're a remarkable couple," she said to him in the lobby.

"I thought the occasion was terribly stiff."

He was not wrong, but tactfully she did not voice her agreement. Instead she proposed a solution. "Tomorrow night, let's take them to al-Quds," she said. It was Tamara and Tab's favorite restaurant, a quiet Arab place where Westerners never went. "There we can relax more."

"Nice idea." Tab frowned. "They don't serve wine."

"Will your folks mind?"

"Maman won't. Papa might want a drink. We could have champagne at my apartment before going to the restaurant."

"And tell your parents to wear really casual clothes."

"I'll try!"

"So," she said, grinning, "did you really work in a restaurant kitchen in California?"

"Yes."

"I imagined that your parents would have bank-rolled you."

"They gave me a generous allowance, but I was young and foolish, and one semester I overspent. I was too embarrassed to ask them for more, so I got a job. I didn't really mind, it was a new experience. I'd never had a job before."

Young, but not so foolish, Tamara thought. He had had the strength of character to solve the problem for himself, rather than run back to Papa and Maman for help. She liked that. "Good-bye," she said. "Let's shake hands. If anyone's watching us we'll look like colleagues, not lovers."

They left. In the back of her car, Tamara could stop pretending. The lunch had been awful. Everyone had felt uncomfortable. Malik might have been all right on his own: he probably would have flirted with Tamara. But Anne had the correct kind of manners that put everyone on their best behavior.

Tamara's relationship with Tab did not depend on his mother's approval, she was sure of that. Anne was a strong character, but not that strong. However, if she took against Tamara it could be an irritant, something that could cause occasional friction between a couple for many years. Tamara was determined not to let that happen.

And there had to be a real woman somewhere inside Anne. She was an aristocrat who had broken out of her social circle and married the Arab son of a shopkeeper: to do that she must have been led by her heart rather than her head. Somehow Tamara would connect with the girl who had fallen head over heels in love with Malik.

She returned to the US embassy and sought out Dexter, who was back at his desk with a large bruise on his forehead and one arm in a sling. He had not thanked her for rescuing him at the refugee camp. "I spoke to Karim about the missing drone," she said.

"Missing drone?" Dexter looked annoyed. "Who told you about the missing drone?"

She was taken aback. "Was I not supposed to know?"

"Who told you?" he repeated.

She hesitated, but Susan would not care what Dexter knew or thought. "Colonel Marcus."

"The women's grapevine," he said scornfully.

"We are all on the same side, aren't we?" Tamara said, letting her annoyance show. The drone story was not top secret. It was just that Dexter liked to control the flow of information. Everything had to pass through him, incoming and outgoing. It was tiresome. "If you don't want to hear what Karim said . . ."

"All right, all right, go on then."

"He said the General doesn't have the drone, but I thought he was lying."

"Why did you think that?"

"Just a hunch."

"Women's intuition."

"If you like."

"You've never been in the military, have you?"

"No."

Dexter had served in the navy. "You don't understand."

Tamara said nothing.

"Ordnance goes missing all the time," Dexter went on. "No one can keep track. There's just too much stuff in too many places being moved too often."

She was tempted to ask how he thought large international airlines managed their fleets, but she continued to hold her tongue.

"Missing gear is missing," he said. "No need for a conspiracy theory."

"If you say so."

"I say so," said Dexter.

On the evening of the next day, Malik and Anne sat on stools in Tab's small kitchen. Tab spread hummus on cucumber slices while Tamara sprinkled olive oil, salt, and rosemary leaves on plain tortilla wraps and crisped them in the oven. As they moved around in the small space they touched one another frequently, as usual. Everyone chatted, but Tamara knew she was being watched, especially by Anne. However, when she caught

Anne's eye she thought she saw a pleased look. Eventually Anne said: "You two are happy together."

It was the first time she had said anything about the relationship between her son and Tamara, and it was positive, which gratified Tamara. And Anne ate all the hot tortillas.

Perhaps one day they could even be friends.

Tamara was a bit nervous about walking into al-Quds with Anne. Tamara could pass for an Arab girl, but Anne was a tall blonde. However, she was not insensitive, and tonight she had put on a headscarf and baggy linen trousers, to be less conspicuous.

The proprietor knew Tamara and Tab and welcomed them cordially, and seemed pleased when Tab introduced his parents and explained that they were visiting from Paris. Al-Quds did not get many customers who were visiting from Paris.

When the food came, Tab began a prepared speech. "My relationship with Tamara is a problem with our bosses," he said. "They don't like us getting too close to officers from other countries' intelligence services. So far we've been discreet, but we can't carry on like this indefinitely."

Anne said impatiently: "Do you have a plan?"

Tab abandoned his script. "We want to live together."

"After one month?"

"Five weeks."

Malik laughed. "Don't you remember how it was with us?" he said to Anne. "After a week we went to bed on a Friday and didn't get dressed until Monday morning."

Anne flushed and said: "Malik! Please!"

Malik was not to be subdued. "They're the same, can't you see?" he said. "That's what true love is like."

Anne did not want to discuss the nature of true love. "Do you want children?" she said.

They had not had this conversation, but Tamara knew how she felt. She said: "Yes."

Tab said: "Yes."

Tamara said: "I want kids and a career, and in that I have two splendid role models: my mother and you, Anne."

"So what will you do?"

Tab said: "I'm going to leave the DGSE, and if you'll have me, Maman, I'd like to work with you in the business."

"I would love that," Anne said instantly. "But, Tamara, how do you fit in?"

"I'd like to stay in the CIA if I can. I'll try to get a transfer to the Paris embassy. If that doesn't work out I'll have to think again. But here's the bottom line: I'd leave the Agency rather than leave Tab."

There was a moment of silence. Then Anne gave the warmest smile Tamara had yet seen on her face. She reached across the table and put her hand on Tamara's. "You really love him, don't you?" she said quietly.

"Yes," said Tamara. "I really do."

Next day Tab called to tell her that the French drone had failed to pick up the radio signal from the consignment and had not sighted a bus anywhere along its route.

Abdul had disappeared.

CHAPTER 22

The Mercedes bus spent five days in a Libyan village with no name, waiting for a new fuel pump to be brought from Tripoli. The inhabitants of the village spoke a Tuareg dialect unknown to anyone on the bus, but Kiah and Esma communicated with the women in gestures and smiles, and managed well enough. Food had to be brought from neighboring villages, because the one settlement could not cope with thirty-nine more mouths to feed, regardless of how much money was offered.

Hakim demanded that everyone pay him extra, because he had not budgeted for this. Abdul said angrily that he was running out of money, and other passengers did the same. Kiah knew that Abdul was pretending, hiding the fact that he had plenty.

They were all used to Hakim and his armed guards now. They were not afraid to argue and negotiate with him about extra payments. The group had survived many setbacks. Kiah was beginning to feel almost safe. She began to think about crossing the Mediterranean, for that was now the part of the journey that scared her.

Strangely, she was not unhappy. The daily privations

and perils had come to seem almost normal. She talked
a lot to Esma, who was about her own age. But she
spent most of her time with Abdul, who had become
fond of Naji. Abdul seemed fascinated by the mental
development of a two-year-old: what the boy understood, what he could not understand, and how much
he learned every day. Kiah asked him if he would have
a son of his own one day. "I haven't thought about that
for a long time," he said. She wondered what he meant.
But she had realized weeks ago that he did not answer
questions about his past.

One day they woke to a thick fog, coating everything in a film of cold dew, something that happened
in the desert, albeit rarely. They could not see from one
house to the next, and the sounds of other people were
muffled, footsteps and snatches of talk heard as if
through a wall.

Kiah tied Naji to her with a strip of cloth, fearful
that if he wandered off he might never be found. She
and Abdul sat together all day, with no one else in sight
most of the time. She asked him what he would do for
a living once they reached France. "Some Europeans
will pay a man to help them keep fit and strong," he
said. "Such men are called personal trainers, and they
can charge up to a hundred dollars an hour. You must
look athletic, but otherwise all you have to do is tell
them what exercises to do." Kiah was baffled by this
notion. It made no sense to her that people would pay
so much money for nothing. She had much to learn
about Europeans.

"What about you?" he asked. "What will you do?"

"Once I get there, I'll be happy to do any work."

"But what would you prefer?"

She smiled. "I'd love to have a little fish shop. I know
about fish. I'm sure they have different kinds in France,
but it won't take me long to learn about them. I'd buy

fresh every day and close the shop when I've sold them all. When Naji's older he can work in the shop and learn the business, then take it over when I'm too old to work."

Next day the fuel pump was at last delivered, by a man on a camel who stayed to help Hakim install it and to make sure it worked properly.

When they set off the following morning they again headed west. Kiah recalled that Abdul had questioned Hakim about their direction previously, but now he kept his mouth shut. However, he was not the only person on the bus who thought the Mediterranean coast did not lie in that direction. Two of the men confronted Hakim at the next rest stop and demanded to know why they were driving away from their destination.

Kiah listened, wondering what he would say.

"This is the way!" Hakim said angrily. "There is only one road."

When the questioners persisted, Hakim said: "We go west, then north. It's the only way, unless you're on a camel." He became sarcastic. "Go ahead, get a camel, we'll see who's first to reach Tripoli."

Kiah said quietly to Abdul: "Do you believe Hakim?"

Abdul shrugged. "He's a liar and a cheat. I don't believe anything he says. But it's his bus, and he's driving, and his guards have the guns. So we have to trust him."

The bus made good progress that day. Toward the end of the afternoon Kiah looked out of the glassless window and noticed the grubby signs of human habitation: dented oil drums, cardboard boxes, a car seat with the foam stuffing bursting out. Looking ahead, she saw in the distance a settlement that did not look like a Tuareg village.

As the bus drew closer she saw details. There were a

few cinder-block buildings and many improvised huts
and shelters made of dried-up tree branches and odd-
ments of canvas and carpet. But there were also trucks
and other vehicles, and parts of the area were closed
off with stout chain-link fencing.

Kiah said: "What is this place?"

"It looks like a mining camp."

"A gold mine?" Like everyone else, she had heard of
the gold rush in the central Sahara, but she had never
seen a mine.

"I guess so," said Abdul.

The place was filthy, Kiah saw as the bus drove
slowly between the huts. On the ground between the
dwellings there were drink cans, discarded food, and
cigarette packets. "Are gold mines always so dirty?"
she asked Abdul.

"I believe that some are licensed by the Libyan government and subject to labor laws, but others are rogue
excavations with no official status and no rules. The
Sahara is too big to be policed. This place must be unofficial."

Ragged men looked incuriously at the bus. Among
them were a few guards, bearded young men with
rifles. Security guards would be needed at a gold mine,
Kiah guessed. She noticed a tanker and a man with a
hose dispensing water to people with jugs and bottles.
In the desert most settlements were built around oases,
but mines had to be where the gold was, Kiah reasoned, so water would have to be trucked in to keep the
miners alive.

Hakim stopped the bus, stood up, and said: "This is
where we will spend the night. They will give us food
and somewhere to sleep."

Kiah was not in a hurry to eat anything prepared in
such a place.

Hakim went on: "Security is strict, because this is a

gold mine. Stay out of the way of the guards. Whatever you do, don't climb over a fence into one of the restricted areas. If you do, you could be shot."

Kiah really did not like it here.

Hakim opened the bus door. Hamza and Tareq got out and stood with their guns in their hands. Hakim said: "We are in Libya, and as previously agreed, you will now pay me the second installment of your fare before you get off the bus. One thousand American per person."

Everyone rummaged in their luggage or fumbled under their clothing for their cash.

Kiah parted with her money reluctantly, but she had no choice.

Hakim counted every note, in no hurry.

When they were all off the bus, a guard approached. He was a few years older than most, somewhere in his thirties, and instead of a rifle he had a holstered pistol. He looked over the bus passengers with an expression of contempt. Kiah thought: What have we done to you?

Hakim said: "This is Mohammed. He will show you where to sleep."

Hamza and Tareq got back on the bus, and Hakim drove off to park. The two jihadis often slept in the vehicle overnight, perhaps fearful that it might be stolen.

Mohammed said: "All of you, follow me."

He led them on a zigzag between the makeshift dwellings. Kiah was right behind him with Esma and her family. Esma's father, Wahed, spoke to the man. "How long have you been here, brother?"

Mohammed said: "Shut your mouth, you foolish old man."

He led them to a three-sided shelter roofed with sheets of corrugated iron. As they entered, Kiah saw a sand rat with a crust of bread in its mouth wriggle out through a gap in the wall, tail flicking behind it like a carefree good-bye wave.

There were no lights in the shelter. There appeared to be no electric power.

"They will bring you food," said Mohammed, and he went away. Kiah wondered who "they" were.

She made camp, clearing an area of the ground with a brush improvised from a piece of cardboard. She took out her blanket and Naji's, putting them down folded next to her bag to claim her space.

Abdul said: "I'm going to look around."

"I'll come with you," she said, picking up Naji. "There might be somewhere to wash."

It was evening but still light. They found a more or less straight path through the camp and followed it. Kiah liked walking side by side with Abdul, Naji in her arms. They were almost like a family.

A woman looked hard at her, then a man stared, and Abdul said: "Put the cross under your dress. I think there are extremists here."

She had not realized that her silver necklace with the little cross was showing. Unlike Chad, Libya was overwhelmingly Sunni Muslim, and Christians were a tiny minority, she remembered. Hastily she pushed the cross out of sight.

The improvised dwellings were scattered around one large cinder-block building. In front of it was a heavy woman in full black hijab that covered everything but her eyes. She was stirring several large pots over an open fire. The food did not have the usual spicy aroma of African cooking, and Kiah guessed she was making millet porridge. No doubt food was stored inside the building. At the back, a great pile of vegetable peelings and empty cans gave off a stink.

However, the quarter in which the migrants were

lodged was the only part of the establishment that was
like this. The rest of the place consisted of three large
fenced compounds that were clean and tidy.

One was a motor park containing a dozen or more
vehicles. Kiah counted four pickup trucks, presumably used for taking away the gold and bringing back
supplies; two large tankers like the one she had seen
dispensing water; and two gleaming black SUVs,
which she guessed were for important people, perhaps
the owners of the mine. There was also a large articulated gasoline tanker truck. Its side was painted yellow
and gray, and featured a black six-legged dragon and
the letters ENI, signifying the giant Italian oil company.
Kiah presumed it was there to refuel the other vehicles.
She also saw a compressed-air hose for pumping up
tires.

A wide gate for vehicle access was chained and pad-
locked, and there was a small guard hut inside the
fence. A man with a rifle stood by the gate, looking
bored, smoking. Kiah guessed he would go into the hut
after dark: desert nights were cold.

"North Korean," Abdul said, more or less to himself.

"Him?" Kiah said, looking at the guard. "No."

"Not him. His rifle."

"Oh." Guns were among the many things Abdul
knew about.

"This might be an illegal mine, but it's surprisingly
well equipped," he said. "It must be making a lot of
money."

"Of course," she said, laughing. "It's a gold mine."

He smiled. "True. The workers who dig up the gold
don't seem to be getting much of the profit, though."

"The workers never get much of the profit, anywhere, ever." She was surprised that the knowledgeable
Abdul could be ignorant of this basic fact of life.

"So what brings them here?" he said.

That was a good question. From what Kiah had heard, the unofficial gold mines opening up in the desert were every-man-for-himself affairs, with individuals grabbing what they could get and managing their own food and water independently. Life was rough, but there might be big rewards. It looked as if the reward for working here was small.

They moved on, and Kiah heard the aggressive rasp of a jackhammer. She saw that the second compound was an enclosure of two or three acres. About a hundred men were working inside. Kiah and Abdul watched through the fence, studying the activity. In a shallow open pit, a man was breaking up the bedrock with a jackhammer. When he paused, a backhoe scooped up the lumps and moved them to a broad concrete apron. This was where most of the men were toiling, crushing the stones with huge hammers. It looked like backbreaking work under the brutal desert sun.

"Where's the gold?" Kiah said.

"In the rock. Sometimes it's in nuggets, about the size of a man's thumb, that can just be picked up by hand out of the debris of smashed rock. More often it's in flakes that have to be extracted by some more complicated process. It's called alluvial gold."

Behind them a voice said: "What do you think you're doing?"

They turned. It was Mohammed. Kiah disliked him: he had a mean streak.

Abdul said: "I'm looking around. Is that forbidden, brother?"

"Move along." Kiah saw that Mohammed had no front teeth.

Abdul said: "As you wish."

They walked on, with the fence on their left. After a

while Kiah glanced back and saw that Mohammed had disappeared.

The third compound was different again. The fence enclosed several flat-roofed cinder-block buildings in neat rows, presumably barracks for the guards. On the far side were four objects shrouded in desert camouflage, each one the size of an articulated truck. Several men, presumably off duty, sat around drinking coffee or playing dice. To Kiah's surprise, the Mercedes bus was inside the compound.

There was one more enigma: a building with no windows, its only door barred on the outside. It looked horribly like some kind of prison. It was painted light blue, to reflect heat, which would be necessary if people were spending all day inside.

They returned to their shelter. The others had done as Kiah had and cleaned the place up. Esma and her mother had gotten a tub of water and were doing laundry outside. The other passengers were chatting in their usual desultory way.

Three women arrived with large bowls of food and a stack of plastic dishes. Supper was the millet porridge Kiah had seen being cooked. It was mixed with salted fish and onions.

The sun went down as they were eating, and they finished by starlight. Kai wrapped herself and Naji in blankets and stretched out on the ground to sleep.

Abdul lay down nearby.

Abdul was intrigued. Hakim clearly had a purpose in taking this diversion, but what was it? The presence of ISGS here would make it a natural place for Hakim to make an overnight stop—if it were on his route. But it was not.

Unlike the other passengers, Abdul was in no hurry to get to Tripoli. His mission was to gather information, and he was deeply interested in this camp. In particular, he was curious about the truck-sized objects in the guards' compound. The last ISGS hideout he had discovered, al-Bustan, had turned out to have three Chinese howitzers. These things looked bigger.

As he drifted off to sleep his mind kept repeating the word *pit*. The gold-bearing rocks were being extracted from a *pit*. What was the significance of that?

He woke with a start. It was dawn, and the word *pit* was still in his head.

The Arabic word for pit was hufra, which was more usually translated as hole. What was the significance of the *hole*?

When the answer came to him, he was so startled that he sat upright, staring at nothing.

The hideout of al-Farabi, "the Afghan," the leader by general agreement of ISGS, was a place called Hufra. It was a hole. It was a pit. It was a mine.

This was it.

He had found what he was looking for. Now he had to report this to Tamara and the CIA as soon as possible. But, maddeningly, there was no phone connectivity here.

How long would it be before the bus reached civilization?

It was an excellent arrangement for ISGS: a hideout in the middle of the vast desert, with gold in the ground just waiting to be picked up. No wonder al-Farabi had made it his main base. This was a hugely important discovery for the antiterrorism forces—or it would be, as soon as Abdul could report it.

He wondered whether al-Farabi might be here right now.

The migrants were stirring. They got up, folded their

blankets, and washed. Naji asked for leben but made do with breast milk. The women who had brought porridge last night now arrived with breakfast, which was flatbread and domiati, a brined cheese. Then the migrants sat around waiting for Hakim to arrive with the bus.

He did not come.

Abdul began to have a very bad feeling.

After an hour they decided to look for Hakim. They split up into groups. Abdul said he would check out the farthest quarter, where the guards' compound was, and Kiah went with him, carrying Naji. The sun was rising, and most of the men were already at work in the pit, so there were only a few women and children in the camp; Hakim would have stood out. Hamza and Tareq would have been even more conspicuous. None of the three was in sight.

Abdul and Kiah reached the guards' compound and stared through the fence. "Last night the bus was parked just there," Abdul said, pointing. It was not there now. Several men were in sight, but not Hakim or Tareq or Hamza.

Abdul optimistically looked for a tall man with gray hair and a black beard, a man with a piercing gaze and an air of authority, who might be al-Farabi. He saw no one of that description.

A voice said: "You again."

Abdul turned to see Mohammed.

The man said: "I told you to stay away from here." His lack of front teeth gave him a slight lisp.

He had not, but Abdul ignored that. He said: "Where is the Mercedes bus that was parked here last night?"

Mohammed looked startled to be questioned so vehemently. He was probably used to being treated with terrified deference. He recovered quickly and said: "I don't know and I don't care. Get away from the fence."

Abdul said: "Three men called Hakim, Tareq, and Hamza spent the night in that compound, where you live. You must have seen them."

Mohammed touched the pistol at his belt. "Don't ask me questions."

"What time did they leave? Where did they go?"

Mohammed drew his gun, a semiautomatic, nine-millimeter pistol, and stuck the end of the barrel into Abdul's belly. Abdul looked down. Mohammed was holding the gun sideways, and Abdul could see the five-pointed star in a circle stamped on the grip. The gun was a Paektusan, a North Korean copy of the Czech CZ-75.

Mohammed said: "Shut your mouth."

Kiah said: "Abdul, let's go, please."

Abdul could have taken the gun away from Mohammed in a heartbeat, but he could not overcome a whole camp of guards, and he was not going to get any information either way. He took Kiah's arm and walked away.

They circled around, still looking for Hakim. Kiah said: "Where do you think the bus has gone?"

"I don't know."

"Will it come back?"

"That's the big question."

Abdul would find out as soon as he got a chance to look at the tracking device in the sole of his boot. He decided to do that as soon as he and Kiah had reported back to the others at the shelter. He would walk into the desert on the pretense of answering a call of nature, and there surreptitiously check the device.

But it was not to be. When they reached the shelter they found Mohammed there, sitting on a wooden packing case turned upside down. He pointed at Abdul, then at a place on the ground where Abdul should sit. Abdul decided not to argue. They might be about to learn what had happened to their bus.

The last of the search parties arrived back and joined those sitting on the ground. Mohammed counted them and found thirty-six people, not including Naji. Then he spoke.

"Your driver has left with the bus," he said.

The oldest man among the migrants was Wahed, and he automatically became their spokesman. "Where has Hakim gone?" he said.

"How should I know?"

"But he has our money! We paid him to take us to Europe."

"Why are you telling me this?" Mohammed said with an air of exasperation. "You didn't pay me."

Abdul was intrigued. Where was this going?

Wahed said: "What are we supposed to do?"

Mohammed grinned, showing his lack of front teeth. "You can leave."

"But we have no means of transport."

"There is an oasis eighty miles north of here. You could walk there in a few days, if you could find it."

That was impossible. There was no road, just a track vanishing and reappearing between the dunes. Tuareg tribesmen who lived in the desert could find their way, but the migrants had no chance. They would wander around in the sand until they died of thirst.

This was a disaster. Abdul wondered how he was going to contact Tamara and make his report.

Wahed said: "Couldn't you take us to the oasis?"

"No. We operate a gold mine here, not a bus service." He was enjoying this.

A light dawned on Abdul, and he spoke up. "This has happened before, hasn't it?" he said to Mohammed.

"I don't know what you're talking about."

"Yes, you do. You're not troubled or even surprised about Hakim running off. You have your speech ready. You're even bored, because you've said the same words so many times before."

"Shut your mouth."

Hakim was running a scam, Abdul saw. He brought migrants here, took the last of their money, then abandoned them. But what happened to them next? Perhaps Mohammed contacted their families and demanded more money for helping them travel on.

Wahed said: "So we just have to stay here until someone appears who is willing to take us away?"

It will be worse than that, Abdul thought.

Mohammed said: "Your driver paid us to put you up for one night. Today's breakfast was your last free meal. We will not give you any more food."

"You will starve us to death!"

"If you want to eat, you'll have to work."

So that was it.

Wahed said: "Work, how?"

"The men will work in the pit. The women can help Rahima. She's the one in the black hijab who runs the kitchen. We're short of women, this place needs to be cleaned up."

"What's the pay?"

"Who said anything about money? If you work, you eat. If not, not." Mohammed grinned again. "Everyone is free to choose. There's no pay."

Wahed was outraged. "But that's slave labor!"

"There are no slaves here. Look around you. No walls, no locks. You can walk out of here anytime."

It was slave labor all the same, Abdul thought. The desert was more effective than a wall.

And that was the final piece of the puzzle. He had wondered what drew people here, and now he understood. They were not drawn, they were captured.

Abdul wondered how much Hakim had been paid. Perhaps a couple of hundred dollars for a slave? If so he had left here with $7,200. This was nothing compared with the profits from the cocaine, but Abdul suspected that most of those profits went to the jihadis, and Hakim was paid a driver's fee. That would also explain why Hakim had worked so hard to chisel a few extra bucks out of the migrants en route.

Mohammed said: "There are rules. The most important are no alcohol, no gambling, and no filthy homosexual behavior."

Abdul would have liked to ask what the punishment was, but he did not want to call further attention to himself. He feared that Mohammed already had him in his sights.

"Those of you who want to be given supper tonight need to start work now," Mohammed went on. "The women should go to the kitchen and speak to Rahima. The men, come with me." He stood up and walked out.

Abdul followed, and so did all the other men.

They trudged along the littered path, hearing the din of the jackhammer grow louder. Most of them were in their twenties or thereabouts; they might struggle but they could probably do the work. Wahed certainly could not.

An armed guard unchained the gate of the pit enclosure, and they all walked in.

The men working inside had the dead-eyed look of those for whom both hope and despair are things of the past. They did not speak or show any animation, they just hammered a rock until it was crushed, then moved on to the next rock. They all had traditional robes and headdresses, but the clothes were falling apart. Their beards were full of dust. They stopped work periodically to go to an oil drum full of water and rinse out their mouths.

They were all lean and muscular, which surprised Abdul, until he realized that those who were less fit had probably died.

The supervisors could be identified easily by the better quality of their clothes. Many of them were intently watching the rocks as they were crushed.

Mohammed gave the newcomers hammers, each with a long wooden handle and a heavy iron head. Abdul hefted his. It seemed to be well-made and in good condition. The jihadis were pragmatic: poor tools would have slowed the output of gold.

Wahed was the only man not given a hammer, and Abdul felt relieved, assuming Mohammed would give the older man some lighter work. That assumption was wrong. Mohammed took him to the pit and told him, with a grin, to operate the jackhammer.

Everyone watched.

A section of the ground had been marked out with white paint, clearly delineating the area to be dug next, but Wahed was not able to lift the drill to move it into position. He could barely hold the thing upright, which made the young supervisors laugh, though Abdul could see that some of the older ones looked disapproving.

Wahed held the jackhammer vertical, leaning over it, struggling to prevent it from falling over. Abdul had never used a jackhammer, but it was obvious to him that the operator had to stand behind it, not over it, and the tool had to lean slightly back toward him, so that if the blade slipped it would move away. Wahed was almost certain to injure himself.

He seemed to realize that and hesitated to operate the drill.

Mohammed pointed to the lever and showed him the hand-squeezing motion required to set the machine working.

Abdul knew he would get into trouble for intervening, but he did so anyway.

He walked over to the pit. Mohammed angrily
waved him away, but he ignored that. He took hold of
the handles of the jackhammer. It weighed thirty or
forty kilos, he reckoned. Wahed backed away gratefully.

Mohammed said: "What do you think you're doing?
Who told you to do that?"

Abdul ignored him.

He knew that jackhammer operators were trained,
but he would have to improvise. Taking his time, he
shifted the chisel to what looked like a small ridge in
the bedrock and lodged the blade there. He took a
small step back, so that the drill was angled. Gripping
the two handles hard, he pressed down and squeezed
the lever for an instant, then released it. The blade bit
into the rock briefly, and a small puff of dust rose up.
Abdul squeezed the lever again, with more confidence,
and had the satisfaction of seeing the blade chew into
the rock.

Mohammed looked furious.

A new person appeared, and Abdul was intrigued.

The man was East Asian, and Abdul guessed
Korean.

He had on heavyweight moleskin trousers and engineer boots, plus sunglasses and a yellow plastic hard
hat. He was holding a spray can, of the type used by
graffiti artists in New Jersey, and Abdul guessed it was
he who marked out the next section of the pit to be
broken up. He was undoubtedly the geologist.

He shouted at Mohammed in fluent Arabic. "Get
the other men working," he said. "And stop fooling
around." Then he shouted: "Akeem!" and beckoned a
heavyset worker with a baseball cap on a bald head.

The man came over and took the drill from Abdul. The geologist said to Abdul: "Watch Akeem and learn."

The newcomers got down to work and the mine settled into its routine.

Abdul heard someone shout: "Nugget!" One of the men with hammers held up his hand. The geologist examined the rock debris and, with a grunt of satisfaction, picked up what looked like a dusty yellow stone: gold, Abdul presumed. He guessed that event was rare. Most alluvial gold was not so easy to extract. Periodically the debris on the concrete apron was swept up and dumped into a huge tank, presumably containing cyanide salts dissolved in water to leach the gold flakes out of the rock dust.

Work resumed. Abdul studied Akeem's drilling technique. When he was moving the drill to a new area, he supported it on one thigh, taking the strain off his back. He did not immediately go deep into the rock but first made a series of shallow holes, and Abdul guessed this would weaken the rock so that the blade was less likely to get stuck.

The noise was oppressive, and Abdul wished he had some of those foam-rubber earplugs the cabin crew gave out in business class. Such things seemed a world away. Bring me a cold glass of white wine, he thought, and a few of those salty nuts, please, and I'll have the steak for dinner. How had he ever regarded flying as a hardship?

But Akeem had something in his ears, Abdul saw, coming back from his fantasy. After a moment's thought he tore two little strips from the hem of his galabiya, balled them up, and stuffed them in his ears. They were not very effective, but better than nothing.

After half an hour Akeem handed the jackhammer back to Abdul.

Abdul deployed it carefully, not rushing, copying Akeem's technique. He soon felt he had control of the drill, though he knew he was not breaking up the rock as fast as Akeem. However, he had not anticipated how quickly his muscles would begin to fail him. If there was one thing he felt confident about, it was his strength, but now his hands seemed reluctant to grip, his shoulders shook, and his thighs felt so weak he feared he would fall over. If he carried on he might drop the damn thing.

Akeem seemed to understand. He took the drill back, saying: "You'll get stronger." Abdul felt humiliated. The last time someone had told him condescendingly that he would get stronger had been when he was eleven years old, and he had hated it then.

However, his strength returned, and by the time Akeem tired he was ready for another session. Once again he did not last as long as he'd hoped, but he did a little better.

He thought: Why do I care how well I perform for these murdering fanatics? It's my pride, of course. What fools we men are.

Sometime before noon, as the sun was becoming unbearable, a whistle blew and everyone stopped work. They were not allowed to leave the enclosure but rested in a shelter under a broad canopy.

Food was brought by half a dozen women. It was better than what had been served to the migrants the day before. There was an oily stew with chunks of meat—probably camel, which was popular in Libya— and large helpings of rice. Someone had realized that slaves would dig more gold if they were properly fed. Abdul found that he was very hungry, and he shoveled the food in greedily.

After eating they lay down in the shade. Abdul was glad to rest his aching body and found himself dreading the moment he had to go back to work. Some of the men slept, but Abdul did not, nor did Akeem, and Abdul decided this was an opportunity for him to learn more. He opened a conversation, speaking quietly, not wanting to attract the attention of the guards. "Where did you learn to operate a jackhammer?"

"Here," said Akeem.

It was a curt reply, but the man did not seem hostile, so Abdul persisted. "I never touched one before today."

"I could see. I was the same when I got here."

"How long ago was that?"

"More than a year. Maybe two. It seems like forever. It probably will be."

"You mean you'll die here?"

"Most of the men who arrived with me are dead. And there's no other way out."

"Does no one try to escape?"

"I've known a few to walk away. Some come back, half dead. Maybe some make it to the oasis, but I doubt it."

"What about vehicles coming and going?"

"You can ask a driver to take you. He'll say he doesn't dare. They think they'll be shot if they do. I expect it's true."

This was as much as Abdul had guessed, but nevertheless it disheartened him.

Akeem gave him a shrewd look. "You're planning your escape, I can tell."

Abdul did not comment on that. "How did you come to be captured?" he asked.

"I'm from a large village where most people followed the Baha'i faith."

Abdul had heard of it. It was a minority religion in many parts of the Middle East and North Africa. There was a tiny Baha'i community in Lebanon. "A tolerant creed, I've heard," he said.

"We believe that all religions are good, because all

worship the same god, though they give him different names."

"I guess that displeased the jihadis."

"They left us alone for years, but then we opened a village school. Baha'is believe that women should be able to read and write, so the school was for girls as well as boys. That seems to be what angered the Islamists."

"What happened?"

"They came with guns and flamethrowers. They killed older people and children, even babies, and set fire to the houses. Both my parents were murdered. I'm glad I wasn't married. They captured the young men and women, especially the schoolgirls."

"And brought them here."

"Yes."

"What did they do with the girls?"

"Put them in that light-blue-painted building with no windows in the guards' compound. It's called the makhur."

"The whorehouse."

"They were at the school, you see, so they could not be true Muslims."

"Are they still in that building?"

"Some will have died: bad food, untreated infections, or sheer despair. There might be one or two hardy individuals still living."

"I thought that building was a prison."

"So it is. A prison for heathen women. It is not sin to rape such women, so our captors believe. Or pretend to believe."

Abdul thought of Kiah with her silver cross.

All too soon the whistle blew. Abdul struggled to his feet, aching all over. How much longer did he have to handle that jackhammer?

Akeem walked with him and they stepped down into the pit. Akeem lifted the drill. "I'll take the first session," he said.

"Thank you." Abdul had never meant those words more sincerely.

Painfully slowly, the sun crept across the sky and began to go down in the west, and as the heat became less Abdul's aches turned into torture. The geologist left and Mohammed blew the whistle for the end of the shift. Abdul was so glad that tears came to his eyes.

Akeem said: "They'll give you a different job tomorrow. Orders from the Korean. He thinks it's the best way to keep the strong men alive. But the day after tomorrow you'll be back on the jackhammer."

Abdul realized he was going to have to get used to this—unless he could do what no one else had managed and escape.

As they were leaving, walking wearily toward the unchained gate, there was some kind of fracas, the guards seizing and holding one of the workers, a small dark man. Two guards held him, each taking an arm, while Mohammed harangued him. They seemed to be telling him to spit something out.

The other guards ordered the workers to stand in line and wait, and pointed their guns threateningly to deter anyone who thought of intervening. Abdul had a nauseating feeling that he was about to witness a punishment.

A fourth guard came up behind the worker and clubbed him on the back of the head with the butt of a rifle. Something came out of the man's mouth and fell to the ground, and a guard picked it up.

It was about the size of an American quarter, and a dirty yellow color: gold.

The man had been trying to steal a small nugget.

How did he imagine he could ever spend it? There was nothing to buy here. He must have hoped he could use it to bribe his way out.

The guards ripped off his threadbare clothes and threw him down naked on his back. They all reversed their rifles, holding them by the barrels. Mohammed hit the man in the face with the butt of his rifle. The man cried out and covered his face with his arms, then Mohammed clubbed him in the groin. When the man covered his genitals Mohammed hit him in the face again. He nodded at the others, then each of the guards in turn lifted his weapon high and swung it through a long arc in order to hit harder. The rhythm was relentless: they had done this before.

Blood came out of the man's mouth when he screamed. They hit him again and again, going for the head, the groin, the wrists, the knees. Bones cracked and blood flowed, and Abdul saw that this was a beating from which the man was not meant to recover. He curled into a fetal position and his screams turned into animal whimpers. The beating continued remorselessly. The man fell silent and still, but they did not stop. They hammered the unconscious body until it was hardly recognizable as human.

Eventually they tired. Their victim seemed to have stopped breathing. Mohammed knelt down and felt for a heartbeat, then for a pulse.

After a minute he stood up and spoke to the watching workers. "Pick him up," he said. "Take him outside. Bury him."

CHAPTER 23

Early in the morning Tamara got a message on her
phone:

The jeans cost 15 American.

That meant she was to meet Haroun, the disaffected
jihadi, today at 1500 hours, three p.m. They had previously arranged the place, the National Museum, by the
famous seven-million-year-old skull.

She felt an uptick of tension. This could be important. They had met only once before, but on that
occasion he had given her valuable information about
the notorious al-Farabi. What news did he have today?

It was even possible he might know something about
Abdul. If so it was likely to be bad news: Abdul might
have been unmasked, somehow, and taken prisoner,
perhaps killed.

Today was a training day for the N'Djamena station
of the CIA. The subject was IT security awareness.
However, Tamara felt sure she would be able to slip
away early for a rendezvous with an informant.

She watched CNN online while she ate a breakfast
of yogurt and melon in her apartment. She was glad

that President Green was making a fuss about Chinese-made weapons in the hands of terrorists. Tamara had had a Norinco rifle pointed at her by a terrorist on the N'Gueli Bridge, and she had no sympathy with Chinese excuses. Besides, the Chinese never did anything casually. They had a plan for North Africa and, whatever it was, it would not be good for America.

Today's big news was that extreme Japanese nationalists were calling for a pre-emptive attack on North Korean bases by the Japan Aerospace Self-Defense Force, which had more than three hundred combat aircraft. Tamara did not think the Japanese would risk a war with China—but anything was possible, now that the equilibrium had been disturbed.

Tab's parents had gone home, which was a relief. Tamara felt she had broken through Anne's shell, but it had been a strain. If Tamara moved to Paris and lived with Tab, she would have to work hard to get on with his mother. But she could do that.

Walking across the embassy compound in the mild morning air, she ran into Susan Marcus. Susan was in combat dress with boots, instead of the service uniform normally worn in an office. Perhaps there was a reason, or perhaps she just liked it.

Tamara said: "Did you find your drone?"

"No. Have you picked up any whispers?"

"I told you I suspected the General had it—but I haven't been able to confirm that."

"Nor have I."

Tamara sighed. "I'm afraid Dexter doesn't take the problem too seriously. According to him, ordnance is always going missing in the military."

"There's some truth in what he says, but that doesn't make it all right."

"However, he's my boss."

"Thanks anyway."

They headed off in different directions.

The CIA had borrowed a conference room for the training session. CIA officers were more hip than regular embassy staff, or thought they were, and some of the younger ones had deliberately dressed down today, wearing band T-shirts and distressed denim rather than the more usual hot-weather outfits, chinos and short-sleeved dress shirts. Leila Morcos's T-shirt said: IT'S NOT PERSONAL, I'M A BITCH TO EVERYONE.

In the corridor Tamara met Dexter and his boss, Phil Doyle, who was based in Cairo but had responsibility for all of North Africa. They were both in suits. Doyle said to Tamara: "Any word from Abdul?"

"Nothing," she said. "He may be stuck at some oasis in a broken-down bus. Or he could be driving through the outskirts of Tripoli right now, trying to get a phone signal."

"Let's hope so."

"I'm looking forward to this course today," Tamara lied. Turning to Dexter she said: "But I'll have to leave early."

"No, you won't," he said. "This is compulsory."

"I have a rendezvous with an informant at three o'clock this afternoon. I'll be here for most of the day."

"Change the rendezvous."

Tamara suppressed her feeling of frustration. "It may be important," she said, trying not to sound exasperated.

"Who's the informant?"

Tamara lowered her voice. "Haroun."

Dexter laughed. He said to Doyle: "He's not exactly crucial to our operation." Turning back to Tamara he said: "You've only had one meeting with him."

"At which he gave me valuable intelligence."

"Which was never confirmed."

"My instinct tells me he's genuine."

"Women's intuition again. Sorry. Not good enough. Postpone." Dexter ushered Doyle into the meeting room.

Tamara took out her phone and wrote a one-word reply to Haroun:

Tomorrow.

She went into the meeting room and sat at the conference table to wait for the training session to begin. A minute later her phone vibrated with a message:

Your jeans are now 11 American.

Eleven o'clock tomorrow morning, she thought. No problem.

The museum was about three miles north of the American embassy. Traffic was light and Tamara was early. The museum was a new modern building in a landscaped park. There was a statue of Mother Africa in a fountain, but the fountain was dry.

She took out the blue scarf with orange circles, put it over her head, and tied it under her chin, just in case Haroun had forgotten what she looked like. She wore a scarf most of the time: with her usual dress and trousers she did not look noticeably different from a hundred thousand other women in the city.

She went inside.

This had not been a good choice for a clandestine rendezvous, she saw immediately. She had imagined that the two of them would be lost in a crowd, but there was no crowd. The museum was almost empty. However, the few visitors all looked like genuine tourists, so with luck no one would recognize Tamara or Haroun.

She went upstairs to the skull of the Toumai Man. It looked like a lump of old wood, almost shapeless, barely recognizable as a head. Perhaps that was not surprising as it was seven million years old. How could something have been preserved that long? As she was puzzling over this, Haroun appeared.

He was wearing Western clothes today, khakis and a plain white T-shirt. She felt the intensity of his dark-eyed gaze as he looked at her. He was risking his life, again. Everything he did would be extreme, she thought. Having been a jihadi, he was now a traitor to the jihadis, but he would never be anything in between.

"You should have come yesterday," he said.

"I couldn't. Is this urgent?"

"After the ambush at the refugee camp, our friends in Sudan are thirsty for revenge."

It never ends, Tamara thought. Every act of vengeance has to be avenged. "What do they want?"

"They know the ambush was the personal plan of the General. They want us to assassinate him."

No surprise there, Tamara thought, but it would not be easy. The General's security was tight. However, such things were never impossible. And if the attempt succeeded, Chad would be plunged into chaos. She had to sound the alarm about this.

She said: "How?"

"I told you that the Afghan taught us how to make suicide bombs."

Oh, Christ, she thought.

Two tourists came into the room, a middle-aged white couple in hats and sneakers, speaking French. Tamara and Haroun were speaking Arabic, which the visitors almost certainly could not understand. However, the newcomers strolled across to where Tamara and Haroun stood, by the cabinet containing the skull. Tamara smiled and nodded to them, then said quietly to Haroun: "Let's move."

The next room was empty. Tamara said: "Go on, please. How will this take place?"

"We know what the General's car looks like."

Tamara nodded. Everyone knew. It was a stretched Citroën like that used by the French president. There was only one in the country and, as if that were not enough, it had a small flagstaff on the fender flying a tricolor of blue, gold, and red in vertical stripes, the banner of Chad.

Haroun went on: "They will wait in the street near the Presidential Palace, and when he drives out they will throw themselves at the car, detonate their explosives, and then, they believe, go straight to heaven."

"Shit." It could work, Tamara thought. The palace complex was heavily defended, but the General had to come out sometime. His car might have been bullet-proof but it probably was not bombproof, especially if the suicide vests carried a large charge.

However, now that she had found out about the plot, the CIA could warn the General's security people, who could take extra precautions. "When are they planning to do this?"

"Today," said Haroun.

"Fuck!"

"That's why you should have met me yesterday."

She took out her phone. She paused for a moment. What other details did she need? "How many bombers?"

"Three."

"Can you describe them?"

Haroun shook his head. "I wasn't told who had been chosen—just that I had not."

"Men?"

"One could be a woman."

"How would they be dressed?"

"Traditionally, I expect. The robes hide the suicide vests. But I don't know for sure."

"Anyone else involved, in any way, over and above the three?"

"No. Extra people just create extra risk."

"What time will they go to the palace?"

"They may be there now."

Tamara called the CIA station in the embassy.

The call did not go through.

Haroun said: "The Afghan also taught us how to temporarily disable phone connectivity in the city."

Tamara stared at him. "You mean ISGS turned off everybody's phones?"

"Until someone figures out how to fix them."

"I have to go." She hurried from the room.

Behind her, she heard Haroun say: "Good luck."

She ran down the stairs and out to the parking lot. Her car was waiting, engine running. She jumped in and said: "Back to the embassy, fast, please."

As the car pulled away she had second thoughts. At the embassy she could report personally to the CIA station, but what could they do with no phones? It would be better to go straight to the Presidential Palace, but she was not well enough known to be admitted without delay—and would the guards at the gate believe a girl who said the General's life was in danger?

Then she thought of Karim. He would have immediate entry to the palace and could quickly get the ear of the General's head of security. But where would she find Karim? It was not yet noon: he might still be at the Café de Cairo, which was near the museum. She could try there first, and failing that drive into the town center and go to the Lamy Hotel.

She prayed the General would not drive out of the palace in the next few minutes.

She changed her instructions to the driver, and they reached the café in a couple of minutes. She hurried inside and saw, with great relief, that Karim was still there. She was only just in time: he was putting on his jacket preparatory to leaving. She had the irrelevant thought that he was getting fatter.

"I'm so glad I caught you," she said. "The phones have been cut off by ISGS."

"Really?" Shrugging on his jacket, he fished in the pocket for his phone, looked at the screen. "You're right. I didn't know they could do that."

"I just talked to an informant. They're planning to assassinate the General."

His mouth dropped open in shock. "Now?"

"I thought you were the best person to raise the alarm."

"Of course. How do they plan to do it?"

"Three suicide bombers outside the palace gates, waiting for his car."

"Clever. A route he must use, a moment when the vehicle must move slowly—he's at his most vulnerable." He hesitated. "How reliable is the information?"

"Karim, no informant is totally trustworthy— they're all deceivers at heart—but I think this tip might be true. The General should certainly take special precautions."

Karim nodded. "You're right. Such a warning must not be ignored. I'll go at once. My car is out back."

"Good."

He turned away to leave, then turned back. "Thank you."

"You're welcome."

Tamara left by the front door and got back into her car.

Again she thought about going to the embassy; again she decided there was nothing to be done there. The operations manual did not have a protocol for a combined assassination attempt and telephone breakdown. She briefly entertained the idea of getting Susan Marcus to lead a squad to the neighborhood of the palace to hunt down the bombers. But the US Army could not act independently of the local army and police—the confusion would be disastrous. And by the time they got the chain of command sorted out it would be too late.

She decided to go there herself. At least she could reconnoiter the street and try to identify the jihadis.

She directed the driver south on the freeway and right onto the Avenue Charles de Gaulle. There was no stopping outside the palace, so she got out of the cab a couple of hundred yards short of the entrance and told the driver to wait.

She checked her phone again. There was still no signal.

She looked along the broad boulevard ahead. The big iron gates of the palace were on the right-hand side of the road, guarded by rifle-toting soldiers of the national guard in their uniforms of green, black, and tan desert camouflage. Opposite were a monument park and the cathedral. The no-parking rule was enforced strictly here, so the jihadis would be on foot.

A black Mercedes squealed to a halt in front of the gates and was admitted immediately. She hoped that was Karim.

She thought for the first time about how dangerous this was for her. Anytime soon, anywhere along this street, a bomb could explode, and if she were nearby it would kill her.

She did not want to die, not when she had just found Tab.

Death was not the worst thing that could happen. She could be maimed, blinded, paralyzed.

She tied her scarf more firmly under her chin. She murmured to herself: "What the hell am I doing?" Then she walked briskly toward the palace.

On the palace side of the street there was no one but

the guards: everyone steered clear of men with rifles.
On her side a hundred or so people were in the monument park, tourists looking at the grandiose sculptures
and locals enjoying the space, eating their lunch or just
hanging out. I must try to identify the bombers, she
thought, and I don't have much time!

A contingent of armed police, led by a mustached
sergeant, watched the crowd. The cops were dressed in
a camouflage pattern slightly different from that of the
national guard. Tamara knew from experience that
their main job was to enforce a rule against photo-
graphing the palace, and she doubted that they would
be quick to spot a real terrorist.

Making herself calm, she carefully scanned the
people in the park. She ignored middle-aged and elderly men and women: jihadis were always young. She
also dismissed anyone wearing close-fitting modern
clothing such as shirts and jeans, because they had nowhere to hide a suicide vest. She concentrated on men
and women in their late teens or twenties wearing traditional robes, and on women in the hijab.

She made a mental note of each of the remaining
possibilities. A young man in white robes and a white
cap was sitting on the edge of a plinth reading the
newspaper *Al Wihda*: he looked too relaxed to be a terrorist, but Tamara could not be sure. A woman of
uncertain age had lumps under her black hijab, but
that might just have been her figure. A teenage boy in
orange robes and a turban was squatting at the roadside mending his Vespa motor scooter, the front wheel
detached and lying on the dusty ground amid a scatter
of nuts and bolts.

To one side of the park she noticed a bearded young
man standing in the shade of a tree, perspiring. He
wore a floor-length robe of the type called a thawb, a
galabiya, or a dishdasha, but over it he had a shapeless

loose-fitting cotton jacket buttoned to the neck. He was near the side street next to the park, and he glanced every now and again at the narrow road, where there was nothing to look at. He smoked nervously, with repeated quick puffs, burning the cigarette down fast.

When the president's car emerged from the palace complex it would probably turn left or right on the wide Avenue Charles de Gaulle, but it could go straight across to the side street that ran down toward the river. Logically there should be one suicide bomber this side of the entrance, one the other, and one near the side street.

She crossed the side street to the cathedral.

She looked across the avenue to the palace gates as she drew level with them. She could see the long straight driveway that led majestically up to the distant building, which looked more like a modern office than a palace. There were half a dozen more soldiers inside the gates, but they were simply lounging around, talking and smoking. Tamara was disappointed: if Karim had raised the alarm, surely by now a squad would be assembling to clear the area and protect the public in case of an explosion? But the street was busy, and cars and motorcycles continued to pass in both directions. A bomb here might kill hundreds of innocent bystanders. Was Karim's warning being ignored in there? Or were they perhaps concerned about the General but not the public?

The Cathedral of Our Lady of Peace was a spectacular modern church. However, the site was fenced and the gates were closed. There was no one in the grounds except for a gardener, in dark robes and a headdress, planting a small tree on the west side, close to the fence, only a few yards from Tamara. From his position he could clearly see the palace gates and the long driveway up to the building, and he could quickly cross the fence to the side street. Could he be an impostor? If so, he was taking a risk: a priest might say to him: "Who told you to plant a tree there?" On the other hand, there did not seem to be any priests around.

She returned to the monument park.

It was a matter of probabilities, but she thought the assassins were the boy mending the scooter, the sweating man under the tree, and the cathedral gardener. Each fit the profile, each had room under his robes for a sizable bomb.

Could they be arrested? Some suicide devices had dead man's ignition, a system in which the bomb would go off when the bomber released a cord, which guaranteed an explosion even if the bomber was killed. However, all three of her suspects were using their hands: one to mend a scooter, one to light cigarettes, and one to plant a tree. That meant they could not have dead man's ignition.

All the same they would have to be handled carefully. They had to be immobilized before they could reach the trigger. It would be a matter of a second or two.

She checked her phone. Still no signal.

What should she do? Probably nothing. Karim would make sure the General stayed out of harm's way. Sooner or later the police would close the monument park and clear the street. The assassins would slip away with the crowds.

But then they could try again tomorrow.

She told herself it was not her problem. She had provided the information: that was her job. The local police and the army must make the decisions.

She should probably leave.

She looked across the avenue and saw the General's distinctive limousine coming slowly down the driveway toward the gates.

She had to act.

She took out her CIA card and approached the police sergeant with the mustache. "I'm with the American military," she said, speaking Arabic and showing him the card. She pointed to the man under the tree. "I think that man has something suspicious under his jacket. You might want to check it out. I advise you to grab both his hands before speaking to him, in case he has a weapon."

The sergeant looked at her with suspicion. He was not going to take orders from an unknown woman, even if she did have an impressively official-looking plastic identity card with her photograph on it.

Tamara suppressed a rising panic and tried to keep her cool. "Whatever you do, you need to be quick, because the General seems to be coming."

The sergeant looked across the avenue, saw the limousine on the drive approaching the gates, and made a decision. He barked orders to two of his men and they marched across the park toward the smoker under the tree.

Tamara sent up a prayer of thanks.

The palace guards stepped out into the avenue and stopped the traffic.

The boy mending the scooter got to his feet.

Across the side street, the gardener in the cathedral grounds dropped his spade.

The palace gates opened.

Tamara approached the boy mending the scooter. He hardly noticed her, he was concentrating so hard on the limousine. She smiled at him and put her hands firmly on his chest. Through the orange cotton robes she felt a hard object with cables attached, and fear seized her. She forced herself to keep her hands there a moment longer. She felt three cylinders, undoubtedly containing charges of C4 explosive buried in small steel ball bearings, with wires connecting the cylinders to one another and to a small box that would be the detonator.

She was a heartbeat away from death.

The boy was surprised and confused by her sudden appearance. He pushed at her ineffectually and stepped back.

In the split second it took him to realize what was happening, she kicked his legs from under him.

He fell on his back. She dropped on him, knees in his belly, knocking the wind out of him. She grabbed the neck of his robe and ripped it open, exposing the black plastic and metal of the device strapped to his chest. Dangling from the detonator box she saw a cable that terminated in a simple green plastic trigger switch. Four dollars and ninety-nine cents at the hardware store, she thought stupidly.

She heard a nearby woman scream.

If he got his hands on that switch, he would kill himself and Tamara and a lot of other people.

She managed to grab both his wrists and push his arms to the ground, leaning forward to use all her weight. He bucked, trying to throw her off. The police nearby were staring in shock. She yelled: "Hold his arms and legs, before he blows us all up!"

After a stunned moment they did as she said. In normal circumstances they would not have followed her orders, but they could see the device and they knew what it was. Four cops grabbed the bomber's limbs and held tight.

Tamara stood up.

All around her the bystanders were backing away, some running.

In the far corner of the park, the nervous smoker was being handcuffed.

The palace gates opened and the limousine came through.

In the cathedral grounds, the gardener ran at the fence.

The car crossed the avenue, picking up speed, and headed down the side street.

The gardener vaulted the fence onto the sidewalk. He reached inside his galabiya and drew out a green plastic trigger switch.

Uselessly, Tamara yelled: "No!"

He ran into the road and threw himself at the car. The driver saw him and slammed on the brakes, too late. The bomber hit the windshield and seemed to bounce, then there was a terrific bang and a flash. The windshield shattered and the bomber was thrown into the road. The car continued to roll forward, leaving the corpse in the middle of the street. It veered to the right and crashed into the fence surrounding the cathedral. The fence was flattened but the car came to a stop.

No one got out.

Tamara ran across the park to the crashed vehicle. Others had the same idea and were close behind her. She threw open the passenger door and looked inside.

The back of the car was empty.

There was a smell of fresh blood. In the front was just one man, the driver, slumped and motionless. His face was too damaged and bloody to be recognizable, but he was small and thin with gray hair, and therefore not the General, who was massive and bald.

The General was not in the car.

For a moment Tamara was bewildered. Then she reasoned that the driver might simply have been going to get fuel. A darker thought was that he had been sent out as a test, to see whether the threat was real, in which case his life had been sacrificed. It was grim but possible.

There were holes in the bodywork and steel balls all over the floor.

Tamara had seen enough. She turned away and walked back to the monument park.

I saved the General, she thought. I nearly lost my life. Was it worth it? Who the hell knows?

But she had not finished. Haroun had said that the government of Sudan was behind this. If true, it was important, but she wanted confirmation.

The boy with the scooter had been relieved of his suicide vest—Tamara would have waited for the bomb squad, if the choice had been hers—and now the police were putting handcuffs and leg restraints on him.

Tamara approached, and a cop said: "What are you doing?"

"I gave the alarm," she said harshly.

Another cop said: "It's true, she did."

The first cop shrugged, and she took that for permission.

She moved closer to the bomber. He had light brown eyes. She could see the wisps of adolescent hair on his cheeks: he was terribly young. Her closeness to him was a contradictory message, both intimate and threatening, and it confused him.

She spoke in a low voice. "Your friend in the cathedral garden is dead," she said.

The bomber looked at her, then looked away. "He is in heaven."

"You did this for God."

"God is great."

"But you were helped." She paused, staring hard into his eyes, trying to get him to look back at her, to make a human connection. "You were taught how to make the bombs."

At last he looked at her. "You know nothing."

"I know that you were taught by the Afghan."

She saw the surprise in his eyes.

She pressed her advantage. "I know that you got the materials from the friends in Sudan."

She did not know this, though she strongly suspected it. His expression did not change. He continued to be startled by how much she knew.

She said: "It was the Sudanese friends who told you to kill the General."

She held her breath. That was what she needed to confirm.

At last he spoke. His tone of amazement was unmistakably genuine. "How do you know?"

It was enough. Tamara walked away.

Back at the embassy she went to her room. Suddenly feeling completely wiped out, she lay down on her bed. She slept for a few minutes, then her phone rang.

Service had been restored.

She answered. Dexter's voice said: "Where the hell are you?"

She almost hung up. She closed her eyes for a moment, summoning her patience.

He said: "Are you there?"

"I'm in my room."

"What are you doing there?"

She was not going to tell him that she was recovering from an ordeal. She had learned long ago not to admit weakness to a male colleague. They would never tire of reminding you about it. "I'm freshening up," she said.

"Get over here."

She hung up without answering. She had come close to losing her life, and she could no longer take Dexter seriously. She walked unhurriedly across the compound to the CIA station.

She found Dexter sitting at his desk. Phil Doyle was with him. By this time Dexter had learned more. "They're saying a CIA woman arrested a suspect!" he said. "Was that you?"

"Yes."

"What are you doing arresting people? What possessed you, for Christ's sake?"

She sat down uninvited. "Do you want me to tell you what happened, or would you prefer just to yell at me?"

Dexter bristled but he hesitated. He could not deny that he had been shouting, and his boss was there. Even in the CIA it was risky for a man to open himself to the accusation of bullying. "All right," he said. "Make your case."

"Make my case?" She shook her head. "Am I on trial? If so, we'd better be formal. I'll need a legal representative."

Doyle spoke in a reasonable voice. "You're not on trial," he said. "Just tell us what happened."

She told them the whole thing, and they listened without interruption.

When she had finished, Dexter said: "Why did you go to Karim? You should have reported to me!"

He was angry that he had been left out of the drama. Tamara was exhausted from the tension, but she forced her brain into gear and re-created the thought process she had gone through. "My informant said the assassination was imminent. But the phones were not working. I had to decide what was the fastest way to get the warning to the General. If I had gone to the palace myself I probably couldn't have gotten in. But Karim could."

"I could have gone there."

Why couldn't he work this stuff out for himself? She said wearily: "Even you wouldn't have gotten in immediately. You would have been subjected to questions and delays. Karim has instant access to the General. He was able to sound the alarm faster than people here at the embassy, in fact faster than anyone else I can think of."

"All right, but why didn't you report to me after you had seen Karim?"

"No time. I would have had to tell you the story. You would have been skeptical, and we would have had a long conversation very like this one. Finally you would have believed me, but then it would have taken you time to assemble a team and brief them, and only then would you have set out for the palace. It was obviously better for me to go to the scene right away and try to spot the bombers. Which I did. Successfully."

"I could have done that more efficiently with a team."

"Except that you would not have gotten there until after the explosion. The assassination attempt took place within minutes of my arrival. In those few minutes I correctly identified all three bombers. Two are now in custody and the third is dead."

Dexter changed his line. "And it was all for nothing, because the General wasn't in the car." He was determined to diminish her achievement.

Tamara shrugged. She hardly cared what Dexter thought. She was realizing that she could not work under him much longer. "Probably he wasn't in the car because Karim warned him."

"We don't know that."

"True." She was too tired to argue.

But Dexter was not finished. "A pity your informant didn't tell us sooner."

"That was your fault."

Dexter sat upright. "What are you talking about?"

"He wanted to see me yesterday. I told you I had to leave the training session early. You ordered me to postpone the meeting instead."

She saw that Dexter had not connected the two events. Now he was worried. It took him a few moments to respond. Then he said: "No, no, that's not how it happened. We had a discussion—"

"Crap," she said, interrupting him. She was not having this. "There was no discussion. You ordered me not to meet him at the appointed time."

"You're misremembering this."

Tamara directed a hard look at Doyle. He had been there. He knew the truth. He looked uncomfortable. She guessed he felt an impulse to lie, in order to avoid undermining Dexter's authority. If he did that, Tamara decided, she would resign on the spot. She kept her gaze on him, saying nothing, just waiting for him to speak.

Eventually he said: "I think you're the one who's misremembering, Dexter. My recollection is that the conversation was brief and you gave an order."

Dexter looked as if he would explode. He reddened and his breath came fast. Struggling to control his anger, he said: "I guess we'll have to agree to differ, Phil—"

"No, no," said Doyle firmly. "I'm not agreeing to differ." Now he was in the position of imposing discipline, and it seemed he was not going to fudge the issue. "You made a judgment call and it turned out badly. Don't worry, it's not a capital offense." He turned to Tamara. "You may leave us."

She stood up.

Doyle said: "You did good work today. Thank you."

"Thank you, sir," said Tamara, and she went out.

"The General wants to give you a medal," Karim said to Tamara the following morning at the Café de Cairo.

He was looking pleased with himself. She guessed that his warning had earned him the General's profound gratitude. In a dictatorship, that was better than money.

"I'm flattered," Tamara said. "But I'll probably have to refuse. The CIA doesn't like its officers to get publicity."

He smiled. She guessed that he did not mind her refusal: it meant he would not have to share the spotlight. "I suppose you are supposed to be *secret* agents," he said.

"All the same, it's good to know that the General appreciates our work."

"The two surviving bombers have been under questioning."

I bet they have, Tamara thought. They will have been kept awake all night, denied food and water, grilled by alternating teams of interrogators, and probably tortured too. "Will you share the interrogators' full report with us?"

"I should think it's the least we can do."

Which was not a yes, Tamara noted, but Karim probably did not have the authority to give a definite answer.

Karim said: "My friend the General is furious about the assassination attempt. He takes it very personally. He looked at the body of the chauffeur and said: 'That could have been me.'"

Tamara decided not to ask whether the driver had been sacrificed in a test. She said: "I hope the General isn't going to do anything rash." She was thinking of the elaborate ambush he had set up at the refugee camp, all in retaliation for a minor skirmish at the N'Gueli Bridge.

"So do I. But he will have his revenge."

"I wonder what he will do."

"If I knew I couldn't tell you—but, as it happens, I don't know."

Tamara felt Karim was telling the truth, but that made her more apprehensive. Why would the General keep his intentions secret from one of his closest associates, the man who had just saved his life? "I hope it's not dramatic enough to destabilize the region."

"Unlikely."

"I wonder. The Chinese are deeply involved in Sudan. We don't want them to start flexing their muscles."

"The Chinese are our friends."

The Chinese had no friends, in Tamara's opinion. They had clients and debtors. But she did not want to argue with Karim. He was a conservative old man who would only take so much from a girl. "That's something to be grateful for," she said, trying to make it sound sincere. "And I'm sure you'll urge caution."

He looked smug. "I always do. Don't worry. It will be all right."

"Inshallah," said Tamara. "God willing."

The next day, toward the end of the afternoon, CNN began to report a serious fire in Port Sudan, the unimaginatively named major port in Sudan. Ships in the Red Sea had first reported the fire, said CNN. They broadcast a crackly radio interview with the captain of an oil tanker who had decided to stand offshore while he tried to find out whether it was safe to enter the harbor. There was a huge cloud of blue-gray smoke, he said.

Virtually all Sudan's oil was exported from Port

Sudan. Most of it arrived through a thousand-mile pipeline that was majority-owned and operated by the China National Petroleum Corporation. The Chinese had also built a refinery, and they were in the process of creating a new multibillion-dollar tanker dock.

The CNN report was followed by a government announcement that the fire service expected to have the blaze under control shortly, which meant it was out of control, and that a full investigation would be carried out, which meant they had no idea what had caused it. Tamara had a dark suspicion in the back of her mind that she did not yet voice to anyone.

She began to monitor the jihadi websites, the ones that celebrated beheadings and kidnappings. On her first sweep they were all quiet.

She called Colonel Marcus and asked: "Do you have any satellite of Port Sudan just before the fire?"

"Probably," said Susan. "There's never much cloud over that part of the globe. What time frame?"

"CNN reported it around four thirty, and there was already a pall of smoke. . . ."

"Three thirty or earlier, then. I'll take a look. What do you suspect?"

"I don't really know. Something."

"Fair enough."

Tamara called Tab at the French embassy. "What do you know about the fire at Port Sudan?"

"Only what's on TV," he said. "I love you too, by the way."

She stifled a giggle. In a lowered voice she said: "Knock it off. I'm in an open-plan office."

"Sorry."

"I told you last night what I'm afraid of."

"You mean the revenge theory."

"Yes."

"You think this could be it?"

"I do."

"There'll be trouble."

"You bet your sweet ass." She hung up.

No one but Tamara was worried about this, and around five o'clock people started to drift away from their desks.

Soon afterward the government in Khartoum, Sudan's capital, added to their original announcement, saying that some twenty people had been rescued from the fire, including four Chinese engineers who had been working on the construction of the new dock. Some Chinese women and children, the families of the engineers, had also been rescued. CNN explained that the dock was being built with Chinese expertise as well as money, and that something like a hundred Chinese engineers were involved in the project. Tamara wondered about the people who had *not* been rescued.

Still there was no suggestion of sabotage, and Tamara was beginning to hope that this would turn out to be a genuine accident, with no political implications.

She scanned the web again, and this time she stopped at a site operated by a group calling itself Salafi Jihadi Sudan. She had not heard of them before. The group condemned the backsliding government of Sudan, especially as symbolized by the corrupt Chinese-led tanker dock project. It congratulated heroic SJS fighters for bringing off today's attack.

Tamara called Susan, who said: "It was my fucking drone—the one that went missing."

"Shit."

"It dropped bombs on the refinery and the half-built new dock, then crashed."

"Chinese engineers were building that dock."

"They struck at thirteen twenty-one."

"An American drone has killed Chinese engineers. There's going to be hell to pay."

Tamara hung up, then sent Dexter the link to the SJS site. She sent the same to Tab.

Then she sat back and thought: What will the Chinese do now?

CHAPTER 24

Chang Kai's phone was ringing but, to his intense
frustration, he could not find the instrument. He
woke up and realized he had been dreaming, but
his phone was still ringing. He found it on the bedside
table. The caller was Fan Yimu, the overnight manager
at the Guoanbu office. He said: "I'm sorry to wake you
in the middle of the night, sir."

"Oh, hell," said Kai. "North Korea has blown up."

"No, nothing like that."

Kai was relieved. The rebels and the regime had
been stalemated for ten days, and he was hoping the
situation would somehow get resolved without civil
war. "Thank God for that," he said.

Ting snuggled up to him without opening her eyes.
He put his arm around her and stroked her hair. "So
what has happened?" he said to Fan.

"Approximately one hundred Chinese people have
been killed by a drone in the city of Port Sudan."

"Where we're building a tanker dock for billions of
dollars, as I recall."

"Just so. Chinese engineers are working on the project. The dead are mostly men, but with a small number

of women, plus children who belonged to the engineers' families."

"Who did this? Who sent the drone?"

"Sir, the news has just come in and I thought it best to inform you before making further inquiries."

"Send a car for me."

"I already have. Monk should be outside your building any minute now."

"Well done. I'll be with you as soon as I can." Kai hung up.

Ting mumbled: "Would you like a quick one?"

"Go back to sleep, my darling."

Kai washed quickly and dressed in a suit and a white shirt. He put a tie in one pocket and his electric shaver in the other. Looking out of the window, he saw a silver Geely compact sedan waiting at the curb with its headlights on. He picked up his overcoat and went out.

The air was frosty and there was a cold wind. He got into the car and started shaving while Monk drove. He called Fan and told him to summon some key people: his secretary, Peng Yawen; Yang Yong, a specialist in interpreting surveillance photographs; Zhou Meiling, a young woman expert on the internet; and Shi Xiang, Arabic-speaking head of the North Africa desk. Each of them would call in support staff.

He wondered who could be responsible for the attack on Port Sudan.

The Americans were automatically prime suspects. They were threatened by China's drive to forge trading links across the world, what was called the Belt and Road Initiative, and they realized that China wanted control of Africa's oil and other natural resources. But would they deliberately murder a hundred Chinese people?

The Saudis had drones, sold to them by the US, and they were only two hundred kilometers from Port Sudan across the Red Sea, but the Saudis and the Sudanese were allies. It could have been an accident, but that seemed unlikely. Drones had direction-finding computers. This had been targeted.

That left terrorists. But which ones?

It was now his job to find out, and President Chen would want answers in the morning.

He reached Guoanbu headquarters. Some of his team were already there and others arrived in the next few minutes. He told them to gather in the conference room. He had acquired the coffee habit recently, like millions of Chinese people, and he got a cup and carried it with him.

On one of the screens around the walls of the room, the Al Jazeera news channel was showing live footage of the fire in Port Sudan, apparently taken from a ship. Night had now fallen in East Africa, but the flames illuminated the smoke cloud.

Kai sat at the head of the table. "Let's see what we've got," he began. "I assume that some of the engineers are Guoanbu assets?" Every overseas venture was kept under close observation by Kai's agents.

Shi Xiang answered him. "Two of them, but one was killed by the bombing." Shi, head of the North Africa desk, was a middle-aged man with a gray mustache. He had married an African girl, years ago during his first posting overseas, and they had a daughter now at the university. "I have a report from the surviving agent, Tan Yuxuan. The dead include ninety-seven men and four women, all of whom were on the dock when the drone struck. It was the heat of the day, when people take a long break in that part of the world, and they were all inside an air-conditioned hut, eating lunch or resting."

"This is terrible," Kai said.

"The drone fired two air-to-ground missiles that

badly damaged the partly built dock and set fire to
nearby oil tanks. There were also two children killed.
We don't normally allow people working overseas to
take their children with them but the chief engineer
was an exception, and yesterday he happened to bring
his twin sons to see the project, tragically."

"What's the government in Khartoum saying?"

"Nothing substantive. They made an announcement two hours ago claiming that they were getting the
fire under control and would investigate the cause. It's
a typical holding statement."

"Anything from the White House?"

"Not yet. It's now early afternoon in Washington.
They may react before the end of the day."

Kai turned to Yang Yong, an older man with a lined
face, experienced with satellite imagery. "We have the
drone on camera," Yang said, touching keys on his
laptop. A picture appeared on one of the wall screens.

Kai leaned forward, trying to make sense of what he
was looking at. "I can't see anything," he said.

Yang was an expert and had probably started out
peering at high-altitude airplane photos, before the
days of satellite photography. He picked up a laser
flashlight and shone a red dot on the image. With that
assistance Kai was able to make out a silhouette. He
might have taken it for a seagull.

Yang said: "It's over a highway." He moved the red
dot. "That smudge is a truck."

"Can we tell what type of drone it is?" Kai asked.

"It's big," Yang said. "I'd say it's an MQ-9 Reaper,
made by General Atomics in the US but sold to a dozen
other countries, including Taiwan and the Dominican
Republic."

"And probably available on the black market."

"It's possible."

Yang changed the image. Now the seagull was over

a city, presumably Port Sudan. Kai said: "Did the Sudanese react to this?"

Shi answered. "Air traffic control must have picked it up, and they probably stopped take-offs and landings for a time—I'll check."

"Their air force could have shot it down."

"I guess they did not assume it was hostile. It might have been civilian, or perhaps a Saudi drone that had strayed across the Red Sea."

Yang changed the picture again. "This is just before the drone fired its missiles. I've zoomed the image. You can see the dock. The aircraft is flying very low." He touched his keyboard again. "And this is just after the explosion."

Kai could see the collapsing masonry and a huge pall of smoke rising. The seagull had tilted as if blown by a wind. Yang said: "The drone was so low that the blast damaged it fatally. Such a mistake might be made by an inexperienced controller."

Kai said: "We can assume the Americans' satellites have shown them similar pictures."

"Certainly," said Yang.

Kai looked at Zhou Meiling. She was young and lacked confidence except when she was talking about her specialty. Kai said: "What have you got, Meiling?"

"A group calling itself Salafi Jihadi Sudan claims responsibility, but we know little about them—suspiciously little. The site has been up for only a few days."

"A new group that no one has ever heard of," Kai said. "Formed just for this one outrage, probably. Or it could be a fake."

"I'm checking."

"Have other sites commented?"

"Just general hate speech—except for the Uighurs in China. As you know, sir, there are several illegal sites claiming to represent Uighur Muslims in Xinjiang, though some or all of them could be fake. However, the fact is that most of these sites are celebrating the killing of repressive Chinese Communists by freedom-loving African Muslims."

Kai was scornful. "The Uighurs ought to try life in Sudan. They'd soon be begging to come back to authoritarian China." He was angry because the rejoicing of the Uighurs might provoke the Communist old guard to rash reactions. Men such as his father would be clamoring for retaliation.

"All right," he said after a pause. "Meiling, see what more you can find out about Salafi Jihadi Sudan. Yang, go through previous satellite pictures and track the drone back to its launch point. Shi, have our man in Port Sudan look for the wreckage of the drone and see if he can identify the source. Everyone, keep an eye on the Arab and American news channels for government reactions. I'll have to brief the foreign minister first thing in the morning and probably the president before the end of the day, so make sure I've got all the information available."

The meeting broke up and Kai returned to his office.

His secretary, Peng Yawen, brought him tea. She disapproved of coffee, which she regarded as a young people's fad. On the tray was a plate of nai wong bao, steamed buns with a custard filling. He realized he was hungry. "Where did you get these, at this time of night?" he asked.

"My mother made them. She heard I was working all night and sent them in a taxi."

Yawen was in her fifties, so her mother must have been in her seventies, Kai thought. He bit into a bun. The bread was light and fluffy, the custard deliciously sweet. "Your mother is a blessing from heaven," he said.

"I know."

Kai took a second bun.

Yang Yong hovered in the doorway, a large sheet of paper in his hand. "Come in," Kai said.

Yawen left as Yang entered. He came around Kai's desk and unfolded the paper, which was a map of northeast Africa. "The drone was launched from an uninhabited area of desert a hundred kilometers from Khartoum." He put his finger on the map at a point west of the river Nile. Kai noticed the ropy veins on the back of his elderly hand.

"You were quick," Kai said in surprise.

"These days you can set the computer to do the tracking for you."

"How far is that spot from the border with Chad?"

"More than a thousand kilometers."

"So this supports the theory that the perpetrators are local Sudanese insurgents, rather than Islamist terrorists."

"The same people can be both."

Just to make things more complicated, Kai thought. He said: "Can you track the drone back farther?"

"I can try. It might have been transported disassembled, of course, in which case it won't be visible. Otherwise it must have flown in. And we don't know how long ago. I'll see what I can find, but don't hold your breath."

A few minutes later Zhou Meiling appeared, her young face alight with eagerness. "Salafi Jihadi Sudan seems genuine," she said. "It's a new name, but they have posted photographs of the members—heroes, as they call them—and some are known extremists that we've seen before."

"Are they Sudanese rebels or Islamic terrorists?"

"The rhetoric suggests both. In either case it's hard to imagine how they got hold of an MQ-9 Reaper. They cost thirty-two million dollars to buy."

"Any indication of where the group is based?"

"The website is hosted in Russia, but SJS obviously isn't there. They can't be in one of the refugee camps, which have no connectivity. They could be holed up in a city, either Khartoum or Port Sudan."

"Keep looking."

It was another hour before Shi Xiang reported, but he had the most important information of all. He walked in carrying a laptop computer. "We just received a photo from Tan Yuxuan in Port Sudan," he said excitedly. "It's a fragment of the wreckage."

Kai looked at the screen. The picture had been taken at night with a flash, but it was perfectly clear. In among the debris of corrugated iron and drywall was a piece of scorched and twisted Kevlar-type composite, the kind of lightweight material that drones were made of. Clearly visible was a white star in a blue disk, with red, white, and blue stripes extending either side—the roundel of the United States Air Force.

"I'll be damned," said Kai. "It was the motherfucking Americans."

"It certainly looks that way."

"Make me twenty high-quality prints of this, please."

"Right away." Shi went out.

Kai sat back. He had enough now to brief the politicians. But the news was bad news. The Americans were involved in the slaughter of more than a hundred innocent Chinese people. This was a major international incident. The explosion on the Port Sudan waterfront was going to send shock waves around the world.

He needed to know what the Americans had to say.

Kai called his CIA contact, Neil Davidson. The call was picked up immediately. "This is Neil." He sounded alert and fully awake, even with his laid-back Texas drawl. Kai was surprised.

"This is Kai."

"How did you get my home number?"

"How do you think?" The Guoanbu had the private phone number of every foreigner in Beijing, naturally.

"My mistake, stupid question."

"I expected you to be asleep."

"I'm awake for the same reason you're awake, I guess."

"Because one hundred and three Chinese citizens have been killed in Sudan by an American drone."

"We did not fire that drone."

"The wreckage bears the symbol of the United States Air Force."

Neil went quiet. Clearly this was news to him.

Kai added: "A white star in a blue disk, with stripes on both sides."

"I can't comment on that, but I'm telling you definitely that we did not send a drone to bomb Port Sudan."

"That doesn't exempt you from responsibility."

"Doesn't it? Remember Corporal Ackerman? You refused to take responsibility when he was murdered with a Chinese weapon."

He had a point, but Kai was not going to admit it. "That was a rifle. How many million rifles are there in the world? No one can keep track of them, whether they're made in China or the US or anywhere else. A drone is different."

"The fact remains that the US did not send that drone."

"Who did?"

"Responsibility has been claimed—"

"I know who's claiming responsibility, Neil. I'm asking you who launched the thing. You should know, it's your fucking drone."

"Calm down, Kai."

"If a Chinese drone had killed a hundred Americans, how calm would you be? Would President Green deal with the incident in a calm and unemotional manner?"

"Point taken," Neil said. "All the same, it's no use us yelling at one another over the phone at five o'clock in the goddamn morning."

Kai realized Neil was right. I'm an intelligence officer, he told himself; my job is to gather information, not let off steam. "All right," he said. "Accepting, for the sake of argument, that you did not launch the drone, how do you account for what happened in Port Sudan?"

"I'm going to tell you something off the record. If you repeat it publicly we will deny it—"

"I know what 'off the record' means."

There was a pause, then Neil said: "Strictly between you and me, Kai, that drone was stolen."

Kai sat upright. "Stolen? From where?"

"I can't give you details, I'm sorry."

"I suppose it was taken from American forces in North Africa that are part of your campaign against ISGS."

"Don't press me. All I can do is steer you in the right direction. I'm telling you that someone purloined that drone."

"I believe you, Neil," said Kai, although he was not sure he really did. "But no one here is going to credit the story without details."

"Come on, Kai, be logical. Why would the White House want to murder a hundred Chinese engineers? Not to mention their families."

"I don't know, but it's hard for me to believe that the US is completely innocent."

"Okay." Neil sounded resigned. "If you guys are determined to start World War Three over this I can't stop you."

Neil had voiced an anxiety that Kai shared. It lay at

the back of Kai's mind like a sleeping dragon, full of
latent menace. Kai would not admit this, but he shared
Neil's fear that the Chinese government would overreact
to the Port Sudan bombing, with severe consequences.
However, he spoke in a normal voice. "Thank you, Neil.
Let's stay in touch."

"You got it."

They hung up.

Kai spent the next hour composing a report summarizing all he had learned since his phone had woken
him. He filed the memorandum under the code name
Vulture. He looked at the clock: it was six a.m.

He decided to call the foreign minister personally.
He should really report to Security Minister Fu Chuyu,
but Fu was not yet in the office; this was a flimsy excuse,
but it would do. He dialed Wu Bai's home phone.

Wu was awake and up. He answered with: "Yes?"
Kai heard a buzz in the background and guessed that
Wu was using an electric shaver.

"This is Chang Kai, and I apologize for calling so
early, but one hundred and three Chinese people have
been killed in Sudan by an American drone."

"Oh, hell," said Wu. The buzzing stopped. "This
will be a shit storm."

"I agree."

"Who else knows?"

"Right now, no one in China outside the Guoanbu.
The TV news is saying only that there is a fire at the
docks in Port Sudan."

"Good."

"But obviously I must inform the military as soon
as I've briefed you. Shall I come to your apartment?"

"Yes, why not, that will save time."

"I'll be there in half an hour, if that suits you."

"See you then."

Kai printed copies of the Vulture file and put them

in a briefcase with some of the photos Shi had printed that showed the USAF roundel on the wrecked drone. Then he went downstairs to his waiting car. He gave Monk the home address of Wu. He took his tie from his pocket and knotted it as they drove.

Wu lived in Chaoyang Park, the swankiest neighborhood in Beijing. His building overlooked the golf course. In the glittering lobby Kai had to prove his identity and pass through a metal detector before he went up in the elevator.

Wu opened the apartment door dressed in a pale gray shirt and the trousers of a pin-striped suit. His cologne had a vanilla note. The place was luxurious, though nothing as large as some of the apartments Kai had seen in the US. Wu took him through to a dining room where breakfast was laid out with gleaming silverware on a white linen cloth. Bone china dishes held steamed dumplings, rice porridge with prawns, fried dough sticks, and paper-thin crepes with a plum sauce. Wu believed in living well.

Kai drank some tea and talked while Wu ate porridge. He ran through the tanker dock project, the bombing, the drone, the claim of responsibility by SJS, and the American allegation that the drone had been stolen. He showed Wu the photograph of the drone wreckage and gave him a copy of the Vulture file. All the while, the aroma of spicy food was making his mouth water. When he had finished speaking Wu told him to help himself to breakfast, and he gratefully took some dumplings and tried not to wolf them.

Wu said: "We have to retaliate."

Kai had expected this. He knew it would be pointless to argue for no reprisals: that would never fly. So he began by agreeing. "When just one American is killed the White House reacts as if there has been a holocaust," he said. "Chinese lives are equally precious."

"But what form should our retaliation take?"

"Our response should balance yin and yang," he said, edging toward an argument for moderation. "We must be strong but not foolhardy, restrained but never weak. The word should be *retaliate*—not *escalate*."

"Very good," said Wu, who was a moderate out of laziness rather than conviction.

The door opened and a dumpy middle-aged woman came in. When she kissed Wu, Kai realized she was Wu's wife. He had not met her before, and he was surprised that she was not more glamorous. "Good morning, Bai," she said to her husband. "How is breakfast?"

"Delicious, thank you," Wu said. "This is my colleague Chang Kai."

Kai stood up and bowed. "I'm delighted to meet you," he said.

She smiled pleasantly. "I hope you got something to eat."

"The dumplings are wonderful."

She returned her attention to Wu. "Your car is here, my dear." She left the room.

She was a complete contrast to Wu, thought Kai, but they were clearly a fond couple.

Wu said: "Have some more breakfast while I'm putting my tie on." He went out.

Kai took out his phone and called Peng Yawen, his secretary. "There's a file called 'Vulture' in my Africa folder," he said. "Send it immediately to Fu Chuyu, with copies to List Three—that's the one with all ministers, generals, and senior Communist Party officials. Attach the photo of the drone wreckage. Do it right away, please—I want these people to get the news from me, not from anyone else."

"The Vulture file," she said.

"Yes."

"And the drone photo."

"That's what I said."

There was a pause, and Kai could hear her tapping her keyboard.

"To Fu Chuyu, with copies to List Three."

"Correct."

"It's done, sir."

Kai smiled. He loved efficient staff. "Thank you." He hung up.

Wu returned in a jacket and tie, carrying a slender document case. Kai went down in the elevator with him. The two government cars were waiting outside the building. Wu said to Kai: "When will you report to everyone else?"

"I did it while you were getting ready."

"Good. I'll probably see you later. The ructions will go on all day."

Kai smiled. "I'm afraid so."

Wu hesitated, evidently deciding just how to phrase what he wanted to say. His face changed: the mask of the bon vivant vanished, and suddenly Kai saw a worried man. "We can't let them kill Chinese people with impunity," he said. "That move isn't on the board."

Kai just nodded.

"What we must do," Wu said, "is stop the warriors on both sides from turning this into a bloodbath." He got into his car.

"You said it," Kai murmured as the car drove away.

It was half past seven. Kai needed a shower and clean clothes and his best suit—the armor of political combat. If he was going to get home today, now was the time. He told Monk to return to the apartment building. Meanwhile he called the office.

Shi Xiang, the head of the North Africa desk, wanted to speak to him. "An interesting story from my people in Chad," he said. "It seems that the US military there has lost a drone, and everyone thinks it was stolen by the Chad National Army."

Perhaps Neil had been telling the truth. "That sounds horribly plausible."

"The theory is that the president of Chad—he's called the General—gave the drone to a Sudanese rebel group, knowing it would be used against the Sudan government."

"Why the hell would he do a thing like that?"

"My people there think it might be the General's revenge for a recent attempt on his life by suicide bombers connected with Sudan."

"A Saharan idol drama," Kai observed. "I bet it's true."

"That's what I think."

"The White House hasn't commented yet, but I've heard from a CIA contact that the drone was stolen."

"Then it's probably true."

"Or an elaborate cover story," Kai said. "Keep me updated. I'm going home to freshen up."

He almost got there. He was a few minutes away from his building when Peng Yawen called. "President Chen has read the Vulture file," she said. "You're summoned to the Situation Room at Zhongnanhai. The meeting begins at nine."

In rush-hour traffic it might take an hour to get there. Kai could not risk being late. There was no time to go home. He told Monk to turn around.

Suddenly he was tired. He had done almost a day's work already. Now, when ordinary people were rising and getting ready for work, he wanted to go back to bed. This would not do. He was going to advise the president during a crisis. He wanted to steer China toward a conciliatory approach. He needed to be alert.

He could rest for a few minutes now, though. He closed his eyes. He must have dozed, for when he opened his eyes the car was driving through the Gate of the New China into the Zhongnanhai campus.

At the entrance to Qinzheng Hall, the presidential building, the dapper head of presidential security, Wang Qingli, was supervising the security operation. He greeted Kai amiably. The metal detector in the lobby beeped at the shaver in Kai's pocket and he had to leave it with security. However, his name was on the list of people who were allowed to keep their phones.

The Situation Room was a bombproof underground vault. In a room like a sports hall, a conference table on a raised stage was surrounded by fifty or more desks, each with multiple screens. In addition there were giant screens all around the walls. Several of them were showing the fire in Port Sudan, where it was still dark.

Kai took out his phone and saw that he had a good signal. He called the Guoanbu and said to Peng Yawen: "Tell everyone to message me with developments. At this point I need to know everything in real time."

"Yes, sir."

He crossed the room and stepped up onto the central stage. His boss, Security Minister Fu Chuyu, was already there, talking to General Huang Ling, who was in full uniform. They were the leaders of the old guard, and they believed in bold, assertive action. Fu pointedly turned his back on Kai: he was undoubtedly angry that Kai had gone on his own to see Wu Bai.

However, President Chen greeted Kai affably. "How are you, young Kai? Thank you for your report. You must have worked all night."

"We did, Mr. President."

"Well, I'm sure you'll be able to take a nap while I'm talking."

It was a self-deprecating joke, and to agree or disagree would have been equally impolite, so Kai laughed and said nothing. Chen often tried to put people at ease with humor, but he was not very good at it.

Kai nodded to Wu Bai and said: "Our second meeting today, Foreign Minister, and it's not yet nine o'clock."

Wu said: "The food's not as good at this one." In the middle of the conference table, along with the usual bottles of water and trays of glasses, were plates of sachima pastries and green bean cake that looked several days old.

Kai's father, Chang Jianjun, was honored with a vigorous handshake from President Chen. Jianjun had helped to get him made president, but since then Chen had disappointed Jianjun and his cronies with his caution and restraint in international affairs.

Jianjun smiled at Kai, and Kai bowed his head, but they did not embrace: both felt that displays of family affection looked unprofessional on occasions such as this. Jianjun sat down with Huang Ling and Fu Chuyu, and they all lit cigarettes.

Aides and junior officials sat at some of the desks on the lower level, but most remained unoccupied. The big room would probably not be filled for any event short of war.

The young national defense minister, Kong Zhao, came in, his hair stylishly disarranged as usual. He and Wu Bai sat together opposite the old guard. Battle lines were being drawn, Kai saw, like troops with swords and muskets facing each other across a field in the Opium Wars.

The commander of the People's Liberation Army Navy, Admiral Liu Hua, was also part of the old guard, and after paying his respects to the president he sat next to Chang Jianjun.

Kai saw that President Chen's gold Travers fountain pen had been laid on a leather-bound notepad at one end of the oval table. Kai placed himself at the opposite end, far from the president but equidistant from the rival factions. He belonged to the liberal bloc, but he pretended neutrality.

The president moved to his seat. A moment of danger was approaching. Kai remembered Wu's parting remark two hours ago: *What we must do is stop the warriors on both sides from turning this into a bloodbath.*

Chen held up a document that Kai recognized as his Vulture file. "You've all read this excellent and concise report from the Guoanbu." He turned to the security minister. "Thank you for that, Fu. Do you have anything to add?"

Fu did not bother to say that he had had nothing to do with the Vulture file and in fact had been fast asleep while all the work was done. "Nothing to add, Mr. President."

Kai spoke up. "In the last few minutes we've heard something—only a rumor, but an interesting one."

Fu glared at him. Kai had shown that he was more up to speed in the crisis. That will teach him to use my wife against me, Kai thought with satisfaction. Then he had a more cautious thought: I must be careful, I shouldn't overdo it.

He went on: "People in Chad believe their army stole the drone from the Americans and gave it to Salafi Jihadi Sudan, as revenge for an attempt on the president's life. It's just possible that the rumor is true."

"Rumor?" General Huang growled. "It sounds to me like a feeble American excuse." His northern Mandarin accent sounded especially harsh today, the "w" changed to "v," an "r" added to the end of some words, a nasal intonation to the "ng" sound. "They've done something criminal and now they're trying to evade responsibility."

"Perhaps," Kai said. "But—"

Huang persisted. "They did the same thing in 1999, when NATO bombed our embassy in Belgrade. They pretended that was an accident. They made the ludicrous excuse that the CIA got the address of our embassy wrong!"

The old guard around the table were nodding. "They believe our lives are worthless," Kai's father said angrily. "They think nothing of killing a hundred Chinese people. They're like the Japanese, who massacred three hundred thousand of us in Nanjing in 1937." Kai suppressed a groan. His father's paranoid generation never ceased to bring up Nanjing. Jianjun went on: "But Chinese lives are precious, and we must show them that they cannot kill us without grave consequences."

How far back in history are we going to go? Kai thought.

Defense Minister Kong Zhao tried to bring them back to the twenty-first century. "The Americans are clearly embarrassed by this," he said, pushing his hair out of his eyes. "Whether the incident is something they planned that went too far or an accident they never intended, the fact remains that they're on the defensive—and we should be thinking about how to profit from that. We might gain some advantage."

Kai knew that Kong would not say that unless he had a plan.

President Chen frowned. "Gain advantage?" he said. "I don't see how."

Kong took his cue. "The Guoanbu report mentions that the chief engineer's twin sons were killed. There must be a photograph somewhere of those two boys. All we have to do is give that photo to the media. Twins are cute. I guarantee the picture will appear in television news broadcasts and on front pages all around the world: the children killed by an American drone."

That was clever, Kai thought. The propaganda value would be enormous. The story running alongside the photo would be a denial of responsibility by the White House—which, like all denials, would suggest guilt.

But the men around the table would not like the idea. Too many of them were old soldiers.

General Huang made a scornful noise and said: "International politics is a power struggle, not a popularity contest. You don't win with pictures of kids, no matter how cute."

Fu Chuyu spoke for the first time. "We must retaliate," he said. "Anything else will be seen as weakness."

Most of them seemed to agree. As Wu Bai had anticipated, retaliation was inevitable. President Chen appeared to accept that. He said: "Then the question is what form our retaliation should take."

Wu Bai spoke up. "Let us remember our Chinese philosophy," he said. "We should balance yin and yang. We must be strong but not foolhardy, restrained but never weak. The word should be *retaliate*, not *escalate*."

Kai smothered a smile: it was what he had said to Wu only a couple of hours ago.

Kai's father was in a belligerent mood. "We should sink an American navy ship in the South China Sea," he said. "It's time we did that anyway. The Law of the Sea does not oblige us to put up with destroyers armed with missiles threatening our shores. They've been told time and time again that they have no right to be there."

Admiral Liu agreed with this. The son of a fisherman, he had spent much of his life at sea, and his weathered skin was the color of old piano keys. "Sink a frigate, rather than a destroyer," he said. "We don't want to overdo it."

Kai almost laughed. Destroyer or frigate or dinghy, the Americans would erupt.

But his father agreed with Liu. "Sinking a frigate would probably kill about the same number of people as the drone at Port Sudan."

"About two hundred, on a US frigate," said Admiral Liu. "But it's in the same neighborhood."

Kai could hardly believe they were serious. Did they not realize it would mean war? How could they talk so casually about igniting the apocalypse?

Fortunately Kai was not the only person to have that thought. "No," said President Chen firmly. "We're not going to start a war with the US, not even after they have killed a hundred of our people."

Kai was relieved, but others were dissatisfied. Fu Chuyu repeated what he had said before: "We must retaliate, otherwise we look feeble."

"That point has been agreed on," Chen said impatiently, and Kai had to smother a smile of satisfaction at Fu's humiliation. Chen went on: "The question is how to retaliate without escalating."

There was a moment of silence. Kai recalled a discussion at the Foreign Ministry a couple of weeks ago, when General Huang had proposed sinking a Vietnamese oil exploration vessel in the South China Sea, and Wu Bai had refused. But it gave Kai an idea, and he said: "We could sink the *Vu Trong Phung.*"

Everyone looked at him, most not knowing what he was talking about.

Wu Bai explained: "We protested to the government of Vietnam about a ship of theirs that was prospecting for oil near the Xisha Islands. We considered sinking the ship but decided to try diplomacy first, especially as there are probably American geology advisors aboard."

President Chen said: "I remember. But did the Vietnamese respond to our protest?"

"Partially. The vessel moved away from the islands, but it is now prospecting in another area, still within our exclusive economic zone."

Jianjun spoke in frustrated tones. "It's a game they play," he said. "They defy us, then back off, then defy us again. It's maddening. We're a superpower!"

General Huang agreed. "It's time we put a stop to it."

"Consider this," said Kai. "Officially, our sinking the *Vu Trong Phung* would have nothing to do with Port Sudan. We would kill some Americans, but they would be collateral damage. We could not be accused of escalation."

President Chen said thoughtfully: "This is a subtle proposal."

And a lot less provocative than sinking a US Navy frigate, Kai thought. He said: "Unofficially, the Americans would know that this is retaliation for their drone attack, but it is also very modest retaliation—two or three American lives for more than one hundred Chinese."

Huang protested: "It's a timid response." But his opposition was half-hearted: clearly he sensed that the mood of the meeting was leaning toward a compromise.

President Chen turned to Admiral Liu. "Do we know where the *Vu Trong Phung* is now?"

"Of course, Mr. President." Liu touched his phone and put it to his ear. "The *Vu Trong Phung*," he said. Everyone watched him. After a few moments he said: "The Vietnamese ship retreated fifty miles south, still within our territory. It's being tracked by the People's Liberation Army Navy ship *Jiangnan*. We have video

from our ship." He looked to the area below the stage
and raised his voice. "Which of you is the technician
managing the images on the giant screens?" A young
man with spiked hair stood up and raised his hand. Liu
said: "Take my phone and talk to my people. Get the
video from the *Jiangnan* on the big screens here."

The kid with the spiked hair sat at his workstation
with Liu's phone held between his shoulder and his jaw,
saying: "Yes . . . yes . . . okay," his fingers flying over
the keyboard all the while.

Liu said: "The *Jiangnan* is a multi-role four-
thousand-ton frigate, one hundred and thirty-four
meters long, with a crew of one hundred and sixty-five,
and a range of more than eight thousand nautical miles."

The picture on the big screens showed the gray fore-
deck of a ship, its pointed prow scything through the
water. It was the time of the northeast monsoon, and
the ship rose and fell precipitously in the waves, so that
the horizon went up and down on the screen, making
Kai feel slightly seasick. Otherwise, visibility was
good, a clear day with bright sunshine.

Liu said: "These pictures are being shot from the
Jiangnan."

An aide returned his phone to him.

Liu said: "You can just about see the Vietnamese
ship on the horizon, but it's five or six kilometers away."

Kai peered at the big screen and thought he could
see a gray smudge on the gray sea, but it might have
been his imagination.

Liu spoke into the phone. "Yes, show us the satellite
picture."

Some of the screens showed a distant aerial shot.
The person operating the screens zoomed in. Two vessels were just discernible. "The Vietnamese ship is the
one at the bottom of the screen," said Liu.

Kai looked back at the video feed from the *Jiangnan*.

It was closer to its target now, and Kai could see the
Vietnamese vessel better. It had a drilling tower amidships. He said: "Does the *Vu Trong Phung* have any
armament?"

"None visible," said Liu.

Kai realized they were contemplating sinking a defenseless ship, and he felt a shiver of guilt. How many
people would drown in that cold sea? It had been his
idea, but he had only wanted to prevent something
worse.

Liu said: "The *Jiangnan* is armed with antiship
cruise missiles, guided by active radar, each with a
high-explosive fragmentation warhead." He turned to
the president. "Should I order the crew to prepare to
fire?"

Chen looked around the room. Several men nodded.

Kong Zhao said: "Isn't this a bit hasty?"

Chen answered him: "It's now more than twenty-
four hours since the drone killed our people. Why
should we wait?"

Kong shrugged.

"I think we're all agreed," Chen said in a somber
voice.

No one dissented.

Chen said to Liu: "Prepare to fire."

Liu spoke into his phone. "Prepare to fire."

The room fell silent.

After a pause, Liu said: "Ready to fire, Mr. President."

Chen said: "Fire."

Liu said into the phone: "Fire."

Everyone watched the screens.

The missile flew over the prow of the *Jiangnan*. It
was six meters long and it trailed a spurt of thick white
smoke. It shot away from the *Jiangnan* at astonishing
speed.

Liu said: "We're getting video from the missile's

onboard camera." A moment later a new image appeared. The missile's speed over the waves was blinding.
The Vietnamese ship grew larger every second.

Kai looked back to the view from the *Jiangnan*
again. A second later the missile hit the *Vu Trong Phung*.

The screens whited out, but only momentarily.
When the picture came back Kai saw a huge blaze of
white, yellow, and red fire bursting from the middle of
the ship. The flames were chased by black and gray
smoke and showers of debris. The noise arrived moments later, picked up by the camera's microphone, a
bang, then a roar of burning. The flames died down as
the smoke bloomed. It rose high in the air, and so did
fragments of the hull and the superstructure, heavy
lumps of steel flying like leaves from a tree in a gale.

Much of the ship was still visible above water. The
middle was smashed and the drilling tower was slowly
sinking, but the prow and stern seemed intact, and Kai
thought some of those aboard might have survived—
so far. Was there time for them to find life jackets or
launch lifeboats before the ship sank?

President Chen said: "Order the *Jiangnan* to rescue
survivors."

Liu said: "Prepare to lower rescue boats."

Moments later the Chinese ship picked up speed
and began to race through the waves. Liu said: "Its top
speed is twenty-seven knots. It will get there in about
five minutes."

The *Vu Trong Phung* remained miraculously afloat.
It was sinking, but slowly. Kai asked himself what he
would have done if he had been aboard and survived
the blast. He thought the best course would have been
to put on a life jacket and then abandon ship, either in
a lifeboat or simply by jumping into the sea. The ship
would go down sooner or later, and anyone still on
board would go down with it.

The *Jiangnan* curved away, then approached the *Vu Trong Phung* on a parallel course but at a safe distance. On the surface of the sea the camera showed one lifeboat and several heads of people floating on the waves. Most of them had life jackets on, so it was difficult to know whether they were dead or alive.

A minute later three of the *Jiangnan*'s boats appeared, going to the rescue.

Kai peered more closely at the heads in the water. All were dark, he saw, except for one, which had long blond hair.

CHAPTER 25

President Green paced up and down in front of the desk in the Oval Office, seething. "I'm not going to stand for this," she said. "Corporal Ackerman was one thing; that was terrorism, even if they did have Chinese guns. But this? This is murder. Two Americans are dead and one is in the hospital because the Chinese deliberately sank a ship. I can't take this lying down."

"You may have to," said Chester Jackson, the secretary of state.

"I must protect American lives. If I can't do that, I'm not fit to be president."

"No president can protect everybody."

The news of the sinking of the *Vu Trong Phung* had just come in. But this was the second crisis of the day. Earlier there had been a Situation Room meeting about the drone that had attacked Port Sudan. Pauline had ordered the State Department to assure the governments of Sudan and China that this was not an American attack. The Chinese refused to believe it. So did the Russians, who traded with Sudan and sold them costly arms; the Kremlin had protested loudly.

Pauline had established that the drone had "gone

missing" during an exercise in Chad, but this was too embarrassing to be admitted publicly, so the press office had announced that the army was conducting an investigation.

And now this. Pauline stopped pacing, sat on the edge of the ancient desk, and said: "Tell me what we know."

Chess said: "The three Americans aboard the *Vu Trong Phung* were employees of American corporations on loan to Petrovietnam, the government oil company, under a State Department scheme to help third-world countries develop their own natural resources."

"American generosity," said Pauline angrily. "And see how we're rewarded."

Chess was not as agitated as she was. "No good deed ever goes unpunished," he said equably. He looked at the sheet of paper in his hand. "Professor Fred Phillips and Dr. Hiran Sharma are presumed drowned—their bodies have not been recovered. The third geologist was rescued: Dr. Joan Lafayette. They say she's in the hospital for observation."

"Why the hell did the Chinese do this? The Vietnamese ship was unarmed, wasn't it?"

"Yes. There's no immediate reason that we can think of. Of course, the Chinese don't like the Vietnamese looking for oil in the South China Sea, and they've been protesting about it for years. But we don't know why they decided to take such drastic action now."

"I'm going to ask President Chen." She turned to her chief of staff. "Put in a call, please."

Jacqueline picked up the phone on the desk and said: "The president would like to speak with President Chen of China. Schedule it as soon as possible, please."

Gus Blake said: "I can guess why they did it."

Pauline said: "Do tell."

"It's retribution."

"For what?"

"Port Sudan."

"Oh, shit, I never thought of that." Pauline tapped her forehead with the heel of her hand, in a gesture that meant *How could I be so dumb?* She looked at Gus, thinking how often he turned out to be the smartest person in the room.

"It's possible," Chess said. "They will say they never intended to kill American geologists, just as we say we never wanted our drone to be used to kill Chinese engineers. We'll say it's not the same, and they'll say what's sauce for the goose is sauce for the gander. Neutral countries will shrug and say these superpowers are all the goddamn same."

It was true, but it angered Pauline. "These are people, not debating points. They have families who grieve for them."

"I know. As they say in the Mafia, whaddaya gonna do?"

Pauline clenched her fists. "I don't know what I'm going to do."

At her desktop workstation, there was a tone indicating a video call. Pauline sat behind the desk, looked at the screen, and clicked her mouse. Chen appeared. Although he was as smart as ever, in his usual blue suit, he looked tired. It was midnight there, and he had probably had a long day.

But she was not in a mood to inquire how he was. She said: "Mr. President, the action of the Chinese navy in sinking the Vietnamese ship *Vu Trong Phung*—"

To her surprise he interrupted her rudely and loudly in English. "Madam President, I protest in the strongest possible terms about criminal activities by Americans in the South China Sea."

Pauline was astonished. "*You're* protesting? You just murdered two Americans!"

"It is against the law for foreign nations to drill for oil in Chinese waters. We do not drill in the Gulf of Mexico without permission; why do you not give us the same respect?"

"It's not against international law to explore for oil in the South China Sea."

"It's against our law."

"You can't make up international law to suit yourselves."

"Why not? It's what the Western nations did for centuries. When we made opium illegal, the British declared war on us!" Chen smiled maliciously. "Now the boot is on the other foot."

"That's ancient history."

"And you might prefer it to be forgotten, but we Chinese remember."

Pauline took a deep breath to help her keep her temper. "The Vietnamese activities were not criminal, but even if they had been, that would not have justified sinking the ship and killing those on board."

"The illegal drill ship refused to surrender. Police action was necessary. Some of the crew were arrested. The ship became damaged and some of those on board regrettably drowned."

"Bullshit. We have satellite photos. You sank the ship with a cruise missile fired from three miles away."

"We enforced the law."

"When you discover people doing something you think is illegal, you don't kill them, not in a civilized country."

"What do police officers do when a criminal refuses to surrender in the *civilized* United States? They shoot him—especially if he's nonwhite."

"So next time a Chinese tourist is caught shoplifting

tights in Macy's, you would be perfectly happy for the security guard to shoot her dead."

"If she's a thief we don't want her back in China."

This was a remarkable conversation to have with a Chinese president, and Pauline paused for a moment. Chinese politicians could be politely aggressive, and Chen seemed to have lost his cool. She resolved to keep hers.

Then she said: "We don't shoot shoplifters, and neither do you. But we don't sink unarmed ships even if they violate our rules, and it's unacceptable for you to do so."

"This is an internal Chinese matter, and you may not interfere."

Jacqueline held up a sheet of paper with the words ASK ABOUT DR. LAFAYETTE.

Pauline said: "Perhaps we should talk about the surviving American, Dr. Joan Lafayette. She must be allowed to come home."

Chen said: "I regret that will not be possible at this time. Good-bye, Madam President." To Pauline's amazement, he hung up. The screen went blank and the phone became silent.

Pauline turned to the others. "I fucked that up royally, didn't I?" she said.

"Yeah," said Gus. "You did."

Pauline left the Oval Office and went to the Residence to say good-bye to her daughter and husband.

Pippa was leaving on a three-day school trip to Boston, staying two nights at a budget hotel. The pupils would visit the Kennedy museum as part of their history course. The trip included tours of Harvard University and the Massachusetts Institute of Technology. Former pupils of Foggy Bottom Day School who were now college students would show them around. Foggy Bottom parents were very keen on elite universities.

The school had asked for two parents to accompany the group and act as supervisors and marshals, and Gerry had volunteered. He and Pippa would each be accompanied by a Secret Service team, as always. The school was accustomed to bodyguards: several pupils were the children of high-profile parents.

Gerry had one small suitcase. He would wear the same tweed suit for three days, changing only his shirt and underwear. Pippa had packed at least two outfits per day, and needed two suitcases plus an overstuffed carry-on bag. Pauline made no comment on the luggage. She was not surprised. A school trip was an exciting social occasion, and everyone wanted to look cool. Romances would begin and end. The boys would bring a bottle of vodka, which would result in at least one girl's making a fool of herself. Someone else would try smoking cigarettes and throw up. Pauline just hoped no one would get arrested.

"How many grown-ups are going?" Pauline asked Pippa as she hauled her bags into the Center Hall.

"Four," said Pippa. "My unfavorite teacher, Mr. Newbegin; his mousy wife, who's coming as a volunteer parent; Ms. I-know-best Judd; and Daddy."

Pauline glanced at Gerry, who was busying himself putting a strap around his case. So he was going to spend two nights in a hotel with Ms. Judd, concisely described by Pippa as small and blond with big tits.

Making her voice casual, Pauline said: "What does Ms. Judd's husband do? Schoolteachers often marry schoolteachers. I bet Mr. Judd is a teacher too."

Without looking at Pauline, Gerry said: "No idea."

Pippa said: "I think she's divorced. Anyway she doesn't wear a wedding ring."

Just fancy that, Pauline thought.

Was this why Gerry had changed—because he had fallen for someone else? Or was it the other way around? Had he become disaffected with Pauline and then gotten interested in Amelia Judd? Probably the two things had worked together, his disenchantment with Pauline heightened by a growing attraction to Ms. Judd.

A White House porter took the baggage away. Pauline hugged Pippa and felt a sense of loss. This was the first time Pippa was going on a trip that was not a family vacation. Soon she would want to spend a summer touring Europe by rail with girls of her own age. Then she would go to college and live in a dorm, then she would want to share an apartment off campus for her sophomore year, and then how soon would it be before she moved in with a boy? Her childhood had gone by too fast. Pauline wanted to live through those years again and relish them more the second time.

"Have a great trip, but don't misbehave," she said.

"My daddy will be watching me," Pippa said. "While the others are playing strip poker and snorting cocaine, I'll have to be drinking warm milk and reading a book by Scott frigging Fitzgerald."

Pauline could not help laughing. Pippa could be a pain in the neck but she was funny too.

Pauline went to Gerry and tilted her face for a kiss. He brushed his lips against hers as if he was in a hurry. "Good-bye," he said. "Keep the world safe while we're gone."

They left, and Pauline retreated to her bedroom for a few minutes of quiet. Sitting at her dressing table, she asked herself whether she really thought Gerry was having an affair. Dull old Gerry? If so she would soon know. Illicit lovers usually thought they were being rigorously discreet, but an observant woman could always read the signs.

Pauline had never met Ms. Judd but had spoken to her on the phone and found her intelligent and thoughtful. It was hard to believe she would go to bed with someone else's husband. But women did, of course, all the time, millions of them, every day.

There was a tap at the door and she heard the voice of Cyrus, the butler, a longtime member of the White House domestic staff. "Madam President, the national security advisor and the secretary of state are here for lunch."

"I'll be right there."

Her two most important advisors had spent the last hour or two trying to find out more about Chinese intentions, and the three of them had agreed to meet at lunch to decide what to do next. Pauline got up from her dressing table and walked along the Center Hall to the Dining Room.

She sat down to a plate of seafood in a cream sauce with rice. "What have we learned?" she said.

Chess said: "The Chinese won't speak to the Vietnamese. I've had the Vietnamese foreign minister almost in tears telling me that Wu Bai won't take his calls. The British have proposed a UN Security Council resolution condemning the sinking of the *Vu Trong Phung*, and the Chinese are furious that there's no motion against the drone attack."

Pauline nodded and looked at Gus.

He said: "The CIA station in Beijing has a more or less amiable relationship with Chang Kai, the head of the Guoanbu, the Chinese intelligence service."

"I've heard that name before."

"Chang has let us know that Joan Lafayette is in good shape and has no real need of hospital treatment. She has been questioned about what she was doing in the South China Sea, she has answered frankly, and, off the record, they don't think she's any kind of spy. She clearly knows everything there is to know about prospecting for oil and very little about international politics."

"Pretty much what we would have guessed."

"Yes. All this is unofficial, of course. The Chinese government may well say the opposite in public."

Chess put in: "They're taking an aggressive line. The Foreign Ministry refuses to discuss Dr. Lafayette's return home or anything else to do with her unless we admit that the *Vu Trong Phung* was engaged in illegal activity."

"Well, we can't do that, even to rescue an American," Pauline said flatly. "We would be stating that the South China Sea is not international waters. That would violate every maritime agreement and undermine our allies."

"Precisely. But the Chinese won't discuss Dr. Lafayette until we do."

Pauline put down her fork. "They've got us up against the fucking wall, haven't they?"

"Yes, ma'am."

"Options?"

Chess said: "We could increase our presence in the South China Sea. We already carry out FONOPs, Freedom of Navigation Operations, sailing battleships through the waters and overflying. We could simply double our FONOPs."

Pauline said: "The diplomatic equivalent of a gorilla beating its chest and tearing up the vegetation."

"Well, yes."

"Which would get us nowhere, though it might make us feel better. Gus?"

"We could arrest a Chinese citizen here in the

States—the FBI keeps tabs on them all, and there's always someone breaking the law—then we could offer to trade."

"It's what they would do in parallel circumstances, but it's not our style, is it?"

Gus shook his head. "And we don't want to escalate. If we arrest a visiting Chinese person, they might arrest two Americans in China."

"But we have to get Joan Lafayette back."

"If you'll forgive me for being mundane, bringing her home would also give your popularity a boost."

"Don't apologize, Gus—this is a democracy, which means we should never stop thinking about public opinion."

"And public opinion likes James Moore's nuke-'em-all approach to international diplomacy. Your Timid Jim remark didn't have the same traction."

"I should never descend to name-calling—it's not really me."

Chess said: "Then it looks as if poor Joan Lafayette is going to spend the next few years in China."

"Wait," said Pauline. "Perhaps we haven't thought hard enough about this."

The other two looked puzzled, evidently wondering what she would come up with.

She said: "We can't do what they're asking—but they must know that. The Chinese aren't stupid. They're the opposite of stupid. They've demanded something they know we can't give. They don't expect us to do it."

Chess said: "I guess that must be true."

"So what do they really want?"

"They're making a point," said Chess.

"Is that all?"

"I don't know."

"Gus?"

"We could just ask them."

"One possibility," said Pauline, thinking aloud. "They don't expect us to support their claim to the entire South China Sea, but perhaps they just want to muzzle us."

"Explain," said Gus.

"They may be seeking a compromise. We don't accept that the *Vu Trong Phung* was doing something illegal, but at the same time we don't accuse the Chinese government of murder. We just shut up."

Gus said: "Our silent acquiescence in exchange for Joan Lafayette's freedom."

"Yes."

"It sticks in my throat."

"And mine."

"But you'll do it."

"I don't know. Let's find out whether your guess is right. Chess, ask the Chinese ambassador, off the record, whether Beijing might consider a compromise."

"Okay."

"Gus, get the CIA to ask the Guoanbu what the Chinese really want."

"Right away."

"We'll see what they say," said Pauline, and she picked up her fork again.

Pauline's guess was right. The Chinese were satisfied with a promise by her not to accuse them of murder. Not that they cared about a charge of murder. They wanted her to refrain from implying that they did not have sovereignty over the South China Sea. In that long-running diplomatic conflict, they would consider American silence a significant victory.

With a heavy heart, Pauline gave them what they wanted.

Nothing was written down. All the same Pauline had to keep her promise. Otherwise, she knew, the Chinese would just arrest some other American woman in Beijing and reboot the whole drama.

Next day Joan Lafayette was put on a China Eastern flight from Shanghai to New York. There she was put on a military plane and debriefed en route to Andrews Air Force Base near DC, where Pauline met her.

Dr. Lafayette was an athletic middle-aged woman with blond hair and glasses. Pauline was surprised to see her looking refreshed and immaculately dressed after her fifteen-hour flight. The Chinese had given her smart new clothes and a first-class suite on the plane, she explained. That was clever of them, Pauline thought, for now Dr. Lafayette showed little sign of having suffered at their hands.

Pauline and Dr. Lafayette did a photo call in a conference room crowded with television and still cameras. Having made an unpleasant diplomatic sacrifice, Pauline was keen to get media credit for bringing the prisoner home. She needed some positive coverage: James Moore's supporters were hammering her every day on social media.

The American consul in Shanghai had explained to Dr. Lafayette that the media back in the States would be less likely to chase and harass her if she gave them the pictures they wanted as soon as she landed, and she had gratefully agreed.

Sandip Chakraborty had announced in advance that they would pose but would not answer questions, and there were no microphones. They shook hands and smiled for the cameras, and then Dr. Lafayette impulsively hugged Pauline.

As they were leaving the room, an enterprising

journalist taking pictures on his phone shouted: "What's your policy on the South China Sea now, Madam President?"

Pauline had anticipated this question and discussed it with Chess and Gus, and they had agreed on a response that did not break her promise to the Chinese. She kept her face stonily expressionless as she said: "The US continues to support the United Nations position on freedom of navigation."

He tried again as Pauline reached the door. "Do you think the sinking of the *Vu Trong Phung* was retaliation for the bombing of Port Sudan?"

Pauline did not answer, but as the door closed behind them Dr. Lafayette said: "What did he mean about Sudan?"

"You may have missed the news," Pauline said. "A drone attack on Port Sudan killed a hundred Chinese people, engineers building a new dock plus some members of their families. Terrorists were responsible but somehow they had gotten hold of a US Air Force drone."

"And the Chinese blamed America for that?"

"They say we shouldn't have allowed our drone to fall into terrorist hands."

"So that's why they killed Fred and Hiran?"

"They deny it."

"That's evil!"

"They probably think that taking two American lives in exchange for one hundred and three Chinese lives is a restrained reaction."

"Is that the way people think about this kind of thing?"

Pauline decided she had been too frank. "I don't think that and nor does anyone on my team. For me, one American life is very precious."

"And that's why you brought me home. I can never thank you enough."

Pauline smiled. "It's my job."

That evening she watched the news with Gus in the former Beauty Salon at the Residence. Joan Lafayette led the bulletin, and the pictures of her with Pauline at Andrews looked good. But the second lead story was a press conference given by James Moore.

"Determined to upstage you," Gus said.

"I wonder what he's got."

Moore did not use a lectern: it did not suit his folksy style. He sat on a stool in front of a crowd of reporters and cameras. "I've been looking at who gives money to President Green," he said. His tone was chatty and intimate. "Her biggest political action committee is run by a guy who owns a company called As If."

It was true. As If was a smartphone app hugely popular with teenagers all over the world. Its founder, Bahman Stephen McBride, was an Iranian American, the grandson of immigrants, and a top fundraiser for Pauline's reelection campaign.

Moore went on: "Now, I've been wondering why our lady president is kinda soft on China. They murdered two Americans and nearly killed a third, but Pauline Green really hasn't laid into them. So I ask myself: do they have some kind of hold over her?"

Pauline said: "Where the hell is he going with this?"

Moore said: "Turns out As If is part owned by China. Now, ain't that interesting?"

Pauline said to Gus: "Can you check that?"

He already had his phone out. "On it."

"Shanghai Data Group is one of the biggest Chinese

corporations," said Moore. "Course, they pretend it's an independent company, but we know that every Chinese business takes orders from the all-powerful President Chen."

Gus said: "Shanghai Data has a two percent stake in As If, and no directors on the board."

"Two percent! Is that all?"

"Moore hasn't mentioned the figure, has he?"

"No, and he won't. It would spoil his smear."

"Most of his supporters have no idea how stocks and shares work. A lot of them are going to believe you're in Chen's pocket."

Cyrus, the butler, put his graying head around the door and said: "Madam President, your dinner is ready."

"Thank you, Cy." On impulse she said to Gus: "We could continue this discussion over dinner."

"I have no plans."

She turned back to the butler. "Do we have enough for two?"

"I believe we do," he said. "You ordered an omelet and a salad, and I'm sure we have more eggs and more lettuce."

"Good. Open a bottle of white wine for Mr. Blake."

"Yes, ma'am."

They moved into the Dining Room and sat opposite one another at the round table. Pauline said: "We can put out a low-key statement early tomorrow clarifying the Shanghai Data stake."

"I'll speak to Sandip."

"Whatever he says should be cleared with McBride."

"Okay."

"This will blow over quickly."

"True, but then he'll come up with something else. What we need is a strategy for presenting you as the smart problem solver who understands the issues, by contrast with the blowhard who just says what he thinks people want to hear."

"That's a good way to put it."

They brainstormed over dinner, then moved to the East Sitting Hall. Cyrus brought the coffee and said: "The domestic staff will retire now, Madam President, if that's all right with you."

"Of course, Cy, thank you."

"If you should need anything later, you only have to call me."

"I appreciate that."

When Cy had gone, Gus sat next to Pauline on the couch.

They were alone. The staff would not return unless summoned. On the floor below were the Secret Service detail and the army captain with the briefcase called the atomic football. Those people would not come upstairs unless there was an emergency.

The mad thought occurred to her that she could take him to her bed now and no one would know. It's a good thing that will never happen, she thought.

He looked at her face, frowned, and said: "What?"

She said: "Gus . . ."

Her phone rang.

Gus said: "Don't answer."

"The president has to answer."

"Of course. Forgive me."

She turned away from him and answered the call. It was Gerry.

She wrenched herself out of her mood and said: "Hi, how's the trip going?" She stood up, turned her back on Gus, and walked a few steps away.

Gerry said: "Pretty good. No one hospitalized, no one arrested, no one kidnapped—we're batting three for three."

"I'm so glad. Is Pippa enjoying it?"

"She's having a great time."

Gerry sounded ebullient. He was having a great time too, Pauline guessed. "Did she like Harvard or MIT best?"

"I'd say she'd have trouble choosing. She loved them both."

"Then she'd better focus on those grades. How are the other supervisors?"

"Mr. and Mrs. Newbegin are complainers. Nothing is up to the standard they expect. But Amelia's a good sport."

I bet she is, Pauline thought sourly.

Gerry said: "Are you okay?"

"Sure, why?"

"Oh, I don't know, you sound . . . tense. I guess you are. There's a crisis."

"There's always a crisis. I have a tense job. But I'm heading for an early night."

"In that case, sleep well."

"You too. Good night."

"Good night."

She ended the call, feeling strangely breathless. "Wow," she said, turning around. "That was weird."

But Gus was gone.

Sandip called Pauline at six a.m. She assumed he was going to talk about Shanghai Data, but she was wrong. "Dr. Lafayette gave an interview to her local newspaper in New Jersey," he said. "Apparently the editor is her cousin."

"What did she say?"

"She quoted you as saying that two American lives in exchange for one hundred and three Chinese lives was a good bargain."

"But I said—"

"I know what you said, I was there, I heard the conversation. You were speculating about how the Chinese Communist government might view the matter."

"Exactly."

"The newspaper is very proud of its exclusive and is promoting this week's issue on social media. Unfortunately James Moore's people have picked it up."

"Oh, hell."

"He's tweeted: 'So Pauline thinks Chinese murder of 2 Americans is a bargain. I don't.'"

"What a fuckwit."

"My press release begins: 'Small-town newspapers sometimes make mistakes, but a presidential candidate should know better.'"

"Good start."

"Do you want to hear the rest?"

"I can't bear it. Send it out."

Pauline watched the news while she drank her first cup of coffee. They were still showing the footage of Joan Lafayette's arrival at Andrews, but James Moore's bargain story was the second lead, taking the shine off Pauline's triumph.

Her mind kept returning to the previous evening. She shuddered when she remembered thinking that no one would know if she took Gus to her bed. It would be impossible to keep such an affair secret in the White House. For Gus would have had to leave her in the middle of the night and make his way through the corridors and walkways to his car, then drive out of the gate, and he would surely have been seen by half a dozen security guards and Secret Service agents, not to mention cleaners and maintenance people, and every one of them would have wondered who he had been with and what he had been doing there so late at night.

Even his departure at nine p.m. had probably raised a few eyebrows among people who knew that Gerry and Pippa were out of town.

She put that out of her mind and focused on keeping America safe.

She spent the morning in meetings with her chief of staff, the Treasury secretary, the chairman of the Joint Chiefs, and the House majority leader. She made a speech to small business owners at a fundraising lunch, and as usual she left before the meal.

Her lunch was a sandwich with Chester Jackson. He told her that the government of Vietnam had announced that all oil exploration vessels would in the future be escorted by ships of the Vietnamese People's Navy equipped with Russian-made antiship missiles and instructed to return fire.

Chess also reported that North Korea's supreme leader was claiming that peace had been restored after the American-fomented trouble in army bases. However, Chess said, the truth was that the rebels still controlled half the army and all the nukes. He thought the apparent peace was a temporary illusion.

In the afternoon Pauline did a photo call with a visiting group of school pupils from Chicago and had a discussion with the attorney general about organized crime.

At the end of the afternoon she ran over the day's events with Gus and Sandip. Social media had been taken up with James Moore's accusation. All the internet trolls said Pauline thought two dead Americans was a bargain.

A new opinion poll showed that Pauline and Moore were now equal in popularity. It made Pauline want to give up.

Lizzie told her that Gerry and Pippa were back, and she went to the Residence to welcome them home. She found them in the Center Hall, unpacking with the help of Cyrus.

Pippa had a lot to tell her mother. The photos of President Kennedy and Jackie in Dallas had made her cry. One of the Harvard boys had asked Lindy Faber to go out with him over Christmas vacation. Wendy Bonita had thrown up twice on the bus. Mrs. Newbegin had been a pain.

"How about old Judders?" Pauline asked.

"Not as bad as expected," said Pippa. "She and Daddy were great, actually."

Pauline glanced at Gerry. He seemed happy. Making her voice casual, she said: "Did you enjoy yourself too?"

"Yeah." Gerry handed a bag of laundry to Cyrus. "The kids were well behaved, somewhat to my surprise."

"And Ms. Judd?"

"I got on with her fine."

He was lying, Pauline could tell. His voice, his stance, and the look on his face all gave it away by being just a touch unnatural. He had slept with Amelia Judd, in a budget hotel in Boston, with his daughter in the same building. Although Pauline had been wondering about the possibility, she was shocked by the sudden intuitive knowledge that her suspicions had been right. She shivered. Gerry gave her a look of curiosity. "I felt a cold draft," she said. "Maybe someone left a window open."

He said: "I didn't notice it."

For some reason, Pauline did not want Gerry to know what she had realized. "So, you had a good time," she said brightly.

"I sure did."

"I'm so glad."

Gerry took his suitcase into the master bedroom. Pauline knelt on the polished wood floor and began to help Pippa with her clothes, but her mind was elsewhere. Gerry's fling with Ms. Judd might be a passing thing, a one-night stand. All the same, she asked herself if it was her fault. She had been sleeping in the Lincoln Bedroom more often. Had she become indifferent to sex? But Gerry himself had never been very demanding. Surely that was not the issue.

Cy came in with a lipstick in his hand. "This was in the First Gentleman's laundry," he said. "Must have dropped in there somehow." He offered it to Pippa.

Pippa said: "I don't use that stuff."

Pauline stared at the little gold-colored tube as if it were a gun.

It was a color she never wore and a brand she did not use.

After a moment she pulled herself together. Pippa could not suspect. She took the lipstick from Cyrus's outstretched hand. "Oh, thanks," she said.

Then she quickly dropped it into the pocket of her jacket.

CHAPTER 26

Men did not live long in the mining camp. Women did better, not having to work in the pit, but a man died every few days. Some just dropped where they stood, victims of the heat and the backbreaking toil. Others were shot for disobeying the rules. There were accidents: a rock falling on a sandaled foot, a hammer slipping from a sweaty grasp, a sharp-edged shard flying through the air and slicing into flesh. Two of the women happened to have some nursing experience, but they had no drugs or sterile dressings, not even a Band-Aid, and anything more than a minor wound could be fatal.

A dead man would remain where he lay until the end of the working day, whereupon the backhoe would be driven out into an area of gravelly sand to dig a grave alongside many others. The man's coworkers were left to carry out any funeral rites if they wished or, if not, to leave the grave unmarked and the man unremembered.

The guards showed no concern. Abdul assumed they were confident that more slaves would soon arrive to replace the dead.

He had to escape. Otherwise he would end up in that desert graveyard.

Within twenty-four hours of arriving, Abdul had become convinced that the mine was run by the Islamic State. It was obviously unlicensed but certainly not informal. The people managing the place were slavers and murderers, but they were also highly competent. There was only one criminal enterprise in North Africa that could achieve this level of organization, and that was ISGS.

Abdul was desperate to flee but he spent several more days gathering crucial data. He calculated the number of jihadis living in the compound, estimated how many rifles they had in total, and guessed at what other armaments they possessed—the shrouded vehicles in the compound looked to him as if they might even be missile launchers.

He discreetly took photographs with his phone, not the cheap one in his pocket but the highly sophisticated device hidden in the sole of his boot, which still had power remaining. He put all the numbers into a document ready to be sent to Tamara as soon as he reached a place where there was connectivity.

He spent a long time thinking about how to escape.

His first decision was not to take Kiah and Naji with him. They would slow him down, perhaps fatally. It would be difficult enough alone. And if he was caught he would be killed, and they would be too if they were with him. They were better off waiting here for the rescue team that Tamara would dispatch as soon as she got Abdul's message.

His yearning for his own freedom was only part of what drove him. He also longed to bring about the destruction of this evil place, to see the guards arrested and the weapons confiscated and the buildings flattened until the whole area went back to being barren desert.

Again and again he thought about just walking away; again and again he rejected the idea. He could navigate by the sun and stars, so he could head north and avoid the danger of going around in a circle, but he did not know where the nearest oasis was. Riding in Hakim's bus had taught him that it was even difficult to see the road at times. He had no map, and probably there was no map in existence that showed the small oasis villages that saved the lives of people traveling on foot or by camel. All that, and he would be carrying a heavy container of water under the desert sun. The chances of survival were just too poor.

He studied the vehicles going in and out of the camp. Observation was not easy, for he worked in the pit twelve hours every day, and the guards would notice anything more than a glance at passing vehicles. But he could recognize the ones that called regularly. Tankers brought water and gasoline, refrigerated trucks supplied food to the kitchens, pickup trucks left with gold—always accompanied by two guards with rifles—and came back with sundry supplies: blankets, soap, and gas for the kitchen fires.

In the late afternoon he sometimes had the chance to watch the vehicles being searched as they left. The guards did not skimp, he noted. They looked inside empty tanks and underneath tarpaulins. They checked below seats. They looked beneath the vehicles in case someone was clinging to the underbody. A man they caught hiding in a refrigerated food truck was beaten so badly that he died the next day. They knew that one escapee might bring about the destruction of the entire camp—which was exactly what Abdul wanted to do.

As his escape vehicle Abdul picked the candy truck. An enterprising vendor called Yakub had a small business driving from oasis to oasis selling items the villagers could not make for themselves or buy anywhere within a hundred miles. He had the favorite Arab sweets, foot-shaped lollipops and soft chocolate in a tube like toothpaste. He offered comic books featuring Muslim superheroes: Man of Fate, Silver Scorpion, and Buraaq. There were Cleopatra cigarettes, Bic ballpoint pens, batteries, and aspirins. His goods were kept in the back of his ancient pickup in locked steel boxes except when he was selling. He sold mainly to the guards, for most of the workers had little or no money. His prices were low and his profits must have been measured in pennies.

The candy truck was examined as carefully as all the rest when leaving, but Abdul had thought of a way to avoid the search.

Yakub always came on Saturday afternoon and left early on Sunday morning. Today was Sunday.

Abdul left the camp at first light, before breakfast was served, not speaking to Kiah. She would be shocked when she realized he had gone, but he could not risk warning her. He took nothing with him but a large plastic bottle of water. It would be an hour or so before the men began work in the pit, and soon after that someone would realize that he was missing.

He hoped Yakub did not decide to leave later than normal today.

Before he had gone more than a few yards he heard a voice say: "Hey, you! Come here."

He noticed the slight lisp and realized the speaker was Mohammed, who had no front teeth. He groaned inwardly and slouched back. "What?"

"Where are you going?"

"To take a shit."

"Why do you need a bottle of water?"

"To wash my hands."

Mohammed grunted and turned away.

Abdul headed toward the men's latrine area, but as soon as he was out of sight of the camp, he changed direction. He followed the road until he came to a junction, marked by a pile of stones but otherwise hardly visible. On close inspection it was possible to see one track heading straight on, back the way Hakim's bus had come; it went all the way to the border and Chad. Abdul could discern a second track, to the left, heading north, across Libya. He knew from studying maps that it should lead to a paved highway that went all the way to Tripoli. There were few villages to the east, and Abdul was fairly sure Yakub would take the northbound track.

Abdul headed that way, looking for rising ground. Yakub's pickup would be even slower going uphill. Abdul's plan was to run after the truck while it was at its lowest speed and leap into the back. Then he would cover his head with his scarf and settle down for a long and uncomfortable ride.

If Yakub happened to look in his mirror at the wrong time, stop the truck, and confront Abdul, then Abdul would offer him a choice: a hundred dollars to drive on to the next oasis, or death. But there was never much reason to look in the rearview mirror while driving in the desert.

Abdul reached the first hill a couple of miles from the camp. Near the top of the rise he found a place where he could hide. The sun was still low in the east and he was able to find shade behind a rock. He drank some water and settled to wait.

He did not know where Yakub might be going, so he could not plan exactly what he would do when he got there, but he considered possibilities while he waited. He would try to jump out of the truck as soon as the destination appeared in the distance, so that he could walk into the village as if he had no connection with

Yakub. He would need to tell a story to explain himself. He could say he had been with a group that had been attacked by jihadis, and he was the only person to escape, or that he had been traveling alone on a camel that had died, or that he was a prospector who had been robbed of his motorcycle and his tools. His Lebanese accent would not be noticed: the desert dwellers spoke their own tribal languages, and those who had Arabic as a second language would not recognize different accents. He would then approach Yakub and beg a lift. He had never bought anything or even spoken to the man, so he was confident that he would not be recognized.

By midday today the jihadis would send out search parties, one to go east toward Chad and another to go north. He would have a good start on them, but to stay ahead he needed a car. He would buy one as soon as he got the chance. And then he would be vulnerable to punctures and other mechanical failures.

There was a lot that could go wrong.

He heard a vehicle and looked up, but it was a newish Toyota with a healthy-sounding engine, definitely not Yakub's jalopy. Abdul sank back into the sand and pulled his gray-brown robes tighter around him. As the Toyota went by he saw two guards sitting in the open back, both holding rifles. They must have been escorting gold, he reasoned.

He wondered speculatively where the gold went. There must have been a middleman, he thought, perhaps in Tripoli; one who turned the gold into money in numbered bank accounts ISGS could use to pay for weapons and cars and anything else they needed for their mad schemes to conquer the world. I'd like to find out the name and address of that guy, Abdul thought. I'd tell him about the place his money comes from. Then I'd tear his fucking head off.

As Kiah washed Naji, a task she performed automatically, she was having an argument in her head with the ghost of her mother, whom she called Umi.

"Where's that handsome foreigner gone?" said Umi.

"He's not a foreigner, he's Arabic," Kiah said with irritation.

"What kind of Arab?"

"Lebanese."

"Well, at least he's a Christian."

"And I have no idea where he is."

"Perhaps he's escaped and left you behind."

"You're probably right, Umi."

"Are you in love with him?"

"No. And he certainly isn't in love with me."

Umi put her hands on her hips in a characteristic combative gesture. In Kiah's imagination Umi had been baking, and now she made floury fingerprints on her black dress, just as she used to before she became a ghost. In a challenging tone she said: "Then tell me, why is he so nice to you?"

"He's quite cold and unfriendly some of the time."

"Really? Is he being coldhearted when he protects you from bullies and tells stories to your child?"

"He's kind. And strong."

"He seems to love Naji."

Kiah dried Naji's damp skin gently with a rag. "Everyone loves Naji."

"Abdul is an Arab Catholic with plenty of money—just the kind of man you ought to marry."

"He doesn't want to marry me."

"Aha! So you have thought about it."

"He comes from a different world. And now he's probably gone back to it."

"What world has he gone back to?"

"I don't really know. But I don't believe he was ever really a vendor of cheap cigarettes."

"What, then?"

"I think he might be some kind of policeman."

Umi made a scornful noise. "The police don't protect you from bullies. They are the bullies."

"You have an answer for everything."

"So will you when you're my age."

After about an hour Abdul saw Yakub's pickup. It came wheezing up the slope, going ever slower, trailing a cloud of dust. The dust might help conceal Abdul as he jumped into the back.

He remained motionless, waiting for the right moment.

He could see Yakub's face through the windshield, concentrating on the track ahead. As the vehicle passed Abdul's hiding place and its dust cloud spread and enveloped him, he leaped to his feet.

Then he heard another vehicle.

He cursed.

He could tell by the engine note that the second vehicle was newer and more powerful, probably one of the black Mercedes SUVs he had seen in the secure parking lot. It was moving fast, and its driver evidently intended to overtake Yakub.

Abdul could not risk exposure. The dust might hide him, but it might not, and if he was seen his escape attempt would be over, and so would his life.

He sank back to the ground, pulled his headdress over his face, and blended back in with the desert as the Mercedes roared by.

The two vehicles climbed the rise and disappeared

over the hill, leaving behind a tan-colored fog, and
Abdul began to trudge back to the camp.

He could at least try again. His plan was still good.
He had just been unlucky. It was unusual for two vehicles to leave the camp together.

He would have another opportunity in a week's
time. If he was still alive.

He was made to work through the midday break as a
punishment for arriving late at the pit. He guessed that
the penalty would have been worse had he not been
such a strong worker.

That evening he was tired and disheartened. Another
week in hell, he thought. He sat on the ground outside
the shelter, waiting for supper. As soon as he had satisfied his hunger he would sleep.

He heard the throb of a powerful engine. A Mercedes
arrived and moved slowly through the quarter. The
black paintwork was brown with dust.

In the fenced parking lot opposite the shelter, the
guard unchained the high gate with a loud metallic
rattle.

The car drove in and stopped, and two guards with
rifles got out. Then two more men emerged. One was
tall, wearing a black dishdasha and a white taqiyah
cap. Abdul's pulse quickened as he saw that the man
had gray hair and a black beard. He turned slowly
around, surveying the encampment with a coldly unemotional gaze, showing no reaction to the ragged
women, the exhausted men, or the ramshackle shelters
where they lived; he might have been looking at be-
draggled sheep in a barren landscape.

The second man was East Asian.

Abdul palmed his good phone and surreptitiously took a photo.

Mohammed came hurrying along the path, a look of delighted surprise on his face, and said: "Welcome, Mr. Park! How pleasant to see you again!"

Abdul noted the Korean name and took another picture.

Mr. Park was well-dressed, in a black linen blazer, tan chinos, and heavy-duty ankle boots with ridged soles. He wore sunglasses. His hair was thick and dark, but his round face was lined, and Abdul guessed he was about sixty.

Everyone around treated the Korean with deference, even his tall Arab companion. Mohammed kept smiling and bowing. Mr. Park ignored him.

They began to walk along the litter-strewn path toward the guards' compound. The tall Arab put his arm around Mohammed, and Abdul was able to see his left hand on Mohammed's shoulder. The thumb was a shortened stump with a gather of twisted skin. It looked like a combat wound that had never been properly treated.

There was no further doubt. He was al-Farabi, the Afghan, the most important terrorist in North Africa. And this was the Hole, Hufra, his headquarters. Yet he seemed to defer to a Korean superior. And the geologist was Korean too. The North Koreans seemed to be running the gold mine. Clearly they were more deeply involved in African terrorism than anyone in the West suspected.

Abdul had to share this information before he was killed.

Watching the group walk away, he noticed that al-Farabi was the tallest, and the cap added another inch or two: he understood the power symbolism of height.

Then he saw Kiah coming in the other direction, toting a plastic demijohn of water on her shoulder, one hip thrown sideways for balance. She was young, and despite having spent nine days in a slave camp she looked vigorous and supple as she carried her burden with little apparent effort. She glanced at al-Farabi, saw the two men with rifles, and moved to give them a wide berth. Like all the slaves, she knew that no encounter with guards ended well.

However, al-Farabi stared at her.

She pretended not to notice and quickened her step. But she could not help looking alluring, for she had to walk with her head high and her shoulders back to carry the weight, and her thighs moved strongly under the thin cotton robes.

Al-Farabi kept walking but looked back over his shoulder, and his deep-set dark eyes followed her as she hurried away, no doubt appearing just as attractive from behind. That look troubled Abdul. There was cruelty in al-Farabi's eyes. Abdul had seen such an expression on the faces of men looking at guns. Oh, Christ, he thought, I hope this doesn't get nasty.

At last al-Farabi turned and faced forward. Then he said something that made Mohammed laugh and nod.

Kiah reached the shelter and set down the heavy water container. Straightening up, she looked flustered and said: "Who was that?"

"Two visitors, both apparently very important," Abdul replied.

"I hate how the tall Arab looked at me."

"Stay out of his way if you can."

"Of course."

There was a noticeable uptick in the discipline of the guards that evening. They walked around the camp briskly, rifles in hands, not smoking or eating or laughing at jokes. Vehicles were searched coming in as well

as going out. Sandals and sneakers disappeared and
they all wore boots.

Kiah wrapped her headscarf around her face, leaving only her eyes visible. Several of the women covered
their faces for religious reasons, so she was not conspicuous.

It did no good at all.

Kiah was afraid the tall man would send for her, and
she would be locked in a room with him and forced to
do whatever he wanted. But she had nowhere to go.
The camp had no hiding places. She could not even
leave the shelter, for Naji would cry for her if she was
away long. Darkness fell and the day cooled, and she
sat at the back of the shelter, alert and scared. Esma
took Naji on her lap and told him a story, in a quiet
voice to avoid disturbing the others. Naji put his thumb
in his mouth. In a few minutes he would be asleep.

Then Mohammed walked into the shelter followed
by four guards, two armed with rifles.

Kiah heard Abdul give a grunt of alarm.

Mohammed looked around and his gaze rested on
Kiah. He pointed at her without speaking. She stood
up and pressed her back against the wall. Naji sensed
the fear and began to cry.

Abdul did not leap to Kiah's defense. He could not
have prevailed against five men; they would have shot
him without a second thought, Kiah knew. He remained sitting on the ground, watching what was
happening with an expressionless face.

Two guards grabbed Kiah, each taking an arm.
Their hands hurt her, and she cried out. But the humiliation was worse than the pain.

Esma screamed: "Leave her alone!"

They ignored her.

Everyone backed away hastily, not wanting to get involved.

When the guards had Kiah firmly in their grip, Mohammed approached her. He grabbed the neckline of her dress and pulled hard. She cried out and her head jerked forward, then the fabric ripped, revealing the slender chain around her neck and the little silver cross that hung from it.

"An infidel," said Mohammed.

He looked around until he saw Abdul. "We will take her to the makhur," he said, watching Abdul for a reaction.

Everyone looked at Abdul. They knew he had grown close to Kiah, and they had seen how he had stood up to Hakim and his armed men on the bus. Eventually Wahed, the father of Esma, muttered: "What are you going to do?"

Abdul said: "Nothing."

Mohammed seemed to want a response from Abdul. "What do you think of that?" he jeered.

"A woman is only a woman," said Abdul, and he looked away.

After a moment Mohammed gave up. He gestured at the guards and they dragged Kiah out of the shelter. She heard Naji begin to scream.

Kiah did not struggle. They would only hold her harder. She knew she could not escape. They took her to the guards' compound. The sentry at the gate opened it for them and locked it after them. They took her to the light blue house they called the makhur, the brothel.

Kiah began to cry.

The door was barred on the outside. They opened it, marched her in, released her, and left.

Kiah wiped her eyes and looked around.

There were six beds in the room, each with curtains that could be drawn for privacy. Three women were there, all dressed in humiliatingly skimpy clothing, Western-style lingerie. They were young and attractive but they looked miserable. The room was lit by candles but was not in the least romantic.

Kiah said: "What will happen to me?"

One of the women said: "What do you think? You're going to be fucked. That's what this place is for. Don't worry, it won't kill you."

Kiah thought about sex with Salim. At first he had been a bit clumsy and rough, but in a way she did not mind that, for it told her that he had not been with other women, at least not often. And he had been thoughtful and caring: on their honeymoon night he had asked her twice whether it was hurting her. Both times she had said no, although that was not really true. And she had soon learned the joy of giving and taking this pleasure with someone who loved her as she loved him.

And now she had to do it with a stranger who had cruel eyes.

The woman who had spoken was reprimanded by another, who said: "Don't be horrible, Nyla. You were upset when they dragged you in here. You cried for days." She turned to Kiah. "I'm Sabah. What's your name, dear?"

"Kiah." She began to sob. She had been separated from her child, her hero had failed to protect her, and now she was going to be raped. She was in despair.

Sabah said: "Come and sit by me, and we'll tell you what you need to know."

"All I want to know is how to get out of here."

There was a moment of silence, then Nyla, the woman who had spoken first, the mean one, said: "There's only one way I know. You leave when you're dead."

CHAPTER 27

Abdul's mind was in a ferment. He had to rescue Kiah and flee from the camp, and he had to do both immediately, but how?

He divided the problem into stages.

First, he had to free Kiah from the makhur.

Second, he had to steal a car.

Third, he had to prevent the jihadis from following him and catching him.

Considered like that, the challenge seemed three ways impossible.

He racked his brains. The others went to the cookhouse and got plates of semolina and stewed mutton. Abdul ate nothing and spoke to no one. He lay still, making plans.

The three adjacent compounds that formed one half of the camp were each fenced with stout steel-framed panels of galvanized wire mesh, standard for security barriers. The pit fence also had rolled barbed wire on top of the fencing panels, to discourage both slaves and jihadis who might try to steal gold. But Abdul did not need to get to the pit: Kiah was in the guards' compound and the cars were in the parking lot.

An armed man guarded the parking lot. Inside the fence was a small wooden hut where he spent most of the cold night. No doubt the vehicle keys were kept in the hut. The cars were fueled from a tanker next to the hut; when the tanker was getting low, another arrived.

A plan slowly took shape in Abdul's mind. It might not work. He would probably be killed. But he was going to try.

First he had to wait, and that was hard. Everyone was still awake, slaves as well as guards. Al-Farabi would be with his men, talking and drinking coffee and smoking. Abdul's best chance would come in the middle of the night, when they were asleep. The hard part was that Kiah had to spend several hours in the brothel. There was nothing he could do about that. He just hoped al-Farabi would be tired from his journey and retire early, postponing his visit to Kiah to another night. If not, she would suffer his attentions. Abdul tried not to think about it.

He lay in his place in the shelter, refining his plan, foreseeing snags, waiting. His companions lay down. Naji kept trying to leave the shelter and go in search of his mother, and Esma had to hold him down. He cried inconsolably but eventually dropped off, lying between Esma and Bushra. The night became cold and they all wrapped themselves in blankets. The exhausted slaves went to sleep early. The jihadis probably stayed awake longer, Abdul guessed, but eventually they too would go to bed, leaving just a few on guard.

Tonight Abdul would almost certainly have to kill people, for the first time in his life. He felt surprised that the prospect did not dismay him more. He knew the names of many of the guards at this camp, just from listening to their conversations, but that did not make him feel any empathy. They were brutal slavers and murderers and rapists. They deserved no mercy. It was the effect on himself that worried him. In his fighting career he had never inflicted a fatal blow. He felt there must be a big difference between a man who had killed and one who had not. He would be sorry to cross that line.

Deep sleep, during which it was difficult to wake the sleeper, generally occurred in the first half of the night, he knew. The best time for clandestine activity was around one or two o'clock, according to his training. He lay awake until his watch said one a.m., then he quietly got to his feet.

He made little noise. In any case there were always sounds in the shelter: snores, grunts, incomprehensible phrases muttered in dreams. He did not expect to wake anyone. However, when he glanced at Wahed he noticed that the man was fully awake, eyes wide open, lying on his side, watching him, his cigarettes on the ground beside his head as always. Abdul nodded, and Wahed nodded back, then Abdul turned away.

He looked outside. There was a half-moon, and the camp was brightly lit. The window of the hut in the parking lot shone with a yellow glow. The guard himself was not in sight, so he had to be inside.

Abdul moved deeper into the slave quarters, then turned, walking parallel to the fence but keeping out of sight behind the shelters. He trod softly, scanning the ground for obstacles that might cause him to stumble and make a noise.

He kept his eyes peeled for guards. Looking between the shelters to the fence, he saw the flash of an electric torch and froze. A guard was being conscientious, patrolling his beat and shining a light into dark zones. The guard inside the pit compound came to the fence to talk to his comrade. Abdul watched, silent and still. The two guards parted, neither having looked toward the slave quarters.

Abdul moved on. He came across a gray-haired man urinating, eyes half closed, and went by without speaking. He was not worried about other slaves' seeing him. None of them would do anything even if they guessed he was planning to escape. No slave ever had contact with a guard unless it was unavoidable. The guards were violent men who were bored, a dangerous combination.

He drew level with the guards' compound. Three hundred yards farther along were two gates, a wide one for vehicles and a regular-size one for people. Both were chained up and a guard stood just inside. From where Abdul stood, half-hidden by a tent, the guard was a dark shape, upright but still.

The makhur stood inside the fence between Abdul and the gate, but closer to the gate. It was white, rather than pale blue, in the moonlight.

At this point Abdul had to start taking serious risks.

He walked quickly to the fence and, without hesitation, scrambled up the wire mesh and jumped over the top of the panel and landed on both feet and lay flat on the sandy ground.

If he was spotted now, he would be killed, but that was not the worst of his fears. If this attempt failed, Kiah would spend the rest of her life as a sex slave to the jihadis. That was the prospect Abdul could not bear to contemplate.

He listened for a sound, a cry of surprise or a shout of warning. He lay still, and he seemed to hear his heart beating. Had the guard seen movement out of the corner of his eye? Was he now looking in this direction, wondering about a dark smudge on the ground that was about the size of a tall man? Was he hefting his rifle just in case?

After a few moments Abdul raised his head cautiously and looked in the direction of the gates. The

dark shape of the guard was motionless. The man had
not seen anything. Perhaps he was half-asleep.

Abdul rolled along the ground until he had put the
makhur between himself and the guard. Then he stood
up, moved to the blank wall of the building, and peeped
around the corner.

To his surprise he saw a woman approaching the gate
from the outside. He cursed: what was this? She said a
few words to the guard and was admitted. She walked
toward the makhur. Abdul thought: What the hell?

She moved like an older woman, and she was carrying a pile of something in both hands, but in the
moonlight Abdul could not make out what it was.
Perhaps a pile of clean towels. He had never been to a
brothel, in any country, but guessed that such institutions might use a lot of towels. His heartbeat returned
to normal.

He remained concealed and listened as the woman
went to the makhur door, opened it, and stepped
inside. He heard voices as she exchanged a few words
with the girls. There seemed to be no men present. The
old woman left empty-handed and returned to the
gate. The guard let her out.

Abdul began to feel calmer. If there were no men
inside, and no used towels to be taken away, perhaps
Kiah had been lucky tonight.

The guard leaned his rifle against the fence and
stood looking out, toward the slave quarters.

There was nowhere to hide between the makhur and
the gate. Abdul would be in plain sight while he covered the distance of about a hundred yards. The guard's
gaze was to the outside. Would he glimpse Abdul out
of the corner of his eye, or even just randomly turn
around? If so, Abdul would say: "Can you give me a
cigarette, brother?" The guard would assume that
someone inside the compound was a jihadi, and it

might take him a fatal few moments to notice that Abdul was dressed in the ragged attire of a slave and realize that he must be a slave and an intruder.

Or he might give the alarm instantly.

Or he might shoot Abdul dead.

This was the second major risk point.

The sash that Abdul had gotten from Tamara had been tied around his waist for six weeks or so. Now Abdul untied it and stripped away the cotton covering, leaving a one-meter length of titanium wire with a handle at each end. What he now held in his hands was a garotte, the centuries-old weapon of silent assassination. He coiled up the wire and held the ensemble in his left hand. Then he looked at his watch: fifteen minutes past one.

He spent a few moments easing himself into combat mode, as he always had before a mixed-martial-arts bout: high alert, low emotion, violent intent.

Then he left the shelter of the building and stepped into open space in the moonlight.

He walked toward the gate, quiet footed but acting casual, staring at the guard. At the back of his mind he knew his life was on the line, but his gait betrayed no fear. As he got closer he realized the guard was half-asleep standing up. Abdul circled to come up behind him.

When he was almost there he silently uncoiled the wire, held both handles, and made a loop. At the last moment the guard seemed to sense his presence, for he made a startled noise and began to turn. Abdul glimpsed a smooth cheek and a sparse mustache and recognized a young man called Tahaan. But Tahaan had moved too late. The loop dropped over his head and Abdul instantly pulled the wire tight, heaving on both wooden handles with all his might.

The wire dug into Tahaan's neck, compressing his

throat. He tried to cry out but no sound came, for his windpipe was squeezed closed. His hand went to his neck and he scrabbled to loosen the wire, but it was too deep in his flesh and beginning to draw blood from his skin, and his fingers found no purchase.

Abdul pulled tighter, hoping to cut off the blood supply to the brain as well as the air to the lungs, so that Tahaan would pass out.

The guard dropped to his knees but continued to writhe. He flailed behind him, trying to reach Abdul, but Abdul easily avoided his hands. The movements became weaker. Abdul risked a look back over his shoulder, across the compound to the dormitory buildings, but nothing was moving. The jihadis were sleeping.

Tahaan lost consciousness and became a dead weight. Without releasing the tension in the wire, Abdul lowered him to the ground and knelt on his back.

He managed to turn his wrist and look at his watch: eighteen minutes past one. To be sure of death, the CIA trainers had said, the victim needed to be strangled for five minutes. Abdul could easily pull the wire for another two minutes but he was worried that someone might appear and ruin everything.

The camp was quiet. He looked all around. Nothing moved. Just a little longer, that's all I need, he thought. He looked up. The moon was bright but it would set in an hour or so. He checked his watch again: one minute to go.

He looked at his victim. I didn't expect one so fresh-faced, he thought. Young men were quite capable of brutality, of course, and this one had chosen a career of cruelty and violence, but still Abdul wished he did not have to end a life that had hardly begun.

Half a minute. Fifteen seconds. Ten, five, zero. Abdul released his hold and Tahaan fell lifeless to the ground.

Abdul wound the wire lightly around his waist with a loose knot held in place by the wooden handles. He picked up Tahaan's rifle and slung it across his back. Then he knelt down, manhandled the corpse onto his shoulder, and stood up again.

He walked quickly to the far side of the makhur and dropped the body to the ground up against the wall of the building. There was no way to hide it, but at least it was unobtrusive.

He dropped the rifle beside the corpse. It was no use to him: one shot would wake every jihadi, and that would be the end of the escape bid.

He found the door of the makhur. The bar was in place, confirming that there were no jihadis inside, just slaves. That was good. He wanted to avoid any kind of fracas that might make a noise. He had to take Kiah away without alerting the guards, for he had much to do before they could flee.

He listened for a moment. The voices he had heard earlier were silent now. He lifted the bar noiselessly, opened the door, and stepped inside.

There was a smell of unwashed people living close together. The room had no windows and was dimly lit by a single candle. It had six rumpled beds, four of which were occupied by women. They were awake and sitting up—such women kept late hours, he guessed. Four unhappy faces looked at him with apprehension. At first they would assume he was a guard who had come here for sex, he supposed. Then one of them said: "Abdul."

He made out Kiah's face in the faint light. He spoke to her in French, hoping the other women would not understand. "Come with me," he said. "Quickly, quickly." He wanted to get her out before the others realized what was going on, otherwise they might want to escape too.

She leaped from the bed and crossed the room in a trice. She was wearing her clothes, as everyone did in the cold Saharan nights.

One of the women stood up and said: "Who are you? What's happening?"

Abdul looked outside, saw that no one was stirring, and ushered Kiah out. As he did so he heard one of the others say: "Take me too!" Another said: "We can all go!"

He quickly closed the door and barred it. He would have liked to let the women escape but they might have awakened the guards and ruined everything. The door rattled as they tried to open it, but they were too late. He heard cries of despair and hoped they were not loud enough to wake anyone.

In the guards' compound all was still. He looked into the mining area. There was no torchlight, but he made out the glow of a cigarette. The guard there appeared to be sitting down. Abdul could not tell which way he was looking. This was as safe as it would ever be, he thought. He said to Kiah: "Follow me."

He walked quickly to the chain-link fence and climbed it to the top. He paused there in case she needed help. It was difficult to cling on, for the holes in the wire mesh were only a couple of inches square, and he was not sure he could maintain his grip and pull her up too. He need not have worried. She was agile and strong, and she climbed the fence faster than he had and jumped to the ground on the other side. He followed her down.

He led her into the slave quarters, where they would be less likely to be spotted by guards, and they hurried between the huts and tents toward their shelter.

Abdul wanted to know what had happened to her in the makhur. This was no time for questions, and they needed to remain quiet, but he had to ask. He whispered: "Did the tall man visit you?"

"No," she said. "Thank God."

He was not satisfied. "Did anyone . . . ?"

"No one came, except the towel woman. The other girls said that happens sometimes. When no guards visit they call it a Friday, like a day of no work."

A weight lifted from Abdul's mind.

A minute later they reached the shelter.

Abdul whispered: "Get blankets and water, and pick up Naji. Settle him to sleep in your arms. Then wait, but be ready to run."

"Yes," she said calmly. She showed no bewilderment or anxiety. She was cool and resolute. What a woman, he thought.

He heard someone speak to Kiah. The voice was that of a young woman, so it had to be Esma. Kiah shushed her and whispered a reply. The others slept on undisturbed.

Abdul looked around outside. There was no one in sight. He crossed to the parking lot and peered through the fence. He saw no movement, no sign of the guard, who was undoubtedly in the hut. He climbed over the fence.

When he hit the ground his left foot landed on something he had not seen, and it made a metallic noise. Kneeling down, he saw that it was an empty oil can. The sound had been the metal buckling under his weight.

He crouched low. He did not know whether the noise of the can could have been heard inside the hut. He waited. There was no sound from the hut, no sign of movement. He waited a minute, then stood up.

He had to sneak up on the guard here as he had with Tahaan, and silence him before he could sound the alarm, but this time it would be more difficult. The man was inside the hut, so there was no way to creep up behind him.

The hut might even have been locked from the inside. But he thought not. What would be the point?

He walked silently across the parking lot, zigzagging between the vehicles. The one-room hut had a small window, so that the guard could watch the cars from the inside, but as Abdul drew nearer he saw that there was no face in the window.

Approaching at an angle, he could see a rack of labeled keys on a wall: good organization, as he had come to expect. There was a table with a bottle of water and some thick glass tumblers, plus a full ashtray. Also on the table was the guard's gun, a North Korean Type 68 assault rifle based on the famous Russian Kalashnikov.

Staying a couple of yards back, he moved sideways to widen his view. Right away he saw the guard, and his heart missed a beat. The man was sitting in an upholstered chair with his head thrown back and his mouth open. He was asleep. He had a bushy beard and a turban; Abdul recognized him. His name was Nasir.

Abdul took out the garotte, uncoiled it, and made a loop. He calculated that he should be able to throw open the door, enter, and overpower Nasir before the man had time to pick up his weapon—unless Nasir was very quick.

Abdul was about to move to the door when Nasir woke up and looked straight at him.

With a shout of surprise Nasir rose from his chair.

Abdul suffered a moment of shocked paralysis, then he began to improvise. "Wake up, my brother!" he called in Arabic, then he hurried to the door.

It was not locked.

He opened it, saying: "The Afghan wants a car." He stepped inside.

Nasir stood with his rifle in his hand, staring at Abdul, momentarily confused. "In the middle of the night?" he said blearily. No one with any sense drove at night in the desert.

Abdul said: "Look lively, Nasir, you know how impatient he is. Does the Mercedes have a full tank?"

Nasir said: "Do I know you?"

That was when Abdul kicked him.

He jumped and then kicked out in midair, at the same time rolling over to land on all fours. His dropkick had won him several contests in his fighting days. Nasir flinched back but he was too slow, and anyway there was not enough room for him to dodge. Abdul's heel smashed into Nasir's nose and mouth.

Nasir gave a cry of shock and pain as he fell back, dropping his rifle. Abdul landed with both feet and both hands on the ground, spun around, and grabbed the gun.

He did not want to fire it. He was not sure how far away the shot might be heard, and he had to avoid waking the jihadis. As Nasir tried to get up, Abdul reversed the rifle and swung it, hitting the side of Nasir's face, then he lifted it high and brought it down on top of the man's head with all the strength he could muster. Nasir collapsed unconscious.

Abdul had let the garotte fall to the floor when he drop-kicked Nasir. Now he picked it up, looped it over the man's head, and strangled him.

He listened as he waited for the silent Nasir to die. The man had cried out, but had anyone heard? It would not matter if a slave or two had been awakened: they would lie still and quiet in their beds, knowing that it was best to do nothing that brought them to the attention of the jihadis. The only other guard anywhere near was the man in the mining area, and Abdul reckoned he could not have heard. But perhaps a patroling guard might have been within earshot, by bad luck. However, there was no sound of alarm, not yet.

Nasir did not regain consciousness.

Abdul kept up the pressure for five full minutes, then removed the garotte and once more tied it around his waist.

Then he looked at the key rack.

The well-organized terrorists had labeled each key and each hook, so that it was easy to find the one required. Abdul first located the gate key. He took it off the hook, stepped over the corpse of Nasir, and left the hut.

To keep out of sight as much as possible he tried to stay behind the big trucks as he crossed the parking lot to the gate. He undid the simple padlock, then removed the chain as quietly as possible.

Then he surveyed the vehicles.

Some were badly parked, so that one could not be driven until another was moved out of the way. There were four SUVs in the compound, and one was in a place where it could easily be moved. It was covered in dust, so it had to be the one al-Farabi had arrived in a few hours ago. Abdul checked its license plate.

He returned to the hut and put the padlock key back in the rack.

It was easy to recognize the SUV keys, for they were all attached to distinctive Mercedes fobs. Each had a tag with the license number of the car. Abdul picked the right one and went outside again.

All was quiet. No one had heard Nasir cry out. No one had yet noticed Tahaan's body on the ground up against the back wall of the makhur.

Abdul got into the Mercedes. The interior lamps came on automatically, lighting him up for anyone outside to see. Abdul did not know where the switch was and did not have time to search for it. He started the engine. That was an unusual sound in the middle of the night, but it could not be heard from the jihadi compound, which was half a mile away. What about the guard at the pit? Would he hear it? And if he did, would he feel it was something he needed to investigate?

Abdul could only hope not.

He looked at the fuel gauge. The tank was almost empty. He cursed.

He drove the car to the gasoline truck and turned the engine off.

He searched around the dashboard and found the switch that opened the filler cap. Then he jumped out. The interior lights came on again.

The tanker was fitted with a regular gas station type of hose and nozzle. Abdul put the nozzle into the fuel pipe of the car and squeezed the handle.

Nothing happened.

He squeezed repeatedly with no effect. He guessed it worked only when the tanker's engine was turning over.

"Shit," he said.

He noted the license plate of the tanker, returned to the hut, found the keys to the truck, and came back. He climbed into the cab, and the inside lights came on. He started the engine. It came to life with a throaty rumble.

He was no longer inconspicuous. The noise of the big engine would carry to the jihadis' compound. It would be a distant sound, and might not wake men who were sleeping fast, but someone was sure to notice it within the next few seconds or minutes.

Their first reaction would be puzzlement: Who was starting vehicles in the middle of the night? Someone must be about to leave the camp, but why now? One man might wake another, saying: "Do you hear that?" They would not jump to the conclusion that a slave was escaping—it was too unlikely—and they might not even consider the matter urgent, but they would want to find out what was happening, and after a short discussion they would decide to follow the sound to its source.

Abdul jumped down from the cab, returned to the Mercedes, put the nozzle in the filler pipe, and squeezed. The gasoline began to flow.

He kept looking around, scanning through 360 degrees. He listened too for the kind of hubbub that might occur if the jihadis were alerted. At any second he might hear shouts and see lights.

When the tank was full the pump clicked off automatically.

Abdul replaced the filler cap, returned the nozzle to its hook, and drove the car to the gate. Still no one had reacted.

He returned to the tanker and took down the nozzle again. He removed the garotte from around his waist and wound the wire tightly around the handle, fixing it open so that the pump worked constantly and gasoline poured out onto the ground.

He dropped the nozzle. The gasoline ran under the cars, spreading left and right and toward the fence. He ran back to the car.

He opened the gate. It was impossible to do so silently: the whole thing was rusty, and it creaked and groaned as it moved on unlubricated hinges. But Abdul needed only a few more seconds.

A pool of gasoline was spreading through the parking lot and the smell filled the air.

He drove the car out through the gate. Ahead of him he could see the moonlit track through the desert.

Leaving the engine running, he raced to the shelter. Kiah was waiting, with Naji in her arms, fast asleep. By her feet was a demijohn of water and three blankets, plus the capacious canvas bag she had had with her since they left Three Palms. It contained everything Naji needed.

Abdul picked up the water and the blankets and ran back to the car, and Kiah followed.

He tossed everything in the back. Kiah put Naji down on the backseat, still wrapped in his blanket. He turned over and put his thumb in his mouth without opening his eyes.

Abdul ran back to the parking lot, now flooded with gasoline. But he was not yet confident of starting a big enough conflagration. He needed to be sure the jihadis had no way of coming after him, not a single usable vehicle. He picked up the hose and began to spray the vehicles. He soaked the SUVs and the pickup trucks and the gasoline tanker itself.

He saw Kiah leave the car and approach the fence. The gasoline was now spreading under the fence and over the path, and she trod cautiously to avoid it. In a low, urgent voice she said: "What are we waiting for?"

"One more minute." Abdul soaked the wooden guard hut with gasoline to destroy the keys.

A male voice called out: "What's that smell?"

It was the guard in the mining section. He had come to the fence and was shining his flashlight at the vehicles. Now it would be only a minute or so before the alarm was given. Abdul dropped the hose. It continued to spurt fuel.

The voice said: "Hey, there must be a gasoline leak!"

Abdul bent over and ripped a length of cotton from the hem of his robe. He soaked the cloth in the lake of gasoline, then retreated several yards. He took out his red plastic lighter and held the gasoline-soaked rag over it.

The pit guard called out: "What's happening, Nasir?"

Abdul said: "I'm dealing with it." He flicked the lighter.

Nothing happened.

"Who the hell are you?"

"I'm Nasir, you fool." Abdul flicked the lighter

again, and again, and again. No flame appeared. He realized it had run out of fuel, or dried up.

He had no matches.

Kiah, outside the compound, could get to the shelter faster than Abdul could. He said: "Quickly, run to the shelter and get some matches. Wahed always has some. Don't step in the gasoline. But hurry!"

She ran across the path and into the shelter.

The guard said: "You're a liar. Nasir is my cousin. I know his voice. You're not him."

"Calm down. I can't speak normally in these fumes."

"I'm going to sound the alarm."

Suddenly there was a new voice. "What the hell is going on here?" Abdul heard the slight lisp and realized it was Mohammed. That made sense: the slaves seemed to be his responsibility, and someone had sent him to find out what was happening. He had crept up unseen.

Abdul turned around and saw that Mohammed had drawn his gun. It was a nine-millimeter pistol and he was holding it in a professional double-handed grip. Abdul said: "I'm glad you're here. I heard the sound of fighting and came to look, and the gates were open and gasoline leaking." Out of the corner of his eye he saw Kiah come out of the shelter. He took a few steps to the right, to put Mohammed between him and Kiah, so that he would not see her.

"Don't come any closer," Mohammed said. "Where's the vehicle guard?"

Kiah came to the fence behind Mohammed. Abdul saw her bend and pick something up from the ground. It looked like a discarded Cleopatra cigarette packet.

"Nasir?" he said. "He's in the hut, but I think he's hurt. I don't really know, I just got here."

Kiah struck a match and lit the cigarette packet in her hand.

The pit guard called out: "Mohammed, watch out behind you!"

Mohammed turned, his gun swiveling with him. Abdul leaped at him and kicked his legs from under him, and Mohammed fell into the pool of gasoline.

Kiah knelt down with her blazing cigarette packet and set fire to the fuel.

It flared up with terrifying speed. Abdul backed away fast. Mohammed rolled over and aimed at him, but he was off balance and shooting one-handed, and he missed. Mohammed struggled to his feet but the flames reached him before he was upright. His clothes were soaked in gasoline and they blazed instantly. Mohammed screamed in fear and agony as he turned into a human torch.

Abdul ran. He could feel the heat, and he feared he might have left it too late to escape the inferno. He heard a shot and guessed that the pit guard was firing at him. He dodged between the cars, for cover, and ran for the gate. He reached the car and leaped in.

Kiah was already there.

He put the car in gear and drove.

As he sped away he looked into his rearview mirror. The flames had spread all over the parking lot. Would all the cars be immobilized? At a minimum all their tires would be destroyed. And the keys were melting as the guard hut burned down.

He turned on the headlights. They and the moonlight helped him to locate the road. He saw the pile of stones that marked the junction and turned north. After two miles he came to the hill where he had earlier hoped to jump into the back of Yakub's candy truck. He stopped at the top of the rise, and they both looked back.

The blaze was tremendous.

He checked his phone, but as he expected, there was

no signal. From the other boot he took the tracking device, but Hakim and the cocaine were far out of range.

He opened the storage bin in the center console and found, as he'd hoped, a phone-charging connection. He plugged in the better of his two phones.

Kiah was watching him. Before now she had not seen the special compartments in his shoes and the devices hidden there. Now she gave him a cool, intelligent look and said: "Who are you?"

He looked back to the camp. As he did so there was a terrific boom and a huge gout of flame shot up into the air. He guessed the gasoline tanker had heated up and exploded. He hoped none of the slaves had been foolish enough to go close to the fire.

He drove on. The car's heater warmed the interior. With no fear of pursuit, he could afford to go slowly and take care that he did not wander away from the track.

Kiah said: "I'm sorry I asked you that question. I don't care who you are. You saved me."

"You saved me too," he said. "When Mohammed was pointing his gun at me."

But he could not help thinking about her question. What was he going to tell her? What was he going to do with her and her child? He had to report to Tamara as soon as he got a phone signal, but he had no further plans, now that he had lost the signal from the cocaine shipment. And what would she want to do? She had paid for passage to France but she was a long way from there and out of money.

However, there was an upside. For now Kiah and Naji were an asset. Hostile tribesmen, suspicious army patrols, and officious policemen would see the three of them as a family. While he was with them, no one would imagine he was an American CIA officer.

In Tripoli there was a station of the French DGSE,

Tab's outfit, thinly disguised as a trading company called Entremettier & Cie. Abdul could dump Kiah and Naji there and make them someone else's problem. The DGSE could return them to Chad—or, if they were feeling generous, they could easily get them to France. He knew which Kiah would prefer. Yes, he decided, he would drive to Tripoli.

It was about seven hundred miles.

After a while the moon went down, but the powerful headlights illuminated the road ahead. The strain on Abdul began to lift when a line of light appeared on the horizon to his right and day came to the desert. He was able to increase speed a little.

Soon afterward they came to an oasis where a makeshift store offered gasoline in cans, but Abdul decided not to stop. The fuel tank was still three-quarters full. He was driving slowly and not covering much ground, so fuel consumption per hour was low.

Naji woke, and Kiah gave him water and some bread from the big canvas bag. Soon he was lively. Abdul found the switch that activated the child locks, which prevented the rear doors and windows from opening, so that Kiah could let Naji romp on the spacious backseat. She produced his favorite toy, a yellow plastic pickup truck, and he played with it contentedly.

As the sun rose higher the car's air-conditioning came on automatically, and they were able to continue driving through the heat of the day. At the next oasis they bought food and filled the tank. Abdul checked his phone but there was still no signal. The three of them ate flatbread and figs and yogurt as they drove on. Naji went quiet, and Abdul glanced back and saw that the little boy was stretched out on the backseat, asleep.

Abdul was hoping they would reach a real road and find someplace where they could get beds for the night, but the sun began to go down and he realized they would have to sleep in the desert. They came to a flat plain where geological activity had thrown up jagged rocky hills. Abdul checked his phone and saw that he had a signal.

He immediately sent Tamara the reports and photos he had prepared during his ten days at the slave camp. Then he phoned her, but she did not pick up. He left a message to supplement his reports, saying that he had disabled the jihadis' transport but they would get hold of fresh vehicles sooner or later, so the military should attack the place in the next day or two.

Leaving the road, he drove cautiously to one of the rocky hills and stopped behind it, so that the car could not be seen from the road.

"We can't run the heater all night," he said. "We'll all have to sleep together in the back for warmth."

Abdul and Kiah got into the backseat with Naji between them, sucking his thumb. Kiah covered all three of them with the blankets.

Abdul had now been awake for thirty-six hours and driving for half that time, and he was exhausted. He would probably have to drive all day tomorrow. He turned off his phone.

He sat back with the blanket over his knees and closed his eyes. For a while he seemed still to be scrutinizing the road ahead, trying to discern its edges and at the same time scanning for sharp rocks or anything else that might puncture a tire. But when the sun disappeared and the desert went dark he fell fast asleep.

He dreamed about Annabelle. It was the happy period before her narrow-minded family poisoned their relationship. They were in a park, lying on a lawn of lush grass. He was on his back, and Annabelle was beside him, propped up on one elbow, leaning over him, kissing his face. Her lips caressed him gently: his forehead, cheeks, nose, chin, mouth. He luxuriated in her touch and the love it expressed.

Then he began to understand that he was dreaming. He did not want to wake up, the dream was too delicious, but he found he could not remain asleep, and Annabelle and the green grass started to fade. However, when the dream vanished the kissing went on. He remembered he was in a car in the Libyan desert, he reckoned that he had slept for twelve hours, and he realized who was kissing him. He opened his eyes. It was early, and the daylight was still pale, but he clearly saw the face of Kiah.

She looked anxious. "Are you angry?" she said.

In some distant corner of his mind he had been longing for this moment for weeks. "Not angry," he said, and kissed her. It was a long kiss. He wanted to explore her in every possible way, and he sensed that she felt the same about him. He thought he had never had a kiss like this before.

She broke away, panting.

Abdul said: "Where's Naji?"

She pointed. He was in the front seat, wrapped in a blanket, fast asleep. She said: "He will wake in an hour."

They kissed again, then Abdul said: "I have to ask you."

"Ask me."

"What do you want? I mean right here, right now. What do you want us to do?"

"Everything," she said. "Everything."

CHAPTER 28

Late on Tuesday afternoon Chang Kai was alarmed by a breaking story on CCTV-13, the all-news channel on Chinese television.

He was in his office at the Guoanbu when his young Korea specialist, Jin Chin-hwa, came in and suggested he turn on the set. Kai saw the supreme leader of North Korea, resplendent in some kind of military uniform, standing in front of jet fighter planes at an air base but obviously reading from a teleprompter. Kai was surprised: it was unusual for Supreme Leader Kang U-jung to speak live on TV. This must be serious, he thought.

North Korea had worried him for years. The government was volatile and unpredictable, which was dangerous in a strategically important ally. China did what it could to steady the regime, but it seemed always to be on the edge of some crisis. North Korea had been quiet for two and a half weeks, since the rebellion by the ultra-nationalists, and Kai had been optimistic that the revolt might fizzle out.

But the supreme leader was nothing if not vengeful. Although he had a round face and smiled a lot, he was part of a dynasty that ruled by terror. It would not be enough for him merely to see the insurrection fade away. Everyone had to see him crush it. He needed to terrify anyone else with such ideas.

CCTV-13 added Mandarin subtitles to the Korean soundtrack. Kang said: "The courageous and loyal troops of the Korean People's Army have combated an insurrection organized by the South Korean authorities in cahoots with the United States. The murderous attacks of the American-inspired traitors have been crushed and the perpetrators are under arrest and face justice. Meanwhile, mopping-up operations are in progress as the situation returns to normal."

Kai muted the sound. The accusation against the United States was routine propaganda, he knew. Like the Chinese, the Americans valued stability and hated unpredictable turmoil, even in the countries of their enemies. It was the rest of the statement that bothered him.

He looked at Jin, who was drop-dead cool today in a black suit with a skinny tie. "It's not true, is it?"

"Almost certainly not."

Jin was a Chinese citizen of Korean ethnicity. Foolish people thought that the loyalties of such men were suspect and they should not be allowed to work for the secret service. Kai believed the opposite. The descendants of immigrants often had exaggerated affection for their country of adoption and sometimes even felt they had no right to disagree with the authorities. They were usually more passionately loyal than the majority of Han Chinese, and the strict vetting system of the Guoanbu quickly weeded out any exceptions. Jin had said to Kai that China allowed him to be himself, a feeling that was not shared by every Chinese citizen.

Jin said: "If it was true that the rebellion was over, Kang would be pretending it had never happened. The fact that he's saying it's over suggests to me that it's not. This may be an attempt to cover up their failure to suppress it."

"That's what I thought."

Kai nodded thanks, and Jin left.

He was still pondering the news when his personal phone rang. He answered: "This is Kai."

"This is me."

Kai recognized the voice of General Ham Ha-sun who had to be phoning from North Korea. Kai said: "I'm glad you called." He meant it. Ham would know the facts about the rebellion.

Ham got straight to the point. "Pyongyang's announcement is shit."

"They haven't crushed the insurrection?"

"The reverse. The ultras have consolidated their position and they now control the entire northeast of the country, including three ballistic missile facilities as well as the nuclear base."

"So the supreme leader lied." As Kai and Jin had guessed.

"This is no longer an uprising," Ham said. "It's a civil war, and no one can predict who will win."

That was worse than Kai had thought. North Korea was boiling up again. "This is a very important steer," he said. "Thank you."

Kai intended to bring the conversation to a close then, knowing that every second added to the danger Ham was in. But the general had not finished. He had an agenda of his own. He said: "You know that I remain where I am for your sake."

Kai was not sure that was entirely true, but he did not want to argue. "Yes," he said.

"When this is over you have to get me out."

"I'll do my best—"

"Forget about doing your best. I need your promise.

If the regime wins they will execute me for being a senior officer on the wrong side. And if the rebels ever suspect that I talked to you they will shoot me like a dog."

It was true, Kai knew.

"I promise," he said.

"You may have to send a special forces team across the border in helicopters to get me out."

Kai might struggle to make that happen for the sake of one spy whose usefulness was at an end, but this was no time to confess to doubts. "If that's what it takes, we'll do it," he said, with all the sincerity he could fake.

"I think you owe me that."

"I certainly do." Kai meant it, and hoped he would be able to pay his debt.

"Thank you." Ham hung up.

The implication Kai and Jin had drawn from the speech of the supreme leader had been confirmed by the most trustworthy spy Kai had ever had. He had to share the news.

He had been looking forward to a quiet evening at home with Ting. They both worked hard and at the end of the day neither of them wanted to dress up and go to fashionable places where they would see and be seen. Quiet evenings were their delight. In their neighborhood a new place had opened called Trattoria Reggio. Kai had been looking forward to some penne all'arrabbiata. But duty called.

He would tell the vice chairman of the National Security Commission, who was his father, Chang Jianjun.

There was no answer from Jianjun's personal phone, but he would probably be at home by now. Kai dialed the number and his mother answered. Kai spent a few moments patiently answering her questions: he was not getting sinus headaches and had not suffered them for some years now; Ting had had her annual vaccination for influenza and had suffered no side effects from the jab; Ting's mother was very well for her age and not suffering any more than usual from her old leg injury; and finally he did not know what was going to happen next on *Love in the Palace.* Then he asked for his father.

She said: "He's gone to the Enjoy Hot restaurant to eat pigs' feet with his comrades and he'll come home stinking of garlic."

"Thank you," said Kai. "I'll catch him there."

He could have phoned the restaurant, but the old man might have resented being called to the phone during a dinner with old companions. However, the place was not far from Guoanbu headquarters, so Kai decided to go there. It was always better to talk to his father in person rather than on the phone, anyway. He told Peng Yawen to notify Monk.

Before leaving he told Jin what he had learned from General Ham. "Now I'm going to brief Chang Jianjun," he said. "Call me if anything happens."

"Yes, sir."

Enjoy Hot was a large restaurant with several private rooms. In one of them Kai found his father dining with General Huang Ling and Kai's boss, Fu Chuyu, the minister for state security. The room was full of the steamy odors of chili, garlic, and ginger. All three men were members of the National Security Commission: they formed a powerful conservative group. They looked sober and serious, and seemed irritated to be disturbed. Perhaps this was more than a convivial get-together. Kai would have liked to know what they had been discussing that required privacy from other diners.

Kai said: "Some news from North Korea that won't wait until the morning."

He expected them to tell him to pull up a chair, but they thought such courtesy was not necessary toward a younger man. Fu Chuyu, his boss, said: "Carry on."

"There's strong evidence that the regime of Kang U-jung is losing its grip on the country. The ultras now control the northeast as well as the northwest—in other words, half the country. A reliable informant describes the situation as civil war."

Fu said: "That changes the game."

General Huang looked skeptical. "If it's true."

Kai said: "That's always a question with secret intelligence. But I would not have brought you this information if I did not have confidence in it."

Chang Jianjun said: "If it's true, what do we do?"

Huang was aggressive, as ever. "Bomb the traitors. In half an hour we could flatten every base they've taken over and kill them all. Why not?"

Kai knew why not, but he kept quiet, and his father answered the question, with a touch of impatience. "Because in that half hour they might launch nuclear missiles at Chinese cities."

Huang bristled. "Are we scared of a rabble of Korean mutineers now?"

"No," said Jianjun. "We're scared of nuclear bombs. Anyone in his right mind is scared of nuclear bombs."

This kind of talk infuriated Huang. He thought it made China weak. He said: "So anyone who steals a few nukes can do whatever he likes and China will be powerless to resist!"

"Certainly not," said Jianjun crisply. "But bombing is not our first move." After a moment he added thoughtfully: "Though it might well be our last."

Huang shifted his ground. "I doubt whether the situation is as bad as it's been represented. Spies always exaggerate their reports in order to pump up their own importance."

Fu said: "That's certainly true."

Kai had done his duty and did not want to argue with them. "Excuse me, please," he said. "If I may, I will leave you older and wiser men to discuss the matter. Good night."

As he left the room his phone rang. He saw that the caller was Jin, and he stopped outside the door to answer. "You told me to let you know of developments," said Jin.

"What's happened?"

"KBS news in South Korea says the North Korean ultras have taken control of the military base at Hamhung, a couple of hundred miles south of their original base at Yeongjeo-dong. They've advanced farther than we imagined."

Kai pictured in his mind a map of North Korea. "Why, that means they now have more than half the country."

"And it's symbolic too."

"Because Hamhung is North Korea's second city."

"Yes."

This was very serious.

"Thanks for letting me know."

"Yes, sir."

Kai hung up and went back into the private room. The three men looked up in surprise. "According to South Korean TV, the ultras have now taken Hamhung."

He saw his father go pale. "That's it," he said. "We have to tell the president."

Fu Chuyu took out his phone. "I'll call him now."

CHAPTER 29

The helicopters flew across the Sahara overnight, aiming to arrive at the gold mine at dawn, a little more than thirty-six hours after Abdul had reported. Tamara and Tab, as the lead intelligence officers, rode in the command chopper with Colonel Marcus. While they were in the air, dawn broke over a featureless landscape of rock and sand, without vegetation or any sign of the human race. It looked like another planet, uninhabited, Mars maybe.

Tab said: "Are you okay?"

She was not really okay. She was scared. She had a pain in her stomach and she had to clasp her hands together to stop them from shaking. She was desperate to hide this from the others in the chopper. But she could tell Tab. "I'm terrified," she said. "This will be my third gunfight in seven weeks. You'd think I'd be used to it."

"Always with the wisecrack," he said, but he discreetly squeezed her arm in a gesture of sympathy.

"I'll be all right," she said.

"I know you will."

All the same she would not have missed this. It was

the climax of the whole Abdul project. Abdul's report had electrified the forces fighting ISGS in North Africa. He had found Hufra and, even better, al-Farabi was there. He had revealed the role of North Korea in arming African terrorists. He had also discovered a gold mine that had to be a major source of income for the jihadis. And he had uncovered a slave labor camp.

Tamara had quickly confirmed the exact location. Satellite images showed numerous mining camps in the general area, all quite similar from six thousand miles up, but Tab had organized a surveillance flight by a Falcon 50 jet of the French air force, six miles up instead of six thousand, and Hufra was easily identified by the large black square of burn damage caused by Abdul's gasoline fire. They now understood why the drone search for the bus had failed: they had assumed the bus would head north as the quickest way to a paved road, but in fact it had gone due west to the mine.

It had been a challenge to alert everyone and coordinate plans with American and French armed forces in such a short time, and there had been moments when the unflappable Susan Marcus looked almost flustered, but she had succeeded, and they had set out in the early hours of this morning and made a rendezvous in the starlit desert an hour ago.

It was the largest operation yet by the multinational force. The rule of thumb for offensive operations was three attackers per defender, and Abdul had estimated a hundred jihadis at the camp, so Colonel Marcus had mustered three hundred soldiers. The infantry were now in place just out of sight. With them was a Firepower Control Team in charge of coordinating air and ground attacks so that no one shot at their own side. The air assault was led by Apache attack helicopters armed with chain guns, rockets, and Hellfire air-to-surface missiles. Their mission was to crush jihadi resistance rapidly in order to minimize casualties among the attacking force and the noncombatants in the slave quarters.

The last aircraft in the fleet was an Osprey helicopter carrying medical staff with their supplies plus social workers fluent in Arabic. They would take charge when the fighting was over. The slaves would have to be cared for. They would have health problems that had never been addressed. Some would be malnourished. All would have to be returned to their homes.

Tamara saw a smudge on the horizon that quickly resolved into a habitation. The fact that there was no greenery indicated that it was not a normal oasis village but a mining camp. As the fleet drew nearer she saw a mess of tents and improvised shelters contrasting vividly with the three neatly fenced compounds, one containing the carcasses of burned-out cars and trucks, one with a pit in the middle that was obviously the gold mine, and the third with cinder-block buildings and what might have been missile launchers under camouflage covers.

Susan said to Tamara: "I think you said that the jihadis go to great lengths to keep the slaves out of the fenced areas."

"Yes. They can be shot if they climb fences, Abdul said."

"So everyone inside the fence is a jihadi."

"Except for those in the light-blue-painted building. They're the kidnapped girls."

"That's helpful." Susan flicked a switch to talk to the entire force and said: "All personnel inside the fenced areas are enemy soldiers, except those in the light-blue-painted building, who are prisoners. Do not fire on the light blue building. All other friendlies are outside the fenced area." She clicked off.

The place was dismal. Most of the shelters looked barely adequate to keep the sun off. The pathways were filthy with litter and other kinds of waste. It was only just first light, so few people were in evidence, just a handful of ragged men fetching water and a small group relieving themselves a short distance from the camp at what was obviously the latrine.

The noise of the choppers reached the camp and more people quickly appeared.

The lead aircraft was equipped with a powerful public address system, and a voice now said in Arabic: "Move into the desert with your hands on your head. If you are unarmed you will be in no danger. Move into the desert with your hands on your head."

People in the slave quarter ran out into the desert, in too much of a hurry to put their hands on their heads, but they were obviously unarmed.

It was different in the third compound. Men poured out of the barracks buildings into the open. Most had assault rifles and some carried handheld missile launchers.

All the helicopters quickly gained height and moved away. Apache fire was accurate from as far as five miles. Explosions peppered the compound and destroyed some of the barracks buildings.

Most of the infantry approached from the desert side, to draw fire away from the slave quarters. There was little cover, but a squad set up a mortar battery in the pit and began to lob shells into the compound. Someone in the air must have been giving them guidance, because their aim rapidly became devastatingly accurate.

Tamara was watching from a distance, though to her it did not seem a very safe distance, given the sophisticated targeting systems of shoulder-launched missiles. However, she could see that the jihadis had no chance of victory. Not merely outnumbered, they were fenced into a clearly defined space with nowhere to hide, and the carnage was dreadful.

One of their missiles found its target, and an Apache blew up in midair, its disembodied parts falling to the ground. Tamara cried out in dismay and Tab cursed. The attacking forces seemed to redouble their efforts.

The compound became a slaughterhouse. The ground was littered with the dead and wounded, often on top of one another. Those still unhurt began to drop their weapons and leave the compound, holding their hands on their heads to indicate surrender.

Without Tamara's noticing, a squad of infantry had approached the compound through the slave quarters and had taken cover near the gate, and they now trained their weapons on those surrendering and ordered them to lie flat, facedown, on the path.

Returning fire died down and the infantry swarmed the compound. Every soldier on the mission had seen Abdul's color photograph of al-Farabi with the North Korean man in the black linen blazer, and they all knew to take both alive if possible. Tamara thought the chances were slim: few of the jihadis were left alive.

The helicopters retreated and landed outside in the desert, and Tamara and Tab got out. The shooting petered out. Tamara felt good, and realized that the fear had left her as soon as the battle began.

As they walked back through the encampment, Tamara marveled at what Abdul had achieved: he had found this place, he had escaped, he had sent the information home, and by setting fire to the parking lot he had prevented the jihadis from getting away.

By the time she reached the compound they had found al-Farabi and the North Korean man. The two high-value prisoners were being guarded by a young American lieutenant who looked proud. "These are your guys, ma'am," he said to Tamara in English. "There's another Korean dead, but this is the one in your photo." He had separated these two from the other prisoners, who were in the process of having their hands tied behind their backs and their feet hobbled so that they could walk but not run.

She was momentarily distracted by the sight of three young women wearing absurd lacy lingerie, as if auditioning for a cheap porno film; then she realized they must be the inhabitants of the light blue building. The social work team would have clothes for them, and for the rest of the slaves, most of whom were wearing rags that were falling off them.

She returned her attention to the prize captives. "You are al-Farabi, the Afghan," she said, speaking Arabic.

He made no reply.

She turned to the Korean. "What is your name?"

"I am Park Jong-hoon," he said.

She turned to the lieutenant. "Set up a shade of some kind and see if you can find a couple of chairs. We're going to interrogate these men."

"Yes, ma'am."

Al-Farabi evidently understood English, for he said: "I refuse to submit to interrogation."

"Better get used to it," she said to him. "You're going to be questioned for years."

CHAPTER 30

Kai got a message from Neil Davidson, his contact at the CIA station in Beijing, requesting an urgent meeting.

For discretion, they varied the venue of their meetings. This time Kai told Peng Yawen to call the managing director of the Cadillac Center and say that the Ministry of State Security required two seats for that afternoon's basketball match between the Beijing Ducks and the Xinjiang Flying Tigers. A bicycle messenger delivered the tickets an hour later, and Yawen sent one to Neil at the American embassy.

Kai assumed Neil wanted to talk about the looming crisis in North Korea. That morning there had been another worrying sign: a collision in the Yellow Sea, off the west coast of Korea. It happened to be a clear day in that zone, and there were good-quality satellite photographs.

As always, Kai needed help interpreting the pictures. The vessels were mainly visible by their wakes, but it was clear that the larger one had struck the smaller. Yang Yong, the expert, said that the larger

CHAPTER 30   575

ship was a naval vessel and the smaller a fishing trawler, and he could make a good guess at their nationalities. "In that area, the navy ship is almost certainly North Korean," he said. "It looks very much as if it rammed the trawler, which is probably South Korean."

Kai agreed. The disputed maritime border between North and South Korean waters was a flashpoint. The line drawn by the United Nations in 1953 had never been accepted by the north, who in 1999 had declared a different line, one that gave them more of the rich fishing grounds. It was a classic territorial squabble and frequently led to clashes.

At midday, South Korean TV broadcast a video made by one of the sailors aboard the trawler. It clearly showed the red-white-and-blue ensign of the North Korean navy flapping in the wind on a ship heading straight for the camera. As it came closer without turning aside, there were cries of fear from the trawler crew. Then there was a loud crash followed by screams, and the film ended. It was dramatic and scary, and within minutes it had gone around the world on the internet.

Two South Korean sailors had been killed, the newsreader said: one drowned and one struck by flying debris.

Soon afterward Kai left for the Cadillac Center. In the car he took off his jacket and tie and put on a black Nike puffer jacket, the better to blend in with the other spectators.

The crowd in the arena was mostly Chinese but with a generous sprinkling of other ethnicities. When Kai arrived at his seat, with a couple of cans of Yanjing beer in his hands, Neil was already there, wearing a reefer jacket with a black knitted beanie pulled low over his forehead. The two of them looked like all the other spectators.

"Thanks," said Neil, accepting a can. "You got good seats."

Kai shrugged. "We're the secret police." He popped his can and drank.

The Ducks were in their all-white home uniform, the Tigers in sky blue. "Looks just like a game in the States," said Neil. "Even some Black players."

"They're Nigerian."

"I didn't know Nigerians played basketball."

"They're very good."

The game began, and the noise of the crowd became too loud for conversation. The Ducks went ahead in the first quarter, and by halftime they were up 58–43.

In the interval, Kai and Neil put their heads together to talk business. Neil said: "What the fuck is going on in North Korea?"

Kai thought for a moment. He had to be careful not to give away any secrets. That said, he believed it was in China's interest that the Americans should be well informed. Misunderstandings so often led to crises.

"What's going on is civil war," he said. "And the rebels are winning."

"I thought so."

"That's why the supreme leader is doing stupid things such as ramming a South Korean fishing boat. He's trying very hard not to look as weak as he is."

"Frankly, Kai, we can't understand why you don't do something to solve this problem."

"Such as?"

"Intervene with your own military and crush the rebels, for example."

"We could do that, but while we're crushing them they might fire nuclear weapons at Chinese cities. We can't risk that."

"Send your army to Pyongyang and get rid of the supreme leader."

"Same problem. We would then be at war with the rebels and their nukes."

"Let the rebels form a new government."

"We think that will probably happen without our intervention."

"Doing nothing can be dangerous too."

"We know that."

"There's something else. Were you aware that the North Koreans are supporting ISGS terrorists in North Africa?"

"What do you mean?" Kai knew exactly what Neil meant, but he had to be cautious.

"We raided a terrorist hideout called Hufra, in Libya near the Niger border. It has a gold mine operated by slaves."

"Well done."

"We arrested al-Farabi, the man we think is the leader of the Islamic State in the Greater Sahara. With him was a Korean man who told us his name is Park Jung-hoon."

"There must be thousands of Korean men called Park Jung-hoon. It's like John Smith in America."

"We also found three truck-mounted Hwasong-5 short-range ballistic missiles."

Kai was shocked. He knew the North Koreans sold rifles to terrorists, but ballistic missiles were something else. He concealed his surprise and said: "Armaments are their only successful export industry."

"Still . . ."

"I agree. It's crazy to sell missiles to those maniacs."

"So it's not done with Beijing's approval."

"Hell, no."

The teams came back. As the game restarted, Kai shouted: "Go, you Ducks!" in Mandarin.

Neil said in English: "You want another can of Yanjing?"

"You bet," said Kai.

That evening there was a dinner for the visiting president of Zambia in the State Banqueting Room of the Great Hall of the People in Tiananmen Square. China had invested millions in Zambia's copper mines, and Zambia supported China at the UN.

Kai was not invited but he attended the predinner drinks. Nursing a glass of Chandon Me, China's answer to champagne, he spoke to Foreign Minister Wu Bai, who was the height of elegance in a midnight-blue suit.

Wu said: "The South Koreans are sure to retaliate against the attack on their fishing boat."

"And then North Korea will retaliate against their retaliation."

Wu lowered his voice. "It's probably a good thing the supreme leader no longer has control of nuclear weapons. He'd be tempted to use them against South Korea, and then we'd have the Americans involved in a nuclear war."

"It doesn't bear thinking about," Kai said. "But remember, he has other weapons almost as fearsome as nukes."

Wu frowned. "What do you mean?"

"North Korea has two thousand five hundred tons of chemical weapons—nerve gas, blister agents, and emetics—and biological weapons: anthrax, cholera, and smallpox."

Wu looked panicked. "Fuck, I didn't think of that," he said. "I knew, but it slipped my mind."

"We probably should do something about it."

"We must tell them not to use those weapons."

"And say that if they do, we will . . . what?" Kai was trying to lead Wu to the inevitable conclusion.

"Cut off all aid, perhaps," said Wu. "Not just the emergency package, but everything."

Kai nodded. "That threat would force them to take us seriously."

"With no aid from us, the Pyongyang regime would collapse in days."

That was true, Kai thought, but the supreme leader would probably think it was an empty threat. He knew how crucial North Korea was to China strategically, and he might decide that, when push came to shove, the Chinese would find it impossible to abandon their neighbor. And he might be right.

However, Kai kept this thought to himself and said neutrally: "It's certainly worth putting pressure on Pyongyang."

Wu did not notice his lack of enthusiasm. "I'll talk to President Chen about it, but I think he'll agree."

"The North Korean ambassador, Bak Nam, is here tonight."

"An awkward customer."

"I know. Shall I let Ambassador Bak know that you need to speak to him?"

"Yes. Tell him to come and see me tomorrow. Meanwhile, I'll try to have a quick word with Chen this evening."

"Good." Kai left Wu Bai and looked around. There were a thousand or so people in the room, and it took him a few minutes to locate the North Korean contingent. Ambassador Bak was a thin-faced man in a well-worn suit. He held his glass in one hand and a cigarette in the other. Kai had met him several times. Bak did not look thrilled to renew the acquaintance.

Kai said: "Mr. Ambassador, I trust our emergency shipments of rice and coal are arriving smoothly?"

Bak replied in perfect Mandarin with a hostile tone. "Mr. Chang, we know it was you who imposed the delay."

Who had told him that? The who-said-what of a policy discussion was always confidential. The revelation of contrary opinions could undermine the final decision. Someone had broken that rule—presumably to get at Kai.

He set the question aside for the moment. "I bring you a message from the foreign minister," he said. "He needs to speak to you. Would you kindly make an appointment to visit him tomorrow?"

Kai was being polite. No ambassador would refuse such a request from a foreign minister. But Bak did not assent immediately. He said haughtily: "And what would he like to discuss?"

"North Korea's stockpile of chemical and biological weapons."

"We have no such weapons."

Kai suppressed a sigh. The tone of a government was set by those at the very top, and Bak was only aping the style of the supreme leader, who had the righteous obstinacy of a religious bigot. *Just say yes, motherfucker,* he thought wearily, but he said: "Then it may be a short discussion."

"Perhaps not. I was about to request a meeting with Mr. Wu on another topic."

"May I ask what?"

"We may need your help in stamping out this American-organized insurrection at Yeongjeo-dong."

Kai did not respond to the mention of the US. It was boilerplate propaganda and Bak did not believe it any more than Kai did. "What did you have in mind?"

"I shall discuss that with the minister."

"You must be thinking about military aid."

Bak ignored that. "I will call on the minister tomorrow."

"I'll let him know."

Kai found Wu again just as the guests were summoned

to their seats for dinner. Wu said: "President Chen agrees with my suggestion. If North Korea deploys chemical or biological weapons we will cut off all aid."

"Good," said Kai. "And when you meet Ambassador Bak tomorrow to tell him that, he's going to ask you for military aid against the rebels."

Wu shook his head. "Chen won't send Chinese troops into battle in North Korea. Remember that the rebels have nuclear weapons. Even North Korea isn't worth a nuclear war."

Kai did not want Wu to turn Bak's request down flat. "We could offer limited aid," he suggested. "Arms and ammunition, plus intelligence, but no boots on the ground."

Wu nodded. "All for short-range battlefield use, nothing that could be used against South Korea."

"In fact," said Kai, thinking aloud, "we could offer aid on condition that North Korea ends its provocative incursions into disputed maritime territory."

"Now, that's a good idea. Limited aid, given on condition they behave themselves."

"Yes."

"I'll suggest it to Chen."

Kai looked into the banqueting hall. A hundred waiters were already bringing the first course. He said: "Enjoy your dinner."

"Aren't you staying?"

"The government of Zambia does not consider my presence to be essential."

Wu smiled ruefully. "Lucky you," he said.

They met the following morning at the Foreign Ministry. Kai arrived first, then Ambassador Bak with four aides. They sat around a table where tea was waiting in cups with porcelain lids to keep it hot. Pleasantries were exchanged, but despite the courtesies the atmosphere was tense. Wu began the discussion by saying, "I want to talk to you about chemical and biological weapons."

Bak immediately interrupted, repeating what he had said to Kai last evening. "We have no such weapons."

"To your knowledge," said Wu, giving him a way out.

"To my certain knowledge," Bak insisted.

Wu had a response prepared. "In case you should acquire any in the future, and in case the military should in fact have such weapons without your knowledge, President Chen wants you to have a clear understanding of his views."

"The president's views are well-known to us. I myself—"

Wu raised his voice and spoke over Bak. "He has asked me to make sure!" he said, letting his anger show.

Bak shut up.

"North Korea must never use such weapons against South Korea." Wu held up a hand to stop Bak from interrupting again. "If you should defy this ruling, or overlook it, or even break it by accident, the consequences will be immediate and irrevocable. Without further discussion or even warning, China will withdraw all aid of every kind from North Korea, permanently. No more. Nothing."

Bak looked defiant, but it was evident to Kai that beneath the slight sneer he was shocked. He attempted a skeptical tone as he said: "If you were to fatally weaken North Korea, the Americans would try to take over, and I'm sure you don't want them for neighbors."

"I have not called you here for a discussion," Wu said firmly. He had now completely dropped his usual urbane manner. "I'm giving you the facts. Think what you like, but leave those appalling and uncontrollable weapons wherever they are currently hidden, and don't even think about deploying them."

Bak recovered his composure. "That's a very clear message, Foreign Minister, and I thank you."

"Good. Now you have a message for me."

"Yes. The insurrection that began in Yeongjeo-dong is proving more difficult to deal with than my government has so far admitted publicly."

"I appreciate your frankness," said Wu, becoming charming again.

"We believe that the quickest and most effective way to end this would be a joint operation between the North Korean and Chinese armies. Such a show of force would demonstrate, to the traitors, that they face overwhelming opposition."

"I see the logic of that," said Wu.

"And it would show their supporters in South Korea and the US that North Korea too has powerful friends."

Not very fucking many, Kai thought.

Wu said: "I will certainly pass this message to President Chen, but I can tell you right now that he will not send Chinese troops to North Korea for that purpose."

"This is very disappointing," Bak said stiffly.

"But don't despair," said Wu. "We may be able to give you arms and ammunition, and such intelligence as we can gather about the rebels."

Bak clearly scorned this offer, but he was too shrewd to reject it outright. He said: "Any help would be welcome, but that would hardly be enough."

"I must add that such help would be given conditionally."

"What conditions?"

"That North Korea ceases its confrontational incursions into disputed maritime waters."

"We do not accept the so-called Northern Limit Line imposed unilaterally—"

"Nor do we, but that's not the issue," Wu interrupted. "We simply think that this is a bad moment for you to make your point by ramming fishing boats."

"It was a trawler."

"President Chen wants you to defeat the rebellion, but he thinks that provocative actions against South Korea are counterproductive."

"The Democratic People's Republic of Korea," said Bak, pompously using the full official name of North Korea, "will not submit to bullying."

"We don't want you to," said Wu. "But you should deal with one problem at a time. That way you have a better chance of resolving both." He stood up to indicate that the meeting was at an end.

Bak took the hint. "I will pass your message on," he said. "On behalf of our supreme leader I thank you for seeing me."

"You're welcome."

The Koreans filed out of the room. When the door closed, Kai said to Wu: "Do you think they'll have the sense to do as we ask?"

"Not a chance," said Wu.

DEFCON 3

INCREASE IN FORCE READINESS.

AIR FORCE ABLE TO MOBILIZE
IN 15 MINUTES.

(US ARMED FORCES WERE AT DEFCON 3
ON SEPTEMBER 11, 2001.)

CHAPTER 31

G us came into the Oval Office with a map in his hand. "There's been an explosion in the Korea Strait," he said.

Pauline had visited Korea when she was a congresswoman. The photographs of her trip had endeared her to the 45,000 Korean Americans in Chicago. She said: "Remind me exactly where the Korea Strait is."

He came around the desk and put the map in front of her. She breathed in his distinctive aroma, woodsmoke and lavender and musk. She resisted the temptation to touch him.

He was all business. "It's the channel between South Korea and Japan," he said, pointing. "The explosion was at the western end of the strait, near a large island called Jeju. It's a vacation resort with beaches, but it also has a medium-size naval base."

"Any US troops at the base?"

"No."

"Good." When in Korea she had talked to a few of the 28,500 American soldiers there, some from her congressional district, and asked them how they felt about living on the other side of the world. They liked Seoul's vibrant nightlife, they said, but Korean girls were shy.

Those young men were her responsibility.

Gus's pointing finger rested on the map just south of the island. "The explosion was not far from the naval base. It was nowhere near as big as an earthquake or a nuclear bomb, but it did register on seismic sensors nearby."

"What could have caused it?"

"It wasn't a natural phenomenon of any kind. It might have been an ancient unexploded bomb, like a torpedo or a depth charge, but they think it was larger than that. The overwhelming likelihood is that a submarine blew up."

"Any intelligence?"

Gus's phone rang and he took it out of his pocket. "Coming in now, I hope," he said. He looked at the screen. "This is the CIA. Shall I answer?"

"Please."

He spoke into the phone. "Gus Blake." Then he listened.

Pauline watched him. A woman's heart can be an unexploded bomb, she thought. Handle me delicately, Gus, so that I don't detonate. If you just bring together the wrong pair of wires I could blow up, destroying my family and my reelection hopes and your own career too.

Such inappropriate thoughts were coming to her more often.

He hung up and said: "The CIA talked to the National Intelligence Service in South Korea."

Pauline grimaced. The NIS was something of a rogue agency, with a long history of corruption, interference in elections, and other illegal activities.

"I know," said Gus, reading her mind. "Not our favorite people. But here goes. They say an underwater vessel was detected in South Korean waters and identified as a Romeo-class submarine, almost certainly Chinese built and part of the North Korean navy. Such vessels are thought to be armed with three ballistic missiles, although we don't know for sure. When it began to approach the base at Jeju, the navy sent out a frigate."

"Did the frigate try to warn the submarine?"

"There's no normal radio transmission underwater, so the frigate dropped a depth charge at a safe distance from the sub, which is pretty much the only way of communicating in those circumstances. But the sub continued to approach the base, and was therefore judged to be on some kind of attacking mission. The ship was ordered to fire one of its Red Shark antisubmarine missiles. It scored a direct hit and destroyed the sub with no survivors."

"It's not much of an explanation."

"I don't necessarily believe the story. More likely the sub strayed into South Korean waters by accident and they decided to prove they could be just as tough as the north."

Pauline sighed. "The north attacks a fishing trawler. The south destroys a northern submarine. Tit for tat. We need to knock it on the head before it gets out of control. Every catastrophe begins with a little problem that doesn't get fixed." This kind of thing scared her. "Tell Chess to call Wu Bai and suggest that the Chinese restrain the North Koreans."

"They may not be able to."

"They can try. But you're right, the supreme leader probably won't listen. The trouble with being a tyrant is that your position is so insecure. You can't relax your grip for an instant. As soon as you show weakness, the smell of blood is in the air and the jackals gather. Machiavelli said it's better to be feared than loved, but he was wrong. A popular leader can make mistakes and survive, up to a point. A tyrant can't."

"Maybe we can get South Korea calmed down."

"Chess can talk to them too. They might be persuaded to make some kind of peace offering to the supreme leader."

"President No is a hard case."

"Yeah." No Do-hui was a proud woman who believed in her own brilliance and felt she could overcome all obstacles. A populist politician, she had won election by vowing that North and South Korea would be reunited; asked when that would happen, she had replied: "Before I die." Cool South Korean kids had taken to wearing T-shirts that said: "Before I die," and it became her defining slogan.

Pauline knew that reunification would never be so simple: the cost would be huge in dollars and immeasurable in social disruption, as twenty-five million half-starved North Koreans realized that everything they had believed in was a lie. Presumably No understood that. She probably calculated that the Americans would pay the financial bill, and the momentum of her triumph would overcome all other problems.

Chief of Staff Jacqueline Brody came in and said: "The secretary of defense wants a word."

Pauline said: "Was he calling from the Pentagon?"

"No, ma'am, he's right here, on his way to the Situation Room."

"Send him in."

Luis Rivera had been the youngest admiral in the US Navy. Although he was wearing a standard Washington dark blue suit, he managed to look as if he were still in the military: his black hair was buzz cut, his tie was tightly knotted, and his shoes gleamed. He greeted Pauline and Gus with brisk courtesy and said: "The

Eighth US Army in Korea has suffered a major cyber-attack."

The Eighth Army was the biggest component of the US military in South Korea.

Pauline said: "What kind of attack?"

"DDoS."

This was a test, Pauline knew. He used jargon to see whether she would understand. But she knew this acronym. "Distributed denial of service," she said, making it a statement rather than a question.

Rivera gave her a nod of acknowledgment: she had passed the test. "Yes, ma'am. Starting early this morning, our firewalls were breached and our servers were flooded with millions of artificial requests from multiple sources. Workstations slowed down and our intranet was disabled. All electronic communication ceased."

"What did you do?"

"We blocked all incoming traffic. We're restoring the servers now and developing filters. We hope to have comms up again within an hour. I should add that weapons command and control, which is ring-fenced in a different system, was not affected."

"Something to be thankful for. Who was responsible?"

"The incoming flood was from many servers around the world, but mostly Russia. The true origin was almost certainly North Korea. Apparently there's a detectable signature. However, I'm now at the limit of my understanding. I'm reporting the findings of specialists at the Pentagon."

"In the nursery, probably," Pauline said, and Gus chuckled. "But why now?" Pauline asked. "North Korea has been hostile to us for decades. Today they suddenly realized it was time to attack our systems. What's their thinking?"

Luis said: "All strategists agree that cyber warfare is an essential prelude to the real thing."

"So this means that the supreme leader thinks North Korea will soon be at war with the US."

"I'd say they think they *may* soon be at war, more probably with South Korea, but given the close US–South Korea alliance they would like to weaken us as a precaution."

Pauline looked at Gus, who said: "I agree with Luis."

"So do I," she said. "Are we planning to retaliate with our own cyberattack, Luis?"

"The local commander is mulling it, and I haven't forced the issue," Luis said. "We have massive cyber-war resources, but he's reluctant to show his hand."

Gus put in: "When we deploy our cyberweapons we want it to be a terrific shock to the enemy, something for which they haven't adequately prepared."

"I get that," said Pauline. "But the government in Seoul may not be so restrained."

Luis said: "Yes. In fact I suspect they may have hit back already. Why did that North Korean submarine approach the naval base at Jeju? Perhaps its systems were down and it had lost navigation."

Pauline said sadly: "All those men dead for no damn reason." She looked up. "All right, Luis, thank you."

"Thank you, Madam President." Luis left.

Gus said: "Do you want to talk to Chester before he calls President Chen and President No?"

"Yes. Thank you for reminding me."

"I'll bring him in."

Pauline watched Gus as he talked on the phone. She was thinking about what had happened when Gerry and Pippa were away. Gerry had gone to bed with Amelia Judd, and Pauline had thought about going to bed with Gus. Her marriage could be rescued, she knew, and she would try to make that happen—she had to, for Pippa's sake—but in her heart she wanted something else.

Gus hung up and said: "Chess is across the street in the Eisenhower building. He'll be here in five minutes."

The White House was like this. Work was intense for hours, and while that was happening her concentration was unshakable; then suddenly there was a pause, and the rest of her life came flooding back in.

Gus said quietly: "In five years you'll be out of this office."

"Maybe in a year," she said.

"But more likely five."

She studied his face and saw a strong man struggling to express deep emotion. She wondered what was coming. She felt shaky. That surprised her: she never felt shaky.

He said: "Pippa will be at college in five years."

She nodded. She thought: What am I scared of?"

He said: "You'll be free."

She said: "Free . . ."

She began to see where this might be going, and she felt both thrilled and apprehensive.

Gus closed his eyes, getting control, then opened them and said: "I fell in love with Tamira when I was twenty."

Tamira was his ex-wife. Pauline pictured her: a tall Black woman in her late forties, confident, well-dressed. Once a champion sprinter, she was now a successful manager of sports stars. She was beautiful and smart and completely uninterested in politics.

Gus said: "We were together a long time, but we slowly grew apart. I've been single for ten years now." There was a note of regret, and it told Pauline that the life of a bachelor had never been Gus's ideal. "I haven't been living like a monk—I've dated. I've met one or two terrific women." Pauline did not detect any trace of boasting. He was just stating the facts. In the interest of full disclosure, she thought, and she was briefly amused at her own legalese. He went on: "Younger, older, in politics, out of it, mostly Black, some white. Smart, sexy women. But I didn't fall in love. Not even close. Until I got to know you."

"What are you saying?"

"That I've waited ten years for you." He smiled. "And if I have to I can wait another five."

Pauline felt overcome with emotion. Her throat seemed to constrict and she could not speak. Tears came to her eyes. She wanted to throw her arms around him and put her head on his chest and cry into his chalk-striped suit. But her secretary of state, Chester Jackson, came in, and she had to pull herself together in a second.

She opened a desk drawer, pulled out a handful of tissues, and blew her nose, turning away. She looked out of the window and across the South Lawn to the National Mall, where thousands of elm and cherry trees blazed their fall colors, every glorious shade of red, orange, and yellow, reminding her that although winter was coming there was still time for joy.

"I hope I'm not getting an autumn cold," she said, surreptitiously blotting stray tears. Then she sat down and faced the room, embarrassed but happy, and said: "Let's get down to business."

That evening, at the end of dinner, Pippa said: "Mom, could I ask you a question?"

"Sure, honey."

"Would you fire nuclear weapons?"

Pauline was taken by surprise, but she had no hesitation. "Yes, of course. How did this come up?"

"We were talking about it at school, and Cindy Riley said: 'Your mom is the one who will push the button.' But would you?"

"I would. You can't be president if you're not willing to do that. It's part of the job."

Pippa turned in her seat to face Pauline. "But you've seen those pictures of Hiroshima, you must have."

Pauline had work to do, as she did every evening, but this was an important conversation, and she was not going to rush it. Pippa was troubled. Pauline thought nostalgically of the time when Pippa had asked easy questions, such as, where does the moon go when we can't see it? She said: "Yes, I've studied those photographs."

"It's, like, flattened—by one bomb!"

"Yes."

"And all those people killed—eighty thousand!"

"I know."

"And the survivors had it even worse—awful burns, then the radiation sickness."

"The most important part of my job is to make sure it never happens again."

"But you say you would fire nuclear weapons!"

"Look. Since 1945 the US has been involved in numerous wars, big and small, some involving another nuclear-armed country—but nuclear weapons have never been used again."

"Doesn't that prove we don't need them?"

"No, it proves that deterrence works. Other nations are afraid to attack the US with nuclear weapons because they know we will retaliate and they can't win."

Pippa was getting upset. Her voice rose in pitch. She said: "But if that happens, and you press the button, we'll all be killed!"

"Not all of us, not necessarily." Pauline knew this was the weak part of her argument.

"Why don't you just say you'll press the button, like with your fingers crossed behind your back?"

"I don't believe in faking things. It doesn't work. People find you out. Anyway, I don't need to pretend. I mean it."

Tears came to Pippa's eyes. "But, Mom, nuclear war could be the end of the human race."

"I know. So could climate change. So could a comet, or the next virus. These are the things we have to manage in order to survive."

"But when would you press the button? I mean, what circumstances? What could possibly drive you to risk the end of the world?"

"I've thought about this a lot, over many years, as you can imagine," Pauline began. "There are three conditions. First, whatever the problem is, we have tried all possible peaceful means of solving it—all diplomatic channels—but they have failed."

"Well, okay, like, obviously."

"Be patient, honey, because all of this is important. Second, the problem can't be solved using our vast arsenal of nonnuclear weapons."

"Hard to imagine."

It was not hard at all, but Pauline did not go down that side road. "Third, and finally, Americans are being killed, or are about to be killed, by enemy action. So, you see, nuclear war is the last resort when all else has failed. That's where I part company with people such as James Moore, who treats nuclear weapons as a first option—after which there's nothing left in the cupboard."

"But if all your conditions are fulfilled, you will risk wiping out the entire human race."

Pauline did not think it was that bad, but it was bad enough, and she was not going to quibble. "Yes, I would. And if I couldn't answer yes to that question, I couldn't be president."

"Wow," Pippa said. "That's awful." But she was not so emotional. Knowing the facts helped her face the nightmare.

Pauline stood up. "And now I have to go back to the Oval Office and make sure it doesn't happen."

"Good luck, Mommy."

"Thanks, honey."

The temperature was falling outside. She had felt it earlier. She decided to go to the West Wing via the tunnel President Reagan had built. She went down to the basement, opened a closet door, entered the tunnel, and walked briskly along the dark tan carpet. She wondered whether Reagan had imagined he would be safe from nuclear attack down here. More likely he just didn't like getting cold as he walked to the West Wing.

The monotony of the walls was relieved by framed photographs of American jazz legends, probably chosen by the Obamas. I doubt whether the Reagans liked Wynton Marsalis, she thought. The tunnel followed the route of the colonnade above, turning at a right angle halfway. It led to a staircase leading up to a concealed door outside the Oval Office.

But Pauline bypassed the Oval Office and entered the comfortable small study, a workplace with no atmosphere of ceremony. She read the full report of the raid on Hufra in the Sahara Desert, noting the reappearance of two effective women, Susan Marcus and Tamara Levit. She mulled over the North Korean weaponry found at the camp, and the mystery man who called himself Park Jung-hoon.

Her mind returned to the conversation with Pippa. Thinking back over what she had said, she did not want to change any of it. Having to justify yourself to a child was a good exercise, she reflected; it cleared the mind.

But the overwhelming feeling she was left with was loneliness.

She would probably never have to make the decision Pippa had asked about—heaven forbid—but every day confronted her with heavy questions. Her choices brought people wealth or poverty, fairness or injustice, life or death. She did her best but she was never 100 percent sure she was right.

And no one could share her burden.

The phone woke Pauline that night. Her bedside clock said it was one a.m. She was sleeping alone in the Lincoln Bedroom, again. She picked up and heard Gus's voice. "We think North Korea is about to attack South Korea."

"Shit," Pauline said.

"Soon after midnight our time, signals intelligence noticed intense communications activity around the Korean People's Army Air and Anti-Air Force headquarters at Chunghwa, North Korea. Senior military and political staff were notified and are now waiting for you in the Situation Room."

"On my way."

She had been in a deep sleep, but she had to clear her head fast. She pulled on jeans and a sweatshirt and pushed her feet into loafers. Her hair was a mess and she paused to tuck it into a baseball cap, then she hurried to the basement of the West Wing. By the time she got there she felt fully alert.

When the Situation Room was in use it was usually full, with every chair around the long table taken and aides in the seats ranged along the walls, under the screens, but now just a handful of people were present: Gus, Chess, Luis, Chief of Staff Jacqueline Brody, and Sophia Magliani, the director of national intelligence, with a handful of aides. There had not been time for others to assemble.

At every place there was a computer workstation and a telephone headset. Luis was wearing his headset, and as soon as Pauline walked in he began speaking, without preamble. "Madam President, two minutes ago one of our infrared early-warning satellites detected the launch of six missiles from Sino-ri, a military base in North Korea."

Pauline did not sit down. She said: "Where are the missiles now?"

Gus put a mug of coffee in front of her, dark with a splash of milk, just how she liked it. "Thanks," she murmured. She sipped gratefully while Luis continued.

"One missile misfired and came down in seconds. The remaining five headed into South Korea. Then another broke up in flight."

"Do we know why?"

"No, but missile failures aren't unusual."

"Okay, carry on."

"At first we thought they were aimed at Seoul—the capital seemed the logical target—but they have now passed over the city and are approaching the south coast." He pointed to a wall screen. "The graphic, built up from radar and other inputs, gives a picture of where the missiles are."

Pauline saw four red arcs superimposed on a map of South Korea. Each arc had an arrowhead that crept slowly southward. "I see two likely targets," she said. "Busan and Jeju." Busan, on the south coast, was South Korea's second city, with three and a half million people and a huge naval base for both Korean and American forces. But the much smaller Korean-only base on the vacation island of Jeju might have symbolic importance because it was where the North Korean submarine had been destroyed yesterday.

Luis said: "I agree, and we'll soon know which." He held up a hand, asking everyone to wait while he listened to his headset, then he said: "The Pentagon says the missiles are now more than halfway across South Korea and they should reach the coast in two minutes."

The speed at which the missiles traveled a hundred miles was breathtaking, Pauline thought.

Chess put in: "There is a third possibility, which is no target at all."

"Explain," said Pauline.

"The missiles could be meant only as a demonstration, to scare South Korea, in which case they could overfly the entire country and come down in the sea."

"Something to hope for, but somehow I don't think that would be the supreme leader's style," Pauline said. "Luis, are those ballistic missiles or cruise missiles?"

"We think we're looking at medium-range ballistic missiles."

"High explosive or nuclear?"

"High explosive. These missiles came from Sino-ri, which is controlled by the supreme leader. He has no nuclear weapons now—they're all at bases controlled by the rebel ultras."

"Why are those missiles still flying? South Korea has anti-missile missiles, doesn't it?"

"Ballistic missiles can't be shot down in midflight—they're too high and too fast. The South Koreans' Cheolmae 4HL surface-to-air system will engage them in their descent phase, as they approach their target, when they slow down. The system couldn't hit them when they passed over Seoul."

"But it should now."

"Any second."

"Let's hope so." She turned to Chess. "What have we done to stop this?"

"I called the Chinese foreign minister, Wu Bai, as soon as we got the warning about signals activity. He gave me some bullshit but it was clear that he had no idea what the supreme leader was up to."

"Did you talk to anyone else?"

"The South Koreans don't know why they're under attack. The North Korean envoy to the UN didn't return my call."

She looked at Sophia. "Anything from the CIA?"

"Not from Langley." Sophia usually looked glamorous, but tonight she had dressed in a hurry: her long wavy hair was scraped back and tied up in a bun, and she had put on a yellow warm-up jacket and green running pants. But her brain was working. "Their best man in Beijing, Davidson, is desperately trying to speak to the head of the Guoanbu, whom he knows well, but he hasn't reached him yet."

Pauline nodded. "Chang Kai. I've heard of him. If anyone in Beijing knows what's going on, he will."

Luis was listening to his headset again. "The Pentagon is now certain the target is Jeju," he said.

"That settles it," said Pauline. "This is retaliation. The supreme leader is punishing the naval base that destroyed his submarine. You'd think he had enough to do combating the rebels in his own country."

Gus said, "He's failed to crush the rebellion, which makes him seem weak, and the sinking of the submarine makes it worse. He's desperate for something that makes him look tough."

Luis said: "We've accessed video from the base. It's not public, they must have hacked it." A picture came up on a wall screen, and Luis said: "It's closed-circuit television, security surveillance footage."

They saw a large harbor enclosed by a man-made seawall. Within the wall were a destroyer, five frigates, and one submarine. The picture changed, presumably to a different CCTV camera, and now they saw sailors on the deck of a ship. Someone in a backroom was looking at multiple feeds and selecting the most informative ones, for the shot changed again, and they saw roads around low office and apartment buildings. This picture also showed frenetic activity: men running, cars driving fast, officers shouting into phones.

Luis said: "The anti-missile battery has fired."

Pauline said: "How many missiles?"

"The launcher fires eight at a time. Wait . . ." There was a pause, and Luis said: "One of the eight crashed seconds after firing. The other seven are in flight."

After a minute seven new arcs appeared on the radar graphic, on an intercept course with the incoming missiles.

"Thirty seconds to contact," said Luis.

The arcs on the screen moved closer.

Pauline said: "If the missiles explode over a populated area . . ."

Luis said: "The anti-missile missile has no warhead. It destroys the incoming ordnance just by crashing into it. But the incoming warhead might explode when it hits the ground." He paused. "Ten seconds."

The room was silent. Everyone stared at the graphic. The dots came together.

"Contact," said Luis.

The graphic froze.

"The sky is full of debris," said Luis. "The radar is unclear. We have hits, but we don't know how many."

Pauline said: "Shouldn't we have gotten them all—with seven interceptors to destroy only four incoming?"

"Yes," said Luis. "But missiles are never perfect.

Here we go. . . . Shit, only two hits. There are still two missiles heading for Jeju."

Chess said: "For Christ's sake, why didn't the battery fire everything they've got?"

Pauline replied: "Then what would they do if the North Koreans sent over another six?"

Chess had another question. "What happened to the five anti-missile missiles that didn't hit their targets? Can they try again?"

"At that speed they can't turn around. Eventually they'll slow down and fall out of the sky, hopefully into the sea."

Luis said: "Thirty seconds."

Everyone watched the TV pictures of the naval base that was the target.

The people there would probably not see the missiles, which must have been moving too fast for the human eye, Pauline thought. But they clearly knew they were under attack: everyone was running, some in a brisk, purposeful way, others in a blind panic.

"Ten seconds," said Luis.

Pauline wished she could look away. She did not want to watch people die. But she knew she must not flinch. She had to be able to say that she saw what happened.

She was looking at a row of low buildings when the screen showed several flashes, five or six all at the same time. She just had time to realize that the missiles must have had multiple warheads, then a wall collapsed, a desk and a man flew through the air, a truck crashed into a parked car, and then the scene was engulfed in thick gray smoke.

The picture switched to the harbor and she saw that the other missile had sprayed its bomblets over the ships. This was luck, she guessed: ballistic missiles were not so accurate. She saw flames and smoke and twisted metal and a sailor jumping into the water.

Then the screen went blank.

There was a long moment of stunned silence.

Eventually Luis said: "We've lost the feed. They think the system has been destroyed—not surprisingly."

Pauline said: "We've seen enough to know that there will be dozens of dead and wounded plus millions of dollars' worth of damage. But is that the end of it? I presume we would have heard if any more missiles had been launched anywhere in Korea."

Luis asked the Pentagon, waited, then said: "No, nothing more."

Now for the first time Pauline sat down, taking the chair at the head of the table. She said: "Ladies and gentlemen, that was not the outbreak of a war."

They took a moment to absorb that. Then Gus said: "I agree, Madam President, but would you explain your thinking?"

"Of course. One: this was a strictly limited strike— six missiles, one target—no attempt to conquer or destroy South Korea. Two: they have been careful not to kill Americans, striking a naval base that is not used by American ships. To sum up, everything about this attack suggests restraint." She looked around and added: "Paradoxically."

Gus nodded thoughtfully. "They've hit back at the base that destroyed their submarine, and that's all. They want this to be seen as a proportionate response."

"They want peace," Pauline said. "They're struggling to win a civil war, and they don't want to have to fight South Korea as well as the ultras."

Chess said: "Where does that leave us?"

Pauline was thinking on her feet, but she was a few

steps ahead of the group. "We must prevent South Korea from retaliating. They won't like it, but they'll have to suck it up. They have an agreement with us, the Mutual Defense Treaty of 1953. In article three that document obliges them to consult us when they're threatened by external armed attack. They have to check with us."

Luis looked skeptical. "In theory," he said.

"True. It's a basic law of international relations that governments fulfill their treaty obligations only when it suits them. When it doesn't they find excuses. So what we have to do now is nail it down."

Chess said: "Good idea. How?"

"I'm going to propose a cease-fire and a peace conference: North Korea, South Korea, China, and us. It will be hosted by an Asian country, somewhere more or less neutral—Sri Lanka might work."

Chess nodded. "The Philippines, perhaps. Or Laos, if the Chinese prefer a Communist dictatorship."

"Whatever." Pauline stood up. "Set up calls with President Chen and President No, please. Keep trying to reach the North Korean envoy at the UN, but I'll also ask Chen to call the supreme leader."

Chess said: "Yes, ma'am."

Luis said: "The families of military personnel in South Korea should be evacuated."

"Yes. And there are a hundred thousand American civilians there. They should be advised to leave."

"One more thing, Madam President. I think we need to raise the alert level to DEFCON 3."

Pauline hesitated. This would be a public acknowledgment that the world had become a more dangerous place. It was never done lightly.

The decision about alert levels had to be made by the president and the secretary of defense together. If

Pauline and Luis agreed, the announcement would be made by the chairman of the Joint Chiefs of Staff, Bill Schneider.

Jacqueline Brody spoke for the first time. "The trouble is that it gets the public all antsy."

Luis was impatient with talk about public opinion. He was not much of a democrat. "We need our forces to be ready!"

"But we don't need to panic the American people," Jacqueline said.

Pauline settled the issue. "Luis is right," she said. "Raise the DEFCON level. Have Bill announce it tomorrow at the morning press conference."

"Thank you, Madam President," said Luis.

"But Jacqueline is also right," Pauline said. "We need to explain that this is a precaution and the public in the United States is not in danger. Gus, I think you should appear alongside Bill to reassure people."

"Yes, ma'am."

"I'm going to take a shower now, so schedule the phone calls for a little later. But I want to get this under way before East Asia closes down for the day. I won't be going back to bed tonight."

James Moore was interviewed on breakfast TV. He appeared on a channel that did not even pretend to report objectively. He was interviewed by Caryl Cole, who described herself as a soccer-mom conservative, but really she was just a bigot. Pauline got up from the table and went into the former Beauty Salon to watch. After a minute Pippa came in, dressed for school and toting her backpack, and stayed to watch.

Pauline expected Caryl to give Moore an easy ride, and that was what happened.

"The Far East is a bad neighborhood," he said in his folksy style. "It's run by a Chinese gang who think they can do anything they want."

"What about Korea?" said Caryl.

Pauline commented: "Not exactly a challenging question."

Moore said: "The South Koreans are our friends, and it's good to have friends in a bad neighborhood."

"And North Korea?"

"The supreme leader is a bad hombre, but he doesn't ride alone. He's part of a gang and takes his orders from Beijing."

"Hopelessly simplistic," said Pauline, "but terribly easy to understand and remember."

Moore said: "The South Koreans are on our side, and we have to protect them. That's why we have troops there. . . ." He hesitated, then said: "Some thousands of troops."

Pauline said to the TV: "The number you're searching for is twenty-eight thousand five hundred."

Moore said: "And if our boys weren't there, the whole of Korea would be overrun by the Chinese."

Caryl said: "That's a sobering thought."

"Now," said Moore, "last night the North Koreans attacked our friends. They bombed a naval base and killed a lot of people."

Caryl said: "President Green has called for a peace conference."

"The heck with that," said Moore. "When someone punches you in the mouth you don't call a peace conference—you hit back."

"And how would you hit back at North Korea, if you were president?"

"A massive bombing attack that would take out every military base they have."

"Are you talking about nuclear bombs?"

"There's no point having nuclear weapons if you never use them."

Pippa said: "Did he really say that?"

"Yes," Pauline said. "And you know what? He means it. Isn't that terrifying?"

"It's stupid."

"It may be the stupidest thing anyone has said in the history of the human race."

"Won't it damage him?"

"I hope so. If this doesn't derail his presidential campaign, nothing will."

Later she repeated the remark to Sandip Chakraborty, and he asked if he could put it in the press release about the peace conference. "Why not?" said Pauline.

Every television newscast for the rest of the day featured two quotes:

There's no point having nuclear weapons if you never use them.

and:

It may be the stupidest thing anyone has said in the history of the human race.

CHAPTER 32

The Libyan oasis town of Ghadamis was like an enchanted castle in a fairy tale. In the deserted old center the white houses, made of mud and straw with palm trunks, were all linked together like one great edifice. At ground level were shady arcades between buildings, and the rooftops, traditionally reserved for women, were connected by little bridges. In the white interiors the window openings and arches were gaily decorated with elaborate patterns in red paint. Naji ran around in delight.

It suited the mood of Abdul and Kiah. For almost a week now no one had told them what to do, or tried to extort money from them, or pointed guns at their heads. Their progress was deliberately slow. They were in no hurry to get to Tripoli.

They were at last coming to believe that their nightmare was over. Abdul continued to be vigilant, checking his rearview mirror to make sure they were not being followed, watching to see if another car pulled up nearby when he was parking, but he never saw anything sinister.

ISGS might have put the word out to friends and

associates to look out for the escapees, but they were a young Arab couple with a two-year-old child, and there were thousands like them. All the same, Abdul kept his eyes open, looking out for the hard-faced, battle-scarred jihadi profile. He had not seen anyone remotely suspicious.

They slept in the car or on someone's floor. They pretended they were a family. Their story was that Kiah's brother had died in Tripoli, where he had no relations, and they had to settle his affairs, selling the house and car, and take the money home to Kiah's mother in N'Djamena. People sympathized and never doubted it. Naji was a help: no one suspected a couple with a kid.

The weather in Ghadamis was searingly hot and the place received about an inch of rain per year. Many of the people did not speak Arabic: they had their own language, a Berber tongue. But the town had hotels, the first Abdul and Kiah had seen since leaving Chad. After they had gone around the magical old center they checked into a place in the modern new town, taking a room that had a large bed and a cot for Naji. Abdul paid cash and showed his Chadian passport, which sufficed for them all, which was fortunate, for Kiah had no papers of any kind.

He was overjoyed to find that the room had a shower—crude, with cold water only, but the height of luxury after what he had been through. He stayed under the spray for a long time. Then he stepped out and looked around for a towel.

When Kiah saw him naked she gasped with shock and turned away.

He smiled and said gently: "What's wrong?"

She half turned, covering her eyes, but then she giggled, and he relaxed.

They had dinner in the café next door to the hotel.

The place had a television set, the first Abdul had seen for weeks. It was showing an Italian soccer match.

They put Naji to bed and made love as soon as he had gone to sleep. They did it again in the morning before he woke up. Abdul had some condoms, though he would soon run out at this rate. Such things were not often used in this part of the world.

He was in love with Kiah, there was no doubt about that. His heart had been captured by her beauty and her courage and her lively intelligence. And he was quite sure she loved him back. But he mistrusted their emotions. These feelings might be little more than the product of the way they had been thrown together. For seven long weeks they had helped one another through intense discomfort and serious danger, all day and all night. He recalled the way she had set fire to the gasoline in the parking lot with no apparent fear for herself. She had saved Abdul's life by killing Mohammed. She had since shown no remorse. He admired her grit. But was that enough? Would their love survive the return to civilization?

And then there was a cultural gulf as wide as the Grand Canyon. She had been born and brought up on the shore of Lake Chad, and until a few weeks ago she had never traveled farther than N'Djamena. The narrow, repressive mores of that poor rural society were all she knew. He had lived in Beirut and Newark and the suburbs of Washington, DC. At high school and college he had learned the permissive morality of his adopted country. And so, even though they were sleeping together, she was shocked when he did something as normal to him as walking around a hotel room naked.

And he had misled her. She had thought he was a cigarette vendor from Lebanon—though by now she clearly suspected the lie. Sooner or later he would have to confess that he was an American citizen and an agent of the CIA, and how would she feel about that?

They lay facing each other in the simple room, Naji still asleep in the cot, with the shutters closed against the heat, and he delighted in the arch of her nose and the brown of her eyes and the color of her skin. Caressing her body, he toyed idly with her pubic hair, but that made her flinch, and she said: "What are you doing?"

"Nothing. Just touching you."

"But it's disrespectful."

"How can it be? It's affectionate."

"It's the kind of thing you'd do to a prostitute."

"Is it? I've never met a prostitute."

There was another gulf. Kiah loved sex—that had been clear from the very first time, when she had been the one to take the initiative—but she had grown up with ideas about modesty that were startlingly different from those of someone raised in an American city. Would she adjust? Would he?

Naji stirred in his cot, and they realized it was time to move on. They washed and dressed the child, then went back to the café for breakfast, and that was when they saw the news.

Abdul was about to sit down when his eye was caught by film of missiles being launched. At first he thought he must be looking at a test, but there were so many missiles—several dozen—that it seemed too costly for a mere exercise. This was followed by shots taken from the ground of missiles in the air, mainly visible by their white contrails, and Abdul realized they must be cruise missiles, for ballistic missiles flew too fast and too high for such filming.

Kiah said: "Why don't you sit down?"

But he remained standing, staring at the television screen, full of fear.

The commentary was in a language he did not recognize, though he thought it sounded East Asian. Then it was faded out and replaced by a translation in Arabic, and he learned that the missiles had been fired by the South Korean army, which had made this film, and that their action was in retaliation for an attack on a naval base of theirs by missiles from North Korea.

Kiah said: "What do you want to eat?"

Abdul said: "Hush."

Next came film of an army base, with a characteristic grid of straight roads connecting low buildings. The signs were in hieroglyphs, and the Arabic translation identified the base as Sino-ri in North Korea. There was frantic activity around what looked like surface-to-air missile launchers. The pictures might have been taken by surveillance aircraft or perhaps a drone. Suddenly there were explosions, gouts of flame followed by clouds of smoke. More explosions burst in the air near the camera: the ground forces were firing back. But the damage down there was tremendous. Clearly the assault was intended to completely wipe out the target.

Abdul was horrified. South Korea was attacking North Korea with cruise missiles, apparently in revenge for an earlier incident. What had happened to cause this disaster?

Naji said: "I want leben."

Kiah said: "Be quiet, Daddy wants to listen to the news."

A part of Abdul's mind registered that he had just been called "Daddy."

The television commentary then added a crucial detail: Sino-ri was the base that had launched missiles against the South Korean naval facility at Jeju.

There was a whole tit-for-tat history to this that he had missed while out of contact in the desert. But this well-made film showed that South Korea wanted the world to know that it had struck back.

How had the Americans and the Chinese allowed this to happen?

What the hell was going on?

And where would it lead?

CHAPTER 33

hang Kai asked Ting to leave town.

He contrived to slip away from the frantically busy Guoanbu office and meet Ting and her mother, Anni, at their gym. They went whenever Ting had a free day. Anni did physiotherapy exercises for her old leg injury, and Ting ran on the treadmill. When they came out of the changing room today he was waiting in the café with tea and lotus paste buns. As soon as they sat down and sipped their tea he said: "We need to talk."

"Oh, no!" said Ting. "You're having an affair. You're leaving me."

"Don't be silly," he said, smiling. "I'll never leave you. But I want you to get out of town."

"Why?"

"Your life is in danger. I think there's going to be a war, and if I'm right then Beijing will be bombed."

Anni said: "There's a lot about that on the internet. If you know where to look."

Kai was not surprised. A lot of Chinese people knew how to get around the government firewall and access news from the West.

Ting said: "Is it really that bad?"

It was. The South Korean bombardment of Sino-ri had taken Kai by surprise, he who was supposed to know everything. President No was obliged to consult the Americans before taking such action. Had the White House approved the attack? Or had President No just decided not to ask? Kai ought to know, but he did not.

However, he did have a strong sense that nobody told No Do-hui what to do. He had met her, and he called to mind a thin, hard-faced woman with iron-gray hair. She had survived an assassination attempt orchestrated by the regime in North Korea. The attempt had killed a senior advisor who—Kai and a small number of insiders knew—had been her lover. This undoubtedly contributed to her hatred of the supreme leader.

Sino-ri had been flattened, and President No had triumphantly announced that no more missiles would be launched by that North Korean base. She talked as if that ended the matter, but of course it did not.

Supreme Leader Kang's ability to retaliate was limited but, in a way, that made matters worse. Half the North Korean army was already under rebel control, and the other half had now been further weakened by the destruction of Sino-ri. Two or three more strikes like that would leave the supreme leader almost powerless against South Korea. He had phoned President Chen and demanded reinforcements of Chinese troops, but Chen had told him to attend President Green's peace conference instead. Kang was desperate, and desperate men were reckless.

World leaders were fearful. Russia and the UK, normally on opposite sides, had joined forces at the UN Security Council to press for a cease-fire. France had backed them up.

There was a slim chance that the supreme leader

would accept President Green's proposal, hold his fire, and attend the peace conference, but Kai was pessimistic. It was hard for a tyrant to de-escalate. It looked weak.

When Kai thought about all-out war, what he feared most was that some harm would come to Ting. He was responsible for the security of all China's 1.4 billion people, but he mainly cared for just one of them.

He said: "China and the US have lost control of events."

Ting said: "Where do you want me to go?"

"To our house in Xiamen. It's more than a thousand miles away from here. You'd have at least a chance of survival." He looked at Anni. "You both should go."

Ting said: "It's out of the question. You know that. I have a job—a career."

He had expected her to resist. "Call in sick," he said. "Go home and pack. Leave tomorrow morning in your beautiful sports car. Stop somewhere overnight. Make a vacation of it."

"I can't call in sick. You know enough about our industry to realize that. There are no excuses in show business. If you don't show up they find someone else."

"You're the star!"

"That doesn't count for as much as you think. I won't be the star for long if I don't appear on the screen."

"It's better than dying."

"All right," she said.

He was surprised. He had not expected her to give in so quickly.

But she was just being theatrical. She said: "I'll go—if you come with me."

"You go, and I'll join you when I can."

"No. We must go together."

That was not going to happen, and she knew it. He said: "I can't."

"But you can. Resign from your job. We've got enough money. We could live for a year or more without running short, longer if we were careful. We could return to Beijing as soon as you think it's safe."

"I have to try to prevent this war from happening. If I can, it's the best way to protect my family and my country. And it's not just a job, it's my life. But I have to be here to do it."

"And I have to stay here because I love you."

"But the danger—"

"If we're going to die in a war, let's die together."

He opened his mouth to speak, but he had nothing to say. She was right. If there was going to be a war they should face it together.

He said: "Would you like some more tea?"

When he got back to the office there was a message on his screen from his boss, the minister for state security, Fu Chuyu, announcing his resignation. He was leaving in a month.

Kai wondered why. Fu was in his midsixties, which in itself was not a reason for retirement in the upper levels of the Chinese government. Kai spoke to Yawen, his secretary. "Have you seen the minister's message?"

"Everybody got it," she said.

That was a significant snub to Kai, who as one of Fu's two deputies would have expected a heads-up. Instead he had been informed at the same time as the secretaries.

Kai said: "I wonder why he's going."

"His secretary told me the reason," said Yawen. "He's got cancer."

"Ah." Kai thought of Fu's ashtray, made of a

military shell case, and his brand of cigarettes, Double Happiness.

"He's known for a while that he had prostate cancer, but he refused treatment and told only a few people. Now it's gone to his lungs and he has to be treated in the hospital."

This explained a lot. Specifically, it accounted for the smear campaign against Ting and, by association, against Kai himself. Someone who wanted Fu's job had been tipped off in advance and had tried to discredit the leading candidate. The villain was probably the domestic intelligence chief, Vice Minister Li Jiankang.

Fu was a typical old Communist, Kai thought. The man is dying, but he's still plotting. He wants to make sure his successor is someone as rigidly orthodox as himself. These people don't stop until they drop.

How much danger was Kai in, personally? It seemed a trivial question when Korea was on the brink of all-out war. How can I be vulnerable to this kind of crap, he asked himself, when my father is vice chairman of the National Security Commission?

His personal phone rang. Yawen left the room and he picked up. It was General Ham in North Korea. "Supreme Leader Kang is fighting for his political life," he said.

Kai thought Kang was probably fighting for his literal life too. If the South Koreans did not kill him, the ultras probably would. But he said: "What makes you say that right now?"

"He can't defeat this rebellion. He's fought them to a temporary standstill, but he's running out of weapons, and they have the upper hand. The only reason the rebels haven't yet wiped out the remaining government forces is that they think the South Koreans are going to do the job for them."

"Does the supreme leader know that?"

"I believe he does."

"So why is he provoking a war with South Korea? It seems suicidal."

"He thinks China can't afford to let him lose. You're going to save him. That's a fixation with Kang. He believes you'll have to send him reinforcements—you have no choice."

"We can't send Chinese troops into North Korea. It would embroil us in a war with the US."

"But you can't let South Korea conquer North Korea."

"That's true too."

"Kang thinks there's only one way for this to end: you will help him hold off South Korea *and* defeat the ultras. The more he's damaged, the greater the pressure on China to come to the rescue. That's why he doesn't think he's being reckless."

Kang felt invulnerable. Anybody who called himself supreme leader might convince himself of that delusion.

Ham said: "He's not crazy. He's logical. He can't fight a long slow war—he doesn't have the resources. He must make a big win-or-lose gesture. If he wins, he wins. And if he loses, you have to save him, so he wins again."

That was true too.

Kai said: "Does he have any missiles left, after the attack on Sino-ri?"

"More than you'd think. They are all truck mounted. After he fired those six at Jeju, he sent all the launchers away from the bases and hid them."

"Where the hell do you hide those trucks? The small ones are nearly forty feet long."

"All over the country. They're parked in places where they can't be seen from above, mostly in tunnels and under bridges."

"Clever. Makes it almost impossible to hit them."

Ham said: "I have to go, sorry."

"Take care of yourself," Kai said, but Ham had already hung up.

Kai reflected somberly on the conversation as he made a note of its details for the record. Everything Ham had said made sense. The only way to avoid war now was for China to restrain North Korea and the US to restrain the south. But it was easier said than done.

After a few minutes' reflection he thought he saw a way to nudge the Americans. He decided to try it out first on a member of the Communist old guard. He phoned his father. He would talk about something else, then slip his idea into the conversation.

"You're a friend of Fu Chuyu's," he said when he got through. "Did you know he's dying?"

There was a hesitation that told him the answer. Then Jianjun said: "Yes, I found out a few weeks ago."

"I wish you'd told me."

Jianjun clearly felt guilty about keeping this to himself, but he pretended otherwise. "I was told in confidence," he blustered. "Does it matter?"

"There's been a nasty little campaign of malicious gossip against your daughter-in-law. It was intended to damage me. Now I see why. It's about who will succeed Fu as minister."

"This is the first I've heard of it."

"I think Fu is in cahoots with Vice Minister Li."

"I have—" Jianjun coughed, a typical smoker's throat-clearing spasm, and then resumed: "I have no information."

I hope those damn cigarettes aren't going to kill you too, Kai thought. "My money's on Li, but it could be one of half a dozen others."

"That's the trouble. It's a long list."

"Speaking of trouble, what's your take on the crisis in Korea?"

Jianjun sounded relieved to move away from an embarrassing topic. "Korea? We're going to have to get tough sooner or later."

That was his response to everything.

Kai decided it was time to try out his idea. "I've just talked to our best source in North Korea. He says the supreme leader is up against the wall—running out of weapons and liable to do something desperate. We need to control him."

"If only we could."

"Or get the Americans to restrain South Korea, persuade President No not to retaliate against whatever is Kang's next move."

"We can hope."

Pretending to speak casually, Kai said: "Or we could level with the White House and warn President Green that the supreme leader is so weak that he's desperate."

"Out of the question." Jianjun was indignant. "Tell the Americans how weak our ally is?"

"A situation like this calls for exceptional measures."

"But not downright treason."

Well, Kai thought, I got my answer: the old guard won't even contemplate the idea. He pretended to be convinced. "I guess you're right." He changed the subject quickly. "I don't suppose Mother would consider leaving town? Moving somewhere safer? Somewhere less likely to be bombed?"

There was a pause, then Jianjun spoke sternly. "Your mother is a Communist."

That remark baffled Kai. "Do you imagine I didn't know that?"

"Communism is more than just a theory we accept because the evidence is good, like Mendeleev's periodic table of the elements."

"What do you mean?"

"Communism is a sacred mission. It comes above everything else, including our family ties and our own personal safety."

Kai was incredulous. "So to you, Communism is more important than my mother?"

"Exactly. And she would say the same about me."

This was more extreme than Kai would have guessed. He felt a bit stunned.

His father said: "Sometimes I think your generation doesn't really understand."

You got that right, Kai thought.

He said: "Well, I didn't phone you up for a discussion about Communism. Let me know if you hear anything about these maneuverings against me."

"Of course."

"When I find out who has been trying to get at me through my wife, I'm going to cut his balls off with a rusty knife." Kai hung up.

He had been right to fear that Jianjun would be against the idea of coming clean with the Americans. Jianjun had been raised to see the capitalist-imperialists as lifelong enemies. China had changed, the world had changed, but the old men were stuck in the past.

But that did not mean his idea was wrong, just that it had to be carried out clandestinely.

He picked up his phone and dialed. His call was answered immediately. "This is Neil."

"This is Kai. I need to know whether you gave President No advance consent for her attack on Sino-ri."

Neil hesitated.

Kai said: "We have to be honest with one another. The situation is too dangerous for anything else."

"Okay," said Neil. "But if you quote me I'll deny it."

"Fair enough."

"The answer is no, we did not know in advance, and if we had we would not have approved it."

"Thank you."

"My turn. Did you know Supreme Leader Kang was going to attack Jeju?"

"No. Same thing. No forewarning, or we would have tried to stop it."

"What is the supreme leader thinking?"

"That's what I need to talk to you about. This crisis is worse than you think."

"Christ," said Neil. "That's hard to imagine."

"Believe it."

"Go on."

"The problem is the weakness of the regime in North Korea."

"Their *weakness*?"

"Yes. Listen. Half the North Korean military is controlled by the rebels now. Some of the other half was destroyed at Sino-ri. The supreme leader has scattered his mobile missile launchers around the country—"

"Where?"

"Bridges and tunnels."

"Shit."

"If not for that, what remains of the North Korean military could be wiped out with another two or three missile strikes from the south."

"So Kang is in deep shit."

"And that will make him reckless."

"What will he do?"

"Something drastic."

"Can we stop him?"

"Make sure President No doesn't strike again."

"But the supreme leader might provoke her."

"He *will* provoke her, Neil. He must take revenge for Sino-ri. I want President Green to make sure the escalation stops there and President No doesn't hit back even harder."

"Everything depends on how severe Kang's revenge is. And the only people who can rein in the supreme leader are you guys—the Chinese government."

"We're trying, Neil. Believe me, we're trying."

CHAPTER 34

can't possibly leave the White House," Pauline said
to Pippa and Gerry on the day before Thanksgiving,
standing in the Center Hall, next to the piano, with
suitcases on the polished floor around their feet. "I'm
really sorry."

Gerry's oldest friend, a fellow student at Columbia
Law a lifetime ago, had a horse ranch in Virginia.
Pauline, Gerry, and Pippa had planned to spend
Thanksgiving with him and his wife and their daughter, who was Pippa's age. School was closed for two
days, so they could leave on Wednesday evening and
return Sunday. The ranch was near Middleburg, about
fifty miles from the White House, a drive of an hour,
more in traffic. Pippa was super-excited: she was crazy
about horses, like many girls of her age.

"Don't worry," Gerry said to Pauline. "We're used
to it." He did not look too disappointed.

She said: "If Korea calms down I might make it for
dinner on Saturday night."

"Well, that would be nice. Give me a call, so I can
warn our hosts to set an extra place at the table."

"Of course." She turned to Pippa. "Aren't you going to be cold, riding outside all day?"

"The horse keeps you warm," Pippa said. "It's like the seat heater in a car."

"Well, make sure you wear warm clothes as well."

Pippa made a rapid adolescent switch and became concerned. "Are you going to be okay, Mom—spending Thanksgiving on your own?"

"I'll miss you, honey, but I don't want to spoil your holiday. I know how much you've been looking forward to it. And I'll be too busy saving the world to feel lonesome."

"If we're all going to be bombed to smithereens I want us to be together." Pippa spoke in a light tone, but Pauline suspected a serious worry underneath.

Pauline too had a hidden fear that she might never see her daughter again. But she replied in the same semiserious manner. "That's very sweet of you, but I think I can hold the bombs off until Sunday evening."

A White House porter picked up the bags, and Gerry said to him: "The Secret Service should be waiting."

"Yes, sir."

Pauline kissed them and watched as they went away.

Pippa's comment had touched a nerve. What Pauline was hiding was her belief that bombs might really fall on Washington in the next few days. For that reason she was glad Pippa was going out of town. She only wished her daughter was going farther.

She had been shocked by the bombing of Sino-ri. No one had expected President No to take such drastic action without consulting the US. Pauline was angry too: they were supposed to be allies, committed to acting together. But No had been unapologetic. Pauline feared that the alliance was weakening. She was losing control of South Korea just as Chen was losing control of the north. It was a dangerous development.

She walked to the Oval Office, where Chess was waiting to say good-bye to her. He was dressed in a down coat and sneakers, about to fly to Colombo, Sri Lanka. "How long is the flight?" Pauline asked.

"Twenty hours, including a refueling stop."

Chess was going to the peace conference. China was sending Wu Bai, the foreign minister, who ranked equally with the American secretary of state.

Pauline said: "You've seen the report from the CIA in Beijing."

"I sure have. The Chinese secret service guy was astonishingly candid."

"Chang Kai."

"Yes. I don't think we've ever had such a frank message from the government of China."

"It might not be from the government. I sense that Chang Kai is freelancing. He's afraid of what Supreme Leader Kang is going to do in North Korea and he's worried that some in the Chinese government aren't taking the danger seriously enough."

"Well, I'm about to make the supreme leader an attractive offer."

"Let's hope Kang sees it that way."

They had discussed this earlier in the day at a cabinet meeting. They needed to give Kang something, and had decided to offer a review of the sea boundaries between North and South Korea, a sore point with him. In Pauline's opinion the review was long overdue anyway. The 1953 lines had been drawn when North Korea was defeated and China was weak, and they favored the south, hugging North Korea's coast and giving South Korea all the best fishing in the Yellow Sea. An adjustment was only fair, and it would enable the supreme leader to save face. President No of South Korea was going to squeal, but she would accept it in the end.

"I've got to go. The plane is waiting, with seven diplomatic and military staffers who all want to brief me on the way." Chess stood and picked up a bulging briefcase. "And when they get tired I've got plenty of situation papers to read."

"Safe travels."

Chess left.

Pauline moved into the study, ordered a salad at her desk, and worked through papers, making the most of a time with few interruptions. When she called for coffee she checked her watch and saw that it was nine o'clock. The thought crossed her mind that Chess was now in the air.

She recalled the way she had marshaled other world leaders, a month ago, to prevent the outbreak of war on the border between Sudan and Chad, and she wondered whether her diplomacy would work again this time. She feared that the Korean crisis would be a lot more challenging.

Then Gus came in.

She smiled, happy to see him, glad to be alone with him in the study. She suppressed a stab of guilt: she was not cheating on Gerry, except in her daydreams.

Gus was all business. "I think the supreme leader is about to do something," he said. "We've picked up two indications. One is intense communications activity around North Korean military bases. We can't read most of the messages because they're encrypted, but the pattern suggests that an attack is in preparation."

"This is his retaliation. What's the second?"

"A sleeping virus in the South Korean military network has been activated and is sending out fake orders.

They've had to instruct all forces to ignore electronic messages and obey only telephoned orders from human beings while they try to debug the system."

"This could be the prelude to a major assault."

"Exactly, Madam President. Luis and Bill are already in the Situation Room."

"Let's go." Pauline got up from her desk.

The Situation Room was filling up. Chief of Staff Jacqueline Brody came in, then DNI Sophia Magliani, followed by the vice president.

Several of the screens came to life, showing what seemed like street camera feeds. Pauline saw a city center, probably Seoul. She guessed that an alarm must have been sounding, for the people on the streets were rushing one way and another. She said: "What's happening?"

Bill Schneider, listening to the Pentagon on his headset, said: "Incoming artillery."

Luis explained: "Seoul is only fifteen miles from the border with North Korea—well within range of old-fashioned big guns, like the tank-mounted Koksan hundred and seventy millimeter."

Pauline said: "Targets?"

Bill replied: "Too early to say, but we assume Seoul."

"Responses?"

"South Korean forces are firing artillery in retaliation. American forces await orders."

"Don't deploy American forces without my say-so. Defensive action only right now."

"Yes, ma'am. Artillery impact has begun."

On the video from Seoul Pauline saw a crater suddenly appear in a road, a house collapsing, a car rolling sideways. She felt as if her heart had stopped. The supreme leader had crossed a line. This was not appropriate retaliation, a token attack, a symbolic reprisal. This was war.

Then Bill said: "Satellite surveillance has observed missiles emerging above the cloud cover over North Korea."

Pauline asked: "How many?"

"Six," said Bill. "Nine. Ten. Increasing. All coming from the western half of North Korea, the government-controlled zone. None from the rebel areas."

Another screen lit up, this one showing radar input superimposed on a map of Korea. The missiles were so crowded that Pauline could not count them. "How many now?" she said.

"Twenty-four," Bill replied.

"This is a full-scale attack."

Luis said: "Madam President, this is war."

She felt cold. She had always dreaded this. She had dedicated herself to preventing war, and she had failed.

She thought: Where did I go wrong?

She would be trying to answer that question for the rest of her life.

She pushed it aside. She said: "And we have twenty-eight thousand five hundred American troops in South Korea."

"Plus some of their wives and children."

"And husbands, presumably."

"And husbands," admitted Luis.

"Get President Chen on the phone please."

Chief of Staff Jacqueline Brody said: "I'll handle that." She picked up a phone.

Pauline said: "Why is Supreme Leader Kang doing this? Is he suicidal?"

"No," said Gus. "He's desperate, but he's not suicidal. He's losing his fight with the ultras, and he can't hold out much longer. They will surely execute him in the end, so he's facing his own death. The only way he can change that is with the help of China, but they don't want to send in their troops. He thinks he can force the issue—and he may be right. China won't save him from his rebels, but they may step in to prevent a takeover by South Korea."

Jacqueline said: "They're ready for you, Madam President." Evidently the Chinese had been expecting the call. Jacqueline added: "You can speak on the handset in front of you, ma'am. The other phones in the room will carry the conversation for listening only."

Everyone picked up. Pauline said into her phone: "This is the president."

The White House switchboard operator said: "Please hold for the president of China."

A moment later Chen's voice said: "I'm glad to hear from you, President Green."

"I'm calling about Korea, as you may guess."

"As you know, Madam President, the People's Republic of China has no troops in North Korea and never has."

That was technically true. The Chinese soldiers who had fought in the Korean War of the early fifties had been volunteers, theoretically. But Pauline was not about to get into that discussion. "I do know that, but all the same I'm hoping you might be able to help me understand what the hell North Korea is doing right now."

Chen switched to Mandarin. The translator came on the line with what was obviously a prepared statement. "The artillery and missile strike that appears to have been launched from North Korea does not have the permission nor the approval of the Chinese government."

"I'm relieved to hear that. And I hope you understand that our troops are going to defend themselves."

Chen spoke carefully and the translator did the same. "I can assure you that the Chinese government has no objections as long as US troops are not on North Korean territory, in North Korean airspace, or in North Korean territorial waters."

"I understand." Chen's ostensible reassurance was in fact a warning. He was saying that US troops must stay in South Korea. Pauline hoped to keep them there, but she was not willing to promise. She said: "My secretary of state, Chester Jackson, is on a plane right now flying to Sri Lanka to meet with your foreign minister, Wu Bai, and others, and I very much hope that this conflict can be brought to an end at that conference if not before."

"So do I."

"Please don't hesitate to call me at any time, day or night, if something should happen that you regard as unacceptable or provocative. The US and China must not go to war. That is my aim."

"And mine too."

"Thank you, Mr. President."

"Thank you, Madam President."

They hung up, and General Schneider immediately said: "The North Koreans have now launched cruise missiles, and bomber aircraft are taking off."

Pauline looked around the Situation Room and said: "Chen was very clear. China will stay out of this conflict if we stay out of North Korea. Bill, that must form the basis of our strategy. Keeping China out is the best thing we could possibly do to help South Korea."

Even as she said it she knew how much scorn would be poured on this approach by James Moore and his supporters in the media.

"Yes, ma'am." Bill Schneider was aggressive by nature but even he could see that this made sense. He went on: "US troops are ready to act within Chen's constraints. As soon as you give the word, we will commence artillery attacks on North Korean military facilities. Fighter planes are on the runways, ready to combat incoming bombers. But at this stage we are not sending manned US planes into North Korean airspace."

"Deploy the artillery now."

"Yes, ma'am."

"Put the fighters in the air."

"Yes, ma'am."

More screens came to life. Pauline saw pilots scrambling to jet fighters at a base that she guessed was Osan Air Base, thirty miles south of Seoul. She looked around the room. "Opinions, please. Can North Korea win this?"

Gus answered. "Unlikely, but not impossible," he said, and Pauline saw heads nod around the table. Gus went on: "Their only hope is a blitzkrieg that will quickly close all South Korean ports and airfields, preventing the arrival of reinforcements."

"Just for a moment, let's consider what we can do if that seems to be happening."

"Two things, though both bring fresh hazards. We could massively increase our forces in the region: more battleships in the South China Sea, more bombers to our bases in Japan, more aircraft carriers in Guam."

"But the Chinese might see reinforcements as a provocation. They would suspect the ordnance was directed at them."

"Yes."

"And the other option?"

"Even worse," said Gus. "We could disable the North Korean military with a nuclear attack."

"That will be what James Moore advocates on TV tomorrow morning."

"And it would risk nuclear retaliation, either from the remnants of North Korea's nuclear arsenal or, worse, by China."

"All right. We stick with our present strategy but closely monitor the battle. What we need from the Pentagon now, Bill, is an on-screen running tally of North Korean planes and missiles downed, and those remaining in the air. Gus, I'd like you to talk to Sandip. He should give the media hourly bulletins; please make sure he's kept informed. I need the State Department to brief our foreign embassies. And we need coffee. And sandwiches. It's going to be a long night."

When the sun went down in East Asia and dawn broke over the White House, General Schneider announced that North Korea's blitzkrieg had not worked. At least half the missiles had failed to reach their targets: some had been shot down by anti-missile fire, others had been made to malfunction by cyberattack interference with their systems, and some had crashed for no obvious reason. Several bombers had been brought down by fighter jets.

All the same there had been many casualties among troops and civilians, both American and South Korean. CNN was showing video of Seoul and other cities, some of the footage captured from South Korean television, some taken from social media posts. It showed collapsed buildings, raging fires, and ambulance crews struggling to help the wounded and pick up the dead. However, no ports or military airfields had closed. The attack continued, but the result was no longer in doubt.

Pauline was wired on coffee and tension, but she thought she could see the end in view. When Bill had finished she said: "I think we should now propose a cease-fire. Let's get President Chen on the phone again."

Jacqueline began the arrangements.

Bill said stiffly: "Madam President, the Pentagon would prefer to complete the destruction of North Korean military forces."

"We can't do that remotely," she said. "We would have to have boots on the ground in North Korea, and that would start a new war, one with the Chinese, who would be a hell of a lot more difficult to defeat than North Korea."

There were sounds of agreement around the room, and Bill said reluctantly: "Very well."

Pauline added: "But until the North Koreans agree to the cease-fire I suggest you throw everything you've got at them."

He brightened. "Very good, Madam President."

Jacqueline said: "Chen is on the line."

Pauline picked up. After brief courtesies she said to Chen: "The North Korean attack on South Korea has been defeated."

Chen spoke through the interpreter. "The aggression of the Seoul authorities against the Democratic People's Republic of Korea is unwarranted."

Pauline was taken aback. Last time they spoke he had been reasonable. Now he seemed to be parroting propaganda. She said: "All the same, North Korea lost the battle."

"The Korean People's Army will continue to energetically defend the Republic of Korea from American-inspired attacks."

Pauline put her hand over the phone. "I know Chen. He doesn't believe any of this crap."

Gus said: "I think the hard-liners are in the room with him, telling him what to say."

Several people nodded.

This made it awkward, but she could still deliver her message. "I believe the people of the United States and the people of China can find a way to end the killing."

"The People's Republic of China will of course give careful consideration to what you say."

"Thank you. I want a cease-fire."

There was a long silence.

Pauline added: "I would be grateful if you would pass that message to your comrades in Pyongyang."

Once again there was no immediate reply, and Pauline imagined Chen's holding his hand over the phone and talking to the old Communists who were with him in his lakeside palace at Zhongnanhai. What were they saying? No one in the Beijing government could possibly want this war. North Korea could not win it—the events of last night had proved that—and China did not want to embroil itself in armed conflict with the US.

Chen, playing for time, said: "And can you assure us that this proposal will be accepted by President No in Seoul?"

"Of course not," Pauline said immediately. "South Korea is a free country. But I'll do my damnedest to persuade her."

After another long pause, Chen said: "We will discuss this with Pyongyang."

Pauline decided to push him. "When?"

This time his answer came without hesitation. "Immediately." That was Chen talking, Pauline guessed, not his minders.

She said: "Thank you, Mr. President."

"Thank you, Madam President."

They hung up. Pauline said: "There's been a change in Beijing."

Gus said: "Once the shooting starts, the military assert themselves—and the Chinese military is run by hard-liners."

Pauline glanced at Bill and reflected that most soldiers were hard-liners.

Pauline said: "All right, let's talk to Seoul."

Jacqueline said: "I'll get President No on the line."

The switchboard got through to Seoul and she picked up. She said: "This has been a terrible day for you, Madam President, but South Korean troops have fought bravely and have defeated the aggressors."

She pictured President No, her gray hair pulled severely back from a high forehead, her dark eyes piercing, the lines around her mouth suggesting a history of conflict.

President No replied: "The supreme leader has learned that he cannot attack South Koreans with impunity." The note of profound satisfaction in her voice suggested, to Pauline, that No was thinking of the assassination attempt that had killed her lover as well as the bombardment of the last few hours. No added: "We thank the brave and generous American people for their invaluable help."

That was enough of that, Pauline thought. "Now we must talk about what to do next."

"It's getting dark here, and the exchange of missiles has tailed off, but it will start again in the morning."

Pauline did not like the sound of that. "Unless we prevent it," she said.

"How would we do that, Madam President?"

"I'm proposing a cease-fire."

There was a silence at the other end.

To fill it, Pauline said: "My secretary of state and the Chinese foreign minister will be arriving in Sri Lanka in the next few hours to meet with your foreign minister and his North Korean counterpart. They should discuss the details of the cease-fire immediately, then move on to negotiate a peace settlement."

President No said: "A cease-fire would leave the supreme leader in power in Pyongyang and in possession of what remains of his weapons—so he would still menace us."

That was true, of course. Pauline said: "No purpose is served by continuing the killing."

The reply shocked her. No said: "I cannot agree."

Pauline frowned. This was more opposition than she had anticipated. What did No mean? "You have defeated North Korea," Pauline said. "What more do you want?"

"Supreme Leader Kang started this war," No said. "I'm going to finish it."

Oh, Christ, Pauline thought; she wants unconditional surrender.

Pauline said: "A cease-fire is the first step in ending the war."

"This is a once-in-a-lifetime opportunity to free our countrymen in the north from a murderous tyranny."

Pauline's heart sank. The supreme leader was, indeed, a murderous tyrant, but President No did not have the power to overthrow him against the wishes of the Chinese. "What are you planning?"

"The complete destruction of the army of North Korea and a new, nonaggressive regime in Pyongyang."

"Are you talking about an invasion of North Korea?"

"If necessary."

Pauline wanted to stomp on this idea right way. "The US would not join forces with you."

No's answer surprised her. "We would not want you to."

Pauline was temporarily lost for words.

No Korean leader had talked this way since the 1950s. If the north and south were reunited by this war, the south would somehow have to cope with a sudden influx of twenty-five million half-starved people who had no idea how to live in a capitalist economy. No had campaigned on a promise of reunification in the vague future: her slogan *Before I die* meant *Not never,* but it could also mean *Not now.* However, the economic issue was not her main problem. China was.

Reading her mind, No said: "If you stay out of it we believe the Chinese will do the same. We will say that Korea's problems must be solved by Korea's people, without the involvement of other countries."

"Beijing will not allow you to install a pro-American government in Pyongyang."

"I know. We would discuss the future of North and South Korea with our allies and our neighbors, of course. But we believe the time has come for Korea as a whole to stop being merely a pawn in someone else's game."

This was not realistic, in Pauline's opinion. If they tried it there would be hell to pay. She took a deep breath. "Madam President, I sympathize with your feelings but I believe that what you propose is dangerous to Korea and to the world."

"I have promised to reunite my country. There may not be another moment like this for fifty years. I will not go down in history as the president who missed her chance."

And that was it, Pauline thought. This was about revenge for the murder of her lover, and about keeping her campaign promise, but most of all it was about her legacy. She was sixty-five and thinking of her place in history. This was her destiny.

There was nothing left to say. Pauline said abruptly: "Thank you, Madam President," and hung up.

She looked around the table. They had all heard the conversation. She said: "Our strategy for dealing with the Korea crisis has now collapsed. The north has attacked and lost, and the south is determined to invade. My peace conference has died before it could be born. President No is planning a giant swerve in world politics."

She paused, making sure the gravity of the predicament had time to sink in. Then she turned to practical details.

"Bill, I want you to take the morning conference in the White House press briefing room today." Schneider looked reluctant, but she wanted a man in uniform. "Sandip Chakraborty will be with you." She almost added *to hold your hand* but stopped herself. "Say that we were prepared for the attack and fought it off with minimum damage. Give them as much military detail as you can: numbers of missiles fired, enemy planes downed, military casualties, civilian casualties. You can say that I was in touch with the presidents of China and South Korea throughout the night, but don't answer any political questions: tell them that the situation is still unclear and anyway you're just a simple soldier."

"Very good, ma'am."

"With luck we now have a few hours to reflect. Everyone please get your deputies into this room and go off and get some rest while East Asia is sleeping. I'm going to take a shower. We meet again this evening, when it's dawn in Korea."

She stood up, and the others all did the same. She caught a look from Gus and realized he wanted to accompany her, but she thought it a bad idea to favor him too obviously, so she looked away and left the room.

She returned to the Residence and showered. She felt refreshed but tired: she was desperate for sleep. However, first she sat on the edge of the bed in her terry-cloth bathrobe and called Pippa to ask how the holiday was going.

"The traffic was terrible last night and we took two hours getting here!" Pippa said.

"Bummer," said Pauline.

"But then we all had supper and that was fun. This morning Josephine and I went for an early ride."

"What horse did you have?"

"A nice little pony called Parsley, lively but obedient."

"Perfect."

"Then Dad drove us into Middleburg to buy pump-kin pies and guess who we ran into? Ms. Judd!"

Pauline had a cold feeling in the pit of her stomach. So Gerry had arranged a rendezvous with his lover at Thanksgiving. Boston had not been merely a one-night stand, after all. "Well, well," she said, forcing a cheer-ful tone of voice. But she could not help adding: "What a coincidence!" She hoped Pippa did not detect the sar-casm.

Pippa seemed oblivious. "Turns out she's spending the holiday with a friend who has a winery not far from Middleburg. So Dad had coffee with old Judders while Jo and I shopped for pies. Now we're heading back and we're going to help Jo's mom stuff the turkey."

"I'm so glad you're having a good time." Pauline re-alized she sounded a bit down.

Pippa was young but she had female instincts, and Pauline's faintly depressed tone reminded her that her mother was not having a holiday. She said: "Hey, what's happening in Korea?"

"I'm trying to stop the war."

"Wow. Should we all be worried?"

"Leave it to me. I'll do the worrying for everyone."

"Do you want to talk to Daddy?"

"Not if he's driving."

"Yes, he's driving."

"Give him my love."

"Sure thing."

"Good-bye, honey."

"Bye, Mom."

Pauline hung up with a bad taste in her mouth.

Gerry and Amelia Judd had planned this. Over the weekend Gerry would find an excuse to slip away from his hosts for an assignation. He had deceived Pauline—while she was valiantly resisting temptation.

What had she done wrong? Had Gerry sensed the feelings she was beginning to have for Gus? You can't help your feelings, she thought, and she had not really minded when she began to suspect that Gerry had a little tendresse for Ms. Judd. But you can help your actions. Gerry had cheated, and Pauline had not. Big difference.

It was eight o'clock, prime time for TV news. One of the programs would be asking James Moore about Korea—like he knows anything, she thought sourly. He probably couldn't find Korea on a map. She turned on the set and hopped channels until she found him on a populist morning show.

He was wearing a tan suede jacket with fringes. This was a departure: he was not even pretending to conform. Did people really want a president who looked like Davy Crockett?

He was being questioned by Mia and Ethan. To begin, Ethan said: "You've visited East Asia, so you have firsthand knowledge of the situation there."

Pauline laughed. Moore had taken a ten-day tour of East Asia and had spent exactly one day in Korea, most of it in a five-star hotel in Seoul.

Moore said: "I wouldn't claim to be an expert, Ethan, and I sure can't pronounce all those funny names"—he paused for them both to chuckle—"but I think this is a situation that needs common sense. North Korea has attacked us and our allies, and when you're attacked you have to hit back *hard*."

Pauline said: "The word you're looking for is *escalate*, Jim."

He went on: "Anything less just encourages the enemy."

Mia crossed her legs. Like all women on this channel,

she had to wear a skirt short enough to show her knees. She said: "But what are you talking about, Jim, in down-to-earth terms?"

"I'm saying we could wipe out North Korea with one nuclear attack, and we could do it today."

"Well, that's pretty drastic."

Pauline laughed again. "Drastic?" she said to the screen. "It's insane, that's what it is."

Moore said: "Not only would that solve our problem at a stroke, but it would scare off others. Let's tell people: if you attack America, you're toast."

Pauline could just picture his supporters punching the air. Well, she was going to save them from nuclear annihilation, whether they wanted her to or not.

She turned off the set.

She was ready for bed, but there was something she wanted to do before she slept.

She pulled on sweat clothes and went down the staircase to the floor below. There she found her Secret Service detail and a young army major carrying the atomic football.

It was not a football, of course, but an aluminum Zero Halliburton briefcase inside a black leather cover. It looked like a carry-on suit holder, except for a small communications antenna sticking out near the handle. Pauline greeted the young man and asked his name.

"I'm Rayvon Roberts, Madam President."

"Well, Major Roberts, I'd like to look inside the football, to refresh my memory. Open up, please."

"Yes, ma'am."

Roberts quickly removed the black leather cover, placed the metal case on the floor, flipped the three latches, and lifted the lid.

The case contained three objects and a phone with no dial.

Roberts said: "Ma'am, may I remind you of each of these items?"

"Yes, please."

"This is the Black Book." It was a regular office ring binder. Pauline took it from him and flipped the pages, which were printed in black and red. Roberts said: "That lists your retaliatory options."

"All the different ways I can start a nuclear war."

"Yes."

"You wouldn't think there would be so many. Next?"

Roberts picked up another, similar binder. "This is a list of classified site locations around the country where you could take refuge in an emergency."

Next was a manila folder with a dozen or so stapled pages. "This details the Emergency Alert System that would enable you to speak to the nation on all television and radio stations in the event of a national emergency."

This item was almost obsolete, Pauline thought, in the age of 24/7 news.

"And this phone calls only one number: the National Military Command Center at the Pentagon. The center will pass your instructions to missile launch control centers, nuclear submarines, bomber airfields, and battlefield commanders."

"Thank you, Major," she said. She left the group and returned upstairs. At last she could go to bed. She took off her clothes and slid gratefully between the sheets. She lay with her eyes closed, and in her mind she saw that leather-clad briefcase. What it really contained was the end of the world.

In a few seconds she was asleep.

CHAPTER 35

Tripoli was a big city, the biggest Kiah had ever seen, twice the size of N'Djamena. The downtown area had skyscrapers overlooking a beach, but the rest of the place was crowded and dirty, with a lot of bomb-damaged buildings. Some of the men wore European-style clothes but all the women had long dresses and headscarves.

Abdul took her and Naji to a small hotel, cheap but clean, where none of the staff or guests were white and no one spoke anything but Arabic. Kiah had been intimidated by hotels at first, and when the staff were deferential she had suspected them of mocking her. She had asked Abdul how to deal with them, and he had said: "Be pleasant, but don't be afraid to ask for what you want, and if they seem curious about you, and they ask where you come from and so on, just smile and say you're too busy to chat." She had found that it worked.

When they got up on their first morning there, Kiah began to think about the future. Until this moment she had not quite believed that they had escaped from the mining camp. As they had traveled north through

Libya, driving on gradually improving roads and sleeping in more comfortable places, she had nursed a secret fear that the jihadis would somehow catch them and enslave them again. Those men were strong and brutal and they usually got their way. Abdul was the only man she had ever known who could stand up to them.

The nightmare was over now, God be praised, but what were they going to do next? What was Abdul's plan? And did it include her?

She decided to ask him. He responded with a question of his own. "What do you want to do?"

"You know what I want," she said. "I want to live in France, where I can feed my child and send him to school. But I've spent all my money and I'm still in Africa."

"I may be able to help you. I'm not sure, but I'm going to try."

"How?"

"I can't tell you now. Please trust me."

Of course she trusted him. She had put her life in his hands. But there was an underlying tension in him, and her questions brought it to the surface. He was worried about something. It was not the jihadis: he seemed no longer to fear they might be following him. He still looked behind him occasionally and checked out other cars, but not all the time, not obsessively. So what caused his tension? Was it thinking about their future together—or apart?

She found this frightening. Ever since she had first met him, he had given the impression of being in control, ready for anything, afraid of nothing. But now he admitted he did not know whether he could help her finish her journey. What would she do if he failed her? How could she go back to Lake Chad?

He adopted a bright tone and said: "We all need
some new clothes. Let's go shopping."

Kiah had never "gone shopping" but she had heard
the phrase, and she knew that wealthy women strolled
around stores looking for things to buy with their surplus money. She had never imagined herself doing the
same. Women like her spent money only when they
had to.

Abdul got a taxi and they went to the city center,
where shady arcades were lined with shops that put
half their wares out on the sidewalk. Abdul said:
"Plenty of French Arabs wear traditional dress, but
you might find life easier in European clothes."

They found a shop specializing in children's wear.
Naji reveled in the whole process of choosing colors
and finding his size. He loved putting on a new shirt
and looking in the mirror. Abdul was amused. "Such
vanity in one so young!" he said.

"Like his father," Kiah murmured. Salim had had a
touch of vanity. Then she glanced worriedly at Abdul,
hoping he would not be offended by the mention of her
late husband. A man did not like to be reminded that
his woman had lain with another. However, Abdul was
smiling at Naji and seemed not to mind.

Naji got two pairs of shorts, four shirts, two pairs of
shoes, some underwear, and a baseball cap that he insisted on wearing right away.

At a nearby store Abdul disappeared into the changing room and came out wearing a dark blue cotton suit
with a white shirt and a plain narrow tie. Kiah could
not remember the last time she had seen a man wearing a tie other than on TV. "You look like an American!"
she said.

"Quel horreur," Abdul said in French. How dreadful. But he smiled.

Then it occurred to Kiah that he might really be

American. It would explain all the money. She would ask him, she decided. Not now, but soon.

He returned to the back of the store and reappeared in his usual gray-brown robes, carrying his new clothes in a bag.

Finally they went to a store for women. "I don't want to spend too much of your money," Kiah said to Abdul.

"I tell you what," he said. "Choose two outfits, one with a skirt and one with pants, and get underwear and shoes and everything to go with each one. Don't worry about the price, nothing here is expensive."

Kiah did not really think the prices were cheap, but she had never bought clothes—just the fabric with which to make them—so she did not actually know.

"And don't rush," Abdul said. "We have plenty of time."

Kiah found that not worrying about the cost was a strange feeling. It was pleasant but also a bit unnerving, because she was afraid to believe she really could have anything in the shop. Tentatively she tried on a checked skirt and a lilac blouse. She felt too self-conscious even to step out and show Abdul. She then tried blue jeans and a green T-shirt. The shop assistant offered her black lace lingerie, saying: "He will like it." But Kiah could not bring herself to buy what looked like underwear for prostitutes, and she insisted on white cotton.

She was still embarrassed about what she had done in the car, that first night after their escape. They had slept in each other's arms for warmth, but when daylight came she had kissed his sleeping face, and once she had started she could not stop. She had kissed his hands and his neck and his cheeks until he woke up, and then of course they had made love. She had seduced him. It was shameful. And yet she could not bring herself to regret it, because she was in love with him and she thought he was beginning to love her. All the same she felt worried that she had behaved like a whore.

She had everything put into a bag and told Abdul she would show him when they got back to the hotel. He smiled and said he could hardly wait.

As they left the shop she wondered longingly whether she would ever really wear these clothes in France.

"We have one more thing to do," Abdul said. "While you were trying on clothes, I asked if there was somewhere we could get photos taken. Apparently in the next street there's a travel agency with a photo machine."

Kiah had never heard of a travel agency or a photo machine, but she said nothing. Abdul often referred to things she did not know about, and rather than pester him with questions all the time she waited for the meaning to become clear.

They walked around a couple of corners and entered a store that was decorated with pictures of airplanes and foreign landscapes. A businesslike young woman sat at a desk wearing a skirt and a blouse a bit like the ones Kiah had bought.

To one side was a little booth with a curtain. The woman gave Abdul some coins in exchange for banknotes, and he explained to Kiah how the machine worked. It was easy, but the result seemed like a miracle: within seconds a strip of paper came out of a slot, like a child poking out its tongue, and Kiah saw four color photographs of her face. When Naji saw the photos he wanted the same, which was good because Abdul said they needed pictures of Naji too.

Like any two-year-old Naji did not see the point of sitting still, so it took three tries before they got good photos.

The woman behind the desk said: "Tripoli International Airport is closed, but Mitiga Airport has flights to Tunis, where you can catch planes to lots of destinations."

They thanked her and went out. In the street Kiah said: "Why do we need photographs?"

"So that we can get you travel papers."

Kiah had never had papers. Identifying herself at borders had never been part of her plan. Abdul seemed to think she could enter France legally. As far as she knew that was impossible. Otherwise why would anyone pay smugglers?

Abdul said: "Tell me your date of birth. And Naji's."

She told him and he frowned, memorizing both dates, she guessed.

But there was a worry. She said: "Why didn't you have your photo taken?"

"I already have papers."

That was not really her question. "When Naji and I go to France . . ."

"What?"

"Where will you go?"

The tense look came back. "I don't know."

This time she pushed him. She felt she had to have an answer. She could not stand the anxiety. "Will you come with us?"

But his reply brought her no relief. "Inshallah," he said. "If God wills it."

They had lunch in a café. They ordered beghrir, Moroccan semolina pancakes, drizzled with a sauce of honey and melted butter. Naji loved them.

All through the simple meal, Abdul had a strange feeling that was a bit like the warmth of the sun, something akin to a glass of good wine, and vaguely reminiscent of Mozart. He wondered if it was happiness.

While they were drinking coffee, Kiah said: "Are you American?"

She was very smart. "What makes you say that?" he asked.

"You have a lot of money."

He wanted to tell her the truth, but at this point it was too dangerous. He had to wait until the mission was over. He said: "I need to explain a lot of things to you. Can you wait a bit longer?"

"Of course."

He still did not know what the future held, but by the end of today he hoped to be able to make some decisions.

They returned to the hotel and laid Naji down for his afternoon nap, then Kiah showed Abdul her new clothes. However, when she put on the white bra and panties they both realized they had to make love immediately.

Afterward he dressed in his new suit. It was time to return to the real world. There was no CIA station in Tripoli, but the French DGSE had an office here, and he had an appointment.

"I have to go to a meeting," he told Kiah.

She looked worried but accepted his statement without comment.

He said: "You'll be all right here?"

"Of course."

"And if anything should happen you can phone me." He had bought her a phone two days ago and loaded it with the maximum of prepaid time. She had not yet used it.

"I'll be fine, don't worry."

The hotel had few amenities, but the check-in desk had a small bowl of business cards giving the street

address of the place in Arabic script, and Abdul picked
up a few on his way out.

He took a taxi downtown. He felt great to be wearing American-style clothes again. It was not even a
very good suit, but no one here would know that, and
anyway it reminded him that he belonged to the most
powerful country in the world.

The cab stopped outside a scruffy office building.
On the wall by the entrance was a column of tarnished
brass plates, each with a bell push, a speaker, and the
engraved name of a business. He found the one marked
ENTREMETTIER & CIE. and pressed the bell. There was
no sound from the speaker, but the door opened, and
he stepped inside.

He wanted something from this meeting and he was
not sure of getting it. He was good at having his own
way in a confrontation in the street or the desert, but
he was not an office warrior. He had a good chance of
achieving what he hoped for, better than 50 percent, he
thought. But if they proved stubborn there was not
much he could do.

Signs guided him to a door on the third floor. He
knocked and went in. Tamara and Tab were waiting.

It was a couple of months since he had seen them,
and he felt quite moved. Somewhat to his surprise they
seemed to feel the same. Tab had tears in his eyes as he
shook Abdul's hand, and Tamara threw her arms
around him and hugged him. "You were so brave!" she
said.

Also in the room was a man in a tan suit who greeted
Abdul formally in French, said his name was Jean-
Pierre Malmain, and shook his hand. Abdul presumed
he was France's senior intelligence officer in Libya.

They sat around a table. Tab said: "For the record,
Abdul, the capture of Hufra was the greatest achievement so far of the campaign against ISGS."

Tamara added: "And as well as closing Hufra down we have acquired a huge file bulging with information on ISGS: names, addresses, rendezvous points, photographs. And we've discovered the shocking extent of North Korean support for African terrorism. It's the biggest intelligence haul in the history of North African jihadism."

An elegantly dressed secretary came in with a bottle of champagne and four glasses on a tray. Tab said: "A little celebration—French style." He uncorked the bottle and poured.

"To our hero," Tamara said, and they all drank.

Abdul sensed that the relationship between Tamara and Tab had changed since the day he had met them on the shore of Lake Chad. If he was right, and if they were a couple now, he wanted to get them to talk about it. It was sure to soften their reaction to the demand he was about to make. He smiled and said: "Are you two an item now?"

Tamara said: "Yes," and they both looked pleased.

Abdul said: "But working for the intelligence services of different nations . . ."

Tab said: "I've resigned. I'm working out my notice. I'm going back to France to work in my family's business."

Tamara said: "And I've applied for a transfer to the CIA station in Paris. Phil Doyle has approved my request."

Tab added: "And my boss, Marcel Lavenu, has recommended Tamara to the CIA chief there, who is a friend of his."

"I wish you well," said Abdul. "You're both so handsome, you'll have the most beautiful children."

They looked awkward, and Tamara said: "I didn't say we were getting married."

Abdul was embarrassed. "How old-fashioned of me to make that assumption. I apologize."

"No need," said Tab. "It just hasn't come up, is all."

Tamara changed the subject quickly. "And now, if you're ready, we'll take you back to N'Djamena."

Abdul did not say anything.

She added: "I'm afraid they want to debrief you exhaustively. It may take a few days. But then you're entitled to a long vacation."

Here we go, Abdul thought.

"I'm happy to do the debrief, of course," he said. It was not true, but he had to pretend. "And I'm looking forward to the vacation. But the mission isn't over yet."

"Isn't it?"

"I'd like to try to pick up the trail again. The consignment isn't in Tripoli—I've checked on the tracking device. So it has almost certainly crossed the Mediterranean."

Tamara said: "Abdul, you've done enough."

Tab said: "Anyway, it could have landed anywhere in southern Europe, from Gibraltar to Athens. That's thousands of miles of coastline."

"But some places are likelier than others," Abdul argued. "The south of France, for example, has a long-established infrastructure for the import and distribution of drugs."

"Still a big area to search."

"Not really. If I drive along that coast road—the Corniche, I think it's called—I may pick up the signal. Then we could find out who is at the very end of the cocaine trail. It's an opportunity too good to miss."

Jean-Pierre Malmain said: "We're not here to catch drug dealers. We're after terrorists."

"But Europe is where the money comes from," Abdul persisted. "The whole operation is ultimately financed by kids who buy dope in clubs. Any damage we can do at the French end will damage ISGS's entire smuggling enterprise—which is probably worth more to them even than the gold mine at Hufra."

Malmain said dismissively: "The decision must obviously be made by our superiors."

Abdul shook his head. "We can't afford to lose the time. The radio transmitters will be discovered when they start to open the sacks of cocaine. This may have happened already, but if not—if we're lucky—it could be any day now. I want to leave for France tomorrow."

"I can't authorize that."

"I'm not asking you to. It's covered by my original orders. If I'm wrong, I'll be recalled from France. But I'm going."

Malmain shrugged, giving in.

Tamara said: "Abdul, is there anything you need from us right now?"

"Yes." This was the delicate part, but he had thought about how he would phrase his demand. He patted his pockets, looking for a pen, but realized he had gotten out of the habit of carrying one. "Would someone let me have a pencil and a sheet of paper, please?"

Malmain got up. While he was fetching the writing materials, Abdul said: "When I got away from Hufra two of the slaves escaped with me, a woman and a child, illegal migrants. I've been using them as a cover, pretending we're a family. It's a perfect legend and I'd like to continue with it."

"Sounds like a good idea," said Tamara.

Malmain handed over a pad and a pencil. Abdul wrote *Kiah Haddad and Naji Haddad* and added their dates of birth. Then he said: "I need two genuine French passports, one for each of them." Like every secret service in the world, the DGSE was able to get passports for anyone, as part of its work.

Tamara saw what he had written and said: "They have taken your surname?"

"We're posing as a family," Abdul reminded her.

"Oh, yes, of course," she said, but Abdul knew she had guessed the truth.

Malmain, who clearly did not like Abdul's plan, said: "I'll need photographs."

Abdul drew from his jacket pocket the two strips of photos taken at the travel agency and slid them across the table.

Tamara said: "Oh! The woman at Lake Chad! I thought the name Kiah was familiar." She explained to Malmain. "We met this woman in Chad. She questioned us about life in Europe. I told her not to trust people smugglers."

Abdul said: "It was good advice. They took her money and dumped her in a Libyan slave camp."

Malmain spoke with the hint of a sneer. "So you have befriended this woman."

Abdul did not reply.

Tamara was still looking at the photograph. "She's very beautiful. I remember thinking that at the time."

Of course they all suspected the relationship between him and Kiah. Abdul did not try to explain it. Let them think what they liked.

Tamara was on his side. She turned to Malmain and said: "How long will it take you to produce the passports—an hour or so?"

Malmain hesitated. Clearly he thought Abdul should first return to N'Djamena to be debriefed. But it was difficult to refuse Abdul anything after all he had done—and Abdul was counting on that.

Malmain gave in, shrugged, and said: "Two hours."

Abdul concealed his relief. Acting as if this were what he had confidently expected all along, he handed Malmain one of the business cards he had picked up at the hotel desk. "Please have them delivered to me at my hotel."

"Of course."

He left a few minutes later. In the street he hailed a taxi and gave the address of the travel agency he had visited earlier. On the way he mulled over what he had done. He was now committed to taking Kiah and Naji to France. Her dream was going to come true. But what about him? What were his plans after that? Clearly this question was on her mind as much as his. He had been putting off the day when he had to answer it, with the excuse that he did not know what attitude the CIA and the DGSE would take. But now he knew, and there was no longer any reason to dodge the real issue.

When they got to France, and Kiah and Naji were settled there, would he say good-bye to them, and return to his home in the US, and never see them again? Whenever he thought about this possibility he felt depressed. He thought about their lunch today and how contented he had felt. When was the last time he had experienced such a sense of rightness and satisfaction with his place in the world? Maybe never.

The taxi pulled up and Abdul went into the travel agency. The same smartly dressed young woman was behind the desk, and she remembered him from the morning. At first she looked wary, as if she thought he might have come back without his wife in order to ask her for a date.

He smiled reassuringly. "I need to fly to Nice," he said. "Three tickets. One way."

CHAPTER 36

A harsh wind was blowing across the circular southern lake in the government complex of Zhongnanhai at seven o'clock in the morning. Chang Kai got out of his car and zipped his down coat against the cold.

He was about to meet the president but he was thinking about Ting. Last evening she had asked him about the war and he had told her that the superpowers would prevent escalation. But in his heart he was not sure, and she sensed that. They had gone to bed and clung to one another protectively. Finally they had made love with an air of desperation, as if it might be the last time.

Afterward he had lain awake. As a young man he had tried to figure out who really had the power. Was it the president, the head of the army, or the members of the Politburo collectively? Or the American president, or the American media, or the billionaires? Gradually he had realized that everyone was constrained. The American president was ruled by public opinion, and the Chinese president by the Communist Party. The billionaires had to make profits and the generals had to win battles. Power resided not in one locus but in an immensely complex network, a group of key people and institutions with no collective will, all pulling in different directions.

And he was part of it. What happened would be his fault as much as anyone's.

Lying in bed, listening to the all-night swish of tires on the road outside, he asked himself what more he could do, from his place in the grid, to prevent the Korean crisis from turning into a global catastrophe. He had to make sure that Ting, and his mother, and Ting's mother, and his father, did not die in a storm of bombs and flying debris and falling masonry and lethal radiation.

That thought kept him awake a long time.

Now, closing the car door and pulling up the hood of his coat, he saw two people standing at the water's edge with their backs to him, looking over the cold gray lake. He recognized the figure of his father, Chang Jianjun, wrapped in a black overcoat, looking like a squat statue except that he was smoking. The man with him was probably his longtime pal General Huang, braving the cold in his uniform tunic, too tough to wear a woolly scarf. The old guard is here, Kai thought.

He approached them, but they did not hear his footsteps, probably because of the wind, and he heard Huang say: "If the Americans want war, we will give it to them."

"The supreme art of war is to subdue the enemy without fighting," Kai said. "Sun Tzu said that."

Huang looked angry. "I don't need a lesson in the philosophy of Sun Tzu from a young whippersnapper like you."

Another car drew up and the national defense minister, Kong Zhao, got out. Kai was glad to see an ally. Kong took a red skiing jacket from the trunk of his car and shrugged it on. Seeing the three of them at the waterside, he said: "Why aren't we going in?"

Jianjun answered: "The president wants to walk. He thinks he needs the exercise." Jianjun's tone was mildly disrespectful. Some of these old military types thought that exercise was a young people's fad.

President Chen came out of the palace warmly dressed with gloves and a knitted cap. He was followed by an aide and a guard. He immediately set off at a brisk walk. The others joined him, Jianjun throwing away his cigarette. They headed around the lake clockwise.

The president began formally. "Chang Jianjun, as vice chairman of the National Security Commission, what is your assessment of the war in Korea?"

"The south is winning," Jianjun said without hesitation. "They have more weapons, and their missiles are more accurate." He spoke in the clipped manner of an army briefing, just the facts, one, two, and three, no frills.

Chen said: "How long can North Korea hold out?"

"They will run out of missiles in a few days at most."

"But we are resupplying them."

"As fast as we can. Undoubtedly the Americans are doing the same for the south. But neither of us can keep this up indefinitely."

"So what will happen?"

"The south may invade."

The president turned to Kai. "With American help?"

Kai said: "The White House will not send American troops into the north. But they will not need to. The South Korean army can win without them."

Jianjun said: "And then the whole of Korea will be ruled by the regime in Seoul—which means by the United States."

Kai was not sure the last part was true anymore, but this was not the time to have that argument.

Chen said: "Recommendations for action?"

Jianjun was emphatic. "We have to intervene. It's the only way to prevent Korea from becoming an American colony—on our doorstep."

Intervention was what Kai was afraid of. But before he could say so, Kong Zhao spoke. "I disagree," Kong said, not waiting for the president to ask him.

Jianjun looked angry at being contradicted.

"Go ahead, Kong," said Chen mildly. "Tell us why."

Kong ran a hand through his already messy hair-style. "If we intervene, we give the Americans the right to do the same." He spoke in the reasonable tones of a philosophical discussion, in sharp contrast to Jianjun's bullets of fact. "The important question is not how to save North Korea. It's how to prevent war with the US."

General Huang shook his head vigorously in nega-tion. "The Americans don't want war with us any more than we do," he asserted. "As long as our forces do not cross the border into South Korea, they will stay put."

"You don't know that." Kong shrugged. "No one knows for sure what the US will do. I'm asking whether we can take the risk of a superpower war."

"Life is risk," Huang growled.

"And politics is the avoidance of risk," Kong coun-tered.

Kai decided it was time for him to speak. "May I make a suggestion?"

"Of course," said Chen. He smiled at Jianjun. "Your son's suggestions are often useful."

Jianjun did not really agree. He bowed his head in acknowledgment of the compliment but said nothing.

Kai said: "There is one thing we could try before sending Chinese troops into North Korea. We could propose a reconciliation between the supreme leader in Pyongyang and the ultras based in Yeongjeo-dong."

Chen nodded. "If the regime and the rebels could be reconciled, the missing half of North Korea's army could be deployed."

Jianjun looked thoughtful. "And the nuclear weapons."

That was a problem. Kai added hastily: "The nuclear weapons don't have to be used. The mere fact that they became available to the government in Pyongyang should be enough to bring the South Koreans to the negotiating table."

Chen thought of another snag. "It's hard to imagine the supreme leader sharing power with anyone, let alone people who tried to overthrow him."

"But if he faces a choice between that and total defeat . . ."

Chen considered this. After a minute or two deep in thought, he said: "It's worth a try."

Kai said: "Will you phone Supreme Leader Kang, sir?"

"Right now."

Kai was satisfied.

General Huang was not. He did not like talk of compromise: it made China look weak. President Chen had been a disappointment to him. Huang and the old guard had backed Chen's rise to power, believing that he favored orthodox Communism, but in office Chen had not been as hard-line as they had hoped.

However, Huang knew how to accept defeat and limit the damage, and now he said: "We can't afford any delay. If Kang agrees, President, I suggest, if I may, that you insist he approach the rebels with this offer *today*."

"Good thinking," said Chen.

Huang looked mollified.

The group had circumnavigated the lake and was now almost back at Qinzheng Hall. Jianjun spoke quietly to Kai at a moment when no one else could hear. He said: "Have you spoken to your friend Neil recently?"

"Of course. I speak to him at least once a week. He's a valuable source of insight into White House thinking."

"Hm."

"Why do you ask?"

"Be careful," said Jianjun.

They all went into the building and climbed the stairs.

Chen said to an aide: "Get Kang on the phone."

They took off their coats and rubbed their cold hands. A servant brought tea to warm them up.

Kai wondered what his father had meant. The words had sounded ominous. Did anyone know what he and Neil said to one another? It was possible. They could have been bugged, despite all the precautions they took. Both Kai and Neil routinely reported their discussions, and such reports could be leaked. Had Kai said anything culpable? Well, yes, he had told Neil how weak North Korea was, and that revelation might be considered disloyal.

Kai felt uneasy.

The phone rang and Chen picked it up.

They all listened in silence as the president ran through the points that had been made in their discussion. Kai paid attention to Chen's tone. Although all presidents were theoretically equals in status, in reality North Korea was dependent on China, and this was reflected in Chen's attitude, which was that of a father speaking to an adult son who might or might not obey.

There followed a long silence in which Chen listened.

Finally he said one word: "Today."

Kai's hopes lifted. That sounded good.

Chen said insistently: "It must be done today."

There was a pause.

"Thank you, Supreme Leader."

Chen hung up and said: "He said yes."

As soon as Kai got back to the Guoanbu he put in a call to Neil Davidson. Neil was in a meeting—about Korea, Kai guessed. He tuned in to South Korean television news, which sometimes reported developments first. The north seemed even weaker, firing few missiles, most of which were intercepted, while the South Koreans were energetically clearing rubble and reinforcing bomb-damaged buildings. There was nothing new.

At midday General Ham called.

He spoke quietly and evidently had his mouth close to the phone, as if he were afraid of being overheard. "The supreme leader has fulfilled all my expectations," he said.

It sounded like praise but Kai knew it was the opposite.

Ham went on: "He has completely vindicated the decision I made all those years ago."

He meant the decision to spy for China.

"However, he has now surprised me by attempting to make peace."

Kai knew that, of course, but he did not say so. "When did that happen?"

"Kang phoned Yeongjeo-dong this morning."

Right after he heard from President Chen, Kai calculated. That was quick. "Kang is desperate," he said.

"Not desperate enough," said Ham. "He didn't offer the rebels any incentive other than an amnesty. They don't trust him to keep an amnesty and anyway they want much more."

"Such as?"

"The leader of the rebels, Pak Jae-jin, wants to be made minister of defense and Kang's designated heir as supreme leader."

"Which Kang refused."

"Not surprisingly," Ham said. "Designating a rebel as heir is like signing your own death warrant."

"Kang could have offered a compromise."

"But he did not."

Kai sighed. "So there will be no truce."

"No."

Kai was dismayed, though not much surprised. The rebels did not want a truce. Clearly they thought they only had to wait patiently for the Pyongyang regime to be destroyed, whereupon they would step into the power vacuum. It would never be so simple, but they did not realize that. In any case, why was the supreme leader not trying harder? Kai said to Ham: "At this point, what does Kang actually want?"

"Death or glory," said Ham.

Kai had a heavy sensation in his belly. This was doomsday talk. He said: "But what does that mean?"

"I'm not sure," said Ham. "But keep an eye on your radar." He hung up.

Kai feared that the supreme leader might now be bolder than ever. He had done Chen's bidding, albeit half-heartedly, and offered the rebels a deal, and he might now feel that their refusal vindicated his aggression. Kai's peacemaking suggestion of this morning might even have made matters worse.

Sometimes, he thought, you just can't fucking win.

He wrote a short note saying that the rebels had rejected the supreme leader's peace offer and sent it to President Chen, with copies to all senior government figures. Such a note should really have gone out over the signature of his boss, Fu Chuyu, but Kai was no longer even pretending to defer to him. Fu was plotting against him and that was known by everyone who knew anything. China's leaders needed to be reminded that it was Kai, not Fu, who sent them the crucial intelligence.

He summoned the head of the Korea desk, Jin Chinhwa. Jin needed a haircut, Kai thought; his forelock was over one eye. He was about to mention it when he realized he had seen other young men looking like that, and it was probably a fashion, so he said nothing about it. Instead he said: "Can we watch North Korea on radar?"

"Sure," said Jin. "Our army has a radar feed, or we can hack into the South Korean army's radar, which is probably more tightly focused."

"You need to watch. Something may be about to happen. And put it through here too please."

"Yes, sir. Please tune to number five."

Kai switched channels as instructed. A minute later a radar feed appeared superimposed over a map. However, the skies over North Korea seemed quiet after days of air war.

It was midafternoon before Neil returned his call. "I was in a meeting," he said in his Texas drawl. "My boss can talk longer than a Baptist preacher. What's new?"

Kai said: "Is it possible that anyone could know what you and I discussed last time we talked?"

There was a moment of hesitation, then Neil said: "Oh, fuck."

"What?"

"You're using a secure phone, right?"

"As secure as they get."

"We just fired someone."

"Who?"

"A computer techie. He worked for the embassy, not the CIA station, but he was getting into our files anyway. We found out pretty quickly, but he must have seen my note of our conversation. Are you in trouble?"

"Some of the things I said to you could be misinterpreted—especially by my enemies."

"I'm sorry."

"The techie wasn't spying for me, obviously."

"We think he was reporting to the People's Liberation Army."

Which meant General Huang. That was how Kai's father had learned of the conversation. "Thanks for being straight with me, Neil."

"Right now we can't afford to be anything else."

"Too damn true. I'll talk to you soon."

They hung up.

Kai sat back and reflected. The campaign against him was building. Now it wasn't just gossip about Ting. Someone was trying to paint him as some kind of traitor. What he needed to do was drop everything and go head-to-head with his enemies. He should raise questions about the loyalty of Vice Minister Li, spread rumors that General Huang had a serious gambling problem, and circulate an order that no one was to talk about Fu Chuyu's mental health issues. But that was all bullshit and he did not have time.

Suddenly the radar came alive. The top left corner of the screen seemed to fill with arrows. Kai found it difficult to estimate how many.

Jin Chin-hwa phoned him and said: "Missile attack."

"Yes. How many?"

"A lot. Twenty-five, thirty."

"I didn't think North Korea had that many missiles left."

"It might be just about their entire stockpile."

"The supreme leader's last gasp."

"Watch the lower part of the screen for the South Korean response."

But something else happened first. Another cluster of arrows appeared, also on the North Korean side but nearer to the border. Kai said: "What the hell . . ."

"They could be drones," said Jin. "It might be my imagination but I think they're moving slower."

Missiles and drones, thought Kai; bombers are next.

He switched to South Korean TV. It was broadcasting an air raid warning alternating with news footage of people running for shelter in underground parking garages and the more than seven hundred stations of the Seoul Metropolitan Subway. The high-pitched whine of the siren sounded over the traffic noise. Kai knew that air raid drills were held once a year, but always at three p.m., and as it was now late in the afternoon the South Koreans knew this was the real thing.

North Korean TV was not broadcasting yet, but he found a radio station. It was playing music.

Back on the radar screen, the incoming ordnance was beginning to encounter anti-missile defenses. The sight was oddly undramatic: two moving arrows, one attacking and one defending, met and touched, then both quietly disappeared, with no sound and no indication that millions of dollars of military equipment had just been smashed to pieces.

But it was clear to Kai that, as with every other missile assault, the defenses were not impenetrable. It seemed to him that at least half the North Korean missiles and drones were getting through. Soon they would hit crowded cities. He switched back to South Korean television.

In between the air raid warnings, the shots of city streets now showed something of a ghost town. There was almost no traffic. Cars, buses, trucks, and cycles were parked where they had been abandoned by panicking drivers. Traffic lights at deserted crossroads changed from green to amber to red unwatched. A few people could be seen running, none walking. A red fire engine came slowly along a street, waiting for the fires to start, and a yellow-and-white ambulance followed. Brave people inside, Kai thought. He wondered who was shooting these pictures and decided the cameras might have been remotely operated.

Then the bombs began to fall, and Kai suffered another shock.

The bombs did little damage. They seemed to be loaded with very small amounts of explosive. Some burst in the air, fifty or a hundred feet up. No buildings collapsed, no cars blew up. Paramedics leaped from their ambulances and firefighters deployed their hoses, then they stood staring in bewilderment at the gently fizzing projectiles.

Finally the emergency workers began to cough and sneeze, and Kai said aloud: "Oh, no, no!"

Quickly the people began to gasp for breath. Some fell to the ground. Those who could still move hurried to their vehicles to break out gas masks.

Kai said: "The motherfuckers are using chemical weapons." He was speaking to an empty office.

Another camera showed the scene in a South Korean army camp. Here the poison seemed different: the soldiers were rushing to put on hazmat gear, but already their faces were turning red, some were throwing up, others were too confused to know what to do, and the worst affected were on the ground, jerking in seizure. Kai said: "Hydrogen cyanide."

In a supermarket parking lot, shoppers were jumping out of their gridlocked cars and trying to make it to the store, some with babies and children. Most were too late to reach the doors and they fell to the tarmac, mouths open in screams that Kai could not hear, as mustard gas blistered their skin, blinded their eyes, and destroyed their lungs.

The worst scene was at a US Army base. There a nerve agent had landed. Many of the soldiers seemed to have been wearing protective gear already, a far-sighted precaution. They were desperately trying to help others who had not yet gotten around to it, including a lot of civilians. The stricken men and women were half-blind, streaming with sweat, vomiting, and twitching uncontrollably. Kai thought they must have been exposed to VX, an English invention favored by North Koreans as a murder weapon. It quickly led from agony to paralysis and death by suffocation.

Kai's phone rang and he answered without taking his eyes off the screen.

It was Defense Minister Kong Zhao, who said: "Are you fucking seeing this?"

"They've deployed chemical weapons," Kai said. "And maybe biological too—those act more slowly, we can't tell yet."

"What the fuck are we going to do?"

"It hardly matters," said Kai. "The only thing that counts now is what the Americans will do."

DEFCON 2

ONE STEP FROM NUCLEAR WAR.

ARMED FORCES READY TO ENGAGE IN
LESS THAN SIX HOURS.
(THE ONLY TIME THE ALERT LEVEL
HAS EVER BEEN THIS HIGH WAS
IN THE CUBAN MISSILE CRISIS
OF 1962.)

CHAPTER 37

For a few moments, Pauline was paralyzed by horror. She had turned on the TV while she got dressed, but now she stood in front of the screen in her underwear, unable to look away. CNN was showing nonstop pictures from South Korea, mostly footage taken on phones and posted on social media, also Korean TV coverage, all of it showing a monstrous nightmare beyond anything conceived by the medieval painters of the Day of Judgment.

It was torture at long range. The poison sprays and gases attacked indiscriminately: men and women and children, Koreans and Americans and others. Those out of doors had been most vulnerable, but shops and offices had ventilation systems that sucked in some of the chemicals, and the deadly air could creep into houses and apartments, slipping silently around the edges of doors and windows. It had even drifted down ramps into the underground parking lot where some people had taken shelter, causing horrific scenes of panic and hysteria. Gas masks did not offer complete protection, for—as the more educated news reports pointed out—some of the lethal substances could slowly enter the bloodstream through the skin.

It was the babies and children that got to her: the screams, the desperate gasping for air, the burned faces, the uncontrollable twitching. It would have been hard to watch adults suffering so badly; to see children in such agony was unbearable, and she kept closing her eyes, then forcing herself to look.

The phone rang. It was Gus. She said: "How widespread is this?"

"The three major cities of South Korea are affected—Seoul, Busan, and Incheon—plus most US and Korean military bases."

"Hell."

"Hell is what it is."

"How many Americans killed?"

"There's no count yet, but it's going to be in the hundreds, including some of our troops' family members."

"Is it ongoing?"

"The missile attack is over, but the poisons continue to claim new victims."

There was a bubble of rage in Pauline's throat, and she wanted to scream. She forced herself to be unemotional. She thought for a minute, then said: "Gus, this obviously requires a major response by the United States, but I'm not going to rush that decision. This is the biggest crisis since 9/11."

"It's dark now in the Far East and there may be no further action overnight. Which gives us a day to plan."

"But we'll start early. Get everyone into the Situation Room, at, say, eight thirty."

"You got it."

They hung up, and she sat on the bed, thinking. Chemical and biological weapons were inhuman and against international law. They were unspeakably cruel. And they had been used to kill Americans. The war in

Korea was no longer a local squabble. The world would be waiting for the American response to the outrage. Which meant her response.

She dressed carefully in a somber dark gray skirt suit and an off-white blouse, reflecting her solemn mood.

By the time she got to the Oval Office, the morning news shows were gathering reactions. People did not need a rabble-rousing politician to get them worked up about this. Pauline's fury was shared all over the US. Commuters interviewed at subway stations were enraged. Any attack on Americans angered them; this one made them incandescent.

North Korea did not have an embassy in the US, but it had a permanent mission at the United Nations, with a one-room office at the Diplomat Centre on Second Avenue in New York City, and an angry crowd gathered on the street outside the building, shouting up at the windows on the thirteenth floor.

In Columbus, Georgia, a Korean American couple were shot and killed in their convenience store by a young white man. No money was stolen, though he took a carton of Marlboro Light cigarettes.

Pauline read her overnight briefings and phoned half a dozen key people, including Secretary of State Chester Jackson, just arrived back from his wasted trip to Sri Lanka and the peace conference that had never happened.

Pippa called from the horse ranch, upset. She said: "Why would they do this, Mom? Are they monsters?"

"They're not monsters, but they're desperate men, which is almost as bad," Pauline said. "The man who runs North Korea has his back to the wall. He's under attack from rebels in his own country, from his neighbors to the south, and from the US. He thinks he's going to lose the war, his power, and probably his life too. He'll do anything."

"What are you going to do?"

"I don't know yet, but when Americans are attacked like this I have to do something. Like everyone else, I want to hit back. But I also have to make sure this doesn't turn into a war between us and China. That would be ten times worse, a hundred times worse, than what's happened in Seoul."

In a frustrated tone Pippa said: "Why is everything so complicated?"

Aha, Pauline thought, you're growing up. She said: "The easy problems get solved right away, so only the hard ones are left. That's why you should never believe a politician with simple answers."

"I guess."

Pauline wondered whether to order Pippa to return to the White House a day early but decided that she was marginally safer in Virginia. "I'll see you tomorrow, honey," she said as casually as she could.

"Okay."

Pauline ate an omelet at her desk and drank a cup of coffee, then went to the Situation Room.

There was tension in the air like static electricity. Was that something you could smell? She noted an aroma of furniture polish from the gleaming table, the body heat of the thirty or so men and women around her, and a sweet perfume from an aide somewhere nearby—and there was something else too. The smell of fear, she thought.

She was briskly practical. "First things first," she said. She nodded to General Schneider, chairman of the Joint Chiefs of Staff, who was in uniform. "Bill, what do we know about American casualties?"

"We have four hundred and twenty confirmed American military dead and one thousand one hundred and ninety-one injured—and counting." His voice was a parade-ground bark, and Pauline guessed he was suppressing emotion. "The attack ended about three hours ago and I'm afraid we haven't yet located them all. The final total will be higher." He swallowed. "Madam President, many brave Americans sacrificed their lives or their health for the sake of their country today in South Korea."

"And we all give thanks for their courage and loyalty, Bill."

"Yes, ma'am."

"What about civilian casualties? We had a hundred thousand nonmilitary American citizens living in South Korea a few days ago. How many did we evacuate?"

"Not enough." He cleared his throat and spoke more easily. "We expect about four hundred civilian deaths and four thousand injured, though that's no more than an educated guess."

"The numbers are tragic but the way they died is utterly horrific."

"Yes. Mustard gas, hydrogen cyanide, and VX nerve gas."

"Any biological weapons?"

"Not as far as we can tell."

"Thank you, Bill." She looked at Chester Jackson, in his tweed suit and button-down shirt a contrast with General Schneider. "Chess, why has this happened?"

"You're asking me to read the mind of the supreme leader." Chess was like Gerry, careful to put in all the ifs and buts, and, like Gerry, he demanded patience. "So my answer is a guess, but here goes. I believe Kang is reckless because he thinks that China must rescue him sooner or later, and the more dire the emergency, the sooner it will happen."

The director of national intelligence, Sophia Magliani, chipped in. "If I may, Madam President, that's the view of just about everyone in the intelligence community."

"But is Kang right?" Pauline asked. "In the end, will the Chinese save his ass?"

"Another exercise in telepathy, Madam President," said Chess, and Pauline controlled her impatience. "Beijing is hard to read because there are two factions, the young progressives and the old Communists. The progressives think the supreme leader is a pain in the neck and they would like to see the back of him. The Communists think he's an indispensable bulwark against capitalist imperialism."

"But the bottom line . . . ," said Pauline, nudging him along.

"Bottom line is that both sides are determined to keep the US out of North Korea. For us to trespass on their land, airspace, or maritime territory risks provoking war with Beijing."

"You say it *risks* war, not that it makes war inevitable."

"Yes, and I chose my words carefully. We don't know where the Chinese would draw the line. They probably don't know themselves. They may not make that decision until they're forced to."

Pauline recalled Pippa's saying *Why is everything so complicated?*

All this was preliminary. The group was waiting for her to speak. She was the captain and they were the crew; they would sail the ship, but she had to tell them where to go.

She said: "This morning's attack by the North Koreans is a game changer. Until now, our priority has been to avoid war. That is no longer the main issue. War has happened, despite all our efforts. We did not want it, but it's here."

She paused, then said: "Our task now is to protect American lives."

They looked solemn but also relieved. At least they had a direction.

"What is our first step?" She felt her heart beat faster. She had never done anything like this before. She took a deep breath, then spoke slowly and emphatically. "We are now going to make sure that North Korea will never again kill Americans. I intend to take away their power to do us harm, permanently. We will utterly destroy their military forces. And we will do that today."

The men and women around the table burst into a round of spontaneous applause. Clearly this was what they had been hoping for.

She waited a few moments, then went on: "There may be more ways than one for us to achieve this." She turned to the chairman of the Joint Chiefs again. "Bill, lay out the military options, please."

He spoke with supreme confidence, a complete contrast to the professorial Chess. "Let me start with the maximum," he said. "We could launch a nuclear attack on North Korea and turn the entire country into a moonscape."

That proposal was a nonstarter, but Pauline did not say so. She had asked for the options and Bill was giving them. She dismissed it with a light touch. "It will be what James Moore demands in his next television interview," she said.

Chess said: "However, it's the option most likely to draw us into a nuclear war with China."

Bill said: "I'm not recommending it, but it should be put on the table."

"Quite right, Bill," said Pauline. "What else?"

"Your stated aim could also be achieved with an invasion of North Korea by American troops. A big enough force could take Pyongyang, capture the supreme leader and his entire team, disarm the military, and destroy every missile in the country as well as any remaining stocks of chemical and biological weapons."

Chess said: "And once again we would have to think about the Chinese reaction."

General Schneider spoke with suppressed indignation. "I hope we're not going to let fear of the Chinese dictate our response to this outrage."

"No, Bill, we're not," Pauline said. "We're just looking at options. What's the next one?"

"Third and probably last," Bill said, "is the minimalist approach: a full-scale American air attack on military and government installations in North Korea, using bomber and fighter aircraft as well as cruise missiles and drones, but not ground troops, the aim being to completely destroy Pyongyang's ability to wage war by land, sea, or air—without actually invading North Korea."

Chess said: "Even that would offend the Chinese."

"It would," said Pauline, "but it's borderline. The last time I spoke to President Chen he implied that he would not retaliate against our missile attack on North Korea provided no US personnel entered North Korean land, airspace, or maritime territory. Bill's minimal option involves us violating North Korean sea and air space—but we would have no boots on the ground."

Chess said skeptically: "And you think that Chen would tolerate that?"

"I don't guarantee it," said Pauline. "We'd have to take a risk."

There was a long moment of silence.

Gus Blake spoke for the first time. "For clarification, Madam President, given any one of these three options, would we attack the part of North Korea that is under the control of the rebels?"

"Yes," said Schneider forcefully. "They're North Korean, and they have weapons. We can't do half a job."

"No," said Chess. "Some of their weapons are nuclear. If we attack them with the stated aim of wiping them out, why would they not retaliate with nukes?"

Gus said: "I'm with Chess, but for another reason. When the supreme leader is gone, North Korea will need a government, and it may be wise to give the rebels some part in that."

Pauline made up her mind. "I'm not going to fire on people who have never done anything to harm the US. However, the minute they move against us we wipe them out."

That got general agreement.

"I get the feeling of a consensus here," she said. "Bill's minimalist option is the one we should be talking about."

Once again there were murmurs of agreement.

She went on: "I said today and I meant it. Eight o'clock tonight, our time, will be soon after sunrise in East Asia. Bill, can you do it by then?"

Schneider was energized. "You got it, Madam President."

"Cruise missiles, artillery, drones, bombers, and fighter aircraft. Also deploy US Navy ships to attack North Korean navy vessels anywhere."

"Even in North Korean harbors?"

Pauline thought for a moment, then said: "Even in harbors. The mission is to wipe out the North Koreans as a fighting force. No hiding place."

"And raise the alert level?"

"Certainly. DEFCON 2."

Gus said: "For maximum impact we need also to deploy forces based outside Korea, specifically in Japan and Guam."

"Do it."

"And it would be good to have some of our allies participate, to show that this is an international effort, not just the US."

Chess said: "I believe they'll be keen to join in, the more so because of the use of illegal chemical weapons."

Gus said: "I'd like to get the Australians involved."

"Call them," said Pauline. "And I will address the nation on network television at the moment our attack begins, eight o'clock tonight." Pauline stood up, and they all did the same. "Thank you, ladies and gentlemen," she said. "Let's go get this done."

Back in the Oval Office she summoned Sandip Chakraborty. He told her that the James Moore campaign was already accusing her of timidity. "No surprises from that quarter, then," she said. She told him to book her fifteen minutes on all the networks at eight p.m.

"Good thinking," he said. "The news shows will spend the day speculating about what you're going to do and won't pay so much attention to Moore sniping from the sidelines."

"Good," she said. In truth she hardly cared about Moore any longer, but she did not want to dampen Sandip's enthusiasm.

After Sandip she called in Gus and said: "I want you to walk me through the protocol for declaring nuclear war."

He looked stricken. "Is it going to come to that?"

"Not if I can help it," she said. "But I have to be ready for anything. Let's sit down."

They sat opposite one another on the couches. "You're familiar with the atomic football," he said.

"Yes, although that's really for use when I'm out of the White House."

"Okay, so if you're here, which is likely, the first thing you're supposed to do is meet with top advisors."

"Everybody thinks this is a decision of the president alone."

"In practice it is, because there's not likely to be time for discussion, but if possible you have to do it."

"Well, I guess I'd want to, if I could."

"You might just speak to me. Allow a minute."

"What next?"

"Step two, you call the War Room at the Pentagon, using the special phone in the atomic football if you're not here in the White House. When you reach them, you need to prove your identity. You have the Biscuit?"

Pauline took from her pocket an opaque plastic case. "I'm going to open it," she said.

"The only way to do that is to snap it in two."

"I know." She took the little case in both hands and twisted in opposite directions. It broke easily to reveal a plastic rectangle like a credit card. The card was changed every day.

Gus said: "Whatever is printed on the card is the identification code."

"It says: 'Twenty-Three Hotel Victor.'"

"You read it to them and they'll know it's you giving the order."

"And that's it?"

"Not yet, no. Step three, the War Room sends out an encrypted order to the crews of missile launchers, submarines, and bomber aircraft. Elapsed time is now three minutes."

"And now the crews have to decode the order."

"Yes . . ."

He did not add *obviously*, but a hint of impatience in his voice made Pauline realize that she was interrupting with stupid questions, a sign that the discussion was making her tense. I need to stay very calm today, she thought. She said: "Sorry, dumb question. Go on."

"The War Room's order gives targets, time of launch, and the codes required to unlock the warheads. Unless the emergency has come as a total surprise, those targets will normally have been preapproved by you."

"But I haven't—"

"Bill's going to send you a list in the next hour or so."

"Okay."

"Step four is launch preparation. Crews have to confirm the authentication codes, enter the target coordinates, and unlock the missiles. Up until this point it is possible for you to countermand your order."

"I guess I can recall bombers at any time."

"Correct. But now, step five, missiles are launched, and there is no way to recall them or even redirect them. Time elapsed is five minutes. Nuclear war has begun."

Pauline felt the touch of fate like a cold hand. "God forbid we ever have to do it."

"Amen," said Gus.

She worried about it all day. What she had decided to do was dangerous, and the fact that her colleagues had unanimously agreed on the plan did not relieve her of responsibility. But the alternatives were worse. The nuclear option—which James Moore was calling for, as Pauline had forecast—was even more risky. But she had to strike a fatal blow at a regime that menaced America and the world.

Round and round she went, and always came to the same conclusion.

The television crew arrived in the Oval Office at

seven. Footage from one crew would be shared by all channels. The men and women in jeans and sneakers set up cameras, lights, and microphones, trailing cables across the gold-colored carpet. Meanwhile Pauline put the finishing touches to her speech and Sandip uploaded it to the teleprompter.

Sandip brought her a blouse in light blue, a better color for the cameras. "The gray suit will look black on television, but that's appropriate," he said. A makeup artist worked on her face and a hairdresser styled and sprayed her blond bob.

There was still time to change her mind. She circled around the argument once more. But she arrived back at the same place.

The clock ticked around and at one minute to eight the room went silent.

The producer counted down the last few seconds with his fingers.

Pauline looked into the camera and said: "My fellow Americans."

CHAPTER 38

The conference room at Guoanbu headquarters in Beijing fell silent as President Green said: "My fellow Americans."

It was eight o'clock in the morning. Chang Kai had summoned the heads of departments to watch with him. Some were bleary-eyed and hastily dressed. The rest of the Guoanbu headquarters staff were watching the same pictures in other rooms.

News channels all over the world had been speculating for the last twelve hours about what Pauline Green would say, but nothing had leaked. Sigint showed increased communications activity in the US military, so something was up, but what? Even Kai's well-paid spies in Washington had failed to pick up a hint. President Chen had spoken to President Green twice and learned only that, as he put it, she was a crouching tiger. The foreign ministers of the two countries had been in communication all night. The UN Security Council was in perpetual session.

Of course President Green would respond to the

Pyongyang government's use of chemical weapons, but what would that response be? In principle, she might announce anything from a diplomatic protest to a nuclear bomb. But in practice it had to be big. No country could fail to retaliate that kind of attack on its soldiers and citizens.

The Chinese government was in an impossible position. North Korea was skidding out of control. Beijing would be blamed for Pyongyang's crimes. This dangerous situation could not be allowed to continue for even one more day. But what could China do?

Kai hoped President Green would give him a clue.

"My fellow Americans, in the last few seconds the United States has launched a full-scale air attack on the military forces of Pyongyang, North Korea."

"Shit!" said Kai.

"Those forces have killed thousands of Americans with vile weapons that are banned by every civilized country in the world, and I am here to tell you . . ." She spoke slowly, emphasizing every word. "The Pyongyang regime is now being wiped out."

It occurred to Kai that the little blond woman behind the big desk looked more formidable, right now, than any leader he had ever seen.

"As I speak to you, we are launching nonnuclear missiles and bombs at every military and government target under the control of Pyongyang."

"Nonnuclear," Kai repeated. "Thank heaven and earth."

"In addition, our bomber pilots are scrambling, ready to follow the missiles and ensure that the targets are completely destroyed."

"Missiles and bombs, but no nukes," said Kai. "Someone get the radar feed and satellite views and put both up on our screens."

President Green said: "Within the next few hours, the man who calls himself supreme leader will totally lose any ability to attack the United States. We will leave him utterly powerless."

Kai took out his phone and dialed Neil Davidson's personal number. The call went straight to voicemail, as Kai had expected: Neil would want to watch the president uninterrupted. But Kai wanted to be the first person he called after the broadcast. In the next few minutes Neil would receive a diplomatic briefing from the State Department that would enlarge on Pauline Green's message and answer some of the questions bubbling up in Kai's mind. He waited for the beep and said: "This is Kai, watching your president. Call me." He hung up.

"The decision to attack is momentous," Pauline was saying. "I have always hoped I would never have to make it. I have not chosen this course emotionally, nor in a heated desire for revenge. I've discussed it coolly and calmly with my cabinet, and we are unanimous in thinking this is the only viable option open to the United States as a free independent people."

A screen on the wall came to life, showing a radar picture superimposed on a map. Kai was puzzled, not sure what he was seeing. The missiles seemed to be beyond South Korea, miles away over the sea.

Yang Yong, who was quick to decipher this kind of visual information, muttered: "How the fuck many missiles is that?"

Kai said: "I don't know, but I'm pretty sure the Americans don't have that many missiles in South Korea, not after the last few days."

"No, these aren't coming from South Korea," Yang said confidently. "In fact I think they're originating in Japan." The US had bases in mainland Japan and on the islands of Okinawa, and could launch cruise missiles from its ships and aircraft there. Yang added: "So many!"

Kai recalled that the US had giant submarines that could each carry more than 150 Tomahawk missiles. He said: "This is what happens when you pick a fight with the richest country in the world."

Jin Chin-hwa, the head of the Korea desk, was looking at his laptop. "Listen to this," he said. "A Chinese freighter discharging a cargo of rice in the North Korean port of Nampo has just sent us a message."

Every Chinese vessel, including commercial ships, had at least one crew member whose duty it was to report anything important they saw. They sent messages to what they thought was the Maritime Intelligence Center in the port of Shenzhen but was in fact the Guoanbu.

Jin went on: "They say that an American destroyer, the USS *Morgan*, sailed to the mouth of the Taedong River and fired a cruise missile that hit and sank a vessel of the North Korean navy right before their eyes."

Zhou Meiling, the young internet expert, said: "Already!"

Kai said: "The president wasn't kidding. She's going to annihilate North Korea's military."

"That's not what she said," Yang Yong said pedantically. "Not exactly."

Kai turned to him. Yang did not speak out as often as the younger officers, who were always trying to show how bright they were. Kai said: "What do you mean?"

"She never said she was attacking North Korea, always Pyongyang, and once the supreme leader."

Kai had not noticed that detail. "Well spotted," he said. "It may mean she's leaving the rebel ultras alone."

"Or simply keeping that option open for the moment."

"I'll try to find out when I talk to the CIA."

The president's broadcast came to an end without further revelations. A few minutes later Kai was summoned to Zhongnanhai for an emergency meeting of the Foreign Affairs Commission. He notified Monk, grabbed his coat, and left the building.

He foresaw that, as the group debated the Chinese response to the American attack, they would split into hawks and doves, as usual. Kai would be searching for a compromise that would enable China to save face without starting World War III.

While he was on the way there in the usual heavy Beijing traffic—and the American missiles were still in the air on their thousand-mile flight from Japan to North Korea—Neil Davidson called.

The Texas drawl was not as laid-back as usual; in fact Neil sounded almost tense. "Kai, before anyone does anything in a hurry, we want to be real clear with you all: the US has no intention of invading North Korea."

Kai said: "So you think you can deal with the present situation with measures short of an invasion, but you're not completely ruling out that possibility."

"That's about the size of it."

Kai was greatly relieved, because that meant there was a chance of containing the crisis even now, but he kept the thought to himself. It was never smart to make things too easy for the other side. He said: "But, Neil, the USS *Morgan* has already violated North Korean borders by approaching the mouth of the Taedong River to sink a ship of the North Korean navy with a cruise missile. Are you telling me that's not an invasion?"

There was a silence, and Kai guessed that Neil had not known about the *Morgan*. But he recovered from the surprise and said: "Naval bombardment is not ruled out. But please take it from me that we do not intend to put American troops on the ground in North Korea."

"It's a hairsplitting distinction," Kai said, but in fact he was not displeased. If that was where the Americans wanted to draw the line between assault and invasion, the Chinese government might accept it, at least unofficially.

Neil said: "As we speak, our secretary of state is calling your ambassador in Washington to say the same thing. Our quarrel is with the people who dropped those chemical bombs, not with the folks in Beijing."

Kai put a note of skepticism in his voice. "Are you trying to say that your attack is a proportionate response?"

"That's exactly what I'm saying, and we think the rest of the world will see it that way."

"I don't think the Chinese government will take such a lenient view."

"So long as they understand that our intentions are strictly limited. We have no wish to take over the government of North Korea."

That was important, if true. "I'll pass the message on." Kai's phone was showing a call waiting. That was probably his office to tell him the first missiles had hit. But he needed something more from Neil. "We noticed that President Green did not say she was attacking North Korea but repeatedly referred to the Pyongyang regime. Does that mean you're not bombing rebel military bases?"

"The president will not attack people who have never harmed Americans."

That was a reassurance wrapped around a threat. The rebels were safe only as long as they stayed neutral. They would become targets if they attacked Americans. "Clear enough," said Kai. "I have another call. Stay in touch." Without waiting for a reply, he broke the contact and picked up the waiting call.

It was Jin Chin-hwa. "The first missiles have struck North Korea," he said.

"Where?"

"Several places simultaneously: Chunghwa, headquarters of the North Korean air force outside of Pyongyang; the naval base at Haeju; a Kang family residence—"

Kai had been picturing a map of North Korea in his head, and now he interrupted Jin to say: "All targets in the west of the country, away from the rebel zone."

"Yes."

That confirmed what Neil had said.

Kai's car was passing through the usual elaborate security at the Gate of the New China. He said: "Thank you, Jin," and hung up.

Monk parked in a row of limousines outside the Hall of Cherished Compassion, the building where the important political committees met. In common with most buildings within the Zhongnanhai compound, it was designed in traditional style, with curved roof lines. It had a massive auditorium for ceremonial meetings, but the Foreign Affairs Commission met in a conference room.

Kai got out and inhaled the fresh breeze coming across the lake. This was one of the few places in Beijing where the air was not noxious. He took a few seconds to breathe deeply and oxygenate his bloodstream. Then he went inside.

President Chen was already there. To Kai's surprise he wore a suit with no tie and he had not shaved. Kai had never before seen him look scruffy: he must have been up half the night. He was deep in conversation with Kai's father, Chang Jianjun. Of the hawks, Huang Ling and Fu Chuyu were present, and Kong Zhao represented the doves. The uncommitted middle-of-the-roaders were represented by Foreign Minister Wu Bai and President Chen himself. All looked intensely worried.

Chen told everyone to sit and called on Jianjun for an update. Jianjun reported that North Korean anti-missile defenses had not worked well, partly because of an American cyberattack on their launchers, and it was likely the assault would achieve exactly what President Green intended, namely the complete destruction of the Pyongyang regime. "I need hardly remind you, comrades," he said, "that the 1961 treaty between China and North Korea obliges us to come to the aid of North Korea when it is attacked."

President Chen added: "It is of course the *only* defense treaty that China has with any nation. If we do not honor it we will be humbled before the world."

Fu Chuyu, Kai's boss, summarized the intelligence from Kai's division. Kai then trumped him by adding what he had learned from Neil Davidson in the last few minutes, that the Americans were not planning to take control of the North Korean government.

Fu rewarded Kai with a glare of hatred.

General Huang said: "Let us imagine a situation that mirrors this. Suppose that Mexico had attacked Cuba with chemical weapons, killing hundreds of Russian advisors, and in response the Russians launched a massive air attack designed to wipe out the Mexican government and military. Would the Americans defend Mexico? Is there even the shadow of a doubt? Of course they would!"

Kong Zhao said simply: "But how?"

Huang was taken aback. "What do you mean, how?"

"Would they bomb Moscow?"

"They would consider their options."

"Exactly. In the situation you have imagined, comrade, the Americans would face the same dilemma we have now. Should you start World War Three because of an attack on a second-rank neighboring country?"

Huang let his frustration show. "Every time it is suggested that the government of China should take firm action, someone says it might start World War Three."

"Because the danger is always there."

"We can't let that paralyze us."

"But we can't ignore it either."

President Chen intervened. "You are both right, of course," he said. "What I need from you today is a plan to deal with the American attack on North Korea without escalating the crisis to a higher level."

Kai said: "If I may, Mr. President . . ."

"Go ahead."

"We must confront the fact that North Korea today has not one government but two."

Huang bristled at the idea of treating the rebels as if they were a government, but Chen nodded.

Kai went on: "The supreme leader, nominally our ally, is no longer cooperating with us and has created a crisis we didn't seek. The rebels control half the country and all the nuclear weapons. We must consider what relationship we want with the ultras in Yeongjeo-dong who have become—whether we like it or not—the alternative government."

Huang was indignant. "Rebellion against the Communist Party must never be seen to succeed," he said. "And, in any case, how could we talk to these people? We don't know who their leaders are or how to get in touch with them."

Kai said: "I know who they are and I can contact them."

"How is that possible?"

Kai deliberately looked around the room at the aides in attendance. "General, you are of course entitled to receive information of the highest secrecy, but forgive me if I hesitate to name highly sensitive sources of information."

Huang realized he was in the wrong and backed down. "Yes, yes, forget I asked that question."

President Chen said: "All right, so we can talk to the ultras. Next question: what do we want to say?"

Kai had a very clear idea, but he did not want this meeting to set an agenda that would tie him down, so he said: "The discussion would have to be exploratory."

But Wu Bai was shrewd enough to know what Kai was up to and did not want to give him a free hand. "We can do better than that," he said. "We know what we want: a complete and unconditional end to hostilities. And we can guess what the ultras want: some large part in any new government of North Korea."

Kai said: "And my task will be to find out exactly what they will demand in exchange for ending their rebellion." But he already knew he was going to go farther than just finding out.

Huang repeated his previous objection. "We should not empower people who have defied the Party."

"Thank you for pointing that out, General," said Wu. He turned to the rest of the group. "I believe Comrade Huang's statement is completely correct." Huang looked mollified, but Wu did not really agree with him at all. "We cannot assume these ultras are trustworthy," Wu went on, making a different point. "No agreement with them is possible without clear safeguards."

Huang, oblivious to the subtleties, nodded in vigorous agreement. Wu's charm, denigrated as superficial by hard-liners, was actually a deadly tactic, Kai reflected. Wu had neutralized Huang, and Huang had not noticed.

Chen said: "This is a good plan but not a quick fix. What can we do today, now, to cool the situation?"

Kong Zhao had a suggestion. "Call for a cease-fire by both sides, and at the same time pressure Pyongyang to cease fire unilaterally."

Chen said: "Do they even have any missiles left?"

Kai answered. "A handful, hidden under bridges and in tunnels."

Chen nodded thoughtfully. "All the same, they will think that a unilateral cease-fire is not much different from an admission of defeat."

Kong said: "We could give it a try."

"I agree. Now, how should we word our demand?"

Kai tuned out. This would be a long discussion. The important business of the meeting was done, but now everyone would contribute something of minor significance. He controlled his impatience with an effort and began to plan his meeting with the ultras.

He had to communicate with the rebel leader, not with General Ham. He composed a message on his phone:

For the attention of General Pak Jae-jin

SECRET

A very senior emissary of the People's
Republic of China wishes to visit you today.
He will be alone except for the helicopter pilot,
and both men will be unarmed. His mission
is of the utmost importance to Korea and
China.

Please acknowledge receipt of this message and
indicate your willingness to meet with this
representative.

From the Ministry of State Security.

He sent the message to Jin Chin-hwa with instructions to forward it to any and every internet address he could find for the military base at Yeongjeo-dong. He would have preferred to use a single, secure address, but urgency trumped security.

As soon as the meeting ended he buttonholed his father. "I need an air force jet to take me to Yanji," he said. "And then a helicopter to fly me from there to Yeongjeo-dong."

"I'll arrange it," said Jianjun. "When?"

Kai looked at his watch. It was ten o'clock. "Eleven o'clock departure from Beijing, two o'clock transfer at Yanji, three o'clock touchdown at Yeongjeo-dong, approximately."

"Okay."

It was a relief to be in accord with his father for once, Kai thought. He said: "I've told the ultras that I'll be unaccompanied except for the pilot, and we'll both be unarmed. No guns aboard the chopper, please."

"Good thinking. Once you're in rebel territory you'll always be outnumbered. The only way to stay alive is not to fight."

"That's what I thought."

"Consider it done."

"Thank you."

"Good luck, my son."

It was a clear, cloudless day in North Korea. Flying low over the eastern zone in a helicopter of the Chinese air force, Kai looked down at a landscape lit by winter sunshine. He had the impression of a country operating normally. There were workers in the fields and trucks on the roads.

It was not like China, of course: traffic in towns was

not gridlocked, there was less of the pink haze of pollution, and the apartment towers that sprouted like weeds on the outskirts of Chinese towns were rare here. North Korea was poorer and less crowded.

He saw no signs of war: no collapsed buildings or burned fields or torn-up railway tracks. The initial rebellion had involved skirmishing around the military bases, and then the new rulers of this zone had stayed out of the international conflict. The people probably loved them for that alone. Were these ultras smart? Or just lucky? He would know soon.

There was also no visible sign of the American attack. As promised, they were targeting the west of the country, the territory still ruled by the supreme leader. Perhaps missiles were flying above Kai's head, but if so they were too high and too fast for him to see.

The machinery of government was working well in the rebel zone. Kai's pilot had contacted Korean air traffic control in the usual way and obtained clearance.

Earlier today the rebel leader Pak Jae-jin had replied immediately to Kai's message. He seemed keen to talk. He had agreed to the meeting, given the exact coordinates of the military base, and fixed the time of the appointment for half past three in the afternoon.

While in transit at Yanji military airport, Kai had received a panicky call from General Ham, his spy in Pak Jae-jin's camp. "What are you doing?" Ham had said.

"We have to end the war."

"Are you planning a deal with the ultras?"

"It's an exploratory conversation."

"These people are fanatics. Their nationalism is like a religion."

"They seem to have won a lot of support."

"Their supporters mainly think anyone would be better than the supreme leader."

Kai had paused to think. Ham did not usually

exaggerate. If he was worried, there had to be a reason. Kai said: "Given that I have to meet these people, how should I deal with them?"

Ham's answer was immediate. "Don't trust them."

"Got it."

"I will be at your meeting."

"Why?"

"To translate. There aren't many Mandarin speakers here. Most of the ultras regard your language as a symbol of foreign oppression."

"Okay."

"Just be very careful not to give any sign that you've met me before."

"Of course."

They had hung up.

From the China-Korea border, Kai's chopper was shadowed all the way by a Russian-made helicopter gunship, a model nicknamed the Crocodile for its menacing snout. It had a camouflage paint job but bore the roundel of the Korean People's Army Air and Anti-Air Force, a red five-pointed star inside a double circle in red and blue. The Korean aircraft kept at a safe distance and made no threatening maneuvers.

Kai spent the time worrying over what he was going to say to General Pak. There were a hundred ways to phrase *Can we make a deal?* But which was the best for this occasion? Kai did not generally lack self-confidence—rather the reverse—but this meeting was exceptional. Never in his life had so much depended on his personal success or failure.

Each time he glimpsed the Crocodile he was reminded that he was taking a personal risk too. The rebels might decide to arrest him and put him in a cell and interrogate him. They could say he was a spy. He *was* a spy. But there was no point worrying about that now. He was committed.

Only he knew that he was ready to go beyond the simple finding of facts. He intended to negotiate with the rebels. He had no mandate, but they did not know that. And if he could strike a reasonable deal, he felt sure he could persuade President Chen to endorse it.

It was a risky strategy. But this was an emergency.

The helicopter approached Yeongjeo-dong along a narrow river in a wooded valley. Kai began to see evidence of the battle for control of the base four weeks ago: an aircraft crashed in a stream, a wrecked cottage, a burned stretch of forest. He heard his pilot talking to ground control.

As he descended toward the base, he saw that the ultras had put on a display for his benefit. Six intercontinental ballistic missiles, each more than seventy feet long, were perfectly lined up on their eleven-axle transporter-erector launch vehicles. Kai knew that they had a range of seven thousand miles—the distance from here to Washington, DC. Each was armed with multiple nuclear warheads. The rebels were showing Kai their trump card.

Kai's aircraft was directed to a helipad.

The small welcoming party was heavily armed, but the men relaxed when Kai got out empty-handed, wearing a suit and tie with an overcoat unbuttoned, evidently unarmed. All the same he was thoroughly patted down before being escorted to a two-story building that was undoubtedly headquarters. He noticed bullet holes in the brickwork.

He was shown into the commanding officer's suite, a comfortless space with cheap furniture and a linoleum floor. Badly ventilated and poorly heated, it managed to be both cold and stuffy. Waiting to greet Kai were three men in the uniform of North Korean generals, complete with the oversize cap that always struck Kai as comical. A fourth general stood to one side, and Kai recognized Ham.

The middle one of the three stepped forward, introduced himself as Pak Jae-jin, and named the others, then led the group into an inner office.

Pak took off his hat and sat behind a utilitarian desk with nothing on it but a phone. He waved Kai to a seat facing the desk. Ham took a chair in the corner and the other two stood behind the desk either side of Pak, framing him in authority. The rebel leader was a short, thin man of about forty with receding hair cut short, and he put Kai in mind of pictures of Napoleon in middle age.

Kai assumed Pak must be brave and smart, to have risen to the rank of general at a relatively young age. He guessed Pak would also be proud and touchy, sensitive to any suggestion that he was an upstart. The best approach would be to be as honest as possible while mildly flattering him.

Pak spoke in Korean, Kai in Mandarin, and Ham translated both ways.

Pak said: "Tell me why you're here."

"You're a soldier, you like to get straight to the point, so I'll do the same," said Kai. "I'll tell you the plain truth. The overwhelming priority of the Chinese government is that North Korea should not fall under American control."

Pak looked indignant. "It should not fall under anyone's control, except that of the Korean people."

"We agree," said Kai immediately, though it was not quite true. Beijing would prefer some kind of joint Chinese-Korean rule, at least for a time. But that detail could be left until later. He went on: "So the question is, how can we make that happen?"

Pak's expression became disparaging. "It will happen

without Chinese help," he said. "The regime in Pyongyang is on the point of collapse."

"Agreed, again. I'm glad we're seeing the same picture. This is a hopeful sign."

Pak waited in silence.

Kai said: "That brings us to the question of what will replace the government of the supreme leader."

"There is no question. It will be the Pak government."

No false modesty here, then, Kai thought. But this was a front. If Pak had really believed he had no need of Chinese help, then he would not have agreed to this meeting. Kai looked him in the eye and said simply: "Perhaps." Then he waited for the reaction.

There was a pause. Pak looked angry at first and seemed about to protest. Then his face changed and he hid his ire. "Perhaps?" he said. "What other possibility is there?"

Now we're making progress, Kai thought. "There are several, most of them unwelcome," he said. "The final victor here could be South Korea, or the US, or China, but that doesn't exhaust the field." He leaned forward and spoke intensely. "If you are to have your wish, and North Korea is to be ruled by North Koreans, you need to make an ally of at least one of the other contenders."

"Why would I need allies?" Kai noticed the use of "I," assuming Ham was translating exactly. As Pak saw things, he himself was the rebellion. "I am winning," he said, confirming Kai's thought.

"Indeed you are," said Kai with an admiring tone. "But so far you have fought only the Pyongyang regime, which is the weakest of the forces involved in this conflict. You will finish them off with only a little further effort: today's air assault must have damaged them fatally. But you may find yourself in difficulty when you come into conflict with South Korea or the US."

Pak looked offended, but Kai felt sure the man saw that the logic was undeniable. Stern-faced, Pak said: "You have come here with a proposal?"

Kai had no authority to make proposals, but he did not admit that. "There could be a way for you to take control of North Korea and at the same time give yourself an impregnable defense against future interference from South Korea or the US."

"And that is . . . ?"

Kai paused, choosing his words carefully. This was the crucial moment of the conversation. It was also the point at which he exceeded his orders. He was now sticking his neck all the way out.

He said: "One: attack Pyongyang immediately with all your forces except nuclear, and take over the government."

Pak showed no reaction: this had always been part of his plan.

"Two: be recognized immediately by Beijing as president of North Korea."

Pak's eyes lit up. He was imagining himself as the acknowledged president of his country. He had long dreamed of this, no doubt, but now Kai was offering it to him tomorrow, guaranteed by the might of China.

"And three: declare an unconditional unilateral cease-fire in the war between North and South Korea."

Pak frowned. "Unilateral?"

"That's the price," Kai said firmly. "Beijing will recognize you and *at the same time* you will declare the cease-fire. No delay, no preconditions, no negotiations."

He expected resistance, but Pak had something else on his mind. "I'll need President Chen to make a personal visit to me," he said.

Kai could see why that was so important to Pak. He was vain, of course, but politically shrewd too: the pictures of the two men shaking hands would legitimize him in a way nothing else could. "Agreed," said Kai, though he did not have the authority to agree to anything.

"Good."

Kai began to think he might have achieved what he had hoped for. He told himself it was not yet time to rejoice. He could yet be thrown into a cell. He decided to get out of there while he was winning. "There's no time for formal written agreements," he said. "We're going to have to trust one another." As he spoke, General Ham's words came back to him: *Don't trust them.* But Kai had no choice. He had to gamble on Pak.

Pak reached across the desk and said: "Then let us shake hands."

Kai stood up and shook his hand.

Pak said: "Thank you for coming to see me."

This was dismissal, Kai realized. Pak was already behaving like a president.

Ham stood up and said: "I'll take you to your helicopter." He led Kai outside.

The weather was still cold but sunny, with little wind and no clouds, perfect flying conditions. Kai and Ham walked a yard apart as they crossed the base to the helipad. Speaking out of the corner of his mouth, Kai said: "I think I did it. He agreed to the proposal."

"Let's hope he keeps his word."

"Call me tonight if you can, to confirm that the attack on Pyongyang is going ahead."

"I'll do my best. You need the details of secure contacts with Pak, and he needs the same from you." Ham wrote a series of numbers and addresses on a pad, Kai did the same, and they exchanged.

Ham saluted crisply as Kai climbed into the helicopter.

The rotors began to turn as he was fastening his seat harness. A few minutes later the aircraft lifted, tilted, and veered north.

Kai allowed himself a moment of sheer triumph. If this worked out, the crisis would be over by tomorrow morning. There would be peace between North and South Korea, the Americans would be satisfied, and China would still have the crucial buffer in place.

Now he needed to make sure President Chen agreed.

He would have liked to call Beijing right away, but his phone did not work here and anyway it would be insecure in this country. He would have to wait until he got to Yanji and call from there before boarding his plane to Beijing. He would speak to Chen, but he would slant his report to hide the way he had overstepped his authority.

The biggest danger was that the old guard would talk Chen out of it. Huang was still horrified by the idea of making peace with those who had rebelled against a Communist regime. But surely the price of continuing the war was too high?

Night was falling over the rush-hour traffic of Yanji as the helicopter came down at the military air base next to the civilian airport. Kai was met by a captain who took him to a secure phone.

He called Zhongnanhai and reached President Chen. He began by saying: "Mr. President, the rebel ultras plan to launch their final attack on Pyongyang tonight." He spoke as if this were intelligence he had gathered, rather than a proposal he had made.

Chen was startled. "We haven't heard a whisper about this before now."

"The decision has been made in the last few hours.

But it's the right strategy for the ultras. Today's American air attack must have almost wiped out any capacity Pyongyang has left to resist. There will never be a better moment for them to make their bid for power."

"I think this is a good development," Chen said thoughtfully. "Heaven knows we need to get rid of Kang."

"Pak made me an offer," Kai said, reversing the true roles. "If we recognize him as president, he undertakes to call a unilateral cease-fire."

"That's promising. The fighting would stop. The new regime will begin by making an accord with us, which is a good start to our relationship. I'll have to talk General Huang around, but whole thing looks advantageous to us. Well done."

"Thank you, sir."

The president hung up. Everything is going according to plan, Kai thought.

He dialed his office and spoke to Jin Chin-hwa. "The ultras will attack Pyongyang tonight," he said. "I've told the president, but you need to inform everyone else."

"Right away."

"Any news at your end?"

"The American bombardment seems to have stopped, at least for today."

"I doubt they'll continue tomorrow. There can't be much left to bomb."

"A few missiles still tucked away, I suspect."

"With any luck this will end tomorrow." Kai hung up and boarded his plane. His personal phone rang as the pilot was starting the engines. It was General Ham. "It's happening," he said, sounding surprised. "Helicopter gunships are even now headed for the capital. Arrest squads are on their way to every presidential residence.

Tanks and armored vehicles are following behind the choppers. They're throwing everything at it. This is make or break."

This was dangerously specific over the phone. Ham used a different phone every time and threw each one away after use. Still it was not quite impossible that surveillance by Pyongyang or by Pak's intelligence service might randomly pick up a call. They would realize what was going on, but they would not be able to identify the speakers, at least not immediately. It was a risk, a small but deadly risk. The life of a spy was dangerous.

Ham continued: "The general is worried that Beijing may have set a trap for him. He thinks all Chinese people are malicious and deceitful. But this is his big chance and he had to take it."

"Are you going to the capital?"

"Yes."

"Stay in touch."

"Of course."

They hung up.

The air force jet did not have wi-fi for passengers, so Kai could not use his phone on the flight. That was something of a relief, he felt as he sat back in his seat. He had done all he could for one day, he had achieved what he had hoped for, and he was tired. He looked forward to spending the night in bed with Ting.

He closed his eyes.

CHAPTER 39

Kai was awakened by his phone as the plane came down over Beijing. He rubbed his eyes and took the call.

It was Jin Chin-hwa, who said: "North Korea has bombed Japan!"

For a moment Kai was completely bewildered. He even thought he might be dreaming. He said: "Who has? The rebels?"

"No, the supreme leader."

"Japan? Why the fuck would he attack Japan?"

"He hit three American bases."

Suddenly Kai understood. This was retaliation. The missiles and bombers that had attacked North Korea today had come from American bases in Japan. As he felt his plane's wheels hit the runway he said: "So the supreme leader did have some ballistic missiles left."

"He must have used the last six. Three were intercepted and three got through. There are three US air bases in Japan, and each one was hit: Kadena in Okinawa, Misawa on the mainland, and—worst of all—Yokota, which is actually in Tokyo, so there will be a lot of Japanese casualties."

"This is a catastrophe."

"President Chen is meeting with colleagues in the Situation Room. They're expecting you."

"Okay. Call me with updates."

"Of course."

Kai got off the plane and was led to his car. As it pulled away Monk said: "Home, sir?"

"No," said Kai. "Take me to Zhongnanhai."

The rush hour was over and traffic was moving freely through the city. It was night, but Beijing had three hundred thousand streetlights, Kai recalled.

Japan was a powerful enemy, but the worst of this news, he reflected, was that Japan had a long-standing military treaty with the US, according to which the US had to intervene when Japan was attacked. So the question was not merely how Japan would respond to the bombing but what the Americans would do now.

And how would this affect the deal Kai had just done in Yeongjeo-dong?

He called Neil Davidson.

"This is Neil."

"This is Kai."

"It's a shit storm, Kai."

"Something you need to know," Kai said, taking the plunge. "The regime of the supreme leader in North Korea will have ended by this time tomorrow."

"What . . . what makes you say that?"

"We're installing a new regime." This was aspiration reported as achievement. "Don't ask me for details, please."

"I'm glad you let me know."

"I presume your president Green will be talking to Prime Minister Ishikawa about how Washington and Tokyo are going to respond to the bombing of US bases in Japan."

"Indeed."

"So now you can tell them they can leave it to China to eliminate the regime that launched those missiles."

Kai did not expect Neil to consent to that. As he foresaw, the response was noncommittal. "Good to know," the Texan said.

"Just give us twenty-four hours. That's all I ask."

Neil continued to be carefully neutral. "I'll pass that on."

Kai could do no more. "Thanks," he said, and hung up.

He felt bothered by that conversation. It was not Neil's studied neutrality, which was to be expected, but something else that made him uneasy. However, he could not immediately put his finger on it.

He phoned home. Ting answered, sounding worried. "You normally call me when you're going to be this late."

"I'm sorry," Kai said. "I was in a place where I had no phone connectivity. Is everything all right?"

"Except for dinner, yes."

Kai sighed. "It's good to hear your voice. And to know that someone worries about me when I don't show up. It makes me feel loved."

"You are loved, you know that."

"I like to be reminded."

"Now you've made me wet. When will you be here?"

"I'm not sure. Have you heard the news?"

"What news? I've been learning lines."

"Turn on the TV."

"Just a minute." There was a pause, then she said: "Oh, my God! North Korea bombed Japan!"

"Now you know why I'm working late."

"Of course, of course. But when you've finished saving China, I'll be keeping the bed warm."

"The greatest reward."

They said good-bye and hung up.

Kai's car reached Zhongnanhai, went through security, and parked at Qinzheng Hall. Kai pulled his overcoat closer around him as he walked to the entrance. Beijing was colder than Yeongjeo-dong today.

He went through building security, then ran down the stairs to the basement Situation Room. As before, the large space around the stage was occupied by desks with workstations. The place was more heavily staffed than last time, now on a full war footing. It was hushed, but there was a faint background sound like the murmur of distant traffic. It was not possible that traffic noise could penetrate here, and Kai decided he must be hearing the ventilation system. The air smelled faintly of disinfectant, like a hospital, and Kai guessed that it was rigorously purified, for the room was designed to operate when the city above was infected or poisoned or even radioactive.

Everyone was listening in dead silence to both sides of a phone conversation. One voice belonged to President Chen. Another was speaking a language Kai identified as Japanese, and a third was an interpreter, who said: "I am glad to have this opportunity to talk to the president of the People's Republic of China." It sounded insincere even at second hand.

Chen said: "Mr. Prime Minister, I assure you that the missile attack against Japanese territory perpetrated by the Pyongyang government was carried out without the consent or approval of the government of China."

Clearly Chen was talking to Eiko Ishikawa, the prime minister of Japan. Chen, like Kai, was hoping to forestall an extreme Japanese reaction to the missile attack. China was still trying to prevent war. Good.

While Chen's statement was being translated into Japanese, Kai tiptoed to the stage, bowed to the president, and sat at the table.

A reply came back from Tokyo: "I am most relieved to hear that."

Chen made the key point quickly. "If you wait a few hours you will realize that this assault, grievous though it is, does not merit any reprisal by you."

"What makes you say that?"

Something about that sentence rang a bell with Kai, but he postponed thinking about it and concentrated on listening.

Chen said: "The regime of the supreme leader will come to an end within the next twenty-four hours."

"What will take its place?"

"Will you forgive me if I don't go into all the details? I only want to assure you that the persons responsible for what has happened in Japan today will be removed from power immediately and brought to justice."

"I understand."

The conversation went on in the same vein, Chen being reassuring and Ishikawa being noncommittal, until they hung up.

Kai thought again about the sentence *What makes you say that?* Neil had used the same words. It was evasive, a way of not responding, a sign that the speaker was being guarded, usually because he had something to hide. Both Neil and Ishikawa had expressed little surprise on learning that the Pyongyang regime was about to be overthrown. It was almost as if they already knew that Pyongyang was doomed. But how was that possible? Pak himself had not made his decision until a few hours ago.

Both the CIA and the government of Japan knew something that Kai did not know. That was very bad for an intelligence chief. What could it be?

A possibility occurred to Kai, one that was so surprising that he could hardly formulate it.

General Huang was speaking but Kai was not

listening. He stood up and moved away—an act of dis-
courtesy to Huang that caused eyebrows to be raised
around the table—and stepped down from the stage.
He called his office and spoke to Jin. "Look at the latest
satellite pictures over North Korea," he said, speaking
in a low voice as he walked away from the stage. "The
skies should be clear, they were a few hours ago when
I was there. I want to see from Pyongyang south across
the border to Seoul just on the other side. What I'm
really interested in is what lies between the two cities,
the road they call the Reunification Highway. When
you've got a good picture, put it up on a screen here in
the Situation Room. Make sure it's aligned with north
at the top."

"You got it."

Kai returned to the big table on the stage. Huang
was still speaking. Kai watched the screens. After a
couple of minutes, one of them showed a nighttime picture. The black was relieved by two clusters of lights,
one in the south and one in the north, Korea's two cap-
itals. Between the two was darkness.

Mostly.

Looking more carefully, Kai saw four narrow streaks
of light, far too long to be any kind of natural phenomenon. They had to be caused by lines of traffic. He
calculated that each stretched for twenty to thirty
miles. That meant hundreds of vehicles.

Thousands.

There it was, the explanation of why Neil and Ishikawa
had not been surprised. They had not somehow found
out about Pak's intention to attack Pyongyang, but they
had known that another force was intending to destroy
the regime tonight.

Others around the table followed Kai's gaze, one by
one losing interest in Huang's speech. Even the president looked.

At last Huang dried up.

Chen said: "What am I looking at?"

"North Korea," said Kai. "The streaks of light are convoys, four of them. Those vehicles are heading for Pyongyang."

Defense Minister Kong Zhao said: "Based on just this photograph, I'd say there are two divisions, each moving in two columns, for a total of about twenty-five thousand troops and several thousand vehicles. The Demilitarized Zone between North and South Korea is a minefield two to three kilometers in depth, but they're past that, so they must have swept broad channels through that barrier—an operation planned long ago, I feel sure. At the same time, I'd guess there are airborne forces dropping right now to seize bridgeheads and choke points in advance of the main army, plus beach landings on the coast; we can try to confirm that."

Chen said: "You haven't said whose troops these are."

"I assume they're South Korean."

Chen said: "So it's an invasion."

"Yes, Mr. President," said Kong. "It's an invasion."

Kai finally slid into bed beside Ting a little after one o'clock in the morning. She rolled over and put her arms around him and kissed him passionately, then immediately went back to sleep.

He closed his eyes and ran over the last few hours. There had been a furious argument in the Situation Room over how they should respond to the South Korean invasion. Kai's negotiations with Pak had instantly become an irrelevance. A cease-fire was now out of the question.

China's defense treaty with North Korea left several options open. Kai's father, Chang Jianjun, and General

Huang had proposed a Chinese invasion to protect North Korea from the south. Cooler heads had pointed out that once Chinese troops were there, American troops would swiftly follow, and the Chinese and American armies would meet in battle. To Kai's great relief this danger was recognized, by the majority around the table, as a price too high to pay.

The supreme leader was fatally weakened but Pak and his rebels were strong and were already in the field. With the agreement of the group, Huang personally phoned Pak, told him everything that was known about the invasion, and encouraged him to bomb the approaching South Korean convoys. Radar showed that Pak did so immediately, while continuing his attack on Pyongyang.

The rebels had used few of their missiles so far, and they had plenty; the convoys were halted.

That was a good first step.

Chinese troops would not get involved but, starting at dawn, China was going to give the ultras everything else: missiles, drones, helicopters, jet fighters, artillery, rifles, and unlimited ammunition. The ultras already controlled half the country and could probably take over more in the next few hours. However, the key clash would be the battle for Pyongyang.

This seemed the least bad outcome. If the Japanese were reasonable, the war would remain confined to Korea.

President Chen had retired to bed, and most of the others had done the same, leaving behind only those who needed to work out the logistics of sending massive quantities of armaments across the border into North Korea in a short time.

Kai went to sleep feeling that the Chinese government might have done a lot worse.

As soon as he woke up he called the Guoanbu and

spoke to overnight manager Fan Yimu, who told him
the good news that the rebels had arrested the supreme
leader, and General Pak had set up his headquarters in
the symbolic Presidential Residence in the north of
Pyongyang. However, the South Korean army was a
harder nut to crack, and they had resumed their advance on the capital.

The morning news on Chinese television announced
that Supreme Leader Kang had resigned due to ill
health and had been replaced by General Pak. The
Chinese president had sent Pak a message of support
reaffirming China's commitment to their mutual defense treaty. An incursion by South Korean forces was
being energetically repelled by the brave People's Army
of North Korea.

All that was as Kai expected, but the second lead
story worried him. It showed angry Japanese nationalists massing in the Tokyo dawn to protest against the
bombing. The news reports noted that among Japanese
people there was already a certain amount of dislike of
Koreans, eagerly fanned by racist propagandists, and
only partly countered by the love Japanese youngsters
had for Korean movies and pop music. An ethnic
Korean teacher had been beaten up by a thug outside
a school in Kyoto. The chairman of an extreme right-
wing political group was interviewed and, in a hoarse
and excited voice, called for all-out war against North
Korea.

Prime Minister Ishikawa had ordered a nine o'clock
meeting of his cabinet. The protests would put pressure
on the Japanese government to take drastic action, but
President Green would be doing her best to restrain
Japan. Kai hoped Ishikawa could keep a lid on it.

In the car on the way to the Guoanbu he read army
intelligence reports of the progress of the battle of
Pyongyang. It seemed the South Korean invaders had

moved quickly and were now besieging the capital. He hoped to learn more from General Ham.

In the office he turned on the TV and saw the Japanese prime minister beginning a press conference after his cabinet meeting. "The Pyongyang regime has committed an act of war against Japan, and I have no choice but to order the Japanese Self-Defense Force to prepare to take action to repel aggression by North Korea."

This was doublespeak, of course. Article 9 of the Japanese constitution forbade the government to go to war. However, it could exercise its right to self-defense. Anything the Japanese military did had to be framed as defense.

But the announcement was enigmatic for a different reason. Against whom were they now defending themselves? Two rival armies were contending for North Korea, and neither of them was responsible for yesterday's bombing. The regime that had done that no longer existed.

The head of the Japan desk told Kai what Chinese spies in Tokyo were saying. Japanese and American military bases were bustling with activity but did not seem to be going to war. Japanese jets were conducting surveillance but no bombers were taking off. No destroyers had left harbor and no launchers were being loaded with missiles. Satellite photographs confirmed what the spies said. All was calm.

General Ham called from Pyongyang. "The ultras are losing," he said.

Kai had feared as much. "Why?"

"The South Koreans are too numerous and too well armed. Our supplies from China haven't all arrived yet and our tanks are still on their way here from bases in the east. We're running out of time."

"What will Pak do?"

"Ask Beijing for troops."

"We'll say no. We don't want to bring the Americans in."

"Then we'll lose Pyongyang to the South Koreans."

That too was unthinkable.

Suddenly Ham said: "Got to go," and disconnected.

It must have been humiliating for Pak to beg Beijing for help, Kai thought. But what else could the rebel leader do? Kai's thoughts were interrupted when he was called to the conference room. The Japanese government had acted.

Twelve jet fighters had taken off from Naha base in Okinawa heading west and, minutes later, had begun to patrol the East China Sea between Okinawa and China. Their sweeps were concentrated around a small group of uninhabited islands and rocks called the Diaoyu Islands. These were six hundred miles from Japan but only two hundred miles from China, yet the Japanese claimed sovereignty and called them the Senkaku Islands.

Chinese jets were also in the sky over the East China Sea, and Kai monitored their video feed. He saw the islands, sticking up out of the water as if scattered there carelessly by the ancient gods. As soon as the Japanese planes were in place, two Soryu-class attack submarines surfaced near the islands.

Were the Japanese really choosing this moment to make a point about a bunch of worthless rocks in the sea?

Kai watched as sailors from the Japanese submarines boarded inflatable dinghies and landed on a narrow beach, where they unloaded what might have been handheld surface-to-air missile launchers. They made their way to one of the few patches of level ground and planted a Japanese flag.

Over the next few minutes they began to erect tents and assemble a field kitchen.

The head of the Japan desk called from the floor below to tell Kai that the Japanese military had announced that "as a precaution" they had set up a forward base on the Senkaku Islands—which, they emphasized, were part of Japan.

A minute later Kai was summoned to Zhongnanhai.

On the way in the car he continued to read the reports and study the video footage. At the same time he had one eye on the radar tracks, which he could watch on his phone. There was no fighting. Right now they were all shadowboxing.

In the Situation Room the atmosphere was somber. Kai took his place at the table quietly.

When everyone had arrived, Chen asked Chang Jianjun for an update. Kai noticed that his father was looking old: his hair was thin, his skin seemed loose and gray, and he had not shaved well. He was not yet seventy, but he had been smoking for half a century, as his yellow teeth witnessed. Kai hoped he was all right.

After summarizing the current situation, Jianjun said: "The last two months have seen an escalating series of attacks on China. First of all, the US tightened sanctions on North Korea, leading to the economic crisis and the rebellion of the ultras. Then more than one hundred of our citizens were slaughtered by an American drone in Port Sudan. Next, we caught American geologists—ineffectively concealed aboard a Vietnamese ship—prospecting for oil within our maritime territory. Finally, our close ally North Korea was attacked by South Korean missiles; attacked again by American planes, ships, and missiles; and then invaded last night. And today the Diaoyu Islands—Chinese territory by any fair-minded judgment—have been invaded and occupied by Japanese soldiers."

It was a formidable list, undeniably, and Kai himself felt for a moment that perhaps he had failed to note the pattern.

"And in all that time," Jianjun said with slow emphasis, "what has China done? With the sole exception of the sinking of the *Vu Trong Phung*, we have not fired a single weapon. I put it to you, comrades, that we have encouraged this mounting aggression by our feeble retaliation."

Defense Minister Kong Zhao replied. "You don't kill a man for stealing your bicycle," he began. "Yes, we must respond to this outrageous Japanese invasion—but our response must be proportionate. US officials have repeatedly confirmed that the Diaoyu Islands are covered by the US-Japan military treaty, so that the Americans are obliged to defend the islands. And let's be honest: the occupation presents no threat to us. There is nothing that Japanese soldiers can do there that they could not do better aboard their submarines—except plant a flag. Flags are symbolic, of course—that is their only purpose—and the Japanese action is symbolic, no more. Our response must be calibrated appropriately."

I couldn't have put it better myself, thought Kai. Kong had turned the mood of the meeting right around.

At that point General Huang said: "We have video of the occupied islands, taken by a Chinese drone. It's a couple of minutes. Do comrades wish to see it?"

They did, of course.

Huang spoke to an aide and pointed to a screen.

They saw a small island: just a rocky peak, a patch of level ground covered with sparse shrubbery and coarse grass, and a narrow beach. Two submarines floated in the bay, each displaying the red-and-white sunburst of the Japanese naval ensign. There were about thirty men on the island, mostly young and cheerful looking. A closer shot showed them chatting and smiling as they erected tents. One of them waved at the aircraft that was filming them. Another jabbed a pointing finger at it—a gesture of contempt and antagonism that was highly offensive in Japan and China—and the rest laughed. The film ended.

There were angry mutters around the table. The behavior of the troops was insulting. The normally urbane foreign minister Wu Bai said: "Those young fools are mocking us."

President Chen said: "What do you think we should do, Wu Bai?"

Wu clearly felt offended by the video, and he spoke with uncharacteristic rancor. "Comrade Chang Jianjun pointed out that we have borne a series of humiliations for the sake of peace." The word *humiliation* was loaded: it brought back thoughts of the country's years under the heel of Western colonialism and never failed to raise hackles. "We have to take a stand sometime, somewhere, and in my view this is the time and place. It is the first occasion on which Chinese territory has been invaded." He paused and drew breath. "Comrades, we should make it clear to our enemies that this is where we draw the line."

President Chen surprised Kai by supporting Wu immediately. "I agree," he said. "My basic duty is to protect the territorial integrity of the country. If I fail at that, I fail as a president."

It was a strong statement—and all because a few high-spirited lads had shown disrespect! Kai was dismayed, but he said nothing. He could not possibly prevail against the hard-liners when they were backed by the president and the foreign minister. He had learned long ago to fight only those battles that he could win.

Chen then backtracked slightly. "All the same, our reaction should be measured."

That was a spark of hope.

Chen went on: "One bomb will destroy the little camp the Japanese have built, and probably kill most of the sailors there too. Admiral Liu, what ships do we have in the neighborhood?"

Liu was already consulting his laptop, and he replied immediately. "The aircraft carrier *Fujian* is fifty miles away. The ship has forty-four aircraft, including thirty-two Flying Shark fighter jets. The Flying Shark carries four laser-guided bombs, each of a thousand pounds. I suggest we send two planes, one to drop the bomb and one to film the attack."

"Give the ship the exact target coordinates and tell them to prepare to launch, please, Admiral."

"Yes, sir."

Kai spoke up at last, but he did not argue directly against the bombing. Instead he said: "We should consider the likely American reaction to this. We don't want to be taken by surprise."

Kong Zhao backed him immediately. "The Americans will not stand aside and do nothing. That would make their defense treaty with Japan look meaningless. They have to do something."

Wu Bai adjusted the display handkerchief in his breast pocket and said: "President Green will avoid aggressive action if she possibly can. She was weak about the GIs killed with Norinco rifles in Chad, weak about the American geologists who went down with the *Vu Trong Phung,* and at first weak about the deaths of Americans in South Korea, until our comrades in Pyongyang were so foolish as to use chemical weapons. I don't think she'll go to war over a few Japanese sailors.

There will be some token retaliation, even perhaps a purely diplomatic response."

Wishful thinking, thought Kai, but there was no point in saying it.

Admiral Liu said: "Mr. President, jets are ready."

Chen said: "Order them to take off."

Liu spoke into his phone. "Go," he said. "I say again, go."

The second jet was filming the first, and one of the screens in the Situation Room had a clear picture. Kai saw the rear of the first Flying Shark, with its distinctive upright fins and twin exhausts. A moment later it sped along the deck, swooped up the curved ski-jump take-off ramp at the front of the aircraft carrier, then climbed fast into the sky. The camera followed, and for a moment Kai felt a touch of nausea as it gathered speed and shot off the end of the ramp.

As the two jets accelerated someone said: "How the fuck fast do they go?"

Admiral Liu said: "Top speed is around one thousand five hundred miles per hour." After a pause he added: "They won't reach anywhere near that on this short journey."

The jets climbed until they were too high to see ships, and attention turned back to the video footage from the drone. The picture showed the Japanese sailors in their camp. The tents now stood in a neat row and some of the men appeared to be making lunch. Others were on the tiny beach, horsing around, splashing and throwing sand. One of their number was filming them on a smartphone.

Their blissful ignorance lasted only a few seconds more.

Some of them looked up, perhaps having heard the jets. The aircraft must have seemed too far away to be a threat, and their markings could not possibly be visible from the ground, so the sailors at first just stood there staring.

The first jet banked and turned, followed by the camera in the second plane, and then started its bombing run.

Perhaps the sailors got some kind of warning from their submarine, for suddenly they grabbed automatic rifles and shoulder-mounted missile launchers and quickly took up defensive positions in what looked like a prearranged pattern around the tiny island. Their launchers, the size and shape of sixteenth-century muskets, were probably a Japanese version of the American FIM-92 that fired a Stinger antiaircraft missile.

Admiral Liu said: "The jets are at about thirty thousand feet and flying at five hundred feet per second. Those handheld weapons pose no threat."

For a moment all was still. The sailors on the island held position, and the first jet remained steady in the camera lens of the second. Admiral Liu said: "Bombs away," and Kai thought he detected a flicker that might have been the release of a missile.

Then the little island exploded in flame and smoke. Sand and rocks were flung into the air, emerging from the smoke and falling into the sea, along with pale objects that looked horribly like body parts. A cheer went up from the military men in the Situation Room.

Kai did not join in.

Slowly the debris settled, the smoke cleared, and the surface of the water returned to normal.

No one was left alive.

The Situation Room was quiet.

It was Kai who broke the silence. "And so, comrades," he said, "we find ourselves at war against Japan."

DEFCON 1

NUCLEAR WAR IS IMMINENT OR
HAS BEGUN.

CHAPTER 40

Pauline was not sleeping when Gus called. It was unusual for her to lie awake at night. No previous crisis had stopped her from falling asleep. When the phone rang she did not need to look at the bedside clock, for she already knew the time: twelve thirty a.m.

She picked up and Gus said: "The Chinese bombed the Senkaku Islands. Killed a bunch of Japanese sailors."

"Fuck," she said.

"The key people are in the Situation Room."

"I'll get dressed."

"I'll walk you there. I'm in the Residence, on your floor, in the kitchen by the elevator."

"Okay." She hung up and got out of bed. It was almost a relief to be doing something rather than lying there thinking. She would sleep later.

She put on a jean jacket over a dark blue T-shirt and brushed her hair. She walked the length of the Center Hall, entered the kitchen area, and found Gus where he had said he would be, waiting by the elevator. They got in and he pressed the button for the basement.

Pauline suddenly felt discouraged and tearful. She

said: "All I do is try to make the world a safer place, but it just gets worse!"

There was no security camera in the elevator. He put his arms around her, and she laid her cheek against his shoulder. They stayed like that until the elevator came to a stop, then they separated before the doors opened. A Secret Service agent was waiting outside.

Pauline's moment of discouragement passed quickly. When they reached the Situation Room she was her normal self. She took her seat, looked around, and said: "Chess. Where are we?"

"Up against the wall, Madam President. Our defense treaty with Japan is a cornerstone of stability in East Asia. We're obliged to defend Japan against attack, and two recent presidents have publicly confirmed that this commitment includes the Senkaku Islands. If we don't retaliate it makes our treaty with Japan meaningless. A lot hangs on what we do now."

Doesn't it always, she thought.

Bill Schneider, the chairman of the Joint Chiefs, said: "If I may, Madam President?"

"Go ahead, Bill."

"We need to make a serious dent in their ability to attack Japan. If we look at the east coast of China, that's to say the part nearest to Japan, their main naval bases are Qingdao and Ningbo. I suggest heavy missile assaults on each one, carefully targeted to minimize civilian casualties."

Chess was already shaking his head in disagreement.

Pauline said: "That would be a major escalation."

"It's what we did to the Pyongyang regime—we destroyed their ability to attack us."

"They deserved it. They'd used chemical weapons. The world was on our side because of that. This isn't the same."

"I see it as proportionate, Madam President."

"All the same, let's look for a less provocative option."

Chess said: "We could protect the Senkaku Islands with a ring of steel: destroyers, submarines, and jet fighters."

"Indefinitely?"

"The protection could be scaled down later, when the threat diminishes."

The secretary of defense, Luis Rivera, said: "The Chinese made a film of the bombing, Madam President. They released it to the world—they're proud of what they've done."

"Okay, let's take a look."

The film came up on a wall screen. There was a long shot of a tiny island, a closer shot of some Japanese sailors planting a flag, and then a Chinese jet taking off from an aircraft carrier. Interspersed with further shots of the jet were close-ups of a young sailor making a rude finger-pointing gesture and another of his comrades laughing.

Luis said: "That's the East Asian version of flipping the bird, Madam President."

"I guessed." The gesture would have infuriated the Chinese leadership, Pauline thought. Those men were nothing if not sensitive. She recalled the preparations for a meeting with President Chen at a G20 summit: his aides had demanded changes to a dozen minor details that they said would slight him, from the height of the chairs to the choice of fruit in the bowl on the side table.

In the film, the soldiers became alert and took up defensive positions, then the island seemed to explode. As the debris settled, a shot apparently taken from a drone zoomed in on the corpse of a young sailor lying on the sand, and a voice-over in Mandarin with English subtitles said: "Foreign armies that violate Chinese territory will all suffer a similar fate."

Pauline felt sickened by what she had seen and by the pride the Chinese evidently felt. "That's awful," she said.

Luis Rivera said: "That threat at the end suggests that one ring of steel would not be enough. There are other disputed islands. I'm not sure we could ring them all."

"Okay, but I'm still not going to overreact," Pauline said. "Give me something that's more than a ring of steel but less than a missile onslaught on mainland China."

Luis had an answer. "The jet that dropped the bomb came from a Chinese aircraft carrier called the *Fujian*. We have ship-killer missiles that could destroy it."

"That's true," said Bill Schneider. "Just one of our long-range antiship stealth cruise missiles can sink a ship, although we would fire a whole bunch of them to make sure of something as big as an aircraft carrier. The range is three hundred and fifty miles and we have plenty closer than that. They can be fired from ships and planes and we have both available."

Luis said: "If we do this, we should let it be known that we will respond the same way to any similar attacks. Madam President, China can't afford to see its aircraft carriers destroyed. We have eleven but they have only three, and if we sink the *Fujian* that will leave two. And they can't easily replace them. Aircraft carriers cost thirteen billion dollars each and take years to build. It's my judgment that sinking the *Fujian*, combined with the threat of sinking the other two, would have a massively sobering effect on the Chinese government."

Chess said: "Or it might drive them to desperate measures."

Pauline said: "Can we get the *Fujian* on camera?"

"Of course. We have planes and drones in the air nearby."

Within a minute the vast gray ship was on-screen, seen from above. Its shape was distinctive, with a curved ramp at the front end like a ski jump. Half a dozen jets and helicopters were on deck, clustered near the superstructure, with a few men busy around them, looking at this distance like ants feeding larvae. The rest of the enormous deck was all bare runway.

Pauline said: "How many crew aboard?"

Bill answered. "About two thousand five hundred, including flight staff."

Nearly all of them were belowdecks. The ship was like an office building, almost nobody visible from outside.

The blast would kill some, Pauline thought; a few might survive; most would drown.

She did not want to end 2,500 lives.

Luis said: "We would be killing the people who killed those Japanese sailors. The numbers aren't proportionate, but the principle is fair."

"The Chinese won't see it that way," said Pauline. "They'll retaliate."

"But they can't win that game, and they know it. Played to the end, there's only one possible result: China becomes a nuclear wasteland. China has about three hundred nuclear warheads; we have more than three thousand. Therefore at some point they'll negotiate. And if we do them serious damage now, they'll sue for peace sooner rather than later."

The meeting went quiet. This is how it is, she thought; all information is available, everyone has an opinion, but in the end one person makes the decision—and that's me.

It was the Chinese threat that made up her mind: *Foreign armies that violate Chinese territory will all suffer a similar fate.* They would do it again. That, combined with the treaty that obliged the US to defend Japan, meant that a token protest would not be enough. Her response had to hurt.

"Do it, Bill," she said.

"Yes, Madam President," Bill said, and he spoke into the phone.

A woman in kitchen whites came in carrying a tray. "Good morning, Madam President," she said. "I thought you might like some coffee." She set the tray down next to Pauline.

Pauline said: "It's very good of you to get up in the middle of the night, Merrilee. Thank you." She poured coffee into a cup and added a splash of milk.

"You're welcome," said Merrilee.

There were hundreds of people waiting to fulfill the president's slightest wish, but for some reason Pauline was moved by Merrilee's making her coffee in the middle of the night. "I appreciate it," she added.

"Please let me know if you need anything else." Merrilee left.

Pauline sipped coffee and looked again at the *Fujian* on the screen. It was a thousand feet long. Was she really going to sink it?

A longer shot showed that the carrier was accompanied by several support vessels. Pauline said: "Can any of those smaller ships deflect incoming missiles?"

Bill Schneider said: "They can try, ma'am, but they won't get them all."

There were some pastries on the tray. She picked one up and took a bite. There was nothing wrong with it, but she found she could barely swallow it. She drank coffee to wash it down and put the pastry back.

Bill said: "The cruise missiles are ready to launch,

Madam President. We're firing them from planes as well as ships."

"Go ahead," she said, with a heavy heart. "Fire."

A moment later Bill said: "The first salvo has been launched from the ship. They have fifty miles to go and should hit in six minutes. The plane is nearer and will launch in five minutes."

Pauline stared at the *Fujian*. Two thousand five hundred people, she thought. Not thugs or murderers, mostly just youngsters who chose to join the navy, a life on the ocean waves. They have parents, brothers and sisters, lovers, children. Two thousand five hundred families will be stricken with grief.

Pauline's father had been in the US Navy before he married her mother, she recalled. He had read all of *The Canterbury Tales* in Middle English, he said, knowing that he would never again have so much spare time.

A helicopter lifted off the deck of the *Fujian*. That pilot escaped death by minutes, Pauline thought. Luckiest person in the world.

There was a flurry of activity around what looked like a gun emplacement. Bill said: "That's a short-range surface-to-air missile launcher. It's loaded with eight Red Banner missiles, each six feet long, able to fly just above sea level. Its purpose is to intercept incoming fire."

"So a Red Banner is an anti-missile missile."

"Yes, and this activity tells us that the Chinese radar has seen our ship-killer missiles coming."

Someone said: "Three minutes."

The on-deck launcher swiveled, and a moment later a burst of smoke from its snout indicated that it had fired. Then a high-level shot showed the vapor trails of half a dozen or more incoming missiles approaching incredibly fast, on course to hit the *Fujian* side-on. The on-deck launcher fired again, rapidly, and one of the approaching missiles broke up in pieces that fell into the sea.

Then Pauline noticed another clutch of missiles approaching the *Fujian* from the opposite direction. These had come from the plane, she assumed.

Some of the smaller ships escorting the *Fujian* were now firing, but there were only a few seconds left to impact.

On deck, sailors raced to reload Red Banners, but they could not move fast enough.

The impacts were almost simultaneous. The hits were concentrated amidships. There was a huge explosion. Pauline gasped as the deck of the *Fujian* seemed to lift and snap in the middle, sending all the aircraft sliding into the sea. Flame erupted from within and smoke poured out. Then the two halves of the thousand-foot deck collapsed slowly downward. Pauline watched in horror as the giant ship broke into two halves. Both halves upended, the central parts sinking while the bow and stern rose into the air. She thought she saw human figures, tiny at this distance, flying through the air and into the water, and she whispered: "Oh, no!" She felt Gus's hand touch her arm, squeeze gently, then withdraw.

Minutes passed as the wreckage slowly filled with water and descended deeper. The stern went under first, leaving a brief crater in the sea that immediately filled and spouted foam. The bow sank soon after, with a similar effect. Pauline stared at the surface as it returned to normal. In a while the sea was calm. A few motionless bodies floated amid bits of wreckage: timber, rubber, and plastic. The escort ships lowered boats, doubtless to pick up survivors. Pauline thought there would not be many.

It was almost as if the *Fujian* had never existed.

The men who led China were in shock.

They had little experience of war, Kai reflected. The last time the Chinese military had been involved in serious fighting had been 1979, during a brief and unsuccessful invasion of Vietnam. Most of the people in the room had never witnessed what they had just seen on video, thousands of people being killed deliberately and violently.

The anger and grief of the people in the room would be matched by ordinary citizens, Kai felt sure. The desire for revenge would be strong here and even greater on the streets, among the people whose taxes had paid for the aircraft carrier. The Chinese government had to retaliate. Even Kai thought that. They could not overlook the killing of so many Chinese people.

General Huang said: "At a minimum, we must sink one of their aircraft carriers in retaliation."

As usual Kong Zhao, the young defense minister, sounded the cautious note. "If we do that they will sink another of ours. One more round of that tit-for-tat and we will have none left, whereas the Americans will still have . . ." He thought for a moment. "Eight."

"Will you just let them get away with this?"

"No, but I think we might pause to reflect."

Kai's phone rang. He left the table and found a quiet corner of the room.

It was Ham. He said: "The South Koreans are taking over the city of Pyongyang. General Pak has left."

"Where has he gone?"

"To his original base at Yeongjeo-dong."

"Where the nuclear missiles are." Kai had seen them, the day he visited; six of them, lined up on their giant launch vehicles.

"There's a way you can stop him from using them."

"Tell me, quick."

"You won't like it."

"I bet."

"Get the US to make the South Korean army pull back from Pyongyang."

The suggestion was radical, but it made a kind of sense. For a moment Kai said nothing, thinking.

Ham added: "You have contacts with the Americans, don't you?"

"I'll call them, but they may not be able to do what you want."

"Tell them that if the South Koreans don't withdraw, Pak will use nuclear weapons."

"Would he?"

"It's possible."

"That would be suicide."

"This is his last shot. It's all he has left. He can't win any other way. And if he loses they'll kill him."

"You really think he might use nuclear weapons?"

"I can't see what's stopping him."

"I'll do what I can."

"Tell me something. Give me your opinion. What are the chances that I'm going to die in the next twenty-four hours?"

Kai felt he owed Ham an honest answer. "Fifty-fifty," he said.

"So I may never live in my new house," Ham said with quiet sadness.

Kai felt a tug of compassion. "It's not over yet," he said.

Ham hung up.

Before calling Neil, Kai returned to the stage. "General Pak has left Pyongyang," he said. "The South Koreans are now in possession of the capital."

President Chen said: "Where did Pak go?"

"To Yeongjeo-dong," said Kai. He paused, then added: "Where the nuclear missiles are."

Sophia Magliani, the director of national intelligence, had been speaking on the phone, and now she said: "Madam President, if I may."

"Please."

"You know we have a back channel in Beijing." A back channel was what they called an unofficial, informal means of communication between governments.

"I do, of course."

"We've just learned that the rebels have abandoned Pyongyang. South Korea has won."

"That's good news—isn't it?"

"Not necessarily. All General Pak can do now is deploy his nuclear weapons."

"Will he do that?"

"The Chinese believe he will—unless the South Koreans withdraw."

"Jesus."

"Will you talk to President No?"

"Of course." Pauline looked at Chief of Staff Jacqueline Brody. "Put a call in, please, Jacqueline."

"Yes, ma'am."

"But I don't hold out much hope," Pauline added.

President No Do-hui had achieved her lifetime ambition: she had reunited North and South Korea under one leader—herself. Would she give that up under threat of nuclear attack? Would Abraham Lincoln have given up the South after winning the Civil War? No, but Lincoln was not threatened by nuclear weapons.

The phone rang and Pauline picked up and said: "Hello, Madam President."

No's voice resonated with triumph. "Hello, Madam President."

"Congratulations on your splendid military victory."

"Which you tried to talk me out of."

In some ways it was a disadvantage that No spoke such good English. Her fluency enabled her to be more assertive.

Pauline said: "I fear that General Pak may be about to snatch that victory away from you."

"Let him try."

"The Chinese think he will use his nuclear weapons."

"That would be suicidal."

"He may do it all the same—unless you withdraw your troops."

"Withdraw?" she said incredulously. "I've won! The people are celebrating the long-awaited reunion of North and South Korea."

"The celebration is premature."

"If I order a retreat now, my presidency won't survive the day. The army will revolt and I'll be usurped in a military coup."

"What about a partial withdrawal? You could retreat to the outskirts of Pyongyang, declare it a neutral city, and invite Pak to a constitutional conference to discuss the future of North Korea." Pauline was not at all sure that Pak would accept that as a basis for peace, but it was worth a try.

However, No was not going to give it a chance. "My generals would see that as an unnecessary surrender. And they'd be right."

"So you're willing to risk nuclear annihilation."

"We all risk that every day, Madam President."

"Not like this, we don't."

"In the next few seconds I have to speak to my people on television. Thank you for your call, and please excuse me." She hung up.

Pauline was momentarily stunned. Not many people hung up on the president of the United States.

After a moment she said: "Can we get South Korean TV on our screens, please? Try YTN, it's the all-news cable channel."

A newsreader appeared, speaking Korean, and after a pause real-time subtitles were shown at the bottom of the screen. Somewhere in the White House, Pauline realized, there was an interpreter who could do simultaneous translation from Korean to English and type the result on a keyboard.

The picture changed to an unsteady shot of a bomb-damaged city filmed from a vehicle, and the subtitles said *South Korean forces have taken control of Pyongyang.* A hysterically excited reporter was sitting on a moving tank, holding a microphone and shouting to the camera. He was wearing a military helmet with a suit and tie. The subtitles dried up, perhaps because the interpreter could not make out what the reporter was saying, but commentary was superfluous anyway. Behind the reporter's head Pauline could see a long line of military vehicles on what was evidently a main road into the city. It was a triumphal entry into the enemy capital.

Pauline said: "Hell, I bet Pak is watching this and burning up inside."

The inhabitants of Pyongyang were staring from windows and open doors, and a few bold ones had the courage to wave, but they did not come out onto the streets to celebrate their liberation. They had lived

their lives under one of the most repressive governments in the world, and they would wait until they were
certain of its demise before they took the risk of showing their feelings.

The TV picture changed again, and Pauline saw the
severe gray hairdo and lined face of President No. As
always, she had beside her the South Korean flag,
white with a red-and-blue taegeuk, the emblem of
cosmic balance, surrounded by four equally symbolic
trigrams. But now the blue-and-white Unification Flag
stood on her other side. It was an unmistakable statement: she now ruled both halves of the country.

However, Pauline had been in President No's office,
and this was not it. No was in an underground bunker,
Pauline guessed.

No began to speak, and the subtitles returned. "Our
brave soldiers have taken possession of the city of
Pyongyang," she said. "The artificial barrier that has
divided Korea since 1945 is coming down. Soon we will
be in reality what we have always been in our minds:
one country."

She's doing well, Pauline thought, but let's hear the
specifics.

"United Korea will be a free democratic country
with close, friendly ties to both China and the US."

Pauline commented: "Easier said than done."

"We will immediately set up an election organization secretariat. Meanwhile the army of South Korea
will act as a peacekeeping force."

Bill Schneider suddenly stood up, staring at a screen,
and said: "Oh, Jesus Christ, no!"

Everyone followed his gaze. Pauline saw a radar
graphic showing a single missile launch. Bill said:
"That's North Korea!"

Pauline said: "Where did the missile originate?"

Bill still had his headset on, connected directly with

the Pentagon. He said: "It took off from Yeongjeo-dong—the nuclear base."

Pauline said: "Fuck, he's done it. Pak has launched a nuclear missile."

Bill said: "It's only just above the clouds. The target is near."

Pauline said: "Seoul, then, almost certainly. Put Seoul on the screens. Get some drones in the air."

First she saw a satellite photo of the city, with the broad Han River snaking through it, crossed by more bridges than she could count. An invisible operator zoomed the photo until she could see traffic on the streets and the white lines painted on a soccer field. A moment later several other screens lit up, showing video that presumably came from traffic cameras and other surveillance in the city. It was midafternoon. Cars and buses and trucks were lined up at stoplights and on the narrow bridges.

Ten million people lived here.

Bill said: "The distance is about two hundred and fifty miles, which is a two-minute journey, and the missile has been in the air about a minute, so I'd guess sixty seconds to go."

There was nothing Pauline could do in sixty seconds.

She never saw the missile. She knew it had landed when all the screens showing Seoul whited out.

For several moments they all stared at blank screens. Then a new image appeared, presumably from a US military drone. Pauline knew it was of Seoul, because she recognized the W-shaped meander of the river, but nothing else was the same. In a central area a couple of miles across there was nothing: no buildings, no cars, no streets. The landscape seemed blank. The buildings had all been flattened, she realized, every single one, and the piled debris covered everything else, including bodies. It was ten times as bad as the worst hurricane, maybe a hundred times.

Beyond that central area, fires seemed to have broken out everywhere, some large and some small, fierce gasoline fires from roasted vehicles and random blazes in offices and stores. Cars were overturned and scattered like toys. Smoke and dust hid some of the damage.

There was always a camera somewhere, and now one of the backroom technicians found live video that looked as if it were being taken from a helicopter rising from one of the airports to the west of the city. Pauline saw that a few cars were still moving on the outskirts of Seoul, indicating survivors. There were injured people walking, some stumbling along sightless, presumably blinded by the flash; some bleeding, perhaps from flying glass; some unhurt and helping others.

Pauline was dazed. She had never thought she would see such destruction.

She shook herself: it was up to her to do something about it.

She said: "Bill, raise the alert level to DEFCON 1. Nuclear war has begun."

Tamara woke up in Tab's bed, as she did most mornings now. She kissed him, got up, walked naked to the kitchen, switched on the coffeemaker, then returned to the bedroom. She went to the window and looked out at the city of N'Djamena heating up rapidly under the desert sun.

She would not be looking at this view for many more mornings. She had won her transfer to Paris. Dexter had opposed it, but her record with the Abdul project made her a natural choice to manage agents infiltrating

Arab-French Islamist groups, and Dexter had been overruled. She and Tab were going to move.

The apartment filled with the invigorating aroma of coffee. She turned on the TV. The main news was that the US had sunk a Chinese aircraft carrier.

"Oh, fuck," she said. "Tab, wake up."

She poured the coffee and they drank it in bed while watching. The ship, called the *Fujian*, had been sunk in retaliation for the Chinese bombing of Japanese troops on the disputed Senkaku Islands, said the newsreader.

"That won't be the end of it," said Tab.

"You bet your ass."

They showered and dressed and had breakfast. Tab, who could get a delicious meal out of the contents of a nearly empty refrigerator, made scrambled eggs with grated Parmesan cheese, chopped parsley, and a sprinkle of paprika.

He put on a tropical-weight Italian blazer, she tied a cotton scarf around her head, and Tab was about to turn the news off when they were stopped by an even more shocking report. The North Korean rebels had dropped a nuclear bomb on Seoul, the capital of South Korea.

Tab said: "It's nuclear war."

She nodded somberly. "This could be our last day on earth."

They sat down again.

Tamara said: "Maybe we should do something special."

Tab looked thoughtful. "I have a suggestion," he said.

"What?"

"It's kind of off-the-wall."

"Spit it out."

"We could . . . would you . . . what I mean to say . . . Will you marry me?"

"Today?"

"Of course today!"

Tamara found herself unable to speak. She was silent for a long moment.

Tab said: "I haven't upset you, have I?"

Tamara found her voice. "I don't know how to tell you how much I love you," she said, and she felt a tear run down her face.

He kissed the tear away. "I'll take that as a yes, then."

CHAPTER 41

nformation began to flood into the Situation Room at Zhongnanhai, and Kai took it in while fighting off a feeling of dazed helplessness. In the next few minutes the whole world was shocked. This was the first time nuclear weapons had been used since 1945. The news traveled fast.

Within seconds, stock markets in East Asia went into free fall. People cashed in their shares, as if money would be any use to them in a nuclear war. President Chen closed the Shanghai and Shenzhen stock exchanges, an hour before the regular time. He ordered the Hong Kong market to close too, but Hong Kong refused, and lost 20 percent in ten minutes.

The government of Taiwan, an island that had never been part of Communist China, issued a formal statement saying that they would attack the military forces of any country that violated Taiwanese airspace or surrounding waters. Kai immediately understood the significance of this. For years Chinese jets had buzzed Taiwan, claiming they had the right because Taiwan was really in China, and in response the Taiwanese had repeatedly scrambled planes and deployed launchers—but had never actually attacked the intruders. Now, it seemed, that had changed. They would shoot down Chinese planes.

"This is nuclear war," said General Huang. "And in a nuclear war it is better to strike first. We have land launchers, submarine launchers, and long-range bomber aircraft, and we should deploy them all right from the start. If we allow the Americans to strike first, much of our nuclear ordnance will be destroyed before it can be used."

Huang always spoke as if stating irrefutable facts, even when he was guessing, but in this case he was right. An American first strike would cripple China's military.

Defense Minister Kong Zhao wore a despairing expression. "Even if we strike first, bear in mind that we have precisely three hundred and twenty nuclear warheads, and the Americans have something more than three thousand. Imagine that every one of our weapons destroyed one of theirs in a first strike. They would still have plenty and we would have nothing."

"Not necessarily," said Huang.

Kong Zhao lost his cool. "Don't try to bullshit me!" he shouted. "I've seen the motherfucking war games and so have you. We always lose. Always!"

"War games are games," said Huang contemptuously. "War is war."

Before Kong could reply, Chang Jianjun said: "May I suggest how we might fight a limited nuclear war?"

Kai had heard his father talk about this before. Kai himself did not have faith in limited war. History showed that it rarely stayed limited. However, he remained silent for the moment.

Jianjun said: "We should make a small number of early strikes on carefully selected US targets—no major cities, just military bases in thinly populated areas—then immediately offer a cease-fire."

Kai said: "That might work, and it would certainly be better than all-out war. But isn't there something else we can try first?"

President Chen said: "What did you have in mind?"

"If we can restrict the fighting to nonnuclear weapons, we can defeat all these raids on our territory. We could even push the South Koreans out of North Korea, eventually."

"Perhaps," said the president. "But how would we stop the Americans from resorting to nuclear weapons?"

"By offering first an excuse, then a threat."

"Explain."

"We should tell President Green that the nuclear strike on Seoul was carried out by rogue elements in Korea who are right now being crushed and dispossessed of their nuclear weapons, and no further such atrocities will occur."

"But that might not be true."

"No. But we can hope. And the statement will buy us time."

"And the threat?"

"An ultimatum to President Green. I suggest the wording: 'A nuclear attack by the US on North Korea will be treated as a nuclear attack on China.' It's similar to what President Kennedy said back in the sixties. 'It shall be the policy of this Nation to regard any nuclear missile launched from Cuba against any nation in the Western Hemisphere as an attack by the Soviet Union on the United States, requiring a full retaliatory response upon the Soviet Union.' I think those were his exact words." Kai had once written a college essay on the Cuban Missile Crisis.

Chen nodded thoughtfully. "What it means is, if you nuke North Korea you will be nuking us."

"Exactly, sir."

"It's not that different from our present policy."

"But it makes it explicit. And it may get President Green to hesitate and think again. Meanwhile we can search for ways to avoid nuclear war."

"I think this is a good idea," said President Chen. "If everyone is agreed, I'll do it."

General Huang and Chang Jianjun looked discontented, but no one spoke against the proposal, and it was agreed on.

Pauline called on the chairman of the Joint Chiefs. "Bill, we have to take away General Pak's ability to use nuclear bombs on our allies in South Korea—or anywhere the hell else. What are my options?"

"I see only one, Madam President, and that is a nuclear attack on rebel territory in North Korea, destroying Yeongjeo-dong and every other military base that might have nuclear weapons."

"And how do we think Beijing would react to that?"

"They might see sense," Bill said. "They don't want the rebels to use those nukes."

Gus was skeptical. "Alternatively, Bill, they could take the view that we have begun a nuclear war by attacking their closest ally, which obliges them to launch a nuclear attack on the US."

Pauline said: "Let's make sure we all know exactly what we're talking about here. Luis, give us a rundown on the likely effects of a Chinese nuclear attack on the United States."

"Yes, ma'am." The secretary of defense had the information at his fingertips. "China has about sixty land-based nuclear-armed intercontinental ballistic missiles capable of reaching the US. These are use-it-or-lose-it weapons, likely to be destroyed early in a nuclear war, so they would launch them all immediately. In the Pentagon's last major war game it was assumed that half the ICBMs would be aimed at the ten largest US cities and half at strategic targets such as military bases, ports, airports, and telecommunications centers. We would see them coming and deploy anti-missile defenses, which might take out one in two, at an optimistic estimate."

"And how do you see American casualty numbers at this point?"

"About twenty-five million, Madam President."

"Jesus Christ."

Luis went on: "We would immediately launch most of our four hundred ICBMs, rapidly followed by more than a thousand warheads fired from aircraft and submarines. That would leave us with a similar number in reserve, but they would not be needed because by this time we would have disabled the Chinese government's ability to continue the war. Surrender would follow quickly. In other words, Madam President, we win."

We win, Pauline thought, with twenty-five million people killed or wounded, and our cities turned into wastelands. "God forbid we should ever have such a victory," she said with feeling.

One of the screens was showing CNN, and Pauline's eye was caught by video of familiar Washington streets, still dark but jammed with traffic. "What's going on outside?" she said. "It's four thirty in the morning—the streets should be almost deserted."

Jacqueline Brody came up with the answer. "People are leaving town. There were some interviews, a few minutes ago, with drivers at stoplights. They think that if there's a nuclear war, Washington is ground zero."

"Where are they going?"

"They believe they'll be safer away from cities—the Pennsylvania forests, the Blue Ridge Mountains. New

Yorkers are doing something similar, driving to the Adirondacks. I guess Californians will head for Mexico as soon as they wake up."

"I'm surprised people even know about this yet."

"One of the TV stations sent a drone camera over Seoul. The whole world can see the devastation."

Pauline turned to Chess. "What's happening in North Korea?"

"The South Koreans are attacking every rebel stronghold. President No is hitting them with everything she's got."

"I'm not going to use nuclear weapons unless I have to. Let's give President No the chance to do the job for us."

Jacqueline Brody said: "Madam President, there's a message from the Chinese president."

"Show me."

"On your screen now."

Pauline read President Chen's ultimatum aloud. "'Any nuclear attack by the US on North Korea will be treated as a nuclear attack on China.'"

Chess said: "Kennedy said something similar during the Cuban crisis."

"But does this change anything?"

Luis Rivera said firmly: "Nothing at all. We would have assumed this was their policy, without the statement."

"There's something else that might be more important," Pauline said. "They say that Seoul was nuked by rogue elements in North Korea who are right now being dispossessed of their nuclear weapons, and no further such atrocities will occur."

Luis said: "Do they add 'We hope' at the end?"

"You're not wrong, Luis, but I think we have to give this a chance. If the South Korean army can wipe out the rebel ultras, the problem will be solved without further nuclear attacks. We can't dismiss that possibility just because we think it's unlikely."

She looked around the table. Some of them did not like it, but no one opposed her.

She said: "Bill, please instruct the Pentagon to prepare for a possible attack on the North Korean rebels. Target nuclear weapons on every military base in the rebel areas. This is a contingency plan, but we must be ready. We'll hold our fire until we can see how the battle is moving on the ground."

Bill said: "Madam President, by waiting you're giving the Chinese the chance to launch a nuclear first strike."

"I know," said Pauline.

Ting called Kai. Her voice was high-pitched and shaky. "What's happening, Kai?"

He moved away from the stage and spoke quietly. "The rebels in Korea dropped a nuclear bomb on Seoul."

"I know! We were filming a scene and suddenly all the technicians took off their headsets and left. Work just stopped. I'm on my way home."

"You're not driving yourself, I hope?" She sounded too upset to drive safely.

"No, I have a driver. Kai, what does this mean?"

"We don't know, but we're doing all we can to make sure it doesn't escalate."

"I won't feel safe until I'm with you. What time will you be home?"

Kai hesitated, then told her the truth. "I'm not sure I'm going to get home at all tonight."

"It's really bad, isn't it?"

"It might be."

"I'm going to pick up Mother and bring her to our apartment. You don't mind, do you?"

"Of course not."

"I just don't want to be alone tonight," said Ting.

Pauline took off her clothes in the Lincoln Bedroom and got into the shower. She had a few minutes to freshen up and change: today of all days she could not wear a jean jacket.

When she got out of the shower Gerry was sitting on the edge of the bed, wearing pajamas and an old-fashioned wool dressing gown.

He said: "Are we about to go to war?"

"Not if I can help it." She picked up a towel. Suddenly she felt embarrassed to be naked in front of him. That was odd, after fifteen years of marriage. She told herself not to be so foolish and began to rub herself dry. She said: "You've heard of Raven Rock."

"A nuclear bunker. Are you planning to go there?"

"Somewhere similar but more secret. And yes, we may have to go there today. You and Pippa should be ready."

"I'm not going," said Gerry.

Pauline knew immediately how the rest of the conversation would go. He was going to tell her that their marriage was over. She was half expecting it, but all the same it hurt. "What do you mean?" she said.

"I don't want to go to a nuclear bunker, now or later, with you or without you." He stopped and looked at her, as if he had said enough.

Pauline said: "You don't want to be with your wife and daughter if war breaks out?"

"No."

She waited, but he did not explain why.

She put on her bra, panties, and tights, and felt less uncomfortable.

He was not going to say what needed to be said, so she would have to. "I don't wish to torture you or even cross-examine you," she said. "Tell me if I'm wrong, but I'm pretty sure you want to be with Amelia Judd."

A series of emotions crossed his face: first surprise; then curiosity as he wondered how she knew and decided not to ask; then shame that he had deceived her; and finally defiance. He tilted his chin up. "You're right," he said.

She voiced her greatest fear. "I hope you're not going to try to take Pippa with you."

He looked thankful to be asked an easy question. "Oh, no."

For a moment Pauline was so relieved that she could not speak. She looked down and raised a hand to her forehead, hiding her eyes.

Gerry said: "I don't even need to ask Pippa about it, because I know what she'll say. She'll want to stay with you." He had obviously thought about this and made a decision. "A girl needs her mother. I get that, of course."

"Thank you for that, anyway."

She dressed in her most authoritative outfit, a black skirt suit over a silver-gray merino sweater.

Gerry did not leave. He had not finished. He said: "I don't believe you're innocent."

That took her by surprise. "What do you mean?"

"You've got someone else. I know you."

"It doesn't really matter now but, for the record, I haven't had sex with anyone else since we started dating. I've thought about it lately, though."

"I knew it."

He wanted to squabble but she was not going to do

that. She felt too sad to have an argument. "What went wrong, Gerry?" she said. "We used to love each other."

"I think all marriages run out of steam sooner or later. The only question is whether the couple stay together out of laziness or split up and try again with other partners."

That was so shallow, she thought. It's nobody's fault, really, it's just normal life, and yadda yadda yadda: that was more of an excuse than an explanation. She did not believe it for a second, but she felt no impulse to contradict him.

Gerry got off the bed and went to the door.

Pauline raised a practical issue. "Pippa will be awake soon," she said. "You have to be the one to tell her we're breaking up. You have to explain it to her as best you can. I'm not going to do that for you."

He stopped with his hand on the door handle. "All right." He was clearly unhappy about it, but he could hardly refuse. "Not now, though. Maybe tomorrow?"

Pauline hesitated, but on balance she was glad of the delay. Today of all days she did not want to deal with a traumatized teenager. "Then at some point we have to announce this publicly."

"No rush."

"We can discuss how and when. But please don't let the news slip out. Be discreet."

"Of course. Amelia's worried about it too. It's going to affect her career, obviously."

Amelia's career, thought Pauline; I don't give half a shit about Amelia's career.

She kept that to herself.

Gerry went out.

Pauline took from her jewelry casket a gold necklace with a single emerald and drew it over her head. She checked herself in the mirror quickly. She looked presidential. Good enough.

She left the Residence and returned to the Situation Room. "What's happening?" she said.

Gus answered. "President No is putting more and more pressure on the ultras, but they're holding out. The Chinese still seem to be thinking about how to react to the sinking of the *Fujian*—they haven't done anything yet, but they will. You've had phone calls from the presidents and prime ministers of many nations, including Australia, Vietnam, Japan, Singapore, and India. An emergency session of the United Nations Security Council is about to begin."

"I'd better start returning calls," Pauline said. "Start with Japan."

Jacqueline said: "I'll get Prime Minister Ishikawa."

But the first call Pauline got was from her mother, who said: "Hello, dear. I hope you're okay."

Pauline could hear a car engine. "Mom, where are you?"

"We're on I-90 just outside Gary, Indiana. Your father's driving. Where are you?"

"I'm in the White House, Mom. What are you doing in Gary?"

"We're heading for Windsor, Ontario. I just hope it doesn't snow before we get there."

Windsor was the closest Canadian city to Chicago, but it was still almost three hundred miles away. Pauline's parents had decided America was no longer safe, she realized. She felt dismayed, though she could hardly blame them. They had lost faith in her ability to protect them. So had millions of other Americans.

But she still had a chance to save them.

She said: "Mom, please call me to let me know how you're getting on. Don't hesitate, okay?"

"Okay, dear. I hope you can make everything all right."

"I'll do my best. I love you, Mom."

"We love you too, honey."

As she hung up, Bill Schneider said: "Missile warning from the infrared satellite."

"Where?"

"Wait . . . North Korea."

Her heart sank.

Gus, sitting next to Pauline, said: "Look at the radar."

Pauline saw the red arc. "Just one missile," she said.

Bill was wearing the headset that kept him in permanent contact with the Pentagon. He said: "It's not aimed at Seoul—it's too high."

Pauline said: "Where, then?"

"They're triangulating. . . . Just a minute. . . . Busan."

It was South Korea's second city, a huge port on the south coast with eight million inhabitants. Pauline buried her head in her hands.

Luis said: "This wouldn't have happened if we'd nuked Yeongjeo-dong an hour ago."

Pauline ran out of patience suddenly. "Luis, if all you can say is *I told you so*, why don't you just shut the fuck up."

Luis went pale with shock and anger, but he fell silent.

She said to no one in particular: "Let's see a satellite photo of the target city."

An aide said: "There's scattered cloud but you can see a lot."

The picture appeared on a screen and Pauline studied it. She saw a river delta, a broad railway line, and vast docks. She recalled her brief visit to Busan, when she was a congresswoman. The people had been warm and friendly. They had given her an item of traditional dress, a red-and-gold silk shawl that she still wore.

Bill said: "Radar confirms that there is just one missile."

"Any video?"

One of the screens lit up with film of the city from a distance. By the way the camera rose and fell it was clear that the video was coming from a ship. The sound came on, and she heard the rumble of a big engine and the swish of waves, plus a casual conversation between two men who clearly had no idea what was about to happen.

Then an orange-red dome appeared over the docks. Whoever was filming cried out in shock. The dome grew into a pillar of smoke, which then turned into the dread shape of a mushroom cloud.

Pauline wanted to close her eyes but she could not.

Eight million people, she thought; some killed instantly, others wounded horribly, many poisoned forever by radiation. Koreans and Americans and, in a port city, many other nationalities. Schoolboys and grandmothers and newborn babies. Luis had been right: she could have prevented this and she had not. She would not make that mistake a second time.

The delayed shock wave hit the ship, and the picture became deck, then sky, then blank. Pauline hoped the sailor who had been filming would survive.

She said: "Bill, have the Pentagon confirm that what we've just seen is a nuclear explosion."

"Yes, ma'am."

She did not really doubt it, but radionuclide detectors could verify, and for what she was about to do she could not have too much proof.

General Pak had now done it twice. She could no longer pretend that nuclear war might be avoided. She was the only person in the world who could stop him from doing it a third time.

She said: "Chess, get a message to President Chen any way you can, telling him the US is about to destroy every nuclear base in North Korea but will not attack China."

"Yes, ma'am."

Pauline took from her pocket the Biscuit. She twisted the plastic case to break the seal, then removed the little card from inside.

Everyone in the room was watching her in silence.

Bill said: "It's confirmed. That was nuclear."

Pauline's last faint hope vanished.

She said: "Call the War Room."

Her phone rang and she picked up. A voice said: "Madam President, this is General Evers in the Pentagon War Room."

She said: "General, in accordance with my earlier instructions, you have targeted nuclear weapons on every military base in the rebel-held zone of North Korea."

"Yes, ma'am."

"I am now going to give you the authentication code. When you have heard the correct code you will give instructions to fire the weapons."

"Yes, ma'am."

She looked at the Biscuit and read out the code: "Oscar November three seven three. I say again, Oscar November three seven three."

"Thank you, Madam President. That is the correct code and I have now given the order to fire."

Pauline hung up. With a heavy heart she said: "It's done."

At Zhongnanhai they watched a radar graphic that showed missiles rising into the American sky like a flock of gray geese embarking on their great seasonal migration.

Chen said: "Launch an all-out cyberattack on American communications of all kinds."

This was routine. Kai's best guess was that it would be only partly successful. The Americans had prepared for cyberwar, as the Chinese had, and both sides had fallback plans and counterattack options. The cyberattack would do some damage without being decisive.

Fu Chuyu said: "Where are the rest of the missiles? I see only twenty or thirty."

Kong Zhao said: "It seems to be a limited attack. They're not starting an all-out nuclear war. Which means the target is probably not China."

Huang said: "We can't be sure of that. And we can't take the risk of leaving it too late to counterattack."

Kong said: "We'll know soon. But right now the target could be anywhere between Vietnam and Siberia."

Kai could see from the radar feed that the missiles were already over Canada. He barked: "Someone give us an estimate of arrival time."

An aide said: "Twenty-two minutes. And the target is not Siberia. The missiles are now too far south for that."

Kai realized the target could even be the very building he was in. The Situation Room was armored against anything but a direct hit by a nuclear bomb. If the American missiles were accurate he would be dead in twenty-two minutes.

Less, now.

He had an urge to phone Ting. He resisted it.

The missiles were now over water.

"Fifteen minutes," said an aide. "Vietnam is not a plausible target. It's Korea or China."

It was Korea, Kai felt sure. This was not just wishful thinking. President Green would be crazy to attack China with only thirty missiles. The damage would be survivable, and the Chinese would retaliate with everything they had, destroying much of the American military before it could be deployed. Anyway it was not China but General Pak who had nuked Seoul and Busan.

Foreign Minister Wu Bai said: "I have received a formal communication from the White House saying that they are attacking nuclear bases in North Korea and nothing else."

Huang said: "Could be a lie."

The aide said: "Ten minutes. Multiple targets, all in North Korea."

Assuming it was not a lie, how would the men in the room deal with this? The Americans had now sunk an aircraft carrier, killing two thousand five hundred Chinese sailors, and they were about to turn half of North Korea, China's only military ally, into a radio-active wasteland. Kai knew that his father and the old Communists could not live with that much humiliation at the hands of their old enemy. Their pride in their country and themselves would not stand it. They would demand a nuclear attack on the US. They knew the consequences but they would want it anyway.

"Five minutes. The targets are all in the north and east of Korea, avoiding Pyongyang and the rest of the territory occupied by the South Korean military."

After this, Kai and Kong Zhao would find it diffi-cult to restrain General Huang and his allies, including Chang Jianjun. But President Chen would have the last word, and Kai felt he would in the end lean toward moderation. Probably.

"One minute."

Kai stared at a satellite picture of North Korea. He was overwhelmed by a sense of tragedy, knowing he had failed to prevent this.

The radar graphic showed the missiles landing within a space of a few seconds all over the northeast quarter of Korea. By Kai's calculation there were eleven military bases within that area, and it looked as if President Green had hit every one.

The same picture was even more vivid in the image from the infrared satellite.

Chang Jianjun stood up. "If I may, Mr. President, as vice chairman of the National Security Commission?"

"Go ahead."

"Our response must be tough, and must do real harm to the US, but it should nevertheless be proportional to the offense. I propose three nuclear attacks on American military bases outside the American heartland: in Alaska, Hawaii, and Guam."

Chen shook his head. "One would be enough. One target, one bomb—if we do this at all."

Kong Zhao said: "We have always said we would never be the first to use nuclear weapons."

Jianjun said: "And we will not be the first. If we do as I suggest we will be the third. The North Korean ultras were the first and the US was second."

"Thank you, Chang Jianjun." President Chen looked at Kai, clearly wanting to hear arguments against.

Kai found himself in direct public conflict with his father. "First, note that American aggression against us, sinking the *Fujian*, did not employ nuclear weapons."

"An important point," said Chen.

Kai was encouraged. The president was clearly favoring restraint. Perhaps moderation would prevail. He went on: "Second, the Americans have used nuclear weapons not against us, or even against our friends in North Korea, but against a rogue group of rebels who are not owed loyalty by the People's Republic of China. We might even consider that President Green has done a favor to us and the world by getting rid of a dangerous maverick group of usurpers who have almost started a nuclear war."

An aide whispered in the ear of Foreign Minister Wu Bai. Wu looked angry. "The chief executive of Hong Kong has turned on us," he said gravely. "He formally requests the Chinese military to evacuate its garrison in Hong Kong immediately, all twelve thousand personnel, to ensure that Hong Kong does not become a nuclear target." Wu paused. "He has made this request publicly."

Huang was red-faced. "The traitor!"

President Chen said furiously: "I thought we had that under control! We appointed that chief executive because he was loyal to the Party."

You installed a puppet government, Kai thought privately, and you never expected the puppet to bite you.

"You see?" said Huang. "First Taiwan becomes defiant, then Hong Kong. I keep telling you, it's fatal to appear weak!"

Kai's boss, Fu Chuyu, spoke. "I'm sorry to follow bad news with worse," he said. "But I have a message from the vice minister for homeland intelligence that you ought to hear. It seems there is trouble in Xinjiang." This vast desert province in the west of China had a majority-Muslim population and a small independence movement. "Separatists have seized control of the Diwopu airport and Communist Party headquarters in Urumqi, the capital. They have declared that Xinjiang is now the independent country of East Turkestan and will remain neutral in the present nuclear conflict."

Kai reckoned that rebellion would probably last half an hour. The army in Xinjiang would come down on the separatists like a wolf pack on a flock of sheep.

But at a time like this even a comic-opera military coup was a blow to China's pride.

It was unnerving, as General Huang immediately demonstrated. "This is reactionary imperialism, obviously," he fumed. "Look at what has happened in the last two months. North Korea, Sudan, the South China Sea, the Diaoyu Islands, Taiwan, and now Hong Kong and Xinjiang. It's the death of a thousand cuts, a carefully planned campaign to deprive China of territory bit by bit, and the Americans are behind it every step of the way! We have to stop it now. We have to make the Americans pay the price of their aggression— otherwise they will not stop until China is reduced to the kind of servile colony it was a century ago. A limited nuclear attack is the only possible course for us now."

President Chen said: "We're not yet at that point of desperation. It may come, I know. But for now we must try less apocalyptic methods."

Out of the corner of his eye Kai saw a look pass between his father and General Huang. Naturally, he thought, they would be disheartened at losing the argument.

Then Jianjun stood up, muttered something about a call of nature, and left the room. That was surprising. Kai knew that his father did not suffer from the bladder problems that were common among older men. Jianjun never admitted to health issues but Kai's mother kept him informed. However, Jianjun must have had a strong reason to leave the room in the middle of such a vital discussion. Was he ill? The old man was a dinosaur but Kai loved him.

Chen said: "General Huang, please prepare for the People's Liberation Army to enter Hong Kong in force and take control of the government there."

It was not what Huang wanted, but it was better than nothing, and he agreed without resistance.

Kai noticed Wang Qingli entering the room. Wang was head of presidential security. Although a crony of Huang and Jianjun's, he was much better dressed, and was sometimes mistaken for the president he guarded. Now he stepped up onto the stage and spoke in Chen's ear.

Kai did not like this. Something was going on. Jianjun had left the room, then Wang had come in. Coincidence?

He caught the eye of his ally Kong Zhao. Kong frowned. He too was unnerved.

He looked at the president. Chen, listening to Wang, looked startled, then anxious, and even went slightly pale. He was shocked.

By now everyone around the table had realized that something odd was happening. The discussion came to a halt and they waited in silence.

Fu Chuyu, the security minister and Kai's boss, stood up. "Forgive me, comrades, but I must interrupt our discussion. I have to inform you that a Guoanbu domestic investigation has revealed strong evidence that Chang Kai is an agent of the US."

Kong Zhao burst out: "Ridiculous!"

Fu pressed on. "Chang Kai has been running his own clandestine foreign policy agenda, unknown to his comrades."

Kai could hardly believe this was happening. Were they really moving to get rid of him, in the middle of a global nuclear crisis? "No, no, you can't do this," he said. "China isn't some banana republic."

Fu continued as if Kai had not spoken. "We have proof of three fatal charges against him. One, he informed the CIA about the weakness of the supreme leader's regime in North Korea. Two, that at Yeongjeo-dong he made an agreement with General Pak that he was not authorized to negotiate. Three, that he gave the Americans early warning of our decision to replace the supreme leader with General Pak."

All of that was more or less true. Kai had done those things—not because he was a traitor, but because they were in China's best interest.

But this was not about justice. Such accusations never were. He might just as easily have been charged with corruption. This was a political attack.

He had thought he was armored against his political enemies. He was a princeling. His father was vice chairman of the National Security Commission. He should have been untouchable.

But his father had left the room.

Kai now saw the profound symbolism of that action.

Fu said: "Kai's close partner in these activities has been Kong Zhao."

Kong looked as if he had been punched. "Me?" he said incredulously. He quickly recovered his composure and said: "Mr. President, it's obvious that these allegations have been brought forward at this precise moment because an aggressive warlike faction within your government sees it as the only way to win the argument."

Chen did not reply to Kong.

Fu said: "I have no alternative but to place Chang Kai and Kong Zhao under arrest."

Kai thought: How can they arrest us in the middle of the Situation Room?

But they had thought of that.

The main door opened, and six of Wang's security men came in, in their trademark black suits and black ties.

Kai said: "This is a coup!"

He guessed this was what his father had been plotting with Fu Chuyu and General Huang over their dinner of pigs' feet at the Enjoy Hot restaurant.

Wang spoke to Chen again, but this time loudly enough to be heard by everyone. "With your permission, Mr. President."

Chen hesitated for a long moment.

Kai said: "Mr. President, if you go along with this, you cease to be the leader of our country and become a mere tool of the military."

Chen looked as if he agreed with that. Clearly he thought the moderates had won the argument. But the old guard were more powerful. Could he defy them and survive? Could he defy the army and the collective authority of the old Communists?

He could not.

"Go ahead," said President Chen.

Wang beckoned his men.

Everyone watched in hypnotic silence as the security men crossed the room and mounted the stage. Two stood on either side of Kai and two beside Kong. Both men stood up and were held lightly by the elbows.

Kong spoke furiously. Looking at Fu Chuyu, he yelled: "You will destroy your country, you motherfucking idiots!"

Fu said quietly: "Take them both to Qincheng Prison."

Wang said: "Yes, Minister."

The guards marched Kai and Kong down from the stage, across the floor, and out of the room.

Chang Jianjun was in the lobby, by the elevators. He had stepped outside so that he would not have to witness the arrest.

Kai recalled a conversation in which his father had said, *Communism is a sacred mission. It comes above everything else, including our family ties and our own personal safety.* Now he understood what the old man had meant.

Wang stopped and said uncertainly: "Chang Jianjun, did you wish to speak to your son?"

Jianjun would not meet Kai's eye. He said: "I have no son."

"Ah, but I have a father," said Kai.

CHAPTER 42

Pauline had killed hundreds of people, perhaps thousands, by bombing North Korean military bases, and more would have been maimed by the blast and ravaged by the radiation. In her head she knew she had done the right thing: General Pak's murderous regime had to be closed down. But no amount of reasoning could make her feel all right about it in her heart. Every time she washed her hands she thought of Lady Macbeth trying to get the blood off.

She had spoken to the nation on television at eight o'clock this morning. She had announced that the nuclear threat from North Korea was now over. The Chinese and others should understand that this was the fate that awaited any group that used nuclear weapons against the US or its allies. She had received messages of support from more than half the world's leaders, she reported: a rogue nuclear regime was a threat to everyone. She urged calm but did not assure the audience that everything was going to be all right.

She feared the Chinese would retaliate, though she did not tell them that. The thought filled her with dread.

Telling people not to panic was never effective, and the flight out of American cities grew. Every major town center was gridlocked. Hundreds of cars formed lines at border crossings into Canada and Mexico. Gun stores sold out of ammunition. At a Costco in Miami a man was shot dead in a quarrel over the last box of twelve cans of tuna.

Immediately after the broadcast, Pauline and Pippa got into Marine One to fly to Munchkin Country. Having been up all night, Pauline catnapped on the way. When the helicopter landed she did not want to open her eyes. She would grab an hour or two of sleep later, if she could.

As the elevator took them down, Pauline was grateful to be deep underground, then she felt cowardly for thinking of her own safety, then she looked at Pippa and was glad again.

The first time she came to Munchkin Country she had been a visiting celebrity inspecting a showpiece. Everything had been pristine, the atmosphere calm. It was different today. Now the place was functioning and the corridors were bustling, mostly with people in uniform. Pauline's cabinet and senior Pentagon officers were moving in. Store cupboards were being resupplied, and half-empty cardboard boxes were everywhere. Engineers accessed environmental control machinery, checking and oiling and double-checking. Orderlies were putting towels in the bathrooms and setting tables in the officers' mess. The air of brisk efficiency did not quite mask the undertone of suppressed fear.

Round-faced General Whitfield welcomed her, looking strained. Last time, he had been the amiable curator of a never-used facility; today he bore the crushing weight of managing what might be the last holdout of American civilization.

Pauline's accommodation was modest, for a presidential suite: one bedroom, a sitting room that doubled as an office, a kitchen nook, and a compact bathroom with a combined shower and bathtub. It was appropriately basic, like a midrange hotel, with cheap framed prints and a green carpet. There was a constant background sound of blowers and the unnatural smell of purified air. Wondering how long she would have to live here, she suffered a pang of regret for leaving the opulent palace that was the White House Residence. But this was about survival, not comfort.

Pippa had a single room nearby. She was excited by the move and eager to explore the bunker. "It's like that moment in an old western movie when they circle the wagons," she said.

She assumed that her father would be joining them later, and Pauline did not disabuse her. One shock at a time.

She offered Pippa a soda from the refrigerator. "You have a minibar!" Pippa said. "All I have is bottled water. I should have brought candy."

"There's a store here. You can buy some."

"And I can go shopping without the Secret Service. What a treat!"

"Yes, you can. This is the safest place in the world." Which was ironic, she thought.

Pippa saw the irony too. Her elation evaporated. She sat down, looking pensive. "Mom, what really happens in a nuclear war?"

Pauline recalled asking Gus, less than a month ago, to remind her of the bare facts, and she felt again her own dread as he reprised the litany of agony and destruction. Now she gazed lovingly at her daughter, who was wearing an old PAULINE FOR PRESIDENT T-shirt. Pippa's expression showed curiosity and concern rather than fear. She had never known violence or heartbreak.

She deserves the truth, Pauline thought, even though it will upset her.

All the same she softened the details. *In the first one millionth of a second, a fireball is formed two hundred yards wide. Everyone within it dies instantly.* She changed that to: "First of all, many people are killed instantly by the heat. They would know nothing about it."

"Lucky them."

"Maybe." *The blast flattens buildings for a mile around. Almost everyone in that area dies.* "Then the blast destroys property and brings down debris."

Pippa said: "So what would the, like, authorities be doing?"

"No country in the world has enough doctors and nurses to cope with the casualties from nuclear war. Our hospitals would be overwhelmed and many people would die for lack of medical attention."

"But how many?"

"It depends how many bombs. In a war between the US and Russia, both of which have huge stockpiles of nuclear weapons, probably about a hundred and sixty million Americans would die."

Pippa was bemused. "But that's, like, half the country."

"Yes. The danger right now is a war with China, which has a smaller stockpile, but we still think something like twenty-five million Americans would be killed."

Pippa was good at arithmetic. "One person in thirteen."

"Yes."

She was trying to imagine it. "That's thirty of the kids in my school."

"Yes."

"Fifty thousand inhabitants of DC."

"And that's only the beginning, I'm afraid," said

Pauline. I might as well give her the whole horror, she thought. "The radiation causes cancers and other illnesses for years to come. We know this from Hiroshima and Nagasaki, where the first nuclear bombs exploded." She hesitated, then added: "And what happened in Korea today is like thirty Hiroshimas."

Pippa was close to tears. "Why did you do it?"

"To prevent something worse."

"What could be worse?"

"General Pak nuked two cities. The third might have been in the US."

Pippa looked troubled. "American lives aren't worth more than Korean lives."

"All human life is precious. But the American people chose me to be their leader, and I promised to protect them. I'm doing my damnedest. And I can't think of anything, in the last two months, that I could have done that would have prevented what's happening now. I averted a war on the Chad-Sudan border. I tried to stop countries from selling guns to terrorists. I let the Chinese get away with sinking a Vietnamese ship. I wiped out ISGS camps in the Sahara Desert. I held back from invading North Korea. I can't see one of those as the wrong decision."

"What about the nuclear winter?"

Pippa was relentless, but she was entitled to answers. "The heat from nuclear explosions starts thousands of fires, and the smoke and soot rise high into the atmosphere and block the sunlight. If hundreds of bombs go off, even thousands, the darkening of the sun will cool the Earth and reduce rainfall. Some of our biggest farming regions may become too cold or dry to grow crops. Therefore, many of the people who survived the blast and the heat and the radiation will end up starving to death."

"So it's the end of the human race?"

"Probably not, if Russia stays out of the war. Even in the worst case, a few people will probably live on in places where there is sunshine and rain. But in any scenario it's the end of the civilization that we know."

"I wonder what life will be like then."

"There are a thousand novels about that, and each one tells a different story. The truth is that no one knows."

"It would be better if nobody had nuclear weapons."

"Which isn't going to happen. It's like asking Texans to give up their guns."

"Maybe we could all just have not so many."

"That's called arms control." Pauline kissed Pippa. "And that, my clever daughter, is the beginning of wisdom." She had spent a long time explaining life to Pippa, but she had to take care of all the other Americans too. She picked up the remote for the TV. "Let's watch the news."

An anchor said: "Millions of American homes and workplaces are without electricity this morning after faults developed in the computers of several different power providers. Some commentators suspect that the faults have all been caused by the release of a single software virus."

Pauline said: "It's the Chinese."

"Can they do that?"

"Yes. And we're probably doing similar things to them. It's called cyber warfare."

"Lucky we're okay here."

"This place has an independent power supply."

"I wonder why they decided to attack the power to ordinary homes."

"It's one of a dozen different things they will have tried. Ideally they want to sabotage military communications, so that we can't launch missiles and scramble planes. But our military software is heavily defended. Civilian security systems aren't as good."

Pippa looked hard at Pauline and said perceptively: "Your words are reassuring but your face is worried."

"You're right, honey. I think we can survive the cyberattack. But something else is worrying me. In Chinese military philosophy the cyberattack is a prelude. What follows is real war."

Abdul drove out of Nice heading west along the coast, with Kiah beside him and Naji strapped into a child seat in the back. He had bought a small two-door family car, three years old. The driving position was a bit cramped for his tall frame but it was all right for short distances.

The road ran beside deserted Mediterranean beaches and restaurants shuttered for winter. There were traffic jams in Paris and other big cities as frightened people headed for the countryside, but the Côte d'Azur was an unlikely nuclear target, and although people here were scared, they could not think of anywhere safer to go.

Kiah had little knowledge of global politics and was only vaguely aware of nuclear weapons, so she did not appreciate the awfulness of what might happen, and Abdul did not enlighten her.

He stopped the car at a large marina in a small town. He checked a device in his pocket and was reassured by a signal the same as the one he had picked up on his first visit here, two days earlier.

He parked the little car and he and Kiah got out and inhaled the bracing sea air. They put on the new winter coats they had bought in Galeries Lafayette. The sun was warm, but there was a breeze, and for people used to the Sahara Desert this was cold weather. Kiah had picked a tailored black cloth coat with a fur collar that made her look like a princess. Abdul had a blue reefer jacket that gave him a nautical air.

Kiah got Naji into his new down coat and knitted hat. Abdul unfolded the stroller and they made Naji comfortable in it. "I'll push him," Kiah said.

"I'll do it, I don't mind."

"It's demeaning for a man. I don't want people to think you're henpecked."

Abdul smiled. "French people don't think like that."

"Have you looked around? There are thousands of Arabs in this part of the world."

It was true. The area of Nice in which they were living had a high percentage of ethnic North Africans.

Abdul shrugged. It really did not matter who pushed the stroller, and in time Kiah would probably change her ideas. There was no need to hurry her.

They ambled around the marina. Abdul had thought that maybe Naji would like to see the boats, but it was Kiah who reacted. She was amazed. She had been a boat owner, but she had never seen vessels like this. The smallest cabin cruiser seemed astonishingly luxurious to her. On some of them the owners were cleaning or painting or just sitting having drinks. There was a handful of large oceangoing yachts. Abdul stopped to look at one called *Mi Amore*. Crew in white uniforms were washing the windows. "It's bigger than the house I used to live in!" Kiah said. "What is it for?"

"It's for him." Abdul pointed to a man in a big chunky sweater sitting on the sun deck with two young women who were underdressed for the weather and looked cold. They were drinking champagne. "Just for his pleasure."

"I wonder where he got all that money."

Abdul knew where the man had gotten the money.

They walked around the marina for an hour. There were four cafés, three closed and one open though not

busy. Inside it was clean and warm, with gleaming
silver coffee machines and a briskly efficient proprietor
who smiled at Naji and told them to sit anywhere they
liked. They chose a table by the window with a good
view of the boats, including *Mi Amore*. They took off
their coats and ordered hot chocolate and pastries.

Abdul cooled some of the drink on a spoon and fed
it to Naji. He loved it and asked for more.

If this afternoon went according to plan, Abdul's
mission would be over by nightfall.

After that he could no longer pretend, to his employers or to himself. He would have to face the fact
that he did not want to go home. But he had enough
money for several months of idleness, and he was not
sure the human race had that much time left.

When he looked at Kiah and Naji, he felt sure of one
thing: he was not going to leave them. He had found a
quiet contentment in his life with them, and he would
never give it up. He knew what was happening in
Korea, and however much time he had left—sixty
years or sixty hours or sixty seconds—all he cared
about was spending it with them.

He saw two small vessels enter the marina, a speed-
boat and a fast dinghy, both white with red and blue
stripes and the word POLICE in large letters. They belonged to the Police Judiciaire, which was the national
serious crime force, a bit like the FBI.

A moment later he heard sirens, and several police
cars entered the marina from the road. Ignoring the NO
ENTRY signs, they drove along the quay dangerously
fast. Kiah said: "I'm glad we're not in their way!"

Both cars and boats approached *Mi Amore*.

The police jumped out of the cars. They were heavily armed. They all had pistols in holsters at their belts,
and some of them were carrying rifles. They moved
rapidly. Some spread out along the quayside while

others crossed the gangway quickly and boarded the yacht. This had been planned and rehearsed, Abdul was glad to see.

Kiah said: "I don't like those guns. They might go off by accident."

"Let's stay here in the café. It's probably the safest place."

The white-uniformed crew of the *Mi Amore* all raised their hands in the air.

Several of the cops went belowdecks.

One with a rifle went up to the sun deck. The big man spoke to him, waving his arms angrily. The cop seemed unconcerned, holding his rifle and shaking his head.

Then a big muscular cop came up on deck hefting a large sack made of heavy-duty polythene imprinted with the words CAUTION—DANGEROUS CHEMICALS in several languages.

Abdul recalled a nighttime scene on a dockside in Guinea-Bissau, and men unloading sacks like that by lamplight while a limousine waited, its engine turning over. "Bingo," he said softly to himself.

Kiah heard and looked at him with curiosity, but she did not ask for an explanation.

The crew were handcuffed, led off the yacht, and pushed into the back of a van. The big man and his girls got similar treatment, despite the man's outrage. A few more people emerged from belowdecks and they too were handcuffed and put into vehicles.

The last person to be brought up from below looked familiar.

He was a pudgy young North African man wearing a green sweatshirt and grubby white shorts. Around his neck was a string of beads and stones that Abdul had seen before.

Kiah said: "It can't be Hakim, can it?"

"Looks like him," said Abdul. In fact he knew. The men running the enterprise had decided, for some reason, that Hakim should accompany the consignment all the way to France, and here he was.

Abdul got up and stepped outside to see better. Kiah stayed inside with Naji.

A cop took hold of Hakim's grigri necklace and yanked it hard. The chain broke and the stones fell to the quay. Hakim let out a cry of grief: his magical protection was gone.

The cops laughed as the ornaments bounced on the concrete.

While they were distracted, Hakim dived off the quay into the water and began swimming strongly.

Abdul was surprised that Hakim could swim so well. Not many desert folk could swim at all. Hakim might have learned in Lake Chad.

All the same his escape bid was hopeless. Where could he go? If he came out of the water onto the quay or the beach he would just be seized again. If he swam out of the harbor he would probably drown in the open sea.

In any case he was not going to get that far. The two cops in the dinghy went after him. One steered the inflatable boat while the other took out a telescopic steel baton and extended it to its full length. They caught up with Hakim easily, and the cop with the baton lifted it high, then hit Hakim's head with full force.

Hakim's head went underwater and he changed direction, still swimming fast, but the dinghy followed and the cop hit him again, missing his head but striking his elbow. Blood appeared in the seawater.

Hakim kept struggling, swimming with one arm and trying to keep his head under the surface, but the cop held the baton ready, and as soon as Hakim came up for air the cop hit him again. The officers on the quay cheered and clapped.

Abdul was reminded of a child's game called Whack-a-Mole.

The cop hit Hakim's head again, to further cheers.

At last Hakim went limp, and they pulled him out of the water, threw him into the well of the dinghy, and handcuffed him. His left arm looked broken and his head was bleeding.

Abdul went back inside. A brutal man had suffered a brutal beating. It was rough justice.

The prisoners were driven away and crime scene tape was fixed all around the yacht. More polythene sacks were brought up from belowdecks—depriving ISGS of millions of dollars, Abdul thought with profound satisfaction. The heavily armed police drifted away and were replaced by detectives and what looked like forensic specialists.

"We can go," Abdul said to Kiah.

They paid for their hot chocolate and returned to the car. As they were driving away Kiah said: "You knew that was going to happen, didn't you?"

"Yes."

"Were there drugs in those plastic bags?"

"Yes. Cocaine."

"Is that why you were on the bus with us, all the way from Lake Chad? Because of that cocaine?"

"It's more complicated than that."

"Are you going to explain it to me?"

"Yes. I can now, because it's over. There's a lot to tell. Some of it is still secret, but I can share most of it with you. Maybe tonight, after Naji's gone to sleep. We'll have plenty of time. And I can answer all your questions."

"Good."

It was getting dark. They drove back to Nice and parked outside their building. Abdul loved the place. There was a bakery on the ground floor, and the smell of new bread and pastries reminded him of his childhood home in Beirut.

Abdul carried Naji up to the apartment. It was small but cozy, with two bedrooms and a living room as well as a kitchen and a bathroom. Kiah had never lived in a place with more than one room, and she thought she was in paradise.

Naji was sleepy, perhaps because of the fresh sea air. Abdul fed him scrambled eggs followed by a banana. Kiah bathed him and put him into a clean diaper and pajamas. Abdul read him a story about a koala bear called Joey, but Naji was asleep before he got to the end.

Kiah began preparing their supper, sprinkling sesame seeds and sumac on cubes of lamb. They nearly always ate traditional Arab food. They could buy all the ingredients in Nice, usually from Lebanese or Algerian shopkeepers. Abdul sat admiring her grace as she moved about the kitchen.

"Don't you want to watch the news?" she said.

"No," said Abdul contentedly. "I don't want to watch the news."

Qincheng was for political prisoners, who got better treatment than common criminals. The losers in a political conflict were often jailed on trumped-up charges: it was an occupational hazard for members of the Chinese elite. Kai's cell was only five yards by four, but it had a desk and a TV set and a shower.

He was allowed to wear his own clothes, but they had taken away his phone. He felt naked without it. He could not remember the last time he had been without a phone for longer than it took to shower.

Today's coup in Beijing had caught him by surprise, but he now saw that he should have at least thought of the possibility. He had been focused on persuading President Chen not to start a war, and he had not imagined that the hawks might deprive Chen of the power to choose.

A conspiracy against the president should have been uncovered by the homeland security half of the Guoanbu, but of course the head of that department, Vice Minister Li Jiankang, had been in on the plot, and his superior, Security Minister Fu Chuyu, had been one of the ringleaders. With the military and the secret service behind the coup, it could not fail.

The greatest shock had been his father's betrayal. Of course he had heard Jianjun say that the Communist revolution was more important than anything else, including family ties, but people said that sort of thing without really thinking about it. Or so Kai had always thought. But his father had meant it.

Sitting at the desk, watching the news on the small TV screen, Kai felt how strange it was to be helpless. The fate of China and the world was now out of his hands. With Kong Zhao also in jail there was no one left to restrain the military men. They would probably carry out Jianjun's scheme of a limited nuclear attack. They might bring about the destruction of China. He just had to wait and see.

He only wished he could wait with Ting. He would never forgive his father for separating them for what might well be their last days of life. He was desperate to talk to her. He looked at his watch. It was an hour to midnight.

The watch gave him an idea.

He banged on the door to attract attention. A couple

of minutes later a muscular young prison officer called Liang came in. He took no precautions: the guards had obviously decided Kai was no threat to them, which was true. "Something wrong?" the man said.

"I really want to phone my wife."

"Not possible, sorry."

Kai took off his watch and held it in his hand for Liang to see. "This is a steel Rolex Datejust that cost eight thousand US dollars secondhand. I'll swap it for your watch." Liang was wearing an army-issue officer's watch worth ten bucks.

Liang's eyes glittered with greed but he said cautiously: "You must be corrupt if you can afford a watch like that."

"It was a present from my wife."

"Then she must be corrupt."

"My wife is Tao Ting."

"From *Love in the Palace*?" Liang was thrilled. "I love that show!"

"She plays Sun Mailin."

"I know! The emperor's favorite concubine."

"You could call her for me on your phone."

"You mean I could speak to her?"

"If you want. Then pass the phone to me."

"Oh, wait till my girlfriend hears about this!"

"I'll write down the number for you to dial."

Liang hesitated. "I'll take the watch as well, though."

"All right. As soon as you pass me the phone."

"Agreed." Liang dialed the number Kai gave him.

A moment later Liang said: "Am I speaking to Tao Ting? Yes, I'm with your husband, but before I pass you to him, I just want to say that my girlfriend and I love the show and it's such an honor to speak to you. . . . Oh, you're very kind to say that, thank you! Yes, here he is."

He gave the phone to Kai, and Kai gave him the Rolex.

Then Kai said: "My darling."

Ting burst into tears.

"Don't cry," said Kai.

"Your mother told me they put you in jail—she says it's your father's fault!"

"That's true."

"And the Americans have destroyed half of North Korea with nuclear bombs and everyone says China will be next! Is that true?"

Kai felt that if he answered honestly she would become even more upset. "I don't think President Chen is so foolish as to let that happen," he said, not really telling a lie but not telling the truth either.

"Everything's going crazy," she said. "All the stoplights in Beijing have been turned off and the traffic is gridlocked."

"That's the Americans' doing," he said. "Cyberwar."

Liang took off his old wristwatch and put on his new Rolex. He held up his wrist, relishing how it looked.

Ting said: "When will you get out of there?"

Never, Kai thought, if the old Communists fire a nuclear weapon at the US. But he said: "If you and my mother put pressure on my father, it might not be too long."

Ting sniffed noisily and managed to stop crying. "What's it like in there? Are you cold? Are you hungry?"

"It's a lot better than the average prison," Kai said. "Don't worry about my comfort."

"What's the bed like? Will you be able to sleep?"

Right now Kai could not imagine sleeping, but he supposed nature would take its course sooner or later. "The only thing wrong with my bed is that you're not in it."

That made her cry again.

Liang stopped admiring his watch and said: "Not much longer. The other guards will wonder what I'm doing."

Kai nodded. "Darling, I have to hang up."

"I'm going to put your photo on the pillow next to me so that I can still look at you."

"Just lie still and think about the good times we've had together. That will help you sleep."

"I'm going to see your father first thing in the morning."

"That's a good idea." Ting in person could be very persuasive.

"I'll do everything I can to get you out of there."

"We can hope."

"We must think positively. I'm going to say good night, and see you tomorrow."

"Sleep well," said Kai. "Good-bye, my love."

For the first time, Pauline held a meeting in the Situation Room at Munchkin Country. It was a replica of the one in the White House. The key people were there: Gus, Chess, Luis, Bill, Jacqueline, and Sophia. Tension was high but they still did not know what China was going to do. It was the middle of the night in Beijing and perhaps the government there would make its decision in the morning. Until then there was little the US could do but fight off cyberattacks, which so far had been a nuisance but not crippling.

Pauline returned to her quarters to have lunch with Pippa. They ordered hamburgers from the canteen. Then Pippa said it:

"When will Daddy get here?"

Pauline had been expecting this. She had been trying to reach Gerry but he was not answering his phone. Now she had to tell Pippa the truth. So be it, she thought.

She said: "Daddy and I have a problem."

Pippa was puzzled but also troubled. She could guess that this would be bad. "What do you mean?"

Pauline hesitated. How much would Pippa understand? How much would Pauline herself have understood at the age of fourteen? She was not sure: it was too long ago and anyway her parents had never split up. She swallowed and said: "Daddy's fallen in love with someone else."

Pippa looked bewildered. Clearly she had never imagined this. Like most children, she unthinkingly regarded her parents' marriage as eternal.

She said: "He's not leaving us, is he?"

Pippa would see this as Gerry's abandoning her as well as her mother. But Gerry had not said he was moving out. "I don't know what he's going to do," Pauline said truthfully, though she might have added that she could guess. "All I know is that right now he wants to be with her."

"What's wrong with us?"

"I don't know, honey." Pauline asked herself the question. Was it her job? Was the sex dull? Or did he simply fancy something different? "Maybe nothing," she said. "Maybe some men just need change."

"Who is it, anyway?"

"Someone you know."

"Really?"

"It's Ms. Judd."

Pippa burst out laughing. She stopped just as suddenly. "It's ludicrous," she said. "My father and my school principal. Sorry I laughed. It's not funny. Except it is."

"I know what you mean. There's something grotesque about the whole thing."

"When did it start?"

"Maybe during that trip to Boston."

"In that crappy hotel? Imagine that!"

"I'd rather not dwell on the details, honey, if you don't mind."

"It just feels like everything is falling apart. Nuclear war and Daddy leaving us—what next?"

"We still have each other," Pauline said. "I promise you, that isn't going to change."

Their food arrived. Despite her distress Pippa ate a cheeseburger and fries and drank a chocolate shake. Then she went back to her room.

Pauline finally got Gerry on the phone. "Couple of things I need to talk to you about," she said. She felt stiffly formal, which was strange with the man she had been sleeping with for fifteen years. She wondered whether Ms. Judd was in the room with him. Where was he, anyway? Her place? A hotel? Perhaps they had both gone to the winery in Middleburg owned by her friend. It would be less dangerous than downtown Washington, though not much.

"Okay," he said warily. "I'm listening."

She could tell from his voice that he was happy. *Happy without me. Is it my fault? What did I do wrong?*

She shoved those foolish thoughts aside. "I've told Pippa what's happening," she said. "I had to. She couldn't understand why you weren't here with us."

"I'm sorry. I didn't mean to dump that responsibility on you." He did not sound very sorry. "I've told the Secret Service, not that they hadn't guessed."

She said: "You still need to talk to her. She has a lot of questions and I can't answer them all."

"Is she with you now?"

"No, she's in her own room, but she has her phone, you could call her."

"I will. What was the other thing? You said you had two."

"Yes." Pauline was determined not to quarrel with the man she had loved for years. If it was possible, she wanted them both to think fondly of their time together. "I just wanted to say thank you," she said. "Thank you for the good times. Thank you for loving me as long as you did."

There was a short silence, and when he spoke he sounded choked up. "That's a wonderful thing to say."

"You supported me for years. You deserved more time and attention than I could spare. Too late now, I know, but I'm sorry about that."

"You don't have anything to apologize for. I was privileged to be with you. It was mostly good, wasn't it?"

"Yes," said Pauline. "It was mostly good."

Some people could not tear themselves away from the TV. Others were partying like it was the end of the world. Tamara and Tab were partying.

Against all the odds they had managed to get married within hours of making the decision and had also organized a wedding party.

Tamara had wanted the humanist woman who had officiated at the marriage of Drew Sandberg, the embassy press officer, to Annette Cecil of MI6. She had called Annette and asked for the woman's number.

"Tamara!" Annette had screeched. "You're getting married! Darling, how marvelous!"

"Calm down, calm down."

"Who is he? I didn't even know you were dating."

"Don't get excited, it's not for me, it's for a friend."

Annette did not believe her. "You secretive cow. I'm desperate to know."

"Please, Annette, just give me the contact details."

Annette yielded and produced the information.

The humanist celebrant was called Claire and she was free this evening.

"It's on," Tamara had said to Tab, and she had kissed him exuberantly. "Now, where shall we hold the ceremony and the party?"

"The Lamy Hotel has a lovely private room that looks out onto the gardens. It holds about a hundred people. We could do the ceremony and the party in the same place."

They spent the day organizing everything. The Oasis Room at the Lamy was available. The hotel had large stocks of Travers vintage champagne. Tab booked it.

"Are we going to have dancing?" he said.

"Oh, yes. I fell in love with you when I saw how badly you dance."

The Malian jazz band Desert Funk were free, and Tamara booked them.

They sent the invitations by email.

Late that afternoon Tamara stood at the open door of Tab's closet, looking at his suits, and said: "What shall we wear?"

"We must dress up," he said immediately. "Everyone must know this isn't, like, a Las Vegas wedding, even though it's been organized at the last minute. It's a real marriage, for life."

After that she had to kiss him again. Then she returned to the closet. "Tuxedo?"

"Nice idea."

She noticed a plastic suit cover bearing the words TEINTURERIE DE L'OPÉRA. It came from a dry cleaner presumably situated near the Place de l'Opéra in Paris. "What's in here?"

"White tie and tails. I've never worn that outfit in Chad. That's why it's still in the cleaner's bag."

She took the suit out. "Oh, Tab, you'll look gorgeous in this."

"I have been told it flatters me. But then you'll have to wear a ball gown."

"That's all right. I have the perfect dress. You'll get a hard-on just looking."

At eight o'clock that evening the Oasis Room was packed with about double the number of guests they had invited. No one was turned away.

Tamara wore an ice-pink dress with an eye-popping neckline.

In front of all their friends they vowed to be companions, allies, and lovers for the rest of their lives, however short or long. Claire pronounced them husband and wife, a waiter popped a champagne cork, and everyone clapped.

Desert Funk started to play smooth blues. The waiters removed the covers from the buffet and poured the champagne. Tamara and Tab got the first two glasses and each took a sip.

Tab said: "You're stuck with me now. How does it feel?"

Tamara said: "I never imagined I could be this happy."

Pippa said: "Mom, you told me you had three conditions for using nuclear weapons."

Pauline found Pippa's questions helpful. They made her focus on the basics. "I remember, of course."

"Tell me again what they are."

"First, we've tried all peaceful means of solving the problem—but they have failed."

"And you seem to have done that now."

Had she? She thought hard. "Yes, we have."

"And second?"

"We can't solve the problem with conventional, nonnuclear weapons."

"Was that true in North Korea?"

"I believe it was." Again Pauline paused and reconsidered, but she came to the same conclusion. "After the rebels devastated two cities with nuclear bombs, we had to be sure of completely closing down the rebels' firepower, so that they couldn't ever do it again. No amount of conventional weaponry could have guaranteed that."

"I guess not."

"And third, Americans are being killed or are about to be killed by enemy action."

"And Americans were being killed in South Korea."

"Correct."

"Will you do it again? Launch more nuclear missiles?"

"If I have to, honey; if Americans are killed or threatened, yes."

"But you'll try not to."

"With all my strength." Pauline looked at her watch. "Which is what I'm going to do now. We have a meeting scheduled, and they're just waking up in Beijing."

"Good luck, Mommy."

Heading for the Situation Room, Pauline passed a door marked NATIONAL SECURITY ADVISOR, and on impulse she knocked.

She heard Gus's voice. "Yeah?"

"It's me, are you ready?"

He opened the door. "I'm putting my tie on. Would you like to step inside for a moment?"

While she watched him knotting a somber dark gray necktie she said: "Whatever the Chinese are going to do, they'll do it in the next twelve hours, I think. If they leave it for another day it will seem like an after-thought."

Gus nodded. "So much of this is about looking strong, to your allies as well as to your enemies."

"And that's not just a matter of vanity. If you look strong you're less likely to be attacked, in international affairs as in the school playground."

He turned to her. "My tie okay?"

She adjusted it, though no adjustment was neces-sary. She smelled woodsmoke and lavender. With her hands on his chest she looked up at him. Something she was not planning to say came out of her mouth unbid-den. "We can't wait five years."

She surprised herself. But it was the truth.

"I know," he said.

"We may not have five years."

"We may not have five days."

She took a deep breath, thought hard, and at last said: "If we live to the end of this day, Gus, shall we spend the night together?"

"God, yes."

"Are you sure you want to?"

"With all my heart."

"Touch my face."

He put his hand on her cheek. She turned her head and kissed his palm. Desire swelled inside her. She felt she might lose control. She did not want to wait even until tonight.

The room phone rang.

She stepped back guiltily, as if the caller might be able to see into the room.

Gus turned and picked up the handset. After a moment he said: "Okay," and hung up. Then he said: "President Chen is calling you."

The mood changed in an instant.

"He's up early," Pauline said. It was five a.m. in Beijing.

"I'll take the call in the Situation Room so everyone can hear."

They left the room together.

She put her feelings for Gus aside and focused her mind on what was ahead of her. She had to forget about everyday life now. She was the mother of a teenager, the wife of an unfaithful husband, and a woman in love with a colleague, and she had to leave those relationships behind and be the leader of the free world. And yet she had to remember that if she made the wrong decision, then the consequences would be suffered by Pippa, Gerry, and Gus.

She straightened her back and walked into the Situation Room.

The screens around the walls showed all the available sources of information: satellite, infrared, and the TV news in the US, Beijing, and Seoul. Her most important colleagues and advisors were at the table. It was not so long ago that she had liked to begin cabinet meetings with a joke. Not anymore.

She sat down. "Put him on the speaker." She made her voice friendly. "Good morning, President Chen. This is very early for you."

His face appeared on screens around the room. He was wearing his usual dark blue suit. "Good morning," he said.

Nothing else. No polite preliminaries, no chitchat. His tone was cold. Pauline guessed he had people in the room with him, monitoring every word.

She said: "Mr. President, I think we both have to end the escalation of this crisis. I'm sure you agree."

His reply was instant and aggressive. "China has not escalated! The US has sunk an aircraft carrier, attacked North Korea, and deployed nuclear weapons! You have escalated!"

"You bombed those poor Japanese sailors in the Diaoyu Islands."

"That was defensive. They had invaded China!"

"That's a matter of dispute, but in any case they used no violence. They did not harm one single Chinese person. But you killed them. That's escalation."

"And what would you do if Chinese soldiers occupied San Miguel?"

Pauline had to think for a moment to recall that San Miguel was a large uninhabited island off the coast of Southern California. "I'd be very angry, Mr. President, but I wouldn't bomb your people."

"I wonder."

"In any case, this should end now. I will take no further military action if you will pledge the same."

"How can you say such a thing? You have sunk an aircraft carrier, killing thousands of Chinese, and you have attacked North Korea with nuclear weapons, but now you ask me for a promise of no military action. This is absurd."

"To anyone who wants to prevent world war, it's the only reasonable course."

"Let me make something clear," Chen said, and Pauline had the unnerving feeling that she was hearing the voice of doom. "There was once a time when the Western powers could do as they wished in East Asia with no fear of repercussions. We Chinese call it the Era of Humiliation. Madam President, those days are over."

"You and I have always spoken as equals—"

But he had not finished. "China will respond to your nuclear aggression," he said. "The purpose of this call is to tell you that our response will be measured, proportionate, and non-escalatory. After that, you may ask us for a pledge of no further military action."

Pauline said: "I will choose peace, not war, for as long as I can, Mr. President. But now it is my turn to make something very clear. Peace ends the moment you kill Americans. General Pak learned that lesson this morning, and you know what has happened to him and his country. Don't imagine it would be any different for you."

Pauline waited for Chen's response, but Chen hung up.

She said: "Fuck it."

Gus said: "He sounded as if there was a commissar pointing a pistol at his head."

The director of national intelligence, Sophia Magliani, said: "That may be the literal truth, Gus. The CIA in Beijing thinks there has been some kind of shuffle at the top, maybe a coup. Chang Kai, the vice minister for foreign intelligence, seems to have been arrested. I say 'seems to' because there has been no announcement, but our best agent in Beijing got the information from Chang's wife. Chang is a young reformer, so his arrest suggests that the hard-liners have taken control."

Pauline said: "This makes it more probable that they will act aggressively."

"Exactly, Madam President."

"I read the China Plan some time ago," Pauline said. The Pentagon had war plans for several contingencies. The biggest and most important was the Russia Plan. China's came second. "Let's run over it so that everyone knows what we're talking about. Luis?"

The secretary of defense looked haggard, despite being as carefully groomed as ever. They were all heading for their second night without sleep. Luis said: "Every Chinese military base that has nuclear weapons, or might have, is already targeted by one or more

ballistic missiles armed with nuclear warheads and
ready to be launched from the US. Firing them will be
our first act of war."

When Pauline had reviewed this plan it had been
abstract. She had studied it carefully, but she was
thinking all the time that her real mission was to make
sure the plan was never needed. Now it was different.
Now she knew she might have to do it, and in her mind
she saw the hellish orange-red bloom, the crumbling
buildings, and the horribly charred bodies of men,
women, and children.

But she maintained her tone of brisk practicality.
"The Chinese will see them on their satellite and radar
feeds within seconds, but the missiles will take thirty
minutes or more to reach China."

"Yes, and as soon as they appear the Chinese will
launch their own nuclear attack on the US."

Yes, she thought. The mighty skyscrapers of New
York will collapse, the gleaming beaches of Florida
will turn radioactive, and the majestic forests of the
West will blaze until there is nothing left but a carpet
of ash.

She said: "But we have something the Chinese don't
have—anti-missile missiles."

"We certainly do, Madam President: interceptor
sites at Fort Greely in Alaska and Vandenberg Air
Force Base in California, plus smaller systems of sea-
based interceptors."

"Do they work?"

"They're not expected to be one hundred percent effective."

Bill Schneider, who as always wore a headset that
connected him with the Pentagon, growled: "They're
the best in the world."

"But they're not perfect," Pauline said. "I understand

that if they kill half the incoming ordnance they're doing well."

Bill did not contradict her.

Luis said: "We also have nuclear-armed submarines patrolling the South China Sea. We have fourteen such vessels, and currently half of them are within range of China. Each one is armed with twenty ballistic missiles, and each missile has between three and five warheads. Madam President, any one of those submarines carries enough firepower to devastate any country on earth. And they will immediately open fire on mainland China."

"But presumably the Chinese have similar."

"Not really. They have four or five Jin-class submarines, each carrying twelve ballistic missiles, but the missiles have only one warhead each. The firepower is nowhere near comparable to ours."

"Do we know where their submarines are?"

"No. Modern submarines are very quiet. Our hydroacoustic sensors detect them only when they approach our coasts. Magnetic anomaly detectors, usually mounted in aircraft, can find only submarines that are near the surface. In short, submarines can hide right up until the very last minute."

Pauline had approved the China Plan, and she did not see how it could be improved, but it did not guarantee a quick victory. America would win, but millions would die in both countries.

Suddenly Bill Schneider shouted: "Missile fired, missile fired!"

"Oh, no!" Pauline looked at the screens around the room and saw no sign of it. "Where?"

"Pacific Ocean." Speaking into his mouthpiece he said: "For Christ's sake, be more precise!" Then after a pause: "Eastern Pacific, Madam President." Speaking into the phone again, he said: "Get some camera drones up in the neighborhood, fast!"

Gus said: "Radar on screen three."

Pauline looked at the screen and saw a graphic showing a red arc on a blue sea. Then the image moved, and on the left of the screen was a familiar-looking island.

Bill said: "One ballistic missile, that's all."

Gus said: "Fired from where? It can't have come from China—we would have seen it half an hour ago."

Bill said: "It must have been launched from a submarine that then immediately submerged."

Gus said: "Here comes the drone picture."

Pauline looked hard. The island was mostly forest, but in the south was a built-up area, with a large airport and a natural harbor. Much of the coast was a golden ribbon of beaches. She said: "Oh, my good God, that's Honolulu."

"They're bombing Hawaii," Chess said with incredulity.

Pauline asked: "How far away is the missile?"

Bill answered: "One minute to impact."

"Christ! Does Hawaii have anti-missile defenses?"

"Yes," said Bill, "on land and aboard ships in the harbor."

"Tell them to fire!"

"Already told, but the missile is low and fast and hard to hit."

All the screens now showed different views of Honolulu. It was midafternoon in Hawaii. Pauline could see bright-colored umbrellas in straight rows on Waikiki Beach. It made her want to weep. A big jet was taking off from the Honolulu airport, probably packed with homeward-bound vacationers who might now escape death by seconds. Battleships and submarines of the US Navy were at anchor in Pearl Harbor.

Pearl Harbor, Pauline thought; my God, this has happened before. I don't think I can bear it.

Bill said: "Thirty seconds. Submarine confirmed as Chinese by infrared satellite surveillance."

Pauline knew what she had to do. Her heart was full and she could hardly speak. She managed to say: "Tell the Pentagon to be ready to execute the China Plan on my word."

"Yes, ma'am."

Gus said quietly: "Are you sure?"

"Not yet," said Pauline. "If this missile is armed with conventional explosives we may be able to avoid nuclear war."

"But not otherwise."

"No."

"I agree."

"Twenty seconds," said Bill.

Pauline realized she was on her feet, and so was everyone else in the room. She could not remember standing up.

The drone pictures kept changing, moment by moment showing the vapor trail over forest and cultivated fields, then a highway busy with cars and trucks, all serene in the sunshine. Pauline's heart was breaking. Her mind said: My fault, this is my fault.

"Ten seconds."

Suddenly there were half a dozen new vapor trails as defensive missiles were launched from Pearl Harbor. "Surely one must hit!" she cried.

Then a picture showed the dreadfully familiar orange-red circle of death appearing in the town, east of the harbor and north of the airport.

The circles of fire engulfed people and buildings, then turned into pillars of smoke with mushroom tops. In the harbor a huge wave entirely swamped Ford Island. All the airport buildings were suddenly flat, and the planes at the gates were ablaze. The city of Honolulu was on fire as gas tanks exploded in every car and bus.

Pauline wanted to collapse, to bury her head in her hands, and to weep, but she forced herself back under control. "Put the Pentagon War Room on the speaker, please," she said with only the slightest tremor in her voice.

She took out the Biscuit. She had broken the plastic case this morning; was this really the same day?

On the speaker a voice said: "This is General Evers in the Pentagon War Room, Madam President."

The room was silent. Everyone stared at Pauline.

"General Evers, when you have heard me read the correct authentication code you will execute the China Plan. Is that clear?"

"Yes, ma'am."

"Any questions?"

"No, ma'am."

Pauline looked again at the satellite images. They showed a picture of humanity's nightmare. Half of America will look like that inferno if I don't read out these numbers, she thought.

And perhaps also if I do.

She said: "Oscar November three seven three. I say again, Oscar November three seven three."

The general said: "I have given the order to execute the plan."

"Thank you, General."

"Thank you, Madam President."

Very slowly, Pauline sat down. She put her arms on the table and lowered her head. She thought of the dead and dying in Hawaii, and those who would soon be dying in China, and soon afterward in the great cities of the continental United States. She squeezed her eyes shut, but she could still see them. All her poise and self-confidence drained out of her like blood from an arterial wound. She was possessed by a helpless grief so overwhelming that her whole body shook. She felt that her heart would burst and she would die.

And then, at last, she began to weep.

THE END

ACKNOWLEDGMENTS

My consultants for *Never* were Catherine Ashton, James Cowan, Kim Darroch, Marc Lanteigne, Jeffrey Lewis, Kim Sengupta, and Tong Zhao.

Several people kindly gave me helpful interviews, especially Gordon Brown, Des Browne, and Enna Park.

My editors were Gillian Green, Vicki Mellor, Brian Tart, and Jeremy Trevathan.

Friends and family who helped included Ed Balls, Lucy Blythe, Daren Cook, Barbara Follett, Peter Kellner, Chris Manners, Charlotte Quelch, Jann Turner, Kim Turner, and Phil Woolas.

I'm grateful to you all.

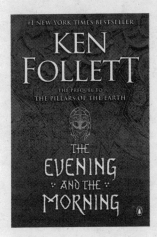

  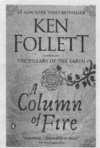

THE KINGSBRIDGE NOVELS
(in historical order)
The Evening and the Morning
The Pillars of the Earth
World Without End
A Column of Fire

THE CENTURY TRILOGY
(in historical order)
Fall of Giants
Winter of the World
Edge of Eternity

WORLD WAR TWO THRILLERS
Eye of the Needle
The Key to Rebecca
Night over Water
Jackdaws
Hornet Flight

OTHER NOVELS
Triple
The Man from St. Petersburg
Lie Down with Lions
A Dangerous Fortune
A Place Called Freedom
The Third Twin
The Hammer of Eden
Code to Zero
Whiteout

EARLY NOVELS
The Modigliani Scandal
Paper Money

NON-FICTION
On Wings of Eagles
Notre-Dame